MW01462958

Love & Nature
Book 1

Ragden Zar

Copyright © 2024 Ragden Zar

All rights reserved.

The characters and events portrayed in this book are fictitious. Any similarity to real persons, living or dead, is coincidental and not intended by the author.

No part of this book may be reproduced, or stored in a retrieval system, or transmitted in any form or by any means, electronic, mechanical, photocopying, recording, or otherwise without express written permission of the publisher.

ISBN: 9798329681741

Printed in the United States of America.

DEDICATION

Thank you to my editor, Saffy Amary'llis, without whom, we would not be here. All the long hours going through every page and line, fixing all the copious errors.

A hearty thanks to the moderators of lushstories.com for the efforts in cleaning up additional errors and typos.

A very special thanks for my wife for her love and support during this creative process. Without you we would not be here. Love you

CHAPTER 1

Tuesday...

For Ragden, it was just another day as he walked through school, dreading what might take place. It was only weeks after his 18th birthday, and school was still torture. School had never been easy for him, but his mild learning difficulties had been compounded by the school bully and her team of "evil witches" that tormented him at every opportunity. The three of them, Aria, Emily, and Sarah, always found new ways to embarrass him as the years progressed. Only a month or two older, they never ceased in their torment of him. Yet, as he walked onto campus that day something felt different.

His first couple of classes were normal enough, and he managed to avoid them- watching around corners and taking different routes if he caught sight of them. Then, just before lunch, he saw them coming down the hall towards his locker. He had no other way to go. Stood up straight and decided that he had had enough.

Aria walked tall and proud before her two friends, spotted Ragden and grinned at the sudden opportunity that presented itself. Her grin widened as she knew everyone present would be watching. They always did, she was the most popular girl in school. The prettiest, the most desired. Her friends were close second and third, but this was her place of power. She spotted Ragden and stopped him in the hall.

"Well, well, well... look at the dweeb," she said haughtily. She tossed her perfect blonde hair and looked over her shoulder at her friends who laughed with her. As she looked back at Ragden, she saw a burning intensity in his eyes she had never seen before.

"You are just jealous because you need someone as cool as me in your life," he quipped back at her. Aria felt a sudden shock to her core. This was not the passive nerd she had been teasing for the last four years.

Aria scoffed and rolled her eyes, "Oh please! You think anyone would

want to be associated with a loser like you? I could have any guy in this school if I wanted!"

She stepped closer to Ragden, and put her arm around his neck, pulled him close to her body, "But hey, maybe there's something I can do to make you feel better about yourself."

Not sure what had come over her, she leaned in and kissed his cheek. Ragden leaned into her, his lips brushing her ear. She could feel the heat that came off him and shivered slightly. Who was this person she had gotten entangled with? Surely not the same dorky nerd she had been picking on for years?

"Are you sure you want your friends to see you getting hot for me? I know you want this. But is now the right time?" he whispered into her ear. Aria's face turned red with embarrassment, but she did not pull back.

"Shut up... Yeah, I guess so," her voice trailed off as she bit her lip nervously. "Fuck my reputation... I don't care... I want this... I want you..."

Aria started to undress Ragden with her hands, revealed his body piece by piece. She pulled his shirt over his head, her hands fumbled with the buckle of his shorts. Between hurried breaths, she sighed huskily, "Take me somewhere private..."

Ragden leaned forward and licked her ear, nibbling on her earlobe. Then he huskily whispered, "Fuck that, I know you want this. Let's put on a show they will never forget."

He grabbed her ass and pulled her fiercely against him. Their groins pressed together; she could feel the heat and pulse of his cock through his clothes. Then he kissed her fiercely, forced his tongue into her mouth, tasting her.

Aria moaned deeply against Ragden. Disbelief floated through her mind. This was not how she imagined this playing out. She wrapped her arms around his neck and pulled him tightly against her, ground against his groin. She could feel her panties going damp against her.

"Fuuuuck...." she gasped between kisses, "This is way too good..."

Her friends stood by watching in shock and awe, unable to believe what they were seeing. Some of them started taking pictures or recording videos on their phones. Ragden then leaned back from her body, grabbed the front of her shirt, and ripped it open. the fragments of cloth dropped to the ground around them. Her simple, white bra was revealed.

"These babies need to be free," Ragden stated simply as he reached behind her. His fingers popped the clasp. Her bra went loose as he slid the straps over her shoulders. She clapped her hands to her chest, as he slid her bra off. She blushed as he pulled her hands off her chest, and revealed her small, round breasts to her stunned friends. She let out a small soft gasp of surprise and pleasure as he leaned forward and clamped his teeth on her neck, then sucked and kissed her.

Ragden's hands slid down her back. He grabbed the back of her skirt and

tugged so hard the fabric gave. She moaned as he pulled the shredded fabric off her body, revealed her tiny white panties, and dropped them to the ground at her feet. Then he ripped her panties in half, held them up, and dropped them to the ground. Her nipples hardened as she felt the cool air across her most private parts. She arched her back slightly, giving his mouth better access to her throat. With her panties discarded in rags on the floor, she stood completely bare before him.

"Ahh... Fuck... ", she moaned between gasps for air, "That feels so good..."

Her friends watched in complete awe, some of them even drooled over the sight of their popular girl being treated like this by the nerd they always made fun of. Ragden moved his mouth to Aria's chest, flicking his tongue over her nipples, while he undid his shorts, and dropped both shorts and boxers to the floor. His large, uncircumcised penis sprang forward. He pulled her against him, trapped his cock against her stomach.

"This is what you really need. Tell me how much you want it..."

Aria's eyes widened in amazement as she saw his massive cock at it stood proudly against her abdomen. She could not believe how big it was, and how much she wanted it. Her hand reached out and grabbed onto the base of it. She felt its warmth and weight.

"Oh god... I need this so bad...," she whispered breathlessly, "I want every inch of you inside me..."

She looked up at Ragden with lust-filled eyes. She craved what he had to offer. He saw her eyes and leaned in to kiss her fiercely again, pushed his tongue deep into her mouth while he wrapped his arms around her and pulled her tight against him. Aria moaned loudly as his tongue plunged into her mouth.

He grabbed her ass, effortlessly lifting her off the ground. She wrapped her legs around him. Aria was overwhelmed as she felt completely vulnerable and helpless. His fingers slid around her ass, pulled her pussy lips wide. The head of his dick slid against her clitoris. A whimper of pleasure slipped from her lips.

"Are you ready for this?" he breathed huskily.

"Yes... I'm ready..."

Ragden slowly lowered Aria onto his cock. The head barely slipped in, her pussy too tight for such a large penis. He leaned forward and sunk his teeth into her neck again, as the head slipped a little deeper into her. Aria let out a soft gasp as that massive, thick cock stretched her walls. The teeth at her neck were another layer of pleasure added to the mix.

"Fuuuuuuck" she breathed heavily, "I've never felt anything like this before..."

She tightened her legs around him and held him as tightly as she could. She was afraid she might lose that incredible sensation. Ragden licked his way up her neck, to nibble on her chin. Aria whimpered in response. The cock

seated within her drove her wild with pleasure. Then he kissed her even more fiercely. She moaned in response. As his cock bottomed out against the back of her vagina, another shiver ran down her spine. Her heart raced faster.

Then he lifted his head and whispered into her ear, "I know you bullied me because you wanted this, and now I'll give it to you, but don't think I've forgiven you..."

"Y-yes... I did it because... I wanted this..."

Ragden bit down on her earlobe as he ground his hips against her. He pressed the head of his cock into her cervix. Then he grabbed her ass, lifted her up and slid half of his massive member out of her. She gasped. Then he lowered her as he thrust his hips forward and drove his cock up into her.

She felt a burning sensation deep inside her. She was filled with pleasure and pain. She gasped and moaned as Ragden latched his mouth onto her neck. Then he lifted and lowered her again, as his teeth marked her. The small crowd watched in awe as his cock slammed into her. Their jaws dropped in disbelief at the scene that unfolded before them.

"Ahh... Fuuuuck..." she breathed heavily. Her voice was weak as she whimpered, lost in the intensity of the moment, "Take me... Take me hard... Make me pay for all those years of torment... I deserve this... I need this... Please..."

Ragden continued to grind his teeth into her neck. A low moan slipped from her lips. He increased the pace of the huge drives into her. Each thrust rocked her body and bounced her small breasts. Aria surrendered herself to the intense sensations as they coursed through her body. She let go of any thoughts or concerns about the consequences of the situation.

"Fuuuuuuuuuck... Yes... Take me harder... Make me pay... I deserve this... I need this... Do whatever you want with me... Just keep fucking me like this..." Her voice trailed off between gasps for air.

Ragden leaned back a hair and altered the angle of penetration. He continued to lift and drop her faster as he thrust deep into her. His hips moved in time to her movement as he lowered her. His groin hit her harder each time. Aria let out a high-pitched gasp at the change. Her pussy clenched and unclenched around him. She tried to hold on to the exquisite pleasure and pain that filled her entire body. Her breath came in short bursts. She cried out in ecstasy and agony. She was lost in the whirlwind of emotions washing over her.

"Fuck... Yes..." She whispered between gasps. Her voice broke as she succumbed completely to the power of the moment. "Do it... Fuck me harder..."

Aria let out a long-drawn-out moan as Ragden shifted position again, and his massive cock slid past her cervix, deeper into her inner depths. His thrusts went deeper, harder, faster. They sent waves of pleasure and discomfort throughout her entire body. She felt his cock as it ripped through her insides. It rearranged her delicate structures. He filled her with a new level of intensity.

She cried out in pleasure and pain. Her voice became raw and primal.

"Ahh... Fuck...," Aria gasped. Her juices flowed freely. She felt overwhelmed by the power, strength, and size of him in her. She felt owned to her very core.

Ragden pulled Aria's ear into his mouth and ran his tongue over it. He grazed it with his teeth. Aria whimpered softly. He continued to slam his groin against hers. Arousal and fear surged through her. She never wanted it to stop. Aria submitted to his dominance.

"Fuuuuck..." she felt the mixture of emotions that swirled within her. It was a confusing blend of desire, submission, fear, and anticipation, "Fuck me harder..."

Ragden growled into her ear with a deep guttural voice, "Cum for me!"

Aria let out a long, low moan in response. He pounded her harder. Her whole body shuddered with each powerful stroke. She was overwhelmed by the intensity of the sensations. Her orgasm built, threatened to consume her as she felt the heat and pressure that built within her core.

As she neared climax, a long, drawn-out cry exploded from her mouth. Her voice rose as the pressure and pleasure exploded within her. She felt her pussy flood with thick, sticky fluid. It poured down over Ragden's cock and groin.

"Cum for you..." she moaned softly.

Ragden growled fiercely into her ear, "Oh... I am not done with you yet..."

Aria whimpered as Ragden spoke. He raked his teeth over her ear again. Then he lifted her off his cock and set her down on her feet. He spun her around and made her face the crowd. She had the sudden urge to cover the faint wisps of blonde hair between her legs. Then he bent her over and placed the head of his cock against her soaked pussy. He grabbed her wrists and pulled her arms back.

He barked at her, "Tell me how much you want this. Tell everyone how much you want this. Make me believe you!"

Aria gasped in surprise. Her eyes widened with fear and excitement. Despite her hesitation, she found herself begging for more. She wanted to fulfill whatever desires he had in store for her. She wanted to prove to herself and everyone else that she truly belonged to him.

"Please... I want this... I need this..."

Ragden slammed his penis into her pussy, ramming it against her cervix. She let out a gasp at the sudden impact. It filled her with pleasure and pain. Her entire body convulsed at the impact. She cried out in delight and agony.

As his cock continued to pound into her, she felt his control over her growing stronger. She welcomed his dominance over her. Ragden transferred her wrists to his left hand, holding them easily in one hand. He pulled them back until she groaned. Then he grabbed her hair with his right hand and pulled her head back. She arched her back further, showing her breasts to the crowd. He slowly withdrew his dick to the edge of her pussy. Aria let out a

low moan. Then he drove it home with one massive thrust that struck her core again.

Each powerful stroke sent shockwaves of pleasure and pain through Aria's body. She felt his cock as it connected with her cervix. Her body trembled and her mind raced. She was unable to resist the pleasure and submission as it overwhelmed her.

The small crowd watched in awe, as he continued to pound into her. Their eyes fixed on the spectacle as it unfolded before them. They could see the look of pure ecstasy and submission etched across Aria's face.

Ragden pulled her head back farther. He continued to slam his cock into her. He relished the vibrations of her body. Aria whimpered as the intensity increased while her body was pulled at new angles. It filled her with pleasure and pain. She surrendered completely to the experience.

He drove deep into her. He ground his hips against her ass and pushed the head of his cock against her depths. She let out a low moan at the sensation of his cock so deep within her. She could feel the heat and pressure as it built again. She knew she was nearing her breaking point.

Ragden growled with the effort, his voice deep and commanding, "Tell me how much you want this!"

Despite the pain and pleasure that surged through her body, she found herself unable to resist the command, "Yes... I want this... I need this..."

Ragden pulled her arms and head back a little further. Then he adjusted his position. His cock slipped deeper into her, filling her again. Aria gasped softly. She felt the thrill of anticipation that built within her. Then he pulled it back and drove it home again, and again. He drove deeper into her than she thought possible. The heat and pressure built within her. She could do nothing but surrender to it. The crowd watched in awe as he continued to pound her. Their eyes fixed on the sight of her exposed body, and the way she submitted to his dominance.

Ragden released her arms. Then he wrapped his arms around her chest and grasped her breasts. He pulled her into a standing position, her back firmly against his chest. She gasped in surprise, feeling the warmth and solidity of his body against hers. She could feel his heartbeat echoing through his chest. She felt a sense of comfort and safety despite the intensity of the situation. He arched his back and drove his cock deep into her abdomen. The bulge in her stomach was clearly visible to the watching crowd. Then he pulled back and drove in again.

The crowd watched in amazement as Ragden continued to highlight his dominance of Aria, their eyes fixed on the sight of her exposed body, and the way she surrendered completely to him.

Ragden took her earlobe with his teeth. Aria whimpered in response as he growled into her ear, "Cum for me!"

His voice echoed in her ear, sending a shiver of pleasure and anticipation through her body. She felt the warmth of his breath against her skin. As he

continued to slam his cock into her abdomen, she felt the heat and pressure hit a breaking point

"Yes..."

The small crowd watched in awe as another orgasm rolled over Aria. Her body convulsed and twitched beyond her control. Her juices flowed freely, splashing on the ground at her feet. The bulge in her stomach twitched.

Ragden released his grip on her chest and grabbed her hips. He pulled her down against his cock. Aria let out a long, drawn-out moan as his cock slid somehow even deeper. As her wrists and hair were free, she felt a sense of freedom and abandonment. She could fully surrender to the pleasure and discomfort that washed over her. As the twitching of her body slowed and stopped from the intensity of her orgasm, she felt the cock still buried inside her. It twitched and pulsed. She felt her boundaries pushed beyond her limits.

"Ahh... Fuck..." she whispered as she rode out the end of her climax, her body came to rest against the solid rock of him against her back.

As her breathing started to calm, Ragden slowly slid his cock from out of her. Until it finally slid free of her. Aria crumpled to the ground. She panted heavily. Her body still quivered with the aftershocks of her orgasm. She felt a sense of emptiness and longing. She knew she could never go back.

The small crowd watched in awe as Ragden stepped back from her. They admired the way Aria half-sat on the ground, barely able to hold herself up. Her body spent. Her pussy still leaked juices over the pavement. The look of satisfaction and dominance etched across Ragden's face.

"You've made me yours," she whispered faintly, "completely."

Ragden chuckled, something deep within his voice, "Oh. I'm not done yet. Are you ready for the next act?"

Aria looked up at him. Her eyes shone with anticipation and submission as she whispered, "Yes... I am ready..."

She lay on the ground, patiently waiting for the next command. She knew that she had nothing left to lose and everything to gain from this moment of total surrender.

Ragden's cock twitched and throbbed in expectation. He reached down and cupped her chin, a small gasp slipped through her lips, as he pulled her to her feet. She felt a sudden rush of anticipation and excitement as it coursed through her body. She saw the determination in his eyes as he grinned savagely at her. Then he spun her round again. He slipped his cock between her legs, sliding the tip along her pussy lips, across her clit, then back to her asshole. She felt the warmth and dampness of her own arousal against the tip of his cock and could not help but whimper softly. He drew a slow circle around that precious hole, his cock vibrating in anticipation as he growled in her ear, "Are you truly prepared? Tell me you want this. Tell me you want this in your ass."

"Yes... I want this... I want you in my ass... Please..."

Ragden pushed the head of his cock against her ass, the massiveness of it

too much to fit. Aria gasped again as his cock pushed against her. She felt the resistance of her tight entrance. She felt the heat and pressure building within her. She knew it was almost impossible for him to fit. He pulled back and slid his cock through her wet folds again, gathering more of her arousal. She felt a new surge of pleasure wash over her and knew that she was ready for anything he might ask of her.

"Yes... Take me... Fill me..."

Ragden again pushed the head of his cock against her asshole. A shiver ran down his back as the first inch slid in. His eyes slipped closed as he felt the impossible tightness wrapped around him. He pulled back, Aria whimpered in response. He almost slipped out. Then he slid back in that inch, and a hair more. She could feel the immense pleasure and fullness of his cock at the edge of her entry, only to have it retreat and then push forward again. She felt it slip farther into her with each incremental movement. She knew that it would be impossible to forget this moment of complete surrender and submission.

"Ahh... Fuck... Just like that... "

The small crowd watched in awe as Aria took that first inch. Then another, and another.

Aria gasped again as Ragden took her hands to her ass cheeks. He forced her to spread herself open further to allow for more of his cock to slide into her. Another inch slid in, back out, then again plus another inch. This was repeated, and again. Each inch sent new waves of pleasure and discomfort that coursed through her body. His massive cock eased deeper into her inches at a time. Until he was finally fully engorged inside her. Every inch, groin to ass, pushed into her.

As the final length slid into her, she felt his pulsing cock against her inner depths. She let out a moan of pleasure and relief. Ragden sighed in contentment.

"Fuuuuuuuccccckkkk..." She whimpered.

Ragden started to build a slow rhythm of movement against her. He continued to slide in and out of her. Each powerful thrust sent new waves of pleasure and discomfort through her. The small crowd watched in awe. They were transfixed, as Aria accepted the size and power of him into her.

Ragden reached down and placed his hands on the lower sides of her thighs. He lifted her with ease into the air. Aria let out a gasp. She felt even more full and overwhelmed as her weight drove her down onto his cock. As he spread her legs, she felt a new level of vulnerability and exposure and she knew everyone was watching her most intimate moments of submission.

"Fuck... I'm so exposed..."

The small crowd watched in awe as Aria's pussy dripped on display for all to see. They could see just how deeply embedded his cock was within her. Aria whimpered softly as Ragden lifted and lowered her. His cock slid even deeper into her. She felt the intensity of his power and speed as it increased with each thrust. Her fluids flowed out of her pussy. She felt vulnerability and

helplessness wash over her as he continued to pound her at a pace that increased with each thrust. She felt even more pleasure and discomfort throughout her body.

"Ahh... Fuck... Faster..." The entire crowd could feel the intensity of the situation as it built while they watched her being driven harder and faster.

Then it stopped. Aria moaned in disappointment as Ragden lifted her off him and set her on her feet in front of him. She stood there, vulnerable, and exposed. Her heart thundered in her chest as she tried to anticipate what would come next. She stood there; her hands clasped in front of her groin. She watched as his cock gently throbbed before her.

"What... are you doing?" She asked hesitantly, "Why did you stop?"

The small crowd watched in anticipation. They waited to see what Ragden would do next. They wondered if he planned to continue his dominance or if he was simply taking a break.

Ragden reached out and placed a hand on her head, gently pushing her towards the ground. She let out a soft gasp of surprise as he forced her to kneel in front of him, "I have more for you. Are you ready?"

Despite her shock, she knew that she had completely surrendered to his will. She felt excitement and anticipation wash over her. Her heart started to beat faster, excited at the prospect of yet another thing to come.

"Yes... I'm ready... What else do you have planned?" she asked nervously, "I'm yours to command."

Ragden knelt in front of her and pushed her back to lie on the ground. She gasped, her eyes a little wild as he crawled over her. He spread her legs with his knees and placed his cock against her ass. The tip slipped in, and he paused.

"Tell everyone how much you love this cock in your ass!!"

Aria's eyes got big as she found herself saying the words. They rushed out of her, "Oh god... I love this cock in my ass..."

Her words were suddenly cut off as her mouth snapped shut as his cock slid into her. One deep savage thrust. Ragden arched against her, muscles strained, every bit of leverage used. His groin was pushed to hers, fully seated against her. Aria gasped loudly as she felt him fill her. She could feel the heat and pressure of it as it filled her inner depths. A moan of submission and pleasure slipped through her lips.

"Fuuuuuuuccccckkk...," she whimpered, "So full..."

Aria moaned in pleasure as Ragden reached up and grasped a breast in each hand and squeezed tightly. He slid out, then back in again. Aria's breasts jiggled in his firm grasp.

"Ahh... Fuck... Squeeze them..."

Ragden continued to slide his cock in and out of Aria. Then he looked up into the crowd. His intense gaze looked at two figures who stood and watched. He pointed at them.

"You and you! Sarah & Emily, right? Get over here!"

Ragden slid his groin against Aria's ass and sat back on his heels. He put a hand down on Aria's stomach, feeling the vibration of her body beneath him. Aria groaned, feeling the throbbing of his cock deep within her. She arched her back and rocked her hips, trying to move herself along his shaft.

Sarah and Emily approached. They kneeled on either side of Aria. They looked down at Aria and saw the sweat on her brow. The look of concentration on her face as she tried to move herself against Ragden's body. They saw the tensing of her muscles and the heaving of her chest with each breath.

Ragden spoke softly, "Would you like to assist me here?"

Sarah and Emily looked at each other, not sure how to respond. Aria looked up at them. She reached out to them, taking their hands in hers.

"Please," Aria begged, "I need this."

Emily looked at Sarah. Then they both looked down at Aria and nodded. Both girls turned to Ragden.

"How can we help?" Sarah asked with a trembling voice. Emily nodded in agreement.

Aria smiled, a warmth spreading through her chest. She had felt embarrassed initially when she heard their names called. Now, affection for them spread through her, knowing that they would be by her side through this experience.

Ragden smiled at them. Then he spoke softly to them, "Lick her chest."

Aria felt them holding her hands. They both leaned in to lick her breasts. Their tongues traced the sensitive nipples of her swollen peaks.

"Mmmph..." Aria moaned in pleasure and submission as she felt their tongues. Her heart thundered in her chest. She felt the powerlessness of the situation as it washed over her again.

Ragden started to slide his cock in and out of Aria's tight ass again.

"Squeeze her breasts."

Aria watched as her two friends reached out tentatively. They squeezed her swollen nipples gently between their fingers. She felt the pleasure of their touch as it added to her already overwhelmed body. The crowd continued to watch. Their mouths agape as Aria's friends squeezed her breasts gently, while she was being fucked by his massive cock. They could see the mixture of pleasure and discomfort as it washed over her face with each powerful thrust.

Aria knew she wanted this; she wanted to be used and dominated. She wanted to feel the power of Ragden's cock as it filled her up completely.

Aria groaned as she felt that massive cock shifting around inside her bowels. Ragden pounded her ass. He pulled her legs against his chest. Aria's breath became ragged gasps with each thrust. Then he slid out of her ass and slammed deep into her pussy. His cock crashed into her cervix. She cried out at the invasion, then moaned in pleasure. Then he slid out of her again and slammed it back into her ass. He closed his eyes as he savored the tightness and slipperiness of her ass. Then he pulled back and drove in again, and again.

Aria moaned in pleasure. Her eyes found her friends where they sat next to her. Their eyes watched her rocking breasts, her flexing stomach, her dripping pussy, her ass so full. She could see the hunger on their faces. She felt humiliated, powerless, and aroused so deeply that she could not contain it. Ragden continued to pound her ass. She could feel the edges of another orgasm. Her eyes started to go wide.

"Cum for me!" Ragden growled between thrusts.

Aria let out a low moan of pleasure and submission. She felt the powerful thrusts as they drove deeper into her ass. She felt helpless.

She moaned as the pleasure crashed over her, as her orgasm claimed her reality. Her eyes squeezed shut. Every muscle in her body clenched. She felt the dam break within her. Ragden pounded her harder and faster. Her climax crashed over her like an avalanche that consumed everything. She felt Ragden release her legs, grab her hips, and pull her against him. Driving his cock even deeper with each world-ending thrust.

Aria let out a loud cry of pleasure as her body surrendered to the waves of pleasure that crashed over her. Ragden reached up and grabbed her breasts and squeezed her nipples. He continued to pound her harder and faster. She felt like his dick was somehow even deeper in her.

Ragden's eyes glazed over as his own climax rolled over him and mixed with hers. His body started to twitch, he started to move even faster against Aria. He continued to drive his cock and in out of her like some kind of savage madman.

Aria let out another loud cry of pleasure and submission. Her body shuddered and twitched as he continued to pound her ass shaking the ground around them.

Aria's arms flailed looking for something to grab onto. Then she grabbed Ragden's hands on her chest, squeezing them fiercely. She forced his fingers to dig into her tender flesh.

Ragden's climax overwhelmed him. He continued to drive into her ass. His rhythm staggered. His body twitched and spasmed. Cum exploded into her ass. It flooded down over his massive cock, pooled on the ground between them. And yet, the movement did not stop. She rocked her hips against his thrusts. She drove him into her. Their bodies seemed to move of their own accord.

Then their pace started to slow. Their bodies flushed and drenched in sweat. Aria's cum flowed freely from her pussy. Her ass leaked his seed. His groin was still firmly seated against her ass cheeks. Aria's breathing started to return to normal. He looked down at her. Grabbed her by the chin and looked her in the eyes.

"No more bullying. If you ever want this again, you will not bully anyone again. Ever."

Aria sighed contently. She felt the massive cock still buried deep in her ass. She internalized the words. She realized that she did indeed want this again

and that she had to do as asked. She nodded her head in agreement.

"Yes..."

As he saw the small nod, Ragden slipped his softening cock from her ass. He crawled over her straddling her chest. He dropped his cock on her chin.

"You can lick it clean now."

Aria hesitated for a moment, unsure if she would obey. Then she decided to accept it. She opened her mouth wide and accepted his dripping cock. She sucked and licked every bit of cum off it. She relished the taste and texture of it. She felt her own submission and the power she had given up.

"Mmm... Thank you..."

She finished cleaning up his cock, then looked up at him with a mix of gratitude and humility in her eyes. She knew that she had accepted her place as a devoted servant. Once his cock was clean, Ragden stood up and started to gather his clothes.

CHAPTER 2

Ragden turned back to Aria. She lay on her side, watching him. He admired her body, the way the curls of her blonde hair framed her face. Her beautiful breasts, as they swayed with each breath. The muscles of her flat stomach quivered slightly from her exertions. The dampness between her legs, the fluid that leaked out of her. The most impressive thing he saw was the look in her eyes. The desire, the contentment, the submission. He smiled. This was not the same woman he had met this morning. This was a new Aria he had helped to form. He wondered what she would want now, given a choice. Would she revert to her past way, or would she embrace this new path?

He looked at her questioningly, "What would you like now?"

Aria hesitated for a moment. She felt his gaze on her body and saw his smile. She felt a warmth in the core of her being that she had never felt before. She felt exposed and vulnerable, but also excited and nervous. She was unsure of what exactly she wanted. Her mind reeled from her experience. She felt the gentle quiver of her muscles. The soft ache inside her. She wanted it again, but more than that, she wanted someone to share in this feeling of submission she had embraced. After a moment of thought, she found the courage to speak.

"Um... Can we... Can we talk about my friends?"

Sarah and Emily had been watching this interchange between Ragden and Aria. They noted that Aria seemed happy in a way that they had never seen before. She almost glowed with the joy of what she had experienced. As they heard her words, they looked at each other; nervous looks of horror crossed their faces.

A wolfish grin filled Ragden's face, and lit him up, "That sounds like an excellent idea."

Ragden placed his clothes back on the ground at his feet. Then he looked at Emily and Sarah. He noted how they sat, kneeling, watching him.

Aria spoke in a rush, "They're both really popular and mean to everyone, especially me."

Ragden stepped over to Emily. He gently placed his hand under her chin and coaxed her to her feet before him. She shivered in anticipation. Her eyes were full of fear and nervousness.

"My dearest Emily, Aria says you bully even her?"

Emily glanced down at Sarah beside her. She realized she had been caught in a trap. She hesitated and licked her lips. Then she spoke, her voice trembling, "Y-yeah... We bullied Aria sometimes. We didn't mean any harm by it, though... It was just... you know, teasing."

Sarah nodded in agreement. Both women could see the uncertainty and fear as they consumed them. Ragden's fierce gaze locked with Emily's eyes. Emily felt like a deer caught in the headlights of an oncoming freight train—trapped, doomed.

"Emily, what do you think of what I did with Aria earlier?"

His voice was soft, almost gentle. She could sense the undertones of power, the hint of something sensual. She felt the gooseflesh rising in her arms. Being the focus of his attention sent a shiver down her back.

Emily's gaze found Ragden's chest, paused on the powerful muscles. She looked up into his face and saw the hard lines of his jaw and the softness of his lips. She wondered what it would be like to kiss them, to feel them on her skin.

She found herself lost in his eyes. Within them, she saw tenderness and affection. A gentleness that defied the scene she had just witnessed. She also saw a hard strength of character that made her shiver again.

"Um... I don't know," she stammered, "It was... intense. I have never seen anything like that before."

Ragden reached out to Aria. She took his hand, feeling his warmth. A swell of pride started to bloom within her at his touch. She stood at his side. He pulled her naked body to his; her side pressed against him. He sighed, feeling the heat and vulnerability that came off her in waves. He placed a hand on her head and pushed her down to her knees. Then leaned down and placed a soft kiss on her forehead.

Aria felt a surge of happiness wash over her. She knew that she had earned his approval and attention. She dropped to her knees obediently. She wrapped an arm around his leg and felt the warmth and strength of him enveloping her. Arousal washed over her, and she knew that she had become completely submissive to him. She felt a sense of excitement.

Ragden turned back to Emily, narrowed his eyes at her, and spoke softly, "Emily. Do you think you can be a good girl?"

Aria looked up at Ragden with hope and anticipation in her eyes. She was eager to see if Emily would submit to him as well. She was excited at the thought of having another person join her in her newfound state of submission. Emily looked at Ragden hesitantly, unsure of what to expect. She

could see the mixture of power and control on his face. She knew she had no choice but to submit if she wanted to experience this incredible sensation as well.

"Um... I... I guess I can try to be a good girl," Emily said uncertainly, "But I don't know if I can be as... Um, obedient as Aria."

Ragden looked at Emily consideringly. His gaze was unflinching. He spoke in hushed tones, soothing, "Oh. That can be taught. I can see your fear and insecurity. I can teach you strength. I can show you safety—if you are willing—even happiness—in places you might not expect."

Aria listened to Ragden's words and watched as hope and eagerness washed over Emily's face. She knew Ragden's words were influencing her. She whispered to herself, "Please, teach us all how to be better people. How to be happy and strong and... and..." She trailed off unable to find the right words to describe the incredible sense of submission and powerlessness that she was feeling.

Ragden reached down and gently caressed Aria's face, kissing her tenderly on the cheek. "I know, darling. But now is not your time. We will have time again soon. Now it is Emily's turn. Please be patient."

Aria's heart filled with happiness and anticipation. She felt a surge of excitement as she watched Ragden focus on Emily. Aria knew she would have plenty of time to spend with Ragden later.

Emily watched the interplay between Aria and Ragden. Her heart thundered in her chest. She felt the prickle of goosebumps down her arms and legs. She wondered what it would be like to submit so completely to someone like that.

Then Ragden turned to Emily with a wolfish grin. Emily shivered under that gaze. A part of her wanted that attention, wanted his hands on her, and more. She shivered again as the thoughts went through her mind. She felt exposed and vulnerable.

"Before we begin, we must first discuss something..." Ragden spoke softly, his voice filling with power and authority. Both girls shivered, as it washed over them. Ragden backed up to stand next to Aria. His hand was on her shoulder, caressing the soft skin. Aria squeezed her arm around his leg, possessively. She leaned her head against his warm skin. There was a look of sublime comfort on her face.

Ragden gestured for Emily and Sarah to join him by Aria. They crawled over, their bodies shivered slightly, aching for more of what he had to offer. Sarah and Emily knelt before him, looked up at his face, and waited for his guidance.

"We need to set a rule. Only one. Particularly important, though..." While he spoke, Ragden disentangled himself from Aria and walked around behind her. He reached down, took her hand, and pulled her to her feet. He stood behind her and pulled her against him. His hands were on her hips. Then he slid his hands up her stomach to gently grasp her breasts. Aria sighed

contently and purred to herself. Ragden's cock slipped between her legs, between her cheeks. It pushed across her asshole, then up through her pussy lips to push against her clitoris. He leaned down and whispered in her ear softly as he nibbled on her earlobe, "Tell them how much you like this... Tell them how good it is..."

Emily and Sarah looked up at Aria. They watched Ragden move against her, the look of pleasure on her face as he pulled her against him. Emily tried to imagine what it would be like to be in her place, to feel his hands on her. A shiver ran down her back at the prospect. She watched his cock throb between her legs. Aria hesitated. Her breath came quickly. Then she spoke up, her voice filled with submission and pleasure.

"It... It feels incredible," Aria breathed.

Ragden kissed Aria's ear and neck. His cock slid back and forth across her clit. She moaned in pleasure, her body shuddering. Her left hand was on her waist above the tip of his cock. Her right hand was between her breasts, trying to calm her heart as it hammered in her chest. He breathed in her ear, "Good, thank you."

Aria's pussy dripped with anticipation. A sublime smile filled her features at the kind words from Ragden. She turned and looked over her shoulder at him, her face filled with beautiful happiness.

"You're welcome," she breathed.

Ragden reached around and cupped Aria's breasts. His fingers found her nipples and tenderly caressed them while his cock slid back and forth through her folds. Ragden looked back at Sarah and Emily, "One rule. And only one. You cum when I tell you to. Not before. Cum early, and you are done. You will never get this. You will only be allowed to watch. Never engage..."

Aria could feel authority and control as it flowed off him. She moaned softly at the pressure between her legs; she ached for him to fill her again. She wanted more. She could feel her pressure and pleasure as it built within her like a wild storm, eager to break free, but she accepted his control. He pointed at Sarah and Emily, "Do you two understand?"

Confusion and curiosity flowed over Sarah and Emily's faces as they tried to understand the incredible power dynamic that was unfolding before them. They watched as Aria completely folded to Ragden's will. Her body hung on every word. Pure blissful joy on her face at the contact with this person they bullied so relentlessly for years. They shivered; fear and lust ran through their veins in equal doses. Sarah and Emily glanced at each other. They saw the same emotions playing on their faces. Then they turned back to Ragden.

"Yes," They said together, "We understand."

Ragden smiled, and they felt the warmth of it upon their skin like sunshine on a rainy day. They felt their hearts flutter. They grew more excited. Their pulses raced.

Ragden spoke, "Excellent... Then we can begin."

He nibbled softly on Aria's ear and neck. He kissed her shoulder as he

stepped backward from her. Eased his cock out from between her legs. Teased her folds. Passed over the opening of her pussy and across her asshole. She groaned; the desire etched strongly on her face. Ragden stepped up next to her and turned to look at her with compassion and care in his eyes, "You may sit, my dear, you have done well. Thank you."

Aria sat down. She felt relief and gratitude as Ragden stepped away from her. He had shown her incredible kindness and support. She watched as Ragden looked at her with compassion and care. She knew that he was now ready to focus on Sarah and Emily.

"Emily. Are you ready?"

Emily nodded hesitantly. Fear and anticipation flooded through her. She stood before him, unsure of what to expect but determined to find out. She looked at him. His strong body, the taught muscles of his chest and stomach. She had never seen him this way before. He had always been the weak one. The geek. The victim. What she saw now was nothing like that. She shivered at this revelation. She felt an almost magnetic attraction to him. A desire to be closer to him, to touch him.

"Yes... I am ready," she said quietly, "Whatever you want."

Ragden smiled, "Now those are magical words. Strip."

Emily gulped. She knew she had committed to this course. She wanted what Ragden had to offer. She looked down at her outfit and gulped. She closed her eyes and took a deep breath. She kneeled and untied her shoes, and slipped them off her feet. Then she stood and pulled her top over her head. With her eyes closed, she imagined she was alone in her bedroom at home. She unzipped her pants and slid them down her legs. She reached around behind her back and unclasped her bra, laying it next to her shirt and pants on the ground. Then she slid her panties off and laid them on the pile.

Emily looked up at Ragden. She held one hand over her groin, the other across her chest. She felt his gaze on her body and blushed. She saw a hungry look in Ragden's eyes. She could feel his desire as an almost palpable thing in the air. She felt herself growing damp. She looked at this throbbing manhood, and she wanted it. She wanted everything he could offer her. She blinked as she realized she wanted this so badly her legs were trembling.

He reached out and took her hand gently. He squeezed her fingers softly and pulled her to him. Emily's heart thundered in her chest. She felt the heat of his body, the power of his presence as it radiated from him. She put a hand on his chest and felt the strong beat of his heart within. She shivered slightly. With her body pulled tight against his, he whispered where only Emily and Aria could hear, "Shall we make Sarah watch or include her in this... lesson?"

Aria murmured, "Including Sarah would be... interesting. I think it would be an effective way to show them the consequences of their actions."

Ragden turned to Sarah, with Emily pressed against his side. "Ms. Sarah. What do you think? Have you been a bad girl? Have you been mean?"

Sarah looked at Ragden. She felt fear and embarrassment as it washed

through her. She was unsure of what to expect. She hesitated for a moment but then nodded her head. "Y-yes," she admitted softly, "I have been cruel. But I didn't think of it as that bad or anything..."

Ragden cocked his head sideways, like a bird considering a worm that just tried to talk to it, "Words are like toothpaste; once you say them, you cannot take them back. Words can leave scars deeper and more painful than any physical wound. Your words and actions have consequences."

Sarah looked at Ragden; realization slipped into her. She saw the mixture of power and control in Ragden's face. She knew that there was nothing she could do to change what she had said or done in the past.

"I understand," she whispered, "I've caused a lot of harm, and now I'm going to learn how to be better."

Ragden raised one arm, to take in all the crowd that were standing and watching. Most were still too shocked to move by the spectacle before them. "And what of these good people here? Shall we show them that you can change, that you can be better?"

Anticipation and excitement filled Sarah. She took a deep breath and looked around at the small crowd with fear and determination. She hesitated for a moment but then spoke up. "I... I am sorry," she said softly, "For being mean. I did not realize how much it hurt people... I... I promise to try harder... to be kinder... to be a better person."

Ragden considered Sarah's words, then said, "Sarah, are you ready to show the people that you can be better? Are you ready to display the depths of your desire?"

Sarah gulped, then nodded. Tears streamed down her face as she struggled to maintain some semblance of composure. She felt small and vulnerable. She knew she was now fully committed to the things to come. "Yes," she whispered, "I'm ready."

"Strip."

Sarah's eyes went wide, but she nodded. She felt the hot tears as they trickled down her face. She looked from Ragden to Emily and Aria. She saw them watching her, waiting to see if she would join them. Her heart thundered in her chest. She saw how happy Aria looked. She saw the nervousness on Emily's face. She gulped and tried to swallow in a dry throat. She nodded again to herself and started peeling off her clothes. She tried to ignore the stares of the crowd behind her. With shaking hands, she neatly piled her clothes next to Emily's. She stood, her arms folded across her stomach, and looked at Ragden.

Ragden looked over Sarah, from head to toe, considering her. He admired the swell of her hips, the small round shape of her breasts, the slickness of her pussy, and the small tuft of dark hair over her groin. He nodded, pleased. Aria watched as Ragden admired Sarah. Aria nodded, whispering to herself, "You look beautiful, Sarah; now, let's show everyone that you are ready to be a better person."

Ragden reached out his right hand to Sarah. She took his hand as he guided her to his side. He turned her around for everyone to see her body. She stood there, naked, and vulnerable, following his lead. She shivered as submission and vulnerability flowed through her. She accepted Ragden's guidance and control.

"This is... new for me," she whispered, "But I want to learn."

Ragden placed his right hand on her ass and pulled her against him. He trapped his large dick against her stomach. A gasp escaped her lips as his hard cock pressed against her. The heat and pressure of it made her squirm with discomfort and arousal. Then he licked her neck and tasted her salt, perspiration, anxiety, and nervousness. He nibbled on her ear as he slipped his hand around the swell of her ass. One finger slipped between her lips, the other caressed her asshole.

"Mmmph!" she said, "Ragden..."

His left hand slid around Emily's ass. A finger slipped into her pussy, and another into her asshole. He leaned over and nibbled on Sarah's ear, then growled, "Are you ready to get fucked in front of this good crowd?"

Aria watched as Ragden continued to assert his control over Sarah, pushing her deeper into a state of submission and vulnerability. She felt a mixture of arousal and power that flowed through her as she saw Sarah respond to Ragden's question. She could see the fear and anticipation on her face.

"Yes," Sarah breathed, "I want to show everyone that I'm changing."

Ragden turned to Emily and kissed her on the forehead. Then the nose and then softly on the lips. He looked her in the eyes and spoke softly to her, "Please prepare Sarah for me. Can you kiss her, love her, and finger her holes for me?"

Emily blushed and felt nervous, but excited and eager to play her part. "Of course," Emily agreed softly, "I'd be honored to do that for you."

Ragden stepped away from Emily and Sarah to stand next to Aria. A hand caressed Aria's cheek tenderly, affectionately. Then he knelt next to her and gently kissed her cheek and ear. He nuzzled her softly while he watched Sarah and Emily. As Ragden stepped back, Sarah sank to the ground, lying on her back, as Emily approached her.

Emily crawled over Sarah. She leaned down and gently kissed Sarah. Her lips pressed against Sarah's in a tender expression of love and care. Then she took her time, carefully inserting her fingers into Sarah's pussy and asshole. She tried to show the crowd the incredible change that Sarah was going to undergo as she learned to accept pleasure and submission. As Emily continued to lovingly touch Sarah, the small crowd watched in amazement, unable to believe what they were witnessing.

Ragden stood as Emily continued to gently administer care to Sarah. He walked around behind her and got down on his knees. He placed his hands on Emily's hips. He cupped her ass tenderly. Then he pressed his rock-hard

manhood between her legs. He slid it up through her lips and across her clit.

Emily's eyes bulged in surprise. Then she sighed at Sarah's mouth as she felt the immense heat and pressure against her folds. She shivered in anticipation, waiting for what would come next. Aria watched as Emily continued to lovingly touch Sarah; the two of them formed a powerful bond of affection and trust as they submitted themselves to Ragden's will. She felt excitement and arousal as she saw Ragden's cock pressed against Emily's pussy and clit.

Ragden leaned over Emily and pressed his chest against her back. His arms wrapped around her to gently caress her breasts. His teeth found her ear. As he nibbled on her, he growled through his teeth, "Are you ready?"

Emily nodded her head and accepted Ragden's request without hesitation. She could feel the mixture of vulnerability and submission as she prepared to accept his cock. She knew it would change her in ways she could not comprehend. She shivered. She was anxious, eager, and afraid of what would come next, but she was committed.

"Yes," Emily breathed, "I'm ready."

Ragden nodded, his movement slow against the back of her body. Emily felt the heat of his breath on her neck, the press of his body against her back. She felt warm and loved, and completely dominated. She ached to feel what he offered. Then he whispered in her ear, "Emily, I want your face in Sarah's pussy. Lick it. Taste it."

Emily moaned, feeling the heavy beat of Ragden's heart against her back. She felt the pressure of his cock against her labia. She nodded. She shifted her position, pressing herself against Ragden so she could lower herself against Sarah's body. She felt Ragden shift behind her, giving her room to move, but keeping himself against her. That incredible heat and comfort against her back, and groin made her feel like anything was possible. She placed her lips around Sarah's entrance. She hesitated for a moment, then opened her mouth, and began to suckle on Sarah's sensitive folds. She used her tongue to tease and pleasure Sarah.

Sarah's eyes closed, sweat breaking out on her brow. Her body tensed as she tried to accept the affection. It was more than she was prepared for. She could hear the crowd around her, watching. She could feel their eyes on her body. They watched every movement, every muscle. She felt exposed, vulnerable, and small. Then Emily's tongue entered her, and her eyes flew open. The pleasure was more than she had expected.

As Ragden watched Emily slip her tongue into Sarah, he tried to slide his massive dick into her. Emily's pussy was too tight. He pulled his cock back and slid it across her lips again, and again until her pussy was dripping wet. Then placed the head against her pussy and slid the tip into her.

Emily closed her eyes, and she gritted her teeth against the pain of the massive meat pushing into her. She gasped as it slid into her. Filled her in ways she never dreamed possible. Her heart hammered in her chest. She heard

the gasps of the crowd. Fear, pain, and pleasure washed over her. She struggled with it and tried to accept it. She knew she had asked for this. She wanted it but was overwhelmed by it.

Pleasure and pain played across Emily's face as Ragden slid deeper into her. Emily then remembered the beautiful pussy before her and hungrily ran her tongue through the folds. Sarah groaned in response and clutched her breasts. Then Ragden started to withdraw from Emily. She groaned, felt her insides collapse around the hole left by his massive dick. She looked over her shoulder and saw Ragden kneeling behind her.

Ragden stood and offered his hand to Emily. She groaned as she saw his massive cock, dripping with her fluids. Her mind reeled at the size of it, the realization that it had been inside her and was still wet, because of her. She swallowed in a dry mouth as she looked up at him. Then she took his hand and stood, a slight tremble running down her legs as she did.

Ragden's gaze took in all of Emily. He looked over her, from head to toe. He raised her hand and spun her around. Then he held her hand for her to face him. He closed his eyes, sniffing the air, sniffing her. A frown crossed his face. He opened his eyes, and his gaze pierced. Emily shivered before that gaze. She felt as if her soul had been pulled out to be examined. She felt his gaze upon her very core.

"Emily, you have taken the first step... Would you like more? Would you accept my help?"

Sarah watched closely. She felt envy and admiration as she saw Emily being offered such an incredible opportunity for change and transformation. She knew that Emily was now at a critical juncture. That her answer would determine whether she too would be able to experience the incredible power and satisfaction that Ragden had to offer. Emily hesitated for a moment. She struggled with the decision. Then she nodded slowly.

"Yes," Emily whispered, "I want... your help."

Ragden leaned down and kissed her softly on the lips, tasted her. Emily sighed in pleasure, feeling the gentleness and love in the soft caress against her skin. Ragden then kissed along her jaw and then her ear. He whispered to her, "Good. Asking for help is but the first step..."

Emily smiled, tentatively, nervous. Aria watched Ragden kiss Emily. She could already see a change in Emily's poise under his attention, something subtle. As if the affection of this one person somehow made her worthy of such attention. That worthiness filled her with the belief that she could be a better person.

Ragden brought Emily's hand up to his face. He kissed her knuckles, softly, then he turned her around. He pulled her body firmly against his own. His penis was now trapped between her ass cheeks, the tip of it pressed against the small of her back. He reached around her and grasped her breasts. He pulled her more tightly against him. She could feel the tremendous heat coming off his body. She felt the steady beat of his heart against her back. She

felt the warmth and the heat. She felt the press of his cock against her back, the massiveness of it spreading her checks. She shivered, vulnerable, yet eager. He squeezed her nipples as he kissed her left ear. He nibbled on her earlobes.

He whispered into her ear, "Do you like this? Do you want more?"

Sarah watched in awe as she saw Emily's response to the incredible sensations. She could see the vulnerability and desire that passed over her friend's face. She knew that Ragden was determined to use every means to transform her into the person she wanted to be. Sarah felt excitement and anticipation as she watched the transformation unfold before her very eyes. She felt a growing sense of envy and desire for the same opportunity.

Emily breathed huskily, her breath hitched, "Yes... Please..."

Ragden drew his hips back from Emily's ass and took a hand to guide his cock between her legs. He slid the tip of it across her asshole. Paused there, circled the tight hole. Emily squeezed her eyes shut, felt the heat against her ass. Then he moved it forward between her labia and pressed against her clit. She felt the pressure against her and moaned softly. He squeezed her breasts between his fingers. Pinched them softly as he put teeth to her neck, applying gentle pressure.

Ragden squeezed Emily's breasts tighter and pinched her nipples more forcefully. She gasped in response. Pleasure and pain coursed through her body. His cock thumped against her clit. It slid up and down as he growled in her ear, "Emily, tell me you like this... Do you want more?"

As she felt the incredible pressure of his cock sliding against her clit, Emily moaned in response.

"Yes..." she breathed, "I want more."

Ragden loosened his grip on Emily's breasts. He still pinched her nipples, but not as hard. He moved his head to the other side of her neck and used his chin to brush her hair out of the way. Then he placed his teeth on her neck. He growled against her skin, "Emily, use your hands. Guide my cock into your pussy..."

As Ragden released his grip on Emily's breasts, Sarah watched as Emily took advantage of the opportunity to guide Ragden's cock towards her pussy. Determination and vulnerability passed across her face. Emily shivered with anticipation and a little fear, not sure she could take something so large into her. Her heart beat faster. She felt this was some kind of test she must pass. Sarah licked her lips, wondering if she could handle the incredible intensity of it when her turn came.

Ragden waited patiently, as Emily slid his massive cock back through her folds. She placed the tip at her entrance. Then he squeezed her breasts again, pinching the nipples gently while he growled against her neck. "Emily, are you ready? Can you accept me into you?"

Emily felt the heat and pressure against her entrance. She felt the size of his meat in her hands. Surely, something so large could not fit into the small hole between her legs. Her heart hammered in her chest. She felt sweat

breaking out on her brow. She looked at Sarah and felt her eyes growing wider as the pressure against her increased. She knew the only way she could survive this was to surrender to it. She forced herself to take a deep breath, to try to calm her frantic heart. Emily nodded her head, showing her readiness. She bit her lip, trying to prepare herself for what came next.

"Yes," Emily breathed, "I'm ready."

Ragden shifted his hips, pushed the head of his cock against her pussy. He forced it to open enough to allow him in. Once inside, he stopped and paused. Emily's eyes watered. Her face flushed with the arousal and pressure inside her. Ragden then released Emily's breasts. He reached across her chest with one arm and pulled her tightly against him. With his other hand, he reached out to Sarah. Holding his hand out, gesturing for her to stand.

Sarah watched in awe as she saw the incredible power and control Ragden exuded as he forced his way inside Emily. She also felt excitement and anticipation as she prepared to stand. She took Ragden's hand. She stood before them; fear and anticipation filled her. Ragden lifted his head from Emily's neck and looked Sarah in the eyes.

"Sarah, kiss Emily on the lips, place your hands on her breasts, feel her as I fill her..."

As the words left his lips, Ragden slid his cock an inch deeper into Emily. He savored the tightness of her tiny pussy. Sarah looked at Emily, then leaned in to kiss her deeply on the lips. She felt the incredible energy that flowed between them as Ragden's cock filled Emily's pussy. She knew that she was about to experience the sensation of being so close to Ragden's incredible member as he continued to fill Emily. As Sarah placed her hands on Emily's breasts, she could feel the warmth and fullness of them. She felt excitement and anticipation as she waited for Ragden's next command.

Emily moaned, feeling the pressure inside her body. The fullness of Ragden's cock filled her. She felt his heart as it beat against her back. She looked at Sarah and saw the intensity in her gaze. Felt her hands on her chest. As they kissed, she felt the softness of Sarah's lips on hers. Her heart hammered in her chest while her pussy dripped with arousal.

While Sarah and Emily kissed, Ragden slid the rest of his cock into Emily. He filled her fully. Sarah and Emily continued to kiss passionately, as they felt the incredible intensity of the moment. Emily slipped a hand between her legs and felt the heat and wetness of her pussy stretched around Ragden's dick. Ragden ground his hips against Emily's ass and pressed his cock against her cervix. Emily gasped at Sarah's mouth; the kiss became fiercer and more needy.

Ragden continued to grind his teeth across Emily's neck while he moved his hands to her hips, to steady her body as he slowly pumped his cock in and out of her. Deep, long strokes. Pulled back to the tip, then he slowly slid in and caressed her cervix with his cock. Pain and pleasure played across Emily's

face as she struggled to maintain her composure in the face of such intense sensations.

Ragden guided Emily's hands into Sarah's groin and slipped them through the wet folds to find her clit. Then Ragden moved his hands up Sarah's abdomen and gently grabbed her breasts. He pulled her against Emily. Sarah moaned into Emily's mouth in response. Meanwhile, he continued his long deep strokes, pumping his cock in and out of Emily. Each stroke, a gentle caress of his cock against her cervix. Sarah and Emily gasped and sighed at each other. They surrendered to the pleasure guided to them by Ragden. Emily's eyes squeezed shut; her body rocked with each gentle thrust inside her. Sarah felt herself grow wetter and more aroused as she watched Emily's body rock against Ragden.

Ragden released Sarah's breasts and moved his hands back to Emily's hips to steady her, as he increased his pace. He pumped his cock faster in and out of her. Each stroke pushed against her cervix, nearly lifting her off the ground. Sarah sighed, disappointed as Ragden released her. She wanted his hands on her, but she felt a growing sense of excitement and arousal as she watched Emily's body respond to his incredible movements. Her eyes went a little wide as Emily was nearly lifted off the ground.

Then Ragden moved his hands under Emily's thighs. He lifted her off the ground, spread her legs for all to see her pussy engorged with his massive cock. The soft spread of her red pubic hair was visible. He lifted her, allowed his cock to slide partially out. Then he lowered her against it and pushed deep into her again. Sarah watched in awe, as she saw Emily's incredibly engorged pussy. Emily closed her eyes as embarrassment and vulnerability flowed through her. She knew everyone could see her most intimate parts. She bit her lip as she rode down his massive cock. She moaned as it hit her deepest parts. She surrendered to it. She embraced the sensations. Her breath came faster.

Ragden pulled his teeth off Emily's neck and locked eyes with Sarah, "Lick Emily's pussy. Feel my cock insider her with your tongue."

Sarah's mouth dropped open; the incredible intensity of Ragden's gaze made her sweat. Her pussy dripped with arousal. She bit her lip, then knelt between Emily's legs. Sarah leaned into Emily's wet pussy and ran her tongue over Ragden's balls and through Emily's folds. The taste of it lingered on her tongue. She moaned against the raw power and intensity of it. She leaned into Emily's snatch. Her hands were on Emily's thighs, spread them wider so she could run her tongue over Emily's folds as Ragden slid in and out of her. Emily gasped in short bursts, "Oh fuck...fuck fuck fuck fuck"

As Sarah licked Emily's incredibly sensitive folds, she felt pleasure and excitement as she tasted the sweet nectar of Emily's pussy. She could feel Ragden's cock as it slid into Emily's cervix. Sarah ran her tongue down through Emily's folds. She found the base of Ragden's shaft. She ran her tongue around it and over his balls as he lifted Emily partially off. Then she slid her tongue up his shaft as Emily slid back down. Her tongue ran up

through Emily's folds to her clit.

Ragden increased the pace of his movements. Huge, deep strokes, each pushed up against her cervix. He raked his teeth across Emily's shoulders, leaving angry red lines as he continued to slide his cock into and out of her.

He continued to pump faster, harder, as deep as he could go. A look of frustration crossed Emily's face. Her body convulsed with the desire to cum but tried to hold it back. Like a dam held with a scramble of branches, she fought it. The incessant pumping inside her drove her wild. Emily gasped for air; tears streamed down her cheeks as she tried to hold back the incredible pleasure. She let out small whimpers of pleasure, betraying her desire to break free from Ragden's control.

"Please... I need to cum..." Emily moaned softly.

Ragden growled against her skin, "Not yet." He withdrew his cock from her incredibly tight pussy and placed her feet back on the ground. He spun her around. She gazed into his eyes; there was no mercy there. Her need and desire were plain to see on her face, but he denied her request, "You do not get to cum yet."

Emily's pussy dripped with desire. Her expression was intense, as she struggled to contain it. Emily gasped for air, her beautiful chest heaving with the effort to contain her pent-up climax and desires. She let out small whimpers of pleasure, "Please... I need to cum..."

Ragden placed a gentle hand on her chest, pushed her towards the ground, and insisted she lay down. He crawled over her, spread her legs, "I know you do, and I will let you... but not yet..."

He spread her legs, pressing the head of his cock against her ass. Then ran it up through her pussy lips, collected her dripping juices, and pushed them around. Then he put his cock against her ass again. Emily continued to gasp for air; her chest heaved with the effort to contain herself as she continued to whimper.

Ragden pushed the head of his cock against her ass, but she was too tight. He grabbed her hips and pulled her against him, forcing her to allow him in. Then the tip slipped in. He released her hips and leaned over her. His cock was only just barely inside of her. He kissed her breasts, one at a time. Then her neck and chin. Then he moved down and clamped his mouth over her right breast, squeezing her nipple with his teeth as he slid his cock fully up her ass.

Emily let out a moan of pleasure, despite her efforts to maintain her composure. She felt Ragden's cock finally enter her incredibly tight ass. It stretched her unbelievably, "Oh fuck..."

With his cock fully into her ass, Ragden ground his hips against her. He pushed his cock around inside her ass, pushed her limits, felt her need. Then he withdrew, and slid home again... then again, faster, and faster. Pain and discomfort washed over Emily. The pleasure she never knew existed. She rocked her hips against Ragden's, meeting each stroke, pushing him deeper

into her.

Ragden increased the pace. He watched in satisfaction as Emily's breasts rocked with each massive thrust. His hips bounced off her thighs. Emily moaned, unable to resist the incredible pleasure that washed over her. She felt Ragden's cock as it drove deep into her incredibly tight ass, pushing her boundaries, "Fuuuck!"

Ragden drove his cock deep into her ass and pushed his massive length all the way home. His hips ground against Emily's tight ass. Ragden leaned forward against her ass and drove his cock into her. He rocked her hips up into the air; her legs now bounced as hard as her breasts with each massive thrust of his cock into her ass. He slid nearly out and then completely in, grounding her organs with his massive cock.

Then Ragden reached down and picked Emily up off the ground. He pulled her legs around him. He used her weight to drive his cock deep into her ass. He licked her face. Kissed her lips fiercely. Then he bucked against her, partially withdrawing his cock, and slid it home again. Then he did it again. He latched his teeth onto her throat, squeezed the soft tissue, and growled against her skin.

Emily's expression intensified as she fought against the sensations, trying to maintain her control. Ragden picked Emily up, off his cock, and set her on her feet in front of him. He kissed her gently on the lips, dipping his tongue in to taste her sweetness. Then he looked her in the eyes. Saw the pain and intensity there.

A tear slipped down Emily's cheek as she bit her lip, "Please... I need to cum."

Ragden gently turned Emily around. He bent her over and beckoned Sarah to come over and hold her hands. Sarah stood in front of Emily and took her hands in her own. She gazed down at Emily's stricken face. Then Ragden placed his hands on her hips and slid his cock into her wet pussy. He gently slid it home, against her cervix, ground it against her. He felt her clench against him.

Emily gasped as Ragden's cock slid deep into her. She felt the immensity of it fill her up as it hit her deepest depths. She could feel her control slipping. It was too much. She clenched Sarah's hands, her knuckles going white. She moaned softly, "Oh god... Please..."

Ragden leaned forward against her. His body leaned against her. Warm, comforting. His heart thundered against her back. He whispered in her ear, against her skin, his breath hot, "Cum now."

Ragden continued to slide his cock deep into Emily's pussy, repeatedly, until she screamed as the climax overtook her. The scream was ripped from her throat as her body shuddered and twitched uncontrollably. Her orgasm was truly a remarkable sight. Her juices overflowed. Cum streamed from between her legs, soaking Ragden's massive cock, still rammed up into her. The massive bulge was there for all to see.

Ragden leaned over Emily's back. He kissed her neck tenderly and comforted her body as she twitched. He grasped her breasts gently as he pulled her body against his. He held her softly as the trembling slowed. Sarah released Emily's hands, as Ragden comforted her. Sarah blinked back tears from the intensity of the climax she just witnessed. She sank to her heels, exhausted just watching it.

Emily's body slowly came down from its intense orgasmic high. She began to catch her breath. Her heart raced, and her body still quivered slightly. She felt Ragden's gentle kisses on her back and neck, which provided a sense of comfort amidst the chaos of emotions that swirled within her. As she regained some measure of control, she realized how much she had given herself over to this incredible experience. She looked up at Ragden; their eyes met for a moment before Emily whispered, "Thank you..."

Ragden whispered against her skin, "You are welcome." Then slowly, inch-by-incredible-inch, slid his cock free of her pussy. It twitched and throbbed between her legs. Ragden held her hand gently to keep her from falling. Then he allowed her to settle to the ground, slowly, gracefully.

Emily looked up at Ragden. Her eyes filled with gratitude and a hint of vulnerability. She felt the warmth and care as he held her hand and ensured her safety after the intense climax. Relief and exhaustion washed over her as she lay on the ground, trying to catch her breath. She tried to come to terms with everything that had happened.

"Thank you," she whispered weakly, her voice barely audible. Ragden nodded.

CHAPTER 3

Ragden turned to Sarah. He locked eyes with her. She shivered under his gaze. Fear and anticipation were stark on her face.

"Sarah. Are you ready?"

She hesitated for a moment. Everything she had just seen played through her mind. She wanted this. She was nervous, anxious, fearful, but ready. She took the next step.

"Yes," she whispered, her voice barely audible.

Ragden took her hand, softly in his. He spun her around to face the crowd. Then pulled her against his chest. He ran his hands across her firm, small breasts. A wave of electricity coursed through her body. She felt fear and anticipation as his hands slid down along her stomach to her groin. Her eyes swept the crowd. She tried to communicate she was ready as his fingers slipped into her folds. He dipped them slightly between them. He felt her moisture. He whispered against her neck. His lips brushed her skin, "Are you ready to show these people here who you CAN be?"

Sarah gasped at the feeling of his breath on her neck. She shivered involuntarily feeling the excitement that built within her. "Yes," she whispered, her voice quiet.

Ragden continued to speak against her neck. His breath was hot on her skin. She felt herself grow damp. Her heart raced.

"Let's show these good people that you aren't the bully you once were, that you can be a better person..."

Sarah nodded, fear and anticipation racing through her. She bit her lip as she tried to mentally prepare herself for what was to come. She knew Ragden had full control over her mind and body. She trusted him to guide her through this incredible journey. She stood tall and lifted her chin proudly as she looked out at the crowd. She was determined to prove to them that she could be a better person and that she was fully committed.

"I'm ready," she whispered.

Ragden placed one hand on her stomach and pulled her against him. His cock was tight between her ass cheeks. It pressed into her back, still slick with Emily's juices. His other hand slipped between her legs. His fingers gingerly slipped through her labia and stroked her clitoris. Ragden's voice was a growl against her skin. It was insistent, commanding. His teeth nipped at her earlobe.

"Louder. Tell these people you want this."

Sarah took a deep breath. She felt Ragden's heart thump against her back, rhythmic and powerful. It consumed her and comforted her. Her voice grew stronger as she spoke to the crowd; her words rang with conviction and determination.

"I want this," she said loudly, her voice carried throughout the hall, "I want to show everyone that I've changed and that I'm no longer the person I used to be."

As Ragden's hand on her stomach pulled her firmly against him, his cock between her cheeks, she moaned softly. She felt the heat and pressure of it against her sensitive skin. She felt his fingers stroke through her pussy, sending waves of pleasure that coursed through her.

Sarah gasped as Ragden's tongue licked her neck, flicked her earlobes, and kissed softly. Shivers of pleasure rolled through her as he whispered in her ear, "Good girl."

She smiled; his praise washed over her, fueling her desire to please him and fulfill his every command. Then he slid his fingers out of her. She groaned, aching for him not to stop. As Ragden guided his big dick between her cheeks, the air hissed out of her lungs as the massive size of it pressed against her ass. She fought not to lift on her toes, to pull away, and almost failed. Then it moved into her pussy lips. It slid up along her. Pressed against her clit. The heat and pressure of it against her drove her wild with anticipation. She turned her head to look up at him. She looked into his eyes and tried to convey her total submission. She realized she was at his mercy and that nothing would stop her from embracing this journey.

"Thank you," she whispered.

Ragden nodded against her. Then he whispered against her neck, "Let's show these good people what your pussy looks like when it is properly filled."

Sarah gasped as Ragden's cock pressed against her pussy lips. The incredible heat and pressure of it drove her wild with desire. She felt his words washing over her. Without hesitation, she spread her legs wide apart. She allowed the audience to get a clear view of her completely exposed pussy. It glistened with arousal and anticipation. The sparse black hair matted to her skin. She bit her lip nervously as she waited for Ragden to finally enter her. To claim her completely. His cock was poised at her opening, but not inside... so close...

"Please...," she whimpered.

She felt the heavy thump of Ragden's heart against her back. His approval seeped from his skin into hers. She closed her eyes, as his lips brushed her skin, "Since you asked so nicely..."

Sarah gasped as Ragden's massive cock finally pushed past her pussy lips. She moaned as it stretched her and filled her. She felt the incredible pressure and heat of it as it filled her to the brim and stretched her walls to their limit. She bit her lower lip even more nervously and felt the mix of pain and pleasure that washed over her.

"Thank you," she whispered.

Ragden whispered huskily against her skin. His voice was deep and seductive. It hinted at things she had yet to experience. Promised they would come, "See what happens when you ask nicely?"

Sarah turned her head and looked at Ragden. Her eyes filled with gratitude and submission as his massive cock filled her. She felt a sense of pride wash over her for having been able to show the crowd that she could do this. That she was no longer the bully she once was.

"Yes," she whispered to Ragden.

In response, he ground his hips against her ass. He slid his cock into her depths. She gasped, as his cock pushed into her cervix, sending a wave of intense pleasure coursing through her body. She could feel his hands under her thighs. As he lifted her feet from the ground. Sarah looked at Ragden with gratitude and submission. She surrendered to him and allowed him to take control. She felt the freedom, the joy of it coursed through her. Her heart hammered in her chest as she whispered to him again, "Thank you."

Ragden spread her legs wide, so the crowd could see her exposed pussy, filled with his massive cock. She felt filled to the brim with it. Embarrassment and vulnerability washed over her as she realized the entire crowd was now fixated on her. They witnessed her transformation. She clutched one hand to her chest and felt her heart as it beat frantically, like a caged animal. The other hand slid down her stomach. Slipped through her folds. She felt how wide she was stretched. Felt the base of Ragden's enormous cock as it filled her. She bit her lip and held her gasp back as she ran her fingers around his girth. Then she looked at the crowd, and whispered to them, "I'm sorry if this makes anyone uncomfortable."

Ragden shifted his position, his cock pushed against her cervix, then slipped past. Sarah's breath was suddenly pushed from her lungs. Her eyes went wild and wide. She struggled to gasp for air and found it harder than she thought. The pressure in her abdomen defied anything she thought possible. Her body tensed up; her muscles fought her. Sarah's hand slid down her chest to the bulge in her stomach. She felt it against her skin. Breathlessly, she whispered, "This is... unexpected."

Ragden's breath against her skin was strained with the effort of his actions. Yet his voice was steady and strong. His lips moved against her, caressing her, "You saw me do this to Aria and Emily. Did you not think I would do the

same for you?"

Sarah's mind raced. She remembered; she could not get the images out of her mind. She had wondered what it would feel like. If she could handle it. Now she was. It made her feel giddy. She tried to inhale, unable to get a full breath. This changed everything. Her heart hammered in her chest, as she choked the word out, "Yes."

Ragden spoke again, his lips against her skin, "Is this what you wanted?"

Sarah nodded. Her eyes swept the crowd. She felt the incredible pressure and heat of his cock as it pushed deeper into her abdomen. Grey started to creep into the edges of her vision. "Yes," she whispered, her voice barely audible. A single tear slipped down her cheek.

Ragden growled against her skin, insistent. His hands gripped her thighs more firmly. She shivered at the intensity of it. His breath was hot on her back. The vibration of his voice made her heart speed up, "I don't think they can hear you."

Sarah looked up at Ragden. She realized that her voice was barely audible. She felt the incredible pressure and heat of his cock as it pushed deep into her abdomen. She tried to take a breath but found herself almost unable to do so. She realized she needed to be heard. She tried to get a good breath, and spoke louder, "Yes, I'm fully committed to this journey."

Ragden nodded against her shoulder. His breath was husky in her ear, "And what do you want?"

Sarah struggled to take another breath. She was overwhelmed by the sensation of her insides pushed around. Her pussy stretched to its limits. Her fingers clutched at the massive bulge in her abdomen, "I want to be your perfect little slut," she said softly, her voice carrying throughout the hall for all to hear, "I want to serve you and fulfill your every need. Please use me however you see fit."

Ragden ground his hips against hers. She gasped. Ragden growled against her skin, "But what do you want right now?"

Sarah spoke softly, voice barely audible again, "I want you to cum inside me. Fill me with your hot, sticky seed. Make me your perfect little whore."

Ragden chuckled softly against her back, "I am not sure you have earned that right. First, I want to see how much you can take before you cum... Are you ready for that?"

Sarah gasped as Ragden ground his hips against her. She felt the position of his cock shift inside her. She felt the heat and pressure of it inside her. She knew she must answer his question honestly if she wanted to continue.

"Yes," she whispered, "I'm ready."

Ragden nodded, "Then let us begin..."

Sarah closed her eyes. She braced herself for the incredible sensations that she was about to experience. Fear and anticipation ran through her. Then she gasped as Ragden slowly raised her. His cock slid inch by inch out of her. She gulped at the air, filling her lungs.

"Please," she whispered, urgently, "Make me your perfect little cum dumpster."

Even though the presence of his cock overwhelmed her, and almost suffocated her as it slid out of her, she ached to feel it again. Then he lowered her back onto it. She took a quick breath and tried to fill her lungs as it slid deeper into her. She felt the air pushed out of her lungs in a rush. She gasped in shock at the intensity of it. Filled, she sighed and embraced the discomfort and vulnerability.

"Oh, God," she whispered, "I'm yours."

Ragden breathed against her back. His voice was deep, soothing, "You always were, you just didn't know it yet..."

He kissed her neck and back as he raised her again. She gasped at the intensity of his passion and domination as it washed over her like a warm wave. Then he slid her back down onto his cock. Slid it just as deep into her again.

"Yes," she whispered, "I'm yours forever."

Ragden whispered against her skin, insistent, "Just follow my one rule..."

He moved more quickly now. In and out. Deep strokes. Filled her body with his cock. Her mind reeled, trying to grasp the situation. The intensity of his cock as it slid in and out of her washed away everything else. There was something important, but the sliding of his cock inside her drove it out of her reach.

"What's your rule?" she asked softly.

Ragden lowered her against his cock and pushed the air out of her lungs again. She gasped for breath as he spoke against her neck, "Have you forgotten already?"

Sarah clutched her chest. She thumped it hard, trying to get enough air to think clearly. Her other hand clutched at the bulge in her abdomen. She could feel the throb of Ragden's cock in her body. Her mind reeled. She scrambled to remember the words he had spoken before. Her legs twitched. Waves of discomfort and pleasure rolled over her.

"No," she breathed, "I haven't forgotten."

Ragden spoke softly against her back, "It is okay, my beautiful little angel; I will remind you..." His voice soothed and comforted her. She struggled to fill her lungs with air but found herself relaxing. Her muscles no longer strained against him, "You cannot cum until I tell you..."

Ragden kissed the back of her neck. Grazed her skin with his teeth. Then he nipped at her earlobe. While he raised her and lowered her down onto his cock again. Pain and pleasure washed over her. Vulnerability and submission consumed her.

"Okay," she whispered, "I won't cum without your permission."

Ragden chuckled at her. He raised her slowly up off his cock; the pressure moved lower in her body but never left it. She took a deep breath, welcome for the relief, but ached to be filled. Unable to believe how badly she wanted it

back in her. The pain and pleasure consumed her desire for breath. His voice licked her back, sending shivers through her, "We shall see if you can keep to that..."

Sarah gasped again as Ragden slid his cock deep inside her. The breath pressed from her lungs. She marveled at the way her pussy stretched around his immensity. Her vagina accommodated something so large. Her guts shifted to allow this invasion of her body. Pain, and pleasure. Mixed to form ecstasy. Vulnerability and discomfort, a mix of emotions she had never expected to feel yet presented to her in a way she could not reject and accept willingly.

"I'll try," she whispered, "I'll do anything for you."

Ragden kissed her back tenderly. Nipped at her flesh with his teeth. His tenderness and passion caused her to gasp in surprise. The insistence of his cock as it slid in and out of her, was in stark contrast with the tenderness of his presence at her back. Unable to reconcile her emotions, Sarah turned her head to Ragden and whispered, "I love you."

Ragden spoke softly against her skin, his voice a gentle, understanding caress, "You don't even know me. I was just another person you bullied at school. No... what you love is this..."

With that, he started to move faster, slid his cock in and out of her. The impact of it caused her breasts to bounce, "And that is okay; I am glad you are enjoying it."

Sarah gasped as Ragden moved faster within her. Built a rhythm. She matched it. She inhaled as he drew out. Exhaled out as he pushed in. She felt the pressure as it built within her and knew she must keep herself under control.

"Yes," she whispered, "I enjoy being with you."

Ragden gently lowered her feet to the ground. Her legs shook. Ragden placed his hands on her hips, braced her, and held her as he slowly slid his cock out of her. Sarah gasped again; she felt the wet trail of stickiness and heat left behind. Pressure and passion washed over her. Sarah's legs trembled, and she placed her hands on him. Felt his strength. She looked over her shoulder and spoke softly, "Thank you."

Ragden smiled a predatory smile. He licked his lips as he gazed at her. His voice was low, sensual. It caressed her skin. It caused her to shiver in anticipation, "We aren't done yet, my dear; we have much yet to do..."

Sarah looked at Ragden, her eyes filled with anticipation and vulnerability. She closed her eyes as the pressure and heat of his passion washed over her like a warm wave. She smiled, eager for whatever would come next.

"What's next?" she asked softly. She heard the need and desire in her voice, surprised by the sound of it.

Ragden stepped in front of her, only an inch between their bodies. Sarah gasped as his cock pressed against her stomach. It twitched and throbbed, as she looked down at it. She marveled at the size of it. Tried to grapple with the

idea that it had been inside her and would again. Ragden slid his hand up her sides, cupped her breasts gently, and squeezed her nipples. Shivers ran down her back at his caress, and she bit her lip as he leaned in to kiss her softly on the lips.

"Mm," she moaned against his lips, feeling her body ache for his touch. Ragden's tongue slipped between her lips and tasted her sweetness. She felt herself go damp at the taste of him and the taste of her on his lips and tongue. She felt his arms pull her against him. She felt his cock pressed against her stomach. It left a wet trail of heat behind that seemed to seep into her skin. She wrapped her arms around his neck and pulled him into her.

"Kiss me harder," she whispered against his lips.

Ragden smiled and whispered back against her, "As you wish..."

Sarah gasped as Ragden's mouth claimed hers in a fierce kiss. His tongue dove deep into her mouth. Explored every corner and taste bud. She felt his cock pressed against her stomach. The incredible heat and pressure of it washed over her like a warm wave.

"More," she whispered.

Ragden wrapped his arms around her, and gently lowered her to the ground. She gasped at the cold, hard feel of the concrete beneath her hands. Ragden knelt between her legs. Leaned against her. His balls resting on her pussy. His cock pressed against her stomach. His chest against her breasts. He kissed her even harder, pressed into her. Sarah trembled at the pressure and heat of him. She squirmed with desire at the pressure of his cock against her. "Kiss me harder," she whispered.

With one hand, Ragden guided the tip of his cock through the slick folds of her pussy. He placed the head of it against her vagina. She gasped and felt the heat and pressure as it surged through her. Desire whipped her inhibitions from her mind. She rocked her hips and tried to pull it inside her but failed. Ragden kissed her harder; his tongue licked every bit of her mouth while his cock teased the edge of her.

"Please," she whispered; the need and desire drove her wild. Her pulse hammered in her chest.

With the slightest of flicks of his hips, Ragden slid the tip of his cock into her. Sarah gasped as it slid in, then gasped again as Ragden grabbed her breasts and squeezed them, pinched her nipples. Then he leaned in and pressed his lips to hers. His tongue invaded her mouth. Her body was driven to the brink of madness from her desire. She tried again to rock her hips, to bring that cock deeper into her, but failed. She reached out and grabbed his ass, desperately tried to pull him into her, to no avail.

"More," she whispered urgently.

Sarah gasped as Ragden's cock started to slide deeper into her vagina. The incredible heat and pressure of it caused her to squirm with desire. She felt his hands still clutching at her breasts. He caused them to ache with pleasure and pain. She felt her climax as it built with each inch of him that slid deeper into

her.

"Please let me cum," she whispered as she felt the incredible passion and heat building in intensity. It threatened to overwhelm her, "Let me cum for you."

Ragden shook his head, "Not yet."

Sarah's heart raced. Her breath became ragged with the strain of it. She fought to maintain some semblance of control, of composure. Still, Ragden slowly slid inch by inch into her. She squirmed, trying to buck her hips against him, anything to make it go faster. Nothing worked. She wanted to scream but knew that even that small release would be too much.

"Please..." she whimpered, "I need to cum."

Ragden closed his eyes, savored the feel of Sarah's tight pussy as it clenched and unclenched along his massive cock as he slid fully inside her. Sarah gasped again, as it slid past her cervix into her abdomen. It filled her like she never believed possible. She had felt it before, but this was somehow different. Pinned to the ground, his weight held her. She thrashed and tried to do something to make it move within her. Ragden held himself still against her. The only thing she could feel moving was the throbbing twitch of his heart beating the length of his cock inside her. That maddening steady rhythm drove her wild.

"Don't cum yet..." he commanded her.

Sarah groaned and moaned, trying to stay strong. She felt her barriers start to slip; her control was almost gone. She could not lose. She must fight; a tear slipped out of her eyes, and it left a cool track across her burning skin. Another sensation added to all of it. It was too much!

"Why?" she whimpered, begging for release, "Tell me why I shouldn't cum."

Ragden looked at her. Watched her fight. Watched her desire ravage her. He spoke slowly, purposefully, "If you cum now, I'll never fuck you again... I'll make you watch while I fuck all your friends, but never you. This is my punishment if you choose to disobey..."

Sarah gasped; her eyes wide as Ragden's words sunk in. Fear and arousal wash over her. She felt his cock buried deep inside her. It twitched and throbbed within her. She squirmed with desire. She fought, and understanding burned within her. To know this, and never be allowed it again. A punishment worse than death. She nodded and bit her lip.

"I understand," she whispered, "I won't cum unless you give me permission."

Ragden nodded solemnly, "Good."

Sarah sighed as Ragden's words confirmed her understanding. Relief and anticipation coursed through her. She continued to squirm; her body still fought her. The edges of her climax threatened to overwhelm her.

"May I cum now," she whispered, "Please say yes."

Ragden drew his cock slowly out of her, to the edge, then slid it home.

Sarah gasped, and the incredible heat and pressure surged inside her. He continued to build a rhythm. Huge, massive strokes, that shook her body. Her breasts rolled beneath his hands. She slid her hands to her abdomen, where she could feel each thrust, the bulge riding up under her hands.

Sarah's breathing fell into a rhythm. Her hips rocked against Ragden's thrusts. Her voice small and vulnerable, begged for release, "Please... I need to cum."

Ragden's response, as he moved with her, as he drove harder, faster, "Not yet..."

Sarah reached out, grasping at Ragden's sweat-slickened body as he continued to slide his cock in and out of her. Her breath was ragged. Her desire and restraint stripped her defenses. Then she cried out as Ragden suddenly pulled himself completely out of her. He poised himself over her, his cock dripped with her juices over her stomach. Her skin tingled at the sensation. Her hips continued to buck.

"You're going to make me wait longer?" she pleaded, agony in her voice, "Can't I cum now? Please?"

Ragden shook his head, "Not yet..."

Then used his hand to guide his cock back through the folds of her pussy. This time lower, to her asshole. She shivered with dread, fear, and excitement. Still dripping with her juices, he drew it around her asshole, teased her. "Are you ready," he asked.

Sarah took a gulp and tried to find her voice. She clutched her chest. Her heart hammered. Her climax was still at the edge of her consciousness. It ached to be released.

"Yes," she whispered, I'm ready."

Still not allowing her anything, Ragden watched her squirm, "Tell me you want this."

Sarah squeezed her breasts. Her muscles clenched with the force of holding herself together. Her breath still ragged as she waited for him to fill her. She could feel his cock, pressed to her ass, but not inside. She ached to be filled, to feel every inch of it in her.

"Yes," she whimpered, "I want this."

Ragden continued to drag the tip of his cock over her asshole, around it, pressed against it. Her body shivered in anticipation and glistened with perspiration. Ragden growled above her, "What do you want exactly? Say the words..."

Fear, excitement, and arousal coursed through every cell of Sarah's being. It overwhelmed her. She bit her lip, tears on her cheeks. She dug her fingers into her breasts, relishing the pain, and bringing her back to reality.

"I want your cock inside my ass," she whispered, "Please... put it inside me."

Ragden pressed harder against her, but still not inside. Her body screamed in anticipation as he whispered to her, "Louder."

Fear and excitement surged through her. She could feel her arousal dripping through her folds. Her as was soaked with it. She could feel the dampness on his cock as it pressed against her.

"I want your cock inside my ass!" she screamed, her voice loud and clear, "Please put it inside me!"

Sarah opened her eyes and sighed as Ragden nodded. A benign smile across his lips. "As you wish."

She blinked the tears from her eyes, and joy swept over her. Her heart thundered. She reached out and grabbed his firm ass in her hands and pulled him against her. He moved only a fraction; the head of his cock throbbed against her ass. It pushed into her. Slowly, it slipped in. A look of concentration and strength passed over his face as Ragden pushed his cock into her ass. The tightness of it overwhelmed him until it finally slid another inch.

Ragden grunted with the effort of it, as his cock slowly slid into her. Inch after inch, it slid deeper into her. Until his groin was firmly seated against her cheeks. His brow glistened with effort. Ragden leaned forward between her legs and laid his body over hers. He leaned in and kissed her softly on the mouth, whispered against her lips, "Is this what you wanted?"

The pleasure and discomfort now familiar to her, she purred contently against his lips.

"Yes," she whispered, her body now full of him, "This is what I wanted."

She wrapped her arms around him and held him against her. He smiled at her, then ground his hips against hers. His cock shifted inside her. She could feel every inch of it as it moved in her bowels. It throbbed inside her. His slow steady pulse filled her and calmed her.

Ragden kissed her softly, and whispered against her lips, "Your ass is incredible. Thank you for this moment."

Sarah blushed, feeling pleasure, embarrassment, discomfort, and pride. Her heart swelled at his compliment. Then he sat back on his heels and dragged his hands across her chest. Then, down her stomach to her thighs. He slid his cock partially out, then slid it back in again. Then again, faster. He built a slow rhythm. He bounced his groin off her hips. His cock slammed deep into her ass. Her breasts rolled with each impact.

Pleasure and discomfort crashed over Sarah. Her eyes rolled wildly. She clutched at her chest. She could feel her climax as it built, fought to hold it off. She had not been allowed that yet.

"Faster," she whispered, "I need more."

Urged by her coaxing, Ragden increased his speed. Slammed his big dick into her harder, faster, deeper. She grunted with each impact, her breath pushed out and sucked in as he drew back. Her body rocking, she begged.

"More. Harder."

Ragden grabbed her hips and rolled into her. He thrust deep into her again, and again. His deep voice rolled over her, "Louder... Make your wishes

heard!"

Sarah gasped again but felt herself responding to his request immediately. "Fuck me hard!" she screamed, "Make me cum!"

Ragden drove as hard and as fast as he could. He slammed her wildly, sending her reeling. Each deep thrust struck the depths of her body. Then he slid a hand down to her pussy. Slipped two fingers in, placing his thumb across her clit, and slid it back and forth.

Sarah felt every sensation as it all pushed her towards a bottomless oblivion of ecstasy she could not comprehend. Her climax threatened to overtake her; she clenched every muscle she could. She squeezed her eyes shut as hard as she could. She tried to blot out everything else. Her heart hammered in her chest like a trapped animal trying to break free.

His cock continued to pound into her ass while his fingers stimulated her clit. His fingers were deep in her pussy, pressing down against where his cock continued to slam into her. Sarah cried out at the new sensations. Her voice was ragged. Filled with need. Her body rocked against his. Tried to get more of him in her, faster.

He slipped his hand out of her, then pinched her clit between thumb and forefinger. Then he slid his other fingers into her pussy. Slid them as deep as he could, spreading them to feel the convulsing of her vagina. She cried out again, her voice broke. Ragden did not slow his pace. He pounded her ass with his massive cock. Rhythmically. Relentlessly.

Ragden placed his other hand on her stomach and braced her. Then he whispered the words she had been waiting for, his voice a caress of her soul. "Now you can cum!"

Her eyes flashed open. Her body convulsed; relief washed over her as she let go of her defenses. As his cock continued to slam into her. His massive thrust shattered her psyche to pieces.

"Oh God... Yes... I'm cumming..." she cried out.

With one final massive stroke, Ragden slammed his cock home against her shuddering body. Rocked her breasts one final time. Her teeth clicked shut with the impact. His cock was fully seated in her bowels; he ground against her as her orgasms rocked her body. He squeezed her clitoris as a hot stream of fluid exploded out of her pussy, soaked his groin.

Sarah's breath was even more ragged; her body still rocked and spasmed with the power of her orgasm. Her hips rocked, slipping, and sliding on Ragden's massive cock. She moved up and down on it ever so slightly as Ragden ground against her.

She continued to moan, her words in time to her breath, "Oh fuck... I'm cumming...."

Ragden sat back on his heels. He watched her body twitch and spasm as the most incredible orgasm of her life rocked her body. Her legs kicked uncontrollably. Her breath was ragged. He continued to pull on her clitoris, milking her. He continued to ground his hips against her ass. His massive

cock still pushed into her bowels.

And still, her words kept flowing, just like the fluids that flowed freely from between her legs, "Oh God... I can't believe how much... I'm cumming..."

Ragden watched as her body twitched. As waves of pressure and pleasure continued to crash over her. The fluid still poured out of her hot drenched pussy. He let go of her clitoris and pulled his hand from her pussy. Drenched, and dripping wet, he placed it upon her lips. While he continued to grind his hips against her. His cock was still deep in her bowels.

Ragden spoke softly, calmingly to her, "Lick my fingers clean. Taste your cum."

Her eyes fluttered open. Noticing as he watched her.

"Okay..." she whispered, her voice barely audible, "I'll taste..."

Ragden slipped his fingers between her lips. He prodded her tongue. Let her fluids flow down his knuckles and fingers into her mouth. Sarah smiled, still feeling the pleasure and discomfort of his cock buried in her bowels. She felt full and satisfied. She accepted the fingers in her mouth, sucking and licking at them.

"Mmm... ", she moaned, savoring the mix of tastes on her tongue. His sweat. Her cum. A symphony of delicious flavors.

Satisfied, Ragden slowly started to withdraw his cock from her ass inch by inch. She closed her eyes and savored the feel of it. She felt every inch as it slid from her. Finally, it slid free of her. Then he knelt over her. His cock was poised over her stomach. Her fluids dripped from it onto her. He kissed her softly on the lips. Licked her lips. Then pressed his tongue gently into her mouth.

Then he whispered against her lips, "Good girl."

"Thank you...," she whispered, his praise filled her heart with happiness, "Thank you... for making me cum.... for making me taste my cum... For making me good... Thank you..."

Ragden smiled at her, "You are welcome."

Sarah smiled up at him, her eyes shining with gratitude and submission, "Can I ask for something else? Can I please have another request?"

Ragden looked at her questioningly. His cock was still poised over her. It dripped with her juices, "What is your request?"

Sarah placed a hand on her stomach. She pushed the fluid around on her. She relished the slick, sticky feeling as it covered her sensitive skin, "Please... Please let me lick your cock clean... Let me show you how much I appreciate everything you've done for me today... Please... Please let me show you much I love being your little whore..."

Ragden nodded slowly and accepted her request. Then he pulled himself to his feet. He offered her a hand, and pulled her up to her knees, "Okay."

His cock throbbed in front of her face, still dripping with her juices. She took it in hand. Ran her fingers along its length. She felt the warmth and

texture of it. She leaned forward and placed her lips around the head. She took it deep into her mouth, sucking gently. She swirled her tongue around the tip, teasing it with her teeth lightly. She moved her hand lower. Wrapped her fingers around the base of his shaft. She held onto it tightly as she continued to suckle on it gently.

"Mmm... This is so delicious. And I love serving you like this... Showing you how much I love being your little whore..." she whispered.

Ragden shook his head slowly, "I did not do this for you to become a whore."

Sarah looked up at him, her eyes filled with determination and vulnerability. Her hands still wrapped around his cock, she spoke slowly, "But now that I am your little whore... I want to be the best little whore possible for you... I want to show you how much I love pleasing you... How much I love serving you..." She licked her lips, then sucked gently on the tip of his cock, then released him, "And I know that being your perfect little slut makes me feel so alive... So full of joy... So happy... Please don't ever take that away from me."

Ragden looked confused and pondered her words. Then spoke slowly, "This was a lesson for you... About how to be a better person. To express your desires more directly, without hurting others. That your joy comes from you, and not from inflicting pain on others. In truth, I want you to be happy, and to express that happiness to others in a healthy way. If having insanely passionate sex, getting fucked silly, makes you happy, then it will be my pleasure to share that with you..."

Sarah smiled at him; her eyes shone with gratitude and submission. "Thank you," she whispered, her voice barely audible. "Thank you for understanding that sometimes... Sometimes, all I need is to be taken over by someone stronger than me... to feel completely powerless and at their mercy... It makes me feel so alive... so full of energy... so happy... And I know that I can be a better person because of that."

Ragden smiled at her, "Then I am happy to help you with that."

Sarah nodded her head in agreement. Her eyes were full of gratitude, and tears started to slip from them. Ragden reached down and gently cupped her chin with one hand. He took her hand with the other and pulled her to her feet. He pulled her shaking body against him, kissed her cheek softly, and hugged her tenderly.

"Thank you," she whispered into his chest, "Thank you for helping me be the best version of myself... For showing me how powerful it can be to submit completely to someone stronger than me... I am so grateful for everything you have done for me today."

Ragden hugged her a little tighter, kissed her cheek, and whispered into her ear, "You are welcome, my dear."

Sarah leaned against his body. Her hands wrapped around his waist. Pulled herself against him. Relished the feel of his flesh under her hands. His heat

and presence washed over her, tears in her eyes. "I am yours... Completely... I will always be grateful for everything you've done for me... And I promise to never forget what it means to be your little whore... To never forget how much, I love being your perfect little slut," she whispered, her voice barely audible, "I will always be here for you... To serve you... To make you happy... No matter what."

CHAPTER 4

Ragden patted Sarah's back reassuringly, then turned to Aria and Emily. He smiled at them. "I would like to climax again. Would any of you like to help?"

Emily hesitated. Then glanced at Sarah, before looking back at Ragden. Her eyes filled with uncertainty and curiosity. Sarah watched closely, filled with anticipation and desire.

"Um. I think... Sarah deserves to receive your cum," Emily said tentatively, her voice soft, "She has been so brave and... and willing to do anything for you. She wants this."

Sarah nodded her head in agreement, her eyes bright with excitement and eagerness. Sarah could not believe her luck; she wanted this. She wanted to feel herself filling with his seed. She licked her lips and looked up at Ragden.

Ragden turned to Aria and offered her his hand. She reached up and took it. She allowed Ragden to gently pull her to her feet. He leaned into her, and kissed her lips gently, whispered against her cheek, "And you, my dear? This all started with you. What do you think?"

Aria hesitated for a moment. She looked at Sarah and then back at Ragden. Her eyes filled with uncertainty and curiosity. She bit her bottom lip nervously, then spoke her voice just above a whisper as she felt the incredible pressure and heat of Ragden's presence., "Well... um... I think... I think if Sarah is willing to receive your cum, then I need to as well... I mean... We are sisters in this, after all... And I want us both to experience this together... To share this special moment with you."

Sarah smiled at Aria, her eyes filled with gratitude and appreciation.

Ragden looked from Aria to Sarah, then back to Aria. "I can only cum in one of you at a time. One now, another later. Who shall be first then?"

Aria hesitated again. She glanced at Sarah before looking back at Ragden. Her eyes filled with uncertainty. She continued to chew her bottom lip

nervously, then spoke up, "Well, I guess, I'd rather go first. I mean... if Sarah is okay with that. Then you can cum for her later."

A look of sadness and longing passed over Sarah's face. Then she smiled, knowing that she would get her turn. Ragden nodded, then kissed Aria on the cheek, the chin, then gently on the lips. She trembled slightly with fear and anticipation as Ragden's tongue darted into her mouth. As he stole the taste of her sweetness. Then he pulled her body against his. Her tight breasts squeezed against his chest. His damp cock pressed firmly against her stomach. One hand slipped down to cup her ass. His fingers traced the edge of her asshole. Inside her pussy lips. Teased her vagina. Teased her clit. He whispered against her cheek, "Where do you want to receive me? Your mouth? Your vagina? Your ass? You have earned your choice..."

Aria trembled with desire as she looked up at Ragden. She stammered, "Um, I-I think. I want to receive you in my vagina. I ... I want to feel your cum inside of me."

Ragden kissed her forehead. Her cheek. Then her lips. He whispered against her, "As you wish."

Aria closed her eyes; her hands reached down to guide Ragden's cock towards her waiting vagina. She could feel the heat and wetness between her legs. She knew she was ready to receive his gift. She bit her bottom lip nervously. Then she opened her eyes and looked at Ragden. Her eyes filled with determination and vulnerability. "Here. Here it is... Please fill me with your cum."

Ragden nodded as he stepped forward, pushed his cock through her pussy lips. It slid across her vaginal opening. Aria gasped in surprise as he reached down and grabbed her thighs. He lifted her. She wrapped her legs around him as he eased his cock into her pussy. She wrapped her arms around his neck and pulled herself close to him. Her body trembled as a moan of pleasure slipped from her lips. His cock slipped into her vagina. It quickly slid deeper into her.

"Oh, God. Oh, God! I can feel you filling me up."

Ragden rocked his hips against her. His cock slid deeper. Hit her cervix and pressed against it, pushed into her. He kissed her breasts. Nipped at the flesh. Licked her nipples. Pinched them between his teeth. Aria gasped in pleasure with her eyes closed. Her body trembled. She bit her bottom lip as Ragden's cock pressed into her deepest depths. A moan of pleasure slipped from her lips as she felt Ragden's attention on her chest. She wrapped her arms around his shoulders and pulled him closer to her. She wanted to feel every inch of him inside her.

"Fuck me."

Ragden arched his back, pressing the head of his cock into her cervix. She felt that incredible pressure deep inside her. His fingers gripped her ass tightly, pulled her lips ever wider around his cock. Allowed it to sink harder into her. She gasped in response, her eyes closed, and her body trembled.

Ragden leaned over her, his mouth on her chest, licked her nipples. His lips brushed them as he spoke into her body, "You are mine. Scream it for the world to know." He lifted her and lowered her in one stroke. Slow and purposeful. It drove his cock into her cervix. It squeezed the breath out of her.

Aria screamed. Her voice echoed through the halls as she felt Ragden's cock sliding deep into her. She bit her bottom lip; tears streamed down her cheeks. Her body trembled with pleasure and ecstasy. She clenched her thighs tightly around his waist. Tried to hold onto him as he drove himself deeper into her.

"Ah. I'm yours."

Ragden's cock throbbed in time to her cries. Twitched deep within her. He lifted her and lowered her. Rocked his hips against her. Drove his cock in and out of her pussy. Deep powerful strokes. He filled her being with all of him.

Aria screamed again. A primal sound filled with longing and desire as she felt Ragden's cock sliding deep into her. She bit her lips. Tears streamed down her cheeks. Her body trembled and twitched with pleasure and ecstasy. She clenched her legs tighter around him. Tried to pull more of him into her.

Ragden matched her rhythm, in time to her screams. Lifted and shifted. Drove and twitch. His climax had started to build in answer to hers. He clamped his teeth down on her nipple. Whispered against her sublime skin, "Cum with me."

Aria screamed again. Her voice echoed through the halls. She felt Ragden's cock as it thumped into her cervix. She blinked through the tears on her cheeks. Clenched as fiercely as she could with her thighs around Ragden.

"Oh! I'm cumming!"

Ragden's eyes glazed over; his climax suddenly overtook him. He lost control; his body thrashed against her. Pounded his cock into her, faster and wilder than before. Aria screamed again with the intensity of her orgasm. Ragden held her tight as his body slammed in and out of her. His cock went rigid as cum exploded within her. It poured up into her in a stream. It filled her and poured out of her pussy. He kept pounding into her, and the stream continued. As did the wild drives into her.

Aria's insides filled with warm intensity as the two orgasms combined. Their bodies continued to thrash, spasm, and twitch against each other as they slowly started to recover. Ragden's legs gave out, and he collapsed to the ground. Aria was still wrapped around his waist. His cock still thrust into her innards. His hips, still convulsed, slid his cock in and out of her.

As he started to regain control of his body, Ragden stopped slamming his cock into her soaked pussy. He slid home one final time. Cock firmly seated as deep as possible. Aria sighed in contented pleasure as he kissed her breasts. Licked the sweat from them. He kissed her chin and her lips. Softly, tenderly. He pulled her against him and kissed her neck and ear. Then whispered to her, "You have been good. My amazing little fuck-star. I look forward to

doing this again."

Aria, still trembling with aftershocks of pleasure, tears on her cheeks, smiled. She was warm, content, and filled with Ragden. She felt fulfilled, and happy. She whispered to Ragden, "Thank you. For filling me with your cum... I can't wait for the next time we'll be together like this."

Ragden leaned his body against hers. Kissed the tears from her face. Soft caresses conveyed his sense of care and respect for how far she had come. He kissed her cheeks, then her lips. Softly parted them to slip his tongue inside. He gently tasted her as she sighed against his lips. His cock throbbed and twitched within her as cum continued to leak from it.

Aria placed her hands on her abdomen. Felt the pressure of Ragden's massive cock still seated inside her. "Your cock is... Still throbbing inside me. It makes me feel so alive... So connected to you."

Ragden winked at her, softly caressing her face with his hands, "That does feel pretty damn good, doesn't it?"

Ragden gingerly ground his hips against her. Aria gasped as she felt his cock pressed harder against her cervix. Ragden kissed her lips again, more passionately. He slipped his tongue inside her mouth. Explored her again. Her body still trembled with aftershocks. She beamed at him, eyes filled with gratitude, "It feels so amazing. Being filled with your cock. Tasting your sweetness. This makes me feel so alive... So addicted to you."

Ragden smiled at Aria and kissed her tenderly again. Then whispered against her lips, "I am glad you feel that way. I look forward to doing this again with you. However, we have others who need attention."

Ragden turned to look at Sarah and Emily who sat in shock. Their bodies trembled slightly from excitement and anticipation. Having watched the scene unfold before them. Aria moaned in disappointment as Ragden gripped her firm ass once more, and slowly lifted her off him. Inch by inch, until his cock slid free of her.

Ragden clambered back to his feet and gripped Aria's hands in his. He then pulled her to her feet. Then against his body. His cock pressed against her stomach again. It left a trail of their mixed cum and body fluids on her perfect little body. Ragden marveled at the feeling of her body against his. He kissed her forehead. Then her nose. Then her lips again. Softly. Tenderly. Lovingly. Then he turned and looked through Aria's hair at Sarah and Emily, "Did you two enjoy the show?"

Ragden disentangled himself from Aria and walked over to Sarah and Emily. They stood as he approached. His erect penis still dripped with Aria's cum and bodily fluids. He reached out and slipped a finger into Sarah's wet pussy. Slipped it across her vaginal opening. Then over her clit. Sarah sighed, her eyes slipped shut, and her legs trembled at the feeling of his touch.

Then he reached out to Emily with his other hand. Slipped that between her legs. His fingers slipped into her wet pussy. Slid across her vagina and clitoris. Her eyes fluttered as she gasped. Her legs trembled. One hand

clutched to her chest; the other spread her lips to allow Ragden's fingers to slip deeper into her.

Ragden stroked them both. Watched them twitch. Then he spoke softly, huskily. His voice was full of lust and desire, "I imagine you would both like to get fucked?"

Sarah and Emily looked at each other. Their desire was plain to read on their faces. Then they both turned back to Ragden, blushed, and nodded. Ragden smiled at them, as he continued to stroke their pussies. His fingers slipped inside them. Stroked inside them. Passed over their clitorises in turn. Both women sighed and stood on trembling legs.

"As I recall," Ragden mused, "Sarah, did seem rather insistent earlier."

Sarah blushed and bit her lip. Her eyes filled with desire, arousal, and anticipation. She nodded vigorously, then looked at Emily in apology. Ragden slipped his fingers out of Emily. She gasped and clutched herself. Then she sank to her knees. Tears in her eyes. Ragden looked back to her, a look of concern in his eyes. He leaned over, kissed her gently on the forehead, and whispered to her, "Do not fret, my dear; your turn will come soon. Be patient. Please."

Emily smiled up at him sadly. She wiped the tears from her face, "I can be patient. Thank you."

Ragden smiled at her again. Then he turned back to Sarah, slipped his fingers deeper into her, and pulled her towards him. She stumbled forward, her legs trembling. Ragden took her other hand in his and steadied her. Ragden leaned into Sarah and kissed her gently on the lips. His tongue darted in to taste her sweetness. Then he smiled at her trembling body. He whispered against her lips, "If you still want it, you can have it..."

Sarah nodded vigorously, her voice lost. Ragden kissed her softly again. His fingers were still inside her. She closed her eyes and let the sensation wash over her. Ragden ran his hand down her trembling back. Placed it on her hip to steady her. Then he kissed her neck, and whispered against her skin, "Where do you want it? Do you wish to swallow my cum? Do you want it to fill your vagina? Or do you want me so far up your ass that your bowels will be filled with cum?"

Ragden pulled Sarah closer. His cock was now pressed against her stomach. A trail of slick wetness collected on her. Sarah trembled. Her hands came up to hold the cock against her stomach. Ragden sighed contently as she slowly ran her fingers the length of his shaft.

Sarah's voice was tentative, nervous, barely audible, "Umm. In my mouth..."

Ragden nodded and kissed her softly on her neck. Then her ear, "As you wish."

He kissed her on the lips and flicked his tongue inside her mouth. Then he drew back from her. Let his cock slide from her hands. She reached out keeping her hands on it as Ragden took a step back. His hand was on her

shoulder. He slipped his finger out of her. He licked it clean and smiled. Then he gently pushed her down to her knees and stepped in front of her. His large dick before her.

Ragden smiled down at her, "Go for it."

Sarah reached out tentatively and grasped his penis. She pulled it to her mouth. She opened her mouth wide and ran her tongue over the massive head. Then she wrapped her lips around it and gently sucked it into her mouth. Ragden sighed and closed his eyes, as she slowly put the head into her mouth. She swirled her tongue around it.

Aria watched in fascination as Sarah opened her mouth and had trouble fitting Ragden's cock in, "Sarah... Take it all in," she whispered to herself, "I hope she likes being filled with his cum."

Sarah opened her mouth as wide as she could and took Ragden's cock in. Her eyes watered from the intense sensation. Ragden closed his eyes as Sarah attempted to take his cock down her throat. She gagged, as her throat bulged. Her eyes watered with effort. He placed a hand on her head, gently. Coaxed her to relax so that it might fit.

She ran her hands along his thick shaft and gently stroked him. She wrapped both her hands around it and squeezed gently. Then she stroked more vigorously. She tasted a bead of precum that formed on her tongue. Then she opened her mouth as wide as she could and tried to fit his cock down her throat. She gagged and choked. She managed to get the head past her gag reflex.

A warm sensation filled her body, as she realized she passed it into her throat. Then she realized she could not breathe. She stroked his cock faster. Ran her hands up and down it. Then she put her hands on his groin and pushed him back. Ragden reached down, grabbed her by her hair, and pulled her head off his cock. It popped out of her mouth. She gasped for breath. Tears slipped from her eyes, but she smiled up at Ragden.

"Thank you, I almost got it. Can I... Can I try again?"

Ragden looked down at her, concern on his face, but he nodded. She felt gratitude welling up from the core of her being as she slipped her hands around his cock again. She ran her tongue over the head and pulled it into her mouth again. Then she started to stroke his cock again. Sucked and licked the head. She felt it throb in her mouth in response. Then she attempted to unhinge her jaw and lean into his cock. Ragden sighed as she grabbed his butt cheeks and pulled him against her. His cock slid down her throat.

This time she did not gag. She was ready for the blockage of all air. Her face went red, but she rocked her body back and forth. Used her throat to fuck his cock. A new sensation filled her body. A sensation of being full in a way she had never imagined. As she started to feel her world go grey, she pressed hard against his groin. Forced his cock out of her throat. Again, Ragden grabbed her hair and popped her head off his cock.

As it popped out of her mouth, she coughed. Greedily gulped air, "Oh,

God! It's... It's amazing."

A small, shocked expression played across Ragden's face as Sarah grabbed at his cock and rammed herself onto it. Forced it into her throat. This time she convulsed on it. Her throat collapsed, squeezed it hard, and she coughed and fell back onto her heels; his cock popped out of her mouth again.

Tears sprang to her eyes, "I'm sorry. I'm sorry. Please... Please let me try again."

Ragden reached down and took her hand. He kneeled in front of her, a look of concern on his face, "It is okay if this is too much for you. Nobody will blame you."

Sarah slapped her other hand down on the ground hard. A look of fierce determination on her face. "No."

She crawled forward and grabbed his cock. She licked the shaft. Ran her tongue over the head. Then she squeezed it fiercely. Her voice was hard and determined, "I will swallow your cum. Please let me swallow your cum. Please..."

Ragden stood up. He nodded and allowed Sarah to take his cock into her mouth again. She stroked the shaft with her hands. One hand cupped his balls. Her tongue swirled around the head. Then she dipped forward. Pulled it into her throat. It slipped down and blocked her airway. This time she was prepared. She took it farther and deeper. She felt the heat of it go down into her chest. Her whole body cried against the invasion, but her determination drove her.

Then she slid forward, pulled his cock back into her mouth. She gulped air around it. She looked up at him, gratitude on her face. Ragden softly caressed her face, "Shall we try this a different way?"

Sarah nodded around his cock. Ragden reached down and gently placed his hands on the sides of her head to steady her. Then he slid his cock forward into her mouth. Sarah relaxed and let him slide into her. His dick slid down her throat. Then he pulled it back and allowed her to breathe. Then he slowly slid it in again, a little farther. Then back out to let her breathe. Then he slid in again. Sarah's eyes bulged with effort. Her face turned red. Then Ragden pulled back and slipped his cock from between her lips.

Sarah looked up at Ragden, tears in her eyes. A huge smile on her lips. Ragden spoke softly, "Is this what you wanted, Sarah?"

"Yes. Yes. This is exactly what I wanted," Sarah gasped between breaths, "It feels incredible. Please continue. Fill me with your cum."

Aria and Emily watched in fascination as Sarah continued to struggle to take Ragden's cock down her throat. Her eyes watered, and her face turned red with the effort. They saw Ragden stopping and withdrawing, then slid it in again. A little farther than before but still came up short of being able to put her lips against his groin. Ragden spoke softly, "You are going to have to help me, my dear."

As Ragden pulled back, Sarah gulped in the air and nodded, "I can do this.

Please let me try."

Ragden slid his cock back into her mouth. Slid it deep, but still not getting there. Before he could withdraw, Sarah grabbed his buttocks and pulled him against her. Sarah's body went rigid. Her eyes bulged. Her legs twitched. Her arms strained. Her knuckles went white. Then something shifted inside her, and Ragden's cock slipped the last couple of inches in. Her lips kissed Ragden's groin, as he groaned at the sensation. Then she pushed him back. Took huge breaths as his cock slipped from her throat.

"Oh, God. Oh God!" Sarah moaned to herself; her pussy started to drip as she pulled his cock back into her mouth. She greedily swallowed him down her throat. She grabbed his buttocks and forced him against her. She squirmed and then slid back. Gasped for breath, then pulled him against her again.

Ragden groaned, his body thrusted with Sarah's movements. His cock slipped in and out of her throat more quickly. His climax started to take hold of him. They worked together, Sarah pulled against him, and Ragden thrust into her. Sarah dug her fingers into his buttocks and urged him to go faster. Ragden responded, thrusting his cock down her throat. Then he drew back and then down her throat again. Timing her breath, Sarah continued to pull against Ragden and felt his climax as it built. She was eager for him to fill her in ways she had only imagined.

Ragden's thrusts sped up, and his cock filled her mouth, throat, and chest. Her pulse pounded against his cock and drove him into ecstasy as his climax exploded over him. A blast of hot cum exploded down Sarah's throat. Too far down to be stopped, she convulsively swallowed. Squeezed his cock even harder, which sent another flood down her throat. Realizing she could not breathe, he pulled back so that she could. Another massive load of cum exploded in her mouth. She coughed, trying to breathe, and spewed cum all over the place.

Then Sarah leaned forward and greedily latched her mouth onto his cock. Ragden's eyes went wide as his throbbing, sensitive cock exploded another load of cum into her mouth. This time she was prepared, and she sucked it down her throat so hard, and with such force, another blast exploded in her mouth. Bits leaked out between her lips. She greedily sucked it back, swallowed as much as she could.

Sarah kept swallowing. His cock throbbed in her mouth, continued to spew cum down her throat. Ragden spasmed forward and inadvertently drove his cock down her throat again. Another load exploded into her that she could not help but swallow. Ragden jerked back, as tears streamed down her face from the effort.

As he felt his orgasm pass, Ragden's cock started to soften in her mouth. She continued to suck every bit of cum that leaked out. It backed out of her throat and gave her room to breathe. His legs shook, and Ragden placed a hand on her shoulder to brace himself. She continued to clean his cock. It was now a more normal, manageable size in her mouth.

Sarah was elated. Her stomach was full of cum, but she continued to suck on his cock. She savored the soft texture in her mouth. This new sensation was somehow even more erotic than before. She knew that this smaller cock, was once so massive she could not get it down her throat, but now was spent, in her, filling her with giddiness and joy. Knowing she did this.

Ragden pulled his clean cock from her mouth. Then he gripped her chin and lifted her to her feet. He softly kissed her on the mouth, tasted a bit of his cum there, "You did well. Thank you."

Sarah sighed with contentment. Her heart raced with excitement. "Thank you," she said weakly. That was amazing."

Ragden smiled at her and pulled her body against his. Kissed her forehead, her nose, her lips, then spoke softly, "And you were amazing, my dear Sarah. I didn't think this," he gestured towards his softened cock, "was going to fit, to be honest."

Sarah smiled, her eyes glittered with pride, "That's good to know," Sarah replied, "I'm glad I could make you happy."

Ragden smiled against her, his voice light, "You did, my dear. But, did it make you happy?"

Sarah rubbed her stomach. Then she cupped her breasts. Looked up at Ragden and smiled. "Yes," Sarah replied softly, "I'm very happy that I could make you feel good."

Ragden leaned into Sarah and pulled her body against his. Her firm nipples pressed against his chest. He grabbed her ass and pulled her groin against his. Ragden's softening cock tickled her clit. He kissed her lips, harder this time. "Is that what you wanted? Or do you want more?"

Aria watched as Ragden leaned into Sarah; jealousy and arousal coursed through her veins. She wondered what it would be like to have her stomach filled with his cum.

"More?" Sarah asked hesitantly, "What do you have in mind?"

Ragden nuzzled her neck softly, "I did not have anything in mind, I wondered if you did..."

Ragden released her from his embrace. Kissed her softly on the lips as he stepped back from her. A look of longing ran down her face. She reached out towards him but pulled her hands back and clasped them in front of her groin. "Well," Sarah said nervously, "There's something I've always wanted to try..."

Ragden looked back at her, "And what is that?"

"I've always dreamed of having your cum inside me," Sarah confessed, "In my belly, and everywhere else."

Ragden cocked an eyebrow at her, "I just came down your throat so hard you coughed it up on me."

Sarah looked up at Ragden. Bashful, and nervous, she trembled slightly, "Yeah, I know. But I still want more."

"Oh," Ragden laughed bawdily, a rich warm sound that sent shivers down

the backs of all three women. There was sex in that laugh, "I see. Well, there will be time for that later."

Sarah smiled. She felt and heard the hint of getting her wishes filled. She knew she must be patient. Her heart beat a little faster. "Okay," Sarah said eagerly, "Whenever you're ready."

Ragden smiled at her, "You must learn patience, my dear."

"I understand," Sarah replied, smiling sweetly, "I'll wait as long as you need me to."

Ragden stepped over to Emily and reached out for her hand. Emily trembled slightly, watching Ragden walk up to her. His cock was still soft, but his body was hard. She longed to touch him, to be near him. She took his hand and allowed herself to be pulled to her feet. "What are we doing now?" Emily asked curiously, "Are you going to use me as a toy for Sarah?"

Ragden lets his eyes look Emily over from head to foot. He took in the sweep of her neck. Her small round breasts. The flatness of her stomach. The touch of red hair over her perfect pussy lips. The sweep of her thighs. The swell of her ass. The taper of her ankles. He stepped closer to her. His cock swelled to full erection. Emily's eyes widened as it grew before her. She sighed, longed to reach for it, but waited. Ragden leaned in and kissed her lips softly. Then he pulled back to look her in the eyes," No, no toys. I only wanted to make you the same offer... If you wanted my essence inside, you..."

Emily smiled, hesitantly. Nervous, and jittering, she trembled. The invitation was too much for her to hope for. "Really?" Emily asked, her voice hitched, "You mean like Sarah just did?"

Ragden smiled at her, his eyes warm and soft. His voice was mellow and sensual, a gentle caress across her skin. It made her long for more, "And Aria before her. Yes. Do you want it?"

Emily's heart skipped a beat. She felt the arousal wash over her. She saw his throbbing cock before her. So close she could touch it, but she mastered herself. Her heart hammered in her throat, and she nodded. "Yes," Emily replied slowly, "I've always been curious about what it would feel like."

Ragden smiled. One hand slid down Emily's back, the other slowly stroked his now-massive throbbing cock. She stared at it, eyes transfixed, unable to look away. His voice a low rumble, "Where would you like it?"

Aria listened as Ragden asked Emily. She remembered her own experience with that cock filling her. She ached for that again. She could still feel his cum as it slipped from inside her. Her juice started to flow again. She watched Emily consider the offer.

Emily smiled, almost giddy. Nervous energy made her twitch. "Inside me," Emily answered softly, "I want your cum to fill my insides."

Ragden nodded and prodded her to be more specific. "Your vagina, or your ass... Your pick. I will fill whichever you want."

Emily hesitated. She pondered the decision. She wanted both but knew this opportunity was for one or the other. "Ass," Emily replied quickly, "I've

always been curious about having someone fill my ass with their cum."

Ragden smiled happily, "If that is what you want, then I will be happy to provide that for you."

Emily smiled and reached out tentatively towards Ragden's cock. Rested a hand on its swollen shaft. She felt the intense heat. It throbbed in her hands. Excitement raced through her. Her heart hammered in her chest. "Thank you," Emily said gratefully, "I appreciate it."

Ragden smiled, enjoying her hand on his cock. He leaned down and gently kissed her cheek. A soft brushing of his lips, as he whispered, "My pleasure. Truly."

Emily slid her hand down his throbbing cock. She wrapped her fingers around its thick base. Her fingers brushed against his balls. She looked back up into his eyes. "Now what?" Emily asks nervously, "Do I just lay down here and wait for you to fill me?"

Ragden stepped forward against Emily and pulled her body against his. Her breasts pressed to his chest. Her groin against his. Ragden's dick pressed against her stomach. He kissed her softly on the lips, slipped a little tongue between them as he slid his fingers over her ass. A finger slipped across her asshole, teasingly. "Do not worry, my dear, we will take this as slowly as you want, or as hard..."

Emily sighed, as the pressure across her asshole sent shivers of ecstasy through her body. She could feel the dampness in her pussy increasing. Her desire increased tenfold.

"Okay," Emily said nervously, "Take it slow."

Ragden pulled Emily firmly against him, picked her up off the ground, and pulled her legs around his back. He trapped his cock between them. Then he lowered her to the ground. He kissed her chest, her collarbone, her throat, her chin, then her lips. She sighed; her heart fluttered. Excitement raced through her. She asked for this. She dreamed of this. And Ragden granted her wish. Then he knelt between her legs, gently pressed the head of his cock against her ass. He looked up at her face and cocked an eyebrow at her questioningly.

Her heart was in her throat. Fear suddenly raced through her. Emily nodded slowly.

"I'm ready," Emily said nervously, "Go ahead."

Ragden pressed the head of his cock against her tiny asshole, which stretched, but not enough. She gasped at the pressure; pain etched on her face. Ragden drew back and slid his dick through her pussy lips, which were dripping in anticipation. Then he placed it against her asshole again. It was damp with her juices. The head slipped through. Emily exhaled sharply.

"It's okay," Emily gasped, "Just go slow."

Ragden turned to notice Aria's intense gaze on his cock slipping into Emily's incredible ass. Aria bit her lip, her pussy damp with arousal.

"Does this make you hot?" he said to Aria, "You have my permission to finger yourself if you want."

He turned back to Emily and slid his cock into her another inch. A soft sigh escaped his lips.

Aria listened as Ragden addressed her while focusing on filling Emily's ass with his throbbing cock. This made her even more excited and nervous. Jealousy and arousal coursed through her. "Hmm?" Aria responded distractedly, "What did you say?"

Ragden turned to look at Aria, and smiled at the condition she was in, "If you are enjoying the view, and it makes you hot, you have my permission to finger yourself as much as you want."

"Oh really?" Aria responded, "Thanks. That sounds nice."

"Go for it, darling."

Aria nodded and slipped a finger down into her wet folds. She gasped at the sensation of it. Jealousy and arousal coursed through her veins. She wondered what it would be like to have her bowels filled with his cum. As she continued to masturbate, she watched closely as Ragden squeezed another inch of his massive cock into Emily's tight ass.

"Mmmph" Aria moaned softly, "This feels good."

Ragden turned back to Emily and smiled down at her. Then he leaned forward between her legs and kissed her chest. Nuzzled her nipples. Took one into his mouth and swirled his tongue around it. Pinched it between his teeth as he slid his cock another inch into her ass. Emily moaned softly; pleasure and discomfort coursed through her. Her mind reeled at the sensation of his penis filling her bowels. She was fearful that she might not be able to take all of it. She wondered how much more would fit into her.

Aria watched, her mouth agape, and her breath came more rapidly. Her fingers slipped over her clit. Her pulse raced as she slipped a finger into her dripping pussy.

"Ahh," Aria gasped, "That's so hot."

Ragden gently clasped Emily's hands in his and pulled them down to her ass. Helped her spread her cheeks so he could more easily fit his massive cock into her. He pushed forward another inch into her, as she moaned. Her eyes squeezed shut, while he continued to pinch and pull on her nipple with his teeth.

Ragden released Emily's nipple from his mouth and moved up her body. Kissed and nipped at her tender flesh. Then he whispered against her cheek, "Is this what you wanted?" His cock slid another inch deeper into her.

Aria watched Ragden, her fingers dipping in and out of her, as her body trembled at the sight of his cock filling Emily's ass. She found herself getting increasingly turned on.

"Yes," Emily breathed heavily, "This is exactly what I wanted."

Ragden placed his hands on Emily's hips and pulled her forcibly towards him, while he thrusted against her. His throbbing cock slid all the way home. His groin grinded against her hips. His cock was now firmly seated in the depths of her bowels. Emily gasped. Her breath came more rapidly. Ragden

whispered against her throat, "Do you like that?"

Ragden ground his groin against her ass and pushed his cock deep into her bowels. Pushed her inner organs around. "Tell me if you like this," he purred against her throat.

Emily moaned softly. "Yes, I love it."

With his hips firmly pressed against her groin, he ground his hips around. Swished his massive throbbing cock around in her bowels. Her purred against her cheek as he kissed her chin," Your ass feels amazing. Are you ready to get going?"

Emily moaned softly. Her arms wrapped around Ragden's neck and gently pulled him against her. "Yes," Emily breathed heavily, "I'm ready."

Ragden lifted his face, looked Emily in the eyes, and smiled happily. Then he darted down and kissed her passionately on the lips. His tongue darted into her mouth as he explored her. Meanwhile, he placed his hands firmly on her beautiful breasts. Squeezed them and pinched her nipples. He drew his cock backward. Emily moaned, feeling his massiveness pulling back out of her bowels. She missed the feeling of him filling her up. Just before his cock slipped out, he drove it back into her. Forcefully pushed it all into her until his groin hit her ass. The impact shook her entire body and drove a gasp of surprise out of her.

"Ahh!" Emily gasped.

Ragden drew back again, slowly, then slammed it back home. He rocked her entire body. He gripped her breasts tightly, kept her body in place as he drew back, and slammed home again. Harder this time. Pushed deeper.

Emily moaned, "This is so incredible."

"Tell me how much you love this."

Ragden drew back and slammed home again, and again. Faster this time, harder. It rocked her body; her breasts vibrated with the impact but held firm under his grasp.

"I... Love... It!" Emily gasped between impacts.

"Louder!"

Ragden released her breasts and dragged his hands across her abdomen. One hand gently pushed on her stomach. Felt the shudders of each massive impact. The other slid down over her pussy. Parted the folds. Slipped two fingers into her pussy while his thumb and forefingers pinched her clit. Another massive thrust hit home and rocked her entire body.

"Yes!" Emily cried out louder between thrusts, "I love this!"

"Louder! What do you love?"

Ragden pinched her clit harder and drove his fingers into her pussy. His cock rammed into her ass again. Filled her bowels with his throbbing member. Her body shuddered. Her breasts rocked. He slammed her again, deeper, harder. Her breath became ragged. She exhaled as each impact rocked her body. Inhaled as he drew back.

"I... LOVE... THIS!" Emily screamed.

Love & Nature

Emily's screams urged him on. He pounded her harder, faster. Probed her pussy with his fingers. His cock slammed into her. Rocked her breasts. Shook her body. His breath was now ragged with the effort. His body glistened with sweat.

The intensity of it washed over Emily, blotted out everything. She no longer saw the crowd watching with mouths agape. Aria, with her fingers buried in her pussy, panting. Need and desire were etched through her features. Sarah, lying on her side, her eyes glazed, watching in fascination. Her hands squeezed her chest. The only thing in Emily's world was Ragden, and his massive throbbing cock as it filled her bowels. Then slid free and slammed home into her. She felt each impact course through her. Waves of pleasure crashed over her, washing everything away.

"OH, GOD!" Emily cried out, "I'm cumming!"

Ragden pounded her faster and harder. He was suddenly overcome by his climax, felt her clenched on him, and his body spasmed, sending him deep into her. His cock throbbed, and a massive stream of cum exploded out of him. Filled her bowels. He pumped her repeatedly. Cum blasted up into her as he spasmed into her. All rhythm lost, all sanity lost; he pounded his throbbing spasming cock in and out of her as more cum exploded into her.

Emily's arms flailed about, searching for something to grab onto. She latched onto Ragden. Pulled him into her. Her fingers dug into his buttocks as she pulled with all her might. Tears on her cheeks as wave upon wave of pleasure and ecstasy washed over her. Hot sticky fluid flowed out of her pussy. It flowed over Ragden's hands, over his groin, pooling around them. Her hips bucked against him, trying to find rhythm, and failing.

Emily cried out again. Ragden drew back and slammed home one last time. His body twitched and spasmed. His groin ground against her hips, uncontrollably, causing his throbbing ejaculating cock to push around in her bowels. More cum poured out of him into her. The sensation more than she could bear, she cried out again, "Oh, God..."

While his groin continued to grind into her hips, his cock pushed around inside of her. He continued to play with her clit and fingered her pussy. Pulled everything out of her as it continued to soak over him. Fluid continued to run out of her.

"I'm... cumming," Emily moaned, softer as she starts to come down from her high.

Ragden smiled at her, "Keep cumming, darling, it's okay." His breath was shaky as his climax started to subside. His body stopped twitching. His cock was still firmly seated, filling her bowels. He let go of her clit and slipped his fingers out of her pussy. He brought them up to her face. He slid them over her lips. Moistening them with her cum. "Taste your cum."

Emily's mouth slipped open. She greedily sucked on Ragden's fingers, moaning in pleasure

Her body still vibrated with the power of her orgasm. Her eyes rolled into

the back of her head. Waves of pleasure rolled over her. Ragden reached down and pulled Emily up against his body. Wrapped his arms around her. He held her limp body against his. Her chest pressed firmly to his. He leaned down and kissed her collarbone, her neck, and her chin. Then he gently pressed his lips to hers. He held her tight and waited for her spasms to pass.

As Emily slowly came back to reality, she realized she had been pulled into a warm comforting embrace by Ragden. His arms gently wrapped around her. She felt at peace. Her heart fluttered, and she wrapped her arms around him and rested her head on his warm shoulder. His heart thumped against her, and she felt such a warm sublime peace. Tears leaked out of her eyes, "Mm. I'm sorry," Emily whispered, "I am so sorry... I didn't know it would be like that..."

Ragden kissed her neck softly, his voice a low purr against her skin, "You do not need to apologize. That was amazing. You are amazing. Are you okay? Was that everything you dreamed it would be?"

Emily hiccupped. Her heart lurched. She could not believe how tender Ragden was with her. After everything, for him to be so caring and tender. It tore her heart asunder. Tears leaked from her eyes. She nuzzled closer to his neck, bathed in the warm comfort of him.

"Yeah. I think so," Emily murmured, "That was everything I ever hoped it could be. Thank you. Thank you so much."

Ragden leaned his head back to look her in the eyes and kissed her softly on the lips. Their lips parted, and he tenderly tasted her mouth. Then he whispered against her lips, "No, thank you. For showing me that you are a better person. Thank you for showing everyone here that you can be a better person. You are amazing, and I love watching the transformation in you."

Tears glistened on Aria's face, as she watched the tender moment between Emily and Ragden. She could not help but feel a little bit jealous, but she was proud of Emily, and her heart soared. Emily looked at Ragden's face with adoration; a hand gently caressed his cheek.

"I hope I can live up to your expectations," Emily whispered, "I want to be the best version of myself for you."

"I think you are off to an incredible start."

Ragden placed his hands under her thighs. He gently lifted her, inch by inch, off his cock. Until eventually, it slid free of her ass. With it came a steady stream of cum that emptied of her bowels. Ragden whistled appreciatively at the pool of cum forming at her feet.

"There we go," Emily said weakly, looking down between her legs at everything coming out. All of it... out."

Emily swayed weakly on her feet. Suddenly lightheaded. Ragden stood quickly and held her steady. Then he stepped next to Emily. One hand on her waist, the other holding her hand to steady her. Then he gazed down at Aria and Sara. A beautiful smile filled his face. His eyes beamed at them. His happiness with them was all-encompassing.

"You three have done marvelously. I am so pleased that we have shared this experience. And I look forward to many more. Though, perhaps without the crowd in the future."

Ragden nodded to the watching crowd. He reached down and took Aria's hand, and pulled her to her feet. Standing next to Aria, he then took Sarah's hand and pulled her to her feet. He stood between them, shoulder to shoulder; they took a bow for the crowd.

"I hope everyone here has enjoyed the show. Thank you for watching."

The audience applauded enthusiastically as they watched the four bow before them. Aria, Emily, and Sarah felt a sense of accomplishment and satisfaction knowing they had completed what was asked of them.

Ragden pulled Aria, Emily, and Sarah around him, in a small circle. He spoke softly so that only they could hear, "You ladies are the most amazing, beautiful, sexy women I have ever had the pleasure of being with. I invite you all to come back to my house to live with me and enjoy each other's company, but... only if that is what you want. I make no demands of any of you. Come or go, it is your decision. It would make my heart warm to have such incredibly strong, powerful women in my life, but I will not force you to do anything you do not wish to do..."

The three women listened attentively to his proposal. Touched by his genuine care and consideration for their well-being and personal choices.

"Thank you for the offer," Emily whispered, "But I think I need some time to process everything that just happened."

Ragden grasped Emily's hands in his own and pulled her to him. He wrapped his arms around her and hugged her gently. Then he kissed her forehead, then her lips. He gazed down into her eyes, a gentle look of compassion on his face, "Emily, take all the time you need. You will always be welcome in my home if you so desire it."

Emily sighed into his embrace, bathed in his warmth. Her heart soared, but she knew she needed to think this through thoroughly before making any decision.

"Thank you," Emily whispered, "I appreciate your understanding."

Ragden gently stepped away from Emily and turned to Sarah. He took her hands in his, and stared into her eyes, "What of you, my dear, will you come with me?"

Aria watched as Ragden turned to Sarah. She found herself intrigued by the idea of being so integrally involved with someone as powerful and influential as Ragden, who seemed to genuinely care about her well-being and desires.

Sarah felt the warm clasp; her heart skipped a beat. She looked up into his eyes and saw the depth of his care and concern. "I... I do not know," Sarah hesitated, "This has been an incredibly intense experience, and I need some time to think about it."

"You do not need to make this decision now. You have all the time you

need."

Ragden pulled Sarah's hands up to his mouth and kissed each one tenderly. Then he hugged her and pulled her body against his. Kissed her on the forehead, and then on the lips, softly, tenderly, like a lover.

"Thank you," Sarah whispered against his chest, hugged him to her, "I really appreciate your understanding."

Ragden stepped away from Sarah, turned to Aria, and smiled. He took her hands in his own and squeezed them gently, "What of you, my dear, beautiful Aria, what would you like?"

Aria watched as Ragden turned to her and expressed his interest in her desires and preferences. She found herself both flattered and nervous by his attention and curiosity towards her. "I... um...," Aria stammered, "I think I need some time to think about it as well."

"As you wish, when you make your decision, you will know where to find me."

Ragden pulled her into a warm embrace, wrapped his arms around her gently caressed her incredible body. He kissed her on the forehead, then gently on the lips. Then he stepped away from her, walked over to his pile of clothes, and casually dressed himself.

Once dressed, he walked back over to the three women and bowed before them. Then he turned and walked towards the parking lot, leaving the school campus.

Aria, Emily, and Sarah watched as Ragden left, dressed once again as any ordinary student. Someone they had once bullied and taunted, but now... somehow, something more. Aria found herself feeling conflicted by her indecision, torn between the incredible power and influence she felt from him, and the potential risks of being associated with him.

Ragden glanced once over his shoulder at them, as he was about to turn the corner. He paused for a moment, considering them. Then he smiled to himself and walked out of sight.

CHAPTER 5

During his walk home, Ragden kept playing out the events of the day in his mind. This was not how he had planned his day going when he rolled out of bed this morning. Parts of him were aghast at what he did. Was he possessed? How was it that he had done those things? Yet, he could still feel their hands on him. His body remembered. His loins stirred at the thought of it all.

As he walked up the quiet path through his yard, his gaze passed over the vibrant bushes and flowers in his yard. The bees buzzed; birds chirped in the air. So much life and love. He brushed his hands over a rose bush, the textures of the leaves playing along his fingers. Then he opened the door and headed inside.

"Mom? Dad? I am home!"

A silent house greeted him. He slipped off his shoes and stored them with all the rest. He noted that his father's boots were not among them. Then he walked through the living room into the kitchen. He felt the absence and quiet stillness of the house. He headed to the back of the house.

The back door opened onto a small 10'x 10' concrete patio. Just beyond was a lush patch of grass, with flower beds all around it. What appeared to be a young woman knelt in the yard; her auburn hair pulled into a bun. A pair of jean shorts tight on her plump ass as she knelt in the dirt, her bare feet in the grass. A small shirt was tied under ample breasts. She turned and smiled as Ragden stepped out of the house. She pulled her hands out of the dirt, stood up, and brushed her hands and her knees off as she stepped towards him.

"Ragden! Son! You are home early." She stepped into his arms and gave him a warm hug. Then she rested her head on his chest. "Is everything okay?"

She looked up into his face and saw the conflicted emotions playing across him. Her look went stern. "What happened at school today?"

Ragden frowned. "A... A lot, Mom. When will Dad be home? I would like

to include him in this conversation."

"Oh honey, he had to go into town. He will not be home until late." She saw the look of concern on Ragden's face, she smiled and patted him on the back. "I won't pry honey. Go in and do your homework. Once I finish this up, I will come in and make something for dinner."

Ragden nodded and turned to head back into the house as his mom walked back over to the fresh garden bed. She sank back to her knees and dug her hands into the soil again. She hummed softly to herself. Ragden went back through the house and made his way upstairs to his room.

He pulled his chair out from his desk and dropped down into it. His mind reeled from all the events of the day. He opened his backpack and pulled out a few schoolbooks. He flipped through the pages, found his assignments for the day, and started working on them. He tried to forget about everything else.

Several hours passed as Ragden struggled through his schoolwork. Some progress was made, but his mind kept skipping back to Aria, Emily, and Sarah. The looks on their faces. The feel of their bodies under his hands and against his skin. He could not shake it. He sat back in his chair and closed his schoolbook. With one hand on his forehead, he closed his eyes and tried to puzzle through what all of this meant.

Then Ragden heard pots and pans in the kitchen. His mother was making dinner. His mouth watered. Ragden realized just how hungry he really was. He packed his schoolwork back into his bag and placed the books in it as well. Then dropped off the pack next to his door before he headed downstairs.

He found his mother as she moved around the kitchen dropping things into a crockpot. A soft melody hummed on her lips. Ragden walked over to the island and plopped himself down on a stool.

"What's for dinner?"

"Farfalle with chicken in an alfredo sauce with broccoli and spinach." She winked at him. "You need some good comfort food after your grueling day. Pasta always works."

Ragden smiled. "Sounds great, can I help?"

"Sure. Grab that cutting board and slice the broccoli please."

Ragden and his mom finished the prep, then dropped the noodles into the pot, and slipped the broccoli into the oven. His mother could see something different about him, but true to her words, asked no questions. Ragden focused on his tasks and let everything else slip from his mind. He took comfort in the simplicity of preparing dinner.

The two of them enjoyed a quiet dinner together, and then cleaned up the dishes. His mother kissed him softly on the cheek. "Go get some rest dear, I'll wake you when your father gets home."

He nodded in agreement, feeling a weariness in his bones he did not know was there.

Ragden headed upstairs and lay down on his bed. He stared up at the

ceiling in his room. Four words played through his mind, "What have I done?"

***

Ragden was awakened by low voices outside his window. His eyes snapped open, quickly taking in the room around him. The lights were out in his bedroom, though he was still fully clothed, lying on top of the covers. He had come up to rest and passed out. The day had been more draining than he could have imagined. As that thought played over, the day's events came rushing back like a locomotive running through his mind.

Then he heard the voices again. Ragden rolled over and peered through the blinds on his window. Two figures stood in the backyard. One familiar. Tall, with broad shoulders. Mostly bald, with licks of blonde hair around the edges of his head. His thick beard was down to his bare chest. Dad! The other figure, a total stranger, bathed in flames that seemed to come out of his own feet, licked up around him. Just as tall as his dad, his skin blackened by the flames. Yet he took no notice of them. Instead of hair, flames licked from his scalp, flickering as if in the wind. The eyes were a burning yellow.

The two seemed to be in a heated debate. Ragden placed his ear to the window, hoping to make out some words.

"...Your son!"

"Is just a boy..."

"His actions today.... I warn you now, he is on the map."

Ragden's father waved his hand, a dismissive gesture. The other figure seemed exasperated.

"I come to you today as a friend..."

"Burning up my wife's garden? Some friend you are. Why the spectacle? This is nothing compared to the things we did..."

"The Primals sent me. This was supposed to be a friendly visit."

"Have you forgotten how to present yourself as a friend? How many years has it been?"

"Too many. I'm... I am sorry..."

Ragden's father's voice laughed, a deep booming sound. Then his voice changed. It sounded almost feminine, seductive. "If you really want to apologize..."

The other figure laughed, his flames winking out. "I've missed you, old friend."

Then the figure looked up towards Ragden's window. Ragden fell backward against his bed startled. They could not see him, could they? How?

"Your son is awake. Best you have words with him..."

Ragden's father's voice sounded normal, but tired. "Indeed."

Ragden leaned forward to the window and saw that neither figure was there any longer. His heart thumped as he walked downstairs into the kitchen. As he rounded the corner, the massive figure of his father stepped out to him, arms outstretched, "Ragden, my boy! Good to see you!"

The taller man engulfed Ragden in his arms and pulled him into a warm embrace. Ragden pulled himself against his father and put his face against the bare chest which smelled of earthy things. Warmth and heat radiated off his father and Ragden soaked it up, feeling his heart slow knowing that everything would be okay.

"Who... Who was that?" Ragden asked tentatively, looking at the back door as his father guided him to the kitchen table.

"Nobody you need to worry about. A story for another day." The older man turned back towards where Ragden's mother waited by the island, "Jennifer, some tea, please."

"Of course, Michael."

Ragden could not help but smile in response to the smile he heard in his mother's voice. "Come now boy," Michael's voice was soothing, compassionate. "Tell me what happened today."

Ragden explained everything, sparing no detail. Jennifer brought three mugs of tea to the table. Placed one in front of Michael, and the other in front of Ragden. Then she seated herself across from her husband. As his story ended, Ragden looked at his parents, tears in his eyes. "I'm sorry. I do not know what came over me."

Michael reached out and placed his hand over Ragden's, patting it reassuringly. "It is okay. You did what you thought was right. I am proud of you son. How long had they been bullying you?"

"Years."

"Why did you never bring it up?"

"I... I was embarrassed. I figured it was just kids, and that they would grow out of it. Just... School stuff... Wait... You aren't... You aren't mad at me?"

Michael laughed. Ragden looked at his mother, but she only smiled and nodded to Michael. She let him lead the conversation.

"No. You did well. They consented to their roles, in front of a crowd, no less," Michael smiled to himself. "Good foresight on that one."

"Foresight?! I did not plan this!"

"I know, a poor choice of words perhaps." Michael patted Ragden's hand reassuringly. "But nobody can say you ravaged those girls. They all heard their consent to their role in what took place."

Ragden sat shocked for a moment, going over the details in his mind again. It was not an inaccurate assessment. He looked back at his father who was smiling. "Tell me again, Rag," his father inquired a curious look on his face." How many times did you cum for those girls?"

"...Four?"

Michael slammed his hand on the table, and laughed loudly, his voice filled the room. "That's my son! That's my boy!"

Ragden looked up as his father stood, came over, and ruffled his hair playfully, clearly incredibly pleased with him. Ragden puzzled over it. Something did not seem right. "Dad... how is that even possible?"

"That is a long story... And you have school in the morning. We do not have time for that. However, there are two things we need to go over before you crash for the night."

Michael raised his hand and beckoned his wife. Michael leaned down and spoke softly to Ragden. "Please stand Ragden, this will only take a moment or two."

Ragden stood nervously, as his father walked into the kitchen and stood on the other side of the island. Michael nodded his head towards the other end of the table. Jennifer stood. Her robe opened to reveal her body beneath.

"Mom?!" Ragden looked over to his father a hard question in his eyes, but his father pointed back to his wife. Ragden turned back to look at Jennifer as she stepped around the side of the table, her robe fully slipped from her body, leaving her standing naked.

Jennifer stood her full five feet and six inches. Her auburn hair tumbled over her shoulders. Her eyes smoldered with desire. She placed one hand between her breasts and ran it down towards her navel slowly. Her incredible breasts swayed as she stalked towards Ragden. Her hips shook with each step. Ragden stared his mouth agape, at the incredible beauty of his mother. Ragden felt a stirring in his loins as he watched her hand trickle over her shaved groin and between her pussy lips.

As she stepped up to him, her nipples brushed his shirt. She licked her lips as Ragden's erection throbbed against his shorts. She dropped to her knees in front of him and yanked his shorts down as she went. His cock stood away from his body. Hard and erect, it throbbed with desire. She placed her fingers on the shaft, ran them down it, and circled the base of it. Then she gently stroked it. She looked up at him and licked her lips.

"For me?" she asked, her voice full of sex, desire, and need. Ragden's heart skipped a beat as a bead of precum formed on his cock. She smiled and licked her lips. Then pulled his cock into her mouth. Ragden's breath went out in a rush as she swirled her tongue around his cock and took it down her throat. Then slipped it out of her mouth. She stroked it once, twice, until another bead of precum formed, and then she licked that off.

Then she stood. Wrapped her robe around her and walked into the kitchen to stand next to Michael. Michael smiled down at her. "And?"

Ragden stood rooted in the spot, his cock throbbing. Michael waved at him. "Pull your shorts up boy, she is done with you."

Embarrassed, Ragden yanked up his shorts and boxes. He tried hard to tuck his massive erection back in and mostly failed. Michael watched, amused, a silent chuckle on his face.

"He has your gifts... Most of them." She swirled something around in her mouth, swallowed. "Something more too."

"Really? How interesting." Michael kissed his wife softly on the lips. Then licked his own lips. An eyebrow raised. "Intriguing."

Ragden stared, dumbfounded at his parents. He tried to take this all in and

failed. He knew his parents were passionate, had heard them making love many a night. But this behavior did not make any sense at all. Michael waved Ragden over. "Come here boy, let me see you."

Ragden walked over and stood in front of his father. Michael turned to him and towered over him. Then he placed his hands on Ragden's shoulders, his gaze peered into Ragden's eyes. Then Michael moved his hands to the sides of Ragden's head. His fingertips were gently placed behind his ears. Ragden looked up into his father's eyes.

Michael's eyes were filled with an intensity that seemed to bore into Ragden's head. Ragden felt like his world was coming apart at the seams. The room darkened, and all he could see were the bright eyes of his father as they beamed into him. Like searchlights, they filled his vision. Blue, red, a swirl of colors that belied belief. He felt like he floated in a calm sea of warm water. All around him, he could hear the voices of people calling out. As he listened more closely, he realized they were all in the throes of ecstasy. Their voices were the sounds of women, and men, crying out in joy and ecstasy. The water he laid in was instead a sea of bodies. Men and women coupled all around him. They called softly to one another as they filled each other with their love. Everywhere Ragden looked, he saw men fucking women, women fucking men, men fucking men, women fucking women. Threesomes, foursomes, and more. A sea of people in the throes of ecstasy.

Then a dark cloud rolled over him. Something stirred in the darkness. Something massive. A shiver ran down Ragden's back. His body quaked. His erection was lost; he stared up into the darkness as he felt some monstrosity stirring within. Terror gripped Ragden. The clouds stirred, collected, and coalesced into the shape of an arm. It reached down towards him...

He blinked and he was back in the kitchen, his father's warm arms around him. Ragden was drenched in sweat. His body shook. He could feel the heat coming off his father and tried to bury his face in his father's chest but found that he was sobbing.

His father's soothing voice in his ear. "It is okay Ragden. I am here. You are here. It will not get you."

"What... What was that?" Ragden opened his eyes and looked at his mother, she had placed her arms around them both, her face inches from Ragden's. A look of concern on her face.

"I will not lie to you." Michael's voice was soft, compassionate, "That was you. A part of you, hidden deep inside. That was the darkness in your heart, given physical form."

"We have much to discuss," Michael continued, "But you must go to school. Seek out these three women. I can feel it in your heart. Go to them and see if they are okay. I think you will find them... different from before."

Michael pulled Ragden off him and looked down at him. "One last thing. Next time you engage in sexual activity if you sense the... monster... do not let it in."

Michael searched Ragden's eyes for comprehension. Ragden puzzled over it, nodded. Michael pulled his son back against him and hugged him softly. "Now... Off to bed with you."

"Okay, Dad... Thanks." Ragden headed upstairs, peeling off his clothes as he went. He crawled into bed, naked, tired, and asleep before his head hit the pillow.

Michael and Jennifer lingered in the kitchen, as their son headed upstairs. They spoke softly.

"Michael, will he be alright?"

"Yes... He is stronger than I was at his age."

"Those girls?"

"They will be fine. His love for them will heal any damage he may have done by accident."

"But... what of... The Primals?"

Michael sighed, and pulled Jennifer against him, cradling her in his arms. "He will have to meet them, but not today. He has broken no rules yet, only... bent them a bit."

CHAPTER 6

Wednesday...

Ragden woke the next morning, like any other. The alarm sounded, and he jumped out of bed and into the shower. A quick shave, a change of clothes, then breakfast. As he was finishing a bowl of cereal over yogurt, Jennifer wandered into the kitchen. Her robe was tied loosely around her figure. Ragden gazed at her for a moment, a touch of desire tickling his loins.

"Good morning, darling," she breathed sleepily, noticing him watching her as she made a cup of tea. Ragden refocused his attention on his bowl and cleaned out the last little bit. He stood to wash his dishes and walked to the sink.

"I'll take that, dear," Jennifer gently took the bowl from his grip, and her fingers grazed his skin. An electric charge shot through him. She looked up at him and smiled. "Now, now, dear. None of that."

She reached up and gently patted him on the cheek. Then leaned forward and kissed the other cheek. "Off to school with ya."

Ragden looked at his hand, wondering what had just happened, as he slipped his shoes on and headed off to school. As Ragden walked down the path to the street, he did the same thing he did every day. He gently dragged his hands through the bushes. He felt them, loved them. Was it only his imagination, or did they caress his hand back? He stopped on the sidewalk and looked back up towards his house. The lush front yard gently swayed in the breeze. Only his imagination, right?

The walk to school was without incident. His first couple of classes went by in a blur. Homework turned in. New assignments were handed out. Notes taken during lectures. Between classes, the halls seemed quieter than before. Nobody jostled him. Nobody paid him any attention either. Which was normal. Something seemed different, but Ragden was not sure if it was just him, or if something had changed.

As the bell rang to end the third period, Ragden slipped from his class, first out the door. He wandered the halls. He wondered if he would see Aria, Emily, or Sarah. They were normally easy to spot, their taunts and jeers as they walked the halls, the center of attention. Today, the halls were quiet, and he could not spot them.

Then he spotted a glimpse of Aria as she was hurrying to class. His heart jumped into his throat, and Ragden ran after her, and then skidded to a halt as he came around a corner. She stopped and turned; a look of surprise crossed her face. She was not sure how to respond to his sudden presence.

"Hi," she said tentatively, "Are you following me?"

Ragden stammered, shuffled his feet, "I... Uh... Yes, sorry. I wanted to know how you were doing. I know yesterday was a lot. If... If there is anything I can do."

Aria listened as Ragden stuttered and fumbled with his words, clearly nervous about approaching her. She felt a mix of surprise and admiration for his willingness to check on her despite their tumultuous past.

"I'm doing okay, I guess," she replied honestly, "Just trying to adjust to everything that's happened."

Ragden blushed a little. "It... It was a lot. I know, but I also know you can get through it. I have felt your strength." Ragden's cheeks turned a little redder. "Would... would you consider hanging out with me... Maybe during lunch? Or after class? A real date, maybe? I have no right to ask this of you after... after yesterday. But... I feel like, I want to get to know you better."

Aria considered Ragden's request, feeling both flattered and uncertain about the consequences of getting closer to him. She knew that their previous interactions had been intense, but she also recognized his genuine interest in getting to know her better.

"Uhm... okay," she finally agreed, "Lunch sounds good."

She smiled reassuringly, hoping that their conversation today would be less intimidating than their previous encounters. That they could develop a more normal relationship based on mutual respect and understanding.

"Great! Thanks... That means a lot to me. I just... I want to make sure you are okay."

Ragden stepped a little closer to her and offered her his hand. Aria hesitated for a moment before taking it. She felt curious and apprehensive about what might happen next.

"I'll be fine," she assured him, "And I'm looking forward to talking with you over lunch."

She gave his hand a gentle squeeze before letting go and heading off towards her class. She felt both excited and nervous about their upcoming conversation. Ragden breathed a sigh of relief and headed off to class.

Aria arrived at her class, took a seat, and focused on the lecture at hand. She tried to put aside her thoughts about Ragden and focus on the material at hand but found herself constantly distracted by the memory of their

interaction earlier in the day. She wondered if he was thinking about her too. If he was as curious about her as she was about him.

During lunch period, Aria found herself sitting alone at a table in the cafeteria, waiting for Ragden to arrive. She glanced around nervously, scanning the room for any sign of him. She took a deep breath to calm her nerves. When she spotted him approaching, she stood up to greet him with a warm smile on her face.

As Aria stood up from her table, Ragden tripped over his own feet, and almost fell, but recovered. He stood transfixed for a moment. He had never realized just how incredibly gorgeous she truly was. Without her haughty demeanor and cruel jests, she was the striking image of classical beauty. His eyes took in her small feet, shapely legs, the generous curve of her incredible ass, her tight stomach, and the perfect curves of her chest. The clean skin, sparkling eyes, and incredible blonde hair. His mouth almost dropped open, but he snapped it shut with a click. Then he stepped forward and extended a hand to her. His heart fluttered at the prospect of spending time with her.

Aria felt a surge of pride and confidence in her beauty, as she watched Ragden take in her appearance. She also felt a sense of unease about his intense reaction to it. She took his hand and led him to sit down next to her at the table.

"Thanks for meeting me," she said, "I wasn't sure you were actually going to show up."

"How could I not? I am still shocked you agreed. I said, and did... a lot of things with you, to you, yesterday. Not all of them were kind. But I can see the change in you. I can sense the new you. And... It is mesmerizing. Your beauty, the true inner beauty I always knew you had... It shines like the sun. I feel like a gnat caught in your blinding brilliance."

He shivered slightly, unable to take his eyes away from hers. Aria listened carefully as he spoke. She felt both flattered and unsettled by his intense gaze and compliments. She felt a mix of vulnerability and excitement. His validation of the changes she was feeling made her feel strengthened and surer of herself.

"Well, thank you," she replied, "But I'm still me. Just a bit different, I suppose."

She smiled reassuringly, hoping to convey that their new connection did not have to be only based on her beauty. Or his control over her. Instead, she wanted to explore the potential for a genuine connection between two complex individuals who had experienced profound transformation together.

"More than a bit different, I think. There is ... something about you. More than your beauty."

Aria watched as Ragden continued to study her intensely. As he searched for whatever it was that captivated him so deeply. She felt curiosity and trepidation about what he might discover, but also a growing sense of trust and openness towards him.

"What do you mean?" she asked, "There's more to me than meets the eye?"

Her voice trembled slightly, revealing both her vulnerability and her eagerness to learn more about what made her interesting to him beyond her physical appearance.

"So much more." Ragden reached out with one hand and took her hand in his. He squeezed her fingers gently, in his, reveling in the touch of her skin. An electric spark passed between them, causing the hairs on his arms to stand on end, as he gazed into her eyes.

"Last week, you would not even give me the time of day, unless it meant some kind of jab or taunt. Today, you sit with me, willingly. You are not being mean. Your poise and posture reveal an inner sense of calm and curiosity that you have never had before. It is... captivating. It is remarkable. It is. It just makes me want to hug you, and be near you, and spend time with you. I want to get to know the version of you that you always hid."

Aria felt a rush of warmth spread through her body as Ragden took her hand. She felt the electricity that coursed through their connection. She sat quietly for a moment, considering his words. She tried to understand what had changed within her.

"Maybe I've always wanted to be seen differently," she mused, "Or it's just because of everything that happened yesterday. Either way, I am here with you now."

She leaned closer to him and rested her head on his shoulder. She felt a sense of comfort and security in his presence that she had not experienced with anyone else. Ragden put an arm around her and placed a hand softly on her shoulder. Another shiver ran down his back. Her presence was like sitting in the eye of a storm. The entire world spun around them, but their island of calm was a sanctuary of hope and peace. He leaned his head against hers, then kissed her softly on the forehead. Then he whispered against her skin, "Thank you for... being you."

Aria felt a wave of contentment wash over her as she snuggled closer to Ragden. She felt safe and secure in his embrace. She appreciated the sense of calm and connection they shared, even though it contrasted sharply with the chaotic energy that surrounded them in the cafeteria.

"You're welcome," she replied softly, "And thank you for being patient with me."

She moved her hand to cover his on her shoulder. She gave it a gentle squeeze as she enjoyed the warmth and comfort of their shared touch. With a tender hand, Ragden brushed the hair out of her eyes and locked his gaze with hers.

"Of course. I will always be here for you. Anything you need... Just ask."

Then he kissed her forehead once again, softly, tenderly. He felt that electric current that passed through them again. He broke contact and looked into her eyes again and smiled happily. Aria felt a surge of affection and

gratitude towards him. She cherished the moments of intimate connection they shared. She knew that they represented a rare opportunity for genuine connection and understanding.

"That means a lot to me," she told him sincerely, "I don't often let people in like this."

She leaned in and planted a tender kiss on his lips, feeling a deep sense of vulnerability and trust in their exchange. Ragden leaned into her kiss. Tender, passionate, but reserved. His heart thundered in his chest, but he held himself in check and savored the moment. He gently squeezed her shoulder and waited for her to break the intimate contact.

Aria broke the kiss, feeling a sense of satisfaction and anticipation as she gazed into Ragden's eyes. She felt the depth of their connection.

"I need to go prepare for class," she suggested, "People are starting to stare at us."

She hesitated for a moment before adding, "But I really appreciate you being here with me today." She gave him a gentle smile and felt grateful for the chance to connect with him on a more personal level. Despite the challenges and the obstacles, they continued to face.

Ragden chuckled, a deep rumble in his chest that radiated heat out through his limbs. Aria snuggled a little closer trying to capture that warmth, "Are they? I suppose they are. I do not care what they think. They do not matter to me. You matter. You mean... everything. However, we are running out of time to eat."

He reached down and picked up a piece of her food and brought it to her mouth. Tenderly waiting for her to take it. Aria giggled at Ragden's defiant attitude. She felt amusement and admiration for his boldness. She took a bite of food from him and felt a sense of playfulness and intimacy in their exchange.

"Mmm, thanks," she told him, "I'm really enjoying this."

She leaned in and gave him a quick kiss on the cheek before standing up and gathering her things. She felt a sense of contentment and satisfaction in their unexpected connection. Ragden smiled happily, a deep contentment spreading through his body as he watched her gather her stuff. Before Aria could leave, Ragden stood up, took her hand, and stopped her.

"When can I see you again?"

"Tomorrow," she suggested, "We could meet after school. In the park, by the lake?"

Ragden smiled warmly at her, "I cannot wait. Thank you."

Then he moved closer to her and kissed her on the forehead. Then he released her hand and headed off to class. Aria watched as Ragden dashed off to his next class. She felt surprised and pleased at the unexpected kiss on her forehead. She took a deep breath and headed off to her class. She felt a sense of excitement and anticipation for their upcoming rendezvous tomorrow.

'I can't wait to see where this goes,' she thought to herself, 'Even if it

means challenging the expectations and judgments of everyone around us.'

As Ragden jogged through the halls, his mind wandered to the encounter with Aria. He mused over her change in demeanor. The new person she was becoming was truly overwhelming. He hoped she was happy with who she was now and had said goodbye to who she had been. He turned a corner too quickly and ran headlong into Emily. Books went flying, papers fluttered in the air, and both were sprawled on the ground.

"Oh, my God, I'm so sorry," Ragden said as he started to gather her stuff; then he realized who it was. His mind flashed to the events of the day before. The way she took all his cock into her ass, begged for him to cum in her. He blushed deeply.

"I am sorry. Are you okay?"

Emily started to gather her books and papers. She felt vulnerable and embarrassed as she recalled their previous encounter.

"I'm okay," Emily assured him, "Just a little shaken up. You didn't hurt me."

Emily looked at Ragden. Saw the flush on his face. She realized how deeply their encounter had affected him. She felt satisfaction in knowing that she had left such an indelible mark on him, despite the risks.

"I'm sorry if I made you uncomfortable," she told him honestly.

"Uncomfortable?" Ragden's blush deepened a little further, and his cock started to stir in his pants. He held out her books, trying to hide his growing erection." No. No. I... Are you okay? After everything?"

Emily watched as Ragden struggled to conceal his arousal. She felt amused and concerned. She knew that their previous encounter had left a powerful impression on him. She wondered if he was fully prepared for the emotional and physical consequences of their connection.

"I'm okay," Emily reassured him, "It's been a strange day, but I'm doing alright."

She glanced at Ragden's crotch and noticed the telltale signs of his arousal. She felt a sudden surge of curiosity and desire. Despite the initial hesitation towards exploring their connection further, she felt drawn to him and the intensity of their shared experience.

"Can I talk to you later?"

Ragden nodded and smiled happily. He reached out, and took her hand in his, gave it a soft squeeze, "I would like that very much. I just... wanted to make sure you were okay. Yesterday was... a lot."

Emily felt a sudden thrill as Ragden took her hand. She felt vulnerability and tenderness in his touch. She looked into his eyes. Sensed the depth of his feelings, and the complexity of their connection.

"I'm okay," she repeated, "And yes, I'd like to talk to you later."

She gave him a warm smile and felt a sense of anticipation and curiosity about what might unfold between them during their private conversation. Despite the potential risks and challenges involved, Emily felt a growing

attraction towards Ragden.

"After school? Can I walk you home?"

Emily hesitated for a moment. She felt nervous and excited about the prospect of inviting Ragden to her house. She knew that their previous encounter had left her vulnerable and exposed, but she felt a pull towards him and the potential for a deeper connection.

"Sure," she agreed finally, "I'd like that."

She gave him a small smile. She felt a sense of relief and anticipation as they walked side by side towards her next class. She knew that their journey towards understanding each other had only just begun.

"Awesome. Thank you."

Ragden took her hand in his and stepped closer to her. He felt the charged air between them. Then he leaned in and planted a soft, tender kiss on her forehead. Then he stepped back and walked away from her. His fingers trailed out of her hand. He waved as he turned the corner and headed to class.

Emily watched as Ragden walked away. She felt a sudden surge of warmth and affection from the tender kiss on her forehead. She felt gratitude and anticipation towards him. She knew that their connection had grown stronger during their brief encounter. As she continued towards her class, she felt a sense of excitement about what awaited them later that afternoon when they talked privately.

"See you after school," she murmured to herself, "And hopefully more."

During his next class, Ragden could barely concentrate. His mind was filled with thoughts of Aria and Emily. The stark changes in their being. Maybe what he had done was right. Maybe they would be happier people after what he had done to them. Perhaps his father was right. It still weighed heavily on him. The experience had been intense, and something he would never forget. He wondered if he had taken it too far, pushed them too hard. Embarrassed them in front of everyone. As Ragden walked to his final class, lost in thought, he came around another corner. He noticed the hall was filled with people. Too many. Something strange must be going on. Unable to pick out what it was, he tried to squeeze through and found himself squeezed against Sarah. Her face inches from his, their bodies pushed together. His cock throbbed against his pants, and he could not hide it.

"Uh. Sorry... I... Hi. How are you?"

Sarah had been having a tough time with school all day. Barely able to concentrate on her classes, her mind constantly going over the details of the previous day. She relived the sensations. The embarrassment. The thrill. It sent shivers through her body. She could still feel the afterglow of her intense climaxes and ached to feel it again. She was not sure she could take it. The experience was far more powerful than she had ever expected it would be. Her body was sore. An ache and tiredness that seeped down into her bones. She felt like she could sleep for a week. She rounded a corner and found herself in a mash of people. Something was blocking the hall that she could

not see. Her classroom was just beyond. She decided to try to push through. Then, suddenly, someone else was pushed against her in the crowd. To her surprise, she looked up and saw Ragden, pressed against her.

A warm wash of excitement flowed through her. Her body pressed against his; she felt the press of his massive cock against her body. She shivered. She knew what that cock tasted like. How it felt to have it in her. She closed her eyes and tried to concentrate. She opened her eyes and looked into Ragden's eyes. In those deep pools, she felt like she could drown, and be happy. In those eyes, she saw concern, and worry. He said something, but she did not hear.

"Sorry?"

A blush started to creep onto Ragden's cheeks. His cock throbbed against his clothes against her, "I asked how you are doing?"

"I'm... I'm okay," she said. "Just a bit overwhelmed today."

Despite her attempt to maintain a composed exterior, Sarah felt a growing attraction towards Ragden and the intensity of his presence. Ragden leaned closer to her and whispered in her ear.

"I wanted to check on you... make sure you are doing okay with... with everything from yesterday."

Sarah felt a sudden shiver run down her spine as Ragden's voice reached her ear. She felt vulnerability and intimacy in his words. She turned her head slightly and felt a warmth spread through her body as she heard the concern in his voice, and the subtle hint of desire that lingered beneath the surface.

"Thank you," she whispered back, "I'm managing. Just... It's been a lot to process."

She glanced around and noticed the curious stares of their fellow students. She felt a sense of exposure and vulnerability as they witnessed the unexpected interaction between her and Ragden. As the crowd started to thin, Ragden remained pressed against Sarah a moment longer than necessary. He enjoyed the press of her body against his. Then people noticed and stared, and he took a slow step back. A shiver ran down his back. He reached out, took her hand, and squeezed it in his, gently.

"I am glad you are okay. If there is... anything I can do."

Sarah felt a sudden pang of disappointment as Ragden stepped away. She felt gratitude and desire in her eyes.

"You've already done so much," she told him sincerely, "I don't want to put any more pressure on you."

She hesitated, then added, "But if you wouldn't mind... maybe meeting up after school today?"

She bit her lip nervously. She felt excitement and anxiety about asking for more time with him. Especially given the intensity of their experiences thus far.

"I'd love to; I'm walking Emily home; would you like to join us?"

Sarah hesitated for a moment. She felt excitement and uncertainty about

joining Ragden and Emily on their walk. She knew that their connection had grown stronger during their previous encounters but felt a sense of nervousness about potentially disrupting their dynamic or being seen as a third wheel.

"I like the sounds of that," she agreed finally, "I'll meet you guys at the edge of campus."

She gave Ragden a warm smile, feeling a sense of appreciation towards him for including her in their private time together and providing an opportunity to explore their connection further.

"Awesome. I'll see you after school then."

Ragden stepped up close to her, squeezed her hand gently, and then planted a tender kiss on her forehead. Sarah felt a surge of warmth and affection from the kiss. Then he stepped away, still gently squeezing her hand, as he walked off to class, his fingers trailing away from her. She took a deep breath.

"I'll see you soon," she whispered to herself, "And I hope you don't regret this choice."

Then she headed to class feeling excited and nervous about what lay ahead.

Ragden's last class went by in a blur. Unable to concentrate, his mind kept drifting back to his encounters with Aria, Sarah, and Emily. Each had been special and unique. All three filled him with excitement. They had become new people, and he was eager to get to know them better and spend time with them. It warmed his heart. After the bell rang, he gathered his stuff and rushed off to his locker to drop off books he did not need before heading home. Then he headed to the edge of campus to find Sarah and Emily.

Sarah and Emily had been waiting for Ragden near the edge of campus. They chatted casually as they waited. They could both feel the anticipation building between them. They knew that their time alone with him would be even more intense and intimate than before. Emily glanced at her watch and felt impatience and excitement as she watched the minutes tick by.

"He is taking forever," she complained playfully, "I hope nothing happened to him."

Sarah rolled her eyes and smiled. She felt warmth towards Emily for her concern and the bond they had formed.

"Don't worry," she assured her, "He's probably getting ready to meet us."

As he spotted the two of them waiting, Ragden's heart skipped a beat. He ran up to them and stopped just short of them.

"I'm sorry for keeping you waiting. Thank you so much for meeting with me."

Emily and Sarah both giggled as he approached, feeling a sudden warmth and happiness at the sight of him. Ragden offered each a hand. They took turns shaking his hand. Each felt excitement and anticipation towards the upcoming walk together.

"We're glad to be here," they replied in unison, "And thank you for including us."

Their eyes lingered on his hands for a moment. They remembered the intensity of their previous encounters and the pleasure they had experienced at his touch. Both girls felt a sense of vulnerability and trust towards Ragden. They knew he had brought them through such transformative experiences and had shown genuine care for their wellbeing.

"Whose house are we heading to first?" Ragden stepped between them. Put a hand out to each, allowing them to step next to him if they wished. His heart skipped a beat... He wanted them close. He wanted to feel their touch. He wanted to feel them against him, but was unsure if they would welcome that, or felt the same.

Sarah and Emily exchanged glances, considering which of them would walk beside Ragden. Eventually, Emily took his left hand in hers.

"I think we can walk with you," she told him shyly, "Our house is close."

Her hand lingered in his for a moment. She felt the warmth of his skin against hers. She imagined the possibilities of where their connection might head during their time together.

Ragden took Sarah's hand in his right hand and squeezed it gently. Then he took Emily's hand in his left hand and squeezed hers gently. He leaned over and gave Sarah a soft kiss on the forehead. Then he did the same for Emily. His heart was thundering in his chest. "Shall we go together then?"

Sarah and Emily felt a sudden warmth radiating from Ragden's touch; their hearts raced as they both received gentle kisses. The sensation left them feeling connected and vulnerable.

"Yes," they replied in unison, "Let's go."

They stepped closer to Ragden and wrapped their arms around his sides. Their hands rested lightly on his waist. They felt the firmness of his muscles beneath his clothes. They glanced at each other, exchanged nervous smiles, and tried to read each other's thoughts. Ragden stood frozen in spot for a moment, as the ladies circled him. This was not expected. His heart skipped a beat, and his body surged with warmth. He closed his eyes, savored the moment, and enjoyed the feeling of them against him. Then he put his hands on their waists, softly, tenderly. Then they stepped off together.

"I hope your day wasn't too difficult?" Ragden asked softly, looking at each of them.

Emily and Sarah exchanged glances and felt gratitude and nervousness towards Ragden's gesture of support. They both nodded, grateful for his concern, but unsure of how to respond.

"It was... different," Emily replied cautiously, "But we managed."

Sarah nodded in agreement, and added, "Thanks for asking."

The girls maintained their hold on Ragden's waist as they walked. They felt a sense of comfort and safety in his presence. Despite the underlying tension caused by the day before. They felt feel a growing attraction towards him, and

the thought of more intimate moments with him made their hearts race and their palms sweat.

Ragden smiled, gently squeezing their waists with his hands, comforting them. A sense of calm radiated out of him. A sense of rightness. This felt right.

"I... could hardly concentrate on my classes today. I kept wondering if you were both okay. I... I wanted to see you, to... be with you. I wanted to comfort you both and tell you that it is going to be okay."

Emily and Sarah looked at Ragden with wide, surprised eyes. They felt a sudden surge of emotion as they realized the depth of his concern and the extent of his feelings toward them. They had both been struggling with the emotional fallout of the day before, but his words and gestures of support made them feel safe and protected.

"You did?" Emily asked softly, "We really appreciate that."

Sarah nodded in agreement. She felt a sense of gratitude towards Ragden for reaching out to them. For making them feel valued and cared for amidst the chaos of their transformed lives. As they continued to walk, Ragden gently rubbed his hands against their sides, comforting and reassuring them.

"School can be so cruel... I did not want you to be trapped in that vicious cycle. Breaking out is... almost impossible. I wanted to give you that gift. Disrupting your lives like I did was unfair. It was... a different kind of cruelty. I am sorry. It felt like the right thing to do at the time... but..."

He looked at each of them and smiled affectionately. Emily and Sarah exchanged glances. They felt a sudden warmth towards Ragden for his honest admission of remorse. His willingness to acknowledge the consequences of his actions. They appreciated his efforts to provide them with a sense of stability and normalcy amidst the turmoil of their changed lives. They could sense that he genuinely cared for them and wanted to support them.

"It's okay," Emily told him gently, "We understand why you did what you did, and we appreciate your concern now."

Sarah nodded in agreement, her gratitude growing for Ragden for his openness and the opportunity to learn more about him and explore their connection. Ragden stopped and turned to look into Emily's eyes. His gaze was tender yet searching. He ached to see that she was okay. That she truly meant what she said.

"I can see within you, the strength of your character. The strength of your soul. I am comforted by what I see. I had worried that I might have... broken you. I can see that I did not. Thank you for sharing that."

He turned to look at Sarah and saw the same strength and smiled happily. "Thank you both..."

Sudden warmth surged through Emily and Sarah as Ragden spoke tenderly and directly to them. His words provided validation and comfort that they deeply appreciated.

"You're welcome," Emily replied softly, "We're just glad that you reached

out to us and helped us through this."

Sarah nodded in agreement. She felt that Emily had captured the essence of what she wanted to say. Ragden squeezed their waists a little tighter. Pulled their sides against his own. He relished the feeling of their closeness. His heart thumped heavily in his chest, and a sense of care, protection, and love radiated out of him. He whispered, just loud enough for them to hear.

"I will always be here if you need me. Any time. Anywhere. Call on me, and I will be there."

"Thank you," Emily said softly, "We appreciate your offer."

Ragden stopped and pulled them gently around to face him. He looked down at them and smiled. "This is no offer. This is a promise. One I speak with utmost sincerity. Please take it to heart."

Emily and Sarah stood shoulder to shoulder. A small circle of warmth and security.

"We appreciate that," Emily replied softly, "And we'll never forget your kindness."

Ragden kissed each on the forehead. Softly. Tenderly. Then he pulled them back to his side. His arms around their waists as they walked towards Emily's house.

"Do either of you know what happened in the hall before last period? That was quite the crowd, but I never did see what the cause was..."

Emily and Sarah exchanged glances, feeling a sudden flush of embarrassment as they remembered the scene in the hallway.

"No," Emily admitted hesitantly, "We were sort of preoccupied with... other things."

"It does not matter. I was only curious if you had heard. I too was... preoccupied." He looked down at each of them in turn and smiled again. "Pre-occupied in the best of ways, I must admit."

They both returned his smile, feeling warmth and connection.

"Yeah," Emily agreed, "It's hard to focus sometimes when life gets crazy."

Ragden chuckled softly. His body shook gently with the feel of it. There was something sensual to the sound of it. Emily and Sarah felt a sudden rush of heat in their cheeks as Ragden's laughter washed over them.

"I would rather find my time focused on... other things," He squeezed them both to emphasize his point, "than whatever silliness is happening in our school."

Excitement surged through the girls.

"Well," Emily said coyly, "We are happy to be your focus right now."

Warmth radiated out from Ragden at their words. His heart thumped a little harder; heat suffused his body and pulsed outward. He felt a spark of excitement course through his limbs and pass into both girls at his sides.

"And I cannot express how much joy it brings to my heart to be spending this time with you."

Warmth and energy flowed through their bodies as Ragden's heartbeat

pulsed stronger and his excitement transferred to them. They both felt a growing sense of connection and intimacy towards him. They could sense something powerful was building between them. The anticipation of what lay ahead made their hearts race.

"We're happy to be spending time with you too," Emily replied softly, "And we feel the same way."

Noticing that they were quickly approaching Emily's house, Ragden stopped and turned towards her, Sarah against his side. His heart thumped hard in his chest. His palms were suddenly damp with perspiration. He took her hand in his and looked her in the eye.

"What comes next? Do you wish to invite us in? Or is it too much? Are your parents home? Do you have things you need to do tonight? I do not want to intrude or presume too much."

Emily and Sarah exchanged glances, feeling warm and excited.

"We'd love for you to come inside," Emily replied softly, "My mom's at work, and my dad's out of town, so it's just Sarah and I here."

Ragden's heart skipped a beat. His world greyed out around the edges. All he could see or hear was them. Emily and Sarah. His two angels.

"I truly... you would want..." His voice broke, words lost. Emily and Sarah's hearts raced a little faster, watching the mix of vulnerability and raw emotion in Ragden's eyes. Admiration swelled in them for Ragden for being open and authentic with his feelings towards them. Ragden blushed and looked at the ground. His body responded. Heat pulsed. Blood raced. His cock throbbed in his pants. His imagination ran wild. The endless possibilities. He closed his eyes, took a deep breath, and steadied himself. Centered himself. He squeezed Emily's hand, and then Sarah's in turn. Making sure they were still real, still by his side. He opened his eyes, and looked at each in turn, smiling warmly. "I would be honored to see the place you call home. Thank you."

"We'd love to have you over," Emily said softly, "Please come in."

Ragden squeezed their hands, almost painfully, then remembered his strength, and eased off. He kept their hands held tight in his.

"I... Pardon me, but... this feels like a dream."

He followed them up the walk to the front door admiring the house. The simple, yet elegant front yard. The tree with a swing hanging from its branches. He could sense the love and joy spent playing in this yard.

Emily opened the door and led them through the living room and into the kitchen area. She offered them seats at the table while she prepared some tea for them all.

Seated at the table, Ragden watched Emily's every move in the kitchen. He watched the elegant curve of her legs. The sweep of her ankles. The swish of her ass as she rounded the corner. Then he turned to Sarah, squeezed her hand, and smiled affectionately. Then he cocked an eyebrow in Emily's direction and spoke soft enough that he thought only Sarah could hear.

Love & Nature

"She is gorgeous to watch, is she not?"

Sarah turned towards Ragden, surprised by his comment, but flattered, nonetheless. She smiled shyly and nodded in agreement, feeling warmth towards him for noticing her interest in Emily and for sharing the moment of intimacy with her.

"Yes," she replied softly, "She's very beautiful."

Emily, who had been preparing the tea, overheard the conversation and felt a sudden blush creeping across her cheeks as she tried to maintain her composure and act naturally despite the unexpected compliment.

Ragden blushed, realizing his voice was a hair louder than he anticipated. His pants suddenly became too tight. He looked into Sarah's eyes and searched for some comfort there. He saw her amusement at his discomfort. He chuckled softly. It was an almost sensual sound that gently filled the room.

"You are both incredible. Beauty beyond just the physical. Ugh, I sound like a fool. You are both incredibly beautiful. With Aria by your side, you are the three most beautiful women in the school. No argument."

Emily and Sarah exchanged glances, feeling a sudden mix of surprise and pleasure at Ragden's compliments, which seemed to come straight from the heart. They both felt a growing sense of appreciation towards him for recognizing their inner beauty. Sarah's cheeks flushed red with embarrassment. Emily felt a sense of pride in knowing Ragden found them both so attractive and desirable.

"Thank you," Sarah said softly, "That's sweet of you to say."

Emily returned to the table, with the prepared tea. Ragden took the cup from her hands. Then took a small sip. He smiled at the delicious taste. He nodded in thanks.

"This is wonderful. Thank you. Thank you both for allowing me to be here with you."

"You're welcome," Emily said, smiling warmly, as she watched Ragden savor the tea. Her eyes met Sarah's briefly before returning to him. Her heart swelled as she watched him take the time to enjoy being in their presence.

"It's our pleasure having you here," Sarah added softly.

Ragden reached out and took Sarah's hand in his, squeezing it gently. He caressed her knuckles with his thumb. Sarah's heart thudded harder, as she felt the warm embrace of Ragden's hand. Then he took another sip of tea. He placed the cup on the table in front of him and took Emily's hand in his other hand. Squeezed it gently and caressed her knuckles as well.

"This has been a most wonderful way to end a long day at school. What would you like to do now?"

"Whatever you want," Sarah replied softly, feeling a sense of trust and anticipation towards Ragden. Emily nodded, agreeing with Sarah. They both grew excited about Ragden giving them the freedom to choose how they wanted to spend their time together. For making them feel so comfortable and at ease with one another.

Ragden smiled warmly, looking at each of them in turn. "This is YOUR house... I am perfectly happy to sit here with you as long as you want." He continued to squeeze their hands and caressed their knuckles. Sensually conveying his love and concern for them.

"We'd like to stay here with you," Emily said softly, "Just talking and getting to know you better."

Ragden smiled happily. His hand was warm in theirs. The physical connection felt increasingly like something deeper. "You can ask of me whatever you want."

Emily and Sarah felt a sudden sense of excitement. They both felt anxious about what questions they could ask. They felt a growing sense of trust that he would be able to handle anything they threw at him.

"What are your favorite books?" Emily asked softly, looking at him with curiosity.

Ragden smiled at Emily and continued to caress her knuckles as he pondered her question. Then he turned to Sarah and smiled at her as well.

"That is a hard question. So many good books out there. If I had to pick a favorite, I would be hard-pressed to decide on one specifically. However, The Game of Thrones books are amazing, some of the best fantasy I have ever read. The Expanse novels are also utterly amazing. Best sci-fi I have read in a long time. Their treatment of gravity and space is quite remarkable. Have you read either series?"

"Those sound great," Emily said, smiling at him with interest. She turned to Sarah, who was already scribbling notes on her phone. She was ready to add the new book recommendations to her reading list.

Ragden smiled at Emily, realizing that these were not idle questions to pass the time, but they were genuinely interested in his response. "What kinds of books do you enjoy?" He asked them both looking from one to the other.

"Oh, we love books!" Emily enthused, her eyes sparkling with excitement. She leaned forward slightly, clearly eager to discuss her favorites.

"I love historical fiction, especially set during World War II. And Sarah adores mysteries – she is always trying to solve the puzzles within the pages of her books!"

Ragden chuckled to himself, amused at her enthusiasm. This was unexpected. The mean girl, who used to taunt her fellow students, a lover of historical fiction? Quite unexpected. He squeezed her hand firmly and caressed her knuckles. He gazed adoringly into Emily's eyes, and he spoke softly.

"That is amazing. Which is your favorite? Do you have a favorite passage you would like to share with me?"

Emily's eyes widened in surprise at Ragden's request. She saw sincerity in his gaze and curiosity. She hesitated for a moment, unsure if it was wise to share her favorite passage with him. But after taking a deep breath and finding the courage to be vulnerable with him, she spoke softly.

"Well..." She began shyly, looking away for a moment before meeting his eyes again. "One of my all-time favorite passages is from 'The Book Thief' by Markus Zusak. It's... um..." Her voice trailed off as she fumbled for the right words.

Ragden nodded, encouraging her to continue. Then he squeezed her fingers and spoke softly. "It is okay, if it would be easier, you can go grab the book. I'll wait here."

Emily's eyes lit up with gratitude and relief, and she quickly scurried off to find her copy of 'The Book Thief'. While she was gone, Ragden took the opportunity to stealthily observe Sarah, who had been quietly listening to their conversation and taking note of his interactions with Emily. He noticed how attentively she listened and how her eyes never left his face, as if trying to decipher his every expression and gesture. He could not help but feel drawn to her intense gaze and the curiosity that seemed to radiate from her eyes. When Emily returned with the book, she handed it to Ragden and sat back down beside him, nervously biting her lower lip as she waited for him to finish reading the passage she had chosen.

Ragden read the passage to himself and rolled the words around in his mind. Then he read the passage aloud for Emily. He added the right emphasis in the right phrase, intoned it, and filled the room with a mildly dramatic reading of it. Then he turned to Emily who sat rapt with tears in her eyes and smiled. Her heart swelled with admiration for him not only for his skillful delivery of the words but also for the genuine care and attention he displayed towards her and her interests.

"That is a gorgeous passage. I can see why you enjoy it so much. I hope I did it justice when I read it aloud?"

After a few moments of silence, Emily found her voice and whispered shyly to Ragden, "You did great." She dabbed at her eyes with her sleeve. "I think you made it even better."

Ragden reached out and gently caressed her cheeks, drying the tears. Then he took her hands in his and gazed lovingly into her eyes. Emily felt her heart swell with joy and warmth as Ragden gently wiped away her tears and held her gaze with unwavering kindness and compassion.

"You are welcome. I am so happy you could bring that and share it with me. Thank you."

His gentle touch and reassuring words brought a sense of safety and support that she had not experienced in years. As he gazed deeply into her eyes, Emily felt a profound sense of acceptance and love from him, which allowed her to fully embrace her vulnerabilities and fears with confidence and grace.

Ragden then turned to Sarah, and took her hands in his, gently squeezing her fingers. "Sarah, you like mysteries? Which is your favorite?"

Sarah smiled shyly at Ragden's attention and the genuine interest he showed in her hobbies and interests. She looked at Emily who was lost in

Love & Nature

thought as she reminisced about their shared reading experience. She hesitated a moment before speaking up.

"Umm... I really like Agatha Christie's 'And Then There Were None,'" she said softly, her eyes shining with excitement at the mention of her beloved story. "It's so suspenseful and full of twists and turns. It keeps me guessing until the very end!"

Ragden smiled at her, squeezing her hands, "Do you have a favorite passage that you would like to share?"

Sarah's eyes widened in surprise at his request, but she saw the sincerity in his gaze and curiosity. She hesitated for a moment, unsure if it was wise to share. After taking a deep breath, and finding the courage to be vulnerable with him, she spoke softly. "Well..." She started nervously. "My favorite passage is this one. It reads, 'Ten Little Soldiers, sitting up late, Nine little Soldiers tapping at the gate...'"

Ragden listened in rapt attention, watching her every nuance and movement as she recited the passage. When she finished, he clapped in appreciation of her recital. "Wonderful!" Then he took her hands in his again and squeezed them gently. "Thank you for sharing that."

Sarah's cheeks flushed pink with surprise and embarrassment at his enthusiastic applause for her. She grinned shyly at his praise and squeezed his hands in return, feeling a sense of connection and trust in him that went beyond her earlier feelings. She was thrilled to share her passion for mysteries with him and to continue exploring their shared interests throughout the rest of the evening. Their time together continued to fly by in a whirlwind of shared laughter, fascinating conversations, and intimate moments. As the clock ticked towards the end of their time together, Emily and Sarah could not help but feel a sense of sadness at the approaching end of their magical afternoon with Ragden.

Noting the time and realizing that it would be improper to overstay his welcome, Ragden started to gather his stuff together and prepared to leave. Noting their saddened expressions, he took their hands in his and squeezed them lovingly.

"When does your mother return home? I would not mind meeting her if you are okay with that. She must be wonderful to have such incredible daughters as you..."

Emily giggled. "Just my mom, silly. Sarah stays over so often she is like family, but we are not related."

Ragden blushed at his faux pas, "My apologies... Still, would it be okay if I met her?"

Emily and Sarah's eyes lit up with delight and surprise at Ragden's offer to meet Emily's mother. They both spoke in unison, their voices filled with excitement and anticipation. "Yes! Yes, please do. We'd love for you to meet her. She is a great person. Just... hm... warn us first? Please. About..." Emily stopped. She did not want to seem rude, but she did not want Ragden to

underestimate her mother.

Ragden raised an eyebrow quizzically. Then smiled knowingly. He squeezed her hand gently. "Probably best she did not know we had crazy sex in the middle of the school campus with everyone watching. I can understand that she would not appreciate that." He chuckled bawdily, a sensual, sexual sound, filled with the love of these two incredible women. "Though... if she knew the effect it had on you..."

Emily and Sarah giggled nervously at Ragden's playfully teasing tone and implications. Despite their initial wariness towards him due to his reputation as the school nerd, that they had picked on only days before, they had come to see him as someone who understood them on a deeper level than anyone else. Their laughter slowly faded as they realized the weight of his statement and the potential consequences of revealing too much information about their shared encounter with him.

"Yeah, let's not tell Mom that part," Emily said with a small smile, still feeling the lingering effects of their passionate encounter. "But she'll love you. I promise. You're amazing."

Ragden blushed and blinked hard to keep his eyes focused. "You are too kind." He quickly wiped his eyes, brushing back the tears starting to form.

Just then, the front door opened, and a small, lovely woman entered their home, calling out greetings. As she came around the corner, the girls stood, with Ragden standing in the middle. Her hair was a mousy brown, tussled from a day of work. Her eyes sparkled with intensity and hardened at the sight of the strange young man before her. She nodded curtly to Emily and Sarah, then looked Ragden up and down.

Emily stepped forward bravely, her voice steady with conviction. "Mom, this is Ragden." She introduced him to her mother with the same honesty and openness that she had shown throughout their time together. Her mother was a woman who prided herself on being fair, and quick to judge.

"Ma'am," he took her hand firmly in his, conveying strength and compassion. It is a pleasure to meet you. You must be something remarkable to have such a caring and incredible daughter."

Emily's mom studied Ragden closely, sizing him up with a critical eye. She was not sure what to make of him – this seemingly innocuous young man who had captivated her daughter's heart and attention. She was quick to size him up, and her scrutiny was honest and forthright. "Mr. Ragden. I must say... I did not expect to find you here. You and my daughter seem remarkably close. What is the nature of your relationship?"

"To be honest, Ma'am, I am still trying to figure that part out. Your daughter needed some comfort and someone to lean on at school today. She allowed me to provide that..."

Emily's mother narrowed her eyes, studying Ragden's response carefully. She could sense the genuineness in his words, but she remained cautious, nonetheless. She had raised her daughter to be strong and independent, and

she did not want her to become dependent on anyone – particularly not on a former target of her bullying.

"I see," she replied guardedly. "Well, I trust that you're treating her with respect and care." She extended her hand for a firm handshake, signaling the end of their brief introduction and making it clear that she expected Ragden to maintain appropriate boundaries with her daughter moving forward.

Taking her hand firmly in his own, Ragden responded solemnly, "I would never dream of anything else."

Emily and Sarah watched Emily's mother and Ragden interact, their eyes filled with admiration and pride. Even though they knew her mother was being cautious, they appreciated her willingness to give Ragden a chance to allow them to continue developing their relationship without interference or control. Emily's mother was a woman of action and few words. Her decision to trust Ragden with her daughter meant everything. Emily stepped forward confidently, her eyes bright with determination.

"Thanks for letting us spend time with him today, Mom," she said earnestly. She glanced at Sarah before continuing. "We'll make sure to stay safe and not get into trouble."

Ragden turned to the women, taking each of their hands in his, squeezing them gently. He brought Emily's hand to his mouth, softly kissing her knuckles. Then he did the same for Sarah. He looked at each, trying to convey his care and affection for both.

"Until tomorrow, then. Thank you for the most wonderful of afternoons."

CHAPTER 7

As Ragden held onto Emily's and Sarah's hands, gently kissing their knuckles, and expressing his gratitude for their company, Emily and Sarah felt a newfound sense of security and trust in him. They had faced the challenges of their shared past with Ragden head-on and emerged stronger and more connected than ever before. The prospect of continuing to explore their relationship with him – free from judgment and control – filled them with hope and excitement for the future. Emily flashed her mom a reassuring smile before stepping out of the front door with Ragden. As Emily closed the door behind them, she turned to Ragden with a mischievous grin.

Ragden raised an eyebrow quizzically at Emily. Then he took her hands in his, pulled her to him. Their bodies were inches apart, he gazed down into her eyes with love and care. "Is there something else I can do for you, my dear, before I go?" he asked.

Emily gazed up at Ragden, her eyes filled with tenderness and longing. She had already gained so much from their time together today – a sense of safety, support, and connection that she had yearned for. Yet, she could not help but wonder what else he could do to further enhance their relationship and deepen their bond. She considered her request carefully, knowing that it would mean something important to her.

"Can I... sleep with you tonight?" she asked shyly. She had lost her virginity the day before to this same man, and the thought of spending the night with Ragden - the guy she had once tormented - made her excited and nervous all at once.

Ragden blinked in surprise while his body throbbed in response. His heart thundered in his chest. His mouth went dry. He blinked slowly, considering the possible consequences.

"Do you think your mom would be okay with this?" he whispered softly.

Emily hesitated for a moment, weighing the risks of involving her mother

in their plans. She decided to err on the side of honesty and openness. She had already shown a willingness to trust Ragden with her daughter's well-being – albeit within certain boundaries. She looked up at Ragden with a mix of caution and determination.

"No. She doesn't need to know about this. This is our secret. Ours." She gazed up into his eyes with a mix of desire and vulnerability. She clearly hoped that he would choose to take the risk with her.

"If this is what you truly want, then nothing would make me happier," he whispered to her. "However, your front step is probably not the best place to get started."

He laughed softly, coyly, teasingly, hinting at things to come. He took her hand in his and led her down the step to the street towards his home. As they walked, he put an arm around her waist and pulled her against him. Ragden's heart thundered in his chest at what possibilities awaited them when they got there.

Emily's heart raced with anticipation as Ragden led her away from her home. She felt a thrill of excitement at the thought of what they were about to do – something illicit and forbidden that only the two of them shared. As they walked together, her body pressed closer against Ragden's, savoring the feeling of his warmth and strength against her own. When they arrived at Ragden's home, Emily followed him inside with eager curiosity and anticipation.

Emily and Ragden walked through the foyer, kicking off their shoes. Jennifer and Michael came around the corner.

"Mom, Dad, this is Emily. She will be sleeping here tonight."

His parents smiled warmly at Emily. Michael shook her hand firmly in greeting, introducing himself. Jennifer hugged her tenderly, also introducing herself. As they headed upstairs, Michael called out behind them.

"Try not to shake the house!"

"No promises, Dad!"

His laughter followed them as they turned the corner and headed into Ragden's bedroom.

Emily and Ragden entered Ragden's bedroom, their eyes locked on each other. As they approached his bed, Emily felt a mixture of excitement and nervousness surge through her veins. She took a deep breath and let it out slowly, trying to calm herself. She looked up at Ragden with a mix of vulnerability and trust.

"This is... really happening," her voice trembled slightly as she spoke. She hesitated for a moment before reaching out and placing her hand on top of his chest, feeling his heartbeat beneath her palm. With each beat, she felt a growing sense of connection between them - a connection that had grown stronger throughout their experiences that day. As they moved towards the bed, Emily's body tensed with anticipation.

"Only if you want it. We can stop at any time." Ragden spoke softly. His

hands on her hips, gently squeezing her comfortingly. "We don't have to do this. Please do not get me wrong. I have wanted this ever since I left school yesterday..." He took his hands off her hips and pulled off his shirt, tossed it to the corner of the room. Then he placed his hands on her hips again, gently caressing her.

Emily watched Ragden remove his shirt, her eyes wide with a mixture of admiration and desire. She felt a sudden rush of heat flood her body as she saw the muscles beneath his skin, the evidence of his dedication to fitness and health despite the taunts of their classmates. As he moved his hands back onto her hips, she felt a renewed sense of trust and vulnerability towards him. She took a deep breath, trying to steady her racing heart.

"I want this," she whispered, looking deeply into his eyes, "I want to be with you."

With that, Emily began to undress herself, revealing her slender frame to Ragden for the first time since their incredibly intimate encounter the day before. As he watched Emily undress herself for the first time of her own desire, Ragden's heart raced. His palms went slick with perspiration. His eyes traced her incredible figure. Her slender ankles. The perfect lines of her calves. The soft swell of her thighs into that incredible ass. Her flat stomach. The swell of her perfect small round breasts. The lines of her shoulders. Her plump lips. Those incredible eyes. He unbuttoned his pants and started to remove them. Then he lost his balance and crashed to the floor, his legs tangled.

Emily gasped in surprise as Ragden crashed to the ground, his pants twisted around his feet. She quickly reached out to help him up, her heart racing with a mix of concern and arousal.

"Are you okay?" she asked, her voice barely above a whisper, even as she tried to suppress the desire coursing through her veins. She stood there in just her underwear. Her body exposed and vulnerable to Ragden's hungry gaze. The sight of her naked flesh sent waves of heat through his body and caused him to struggle to regain control of his thoughts and actions. Ragden finally managed to stand upright, his pants discarded beside him.

Laughing at his own clumsiness, Ragden reached out to Emily and took her hands in his. He stepped up close to her and felt the heat coming off her body. The desire coursed through him. His eyes hungered for her. His body twitched with desire. His cock throbbed painfully in his boxers. Its shape and size were clear.

"Pardon my clumsiness... I... was overcome by your beauty..."

Emily smiled reassuringly at Ragden, seeing how his accident had shaken him. She noticed the incredible heat radiating off his body. The way his eyes were now fixated on hers with intense desire. She stepped closer to him. Her breasts brushed against his chest as she placed her hands on his shoulders. Suddenly, Emily felt bold. Desire coursed through her like an electric current. She leaned in and kissed Ragden. Hard.

Ragden responded to her kiss in kind. His lips parted, and his tongue dipped into her mouth. He tasted the familiar sweetness of her. His arms wrapped around her, pulled her body against his. The flesh-to-flesh contact was electric. He felt energy coursing through his body. The excitement at the contact was almost too much to contain. *Gods, how I've wanted this again.* As their kiss deepened, and got more passionate, Ragden slipped one strap of her bra off her shoulder. He gently unsnapped the clasp around her back with his other hand.

Emily moaned into Ragden's mouth as he touched her. Her body trembled with desire. The sensation of his fingers working at her bra made her shiver with anticipation. She pulled back slightly, panting as she gazed up into his eyes. She helped him finish removing her bra. She felt incredibly exposed and vulnerable before him. But instead of fear, Emily felt a sense of trust and desire that surprised her. Emily leaned in to kiss Ragden again. As their lips met, she ran her hands along his chest and down to his boxers. She grabbed the monstrous cock that throbbed under her grasp.

Feeling her bare chest pressed against his, Ragden's heart raced even faster, thundering in his chest. As her hand wrapped around his cock, it surged, harder than ever. His dick throbbed under her gentle grasp. He moaned against her lips involuntarily. His hands slipped down her back and slid under her panties. They grasped her ass cheeks and pulled her against him harder. They pinned her hand against his groin as he pressed their bodies together. His fingers curled around her ass cheeks, brushed across her asshole, and teased her damp pussy lips.

Emily's eyes widened in shock as she felt Ragden's hands on her ass, pressing her hips against him with force. She gasped again sharply as his fingers teased her entrance; her hand moved to push him away. But as she fought the incredible urge to surrender to his touch, Emily found herself unable to resist. Instead, she continued rubbing his cock, feeling the slick wetness between her fingers as she explored his body with a mixture of curiosity and desire. Their tongues danced together again; Emily's moans muffled by Ragden's lips. She could not believe how good it felt to be this close to him after everything they had been through.

Ragden felt her tense and start to push against him slightly. He slid his fingers away from her tender spots. Instead, sliding her panties off her hips, so that when he released them, they dropped to the floor. Then he drew back from her embrace enough to break his lips from hers.

"I don't think you need these anymore," he whispered against her lips as her panties hit the floor. "Nor do I need these..." Emily's eyes widened as she realized that Ragden was about to expose himself to her fully. He ran his tongue over her lips as his boxers hit the floor.

She felt her heart race with anticipation and desire, and suddenly, she did not want him to stop. She licked her lips and tasted the sweetness of their kisses as she gazed up at him. Her hands reached out to touch him, her fingers

running lightly along his chest and abdominal muscles. Her nipples hardened under the cool air. Emily took a deep breath and broke the spell. She turned to the bed. She climbed up and laid down, inviting Ragden to join her.

Ragden reached out to take her hand as he climbed onto the bed beside her. Then he rolled over on top of her. His knees slipped between hers. Their groins pressed together. His cock lay across her mound, the head of it against her stomach. His hands pressed to the bed beneath her arms, so he could look down at her. He leaned in and kissed her tenderly, lovingly. He lowered himself down to his elbows and laid his chest against hers. He felt her nipples pressed against him.

"You are amazing, you know that?" He whispered softly to her as he kissed her again.

Emily's eyes fluttered shut as Ragden's lips pressed against hers in a tender kiss. She gasped as she felt his cock pressed against her stomach, and her nipples crushed against his chest. She moaned softly, losing herself in the sensations. Emily's body was alive with desire, every fiber of her being focused on him. She nodded her head in agreement with Ragden's words, feeling incredibly touched by them. As he lowered himself to his elbows, Emily swallowed nervously. For the second time in as many days, she was about to let a man penetrate her. But as she thought about it, Emily realized that she wanted this. She wanted Ragden. And nothing would stop her from having him.

Ragden slipped his arms under her shoulders and pressed their bodies together. His chest hitched, a soft sob in his throat. He kissed her shoulder, her neck, her earlobe. Then he whispered against her skin, "I wasn't sure you would ever want this again... after what I did to you yesterday..."

Emily's eyes filled with tears as Ragden spoke to her. She had never expected such incredible honesty and vulnerability from him. Suddenly, it all became so clear. She wanted Ragden too. More than anything. She turned her head to him, captured his lips with hers in a passionate kiss. Emily's heart raced with desire as she moved her hips against his. She wanted him to feel how much she wanted him. She wanted him to know how much she needed him.

He whispered softly against her lips, "Were you a virgin before yesterday?"

Emily's eyes widened in surprise at Ragden's question. It was not the typical smooth-talking line a guy might use to break the ice or get a girl into bed. But it was honest and direct. She nodded her head slowly, her heart racing with anticipation. She licked her lips nervously, wanting to trust him and open up to him completely. "I was..."

A single tear slid down Ragden's cheek. A second sob hitched his chest. He buried his face in her shoulder, pulling her painfully tight against him. "I'm sorry... I'm so sorry..."

Emily's heart ached as she watched Ragden cry against her. She pulled him even closer, wrapped her arms around him, and held him tightly. She could

not imagine causing him so much pain, but she knew that he needed her now, and she would do whatever it took to make him feel better. She stroked his hair gently, whispered soothing words into his ear, and tried to comfort him as much as she could.

"It's okay. I forgive you."

"That's... That's... Kind of you... I wanted to teach a lesson, to change who you were... I was cruel to take that from you. I gave you no choice... I do not regret it... I'm sorry, but I do not. I loved every minute of it, but I am sorry. Sorry if I hurt you. Sorry if I caused you pain."

As he spoke, he raised his head up, the intensity of his gaze boring into her. The desire for her touch, for her presence, overwhelmed him.

Emily's heart swelled with love and compassion as she listened to Ragden's words. She could see the sincerity in his eyes and hear the pain that he was still carrying with him. She knew that he was exposing his vulnerabilities to her out of necessity, hoping she would understand and forgive him. But she also knew that he meant every word he said. His apology came from a genuine place within him. She moved her hand up to cup his cheek, gently feeling the dampness of the tears on his skin. Emily's own eyes filled with tears as she spoke softly.

"You didn't hurt me. You taught me something incredible. About trust and desire and... love. I forgive you."

Ragden leaned forward and kissed the tears from her cheeks. He kissed her jaw and her lips. Tenderly, lovingly. He whispered against her lips.

"Thank you. Thank you for being here with me. Thank you for growing and allowing the lesson to take root in your heart. I can see that I caused you grief, but I can also see the strength you've gained from it."

Emily's heart fluttered with joy at Ragden's words and the tender kisses he bestowed upon her. She felt incredibly grateful to him for teaching her so much about love and trust. She knew that without him, she would not be where she was today – strong and confident in her desires. Emily knew that Ragden was right. She had grown immensely because of him. She smiled up at Ragden, her eyes sparkling with emotion.

"I love you, and I am here because of you. Because of what you did. Because of how it made me feel. How it changed me."

"I... I love you too..." He smiled, realizing his own feelings for her. He rolled over onto his back, pulled her over on top of him. He giggled up at her. Then he went deadly serious. "I think I love all three of you. Are you okay with that? I love Sarah. I love Aria. And I love you..."

Emily's heart swelled with joy at Ragden's confession. She knew that he cared about Sarah and Aria, but hearing him say that he loved her too was incredibly powerful. She smiled down at him, tears welling up in her eyes. She nodded her head, unable to find the words to express how much his words meant to her.

"Ragden, you're amazing. Perfect. Imperfect. Flawed, and amazing..."

Love & Nature

Then she leaned in and kissed him. Ragden, the man who helped her grow. To become the woman, she had always dreamed of being.

Ragden laughed and pulled her down against him, pressing her body against his. He felt every inch of her pressed against him. He shivered, knowing her body. He knew every inch of it. And knowing she was here again, choosing to be with him, after the previous day's events.

"Only human... imperfect and flawed... only human," He laughed again, shaking them both with the humor of it. Then he placed his hands on the sides of her head, and gently pulled her towards him. Once again kissed the tears from her cheeks. Then he kissed her lips, softly, tenderly, as only the closest of lovers would do. His tongue slid between her lips, the taste of her salty tears still upon it.

Emily's heart melted at Ragden's tenderness. She felt his love pouring out of him. It filled her with warmth and security. She felt his hands on her face, guiding her lips towards his, and as their lips met, Emily experienced a sense of completion that she never thought possible. She loved him fiercely, deeply, and with all her heart. She loved him despite his flaws and mistakes because those things only served to make him more human and relatable to her. She wrapped her arms around him. Held him tightly as they shared another soul-stirring kiss. Emily could not imagine life without him now. He was her rock, her anchor, her partner in love and adventure.

Ragden's cock throbbed between them. His desire made his body twitch. He rolled over again, putting himself between her legs, and on top of her. His cock pressed against her groin, her clit, her stomach. He kissed her lips. Then her jaw, her throat, her breasts. He ground his hips against her.

"Do you still want this? Or has all this emotion wearied you? We can sleep if you prefer. I would not fault you for it. But... GODS, woman, I want to be inside you again!"

Emily's eyes gleamed with desire as she watched Ragden move above her. She felt the heat emanating from his body, the weight of his cock pressed against her sensitive folds. She knew that she wanted him inside her again. She wanted to feel that incredible sensation of being filled by him once more. She reached up and caressed his cheek, her voice soft and tender.

"No. I want you. I want all of you."

With that, Emily lifted her hips to meet his, guiding him towards her entrance. Ragden blushed with the intensity of her adoration. Her love. He was not convinced he was worthy of it, but he accepted it, and he loved her back more fiercely for it.

She gasped as he entered her, slowly, savoring each moment of their connection. As his cock slid deeper into her, he moaned. She was so tight, so deliciously, incredibly, achingly tight, and wonderful. As he filled her, Emily looked up at Ragden with adoration in her eyes. With half the length of his throbbing member in her, he paused. He kissed her breasts and suckled her nipples. Then he tenderly kissed her neck and her chin, and then her lips, then

he whispered to her.

"You feel even more amazing than yesterday... how is that possible?"

Emily's eyes flashed with pride at Ragden's praise. She felt incredibly cherished and loved by him. She felt like the most important person in the world to him. She reached down and grabbed his ass, pulled him closer to her, deeper into her. She could not get enough of him. She whispered to him, her voice breathless with desire.

"Because I love you... and you make me feel so amazing. So complete. So perfect."

Her hand on his ass, Ragden slid all the way in, slowly, gently, lovingly. His cock hit the back of her. It pressed against her innermost depths and slid against her cervix like a gentle caress of that deepest part of her. His own voice breathless, contorted with desire, and overcome by how amazing she was, he whispered to her.

"I love you too. Always have, always will."

Emily's heart swelled with happiness. She knew that he had always loved her, even before he took away her choice. She knew that he had always seen something special in her, something worth fighting for. She felt incredibly lucky to have found someone who loved her so deeply, even when she was at her most vulnerable. She wrapped her arms around him, pulled him even closer to her. Emily's heart raced with anticipation as she felt his cock sliding against her inner walls, preparing to bring them even closer together. She looked up at him, her eyes full of adoration and love.

"I love you too... forever."

"And forever more."

He whispered against her neck, as he gently kissed her silky-smooth skin. He ground his hips against her. Pressed his swollen member against her cervix. She gasped at how it felt when it moved within her. His body trembled with the ecstasy of being so deep inside her.

Emily's eyes closed, lost in the moment as Ragden moved within her. She could feel every inch of him, every ripple of his muscles, every grunt of pleasure. She loved the way his cock moved against her cervix, sending waves of electricity through her entire body. She loved the way his weight pressed her into the mattress. She loved everything about him. She loved him. Completely and utterly. She nuzzled her face into his neck. Inhaled his scent, letting the sound of their moans fill the room as they moved together in perfect harmony.

Ragden slowly drew his cock partly out of her vice-like pussy, then slid it back in. Then again, building a slow, tender rhythm. Fighting for control against his urges and desires, he maintained a slow persistent pace, filling her, sliding against her cervix, then withdrawing and doing it again. His body shuddering at the ecstasy of her body against his.

Emily's eyes squeezed shut as Ragden moved within her, sliding his cock along her inner walls in a slow, deliberate pace. She felt every inch of him,

every movement, every ripple of pleasure. She knew that he was fighting to maintain control, and she respected him for it. She loved him even more for it. She nuzzled her face into his neck again, breathing his scent as she matched her movements to his own. Emily knew that they were moving towards something incredible together. Something that neither of them could have experienced alone. She felt connected to Ragden on a level that she never imagined possible.

Feeling her move with him, he could not help but shiver as the ecstasy of it entered an entirely new level for him. Feeling every inch of her pressed against him, he could not help but close his eyes and savor the feel of her skin moving beneath his. Their hips met, then parted, and met again. The pace was still purposeful and steady. He traced his hands along her sides. He felt the swell of her breasts pressed against his chest. The soft tender skin of her abdomen. The swell of her hips pressed against the mattress. He slid his hands along her thighs, marveling at the firm, tender texture of them. He squeezed them gently, feeling the muscles flexing with their movements.

Emily's heart raced with excitement as Ragden moved his hands on her thighs. She felt incredibly exposed and vulnerable, yet incredibly cherished by him. She felt his hands squeezing her thighs, and she knew that he was feeling the same thing she was feeling, the incredible texture and power of her legs. She loved the way his hands felt on her thighs. She loved the way he was exploring her body with such tenderness and care. She loved him. She met his gaze, breathless with desire.

"Ragden..."

He opened his eyes and gazed into hers. His chin against hers, their lips almost pressed together, their noses touching as their bodies moved together, meeting and sliding apart, then meeting again. He slid his hand up her thigh, sliding it along her ass, savoring how tight and perfect it felt.

"Yes, my love?"

Emily's heart pounded with anticipation, as Ragden moved his hands higher up her leg. She felt his fingers brush against her hip, her buttocks. She gasped as he cupped her bottom, feeling the roundness of her cheeks in his palm. She felt his thumb stroke the curve of her rear. Emily felt incredibly exposed and vulnerable before him, but she knew that Ragden was only showing her love and affection. She knew that he saw her fully and completely and accepted her for who she was. She looked up at him, her eyes wide with wonder.

"Ragden... thank you. For everything."

Ragden nodded his head, sweat breaking out on his brow, as they continued to move together, one machine, one rhythm. Two bodies, together, in perfect unison. His penis in her pussy. Sliding deeper, then sliding back, then deeper again. Her hips pressed to his. His pressed to hers. He kissed her lips deeply, passionately, his tongue tasting her.

"You are welcome," he whispered against her lips, breathless. His heart

thumped in his throat with each parting and rejoining of their bodies, "It is I... who must... thank you..."

Emily's heart soared at Ragden's words. She knew that he was struggling with the idea of accepting gratitude, but she also knew that he was incredibly humble and deserved recognition for his actions. She knew that he had given her something utterly amazing – himself – and she appreciated it beyond measure. She knew that Ragden was the most incredible person she had ever met, and she loved him with all her heart. She pulled back slightly from his lips and looked into his eyes. Emily placed her hand on his cheek and felt the warmth of his skin against her fingertips.

"I love you. And you're welcome. Always."

A single tear slid down Ragden's cheek at the warmth of her, the love. He did not deserve it. He could not. But he sighed and accepted it. He kissed her more fiercely, more deeply. Moaned into her lips as he slid deep into her, and pressed against her cervix, then drew back and did it again. Even though it was his cock filling her, he felt filled up with her love. Her adoration. Her thanks. He struggled to accept it. He struggled with his own faults and weaknesses. The things he did that he found difficult to forgive himself for. He felt loved and accepted. His heart started to beat faster and harder. He paused, sliding himself fully into her. Slid against her cervix, pinning her hips to the mattress. Pressed her into place. His hands cupped her ass.

"Thank you," he whispered against her lips, as another tear slid down his cheek.

Emily's heart swelled with love as she watched Ragden struggle with the idea of accepting her gratitude. She knew that he was incredibly humble and did not believe that he deserved anything, but she believed he did. She loved him for his honesty, his vulnerability, his passion, his dedication. She loved him for everything that he was. She pulled back slightly from his lips and looked into his eyes with infinite love and admiration. Emily saw the single tear as it slid down his cheek, and she felt a lump form in her throat. She knew that he was experiencing emotions just as intense as she was. She knew that they were both on a journey together – a journey towards self-discovery, growth, and love.

Ragden kissed her again, more passionately than before, picking up the slow rhythm that they had attained before. He slid his hands from her ass towards her knees, then slid around to the inside of her thighs, tracing a line towards her groin.

As Ragden slid his hands across her thighs, Emily felt a wave of arousal wash over her. She knew that he was seeing her completely, and she was incredibly turned on by the thought of him touching her most intimate parts. She gasped as he traced a path to her groin, felt the heat radiating from there, and the pulse of her blood flowing. She felt incredibly exposed and vulnerable, but also incredibly desired. She looked up at him. Her eyes sparkled with love and lust. His touch ignited a fire within her that burned

hotter than any other physical sensation she had ever experienced. Emily knew that she was falling further in love with him with every passing second.

He kissed her again, pressed his lips against her, dipped his tongue into her mouth, and savored the sweet texture of what was her. He slid his cock fully up into her. Its throbbing massiveness filled her. He pressed against the back of her, his cock pressed into her cervix. A tender, gentle caress of the deepest part of her.

Emily felt Ragden's cock filling her completely, stretching her to the limit. She felt the tip press against her cervix, causing a surge of electrical energy to course through her entire body. She gasped and felt pain and pleasure mingle together in a symphony of sensations. She loved him for his ability to push her boundaries and make her feel alive in ways she never thought possible. She leaned her head back, exposing her throat to him. She felt his breath on her skin, warm and tender. She closed her eyes, feeling safe and secure in his arms.

Ragden wrapped his arms around her as he ground his groin against her. He slid his cock into her cervix, a gentle, tender caress so deep inside her. Emily gasped at the incredible pressure and sensitivity of it. He savored the tight, vice-like grip of her pussy along his throbbing shaft. He pulled her body against his, as he kissed her exposed throat, his teeth gently nipping at the tender skin she bared before him. She felt her body being pulled against his, his teeth grazing her throat in a tender, playful manner. She loved the way he showed his dominance while remaining incredibly gentle and tender with her. She smiled up at him, feeling a sense of peace and contentment washing over her. Emily trusted Ragden completely, knowing that he would protect her and cherish her no matter what happened.

Ragden drew back from her ever so slightly, allowing her room to move beneath him, no longer pressed so hard into the mattress. His body was still against hers, he could feel every muscle move, every slight movement, every hitch of her breath. It was like a warm blanket on a chilly night. Comforting and relaxing. And yet, the feeling of her pussy wrapped around his cock filled him with desire. Desire to please her, to fill her with happiness and love as she so desperately needed and deserved.

Emily felt Ragden's body shift slightly, giving her space to move. She felt incredibly grateful for his consideration, and she appreciated the fact that he was sensitive to her needs. She loved the way he was able to read her body language and respond to it appropriately. Emily felt overwhelmed with emotion as she realized how much she meant to him. She felt incredibly cherished and loved by him. As Ragden continued to grind his cock against her cervix. Emily bit her lip nervously, unsure of where this intense connection between them was leading. But she wanted to follow wherever it took her – because she loved him, and she believed in their bond.

Ragden slid his cock back, then slid deep into her again. He gasped at the feel of her silken insides. Then he did it again, savoring the feel of it. He gazed

into her eyes with each gentle thrust; he kissed her lips tenderly as he slid into her depths.

Emily felt Ragden's cock pull back, then slide deep into her once more. She felt a surge of pleasure shoot through her body. She gasped involuntarily. She gazed into his eyes, saw the intensity of his gaze, and felt his passion and desire for her. She felt incredibly connected to him, and she knew that nothing could tear them apart. She leaned forward, wrapped her arms around his neck, and pulled him closer to her. Emily's lips met his in a deep, passionate kiss. Their tongues intertwined as they moved together in perfect synchronization. She felt the heat of their bodies mixing, creating an explosive combination of emotions and sensations that were impossible to ignore or forget.

Ragden felt her move with him, and he moved a little faster. His body strained against him. Muscles tensed; he felt the wild monster of reckless abandon hovering just beyond the edges of his world. The thing waited, lurked in the shadows, waited for his guard to drop. A shiver of fear trickled through him at the thought of what would happen if it were set loose. The thing in the cloud reached for him. He kissed Emily deeply, passionately, and pushed the monster out of his head, knowing it yet lurked.

Emily felt Ragden's increased pace, and she responded by moving with him, matching his rhythm perfectly. She felt the heat of their bodies mixing, and she felt a sense of wild abandon taking hold of her. She knew that something powerful was happening between them, something that was unlike anything she had ever experienced before. Emily was both terrified and excited by the thought of what might come next. She broke away from his lips, panting heavily.

"Ragden... I feel it too." Her voice trembled with both fear and anticipation. "The monster. I feel it."

Ragden's eyes went a little wide. As they continued to move together, the rhythm increased ever so slightly. He kissed her softly, tenderly, reassuringly. He continued to move at the same pace, muscles moving fluidly, in complete control. He whispered against her lips.

"You do not need to fear the monster... I can keep it at bay..."

Emily found solace in Ragden's words, and she clung to him even more tightly. She felt his warmth and strength as it surrounded her, shielding her from the darkness that threatened to consume them. Emily felt incredibly vulnerable, but she trusted Ragden completely. She knew that he would never hurt her intentionally, and she was grateful for his protection. She whispered back.

"I know you can keep it at bay, Ragden. I trust you. With you, I have nothing to fear."

Ragden continued to move with her, rhythm built on itself, their bodies moving together perfectly, like a symphony of love and sensuality. His body shivered with the ecstasy of it. The wonder, the love, the sensation of being

washed away with it. He could start to feel the climax that built within them both.

As Ragden's pace increased, Emily felt the building pressure within her body. She could feel the waves of pleasure starting to build, and she knew that they were heading towards something incredible. Emily's eyes slipped closed, lost in the sensations that were washing over her. She completely surrendered to Ragden and trusted him completely with her body and her heart. She cried out, unable to contain the emotions that were welling up inside her. Emily's orgasm was incredibly intense and left her feeling drained and fulfilled at the same time. She gasped for air. Emily's heart raced; her mind spun with emotions. Emily's eyes were wet with tears of love.

Ragden continued to move with her body, as she convulsed through her climax. He kissed the tears from her face as his own climax began to wash over him. Deep in the recesses of his psyche, he could sense the monster of reckless abandon being washed away with the waves of Emily's intense orgasm. Followed by his own. Wave upon wave of ecstasy washed over them both. He felt a massive load of cum explode within her, streaming out of him, filling her up. He felt her juices as they flowed freely over him, soaking them both.

As Emily's orgasm reached its peak, she was overwhelmed with incredible sensations. She felt the waves of pleasure crashing over her, leaving her breathless and spent. She cried out loudly; her voice echoed throughout the room. She felt incredible and exposed, but she felt cherished and loved by Ragden. She opened her eyes, looking into his.

"Oh god... oh god! That was incredible!"

She giggled nervously, feeling embarrassed about the sound of her voice, but she was unable to control herself. Emily's heart raced, and she was incredibly turned on by the intensity of the experience.

Ragden laughed with her, their bodies still pressed tightly together, feeling her shake beneath him. The twitches and spasms in his muscles started to slow. He wrapped his arms around her, pulled her tightly against him, and enjoyed the feel of the afterglow of their joined orgasms; his cock still buried deep within. He could still feel his cum leaking into her.

Emily felt Ragden's arms wrap around her, holding her close as they both enjoyed the afterglow of their incredible experience. She could feel his cock still deep within her, and she felt the remnants of their combined release dripping from her. Emily was incredibly grateful for the way that Ragden was able to hold her, comfort her, and cherish her in those moments. She snuggled into him. She felt incredibly safe and loved. Emily was incredibly thankful for the way that Ragden was able to push past her defenses and show her true vulnerability.

Ragden sighed against her and felt her snuggle against him. He did not want this moment to end. The warmth, the love, the security washed over him. Then his stomach grumbled. He opened his eyes and looked down at

her; a small smile played across his lips.

"Excuse me... I... must be hungry."

Emily giggled, finding it incredibly endearing. She was surprised by the sudden change in topic. The intensity of the emotions, that had coursed through them during their lovemaking had been incredible. She found his returning appetite very sexy and exciting. She spoke softly.

"Hey... you're hungry? Well, that's good news."

Ragden chuckled and pulled her tight against him. Then he thought about the afternoon and evening, wondering if they had taken the time to eat before they ran off to bed. He could not recall. Ragden looked down at Emily questioning...

"Are you hungry? I am famished. Shall we go downstairs and see if we can scrounge up some food?"

Emily nodded, feeling incredibly turned on by the way Ragden's voice changed when he talked about being hungry. She found him incredibly attractive and sexy, even when he was talking about something other than sex and emotions. She also found herself drawn to him, regardless of what he was saying or doing.

"Yeah, let's go downstairs and see if we can find something to eat. I'm hungry too."

She gave him a genuine smile. Ragden smiled back, deeply moved by how she made him feel. He caressed her cheek with his hand, then kissed her lips tenderly at first, but then harder, feeling his passion starting to course over him again. Emily kissed him back, with equal passion and intensity. She felt incredibly turned on by the way he was able to make her body react to him. She felt her pussy start to throb with excitement, and she wanted him more than ever right then. Then he broke free from her, breathless. She panted heavily as they parted.

"Mmm... Ragden... I'm so hungry for you." she said, looking into his eyes with a mixture of desire and adoration. Then his eyes widened as his stomach grumbled again.

Ragden laughed; his body shook with the humor of it. He could see the desire in her eyes and knew that it was echoed in his own. He could also feel the weariness in his muscles. Their lovemaking had been very physical, and their bodies needed fuel.

He started to raise himself off her, but as their flesh started to part, he groaned. He did not want to be separated from her. He took a deep breath and tried to prepare himself for the loss. He laughed at himself and kissed her again.

Emily watched him try to rise, feeling a mix of sadness and desire in her heart. She knew that he was going to leave her, but she also knew that he needed to eat. She could see the hunger in his eyes. Emily wanted to be with him, and she wanted to be able to provide for him. Emily looked up at Ragden, her eyes filled with love and admiration.

"Ragden... I want to be with you. I want to be with you, and I want to feed you. Can I cook something for you? For us? You said you were hungry, and I want to make something special for you. Something that will taste amazing."

Ragden smiled happily, still pressed against her. "That sounds lovely. First, we must get there, though."

Watching him smile, Emily melted into him. He laughed again, then he stopped and put a finger to his lips, stilling himself to listen for noises in the house. Faintly, in the distance, he could hear someone in the kitchen.

"I think someone is in the kitchen, maybe we can get lucky, and one of my parents is already there cooking something... Shall we check?"

CHAPTER 8

Emily's heart raced with anticipation, wondering if they would be caught in the act of making love. She found herself turned on by the idea of being discovered by Ragden's family. She was also excited to show them how much she meant to him. She spoke softly.

"Let's check it out. If someone is in the kitchen, we can use it to our advantage. We can pretend to be... you know... just two really hungry people. And I'll cook something for you, and you can eat it, and it'll be... yeah, that's a good plan."

Ragden laughed. "That is a great plan, but my parents are no fools. They will love you; I know. I am also quite sure they know everything that took place here this evening."

Ragden gave her a knowing smile and wink. Then he kissed her passionately, breaking from her breathless again. Emily smiled at Ragden's confidence. She felt a surge of pride in her heart. She was incredibly grateful for the way that Ragden believed in her. The way he was able to express such a strong faith in her abilities. She felt secure in the knowledge that he honestly believed in her.

"Okay... let's go check it out. If your parents know what happened here tonight, then it's only fair that I should be able to cook something for you. And if they don't know... well, then it'll be a surprise. Let's just go downstairs and see what happens."

Ragden smiled at her and slowly raised himself off her. His skin tingled as it pulled away from hers. He groaned, not wanting to part from her. His still mostly firm cock was buried within her. Emily did not want him to leave either. She felt a sharp pain in her heart and knew she was experiencing the beginning stages of withdrawal from his presence. She reached out, and wrapped her arms around his waist, holding him against her. Ragden ground his hips against her. He sighed in pleasure as his mostly firm cock slid around

in her tight pussy.

Emily laughed, feeling Ragden's cock slide around in her pussy. She was incredibly turned on by the sight of him. She spread her legs wider and allowed him to slide deeper into her. A shiver of ecstasy ran down Ragden's back as he did. His cock throbbed gently in response.

Then he raised himself off her. His cock gently slipped out of her. Emily felt a pang of disappointment in her heart. She knew that she wanted him to stay inside her. To remain connected to her. To be a part of her. She also knew that she could not ask him to do that. She respected the boundaries that he set for himself. Ragden shivered again now that his cock was no longer inside her. He felt the most powerful urge to slip it back in. His eyes looked over her body hungrily, desiring her more than he could explain. He took a deep breath, to steady himself. Then rolled off the bed to stand on shaky legs.

Emily lay on the bed, feeling incredibly vulnerable. She was also incredibly turned on by the sight of him standing above her. His body was tense with desire.

"Go ahead... Go downstairs. I'll be right behind you. Don't forget to be hungry..."

He laughed again. "Darling, I'll always be hungry for you."

Then he winked coyly, as his heart skipped a beat. Then he held out a hand to her, to help her off the bed. Emily smiled at Ragden's comment and felt incredibly flattered by his words. She accepted his offer of help and allowed him to lift her from the bed. She felt weak and vulnerable in her heart. But as he held her hand, she could feel the strength of his grip. She knew he would be able to support her and guide her through anything that came their way. She also felt incredibly lucky to have found someone who could make her feel so alive, desired, and so loved.

"You're so sweet, Ragden."

He smiled at her words. Then he looked at the bed, the sweat-stained sheets, the blankets tossed aside and snickered. Then he looked at her. She was radiantly gorgeous. Her tussled hair. Her body was streaked with sweat. Her dried fluids were on her legs. Skin glistened with perspiration. He pulled her against him. Sighed with delight as she pressed against him. He cupped her ass. Pulled her groin against him. His softened cock pressed against her skin. Emily moaned softly against him. Her pussy grew damp as his softened cock pushed against it. He kissed her softly.

"Maybe we need a shower first?"

She felt a sense of vulnerability, knowing that she was completely exposed to him, both physically and emotionally. She replied.

"Shower...yes. We can take a shower together. It will be fun."

He kissed her again. Slipped his tongue into her mouth. Sighed at how sweet she tasted. He pulled her tighter against him, drinking in her warmth, her presence, her love. Then he stepped back, breathless.

"Shower... Food... Priorities." He laughed as he pulled her towards the

door.

Emily laughed along with Ragden. She felt incredibly turned on that he was able to make her laugh and smile. She was grateful for the way he was able to bring joy into her life. Thankful for the way he was able to make her feel like nothing else mattered except for him and her. She stepped forward and followed him towards the bathroom. She felt relief and satisfaction in her heart as she did so.

"Yes, priorities. And you're right, Ragden. Showers first, then I'm going to cook something amazing for you. And I'm going to make you super crazy with desire while I'm doing it, so be prepared."

He turned in the hall, his back to the bathroom door. He pulled her against him, cupped her ass. Pulled her groin against his. His dick throbbing against her. He kissed her passionately. She moaned softly, feeling her pussy twitch with desire as she felt his cock pressing against her. She also felt a sense of relief in her heart, knowing that she had made him hard again. That he was fully prepared to enjoy everything she had to offer. Then he pulled his head back, their lips parted, and he sighed.

"Oh... I am prepared." He winked at her as he nudged the door open behind him.

She stepped forward with him, her own hands reaching down to cup his bare ass. She knew that he was watching every inch of her naked body. She was incredibly proud of the way that she was able to turn him on so easily. She spoke huskily.

"You're such a tease, Ragden. You know that? Always making me want more of you."

He gave her a knowing smile, "It's not a tease if I give it to you..."

Then he stepped into the bathroom and pulled her in with him. He flipped on the light, pulled her in, and closed the door behind her. Then he pulled her against him. His hands trailed down her back, cupped her ass again, and squeezed it gingerly. While he pulled her against him, he kissed her again. Emily closed her eyes, feeling incredibly vulnerable, turned on, and happy. She wrapped her arms around his neck and pulled herself closer to him. She felt the heat of his skin against her own. She could feel the pulsing rhythm of his heartbeat against her chest. She felt a sense of connection, unity, and absolute trust in the depths of her heart. She knew she was able to share everything with Ragden, and that he would accept her completely, without hesitation or reservation. She spoke softly.

"Mm... I'm all yours. Take me however you want."

"Now, who is the tease?" he asked, laughing.

Then he reached over and opened the shower door, pulled her with him, reached in, and turned on the shower. Then he closed the door. Slowly, Emily noticed the size of the bathroom. The massive full wall mirror. The two sinks in the large vanity. Twin medicine chests. The toilet with bidet. The large shower with multiple shower heads canted at different angles. Enough room

for two to easily stand together under the beams of water.

Emily gasped as she took everything in. She felt a sense of wonder and awe as she looked at everything, "This is amazing, Ragden."

"If you think this is wild, you'll have to see my parents shower someday."

He laughed again, trying to imagine the look on her face when she saw that space. "My parents have a... strange idea of what a shared space is supposed to look like."

Emily laughed, feeling turned on by the thought of seeing Ragden's parents' bathroom, and she was very curious what that would be like. She was grateful that he wanted to share this space with her. "Well, that means I'll have to see your parents shower someday. I hope it's as impressive as this one."

Ragden laughed again as he reached in to test the water temperature with one hand.

"Even more so. I will show you one day, but not today."

He winked. Then he stepped into the shower and pulled her gently in with him. He pulled her body against his. He leaned against the wall as the shower cascaded around them. He slid his hands onto her shoulders and circled them around her back. He pulled her gently against him as he kissed her softly. She sighed with pleasure at his touch and the feel of the hot water pouring over her body. She felt vulnerable and exposed but also turned on. And excited, knowing that Ragden was taking control of the situation and that he was leading her through the experience. She trusted him from the depths of her being, knowing that he would never force her to do anything she did not want to do. He would always respect her boundaries and her limits.

"Mm... This feels amazing."

"I know. I love this shower. But do you know what makes this shower even more amazing?" He leaned in and placed his lips against hers, gazing into her incredible eyes. "Being here with you."

She sighed deeply, feeling a rush of pleasure coursing through her veins as she realized that he was speaking the truth. She felt a sense of happiness and a sense of contentment, knowing that she was able to share this moment with him. That he was able to cherish her company as much as she cherished his. She also felt a sense of pride, knowing that she was able to bring such joy and happiness into his life. She was also grateful for the way that he was able to make her feel so incredibly alive, desired, and loved.

"Yes... Being here with you is amazing. And you are right, Ragden. This shower feels incredible."

He kissed her softly on the lips. Then he reached over, grabbed a loofa, and poured body wash on it. He lathered it up, then reached around and pressed it to the back of her neck. He kissed her on the lips as he ran it down her back, scrubbing gently as he went. Then he slid it up her side, ran it under her armpit, down her arm, and out to her fingertips. Then he turned it over and ran it back up the other side of her arm. Gently scrubbing as he went.

Then he kissed her again, as he ran it across her back to her other arm. Down her arm to her fingertips. Then he flipped it over her hand and up into her armpit and down her side.

Emily felt a sense of incredible anticipation, knowing that Ragden was taking his time. That he was savoring every moment of the experience. That he was enjoying the act of pleasuring her while cleaning her. She was grateful for the way it made her feel so incredibly desired and cared for. So incredibly loved.

She whispered, "Mm... Ragden, that feels amazing."

"Well... if we want to make a good impression on my parents, we've got to be clean."

He winked before he kissed her lips again. Then he ran the loofah over her ass, gently massaging the soap into her skin. Then he slid it between her cheeks. Ran it over her asshole and brought it up through her folds over her clit. He kissed her gently on the lips as he dragged the loofah up her groin and swirled it over her waist. Gently scrubbing the sweat and dirt off her body. She felt anticipation building as Ragden took his time, continuing to savor the experience, and used the loofah to pleasure her in ways she had never experienced before. She felt vulnerable, knowing that Ragden was able to see every inch of her naked body. That he was able to touch her in ways that were incredibly intimate and personal. She whispered huskily.

"Mmmm... this is so amazing..."

He kissed her softly, then dropped to his knees before her. He slid the loofah over her right hip and scrubbed the sweat and dried fluids from her thighs. Then he slid it down over her knee, around behind it, and dragged it down across the backs of her calves. Ragden gently picked up her foot and scrubbed between her toes, her ankles, and the arches of her feet. Then he placed a soft kiss on the top of her foot before placing it back on the floor. Then he picked up her left foot and scrubbed it the same way. He worked the loofah up her calf, to her knee. Then he kissed her right knee as he slowly stood and ran the loofah up her thigh. He started from the outside then slid it along her inner thigh, up into her groin. He slid it between her legs, gently scrubbing her pussy, slipping it between her folds, caressing her clitoris with it, before dragging it up to her stomach.

She moaned softly, "Mmmm..."

Then Ragden slid the loofah in a slow gentle circle across her stomach. Gazing into her eyes lovingly, he slid it up between her breasts. He gently dragged the scrubbing action across her breasts, cupping and gently scrubbing each. As he finished with each, he placed a soft kiss on her nipples.

Emily sighed softly, feeling the sense of incredible pleasure at the combination of the loofah on her skin, and his lips against her sensitive nipples. "Mmmm... Ragden, that feels amazing."

He smiled at her, and kissed her on the lips, as he set the loofah back on the shelf where he got it. Then he grabbed a bar of soap and lathered up his

hands.

"Close your eyes" he whispered.

As her eyes closed, he gently rubbed the soap into her face. He softly scrubbed her forehead and massaged her cheeks. Then he gently ran his fingers behind her ears. Tenderly, he turned her face into the water from one of the shower heads washing the soap from her face. Then he kissed her softly.

"You can open your eyes now."

As the water rinsed the soap from her face, she felt refreshed and loved in ways she had never experienced. She watched as he grabbed a bottle of shampoo and poured a small amount into his hands. He kissed her lips softly as he worked it into her hair. Then, satisfied, he gently turned her head so the water could run the shampoo out of her hair.

Then he grabbed a bottle of conditioner and worked that into her hair. He softly rinsed it out once complete. She felt a sense of incredible pleasure. She felt the tension and stress of the day melting away as the water rinsed the shampoo from her scalp. Then he took a step back from her and admired her incredible body. Clean from head to toe, she radiated such beauty that his heart ached. Satisfied, he grabbed the loofah again, filled it with body wash, and started to work it into his skin.

"You look amazing, my dear. I am afraid to touch you before I get myself clean." He spoke softly, almost purring. She smiled and blushed slightly as she felt so incredibly beautiful, sexy, and desirable.

After running the loofah over his arms, chest, and legs, he handed it to Emily and turned his back to her. "Would you mind? Gets hard to reach sometimes."

Emily took the loofah from Ragden and smiled as she worked it into his skin. She felt the incredible texture of his skin beneath her fingers. Felt the way his muscles tensed and relaxed as she ran it over his skin. Felt the incredible sensation of pleasure that flowed through her body as she scrubbed his skin. She felt a sense of trust, knowing that he was allowing her to please him in this way. She could see that he cherished every moment of the experience. It made her feel even more connected and appreciated by him for the care and attention she was able to provide.

As she finished, he turned and kissed her softly on the lips, "Thanks."

Then he grabbed the shampoo and quickly washed his hair. Once that was finished, he stepped into her warm embrace again. He smiled as he licked her lips, and kissed her softly, "All clean and fresh for you, my love."

She smiled at his kisses, feeling a sense of satisfaction and accomplishment. She spoke softly against his lips, "You're welcome, Ragden. You taste delicious."

"So do you" He whispered against her lips as he kissed her more passionately. Emily smiled into the kiss, feeling the intensity of their kiss growing deeper and more passionate. She felt the water cascade over them.

He pulled her body against his. Felt her breasts pressed against his chest. His cock throbbed between them, poking into her stomach. She ached to feel it inside her again. At the same moment, his stomach growled again. He looked down at his cock, and his stomach. He was not sure which to satisfy first.

Emily also felt her stomach growling, and she looked down at her body. She saw her ravenous appetite reflected in the hunger that burned within her belly. She spoke, "Hm. Maybe we should feed our stomachs first."

Ragden laughed. "One last thing I'd like to do first." He winked at her and kissed her lips softly. "If you'll let me?"

Emily felt Ragden's lips on her own, and she smiled, feeling the intensity of their kiss. She felt a sense of anticipation, a sense of desire, as she knew that Ragden was about to ask her something incredibly intimate and personal. She also felt a sense of trust, knowing that Ragden was cherishing every moment of the experience. That he was able to take his time, to make her feel desired, loved, and turned on. She spoke.

"What do you have in mind, Ragden?"

Ragden slid down to one knee before her and looked up at her hungrily. Then he leaned into her groin and gently kissed her pussy. His tongue teased the edges of her. Emily felt a sense of incredible pleasure, feeling his tongue teasing the edges of her sensitive lips. An electric surge ran through his body at the incredible taste of her. Then he looked up at her and asked permission with his eyes.

She spoke softly, huskily, "Go ahead, Ragden. Ask me."

"Can I taste your core? Can I sample your juices? Can I kiss your pussy and taste your vagina?"

Emily felt Ragden's words, a sense of excitement, desire, and vulnerability. She realized that he was asking her to allow him to indulge in some of her most intimate and personal fantasies. She felt a sense of trust.

"Yes, Ragden. Go ahead."

He smiled up at her, then leaned his face into her warm pussy. As the water of the shower cascaded over their bodies, he slipped his tongue between her lips. He dipped it into her. A shiver of ecstasy ran through him at the sheer delicious flavor of her. His cock throbbed between his legs as he gently ran his tongue over her clitoris. Then he gently lifted her left leg and set it on his shoulder, spreading her lips open so he could run his tongue the full length of her.

Emily felt Ragden's tongue exploring her pussy. She felt a sense of incredible pleasure. Felt the electricity that coursed through her body as she felt his tongue gently exploring her depths. She also felt a sense of vulnerability. She knew that Ragden was able to taste her. To sample her essence. To enjoy the incredible sensations that came with indulging in her most intimate desires. She moaned softly, "Ragden... mmm..."

He leaned into her groin and buried his face in her lips. Dipped his tongue into her vagina and ran it along her inner walls. Then he slid up over her. Ran

his tongue over her clitoris, gently pulling it into his mouth to suckle it softly.

Emily felt Ragden's mouth gently wrapping around her clitoris. She felt a sense of incredible pleasure, feeling the electricity that coursed through her body as she felt his tongue gently suckling her most sensitive spot. She felt more vulnerable, knowing that he was able to please her in ways that were incredibly intimate and personal. She moaned softly.

Then he gently placed his hand on her right thigh and lifted her leg. Spread her legs open and her pussy. He slid her up the wall and braced her against the wall as he licked the length of her. His tongue explored every inch of her lips. Dipped inside her pussy to sample her juice. Then up to her clitoris to suckle on it.

Emily's pulse raced as he slid her up the wall. She felt herself at his mercy but trusted in him completely. She clutched her breasts and squeezed them as he continued to savor her most intimate parts. Pulses of pleasure spread out through her body at his gentle actions. She gasped as he dipped his head lower, ran his tongue over her asshole. Teased it softly. Surges of pleasure, the likes of which she had never felt before, spiked through her body. Her muscles twitched in response. Then he dragged his tongue back through her lips. Dipped as deep into her vagina as he could.

Then he dipped back down and slipped his tongue into her asshole. She gasped as he softly, tenderly pushed the tip of his tongue into her. As he felt the tightness of her. Her thighs convulsed. He held them firm as he worked his tongue inside her. Then he slipped it out and licked his lips. Then he ran his tongue up through her pussy again. He deeply explored her vagina with his tongue. She gasped again as he slid up higher and sucked on her clitoris hungrily.

While he still gently held her to the wall, he slid his tongue up her groin. Across her navel, between her breasts up to her chin. He kissed her chin, her jaw, and then her lips. Emily sighed, as she felt Ragden exploring her body with his tongue. She felt the intensity of his passion. Then the head of his cock pushed through her pussy, teasing her vagina, before sliding against her clitoris. She felt the incredible heat of it against her entrance. He kissed her passionately, tasted her sweetness, letting her taste her juices on his tongue.

Ragden whispered against her lips, as his cock throbbed in her labia, at the entrance of her pussy, teasing. It pulsed, causing her muscles to vibrate in response.

"Was that, okay?"

Emily felt Ragden's whisper against her lips, and she nodded. She felt the incredible heat of his member against her wetness. Felt the intensity of his passion, and she spoke.

"It was amazing, Ragden. Please continue."

Then, his stomach rumbled loudly, and he laughed. His body shook with the humor of it. His cock slid against her folds but did not enter her. She laughed with him, feeling the incredible connection that they shared. She felt

the incredible passion that coursed through their bodies. His voice was full of humor; he sighed against her lips.

"Food first? Love later? Or..."

"Food first, love later, Ragden. It's only fair."

He shifted his hips. His cock slid through her lips. Slipped into her vagina. Partly slid up into her. His breath hissed through his teeth. Her tightness wrapping around his cock. He gasped in pleasure, leaned into her, and pushed her against the wall a little harder. He kissed her passionately. His tongue danced across hers.

Emily felt Ragden's cock sliding into her, filling her, but not completely. She could feel he had deeper he could go. She ached for him to finish that, to fill her. She felt a sense of incredible pleasure. She felt the incredible tightness of her body wrapped around his member. She could feel the heat radiating from his shaft, as it throbbed inside her pussy. She felt so loved and cherished, her heart full to bursting.

He slid his cock deeper into her. Ground it into her cervix. Gently caressed that hard wall within her with the head of his cock. She felt a sense of incredible pleasure. She felt the intense pressure against her cervix. He groaned against her. The feeling sent electrical pulses coursing through them both. The air around them suddenly felt charged with power, sex, comfort, and love. He kissed her harder, savored every inch of her wrapped around him, pressed against him.

Slowly, gently, he backed his lips off hers. As they broke apart, he panted, trying to catch his breath. His heart hammered in his chest. She looked into his eyes and saw the incredible passion that still burned within them. He looked down as the warm water of the shower cascaded over their entwined bodies. His cock was firmly seated deep within her. He moaned softly against her.

"God, you feel so amazing."

Then his stomach rumbled again, and he sighed, disappointed. He looked at her. He ached to finish what he had started but also ached for food. Slowly, he eased his dick out of her. Inch by precious inch, slipped from her. Then he gently lowered her feet to the floor of the shower. He smiled sadly at her, then kissed her lips tenderly.

"Later," he promised her. "We will continue this later."

Emily sighed, disappointed. She wanted him to finish, wanted to feel his cock filling her up. Instead, she looked down at his throbbing cock as it slipped from within her. Her juice was gently washed off by the cascading water from the shower. She pouted slightly at him. She could still feel the heat of his cock, so close to her body. It throbbed just out of her reach. For a moment, she considered trying to grab it and slip it back into her incredibly tight, wet pussy.

Then Ragden reached over and shut off the water. He opened the shower door and grabbed a towel. He turned to her and started drying her hair,

carefully, gently, he squeezed the water out. She closed her eyes and enjoyed the intimacy and tenderness of his touch. Then he pulled the towel around her back. He kissed her softly as he pulled it back and forth, drying her back. She opened her eyes, and gazed at him, watching how his muscles flexed and pulled as he took his time drying her. She felt so loved and cherished by this simple act. The sensation of the towel as it gently brushed away the water from her skin, and the tenderness of how he cared for her. Then he ran the towel down her arms, and across her chest. He paid special attention to her breasts. He gently ran the soft fabric over them and under them, drying them thoroughly. As he finished, he kissed each nipple. A soft caress with his tongue. She sighed at his soft touch, her nipples aching for more, and her body throbbed with desire.

Then he slid the towel over her stomach and across her groin. He slid the towel between her legs, drying her as best as possible Then he ran it over her ass, gripping her firm muscles gently as he dried them. Then he dropped to one knee in front of her and ran the towel down her legs, over her knees, around her calves. He picked up a foot, dried it off, then kissed it and placed it back on the shower floor, doing the same with the other.

Emily smiled as she let Ragden run the towel over her body. She felt the incredible sensation of the soft fabric as it brushed against her skin. Felt the incredible tenderness with which he cared for her. She watched the way his cock throbbed while he dried her body. She ached for him to fill her up, to finish what they had started. But she knew, as her stomach growled, that she needed to refuel before engaging in more strenuous activity again. Her muscles ached slightly, though the shower had been marvelous, sensual, and so much more than she had expected; she knew she needed a satisfying meal and rest.

Ragden slowly stood before her now dry, perfect body. Emily watched Ragden stand, admiring the incredible sight of his perfectly toned, wet body. She watched as he hung the towel outside and grabbed a robe for her. He stepped behind her, holding out the sleeves so she could slip into it. She slipped her arms into the sleeves and felt the warm, soft fabric slide up her arms. She pulled it around herself, as Ragden gently lifted her hair out of the back.

Ragden kissed Emily softly on the cheek as he reached for his towel. Draping it over one arm, he held the door open for her with one hand. Offered her the other to step free of the slippery shower. Emily stepped forward and allowed him to take her hand. She felt his warm powerful grip stabilizing her. She stepped out and turned to watch Ragden as he dried himself off. She licked her lips and felt her pulse quicken as he ran the towel over himself unaware of her gaze on him. Then he turned to her and smiled, her pulse quickening. Then he hung up the towel, grabbed a robe, and slipped into it. He left it hanging open in the front. His still erect penis peeked out between fabric. Watching it throb, she felt the desire and passion running

through her.

Ragden stepped out of the shower and up to the mirror. He pulled open a drawer and grabbed a brush. Then he turned Emily to face the mirror. He stood behind her and gently ran the brush through her hair. She felt the incredible sensation of the bristles against her scalp and smiled softly. Ragden gently leaned against her, his lower body pressed against her. His cock pushed against the fabric of the robe. She sighed feeling its pressure against the curve of her ass. He gently continued to brush her hair, ignoring it.

Satisfied with how incredible her hair looked all brushed out. It was dry and bounced against her back. Ragden leaned against her, reached around, and cupped her breasts through the open front of her robe. He kissed her ear, pulled her against him, he whispered in her ear.

"I love you."

Emily shivered with desire at his gentle caresses. She could feel the heat of his cock against her back, and her insides quivered with the desire for it. She bit her lip as he whispered in her ear. She sighed softly. She relaxed her body against his, felt the press of it through the robe, and wanted more.

Then Ragden released his grasp on her breasts and grabbed a comb from a drawer. He quickly ran it through his hair. Got it to lay just where he wanted it, then put the comb away. Then he placed a hand gently on Emily's shoulder and turned her to face him. Their robes flapped open, and their bodies pressed together. Naked flesh to flesh. The electric current surged through them. His cock pulsed and throbbed against her skin. He reached up under her robe and pulled her tightly against him. He savored the feel of her skin against his. He kissed her forehead, her nose, and then her lips, savoring the taste of her.

Emily took a half step back and felt the counter press against her ass. Desire and passion coursed a hot path through her body. Her nerves tingled with need. She reached back and placed her hands on the counter. She smiled wickedly as she hoisted herself up onto the counter and spread her legs to wrap them around Ragden. Then she reached down and guided his cock into her pussy.

"I can't wait," she said huskily into his ear as she pulled him into her.

He rolled his hips into her groin, slid his throbbing cock deep into her. Felt it ground out against her cervix. He gasped as her incredibly tight pussy seemed to part and let him sink into her in one stroke.

"Oh gods..." he whispered into her lips as he kissed her deeply. He ground his hips against her groin. Pushed his cock harder against her cervix. Emily felt the heat, intensity, and passion rolling of Ragden, filling her up. She sighed, as he pushed against her depths, and felt the pressure inside her.

"I thought we were going to get something to eat first?"

He whispered huskily into her ear as he pulled back slightly. He slid his cock almost out of her vice-like vagina. Emily moaned in response. Wrapped her legs tighter around him and pulled him back into her. Her arms wrapped

around him, and grabbed his ass. Pulled him fully into her. She moaned as his cock brushed up against her cervix. She pulled against him, squeezed, and tried to get him deeper into her.

He took a deep breath as he slowly slid partially out, then slid back in. His breath came in gasps as her body pulsed around him. He could feel her heart thumping against his chest. His heart sped up to match hers. Emily moaned in response, feeling her heart beating against Ragden's chest. She felt her body pulsing around his cock; the heat and intensity filled her.

Ragden drew back and slid half his throbbing cock from her incredible vagina. Then slid it back in more quickly. Her entire body pulsed around him. He quickly found himself moving more rapidly, sliding in and out with increased speed. His breath picked up pace as he felt her starting to lose control. Emily moaned louder; her voice echoed throughout the bathroom as Ragden's cock slid in and out of her incredibly tight pussy. She felt the passion that burned within him, felt the incredible desire that coursed through her veins.

To her surprise, Emily could feel her orgasm building rapidly. The sensation of everything that had transpired in the last ten minutes built upon itself and overwhelmed her. Feeling Emily's building orgasm, Ragden's body responded in kind. The tenderness of the shower, the teasing, every incredible sensation built into a symphony of ecstasy. His cock throbbed harder as it slid in and out of her pussy. He never wanted it to end, but knew he was moments from climax.

Emily's eyes rolled back into her head as she felt Ragden's cock slamming into her incredibly tight pussy. She felt the incredible heat that radiated from his member. Their bodies once again worked together. Emily rolled her hips in time to his thrusts. Each thrust pushed into her cervix and shook her body. Her breasts spilled from the open robe. Bounced in time to her heart, in time to each thrust. Her nipples hardened as she felt Ragden's cock slamming into her.

Ragden leaned forward, and latched his mouth onto one breast, one hand on the other. His other hand braced against the vanity as he slammed his cock into her faster and harder. Their rhythm was still building. He could feel the wildness of her heartbeat, like a caged animal. His beating to match. Their breathing was rapid and in sync. He flicked his tongue over her nipple as he slammed his cock in and out of her.

Emily's body trembled as Ragden's mouth captured her breast and suckled her nipple. While his cock continued to pound into her tight pussy. As he felt her tremble, his desire intensified. Their pace increased. The vanity shook beneath them. He flicked and licked her nipple with his tongue as he continued to slam his cock into her even faster. His fingers curled into her. Emily's fingers dug into his ass, pulled him into her with each thrust.

Emily's body shook violently as Ragden's cock pounded into her. Her knuckles went white with the effort of holding onto the vanity. Her eyes

rolled up into her sockets. Her mouth hung open, as she gasped for breath.

At the edges of his psyche, in the back of his mind, Ragden could feel the dark cloud coming closer. He could feel his body starting to succumb, to lose control. 'Release me,' the words crept through his mind, hauntingly, comfortingly; all he had to do was let go... A cold trickle of fear went down his back. He tried to refocus on Emily, his precious beautiful, sexy, wonderful Emily. His cock slammed into her pussy, filled her, worshipped her, loved her. He could still feel the dark cloud just out of sight. He tried to shake his head to lose it. With a massive effort, he shoved it away... Its laughter faded as it disappeared. Ragden's eyes refocused, and he looked down at Emily, his cock still slammed into her, over and over. Their bodies were in a psychotic rhythm of ecstasy.

Emily's head rolled back, her back arched, and every muscle seized as she cried out from the force of her climax. The orgasmic waves suddenly overcame everything she was experiencing. Her heart stampeded in time to the psychotic thrusts of Ragden's hips. His cock slid in and out of her so fast, she could not tell where he began, and she stopped. She cried out as her body shuddered, and shook, gasped for breath as another wave of orgasmic energy crashed over her. Arched her back and threw her head back as she cried out again.

Just as suddenly, Ragden's climax overtook him, blotted out existence. His muscles seized, and his cock slammed into her cervix, as his body locked up, tried to push deeper into her. He pulled her against him and groaned with effort as his heart stampeded in his chest. Every muscle clenched, then he felt it release as cum exploded out of his cock, filling her. His own back arched, pushed against her harder and tried to push his cock deeper into her as more cum poured into her.

Emily's body convulsed, her heart hammered as she screamed out, her orgasm ripped through her very soul. Forcing his eyes to open again, as Emily screamed the force of her orgasm, Ragden felt his body crumple. He reached out and grabbed her limp body as they slid to the floor. He cradled her against him and prevented her from hitting anything as he collapsed, unable to hold his weight. She sagged against him, her strength gone. Her breath was faint, her pulse rapidly slowing. He could feel his cock still buried deep in her pussy, pushing against her cervix. Her vagina clenched on his cock, as more cum poured into her. He wondered when it would stop. He hoped it would not just from the sheer pleasure of it and hoped it would.

Emily's body went limp, completely spent. Her heart slowed and breath slowed, her mind blank. Her pussy still gripped Ragden's cock; her juices flowed out of her as she came. As they lay there, she felt the wetness of his seed as it mixed with her juices. Her thoughts floated on a sea of pure ecstasy; her body felt completely fulfilled. Completely satisfied. Completely overwhelmed by the incredible pleasure that had just taken over her being.

Ragden felt himself starting to soften within her as he cradled her in his

arms. He felt for her pulse and found it weak in her arms. He felt her breathing against him, shallow and faint. His heart thundered in his chest. What had happened? He feared that he had almost killed her, fucked her to death. Was such a thing possible? A small voice in the back of his head said it was. How? Why? He shook his head and tried to clear such thoughts. His heart ached for Emily. He felt the strength slowly returning to his limbs; he caressed her lovingly. Hoping she would recover.

Emily's heart slowed, her breathing slowed even more, and her mind floated in a sea of absolute bliss. She could feel her body slowly starting to come down from the height of her incredible orgasm. She could feel her pussy slowly start to contract, felt her vaginal walls slowly start to close around Ragden's still throbbing cock. She could hear her heartbeat, slowing, her breathing growing shallow. She felt the world slipping away and wondered if she was dying and if that would not be so bad. The experience had been the greatest of her life, and to end it there would not be so bad...

Ragden kissed her forehead softly, brushing of lips against hot skin. "Are you okay?" He whispered. Emily's heart rate continued to slow down; her breathing became slower. Her body started to recover from the incredible orgasm that had just overwhelmed her. She felt Ragden's lips brush against her forehead, and she opened her eyes, looked up at him, and saw his concerned expression. She felt her pussy still clenched on his cock. She could feel the incredible pleasure that had just filled her, and she smiled at him.

Ragden pulled the robe around her, around them both. Feeling its warmth against their skin. He could feel every bit of her pressed against him. The hard floor at his back. He knew if they stayed there much longer, he would be even more sore and that did not sound like much fun. He tried to sit up and found that difficult. He cradled her body against his. Felt her arms slip around him, as he sat up. Her body was still limp against him. Her breath was shallow, and her heart rate was almost undetectable.

"Do you think you can stand?" he asked cautiously, not even sure he could stand.

Emily's body was mostly limp against Ragden's. Her heart rate was still slowing, her breathing shallower. She could feel Ragden's arms wrapped around her, but it felt like something far away. Ragden tenderly brushed the hair from her eyes as he looked for some recognition that she was still there. He leaned down and kissed her forehead.

"Emily," he whispered. "Are you okay?"

Emily's eyes fluttered open, but she did not see Ragden looking at her. Her heart rate continued to slow. Her breath was even more shallow. She could feel Ragden's lips pressed against her forehead, and she closed her eyes again. She felt the warmth of his lips against her skin. It felt like something that happened to someone else. She noticed how her pussy clenched around his throbbing cock, but it was a distant sensation. Something far off, as she swam in bliss.

Cautiously, Ragden tucked his feet under him. Then he lifted himself upward. Using one hand to keep her tucked against him, he braced against the counter and stood. Her legs gently slipped around him, her arms snaked around his chest, tucked her against him. He could feel the faint beat of her heart against his skin. Her breath barely tickled his chest. It was faint and slow. If he did not know better, he would think she was asleep. Ragden leaned against the counter, with her still wrapped around him. He could still feel his cock lodged within her pussy; its walls still clamped down on him. He shuddered at the feeling. It felt so good. Even as his cock started to soften, her body did not let go. He leaned down and kissed her lips softly.

"Emily, are you okay?"

Her eyes fluttered but did not open. She returned the kiss, sluggishly. He smiled at her return kiss. She was still responsive, but only just. He leaned against the counter, held her to him as his cock softened, hoping she would recover. Wishing her to recover. Then something clicked in the back of his head, something shifted internally. He could feel her, all of her. The core of her being. Her soul. His heart leaped in his chest. Love poured out of him. He found her, supported her, and poured his love into her. He could not explain how, or what, but he felt his love pouring into her. It filled her up and returned her energy. The flush of her cheeks darkened. Her breathing steadied. Her heart beat stronger again. Her eyes fluttered open, and he saw something behind them. The strength of who she was. She no longer stared blankly. He saw recognition in her eyes.

Emily felt her heart rate growing stronger, her breathing becoming steady and deep. Her body started to recover from the incredible orgasm that had just overwhelmed her. Everything had a crispness to it, like someone had sharpened the edges of reality. She could feel every inch of Ragden's cock still lodged deep within her pussy. She could feel the incredible pleasure that had just filled her. As she looked at Ragden, she could feel something happening within her. Something deep within her. Something that she could not describe. She could feel her heart rate increasing. Her breath quickening. Her entire body tensed as she felt a rush of incredible emotion filling her. A rush of incredible sensations that flooded her very being. A rush of pure ecstasy that seemed to fill and strengthen her very essence. She gasped as it filled her and flowed through. She felt every pore of her being filled with it.

"Emily," he whispered, seeing the color in her cheeks again. "Are you okay? Can you say something? You're scaring me..."

Emily blinked, slowly. She looked around the room. She tried to curl tighter around Ragden but was already snuggled against his chest. Then she looked up at him and saw the concern on his face. The worry in his eyes.

"Wha...? I'm... I'm sorry... I'm here. I'm... I think I'm okay." She could still feel his cock. Even though it was smaller and softer, deep inside her. She smiled at the sensation of it. Even as it started to get smaller and slip out of her. Then her stomach rumbled again. She looked down at her body and

giggled.

Ragden smiled down at her, then kissed her lips tenderly. He leaned back and gently pulled her legs out from around him. He gripped her ass softly and lifted her off his cock. Let it slide from within her. Then he set her softly on the floor. His hands on her hips to steady her shaky legs.

Emily felt a sense of loss as his cock slipped from her. She missed the feeling of him deep within her. The incredible pleasure that he brought her. Ragden looked down and saw a slow stream of fluid running down her leg from her drenched pussy lips. A mix of her juices and his. He stood up and stepped away from the vanity. He kept a hand on her hip in case she lost her balance. He grabbed a washcloth, dampened it, and then gently ran it up her leg, wiping the fluids from her skin. As he did so, he bent down and smelled it. He touched his tongue to it and shivered at the complex mix of their flavors. Then he finished running the cloth up to her groin, where he held it against her.

Ragden stood and wrapped his arms around her. Pulled her against him. He kissed her forehead softly, then her lips. A tear in his eye as he whispered to her.

"I thought I'd lost you there for a moment..."

Seeing the tear in Ragden's eye, Emily's heart fluttered. She could not clearly remember what had happened. She felt okay. She felt better than okay. She felt amazing. She leaned into Ragden and kissed him tenderly on the lips.

"I'm sorry, love; I didn't mean to scare you."

He smiled down at her, noting something different but not able to put his finger on it. His hands trailed around her waist.

"God... You are so beautiful."

Emily blushed slightly, feeling Ragden's hands on her waist. She felt a newfound confidence. A newfound self-assurance. A newfound beauty that seemed to radiate from within her very being. She felt incredibly sexy, desirable, and attractive. She felt like nothing could compare to the way she felt right now. Nothing could take that away from the incredible pleasure she was feeling. She felt like she belonged to Ragden like she was his, and he was hers.

"Lover," she whispered, her voice soft and sweet, "You make me feel like the most incredible woman in the world. Like I have never felt before."

Ragden felt heat coming down his cheeks. He blinked hard, feeling tears starting to well up. He hugged her fiercely and pulled her against him. Then he whispered to her.

"Shall we go downstairs and get some food then?"

Emily felt Ragden's heat. She knew that he was feeling emotional. She could see the tears in his eyes, and she knew that he was feeling something deep within himself. She wrapped her arms around him and hugged him tightly. She felt the incredible pleasure that was still coursing through her very being.

"Love, please don't cry. I want to make you feel better. I want to make you feel like everything is all right. I want to show you how much I care about you; how much I need you."

Ragden sighed at her, his heart hammered in his chest as he spoke softly. "I feel it."

Then his stomach rumbled again. Echoed by hers.

"I think it's best we eat something, though..."

Then he laughed softly. She laughed along with him. She looked down at herself, and she could see the incredible glow of health and vitality that seemed to radiate from her very being.

Ragden smiled happily. Then he reached over and pulled her robe closed. He grabbed the sashes, and gently tied them in a bow across her stomach. Then he pulled his robe about him and tied it similarly. He took her by the hand. He pulled the door open and walked out into the hall. He pulled her behind him. Then he reached back in and turned off the light.

CHAPTER 9

As they walked down the stairs, Ragden could hear voices in the kitchen and dishes clinking. He checked the clock in the foyer and noted that it was close to midnight. Far more time had passed than he had anticipated. He walked through the living room and into the kitchen with Emily close on his heels. The feeling of her behind him made his heart light with joy. As they rounded the corner, Ragden's Mom and Dad looked up. His dad was in a pair of sweatpants, shirtless. His hair tumbled. His beard was stiff, and he had a huge smile on his face. His mom was in a similar robe to them, pulled tight around her generous figure. Her cleavage just barely showing. For a moment, Ragden wondered what she was wearing underneath if anything.

"We expected that you would be hungry, so we cooked up a little something for you." Michael smiled, "Steak, mashed potatoes, broccoli, and some freshly made biscuits."

Jennifer pointed to the table, where spots had already been laid out. "Have a seat, your timing is perfect, it'll be ready in a minute or two."

Emily followed closely behind Ragden. As they stepped to the table, she suddenly felt ravenously hungry. She looked at Ragden and saw the love in his eyes. She saw the happiness that was reflected in her. She looked in a mirror and saw the incredible beauty she had become. The radiance that surrounded her. The glow that seemed to come from within her very being.

As they approached the table, Ragden pulled out a chair for her and slid it in as she sat down. Then he sat in the seat next to her. He took her hands in his and noticed that she was still trembling. He kissed her hands softly and placed them on the table. Jennifer walked over and sat across from them, gazed at them holding hands, and smiled.

"Looks like you two had a very eventful evening."

Ragden blushed while Emily looked down shyly, trying to hide her blush. Jennifer giggled like a schoolchild. Michael called from the stove, "Emily, how

do you like your steak?"

Emily looked at Ragden and saw the love in his eyes. She felt the incredible connection that they shared. She looked at his hand holding hers. She felt her heart rate increase. She looked at Jennifer and Michael, and she saw the incredible connection between them. All of them. The love that filled the home. She felt like she belonged here, like she was part of this family. Like she was loved and cherished by everyone here.

"Medium is fine. Thanks." Emily responded.

"Perfect, just about done then..."

Jennifer reached across the table and took both of their hands in hers. Her fingers were soft, and she squeezed their hands, smiling. Then she looked at Emily.

"Please tell me you are planning to spend the night. It is quite late."

Emily looked at Jennifer, blushed slightly, then nodded, "Yes, I'd like to spend the night. If that's okay with you."

Jennifer smiled and giggled to herself. She squeezed their hands more firmly, then drew back. "Of course. We would love for you to stay."

Just then, Michael walked out of the kitchen with steaming plates of food. He set down a plate in front of Jennifer and Emily. Then he went back and grabbed two more plates. He set one in front of Ragden and one in front of his place. Then he walked over and kissed Jennifer tenderly on the lips before taking his seat. He looked over at Emily.

"Of course, you can stay, my dear. I insist."

Emily looked down at the plate of food in front of her and realized just how hungry she was. She looked around the home. She felt the love filling the place and marveled at it. Then she looked back to Michael and Jennifer.

"Thank you. That means a lot to me. I appreciate it." Emily said sincerely.

Michael laughed. It was a deep sound that filled the room. "Of course. Now eat. You look as famished as Ragden... Eat! Both of you!"

He laughed again, picked up his silverware, and cut into his portion of steak. Ragden picked up his silverware and did the same. The steak was heavenly. The mashed potatoes, perfect; the broccoli to die for.

"Dad, this is amazing!" Ragden said around a mouthful. Michael waved dismissively.

"You are just hungrier than usual. But I'll take the compliment. Enjoy."

Emily looked at the food, and she knew that she was incredibly hungry. She cut into her steak and watched the juices flowing over her fork. She took a bite and moaned softly.

"This is the greatest steak I've ever had!"

Again, Michael waved his hand dismissively. "It is decent at best, but everything tastes amazing when you are tired and hungry. Happy to provide. Enjoy."

They sat quietly and ate their meal. The food was too delicious for conversation. After they finished their meals, Jennifer collected the dishes and

took them into the kitchen to wash. Michael followed her, helping, and cleaning up the stove, pots, and pans. Ragden turned to Emily and took her hands in his, squeezing them gently.

"Are you okay? You still seem a bit... off?"

Emily looked at Ragden and saw the love in his eyes. She felt the connection that seemed to flow between them. She smiled at the feeling of the meal she had just devoured. Her full belly. It made her feel warm, and content. She sighed happily.

"Yes, I'm okay. Just incredibly full and happy."

Ragden leaned over and softly kissed her on the mouth.

"Hey now, save that for later," Michael called from the kitchen. They broke off the kiss, blushing. "Come on over and give me a hand here, Rag."

Ragden stood, his hands trailing from Emily's. He smiled at her as he walked into the kitchen to help put away dishes. Emily stood and followed Ragden into the kitchen. She stood at the edge of the island, watching how everyone worked together in harmony. She felt the warmth and connection of family and smiled. As she finished washing the plates, Jennifer walked over to Emily and put an arm around her shoulders.

"Dear, come with me; I think we can let the boys finish up."

She led Emily back around the island and sat her on a stool. She noticed the slight stagger in Emily's stride. She reached into her robe, pulled out a small glass bottle, and pressed it into Emily's hands.

"This is a small medical ointment. Rub this into your muscles, particularly your thighs. It'll soothe the soreness. Like tiger balm, but with a few personal ingredients that smell so much better. You will feel right as rain in no time."

Jennifer winked and squeezed Emily's hands softly. Emily smiled at Jennifer and felt everything washing over her. She felt an incredible heat filling her entire body. She knew that she was alive, young, vibrant, incredibly beautiful, and incredibly sexy. All these sensations were washing over her very soul.

Once the dishes were cleaned and put away, Michael walked Ragden out onto the patio in the cool night air. He turned to Ragden and looked at him sternly. "What happened? Your own words."

Ragden described the dark cloud, and how it almost took him. Michael frowned.

"I warned you."

"I fought it off..."

"You let it get too close..."

"But... What happened to Emily? Did I break her? I thought I fucked her to death at first... Is that... Is that possible?"

Michael nodded slowly. "Yes. It is. We aren't normal, Rag. You must be careful; what you did was extremely dangerous. You could have killed her."

Tears filled Ragden's eyes. "I tried to fix it. I ... pushed... myself into her."

"I can see that."

"But... now she seems... off."

"What you did was also very dangerous. She will recover, but it will take time, and she may never be quite the same again. I can see what you did was out of love... You just have to be more careful."

Michael pulled Ragden into a hug and wiped the tears from his eyes. "I will explain this weekend when we go to the beach house. We have much to discuss."

Ragden sighed, feeling as if the weight of the world had dropped on his shoulders. His dad grabbed him by the shoulders and shook him gently.

"Enough of that. Don't mope. You have a beautiful, wonderful young woman in there who wants to be with you. Go. Smile. Love her. Share yourself with her. Just... be mindful of what you do."

Michael chuckled to himself and pushed Ragden back inside. He walked over to where Emily and Jennifer were quietly talking. Emily turned to Ragden as he walked up. He pulled her into a tight embrace and pulled her against him. Tears sprang to his eyes again. He tried to bury them in her hair but could still feel them burning on his face. Jennifer smiled and wiped his face clean.

As Emily looked up at him questioningly, Ragden smiled and kissed her softly on the lips.

"Come..." he spoke softly, "Let's call it a night."

Emily looked up at Ragden and saw the pain and sadness in his eyes. She saw the fear that filled him. She could see the beauty that surrounded him. The radiance that seemed to emanate from within him. She could feel the glow that seemed to pulse from his skin. The heat seemed to pour from his very pores. She could see the desire that drove him. The passion that consumed him. She could see the incredible love that filled every corner of his heart. She felt her heart ache for him. She knew at that moment that she was well and truly in love with him.

Ragden leaned over and kissed his mom on the cheek. "Thanks for dinner, Mom. You are the best."

Jennifer smiled warmly and hugged both Ragden and Emily. She wrapped her arms around both. Then Michael came up behind them and wrapped his long arms around all three of them.

Michael's rich voice washed over and caressed them like a gentle breeze, "Get some rest, you two. If you must... have a little fun... just be mindful of the time, please. You do have school tomorrow..."

"Thanks, Dad. Thanks for dinner; it was awesome. Have a good night."

Ragden walked back through the living room, Emily in tow behind him. He pulled her up next to him, placed his arm around her waist to guide her up the stairs, and made sure she did not fall. They stepped into his bedroom and looked around. The bed was made with fresh sheets. Emily's clothes were clean, in a neat, folded pile on Ragden's desk. He cocked an eyebrow, trying to puzzle over when his mother might have gotten in behind them and cleaned

the room. Then he turned to Emily and pulled her against him, hugging her tightly.

Emily looked at the bed and saw the softness of the sheets. The comfort that seemed to radiate from them. She looked at the clothes and saw the orderliness of them. The care that seemed to have gone into making sure everything was in its proper place.

Ragden reached over and turned off the lights. The room was bathed in darkness. He closed his eyes, while he held Emily against him. He waited for his eyes to adjust. Once he could see, by the soft light filtering in through the partly open window, he leaned in and kissed Emily softly on the lips. Then he untied his robe, and let it slide off his shoulders to the floor.

Emily watched as Ragden removed his robe. Her heart raced with anticipation. Her breath grew shallow. She watched as the robe slid off his shoulders, revealing his naked body. She could see the strength that seemed to flow through every muscle, the power that radiated from his being.

Ragden reached over and untied Emily's robe. Then he slid it off her shoulders for her and watched it fall to the floor at her feet. He watched her shiver slightly, her hands snaking up to cover her breasts and groin. He reached out and stopped her. Pulled her hands into his.

"Please don't cover yourself. You have nothing to hide from me. I love you; I love your body. I love everything about you. You have nothing to hide, nothing to be ashamed of."

Emily smiled, as she felt new confidence in her body. He pulled her naked body against his and felt her breasts press against his chest. The soft heat of her groin against his. He ran his fingers down her back and curled them around her waist. Held her against him as he leaned down and kissed her lips tenderly. Emily's heart raced, her breath grew short, and her body trembled with desire.

Gently, Ragden swept one arm under her knees. The other curled around her back to hold her. He picked her up easily. Her arms circled his neck to hold her head up to his chest. Then he walked over to the bed. He kicked the covers off the side of the bed and crawled onto the bed. He gently laid her head down on the pillows. Then he slid in next to her, rolling her onto her side, away from him, cradling her body against his.

Emily felt his body curl around her, comfortingly. She sighed as the heat of his body washed over her. She felt him slide an arm under her neck. She felt him reach down around her body. Sliding his arm between her breasts. His palm was on her stomach. His other hand slid along her side and pulled her body against his chest. He spooned around her. As her ass slid against his groin, she could feel his cock hardening between her legs. Her heart fluttered in her chest. She could feel his deep, even breathing calming her.

As she felt his body hardening against her, Emily felt her heart beating more quickly. The desire and need for him were building deep within her core. She placed her hands over his and felt a tingle along her skin at the

touch. She sighed as Ragden kissed the back of her neck tenderly. His cock throbbed against her groin. The shaft pressed against her clitoris. Emily felt herself growing wet at the closeness of that massive meat between her legs. Her arousal built deep within her. The need for him to be in her.

Ragden reached around her and gently cupped her breasts as he slid his cock through her folds. He placed the head of his cock right at the entrance of her vagina. He kissed the back of her neck tenderly. She felt his love for her washing over her. It filled her heart. Filled her being. Filled her soul.

As he felt her arousal leaking over him, Ragden gently, slowly, lovingly slid up into her. Slowly slid deeper and deeper into her until the tip of his cock gently pushed against her cervix. He shivered with the ecstasy of how amazing she felt, how alive. Her vagina squeezed around him. He whispered into her ear as he nuzzled her neck.

"Good God, woman, that feels amazing..."

Emily felt Ragden's cock push against her cervix. She could feel the heat that surrounded him pulsing within her. She felt herself growing even more wet. Her arousal deepened and built within her very soul.

As he felt her pulse start to quicken, Ragden felt his beating to match. He gently rolled his hips, slid his cock partially out, then slid back in. Gently. Lovingly. He closed his eyes and savored the feel of her body against his. The electric charge of her body curled against his. The tightness of her vagina clenched around his throbbing cock. He searched his psyche for the darkness and found it lurking nearby. He took all the force of his will and sent it hurtling into the depths. It howled in rage as Ragden locked it behind iron gates and massive walls. No longer feeling its presence, he refocused his attention on Emily; felt her light, and love radiating around him.

Emily felt Ragden's hips roll against hers, and she sighed. This was what she wanted, and the pleasure of it rolled over her. It filled her with love and joy. Ragden continued to gently roll his hips, slowly sliding his cock in and out of her. He cupped her breasts tenderly from behind and kissed the back of her neck. She rolled her hips against his, meeting him halfway. His cock thumped heavily against her cervix. She gasped softly at the impact, as she felt it so deep within her. Her sharpened senses seemed almost overwhelmed by the sensation of it like she was feeling it again for the first time.

Ragden built a slow steady rhythm. He gently held her breasts and tenderly kissed her neck and shoulders as he slid into her depths. Then out, and back in. He felt her heart beating in her chest. Her skin pulsed against his. Her body squeezed tight around his cock as he cradled her body against his. She matched his rhythm, her breath matching his. He felt her heart beating in time to his. She felt so full of life, love, beauty, and confidence. It was overwhelming, and yet everything she wanted, craved, and needed.

As Ragden continued to gently slide his throbbing cock in and out of her, he released his grip on her amazing breasts. He slid his hands to her hips. Then he slid one hand around her waist and slipped it between her legs. He

gently stroked her clitoris as he kissed her neck and shoulders.

Emily sighed contentedly, placing her hands on top of his. She felt their strength and tender touch. The electric charge of it sent shocks of pleasure through her body. His love filled her, made her feel complete. Her pussy clenched and unclenched with each gentle, loving thrust that filled her with his love and compassion. She bit her lip as she felt it building and building within her.

Ragden gently slipped his fingers around her clit; Emily's breath caught in her throat as she felt an electric charge shooting through her groin at his touch. He felt her hand on his. He slid his hand a little lower, felt her spread pussy lips. Soaked with her arousal, around his throbbing cock. The heat of it was a palpable thing between her legs. Then he slid his hand back up to her clitoris, gently stroking it as his cock slid so impossibly deep inside her. Caressed her cervix and slid out and in again. He gasped softly against her back. He felt her tighten around him. She gasped softly at the feeling of him pressed against her deepest parts. Then he kissed her neck and the back of her ear softly and flicked her earlobe with his tongue. Gently pulled it into his mouth to suckle it.

He felt her sigh against him. Ragden's heart rate increased, and his gentle thrusts became more insistent. His fingers worked over her clit a little faster. He felt her skin charged with loving energy; her body pulsed against his. His cock throbbed with each squeeze of her pussy along its shaft as he continued to slide it in and out of her. He kissed the back of her ear and the side of her neck. He gently slid his teeth across her skin. He savored the silky smoothness of it. The taste of it on his tongue was sweet, like a honeyed nectar.

Emily moaned softly as she felt his fingers working over her clit. She felt the incredible heat that surrounded him. She felt his cock sliding deep into her, filling her with incredible pleasure. His strong thrusts drove her closer and closer to the edge of ecstasy. She felt her pussy tingling and clenching around him as he continued to work his magic upon her sensitive flesh.

As Emily moaned and started to move against Ragden, his pace increased. Just a hair faster, more insistent, but still tender, gentle, and loving. His cock slid in and out of her, filled her with his love and compassion. He felt his body throb with each gentle stroke, each gentle caress across her deepest parts. She moaned again as his fingers continued to play with her clit, gently stimulating, caressing. His teeth nipped at her neck, softly, tenderly. His other hand reached up and gently squeezed a breast, gently pinched her nipple, adding pressure and pleasure.

Emily felt the pressure of all his body pressed against her back, her breasts, her clit, and her neck. She continued to move with him, her hips began to undulate. She drove herself further towards the edge of ecstasy. Ragden matched her movement, her rhythm, and matched her thrusts. His fingers moved to her breath and her pulse.

Emily moved with Ragden. She felt his fingers working over her sensitized

clit, felt his cock sliding deep within her. It filled her with incredible pleasure. She felt her pussy tingle and contract around him as she matched his rhythm. Her hips undulating, her movements becoming more powerful and intense. She felt her climax building deep within her, as she felt her body begin to quiver and shudder. Her orgasm was about to explode within her.

Ragden could feel her reaching the edge of what she could contain. His orgasm built with hers. His heart racing with hers. Their bodies worked together like one incredibly beautiful machine. Thrust for thrust. Pulse for pulse. Breathe for breath. His fingers were on her flesh, in time to her heart beat. His breath in her ear matched hers. His cock slid deep, out, and deep again, matching her every movement.

Emily felt Ragden's cock as it slid deep into her, filling her with incredible pleasure. As she matched his movements, her pussy tingled and contracted around him. Her hips undulated in perfect harmony with his. She felt her climax building, as she felt his orgasm building with hers. She felt his fingers working over her sensitive clit, in perfect time with her heartbeats. She felt her breath catch in her throat, and her heart raced with anticipation. She felt her body shudder and quake. She felt her orgasm as it exploded in a torrent of pleasure; her pussy gushed and spasmed around his thick throbbing cock.

As her orgasm exploded, Ragden's exploded over him. It washed away reality. His body spasmed and shuddered in time to hers. He tried to keep moving, to keep stimulating her, to keep sliding in and out, but his muscles seized. His cock slid deep into her, gently pressed against her cervix. He tried to push deeper but could not. He felt his orgasm surge into her, filling her. He could feel her juices mixing with his and flowing out of her and over him. He shivered with ecstasy, sighed, and gasped in time with her. As the orgasm rolled over them, he slid his hand up to her other breast, grasped her gently, and pulled her body firmly against his. Feeling every shudder and heartbeat as they became one being of love and compassion.

Emily felt Ragden's cock as it pulsed and spasmed inside her. She felt her orgasm erupting, flooding her womb with waves of pleasure. She felt his cum mixing with hers. It filled her, as she felt her body convulsing and trembling with pleasure. She felt her heart racing in time to his, and she let out a soft, satisfied moan. She felt her body gush and squirt with pleasure. She felt every shudder and heartbeat as he pulled her against him

Ragden sighed as his muscles slowly started to relax. He let himself sink into the mattress and pulled her body against him. He basked in the afterglow of their joint orgasm. He had dreamed of good sex before and ached to know what that was like, but never had he imagined this. Pure bliss filled every pore of his being. He gently lifted his head and turned her head to look into her eyes. Then he kissed her softly on the lips, tenderly, tasting her, and breaking away breathless.

Emily gazed into Ragden's eyes. She saw the love and passion that seemed to radiate from them. The intensity of the pleasure that they had just shared.

She felt her heart racing, her body trembling, and her mind spinning as she realized that she had just experienced something truly incredible. She felt his lips on hers, kissing her softly, tenderly as if he were savoring her taste. She could still feel her juices from her swollen, sensitive folds still wrapped around his massive throbbing cock.

Ragden kissed her again, softly. His cock still throbbed but starting to soften, deep within her. Then he whispered against her lips. "Are you okay?"

Emily nodded. She smiled softly, looking deeply into his eyes, as she whispered against his lips. "Yes, Ragden. That was amazing. Thank you for sharing that with me."

A single tear slid down his cheek at her words. He kissed her a little harder, felt her body against his, felt her heart beating with his. He smiled at her.

"I'm just... so eternally grateful to you. For being here with me. For accepting me. For your love... I just... I cannot put it into words how happy you make me. Thank you." He kissed her again, tenderly.

Emily felt his cock still throbbing deep within her. She felt her juices still flowing from her swollen, sensitive folds. She saw the tear as it ran down his cheek. She reached up and wiped it away as she kissed him back. She felt the heat and passion that filled every corner of his being. She smiled deeply, feeling the bond that connected them. She felt his love and passion coursing through her veins. She spoke softly, her voice full of love and devotion.

"You are welcome, Ragden. You have given me something incredible too. You have shown me what true love and passion can be, and I am so grateful for having you in my life."

Ragden settled into the mattress again and rested his head on the pillow. He buried his face in her hair. He breathed deeply of the scent of her against him. He gently kept her back firmly pulled against his chest. His cock softened within her. He could still feel her juices flowing. His still leaking into her. A shiver ran down his back at the sheer ecstasy of it. The amazing feeling of being so connected and in love and being loved back. He gently caressed her incredible breasts, feeling the fullness of them. The simple beauty of them. He whispered against the back of her neck.

"I feel so... content. I think I could lie like this all night if you'd let me."

"Mm... That sounds wonderful," she said softly as she felt her body start to relax. Her pussy still gripping and clenching around his thick throbbing member.

"Are you comfortable? Will you sleep this way? I never imagined I'd have the opportunity to sleep with someone as incredible and beautiful, and... loving as you. I want to sleep with you in my arms, wake up with you by my side."

Emily smiled and nodded. She felt her heart race with excitement, as she spoke softly, "That sounds wonderful. To be able to share such intimacy with you, to feel your warmth and love surrounding me... It's a dream come true."

Ragden's breath hitched in his throat. He gently slid his hands off her

breasts and pulled himself away from her just enough to grab the blankets and pull them up and over them. Then he pulled them up onto their shoulders, covering their naked bodies, which warmed them against the cool night air leaking in from the window. He took a glance at the window, still partly open. He took a sniff of the sweet night air. He could smell the flowers from his mother's garden, their scent comforting and relaxing. His eyes started to feel heavy. He laid back down and nuzzled his face into her hair and neck. He buried himself in her sweet scent. He wrapped his arms around her and pulled her body gently against his. Her back against his chest. Her ass was against his groin. His cock was still buried deep in her. He could feel her pussy still clenching and unclenching on him. Like a relaxing, sensual massage on his cock. He could feel the passion stir, and his heartbeat picked up, then sleep started to edge in. He closed his eyes, nuzzled against her, and let his body relax. He felt the world start to drift away.

Emily felt her heart rate slow, and her breathing deepened. Her mind started to drift off into a peaceful tranquil state of relaxation. She felt his cock soft, but large, still deep inside her. It created a sensation of pleasure that lulled her into a state of calm, serene pleasure. She whispered.

"Good night Ragden."

"Good night, my love," he mumbled softly against her back as sleep finally consumed him.

Emily felt Ragden's soft words, as she felt her body start to relax. Her mind started to drift off into a peaceful, dreamless state of rest. She closed her eyes, feeling the weight of her eyelids falling heavily over them. She surrendered herself completely to the peaceful embrace of the night. She felt safe and secure in Ragden's arms. She felt loved and cherished.

"Sleep well, my love," she mumbled softly as she drifted off.

CHAPTER 10

Thursday...

Reality started to seep back into Ragden's awareness. He took a deep breath and his nostrils filled with the scent of Emily. He smiled, remembering the activities of the night before. He felt her gently resting against him, and he felt so warm, happy, and content. He opened his eyes and lifted his head to look around the room. The window was raised a little higher, and the bed felt more occupied. He shifted slightly and noticed a pair of foxes curled up against his back. Just past that, two rabbits lay next to each other against the backs of his thighs. A pair of raccoons just past them. Along Emily's back was a pair of small cats and two small birds. Just past them were a pair of groundhogs followed by a pair of skunks. Ragden took a deep breath, feeling them all around them, at peace, resting, and wondered at it. Their presence was soothing and peaceful. He reached out and gently placed a hand on one of the fox's heads. It opened its eyes and looked at him. It sniffed his hand, then gently rubbed his hand with its head. He scratched behind it's ears, and it looked at him peacefully. As he pulled his arm back under the covers and snuggled up against Emily, the fox rested its head on its mate and snuggled itself back to rest. Ragden felt his cock still within Emily and smiled. Having Emily pulled against him felt so natural, so peaceful, and so exquisitely sensual. His cock throbbed gently, as he snuggled against Emily, pulling her gently against him.

Emily felt Ragden lift his head. She felt his cock still buried deep within her, filling her. She smiled as her body started to twitch and writhe with pleasure.

"Mm... Ragden," she whispered.

Ragden kissed her neck softly, "I'm sorry, did I wake you?"

Emily shook her head slightly as she felt his lips on her neck. She felt her pleasure starting to build once again. Her heart rate was speeding up. She felt

her pussy grip and clench around his throbbing member inside her. She looked around at the peaceful scene around her as her body started to respond to the incredible sensations still coursing through her very soul.

"No, Ragden," she whispered.

"Did you sleep well?"

He whispered against her skin as he gently rolled his hips against her. His cock throbbed into its full size within her. He moaned softly against her as he felt her body respond to his. His heart rate sped up to match hers. Emily sighed as she felt Ragden's hips rolling against her. She felt the sensation of his cock throbbing within her, filling her with pleasure. Her heart rate sped up as she felt her body responding. Her pussy gripped and clenched around him. Her juices started to flow. She quivered and shuddered with pleasure.

"Yes, Ragden, I slept incredibly well," she whispered.

As Ragden rolled his hips against Emily, he could feel the animals starting to stir around them. Each stood and stretched. The fox came over and licked his shoulder, nuzzled him, and then lightly jumped over and out the window. His mate did the same. Ragden stopped moving and lay still. Wrapped around Emily as each animal got up, walked over, offered its thanks, and then left out the window.

"That was.... different," he said as the last of the animals left. Then he turned his attention back to Emily and kissed her softly on the neck, shoulder, and earlobe. He slid his throbbing cock deeper, then back out, and then against her cervix in a gentle caress.

"Mm... yes, it was incredibly different," she whispered.

"Do you mind," Ragden whispered as he sat up and pushed the blankets off their bodies. His groin pushed firmly against hers. His cock pushed against her cervix. "If we change position? I loved being at your back all night, but now I'd like to easily look into your beautiful face."

She nodded softly, as she felt his cock slide into her cervix. The pleasure built within her. The urge to release that pleasure built steadily, "Of course, Ragden."

He gently grasped her left leg and lifted it against his chest. He kissed the back of her knee and her calf as he slid his left knee under her right leg, and then laid her leg back down over his right knee. Sitting on his heels, between her legs, he gazed down at her spread pussy. His groin pushed firmly against it; his throbbing cock pushed deep into her. He leaned forward and planted his hands on the mattress on either side of her waist. He kissed each breast, gently suckling her nipples. Then he kissed her throat and chin. Then he kissed her lips tenderly as he looked into her eyes and winked. Emily sighed softly, letting the sensations wash over her.

Ragden leaned forward and lowered his body against hers, his chest against her breasts. Her firm nipples pressed against him, his groin against hers. He slid his hands up her back and curled around her shoulders. He held her against him as he kissed her more passionately. His tongue parted her lips and

danced with hers. The sweet flavor of her almost overwhelmed him.

"Ragden... oh, God... please," Emily moaned softly against his lips.

He gently rolled his hips away from hers, slid partially out, then gently slid back into her until his cock caressed her cervix again. He kissed her lips, her chin, her throat. He savored the taste of her sweat and her skin. He slid his hands to her sides. Felt the swell of her breasts, the softness of her abdomen, the swell of her ass and hips.

Emily moaned as she felt his cock sliding in and out of her. She could feel the sensation of him rolling away and then gently thrusting back into her. She felt the pressure building up within her, as she felt the pleasure growing stronger with each passing moment. She felt the caress of his hands and the urge to release the pressure building and building within her.

"Please, Ragden... Fuck me harder."

He stopped for a moment, shocked by her sudden request. Then he slid more rapidly inside her. Quickly finding a rhythm to match her frantic heartbeats. His heart skipped a beat, trying to match hers. His breathing sped up to match the frantic pace she set. Emily felt his cock sliding into her. She felt the sensation of his heart as it raced along with her own. The pleasure continued to build within her, as the intensity of his thrusts increased. The force of his strokes. The pressure was still building within her, building, building.

"Fuck me harder, Ragden!"

Feeling her accelerating heart beating against his, Ragden pushed his hands deep into the mattress. He lifted his chest off hers. Ground his hips against hers. Pushed his cock deep into her. Then, from the new leveraged position, he leaned down and kissed her as he slid his cock in and out more forcibly. Harder. He drove into her. Now free, her breasts rocked with each massive thrust.

Emily felt Ragden's cock as it drove into her. She felt the intensity of his movements. The pleasure and pressure built up within her. The force of his strokes, the heat, and the wetness between her legs. The pressure started to overwhelm her. She could feel her orgasm building up with her, and the urge to release it.

"Ragden... Oh, God. FUCK ME HARDER!"

As he felt his orgasm building with hers, he increased the pace to a fevered intensity. He felt her pulse against his cock. Her heart hammered like a wild animal. The energy of her impending orgasm was a palpable thing. His body responded in kind. His heart raced with hers. His breath became ragged as he slid in and out of her faster. Pushed forcefully against her cervix. Her body rocked with each massive thrust. His hips bounced off her thighs, the whole bed rocked with their motion.

Emily felt each massive thrust. Each added to the pressure of her orgasm. Pushed her closer to release. The pleasure and pressure became almost unbearable. She felt the incredible intensity of her climax building as the force

of her orgasm started to overtake her. The need for release built beyond her limits to contain it.

"Ragden... I'm about to cum."

He felt her body start to shake with her orgasm. Her arms and legs trembled with the force of it. His climax started to overtake him. He tried to focus on her, slamming his cock in and out of her faster. Her hips and thighs bounced off the bed. The bed rocked with each massive thrust. Her breasts rocked with each incredible impact. Their breath exploded in and out, gasping with pleasure and ecstasy. The dam was close to breaking. He tried to keep the pace, to keep pushing to keep her in that exquisite state of ecstasy.

Emily felt Ragden driving into her. Her orgasm continued to build. She felt the incredible pleasure consuming her. Her orgasm still building. Ragden moved his hands to her thighs and pinned her legs against the mattress as he increased the pace. Slammed her harder, faster, deeper. His orgasm was only moments from crashing over him. He clenched every muscle. Tried to force it to hold off, to give him just a little longer. He could feel her pussy clenching on his cock, harder, driving him faster within her. He could feel her racing pulse beneath his touch.

"Oh, God... Ragden... I'm going to cum!"

At her urging, He tried to maintain his pace, his orgasm looming over him. He could feel it starting to press down upon him. He drove hard and fast into her. He held her thighs down as he fucked her as hard as she had asked for. His muscles strained to maintain the pace.

Emily felt Ragden's cock driving into her as she felt her orgasm hit it's breaking point. She felt every inch of his massive cock sliding in and out of her, hitting her depths. It shook her body, then slid out and hit her again. She clenched her teeth, feeling her body rock with each impact. Then her orgasm crashed down upon her. She felt her entire body start to shudder and convulse with the incredible force of her orgasm. Her hands grabbed into the sheets, balling them up.

"Ragden... I'm cumming," She moaned loudly.

As her orgasm crashed over her, the force of it washed over Ragden. He felt his response crashing over him. His body convulsed with the force of it. His limbs went rigid. His cock slammed home into her. His hips pressed hard into her thighs. Pinned her to the bed. Pushed his cock forcefully against her cervix. She groaned at the pain and pleasure of it, her pussy clenched on his cock, squeezing it so hard he could feel the explosion of cum inside her, filling her up. Their mixed juices and essences flowed out of her and washed over him. His arms gave out, and he collapsed heavily upon her. He gasped for breath; his face buried in her hair. He gently kissed her ear.

"Ragden," Emily moaned in his ear. Her body twitched and shuddered with the force of her climax. Ragden lay upon her. He felt every inch of her body pressed against him. He felt her arms slowly drag themselves around him, no strength left in them. She hugged him softly against her. He smiled

into her hair and softly kissed her ear. He gently pulled his arms up and slid them down along her sides. Felt her quivering muscles under his hands. Her pussy still clenched on his cock; he could feel himself still emptying into her. He shuddered at the feeling of it. The sensual loving feeling of it.

Emily sighed contentedly as she felt Ragden's cock still filling her. The waves of her orgasm still washed over her. She tried to relax as another wave sent her muscles trembling. Emily could still feel the muscles of her vagina clenching and unclenching on his cock deep inside her. Continuing to milk every drop of cum he could spare. She shivered at the feeling of it filling her up and spilling out of her. She dimly felt a dull ache in her muscles, her thighs where Ragden's hips pinned her to the mattress. It was a comforting pain, letting her know she was alive and loved. She felt every inch of his body pressed against her, and it comforted her. His strong heart beating against her chest. Her breasts pressed against his chest. She gingerly tried to flex her legs, to wrap them around him, but found the muscles still twitching and trembling, unable to move. Instead, she sighed at him and kissed his neck and shoulder.

Ragden laid still upon her. He felt her body still twitching and spasming. His muscles were slowly calming. He savored the feel of her body pressed to his. The sheer, incredible, loving comfort of her heart against his. Her skin against his. He felt like he could die a happy man, there and then. He felt her tender kisses, and he slowly lifted his head. His chest rose ever so slightly off hers to look into her eyes. He kissed her softly on the lips.

"You are amazing," he whispered against her lips, "That was amazing... I loved it and I love being with you, being in you." He kissed her lips again, a little more passion in it. Then he broke free, breathless.

Emily felt Ragden's words and actions. She felt the incredible mixture of pleasure and love that filled her. She felt his cock still filling her. His cum still leaked out of her, as she felt it collecting inside her. She felt his heartbeat against her chest, and she knew she was deeply in love with him. Emily's hand moved up to stroke his cheek, while she looked deeply into his eyes. She felt her heart as it raced with every single emotion that was running through her. She felt her legs finally calming down, as she wrapped herself around Ragden. She embraced him tightly. Her arms encircled his torso, her breasts pressed against his chest. Her thighs intertwined in his, as she felt his cock still filling her up.

Feeling her wrap herself around him, Ragden pulled her closer to him. He snuggled into her. Then he rolled over onto his back and pulled her over on top of him. His cock started to soften and slipped back, but still inside her. He felt her pussy clench on it, trying to keep him within her. He sighed at the sheer ecstasy of it and watched the play of emotions on her face as it happened. He leaned up and softly kissed her lips again. Then he looked to his right at the clock. Plenty of time still to prepare for school. He gently ground his hips up into her, pushed his cock deeper. Then slid back out. As

she felt his cock slip free, she groaned.

"Unfortunately, my love," he smiled up at her sadly, "Today is a school day, and we both have things we must do. As much as I would love to lay here the entire day with you... We need to get going."

Emily's heart rate started to slow down. Her breathing returned to normal. She felt the sensation of her orgasm slowly dissipate. Emily's hand reached down and pulled Ragden's cock out of her pussy. She looked down and saw the last bit of cum ooze out of her.

"Ragden. It's okay, we don't have to do this right now. I don't mind if you stay inside me for a while longer..."

Ragden laughed and smiled at her. Then he closed his eyes, felt her hand on his cock. Still softening but her touch made his heart flutter in his chest.

"I fear if we start again, we may never stop..." He kissed her lips softly. "As much as I would love to do that... we really must get going."

Emily smiled at Ragden's comment. She felt his cock softening. Her pussy clenched without it. She stroked it gently. She saw the desire in his eyes and felt the incredible attraction between them. Emily closed her eyes and took a deep breath before speaking softly.

"But Ragden... I want you to stay inside me for a little longer," she said, as she pulled his softened cock back into her pussy. Her pussy contracted on it, pulling it deeper into her. Emily could feel her orgasm starting to build again, as she looked at Ragden with lustful eyes.

As he felt his cock slide up into her again, guided by her hand, Ragden sighed with pleasure. His cock started to harden within her. It started to fill her up. He rocked his hips gently against her. Slid his now rock-hard cock against her cervix. "Maybe one last quickie?" He winked, ground his hips against hers, his cock pushed into her cervix.

Emily rocked forward, felt Ragden's cock as it slid back and up into her again. She felt her pussy clench and release it, pulling it deeper into her. She could feel her orgasm as it built once more. She felt her muscles tense and her breath hitch. Emily's hand ran along his length. She felt her fluids as they dripped from her pussy, mixing with his cum. She looked at Ragden with lustful eyes, as she spoke softly.

"Yes... just one more quickie..."

He gently thrust up into her and watched her body gently sway with the motion. Her breasts swayed delicately. Her hair bounced slightly. The look in her eyes as his cock slid out and then up against her cervix again, a gentle caress. His eyes slipped closed as her pussy clenched hard around his cock. He reached up and placed his hands on her breasts, grazed her nipples with his thumbs as he gently squeezed them. He looked into her eyes and blew her a kiss.

Emily felt his cock slide up against her cervix. She felt her orgasm building. Her body tensed. Her pussy clenched hard as she felt her breasts being gently squeezed. Emily's eyes rolled back in her head. She let out a low moan as she

Love & Nature

felt her orgasm building. He thrust up into her with a little more force, causing her to bounce against his hips. He gently squeezed her breasts and applied more pressure to her nipples as he drew back and thrust again. He moved a little bit faster. He could feel her pulse under his hands, quickening as her orgasm built. Her pussy clenched harder, squeezing his cock as it slid up into her.

Emily felt his cock slide deeper into her. She felt her orgasm building. Her eyes rolled back in her head as she felt her orgasm start to release. Her pussy clenched and released his cock. Emily's body shook with pleasure, as she let out a low moan. She felt her inner walls clenching and releasing his cock, her pussy being engulfed with pleasure.

As her orgasm started to release, Ragden slid his hands to her ass. He gently spread her cheeks, allowing him to thrust deeper, faster, in time with her orgasm. His orgasm built rapidly in response to hers. He moved his hands back up to her chest and grabbed her breasts with a little more force. His thumbs ran over her nipples and felt them harden. He continued to thrust up into her, feeling her muscles clench tightly around his cock. The sensation caused pulses of pleasure to shoot down his cock into his body.

Another wave of pleasure rolled over Ragden as cum exploded out of his cock into her. He watched the impact of it wash over her. Her body shuddered with it. Ragden reached his arms around her back and pulled her down onto his chest. His cock slid home against her cervix. Cum poured into her, mixed with hers, and washed down out of her. He held her quivering body against his. He felt her heartbeat against his chest, her breasts squeezed against him. He kissed her forehead and her nose, then raised her face to kiss her lips.

She felt the incredible sensation of his cum filling her and mixing with her fluids. She could feel her inner walls as they clenched and released him. She felt her orgasm subside, and her pussy start to fill with his thick, warm, sticky seed. Emily's body shook with pleasure. She felt her pussy being engulfed in pleasure. She felt his heartbeat against her chest, her breasts squeezed tightly against him.

"That wasn't nearly as explosive, but gods it felt good." He kissed her lips tenderly, savoring the feel of her against him. "Thank you."

Emily looked at Ragden, her eyes full of love and desire as she spoke softly, "It was amazing... Thank you for giving me such incredible pleasure."

"That is a two-way street, my love. I give you pleasure; you give me pleasure. In the end, we both get something amazing out of the deal." He winked, a sly look on his face, then kissed her softly on the lips.

"Now, I think it best we prepare for school... Much as I hate to part..."

He gently sat up, still cradling her body against his. He enjoyed the feel of her in his lap, against his chest, wrapped around his cock. Slowly, he lifted her out of his lap. Let his cock slip out of her, then held her up so she could settle her legs to the floor. He held her hips, to steady her, as he swung around and

stood next to her. Emily felt a slight twinge of disappointment, as she felt her orgasm fading away. Her pussy started to become less sensitive. She looked up at Ragden, her eyes filled with love and desire, as she saw him standing beside her. He held her hips and looked down at her with desire, love, and lust in his eyes. Emily's heart raced, as she felt her pussy clench and release, her fluids trickling down her thighs.

"Mm... I suppose you're right," she said softly, sadly.

As he noticed the trickle down her leg, Ragden reached down and wiped it off with his hand. His fingers brushing her pussy lips. Then he licked his fingers and smiled at the taste of her. "Mm... you taste delicious."

As he noticed the slight quiver in her legs, he cocked an eyebrow. Then he kneeled and fished through the pockets of her robe. He grabbed the small jar of ointment his mother had given her last night. Handing it to her, he said.

"Here, rub this into your legs. I'm sure it will help."

"Mm... I'll use it... but only if you tell me what you're thinking about when you taste my pussy."

Ragden laughed lustily. "Things best left unspoken for now. Later, I promise. Remind me after school. Though, that is something we need to talk about... Would you like a shower before we head out?"

Emily watched Ragden laugh. She felt her pussy clench and release, as she felt the incredible sensation of him focusing on her, even after their intense orgasm. Emily nodded, as she spoke softly, "A shower sounds great..."

He grabbed their robes, opened the door, and pulled her across the hall into the bathroom. Once inside, he hung up the two robes and turned on the water in the shower. "Separate, or together?"

Emily thought about it for a moment, as she looked at Ragden, and then decided to speak, "Together... I want us to be together."

She walked into the shower, letting the water cascade over her face and across her shoulders, her heart raced as she waited for him to join her. Ragden smiled happily, then stepped into the shower behind her, pulling the shower door shut.

"No sex this time, we do not have time right now. Just get clean."

He slapped her ass teasingly, marveling at the way it jiggled. Then he stepped next to her in the water, letting it rinse his muscles clean. He grabbed a bar of soap, handed it to her, then grabbed one for himself.

Ragden quickly ran the soap over himself, building a lather, rubbing it into his muscles. Then he rinsed clean. Then he grabbed the shampoo and worked it into his hair. As he let the water rinse it clean, he turned and leaned against the wall, letting the water cascade over him as he watched Emily clean herself. He licked his lips, watching the water run down her breasts and over her navel. He watched the way it curled over her groin and dripped through her lips. The drops fell off her ass, running down her legs. He ached to pull her against him but knew that they did not have time.

Emily watched Ragden clean himself while she did the same. Then she

could not help but blush as he leaned against the wall and watched her. She watched the look on his face as his eyes watched every inch of her body. She felt vulnerable, exposed, and incredibly sexy. Her heart beat a little faster as she could see the desire in his eyes, the way he licked his lips.

"You look like a goddess," he whispered, watching her in the water. Then as she turned to face the water, he grabbed a bar of soap and lathered up his hands. Once lathered, he placed them on her shoulders and massaged the soap into her tired muscles. He kneaded the soap in. Emily's heart raced as she felt his hands. Then he worked down her back and finished by rubbing it into her incredible ass. Once done, he stepped up against her and pulled her body against his. He leaned over her shoulder and kissed her on the lips. She moaned softly against him.

As he noticed that she was clean, Ragden reached around her and turned off the water. Then he stepped back, opened the door, and grabbed two towels. He handed her one and used the other to dry himself off. He watched her every movement, enjoying the sight of her. Once dry, he hung up the towel and stepped out of the shower up to the mirror. He opened a drawer and pulled out a comb and brush. He put the brush on the counter while he ran the comb through his hair, parting it where he wanted it, making sure it flattened out correctly.

Emily followed him, mesmerized as he took care of his appearance. Her eyes traced the lines of the muscles in his back, the firmness of his buttocks, the bulk of his thighs and calves. She felt her desire building. She tried to stifle it and failed. She licked her lips as she stepped up next to him and looked at him in the mirror.

Ragden turned to her and noticed she was still a bit wet. He picked up the towel and dried her off, slowly. Then he hung up the towel and picked up the brush.

"Would you like to brush your hair, or would you like me to?"

Emily bit her lip and realized how incredibly sexy he was, standing before her, fully naked. His cock dangling between his legs, large and soft. Then she noticed the brush in his hands and answered softly, "Do it... I want to watch you brush my hair."

He leaned over and kissed her softly on the lips, "As you wish."

Ragden stepped behind her as she turned to face the mirror, his flesh so close, but not touching. He gently pulled her hair back with his hands and ran the brush through it. He grabbed a hair dryer out of another drawer. He plugged it in and used the dryer in one hand, and the brush in the other. He gently ran through it, as her hair dried. Then he took one hand and gently pulled on her hair as he ran the brush through it. He pulled out the tangles and brushed it until it shined. Then he looked into the mirror and saw her watching him. He put the brush in the drawer and stepped up behind her, gently pressing his body against her back. Her heart raced. He pulled her hair to one side and kissed her shoulder, her neck, her cheek.

"Is that good? You look amazing."

"That's perfect," she breathed softly.

Ragden smiled down at her, then took her by the hand. He pulled the door open and stepped across the hall into his bedroom. He stepped over to his desk and picked up her panties. He stepped up and kneeled before her. He picked up one foot and held her panties open for her to slip into. She stepped into them, and he gently slid them up her calves, over her thighs to her groin. He stood up to her as he did. As he slid them over her ass, he ran his finger around the inside of her waistline and kissed her softly on the lips.

"Perfect."

Emily felt her heart racing. She had never thought getting dressed would make her feel so hot. Her desire burned up inside her.

Then Ragden stepped back to his desk and picked up her bra. He stepped behind her and held it in front of her. She placed her arms through it, and he slid it over her body and fixed the clasp behind her back. Then he reached around her and adjusted it against her chest. Gently cupped each breast to make sure the fit was firm and seated where it was supposed to be. Looking over her shoulder, and down her cleavage, he smiled. Then he pulled her against his chest and kissed her on the cheek.

He whispered, "Perfect."

Emily felt the heat rising in her cheeks; her panties grew damp between her legs. She turned and kissed him deeply on the lips. Then whispered, "You're just playing with me, aren't you?"

"Maybe... " He smiled at her. Then reached around behind her, grabbing her shirt and skirt. "Would that be so bad if I was?"

Emily glared at Ragden or tried to. She felt herself enjoying the tease, she wanted to hate him for it, but her heartbeat was a little too fast, and her skin felt too hot. She felt his love and his gentle tease. She wanted to rip her clothes off and jump him. As she tried to glare, she felt her expression softening. She could not stay mad at him. She reached out and ran her fingers down the length of his cock, smiled wickedly as it responded, and stiffened in her hands. She pulled her hand back and watched him sigh in pleasure. She knew he was driving her wild with desire, and now she could return the favor.

Ragden blushed, blinked hard, and tried to contain himself. His cock throbbed as he held open the skirt for her to slip into. He waited patiently as she stepped into it. Then he slid it up her legs, softly, pulling it around her waist. He pulled up the zipper while softly kissing her on the lips. Then he handed her the shirt as he walked over and pulled open a drawer in his dresser. He pulled out a pair of boxers. Then he turned to her and smiled as he pulled them up over his throbbing erection. Emily giggled to herself as the head of his cock popped through the front of his shorts. Ragden blushed and then adjusted himself so that that did not happen again. Then he pulled out a pair of shorts and a shirt from another drawer. Then he grabbed a pair of socks out of another drawer and slipped his feet into them. Then he spoke

softly, trying to master his voice which had an edge of desire to it.

"Hungry? We can run downstairs and grab some breakfast before we head to school if you want?"

Emily watched Ragden, and giggled softly, feeling her cheeks grow hot. Turnabout was fair play, right? She felt her desire burning within her and struggled to contain herself. Looking over Ragden, dressed for school, she saw his incredible physique. She thought him incredibly attractive, and she could not help but feel a sudden surge of desire. She knew that he was trying to hide his arousal from her but failed miserably. Then she remembered herself, and said huskily, "Yeah..."

Ragden took her by the hand and squeezed gently. He felt her pulse race beneath his hand and led her out to the door. He reached back in to grab his backpack. Then they went down the stairs to the foyer. Ragden dropped his bag by the door and then led Emily through the living room into the kitchen. Jennifer was in the kitchen scrambling some eggs with sausage and bacon in another frying pan. She smiled as the two entered the room.

"How do you like your eggs, Emily?"

Emily looked across at Jennifer; seeing her smile, she felt herself blush again.

"Umm... scrambled, please."

Jennifer looked at Emily, a knowing smile on her face. "I bet you do, but I'd bet you preferred that Ragden scrambled them..."

"Mom!" Ragden barked as he blushed deeply. He pulled Emily over to the island with the stools. Then he walked around the kitchen and opened cabinets and drawers. He grabbed plates and silverware. Jennifer divided the servings across the two plates. Then Ragden walked over and set one plate in front of Emily, the other in front of his stool. Then he sat down next to Emily. His shoulder brushed against hers as he started to eat.

Emily blushed as she ate her food. She watched Jennifer's knowing smile and felt the love the older woman had for Ragden and, surprisingly, for her. She paused and looked at this older woman. With tight firm breasts and a flat stomach, she looked like a supermodel who had gone slightly soft. Still incredibly attractive. How could she be Ragden's mother? She only looked twenty-something. And yet those eyes, Jennifer's eyes, were full of knowledge and wisdom. It felt strange that this woman, whose son had once been the target of her endless taunts but who was now her lover, loved her so incredibly deeply. It boggled her mind. His mother accepted it all with a smile and her blessing. Emily blushed deeper under that gaze. She felt so loved, and at home. She ate her food quietly, stealing glances at Ragden next to her. She watched him hungrily eat, and sneak glances at her. The love in his eyes was a palpable thing that made her feel warm, comfortable, confident, and sexy all at once.

"Oh... Emily", Jennifer went around the island to stand closer to Emily. She rested a hand on her shoulder, "I almost forgot. I called your mom last

night to let her know you were staying here last night."

A look of pure horror crossed Emily's face. Jennifer patted her on the shoulder

"Darling, calm down. It's okay. She understands. We found you out after dark and let you stay here so you could calm down, as you were in no state to get home last night. Everything is fine. Your mother is okay and said it would be fine for you to stay here any time you needed. Calm yourself; everything is okay."

Jennifer wrapped herself around Emily and gave her a comforting hug. She patted her on the back softly. Emily blinked in surprise. She hugged Jennifer back while she tried to find the words. She looked at Jennifer and saw the love and concern in her eyes. Emily felt a surge of gratitude towards this woman, who was allowing her to stay with her son.

"Thank you..."

Jennifer kissed Emily on the forehead, "Of course, my dear. Anyone my son cares about so deeply is always welcome in our home. Michael and I will do anything we can to make your lives more comfortable. If Ragden loves you as much as it looks like he does," She smiled at Ragden, "And if you love him as much as it appears you do... Well, we are not going to get in the way of that. We will do what we can to help."

She hugged Emily again, squeezed her gently, and kissed her on the forehead again.

"Thanks, Mom," Ragden said, a tear in his eye.

Jennifer cleared the dirty dishes, "Go, or you'll be late for school."

Ragden nodded, "Thanks for breakfast, Mom."

Ragden took Emily's hand in his and headed back towards the foyer to grab his backpack. They headed out the door. As they walked down the path to the street, he dragged his hands gingerly through the bushes. He felt the bushes caress his hand as they walked by. He smiled at the tender feeling of affection. Then they turned onto the sidewalk and headed towards school. Holding Emily's hand in his, everything seemed right. He pulled her against his side and slipped his arm around her waist. He enjoyed the feeling of her against him.

"Do we need to swing by your house and pick up anything for school?"

Emily slipped her arm around Ragden's waist, enjoying the feel of him against her side. She smiled up at him and shook her head.

"No, I have everything I need. Thanks for asking, though."

"Okay. No problem. Do you have any plans for your day? I can meet you for lunch, just tell me where... I can't imagine eating lunch without you..."

He squeezed her waist gently, pulling her softly against him as they walked. Emily blushed as she felt his pull, and she felt a sudden surge of desire from his soft voice and the love in it.

"I'll be at my locker at lunch, and I'll be free then. You can come and find me. And I'll be yours."

Ragden leaned over and kissed the top of her head lightly, enjoying the smell of her hair.

"Just... one other thing. I told Aria I would meet her after school in the park. Did you have any plans for after school?"

Emily's heart raced at his touch. She hesitated, feeling torn between wanting to spend time with him, and not wanting to interfere with his other commitments.

"It's okay if you need to meet her. Just promise me something," she whispered. She looked up at Ragden, a pleading look in her eyes.

He stopped and turned to her. His hands on her waist, "Name it."

Emily looked up at Ragden; her heart raced. Her eyes widened with surprise and pleasure, as she saw the hunger in his eyes and the love in his expression. She felt another surge of desire as she felt his hands on her waist.

"Promise me you won't forget about me. Promise me you won't let Aria use you or abuse you. Promise me you'll keep your focus on me and ignore her attempts to flirt with you. Promis-"

Ragden leaned forward and kissed her lips, softly, tenderly, interrupting her.

"Darling. My love. I will always love you. Nothing can take that away. We spoke about this last night, but I know you were overwhelmed with everything. I also have strong feelings for Aria and Sarah. I... I think I love all three of you."

He looked down into her eyes and searched for acceptance. He tried to see if she would be okay with this. He wanted her to accept this.

Emily felt Ragden's love pouring into her, filling her with warmth and tenderness. She knew that he loved her and that he also loved Aria and Sarah. She tried to look inward, to see how she felt about that. Her love for him was deep and powerful. It filled her heart with joy. She did not want to share him, but at the same time, she understood this was part of the package. That he would always love her, regardless of his feelings for Aria and Sarah. That love was not a limited thing. That the bucket it came from was endless. Her heart swelled, and she felt tears in her eyes. She looked up into his face and saw it written there clearly. She nodded vigorously, showing that she understood and accepted.

His voice was soft and tender. It washed over her like a warm comforting blanket on a chilly night. "My love for you will never dwindle. You will always have a place in my heart. Always."

He leaned in and pulled her against him. He felt her body pressed against his. He kissed her fiercely. His lips pressed to her. His tongue slipped into her mouth as he savored her sweetness. His cock throbbed between them. He broke the kiss breathlessly and blushed deeply, the color and heat rising in his cheeks.

"Sorry... I... This isn't the right place for... Ugh, I love you."

Emily felt Ragden's cock pressed against her. She felt a sudden surge of

desire. She felt her heart swelling with love. "Love me back... Please," she whispered.

"Always," he whispered back against her lips. Then he kissed her again and pulled her against him. Then he broke the embrace, breathless. His body throbbed with desire. "Just... after school? If you can wait?"

Emily nodded. Her heart thundered in her chest. She knew she could wait. That she wanted to wait, and she wanted to be with Ragden. She wanted to be alone with him.

"Yes, of course. After school. Be ready for me. Naked. For me."

Ragden laughed lustily. He could see the raw desire in her eyes and knew his echoed her feelings. Then he pulled her against his side and started walking back towards school.

"If you want, you can head straight back to my house after school. I'll meet you there after I meet with Aria. Your call. Though you might want to check in with your mom first so she doesn't freak out."

He squeezed her waist softly. Emily felt Ragden's laughter, and she felt her heart race. They quickly crossed through the streets onto campus. They reached the point where she needed to head off to her first class and he had to go to his. He turned to her and pulled her against him into a warm embrace. He leaned down and gently kissed her on the lips. Then he stepped back, trying to catch his breath.

"Enjoy your classes; I'll see you in a couple hours for lunch at your locker."

As he stepped back, Emily refused to let go of his hands. Their hands slowly slipped apart, and they went to class.

Love & Nature

CHAPTER 11

The first couple of classes for Ragden went smoothly. His third period, History, was always a challenge. Today was not too bad. The fresh thoughts of his time with Emily made everything easier to deal with. After third period, he headed towards his fourth class, math. As he turned the corner, he almost walked straight into Sarah. They stopped just short of colliding. Their bodies were only inches apart.

"Sorry... I... Didn't see you," Ragden blushed slightly as his body responded to the proximity of hers. "How are you today? I had an enjoyable time yesterday. Thanks for that."

Sarah looked at Ragden. She saw something slightly different about him. Something that pulled at her heartstrings. She smiled and blushed slightly.

"Hi... Yeah... Yesterday was great. Thanks for coming over."

Ragden smiled. Then he reached out to take her hand in his. He squeezed it softly and felt the soft texture of her skin. A thrill ran through him.

"Are you... doing anything for lunch?"

Sarah blushed a little more, feeling a sudden surge of warmth fill her. She looked into his eyes and saw the care and compassion, and... something more. She stared into his eyes, seeing the depths of feeling there. The depths of things she had never thought about. A shiver ran down her back. She blinked, then blinked again, realizing he had asked her a question. Her heart beat a little faster. His hand was still in hers. She looked down at it, feeling the warmth spreading up her arm. She looked up and smiled.

"Uh... Lunch? Yeah, I'm free. Why?"

Ragden smiled at her and watched the play of her emotions. He saw the soft sigh on her lips. "I'm meeting Emily at her locker; would you like to join us?"

Sarah's heart skipped a beat, as she felt Ragden's gaze on her, and she felt a sudden flush of desire. "Yeah... sure. That sounds fun."

Sarah licked her lips, then thought for a second, "Emily slipped out last

night; I did not see her leave. Do you know anything?"

Ragden blushed slightly, feeling the heat creep into his face. His body responded. His cock started to harden at the memories of the night before. He looked down at Sarah. He saw her intense stare. The question in her eyes.

"Yeah... I do," He stuttered slightly. "She... came home with me last night."

Sarah's eyes widened as she saw Ragden's reaction. She felt her heart race as she saw his cock harden. She looked down, feeling her desire ratcheting up another notch, as she saw the evidence of his arousal. She looked back up at his face. Her heart raced quicker. She saw the passion, love, and desire in his face.

"You fucked her?" Sarah whispered, her voice barely above a whisper. "Did you cum inside her?"

Ragden pulled her closer to him. His lips were inches from hers. He could feel the desire boiling off her, the heat. "You swallowed buckets of my cum two days ago. Are you jealous of Emily?"

Sarah felt her heart racing. Her memories of the day he mentioned came flooding back. She blushed darkly at it. Her body clenched up. She felt her desire surging and realized that she was jealous of Emily. She nodded, as she realized just how jealous she was.

"Yeah... I'm so fucking jealous of her..."

Ragden pulled her a little closer and closed the gap. His lips brushed against hers as he whispered to her, "What if I told you that I love her?" He sighed against her lips, and kissed her tenderly, "What if I told you that I love you as well?"

Sarah's heart raced, feeling his lips on hers. The confession of his love caused her desire to become something she could barely contain. His confession of love for Emily made her feel intensely jealous, but she realized that he loved them both. She felt a surge of lust. She realized she wanted to be loved by him as well.

"Tell me... Tell me you love me... Say those words to me, Ragden... Please... I need to hear them from you."

Ragden pulled her body against his. Pressed them together. His cock throbbed against her body. His arms wrapped around her. He pulled her into a warm embrace. He could feel her heart as it raced in her chest against his slow, steady, and calming pulse. He lovingly caressed her hair. He gently pulled her hair, pulling her face out of his chest so he could look down into her eyes. A tear on his cheek, he leaned in and kissed her softly on the lips. Then he spoke softly, his lips brushing across hers.

"I've always loved you. From the moment I saw you four years ago. I loved the shine of your hair. The twinkle in your eyes. The way you touch your ear when you are nervous. I loved the way you walked. The swish of your hips. The curve of your ass. When you started teasing, taunting, and bullying me, it broke my heart. But I never stopped loving you..." He kissed

her softly on the lips. "And I love you still. Always will."

Sarah felt Ragden's cock pressed against her stomach. She felt her wetness. She felt her desire as it overcame her sense of reason. His confession of love sent her heart stampeding through her chest. She knew that she was falling deeper and deeper in love with him. She felt her lust overcoming her as she realized that she wanted nothing more than to be used by Ragden. To be taken by him. To be filled by him. To be loved by him.

"Fuck me, Ragden. Fuck me hard. Make me cum for you. Show me how much you love me."

Ragden chuckled softly and caressed her cheek lovingly. Then he kissed her softly on the lips, "Don't you have a class to get to? Now is not the best time, as tempting as that would be. Later. I promise you that." He kissed her lips again, softly, and cupped her cheek with his hand. "Meet me for lunch, and we can discuss plans for later. Okay? Please? Be patient?"

Sarah felt his lips on her lips, her heart beating wildly. His gentle caress on her cheek and her desire was more than she could contain. She felt a rush of wetness between her legs. She realized she was soaking her panties with her fluids. She felt the urge to cum, and she felt the sudden need to be filled.

"Please... I need you now... Please fuck me now."

"Right here? In the middle of the hall? With everyone watching? Surely you jest. Where would we go? Can you think of somewhere private for us to go?"

Sarah felt Ragden's lips on her lips, her mind barely grasping the question. She knew she was begging for something. Knew that she was asking for something she had no right to ask, but her thoughts were a scattered thing consumed by her need. She struggled and found her words.

"No... Right here. Right now. Just fuck me hard."

He saw the raw need on her face, the desire overpowering her sense. He looked around and spotted a janitor's closet nearby. He walked over to it and pulled her along with him. He opened the door and pulled her inside. Then closed the door behind them. The room was dark. He reached over and flipped the switch. The space was small, cramped, and full of cleaning supplies, but room enough for the two of them. Ragden reached over and flipped the lock on the door. Then he turned back to Sarah. He brushed the hair from her face. Pushed it back behind her ear and saw the raw need on her face.

"This... isn't what I wanted... I want to lay you down on a soft bed and worship your body. I want to make love to you in a way that you'll never forget. But if what you really want right now is to get fucked, then we can do that... Just, not quite what I had in mind."

"Fuck me. Make me your dirty little whore. Use me like the filthy cunt I am."

He pulled her body gently against his and felt her racing heart, the desire burning off her like a fever. He kissed her gently on the lips, then whispered

against her lips.

"I will never think of you like a filthy cunt or a dirty whore. You are an angel, a goddess, a woman worthy of worship, but if you want to get fucked like a whore..."

He reached under her skirt and pulled her panties down around her ankles. Then he spun her around in one smooth motion and bent her over. Ragden dropped his shorts and slid his hard dick through the dripping folds of her pussy and pushed it against her clit. "Is this how you want it?"

Sarah gasped feeling the heat of his cock pressed against her pussy. She tried to buck against him, to get it into her, but he held her firm. She knew she was about to get filled, and she could not wait any longer.

"Yes. Yes. Fuck me. Fill me with your hot cum. Make me your dirty little whore. Make me your dirty little slut."

Ragden flipped up her skirt so he could see her lily-white ass. He grasped her firmly by the hips and slid the head of his cock through her lips, and into her vagina. She was dripping wet, but so tight it still took effort to slide even part way in.

Sarah felt his penis enter her tight pussy. Her heart raced, as she felt the pressure of his thick member filling her tight, tight pussy. She felt a sudden surge of pleasure as she felt his large cock filling her. It stretched her tight walls. She knew she was about to get used. Her desire surged again as she felt Ragden's precum leaking from the tip of his cock, and she wanted more.

"Fuck me harder, Ragden. Make me your dirty little whore. Make me your slut."

Ragden grasped her hips and pulled her against him. His cock slid fully into her and pressed against her cervix. He gently turned her body so that she was facing the sink and had something to hold onto. Her hands wrapped around its edge. Her knuckles went white as he slid halfway out, and gently back into her.

Sarah felt Ragden's cock sliding in and out of her tight, wet pussy. She felt her heart race, as she felt his large member filling her. She moaned as she felt her tight walls getting stretched. Her surging desire filled her, as his balls slapped against her clit. She knew she was going to be filled with his hot, sticky cum.

"Fill me, Ragden. Fuck me hard. Make me your dirty little whore."

Ragden gripped her hips more firmly, and slid out and back a little faster, a little deeper. The feel of her stretching around his cock was magnificent and he sighed in pleasure. He felt her racing heart under his hands. Her insistent need. He moved a little faster, pressed more insistently against her cervix.

"Give it to me... Give me your hot, sticky, cum-filled load, Ragden."

Ragden continued to thrust into her, building a slow rhythm. He pulled her hips against his groin with each thrust. Each impact drove deep into her and shook her whole body. Her grip on the sink tightened as she pushed herself back towards him, joining the rhythm, and moving with him. Sarah

could feel her orgasm building with each stroke.

"Oh... Oh, yes."

Ragden could feel her orgasm building within her. His started to take on shape as well. His breath was in time to hers, their hearts beating as one. Thrust, withdraw, thrust again. Harder, his cock pushed into her cervix less gently. Sarah pushed against the sink and pushed herself back with each stroke. His hands on her hips, tight. His fingers dug into her soft flesh, pulling her against his groin as he drove into her.

"Yes! Yes!"

His movements increased in pace, more insistent. His grip on her hips got tighter as he pulled harder. Drove into her faster. In time to her breaths, feeling her push against him with each thrust. Sarah felt Ragden's cock sliding in and out of her tight, wet pussy. She felt her orgasm building and building. She could feel his fingers digging into her, and the pain only heightened her arousal. She felt her pleasure surging with her.

"Oh... Fuck!"

Ragden felt her pulse increasing, he moved faster to match her breaths, her insistence. He matched her hips with his. Drove harder into her. Pushed his cock deep into her and slammed into her cervix with each thrust. The impact jarred her and bounced her breasts. He watched as her head craned back, her back arched. She tried to get more, to drive faster. He pulled harder and pounded into her faster. His climax was upon them. He clenched his eyes, his teeth, every muscle clenched to hold it off. To keep fucking her as hard as she wanted it.

Sarah felt her orgasm building upon itself. She knew that she did not have long to last at this pace. She felt his large member as it filled her and stretched her tight walls. It was so big it hurt. The pain, combined with each impact against her cervix, made her want more. A mix of pleasure and pain she could not get enough of. Ragden's fingers dug into her hips and pulled her against him. Another note in the symphony of ecstasy that threatened to overwhelm her. She did not know how much more she could take, but she wanted it all.

Ragden felt the edges of her climax, driving her body to slam against him. He pulled harder, thrust faster. No longer an elegant caress of her insides, his cock was now a driving jackhammer against her cervix. His breath came out in gasps with each impact. Sent shock waves through his body, and hers. Sarah knew that she was close to reaching her peak.

"Fuck me... Fuck me."

Ragden pulled on her harder and thrust into her with even more force. Her urges drove him to move faster. Her hips and his, driving together. The sound of it a hard slap of noise inside the small room. He dug his fingers in around her hip bones. Pulled her against him, harder. Faster. He slammed his cock into her cervix. Sarah felt her orgasm continuing to build with all the sensations crashing over her. She knew that she needed to cum and needed to cum now.

"""Cum... Cum in me... I want your hot, sticky, cum-filled load!"

At her urging, Ragden drove even harder, slamming into her like a madman. At the edges of his psyche, he could sense the dark cloud approaching, and he shoved it back. Sent it screaming back into the depths of his mind. Then he refocused his energy on Sarah. Let his love and compassion come crashing over her like a tidal wave. His cock slammed into her vice-like pussy, filing her, slamming into her cervix. Her body jerked and shuddered with each impact. The sink on the wall rattled with the force of it. Her arms and legs shook as she thrust herself against him, in time to his thrusts into her. He could feel his energy reaching out to her, increasing her climax. It added new layers to it. Spreading it, turning it into more than just a peak, but a tidal wave ready to come crashing down on them both.

He dug his fingers deeper into her hips, her tender flesh yielding against the strength of his grip. Ragden knew she would have bruises there, but he pulled her harder. He thrust into her. His massive, throbbing cock stretched her to her limits. Filled every inch of her and slammed into her cervix with the force of a Mac truck. Then he jerked back, almost coming free of her, and slammed into her again. The sink rattled with the impact. Her arms shook. Her eyes rolled back into her head. Again, and again.

"Ahh! Ahh! Ahh!"

As she cried out, he pulled her harder. Each cry was punctuated with an impact against her that shook the entire room.

Sarah's voice echoed throughout the room as she felt Ragden's cock slamming into her cervix. She felt her body shuddering and starting to convulse. Her muscles twitched with the energy of her climax. It loomed over her. An orgasm, unlike anything she had ever experienced. She felt her eyes roll back in their sockets as she surrendered to its awe-inspiring presence.

Ragden felt her body start convulsing against his. Her body pitched itself against him. Her hips bucked against his more forcefully as he pulled and thrust into her. His cock slammed into her so hard that the whole room rattled with each impact. His cock seemed to tap into her very soul. He could feel the swelling of her climax as it filled her being and tapped into his. His body started to twitch as an electrical current ran over his skin. Tinging from head to foot, he forced his eyes to stay open as he continued to thrust hard and fast into her.

Sarah's body shook violently. Her muscles contracted with each impact. She knew she was about to cum. Her voice rose above the thunderous roar of the room, as she felt her orgasm building, building, building...

Ragden's grip on her hips tightened even further, keeping her on her feet as her legs twitched and convulsed, and almost gave out underneath her. Still, he pulled her against him and thrust into her. His cock still slammed through every inch of her tight pussy. It smashed into her cervix and shook her body. Her breasts rocked up under her shirt. Her bra was no longer able to contain them. Her skirt was now around her stomach. His hands pulled her against

him, then let her slide forward as he crashed into her. Then pulled her into him again... and again... He felt her orgasm expanding, consuming her reality and his. The light in the room flickered with the energy thrown off from their bodies as they continued to thrash into each other. Bounce off and smash into each other with even more force.

Sarah's body trembled and shook. Her muscles spasmed as she felt Ragden's cock slamming into her. She felt a sudden surge of pleasure, as she felt Ragden's cock tapping into her very soul. Then when she was beyond any limit she could have imagined, her climax crashed down upon her. Her eyes rolled into the back of her head. Her back arched and convulsed, pulling her into an angle she never thought possible. Her stomach stretched. Her breasts thrust forward. Her back was arched. Her hungry mouth pointed to the ceiling. She pushed against the sink and felt it crumple against the wall. Then she screamed as the orgasm rolled over her. Every muscle in her body seized and twitched. She would have fallen, her legs completely useless, had Ragden's grip on her not been so strong. She felt his cock ram home one last time into her cervix. The explosion inside her added a new wave of ecstasy that rocked her again. She felt her breasts slip free of her bra. Felt the cool air across her chest. Another sensation washed over her, adding even more to the symphony of overload in her system.

As he felt Sarah go slack beneath him, Ragden slammed his cock into her cervix one last time. His orgasm rolled over him. The lights went out as a wave of energy rolled off their bodies. He could hear the tools rattle along the walls. He felt her insides filling with his essence as it poured into her, mixed with her own, and came spilling out. Through sheer force of will, he maintained his footing. Kept standing, holding her against him. Kept her from collapsing on her face. As her body went completely limp, he slipped a hand around her stomach and pulled her up against his chest. His cock throbbed painfully against her cervix, still buried inside her. He slid his other hand up to her chest. Brushed across her bare breasts. Felt her thundering heartbeat as he held her against him.

Sarah's mind reeled, trying to process everything that had just happened. She could not move a muscle. She felt the cool air on her chest. The firm hand against her stomach and chest holding her upright. She lolled against him, moaning as she felt her insides filling. Her vagina contracted and squeezed over the massive meat stuffed so deep into her. Every inch of it filled her, touched her cervix, filled her with his essence. She could feel more of her juices pouring out. Her body twitched and shuddered.

"Mm... Fuck."

Ragden felt his body slowly start to relax. He held her gently against him. Cradled her body against his chest. The lights flickered back on. He looked around the room. Saw all the tools that lay strewn about the floor. The sink was half crushed against the wall. A large pool of their mixed fluids collected on the floor at their feet, still pouring out of her.

"Holy fuck," he whispered, "Are you okay?"

Sarah's body was still quivering. Her vagina contracted and released against Ragden's thick, hot, cum-filled cock. She felt her nipples harden in the cool air. She looked down at them, then up at Ragden, and met his gaze. She saw his concern, and she nodded, speaking between contractions as she tried to catch her breath, "Yeah... Yeah... I am good. Just... fucking... Amazing..."

Ragden chuckled softly to himself. "I must agree. You are amazing..."

He turned her head slightly so he could place a soft, tender kiss on her lips. Then he nuzzled her neck softly. "Do you think you can walk after that?" He tensed his leg muscles and found them recovering quickly, given the recent strain he put them through.

Sarah nodded as she spoke between contractions that were starting to fade; as she caught her breath, "Yeah... Yeah... I'll be... fine..."

He started to lower her to her feet, but her legs crumpled beneath her. Ragden gently swept his arm under her legs and held her against his chest. His cock slipped out of her as her arms draped around his neck limply. He could hear the drip of their mixed juices still spilling out of her. For a moment, he ached to be back inside her. His cock softened in the cool air of the room. Then he looked down at Sarah, spent, exhausted, too weak to stand, and he softly kissed her forehead. Then her lips.

"Are you... Are you sure you are, okay?"

Sarah's body still trembled. Her vagina clenched and released. The muscles still spasmed inside her. She sighed sadly as she realized his cock was no longer inside her. She ached for it to be back inside her but knew she could not handle it again so soon. She could feel a dull ache inside her that she had never felt before. That weariness in her muscles made her wish for sleep. And yet, she felt amazing. Energy coursed through her body. Something she had never felt before. Sarah tried to put her mind to it, and the only thing she could produce was... love. The energy that filled her was love. Something she had never felt in such abundance that it filled her every pore of who and what she was. She looked up at Ragden and saw the concern and compassion in his eyes, on his face. His love filled her. She tried to pull him closer to her but found she still did not have the strength. She took a deep breath and felt her body still trembling. The muscles that were still contracting. She spoke softly.

"Mm... Yeah, I'm good. I've never felt better, actually. That was fucking amazing."

Ragden smiled down at her and kissed her lips tenderly; he could feel her heartbeat starting to return to a more normal rhythm. Her breath was more under control. He gently lowered her to her feet, and she staggered but remained standing. He kept a hand on her hip, the other holding her hand as he stepped back to see if she could stand on her own. Sarah's body still trembled. Contractions still rocked her abdomen. She could see his concern and nodded.

"Yeah, I'm okay, just give me a minute. I think I'm good."

Her voice was weak, but she stood straight, supported by his hand on her hip. She looked up at him, her breasts heaved with each breath as she spoke.

"Fuck me again. Make me cum again. I want to feel that amazing feeling. Please..."

Ragden laughed. Then he put a hand on her chest, between her breasts, and felt her heartbeat. He closed his eyes, and behind them, he could see... HER. Feel her very soul. Her energy was chaotic and swirling like a maelstrom. Her need and desire for something so intimately powerful. He felt his energy caress it, and nurture it, helping it find balance and heal from some wound she suffered in the past. Some need she could never have gotten filled before. He felt the weariness in her bones. The ache of her muscles. The clenching and unclenching of her muscles still spasmed with the aftershocks of her orgasm. Ragden shook his head slowly. He looked at her sadly.

"Not yet," he whispered. "Your heart could not take it. If we did that again, I fear it could kill you..."

Sarah's body still trembled, as she looked up at Ragden. She looked down at his hand on her chest. She realized he was seeing something else. She looked up to see his eyes, and she saw that they were closed. She felt his energy. She felt her own as it mixed with his. She felt connected to Ragden on a level she never thought possible. She wanted more. She wanted more of this connection. More of this energy. More of this... Love.

"Please," she begged, tears in her eyes, as she watched him pull up his boxers. His softened cock slipped in. Then he pulled her gently against him. Hugged her tenderly. He could feel the hitch in her breath, the spasm of her muscles. Her deep desire and need. He kissed her shoulder softly, then her neck. He whispered into her ear.

"No. I'm sorry. I love you, but you need to recover." He leaned back to look her in the eyes, "I promise, we will do this again, but you need time to recover, to get your strength back."

She looked up into his face, and her eyes welled up with tears. She felt his energy, and she felt her own. Her heart skipped a beat, and as she looked into his face. She realized she was falling in love with him. She did not care. She loved him. She needed him. She craved him. She wanted him to fuck her again.

With one hand in hers, he stepped back and looked around the room. He found a clean washcloth, knelt in front of her, and gently cleaned the insides of her legs. Gentling wiped away the fluids that spilled out of her. Then he held it softly against her pussy, catching what was still slipping out of her. Then he gathered up her panties and gently slipped her feet through them. Slid them up her legs. Moved the washcloth out of the way and slipped it over her groin and hips. Then he straightened her skirt. Tenderly adjusted her bra. Slipped her breasts back into it. Then he stood back up and gave her a sad smile.

"I know you crave more, and I promise you, I will give it to you, but not

right now. Can you be patient for me?"

Her breath hitched, as she spoke softly, "Yeah... Yeah, I can wait for you."

"Thank you," he whispered as he kissed her tenderly on the lips. Now we need to get to class. Can we meet at Emily's locker for lunch?"

She nodded and stepped forward. Her legs wobbled as she followed Ragden through the halls of the high school. Her breasts jiggled with each step. Her heart raced. She could feel the love that radiated from Ragden. She knew she was falling desperately in love with him, and she did not care. She was in love with him. She was addicted to him—to his energy, to his love.

He stopped and looked at her, watching her walk, "Do you need help? Can you make it on your own?"

She tried to straighten up a little taller, but a hand snapped to her abdomen as another contraction rocked her body. She smiled weakly and stood up tall again.

"Nope, I am good. Thanks..."

Ragden let go of her hand and watched her lose her balance and nearly fall. She grabbed at the wall of lockers to keep her legs from giving out. He raised his eyebrows.

"You don't look good."

He stepped forward and gently swept her off her feet. Cradling her to his chest, he asked quietly, "Where is your next class?"

She whimpered slightly and pointed down the hall. He nodded in response and carried her to the door. Then he gently, slowly, placed her back on her own two feet, one hand on her hip, the other in her hand to brace her. He stepped forward and kissed her softly on the lips again, savoring the feel of her, the smell of her, and the taste of her lips. Then he stepped back slowly, his hands lingering on her hips.

"Take it slow. Deep breaths. I will see you soon..."

Sarah stood trembling but nodded slowly. She willed her legs to carry her, to move. "I will. Thanks."

CHAPTER 12

Ragden nodded, then leaned in and gave her one last kiss before turning and jogging to his classroom. He opened the door softly. He tried to sneak in, but the whole class turned to look at him. The teacher turned and glared, hands on his hips.

"Sorry, I'm late... Had a... Bathroom emergency."

He blushed sheepishly. Some of his classmates giggled. The teacher's expression softened.

"Take your seat, please, Ragden..."

He moved to his seat and pulled out his book to try to catch up with the class. The rest of the class went without incident, though a few of the students gave him curious looks, which he tried to ignore.

His mind raced, thinking about Sarah. He wondered if Jennifer had packed any more of that balm she gave Emily. He opened his backpack to check and found a small bottle tucked in the back of his pack. A small note taped to it which read, 'Just in case.' He smiled to himself and whispered, 'Thanks,' then went back to his book, following along with the class.

The bell rang and he collected his things, stuffed them in his pack, and started to head for the door. The teacher stopped him just before the door.

"Everything all right? Do you need to see the nurse?"

"No sir, I'm good. Just... Took a little longer than I thought. Sorry."

"Alright then. Off with you. Homework is due tomorrow."

"Yes, sir. Thank you."

He slipped out of the classroom and headed for Emily's locker. Walking through the halls, he felt curious glances pointed in his direction. Something felt different, but again, he still could not put his finger on it. As he started to turn the corner, Ragden saw Emily and Sarah standing before Emily's locker deep in conversation. Realizing he could not hear anything from where he was, Ragden stepped around the corner and walked up to them, smiling. Two of his favorite women in the school. His heart swelled. His love for them

filled him up and made him feel like a better person.

"Hey, you two. Shall we get some food?"

Sarah felt the glances of the other students and did not care. She had made up her mind. She was in love with Ragden, and she did not care what anyone else thought. She looked up into his face and spoke softly.

"Yeah, let's go get some food."

Ragden stepped forward and wrapped his arms around both girls, pulling them both against him. He gently felt their bodies pressed against his. He could feel Sarah still trembling. Her body was still not recovered. Sarah and Emily both slipped their arms around his waist, hugging him back. His heart swelled. He kissed Sarah softly on the forehead, then turned to Emily and kissed her softly as well. To Emily, he spoke softly.

"How was your morning, my dear?"

Emily looked up at Ragden and saw the love radiating from him. She pulled herself against him, felt his body against hers, and sighed contentedly. Then she looked over at Sarah. She saw the quiver in her muscles. The twitch in her legs. She furrowed her brow for a moment and peered at Sarah. She reached out and gently felt Sarah's chest. Felt the way her heart fluttered. Sarah looked down at Emily's hand on her breast, a mix of surprise and pleasure on her face. Emily pulled her hand back and looked up at Ragden, saw the love radiating there, and remembered the words he had spoken the night before. His confession of love for her, Sarah, and Aria. She smiled to herself, feeling her own heart swell in response.

"You two fucked like rabbits between classes, didn't you?"

She giggled to herself at the sound of her own words. She searched her feelings and found only a twinge of jealousy. Mostly she felt in awe at the audacity of it. She leaned over and kissed Sarah on the lips. Then she whispered against her lips.

"It felt amazing, didn't it? Tell me!"

Ragden blushed at the sudden fierceness of Emily's words. There was a look of shock and embarrassment on Sarah's face, then she quickly composed herself. Ragden felt Emily's heart thundering in her chest against him. He marveled at it. She was not angry or jealous, she was... inspired. Happy? Sarah bit her lip and nodded. Then the words gushed out of her.

"Oh my god! I've never felt anything like it. So full of... him... Of... His love... his..." She whispered as she blushed madly, "His cum filling me up and pouring out of me..." Sarah shivered at the thought of it, her legs quaked.

Emily blinked, looking at how Sarah's body trembled. She quickly reached into her back pocket and pulled out the jar of balm Jennifer had given her. She looked at the balm, then up to Ragden. She spoke softly.

"Can we find somewhere quiet? Sarah needs this..."

He nodded. "She does; her legs could barely hold her up last I checked."

Emily giggled, then hugged Ragden fiercely. He smiled down at her in response.

"Let's find somewhere to put that on... Do you have any ideas where we could go? I suppose your house isn't far..."

Sarah's legs trembled a bit as she looked curiously at the jar of balm in Emily's hand. She looked at Emily and Ragden. She saw the glow of love between them. She felt included and loved. Her heart skipped a beat. Her body clenched painfully, and she closed her eyes. Then she opened them and looked at the two of them.

"Yeah, my house isn't too far. It's just up the road there, the third house on the left."

"Oh... I didn't realize your house was so close. Let's go then..."

Ragden swept Sarah gently off her feet. She sighed as he pulled her against his chest, cradling her body against his. Emily smiled happily and giggled at the scene. Sarah draped her hands around his neck to help support herself. They walked quickly through campus, getting numerous odd looks, but none of them cared. He was more concerned about getting Sarah home and rested. The walk was quick and quiet. Emily was endlessly amused at the situation. She stole amused glances that caused Ragden's heart to flutter in his chest. She placed her hand on Sarah numerous times to check on her. For her part, Sarah closed her eyes and rested against him. He could feel her slow, even breaths between small spasms as her muscles clenched and released. As they approached her house, Ragden leaned down and kissed her lips softly, whispering to her.

"Will there be anyone home? I think it might be a bit awkward to explain your... problem..."

Sarah's mind drifted. She could feel Ragden against her. She felt his heart beating against hers. She could hear Emily's soft giggles. She felt her heart race a little faster as she looked up to see the love that radiated from all three of them. She felt like the luckiest girl in the world.

"Darling," Ragden whispered to Sarah, "We are quickly approaching your home. Will the door be open? Is anyone going to be home?"

"Uhm... no... Everyone is at school today. You can fuck me on my bed, in my room... No one will hear us." Sarah said softly, her voice a whisper.

Ragden laughed softly and smiled down at Sarah. He saw the confusion in her eyes. Emily pushed the door open, and he followed her in, still carrying Sarah.

"There will be no more fucking today for you, my dear. I'm sorry... You need rest for now." Another spasm passed through Sarah's body, causing her to squeeze her eyes shut. Then open them slightly breathlessly. "That... That right there is why you are not having sex again today..."

Sarah's body shook; her vagina clenched and released, the muscles still spasming. She felt Ragden's words. She saw the love in Emily's eyes. She looked up to see the love in Ragden's eyes. She felt like she was in a dream, and she did not care.

Emily led the way to Sarah's bedroom and opened the door. Ragden

Love & Nature

carried Sarah in and laid her down on the bed. Emily stepped up next to him. Sarah sighed, her eyes closing contentedly as she settled into her mattress. Emily slipped her arm around his waist and hugged him.

"You really did a number on her..." She giggled again.

Ragden sighed and shrugged, "She kept asking for more..."

Emily turned to him and looked into his eyes. Her eyes were full of desire. She licked her lips, and smiled, "And you gave her what she wanted.... I wish I could have seen it..." Her eyes sparkled with curiosity and lust. Ragden felt his loins stirring under that intense stare.

Then Sarah moaned softly as another spasm passed over her. Emily's eyes went wide, and she pulled out the small jar of balm and handed it to him. Ragden popped the jar open, and the room was suddenly full of the scent of Lavender. He dabbed a small amount on the fingers of his right hand, then spread it over his fingertips. He climbed onto the bed with Sarah, gently spread her legs, and lifted her skirt. He placed his fingers on her inner thighs and gently rubbed the balm into her skin. The scent intensified, and Sarah moaned again. He worked the balm into one thigh. Then dabbed a little more and rubbed it into the other. After that, he did the same over her hips, where bruises in the shapes of his fingers were already developing.

Emily smiled the whole time, watching everything intensely. As he worked on Sarah's left leg, Emily crawled up next to him and started to massage Sarah's right thigh. She gently bumped his shoulder and smiled at him. The room slowly filled with the scent of Lavender and love.

"This smells so amazing." Emily breathed huskily.

Sarah sighed contentedly; her eyes fluttered shut. Her body no longer spasmed. Emily and Ragden watched, their hands clasped as Sarah drifted off to sleep. Then they gingerly eased off her bed. Trying their best not to disturb her. As they stood at the door, Emily slipped her arms around Ragden's waist and buried her face in his chest.

Ragden hugged Emily's body against his and pulled her tight against him. He felt every inch of her pressed against him. His loins stirred again, and he could feel his cock starting to harden. He stepped away from Emily slightly. Her hand in his, he pulled her through the door and pushed it gently shut.

Emily followed Ragden as he went down the hall into the living room and sank into the couch. He checked his watch and noted how much longer it was until the next class started. Emily sank onto the couch next to him and pressed her body against his. One hand snaked into his lap and felt his hardon through his shorts. Ragden sighed, a contented smile on his face.

"You really fucked her hard, didn't you?" She breathed huskily, stroking his cock through his shorts. "Anything left for me?" she grinned lustily.

Ragden laughed huskily; his cock throbbed at her touch through the fabric. He reached over and placed his hands on the sides of her head and guided her face to his. He kissed her softly on the lips. He whispered to her. "Always for you, my love." Then he looked into her eyes and searched for her acceptance.

"Are you really okay with this?"

Emily's eyes locked onto Ragden's. She saw the love in his gaze, and she felt her heart race faster. She felt her body tremble. Her pussy twitched. She pulled her hand from his shorts and slid it up to cup his face. She leaned into him and pressed her body between his legs. She ground her hips into his thighs, as she whispered against his lips.

"Of course, I'm okay with this... I saw the love on her face and the love on your face with her. Then and now. I loved watching you fuck those girls... And I want to be the one who gets to ride your big cock when you're done..." Her voice dropped lower, and she licked her lips seductively. "I want to taste all their juices on your thick cock... and I want to make you cum inside me."

He smiled and leaned in to kiss her passionately on the lips. His tongue slipped between her lips to taste her sweetness. He tasted her love and lust. He chuckled softly, "I didn't get a chance to clean up after we finished. I was more worried about getting her to class when she couldn't stand."

Emily's body trembled, her vagina clenched and released, her pussy dripped with excitement. She licked her lips and whispered, "Go ahead, cum in my mouth; I want to taste all of their juices from your thick cock."

She gripped his thighs tightly and pulled him towards her. She looked up to see the love in his eyes, and she felt her heart race faster. She looked down at his shorts, and she could see the evidence of his arousal. She felt her heart race faster. She pulled his shorts down, exposing his fully erect dick. She bent down and put it into her mouth.

Ragden leaned back and let her do what she wanted. He rested his hand on her shoulder and gently caressed her cheek as she slipped her lips over his cock. He shivered with the sensation. Emily took his cock deep into her throat. He felt her throat constrict around it. She sucked and slurped, her tongue playing around the underside of his length. She used her hand to stroke his balls, as her mouth worked expertly around his member. She gagged slightly but continued to work her magic. She pulled off his cock with a wet pop and looked up at him with a hungry expression on her face.

"Mm... Tasty," she said, her voice muffled by the wetness in her mouth. She pulled her hand away from his balls and let them hang below her mouth. She looked up at him, her eyes sparkling with desire. "Now, give me that thick, delicious load."

"Don't stop," He groaned softly, enjoying every moment of her attention.

Emily's eyes lit up with delight, and she eagerly continued to work her magic on his cock. She bobbed her head up and down. Took him deeper into her throat. Used her tongue to play along the underside of his length. She gagged slightly but continued to work her magic. Her hand moved to cup his balls and roll them gently in her palm. She pulled off his cock with a wet pop and looked up at him with a hungry expression on her face.

"Give it to me," she whispered. She looked up at him with a hunger in her eyes. She held out her hand, her mouth opened wide. Waited for him to

unload into her eagerly awaiting mouth.

As if his body bowed to her every whim, cum exploded out of the tip of his cock. His eyes widened in surprise as a massive load burst into her waiting mouth. He gasped slightly at the feel of it as she wrapped her hand around his cock, milking the cum out into her mouth. She greedily gobbled it down.

Emily's eyes gleamed with delight, and she eagerly swallowed every drop of cum that erupted from him. She looked up at him; her mouth overflowed with his seed. She licked her lips, enjoying the taste of him. She eagerly accepted every drop, her eyes locked onto his.

"Mm... Delicious," she said. She pulled her mouth away from his cock. Her hand was still wrapped around it. She looked up at him, her eyes sparkling. "Sarah's juices made you even sweeter."

Ragden smiled and felt his pulse starting to relax a bit. His body calmed after the sudden climax she drew out of him. He reached out and gently caressed her face, softly, lovingly. "Is that what you wanted, my love?"

Emily's eyes sparkled with delight. She nuzzled into his soft caress. Her hand still wrapped around his cock. Her mouth was empty of cum. "Yes, that's exactly what I wanted. To taste Sarah's fluids from your thick, delicious cock." She said, her voice barely above a whisper; she leaned into his caress, eyes closed as she savored the touch. "Thank you."

Ragden cupped her chin and brought her face up to his. She slowly stood, sliding between his legs. She leaned against him. He kissed her passionately on the lips and tasted his cum on her tongue. "You are quite welcome, my love."

Emily stood between his legs. Her hand reached down to stroke his cock. She tasted the remnants of his cum on her tongue. Her body trembled. Her pussy clenched and released involuntarily. She looked at him, her eyes sparkling with desire.

"I love being able to taste your cum, and knowing that it's been inside Sarah," she whispered, her voice barely above a whisper. She reached down and gripped his cock firmly, stroking it slowly. "I love knowing that she came just for you and that I get to taste your delicious seed."

Ragden laughed lustily, as he watched her writhe between his legs. He reached up and slid his hands under her skirt. Pulled her panties down her legs. Emily's body trembled; her vaginal walls clenched and released involuntarily at his touch. Then he ran his hands up her sublime calves, caressing her thighs, then gripping her firm ass. Emily gasped as his fingers curled between her cheeks, teased her asshole, and gently spread her pussy lips.

He stood up. His cock slid up between her legs and brushed against her pussy as he pulled her against him, kissing her passionately. It throbbed against her, fully erect. His dick slid along her folds as he pulled her against him, kissing her. She eagerly awaited the moment when he would slide his thick, rigid cock into her ready pussy. Feeling its head pushing against her entrance, she gripped his shoulders tightly and held onto him as he began to

push into her.

He kissed her. Slipped his tongue into her mouth and explored her fully as his hands gripped her ass. He picked her up off the ground. Her legs wrapped around him, his fingers pulling her lips wide as his cock slipped between them into her waiting pussy. He sighed heavily. His cock slid up into her, her vaginal walls clenched against his cock, stopping him halfway in.

"Oh, God," he whispered against her lips. "That's a good trick."

She giggled against him shyly as her vagina relaxed, and she slid down his cock until the tip gently pushed against her cervix, bottoming out in her. Emily's body trembled; her vaginal walls clenched and released involuntarily as she felt Ragden's cock slip into her, filling her with pleasure. She gasped slightly. Her eyes rolled back in her head as she felt the thick head of his cock press against her cervix. As he lifted her and his cock slid out, she eagerly awaited the moment when he would begin to push back into her again. She wanted to be filled with his thick, delicious meat. She gripped his shoulders tightly and held onto him as he began to slide back into her. Her pussy clenched around him, pulled him deeper into her warm embrace.

He gently lifted her hips, slid her up his cock. Then lowered her slowly, letting his cock slide up into her. It caressed her cervix. Then he did it again, moaning softly as her vaginal walls clenched around his cock, squeezing it tightly within her.

"God, you feel amazing. I will never tire of this."

He kissed her again, his tongue darting in as he slid her up his cock and back down again. Emily's body trembled. She felt his cock slide in and out of her. It caressed her cervix, then pulled back out before pushing back in. She felt filled once again. She moaned softly. Her eyes closed as she felt the pleasure coursing through her veins. She gripped his shoulders tighter and held onto him as he lifted and lowered her.

Ragden slowly lowered her to the floor, laying her down on her back. Balancing on his elbows and knees, he gently slid his cock up into her. Pressed the head of it firmly against her cervix, and gently caressed her insides. He sighed at the sheer incredible pleasure of her tightness. The silky-smooth feel of her wrapped around him. He closed his eyes as he took a moment to enjoy it. Then he gently drew back and slid home. He built a slow steady rhythm. She quickly matched his movements and rolled her thighs and hips against his gentle thrusts. Pushed her cervix into his cock as it slid home within her. Emily's body gently shook with each impact.

Emily's body trembled. She gasped slightly. her eyes fluttered shut as she felt the incredible pleasure of his big cock sliding into her warm, wet pussy. She matched his pace and pushed her thighs and hips against him. She refocused her eyes on his face as he continued to slide in and out of her, kissing him fiercely.

He leaned down and kissed her collarbone and her neck, pulled her earlobe into his mouth, and gently scraped his teeth across the tender skin as

he continued to roll his hips into hers. Emily moaned at the sensation. Her breathing sped up. Her heart started to accelerate. Then he slid his cock back until just the head remained in her and gently slide it back in. As he felt her clenching and unclenching, he slid through her tight folds and shivered with the ecstasy of it.

Ragden kissed her earlobe softly, then her chin. He kissed her softly on the lips as he continued to gently slide his hips against hers. His dick slid gently in and out of her. Their bodies were in a matched rhythm, breathing in time to the gentle strokes. Then he suddenly slid out, completely withdrawing his cock from her folds. Her eyes flashed open. Disappointment burned in her.

He sat back on his heels and placed one hand on his cock to guide the thick head of it through her folds, pressing it against her clitoris. Then slid it through her lips to her asshole. She exhaled sharply and gasped at the pressure. A shiver ran down her back as he slid the tip around her deliciously tight asshole. Then he slid his cock back through her lips. Around her clitoris, then through her lips to the opening of her vagina. Then he leaned forward and kissed her lips softly as he slid it into her, slipping through her clenched vagina and caressing her cervix gently.

They quickly found their matching rhythm again; their hips met gently, pressing his cock to her cervix. Then he slid out and back into her depths again. He softly caressed her face with one hand as the other gently squeezed a breast through her shirt. All the while, their hips continued to meet and part and meet again. His cock slid into her. Filled her completely. Stretched her walls. Caressed her cervix. Then slid back and in to do it again.

Emily's body trembled, shivering with the pleasure of him filling her. She gasped at the incredible pressure that started to build within her.

Ragden sat back on his heels again and slid his cock out of her completely. He watched her look of disappointment and smiled softly. She trembled. She felt empty and wanted more. She looked at him with a mixture of disappointment and curiosity. Then he slid his cock down through her folds again and circled her asshole with it. He gently slipped the tip in circles, pressing into her asshole. Slowly, gingerly working it open. Her eyes went wide with surprise as he started to work his thick, rigid meat in circles around her asshole.

"What are you doing?" she asked softly, her voice barely above a whisper. She watched him carefully, working his cock around her asshole.

"I thought maybe we would try something different." He whispered huskily as the tip of his cock slipped in gentle circles around her asshole, slowly opening it. "I'll stop if this makes you uncomfortable..."

Emily's body trembled; her vaginal walls clenched and released involuntarily as she felt Ragden's cock slide in gentle circles around her asshole. She gasped softly, her eyes rolling back in her head as she felt the incredible sensation of his thick, rigid meat working its way into her tight asshole. She remembered, not two days before, when he had cum in her ass.

The experience had been so intense she was not sure if she wanted that again. The thought of it made her shiver in anticipation. She hesitated briefly, unsure of whether she would let him proceed, but the overwhelming desire to experience new pleasure drove her to nod slightly, permitting him to continue.

"Go ahead," she whispered huskily as she bit her lip.

He gently applied more pressure, her ass not opening enough for more than just the tip to peek in. He continued his slow, gentle circles. Opening her slowly, a fraction of a space wider, then a hair wider, then a hair more. Gently and patiently, he kept working it in small circles, gradually getting bigger, and pressing more of the tip into her.

Emily's body trembled as she felt Ragden's cock press against her tight, puckered asshole, slowly working its way in. She gasped softly, her eyes rolling back in her head as she felt the incredible sensation of his thick, rigid meat pushing against her tight ring of muscles. She could feel her asshole stretching, slowly accommodating his size. Her vaginal walls clenched and released in anticipation of the incredible pleasure that was about to come.

"Fuck... I can't believe how much you're going to fill me up," she breathed huskily.

Ragden kept gently circling her asshole with the head of his cock. Slow, gentle pressure until the tip slipped in. Then a little more than the tip. Then the head slipped in. She gasped louder. Her eyes watered as she felt the incredible pressure of his cock pressed against her anal ring, forcing her asshole to stretch to accommodate his size. He took a deep, shuddering breath. He stopped, leaving just the head in her ass. He could feel her clenching muscles almost pushing him out. His weight and pressure kept it firmly seated. He leaned forward, his arms shaking slightly from the intensity of her ass on his cock. He kissed her on the lips, softly at first, but then becoming more passionate. He had to stop to catch his breath. His heart thundered in his chest. She could not resist the incredible pleasure that came with having such a big dick pushed into her rectum.

"You're going to fuck me in the ass," she whispered, half in awe, half as a request. The desire was plain in her voice.

He kissed her passionately; his hands slid up to her breasts to squeeze them gently. His thumbs ran over her hardened nipples. He pulled back to catch his breath and speak softly, his lips brushing over hers.

"Only if you want me to... I will stop the moment you tell me..."

"Yes," she whispered breathlessly, her voice barely above a whisper. Her face flushed with excitement.

He pressed against her, increasing the pressure. His cock throbbed as it slipped a little deeper into her. Then he slid back to just the head inside, then pushed forward, sliding just a little deeper into her. The pressure caused his heart rate to spike. His breath came in a rush. He could feel his climax starting to scramble at the edge of his psyche.

Emily gasped. Her eyes squeezed shut as she felt the incredible pressure of

his thick, rigid meat forcing its way deeper into her bowels. She felt it filling her with incredible pleasure. She could feel her asshole as it clenched and released around his thick, delicious meat. She could feel her body trying to force it out, but unable to resist the incredible pleasure that came from having such a massive cock buried deep in her rectum.

"Please don't stop," she moaned.

Ragden leaned down and kissed her passionately on the lips as he slid his cock a little deeper into her ass. He shivered as her muscles clenched around him. Then he slid back and slid in a little deeper. His heart thundered in his chest.

Emily's body continued to tremble. Her muscles clenched and released involuntarily as he slipped deeper into her. She gasped softly with each gentle thrust that went a little deeper each time. She could not believe how good it felt. The pain and pressure that filled her bowels.

"Don't stop," she moaned.

Ragden kissed her harder, as he slid more of his cock up her ass. Then he slid it out, and gently slid it back in. Another shiver passed down his back, as she clenched on him again. Then he backed most of the way out and back in a little deeper. He continued to repeat this until, finally, he managed to ease the last few inches into her. His groin was now pressed firmly against her hips. Every inch of his massive, throbbing cock in her bowels.

Emily's body continued to tremble. Her muscles clenched and released, fighting against the enormous invasion in her bowels, but unable to prevent it. She could feel the incredible pressure and pleasure building up inside her.

"Jesus Christ," she whispered, her face flushed with excitement.

Ragden started to build a slow, careful rhythm. He drew back, then gently slid in until fully seated again. His balls gently rested against her ass. His cock was as deep into her bowels as it would go. Then he slid back and in again. She picked up the rhythm and met him halfway. The first gentle bump of her groin against his sent a shiver through his whole body. It was intense, and he almost climaxed at once. Somehow, he managed to stave that off. He could feel precum leaking out.

Emily's body continued to tremble, as she rocked her hips against his. She could feel her asshole stretching further with each gentle thrust. She could feel the pressure building and building within her.

"Oh, Fuck!" she cried out, her voice soft but insistent. She felt herself being driven closer and closer to climax by the incredible pleasure filling her ass.

Feeling her pulse start to quicken, his rhythm picked up in pace. Emily matched it immediately, her hips ground against his, pushing his cock into her.

"Good fucking God," he breathed heavily. The silky smoothness of her bowels stretching and squeezing against his cock threatened to blot out all existence. He could feel the black cloud of reckless abandon looming, and he forced it away into the recesses of his psyche. Its screams of rage dissipated

rapidly. He focused back on Emily, and almost lost the fight to contain his climax. His body shuddered and spasmed. More cum leaked out of him, but he maintained his slow pace. Their hips bumped, forcing his cock deeper into her bowels.

Emily's body trembled more violently, her muscles clenched and released harder, as she felt Ragden's cock slide in and out of her tight, puckered asshole. She felt the pressure building within her. She continued to move with him, matching each thrust. Her body rocked with each impact.

"Fuck yes!" she cried out, as she felt the pleasure in her ass building.

As he felt her enjoyment increasing, his pace started to pick up. Ragden still tried to be careful of hurting her, as he slid into her depths. Then he drew back and gently slid in again, as deep as he could go. Then he slid out and in again. He reached up and gently grasped her breasts. His thumbs rolled across her firm nipples as he gently squeezed and then released as he slid in and out of her.

"God damn it," she cried out, her voice soft, but picking up volume as the intensity increased. The pressure and pleasure continued to build within her. She felt her limits being pushed, the pleasure hitting the point where she did not think she could contain it any longer.

Ragden continued to slide in and out of her, their rhythm matched, their pace even. Each enjoyed the feel of the other. Her ass clenched on his throbbing cock. He slid one hand down over her stomach, and he slipped his thumb over her clit. Gently ran it across her wet folds, then circled her clit. All the while, he continued to slide his dick in and out of her asshole. Pushed until their hips ground together, then slid out and pushed in again.

"Fuck!" she cried out, her voice finding volume as she gasped at the sensation of his fingers across her clitoris. She suddenly found her climax building fast, threatening to overcome her.

As he continued to slide in and out of her ass, his rhythm started to increase as he felt her climax building, his own answering it. Like their bodies and their hearts, their climaxes joined and built upon each other. Their breath became ragged. Their hearts beat faster. Ragden slipped two fingers into her pussy, and gently pinched her clitoris with his thumb and forefinger. His cock continued to slide into her depths, then out, and deep again. Their hips parted and met; each meeting pushed his cock deep into her bowels.

Emily's body trembled even harder, as she felt her climax building rapidly. Her body trembled with anticipation. Her heart raced with excitement. "Ah!" she cried a little louder, as her ass clenched on his throbbing cock, then released and clenched again.

Ragden's pace picked up a little more; their hips parted and met a little faster. Each impact rocked her body. Caused their breaths to burst from their lungs. His cock drove so deep into her bowels. Filled her so completely. Her ass squeezed on his cock. The throbbing was almost painful. Their climaxes continued to build. The intensity of it became a palpable thing. He felt

electrical tingles along his arms and legs. He looked down and saw little sparks of blue energy creeping along his skin and marveled at it. A spark passed down his arm into her clit, causing her to convulse. Her eyes flashed open, and she stared at him in shock. The muscles in her pussy clenched tight on his hand. Her ass clenched hard on his cock, painfully tight, but her hips rocked, and he slid deeper into her.

Emily's eyes went wide as her muscles stopped convulsing; she gasped, "What was that?!"

"I'm not sure," he answered. He continued to slide his cock in and out of her asshole. Her hips met him partway, pushing his cock deeper into her ass. Her eyes rolled into the back of her head, a soft moan slipping from her lips.

"God, don't stop, just... don't... stop..." She rocked her hips against him, drove his cock in and out of her ass, matching his pace again. Feeling the pressure and pleasure as it continued to build, her climax was fast approaching.

Ragden watched in awe as more sparks appeared along his arms, legs, and abdomen. They rolled across his flesh towards her. He continued to slide in and out of her, his pace increasing, as he nervously watched the play of energy across his skin. He continued to slide his throbbing cock in and out of her ass, driving into her. Then sliding out, and back in again. He closed his eyes, savoring the feel of her tight ass wrapped around his cock. Her body clenching and squeezing against him. Then he looked down and watched as the energy pulses suddenly ran down his abdomen and into his cock. They shot up his dick as he thrust into her. The sudden burst of energy out of his cock felt like a miniature climax. His back arched with the force of it. His legs went rigid, and his cock slammed home into her bowels. He found he could not move for a moment. His eyes popped open to see the energy surging through her body, coursing up through her ass and down her legs.

Emily's eyes widened; her mouth dropped open slightly as she felt the incredible sensation of energy flowing through her body. She felt the incredible heat radiating from her asshole, the pleasure intensifying as she felt the energy fill her up. It traveled up her legs and into her pussy, causing her to buck and quiver. Her asshole clenched and released. The incredible pressure drove the energy up her insides and caused her entire body to shake and quake with pleasure. She could not believe how much pleasure she was experiencing, her mind completely blank as she felt the energy fill her up, causing her to erupt in an explosion of ecstasy.

"Fuuuccckkk!"

Ragden watched in fascination as the energy surged through her pussy, then into his arm, causing him to go rigid again; then it raced through his chest, down his abdomen, and exploded out of his cock again. This time he climaxed with it. His body bucked wildly, like on a live current. His hips drew back and slammed into her hard.

"Oh, goddamn. Fucking shit... piss... fuuucccckkk," he yelled as his body

convulsed, and he slammed his cock into her ass so hard the whole room shook. Then he drew back faster, and slammed into her again, picking up pace. He could feel his climax building again, as his body thrust into her repeatedly. He pulled his hands off her and grabbed into the carpet, trying to brace himself as his body continued to slam into her. His eyes went wide as his fingers sunk into the carpet and wood beneath. Then his entire body went rigid, every muscle seized at once. His cock slammed deep into her bowels as his climax exploded out into her. He watched in fascination as a wave of energy rolled through the house. Everything in the room rocked and shook. Then his body went limp and collapsed forward, his arms buckling as he tried to break his fall, so he did not hurt Emily. Her eyes shut against the shuddering of her own body. He collapsed on top of her.

Emily's body shook violently, her vaginal walls clenched and released involuntarily as she felt Ragden's cock slamming into her ass. The incredible pleasure coursed through her entire body. She gasped loudly, her mouth open, as she felt the incredible pressure of his massive cock filling her bowels. The energy pulsed through her very core, causing her to climax with him. She could feel the incredible waves of energy rippling through the air, causing everything in the room to shake and tremble.

Every muscle in Ragden's body twitched. He felt like he had ants crawling all over him. He cradled Emily against him and felt her body pressed against his. Her breasts smashed against his chest. Her hair was in his face. His cock still pressed firmly, deeply into her ass. The base of his groin still pressed hard against her hips. He tried to move and found that his muscles were too sore to move. He groaned, feeling sore and tired. He felt Emily breathing softly against him. He dragged a limp arm up along her side and placed it against her cheek, turning her head to face him.

"Are you... Are you okay?"

"Y-yes," she said softly, her voice barely above a whisper, as she felt the incredible sensations of pleasure still coursing through her body. She smiled as she could still feel his massive cock planted in her bowels, his seed filling her up. She had felt him climax in her ass before, but never like this. She loved every moment of it, but she was not prepared for this new level of intensity.

"Wha-what happened?" she asked softly.

Ragden kissed her lips softly, tasting her. He drew back, startled. She tasted different. Somehow, something in her had changed. He kissed her softly again and slipped his tongue in.

"I... I honestly don't know" He gently cupped her cheek in his hand, feeling the texture of her cheek. "I just wanted to make sure you are okay."

Emily's heart raced, her body still trembled with pleasure, as she felt Ragden's lips pressed against hers, tasting her. She closed her eyes and enjoyed the taste of him, the sensation of his tongue slipping between her lips. She felt his hand caress her cheek, and she looked at him, her green eyes filled with a mixture of desire and confusion.

"That was ... scary..." He breathed softly into her. "But holy fuck, that was amazing."

Emily's eyes widened, and her body trembled with pleasure as she listened to Ragden's words. She knew he was right. She could feel the incredible pleasure that had just been shared. The incredible amount of energy that had been exchanged during the intense sexual encounter. She looked up at him. Her expression filled with wonder and curiosity, as she felt something different within her. She did not know exactly how or why, but she could feel it. She could sense it. She could not help but feel excited by the thought of it.

"Can we... Can we do that again? Please?" she asked softly, her voice barely above a whisper. She gazed into his eyes with a mix of hope and desire.

Ragden laughed, his body shook with amusement. Then he groaned, his muscles still sore

"I think... I need time to recover from that," he smiled softly at her, then kissed her passionately. Slipped his tongue into her mouth, marveling at the new flavor of hers. "I promise we will, but we need to check on Sarah and get back to school."

Emily's heart raced, and her body trembled with desire as she listened to Ragden's words. She gazed into his eyes. Her green eyes were filled with a mixture of desire and uncertainty. She wanted to stay in this position, she wanted to keep making love. To feel the incredible pleasure that they had just experienced. She knew that he was right, they had things that needed doing. She bit her lower lip softly. Then she nodded her head in agreement.

"Okay," she whispered, as she ground her hips against his, feeling his cock sliding deep into her bowels. She leaned up and kissed him deeply. Her tongue teased his lips before she pulled back and looked into his eyes once more.

Ragden closed his eyes and enjoyed the feel of her ass clenched on his cock. A shiver ran down his back. Then he opened his eyes and looked into hers again and kissed her softly on the lips. Then he raised himself off her sublime body. Slowly, gently, he slid back. His softened cock slipped from her ass. He moaned softly as it slipped free, followed by a stream of cum slipping out of her.

Emily's eyes widened, and her body trembled with pleasure as she felt Ragden's cock slide from her ass. She gazed into his eyes, her green eyes filled with a mixture of desire and satisfaction. She watched as a stream of cum shot from his cock, hitting her ass and pooling on the floor below them. She bent her knees slightly, allowing some of the warm liquid to drip into her waiting pussy, feeling the incredible sensation of it spreading inside her.

"Mm," she murmured. She reached her hand down to stroke her pussy and brought some of the mixed fluids to her lips. She tasted the salty, delicious fluid on her lips.

Ragden laughed, then slipped his fingers into her pussy to collect some of the fluid, then tasted it himself. Her body trembled at his touch, her vagina clenched and released. She felt her pussy contract slightly as she watched him

taste her, feeling the incredible pleasure and satisfaction that filled her body. Not what he had expected, there was something flinty and almost spicy to the flavor. He slowly stood on shaky legs and braced himself against the couch. Then he reached down and pulled Emily to her feet. One hand on her hip, he held her steady, as her legs were just as shaky as his.

"Mm," she whispered, as she felt him pull her to her feet. She looked at him, her green eyes filled with admiration and desire as he braced her.

Ragden gathered her panties and handed them to her as he grabbed his boxers and shorts. He slipped them back on. He watched her hungrily as she slid her panties up her incredible legs. Then he checked the time and cursed.

"We barely have enough time to get back to class!!"

She looked at him, her eyes filled with a mixture of disappointment and frustration as she realized that they had to leave. She stood there, her vagina clenched and released, as she felt the incredible afterglow of their encounter wash over her body.

"It's alright," she said softly, "We can always do that again later."

Now dressed, he stepped over and embraced her, feeling his strength returning. He pulled her body against his, his loins stirred at her proximity. He kissed her passionately, marveling at her fabulous flavor. "That we most certainly will. But later..."

He grabbed her hand and quickly ran for the door. She kept a close pace with him, as they jogged down the way they had come, headed back for campus. As they crossed into the halls and reached the point where they had to head in separate directions, he pulled her against him. He kissed her passionately and slipped his arms around her, pulling her body against his. He whispered in her ear.

"Gods, I love you. You are so amazing."

Emily's heart raced, and her body trembled with desire as she felt Ragden's strong arms wrap around her, pulling her body against his. She gazed into his eyes, her green eyes filled with a mixture of desire and adoration. She felt his lips against her ear, his voice echoing in her head as she spoke softly, "I love you too, Ragden. And I cannot wait to make love to you again."

As they separated, Emily looked into his eyes one last time, before heading in opposite directions to their respective classes. She felt a twinge of sadness, knowing that they would be apart for a while, but she also felt a sense of excitement, knowing that when they got together again, things would be different.

CHAPTER 13

Ragden's first class after lunch was a whirlwind. Done and over with before he could fully realize what was going on. His thoughts kept slipping back to the energy that played over him and Emily during their sex. He had to ask his dad what that was about. Dad had warned him before, but not about that. Then the bell rang, and Ragden rushed off to his next class. He searched the halls for Emily as he forgot to mention something. He ran and caught up to her right before she entered another classroom. He caught her hand and spun her around to face him, pulling her body against his. Ragden's heart sang, and his body felt charged in her presence. His energy interacted with hers. He could feel the air around them charged with ozone. He kissed her softly, not caring what anyone had to say about it. His heart thudded heavily in his chest. Then he broke the kiss and whispered in her ear.

"Don't forget... Please check on Sarah after school and talk to your mom. Then, if you want, meet me at my house for dinner..."

Emily's heart raced, and her body trembled with desire as she felt Ragden's strong arms wrap around her, pulling her body against his. She gazed into his eyes, her eyes filled with a mixture of desire and admiration. She felt his lips against her ear, his voice sent shivers down her spine as he whispered.

"I love you Ragden and yes, I will check on Sarah and talk to my mom. Then I will most definitely come to your house for dinner."

She turned and looked into his eyes, her green eyes filled with a mixture of desire and anticipation. She could feel the energy that surrounded them. She could also feel the electricity that danced around them whenever they were near each other.

"Awesome, thanks so much. I can't wait to see you tonight. Love you." He kissed her softly on the lips, then dashed off to his next class.

Emily's heart raced, as she watched him run off to his next class. Her mind raced with thoughts of how incredible their night together would be. She took a deep breath, focusing on her studies, even though all she could think about

was how much she wanted to be with him. She felt the energy surrounding them. She could feel it in her bones and in her soul. It was an electrifying feeling that made her feel alive, that made her feel connected to Ragden on a level that went beyond anything she could ever imagine.

The last two classes of the day dragged for Ragden. Probably because he wanted them over with. As the last bell rang, he went to his locker and put everything away that he would not need overnight. There were only a few assignments he might need to look at that night, and, of course, the homework from 3rd period. Then he slipped his backpack across his shoulders and headed for the park.

***

Emily's afternoon dragged on endlessly. Each class seemed like a special kind of torture to keep her from seeing Ragden again. She could still feel the tingle of his energy across her skin. Her breasts ached for his touch. When she closed her eyes, she could feel his hands on her ass, his dick in her bowels. She could feel his energy coursing through her, filling her with his love and power. She felt her cheeks growing hot, and the dampness between her legs growing.

She blushed and pinched her legs together. She looked around the room, hoping nobody noticed the hot flush on her face. As her last class was done, she ran to her locker and stuffed her books inside it. She could not wait to meet up with Ragden later. Just the thought of that meeting made her legs tremble, and her heart skipped a beat. She felt herself growing damp between her legs again. She groaned, hoping her arousal was not too evident to people walking by. She needed to focus her mind on something else.

As she started to head off campus, Emily remembered she needed to head over to Sarah's house and check on her. She turned and headed that way. Her heart longed to go straight to Ragden's house, and as she changed directions, she groaned. She took a deep breath and focused on putting one foot in front of the other. She remembered the look on Sarah's face, the flush of her skin, the tremble in her legs. Emily laughed as she remembered watching Ragden carry Sarah home.

Emily paused for a moment. She closed her eyes and searched her feelings. How did she feel about this? She had never been a 'good catholic girl.' The idea of monogamy had been ingrained in her since she was a child. How was she okay with Ragden sleeping with her best friend? Her parents had been married for ages, and she had never once seen them interact with other couples, or even hint at any kind of other behavior. She had no model, no comparison, no idea how to wrangle this in her head. Ragden had slept with her best friend. Yet, as she searched her feelings, she found that not only was she okay with this fact, but she also reveled in it. It brought her joy and love. She was not jealous of Sarah. She knew that he loved her and that he also

loved Sarah and Aria. That knowledge made her feel warm, content, and full of joy.

Emily resumed her walk to Sarah's house. As she approached the house, she noticed a car in the driveway. One of Sarah's parents was home from work early. Emily hoped it was Sarah's dad. Her mother was a little strict, but her dad was much more relaxed. Sarah had a history of saying whatever popped into her head, and while her dad would laugh it off, her mother tended to take her more seriously. Emily walked up to the door and knocked.

A moment later, a short, slightly overweight man opened the door and smiled at Emily. His hair was balding, and he had his glasses perched on the tip of his nose. He was clean-shaven, and his eyes sparkled with mischief.

"Is Sarah available?" Emily asked.

"Yes," he answered, stepping back from the door to allow her to come in, "I heard her moving around in her bedroom earlier. Go ahead."

Emily slipped past the older man and went down the hall to Sarah's room. She heard her father go back into the living room and sink into the couch. She thought briefly about what she had done the last time she had been there and blushed. Then she knocked on Sarah's door.

The door was thrown open almost immediately, and Sarah bounded out and wrapped her arms around Emily, hugging her fiercely. She leaned hard into Emily, pushing her body against her with so much force that Emily stumbled backward into the wall. Sarah giggled in Emily's ear as she squeezed her tight. Emily melted into her friend's embrace.

"I am so happy to see you," Sarah gushed as she stepped back, took Emily's hand, and pulled her into Sarah's room. She pushed the door shut behind her, then pulled Emily over to her bed, and the two girls sat down facing each other.

Emily looked Sarah up and down. "Are you feeling better?"

Sarah lit up with joy; her eyes sparkled as she broke into a huge grin. "I feel amazing!"

"Your legs?"

"Totally fine! I feel like I could run a marathon! Where is he? Is he here with you?"

"No. He went to meet with Aria."

"Oh," Sarah pouted, then threw herself back onto the bed, laying on her back. She cupped her breasts and sighed in pleasure. Then she sat up and looked into Emily's eyes. Emily giggled to herself as she watched. Sarah had always been a bit dramatic.

"When can we see him?" Sarah asked.

Emily smiled. "We can head over to his house and wait for him to come home. He invited us over for dinner."

Sarah clapped with joy. Then she jumped to her feet, dragging Emily up with her. "Can we go now? I want to go. Take me with you. Oh, please!"

Emily felt infected with Sarah's giddy joy and nodded in response. Sarah

pulled Emily into a tight hug, and whispered in her ear, "Thank you!"

When Sarah pulled back, she gave Emily a soft kiss on the lips. Then she pulled back and giggled. Emily smiled at Sarah, then asked, "For what?"

"For being willing to share him, of course. You got him first. You lucky bitch! Oh... I love him so much. I just want to hug him and squeeze him and fuck his brains out..."

Emily laughed at Sarah's exuberance. She felt herself being swept up in Sarah's joy. She felt something within her shifting and swelling. It took her a moment to figure out what it was. Then she realized it was her love. Her love for Sarah. Her love for Ragden. She reached out, grabbed Sarah, and pulled her against her. Sarah gasped in surprise and then squeezed Emily tightly.

"How could I not share him?" Emily asked softly. Tears leaked from Emily's eyes as she squeezed Sarah tighter, "Seeing how happy he makes you. I love him so much, and I love you too. I am so happy we can share him."

Sarah laughed again, then stepped back from Emily. As she saw the tears on her face, she reached up and brushed them away. Then she leaned in and kissed Emily hard on the lips. Emily blinked in surprise as she felt Sarah press against her. She felt Sarah's breasts pressed against her own. Her heart beat hard in her chest, and she felt herself growing damp again. Then Sarah slipped her tongue into Emily's mouth, and Emily moaned in pleasure.

Sarah pulled back and licked her lips. She grinned with mischief, "You taste like him. That is so not fair."

Emily blushed, and Sarah laughed again. Then Sarah grabbed Emily by the hand, threw the door open again, and pulled her into the hall. As they headed towards the door, her dad's voice called from the living room, "Leaving so soon?"

"Yeah, going out with Emily."

"Will you be home for dinner?"

"Nope."

"Later?"

"Maybe."

"Okay. Be safe out there."

"Thanks, Dad!"

With that, they left out the front door and headed to Ragden's house. Sarah danced down the driveway, pulling Emily along behind her. Emily had to jog to keep up. Sarah laughed, slowed down, and wrapped her arm around Emily's waist. She looked over at her and stared at her intently.

"Did you do something different with your hair?"

"No," Emily responded, a little surprised by the scrutiny.

"You look amazing today," Sarah said as she looked at Emily and bit her lip, "What did you do?"

Emily raised an eyebrow as she looked at Sarah, "Nothing."

"Oh," Sarah laughed, nudged Emily gently, "His magic dick turned you into a fairy princess. I see it now."

Sarah laughed harder as Emily blushed. Emily shook her head, but as she looked down at her chest, and saw her hair out of the corner of her eyes, she realized things were slightly different. The sex had been amazing. Magical seemed a stretch. She did feel different; maybe it was changing her. If so, this was a change she could embrace.

Emily looked at Sarah and winked, "Maybe."

They laughed together as they kept walking to Ragden's house.

***

Ragden's heart beat a little faster with nervous energy as he walked into the park to meet with Aria. It was time to meet with her. Time to see how she felt. His reunions with Emily and Sarah had been nothing short of amazing. He wondered if Aria would feel similarly, or if he had lost her. He did not want to lose her. He kept puzzling over what he was going to say. How would he explain everything going on? So much had happened since lunch the day before.

Then, before he could figure out what he was doing, he stumbled across her favorite spot in the park, and there she was. Sitting on her favorite patch of grass under the old oak tree, looking out at the lake. An amazingly picturesque view. His heart skipped a beat. She looked beautiful. Her perfect blonde hair hung loosely around her shoulders. Her make-up was pristine. Her blue eyes pierced. A light blouse clung to her chest, her cleavage showing, but modestly. Her flat stomach was exposed over a beautiful knee-length skirt.

Aria's heart raced, and her body trembled with anticipation as she sat on the grass beneath the old oak tree, looking out at the incredible view of the lake. She felt a sense of peace and serenity as she gazed out at the water. She felt a presence beside her, and she glanced over to see Ragden sitting down beside her. She felt a surge of excitement, a mixture of fear and joy coursing through her veins as she gazed into his eyes.

"Hey Aria, ...uh... hi... Sorry, I'm late... I..." He stuttered and blushed, then sank into the grass next to her.

"Ragden..." she whispered, her voice barely above a whisper.

He took her hand in his and squeezed it softly. Then leaned over to kiss her softly on the lips.

"Hey, there, gorgeous. Sorry, I'm late. I hope I did not keep you waiting too long."

Aria's blue eyes sparkled. Her body trembled with anticipation as she felt Ragden's lips against her own. She gazed into his eyes. Her heart raced as she felt his hand take hers, squeezing softly. She felt a surge of excitement and pleasure wash over her body as she gazed into his eyes. She felt a connection that was stronger than any she had ever felt before.

"No, Ragden, you didn't keep me waiting too long. I was enjoying the view. It is incredibly peaceful here." she whispered.

"You always did know how to pick the best spots," Ragden said softly in response. He sat next to her and slipped his arm around her shoulders, allowing her to rest her head on his shoulder if she wanted.

"Thank you for meeting me here. I... was almost afraid you wouldn't show up. I know I... asked a lot of you, but thank you for giving me a chance."

Aria felt Ragden's arm slide around her shoulders. She gazed into his eyes, her heart racing. She felt a sense of intimacy. A sense of closeness that she had never felt with anyone else before. She felt a mix of fear and excitement. A vulnerability that she and never felt before. She gazed into his eyes; her heart raced as she felt a sense of trust and love building within her.

"Ragden, I would never miss the opportunity to be with you. To feel your presence."

Ragden blushed softly. He turned his head and kissed her softly on the lips, "I wasn't... I wasn't sure you felt that way. I'm... flattered."

Aria felt a surge of pleasure wash over her body as she felt his lips against her own. She returned the kiss, pressed her body against his, and felt the incredible energy that surrounded them both.

"Ragden... I feel something incredible when I'm with you. Something that I've never felt before, and I can't seem to resist you."

Ragden's heart thudded in his chest. Had he done something to her? Put her under some kind of compulsion? Was this not her free will? Oh, he wanted her. He loved her, but he wanted her to choose him, not be forced.

"I'm... not sure how to respond to that. I... Maybe this is a bad idea. I'm sorry... I must know you are choosing me. I don't want to force you to do anything; it would break my heart..."

His breath hitched in his throat, and he could not get more words to come out. He looked at her, a tear slipping down his cheek. Aria felt a surge of pleasure over her body as she felt Ragden's hesitation, as he seemed unsure of whether he could continue. She gazed into his eyes, her blue eyes filled with a mixture of desire and admiration.

"Ragden... please don't stop. Don't worry, I'm choosing you. I want to be with you. I want to feel that incredible energy that seems to surround us both."

"Oh God, Aria... I'm sorry... I... I love you. I don't know how else to put this... I've loved you for so long; my chest hurts from it." Tears slipped down his cheeks.

She reached up and wiped them away. She felt a surge of pleasure wash over her own body. She gazed into his eyes, her heart racing as she felt a sense of longing. A sense of desire that consumed her very being.

"Ragden... I love you too."

He reached out and pulled her against him. He lost his balance and fell over into the grass, pulling her down on top of him. He kissed her lips. Slipped a bit of tongue between her lips to taste her. Then he closed his eyes and reached out with his energy, to see if he could tell whether it was truly her

desire. His energy blossomed out like a flower opening under the morning sun, filling the area around them. The grass waved like in a soft breeze, licking his skin, and reassuring him. He felt her on top of him, and her energy. Her soul. His energy caressed it, tested its integrity. He searched for... something amiss and found nothing that did not 'feel' right. His energy licked around her like a fire around a log. He could feel her soul responding with longing and desire. It wanted that warm fire.

Aria felt Ragden's energy envelop her. It filled her with a sense of incredible pleasure. She felt a surge of heat. A wave of desire that washed over her very being. When it had passed, it left her feeling weak and vulnerable, yet incredibly aroused. She felt a sense of longing. A yearning that she could not resist. She felt a mix of fear, excitement, and vulnerability that consumed her very being. She felt her energy intertwining with Ragden's, creating a symphony of pleasure that filled every corner of her being.

He pulled his energy back into himself. He felt the grass return to normal. The breeze faded. The light around them dimmed until it was just the two of them, lying in the grass. Her body pulled down against his. Every exquisite inch of her pressed against him. He felt his loins stirring, his cock started to harden beneath her. It responded to her warmth and desire. He opened his eyes, looked into her sparkling blue eyes, and kissed her passionately.

"I believe you. Thank you... That .... means so much..." He choked on his words, his breath hitching as fresh tears sprung to his eyes. Tears of happiness. She felt gratitude and relief that Ragden believed her, that he accepted her choice without question.

Ragden pulled her down against him, feeling her heart beating against his chest. He squeezed her gently against him, savoring the feel of her. Then he whispered against her cheek.

"I do have one concern, though. Something I must disclose to you." He signed softly. "There is no easy way to say this, so I'll just say ... I love you. And I love Sarah. And I love Emily too..."

Aria felt Ragden's words wash over her. They filled her with a sense of pleasure and delight.

"Ragden... I understand. I love you, and I love that you love Sarah, too, and Emily. It's okay. I want you to be happy. I want you to be with whoever makes you happy."

"You all make me happy—happy beyond description. But do not mistake me—I love you all. I do not place any one of you above the other. My love for them does not diminish my love for you. Nor does my love for you diminish my love for them. I... have so much love to offer you all... if you would accept it and be okay with it."

"Ragden, I love you, and I want you to be happy."

"And I love you too. What would truly make me happy is if you could accept this and join us."

Aria felt a sense of joy and happiness that Ragden had chosen to share his

life with her, Sarah, and Emily. Aria laughed and nodded, "Yes... Yes... I can accept it."

Ragden laughed with her and kissed her more passionately. He wrapped his arms around her and pulled her against him. His cock throbbed against her. He chuckled again.

"Sorry... it seems my dick has a mind of its own. Sorry... Just ignore him..." He kissed her again, softly on the lips.

"Ragden, don't apologize. I love it when you're like this."

He rolled over onto his side, his arm around her, gently lowering her into the grass. Side by side, he gazed out at the lake and smiled at her. "This is a beautiful spot. Now that we have gotten that out into the open, how was your day at school?"

Aria spoke softly, slowly. "It was... interesting. Today was the first day that I really felt like everyone was treating me differently."

"Different good or Bad?" He gazed into her eyes, interested in this new development.

"Both, actually. People were sort of... nice to me today. Like they weren't being as mean as usual."

Ragden cocked an eyebrow at her. She used to be the school bully, and people used to be mean to her? This seemed oddly out of place. "That sounds... nice? How did it make you feel?"

Aria spoke softly, "It was... strange. I didn't know how to react."

"Well, it sounds nice to me." He smiled happily, trying to gauge her reaction. "My day was... a bit on the wild side."

"Wild? In a good way, or a bad way?"

"A bit of both? To be honest. I was expecting to be too sore to move, but..." He flexed his stomach muscles and his thighs. Things he could not move after lunch seemed fully recovered. "I guess I'm going to be fine..."

"What? You're not going to be sore anymore? That's... amazing. Can you show me why? Please?"

"It's... hard to explain. I have done things that I never thought possible, and I'm recovering faster than I would have expected. I'm hoping my dad can explain that to me this weekend when we head to the beach house..."

"But... can you just show me? Please? I want to feel what it is that makes you... not sore."

He laughed, "It's ... kind of a lot to explain, and I'm not sure I can ... show you." He kissed her softly on the lips. Then he whispered huskily, "Though, I suspect I'll be showing you soon enough if that is what you want."

His body responded, his cock throbbing against her leg.

"Please... I want to feel it. Show me." She said with a mix of desperation and need in her voice.

He wrapped his arms around her, and rolled over onto his back again, pulling her over on top of him. His cock throbbed painfully against her groin. He pulled her down against his chest, her nipples pressed into him. He kissed

her passionately and slipped one hand down her back to gently grasp her ass and press her groin against his. He whispered huskily against her lips. "You remember two days ago, in the hall... We put on quite the show... Let's just say that I've never heard of anyone recovering from something that intense that quickly... and I've been active at that kind of level ... ever since?"

"Show me then." She said simply, her tone demanding, her body begging for it.

He laughed lustily. "Here? In the park? Where anyone can see? Have you become that much of an exhibitionist?"

"I don't care. I want to watch you cum."

His body responded to her words. His cock throbbed hard against her. He slipped his hands under her skirt, running them up her thighs to her ass. He grasped it firmly in his hands, savoring the firmness of her.

"Do you want to come back to my house first? Or do you really want to make out right here in the middle of the park?"

Aria sighed, feeling his grip on her ass. Her body trembled with desire and need. She signed softly. "Your house. I want to see where you fuck your girlfriends."

He laughed again and kissed her on the nose. "Unless I'm mistaken, you are my girlfriend now, too—my lover. And I would express that love in the most physical way possible... If you want..."

Aria felt a sense of longing, a sense of desire that consumed her very being, "I want to see you fuck Sarah and Emily."

"And what if they want to watch me fuck you? Would you consent to that?"

"Yes. I want them to watch me get fucked by you, and I want to watch you fuck them."

"Well then, we have an accord."

In one smooth motion, he stood up, pulled her against him, and easily lifted her. He lightly set her on her feet next to him, his hand in hers. "Shall we go then? Or is there anything else you would like to discuss first?"

"Let's go. I want to see you fuck Sarah and Emily."

"We may need to see how they feel about that. Though, if my experiences have taught me anything, I suspect they may agree."

He pulled her against him and kissed her softly on the lips. Then they set off for his house with his arm around her waist.

"They will agree. They are already jealous of us."

As they walked briskly through the park, he looked at her curiously. "What makes you say that?"

"Because every time I talk to them, they act all weird and distant."

"That might be because I have already had wild sex with both of them in the last two days. They may not have known how to react to you."

"Oh, well then. That just means more fun for me. Let's go to your house."

They walked at a brisk pace. Winding through the streets, his arm around

her waist. They noticed a few folks from school who gave them curious looks, but he ignored them.

"What about your parents, do you wish to contact them? Let them know where you are going?"

"No. Don't bother calling my parents. Just let them think I went somewhere with friends or something."

"That seems fair, and not entirely untrue." He smiled happily at her and squeezed her hand gently. "I am not positive Sarah will be there. I know Emily was going to check on her...."

"Doesn't matter. I want to see you fuck Emily."

Ragden squeezed Aria against him gently, feeling the line of her body against his. "As long as Emily agrees, then I am fine with that, but she gets her say as well. This is a mutual thing. No more bossing people around. They have their feelings and opinions, and they matter, just like yours do."

"Emily will agree. She has always wanted you."

Ragden laughed, remembering the activities of the day, "You are more right about that than you know, but I also want to feel your body against mine. I want to see you enjoying yourself. I would very much like to see you get the release you so desperately crave."

"Just watching you cum inside me will be enough for me. But seeing you fuck Emily will be even better."

Ragden cocked an eyebrow at her. "How many guys have you ever seen cum twice that quickly?"

"Not many. Most guys only cum once and then lose control. You are different. You have been controlling things from the start."

He chuckled as they rounded the corner, seeing his house just down the street. "I guess you have been paying attention. That is what has been shocking me. I keep expecting to find the limits of what I can do, and... not finding them. I am excited to share that with you..."

"Please show me. Please fuck Emily while I watch. Make her beg for you to fill her up with your hot seed."

Ragden stopped at the edge of his property around his house and turned to Aria. He pulled her against him. His cock throbbed against her. He kissed her softly on the lips, pulling her into his warm embrace and hugging her against him. "I would love to show you. I would love to see you filled with the pleasure and love we have to offer. It warms my heart beyond description that you have decided to come..."

"I couldn't resist coming over tonight."

"I'm glad you did. Thank you. This means... more to me than I can explain..." He hugged her again, pulling her tight against him.

"It means everything to me too. I want to be here with you. I want to see you cum again."

He turned and started up the walk to the front door of his house. As always, he dragged his hands through the bushes, feeling their soft caress. He

smiled. He opened the front door, stepped in, and pulled off his shoes. Gestured to Aria to do the same.

"Mom! I'm home!" He called out listening for voices and movement in the house.

"Be careful," Aria whispered as she took off her shoes.

Ragden turned to Aria and smiled. "Nothing to worry about; you have not met my parents. Relax."

He turned and started towards the living room as Jennifer came around the corner smiling. She walked over and gave him a warm hug, then winked at Aria.

"Mom, this is Aria; she will be joining us this evening," he said to her.

"Aria, oh, I remember Ragden mentioning you. It's such a pleasure to finally meet you." Jennifer stepped forward and pulled Aria into a warm, motherly hug. She winked at Ragden over Aria's shoulder.

"Hi, Jennifer. Nice to meet you." Aria smiled nervously as she returned Jennifer's hug. Jennifer released Aria and turned to Ragden. Aria blushed slightly.

"Mom, have you seen Sarah or Emily?" He asked.

"Oh darling, we were just talking about you. We are all in the living room. Come..."

Jennifer turned and walked towards the living room. Aria turned to follow her. Ragden gulped and followed.

They walked into the living room. Emily and Sarah were sitting side-by-side on one couch. Jennifer sank into a loveseat opposite them. Aria walked over to Emily and Sarah, hugged each of them, and sat next to Emily. Then they all turned and stared at Ragden, standing awkwardly in the room. He looked for where to sit. He could see desire on all three of their faces. He gulped. Was he ready for this? He was not sure.

Aria's body trembled with desire. She looked over at Ragden, then to Emily and Sarah. She saw the desire in their eyes, the hunger for what was to come. She knew that she wanted to be part of it, to witness it firsthand. She also knew that she wanted to be the center of attention, to be the focus of all their lustful desires. She crossed her legs, waiting for them to make the first move. She looked up to Ragden and spoke softly, motioning to the space beside her.

"Come sit next to me."

Ragden looked at Sarah and Emily, asking for permission. He saw both smile and nod, he walked over to Aria and sat down next to her. Then he looked at his mother.

"So... uh... What were you discussing?"

Jennifer smiled softly, then spoke, "Well, dear, mostly about how you fucked Sarah so hard she couldn't walk." She chuckled softly to herself. "Oh, don't worry, dear; she is fully recovered now. The balm you applied worked its magic."

Jennifer winked at Ragden, who looked at Sarah and smiled, seeing her radiant smile in return.

"Oh, Emily did mention the whole energy spark thing you two pulled off..." Ragden blushed crimson, wondering how much detail Emily had shared of that one. He looked at Emily, who was also blushing darkly. Emily smiled at Ragden and shrugged.

"You are going to want to ask Michael about that one. I've heard of similar stuff, but it has been an EXCEPTIONALLY long time. That is OLD magic. And yes, I know you fucked her in the ass, she didn't mention it, but I figured it out."

Ragden's blush darkened, as did Emily's. Sarah turned to Emily. Her eyes gleamed.

"Really!? Ooohh... I wanna see..."

Jennifer laughed from where she sat. Then spoke softly to Ragden, "I think you might have your hands full with these women. You sure do know how to pick them..." Then she winked.

Ragden blushed again, his jaw working, but not his vocal cords. Jennifer stood and walked over to him. She pulled him to his feet and gave him a soft hug. Then she stepped back and spoke to the room.

"Michael, my husband, will be home in a few hours. The room upstairs is ready for you all. Dinner will be ready... later. And you are all welcome to spend the night. If you need us to reach out to your parents, just let me know."

Ragden reached down and took Aria's hand in his, pulling her to her feet. Then he kissed her lips softly as his mom walked into the other room. Then he turned to Sarah and Emily, reaching out to them.

"Shall we... uh... Head upstairs?"

"Yes, let's go," Aria replied softly, her voice barely above a whisper.

Emily smiled happily as she took his other hand, stood, and crossed over to hug him. Sarah stood shyly and came over and slipped in behind to wrap her arms around Ragden's waist. Aria called out after Jennifer.

"Uh... Jennifer? Can you... Can you call my parents, they know I'm out, but... they are expecting me for dinner... Can you talk to them?"

Jennifer came back over and patted Aria's hand lovingly, "Of course, dear. I will take care of it. Enjoy everything my son has to offer." She winked at Ragden. Then she spoke softly to Aria. "Rest well, dear, you deserve it."

Aria turned back to him, blushed slightly, and took his hand in hers. "Lead the way..."

CHAPTER 14

Ragden stood for a moment, just enjoying the presence of the three wonderful, beautiful women around him; then he took a deep breath and headed upstairs with them right behind him. They reached the landing and walked to the door of his room. He turned the handle and stepped in, the girls following him. He took another step to unblock the doorway, then stopped and scratched his head.

"This bed is larger than I recall," Emily spoke softly. Sarah turned and grinned wickedly at Emily, nudging her in the ribs softly. Emily blushed.

"No... You are right. I do not recall this room having a king-sized bed. I am... not going to complain; the bed we were in last night wouldn't have fit four people."

Emily stepped up next to him and circled his waist with her arms, squeezing him gently. He looked down at her and smiled. Then he leaned down and kissed her softly on the lips. Slowly, he pulled off his shirt. Emily took a step back to admire him. He then noticed all three of them staring at his chest and arms. He cocked an eyebrow.

"What? It's not like you haven't seen me without a shirt before."

All three women blushed, though Emily blushed the deepest. Sarah giggled slightly, then ran over and hugged him tightly, burying her face in his chest. Then she looked up at him and licked his chest. He chuckled, the sensation mildly tickling him. He leaned down and kissed her softly on the lips and cleared his throat.

"How... uh... How do you want to proceed?"

"Can we play a game?" Aria suggested softly, her voice barely above a whisper. She bit her lower lip, hoping that Ragden would agree to her request.

Ragden reached out a hand to Aria and then took her hands in his, pulling her to him. Sarah groaned and moved out of the way, stepping around behind him and keeping her arms around him. Emily blushed slightly, reaching out, then pulling her hands back. He hugged Aria and kissed her on the forehead.

"What is your request, my love? What kind of game do you want to play?"

She looked up at him, her cheeks flushed, her heart racing, "A game of truth or dare. I want to see you be honest with me. I want to make you feel good, make you feel like you have no choice but to obey me. I want to see you strip for me, and I want to hear your thoughts as you do it. I want to know that you are doing this because you want to please me."

Ragden laughed softly, musically. A sound of love and affection flowed over the room. He felt Sarah's arms prickle with goosebumps at the sound of it. Emily shivered and stepped closer to him. He looked down at Aria. "My love, we don't have to play 'truth or dare.' If you have questions, I will tell you the truth. If you want to do something, ask."

"Okay. We do not have to do that. I want you to strip for me, and I want to hear your thoughts as you do it. I want to know that you are doing this because you want to please me. I want to see you lay yourself bare for me, completely naked, so that I can own every inch of your perfect body."

Ragden stepped back from her, his hands on her shoulders, pushing her gently away from his body. Sarah kept herself against him, her arms still circling his waist. He spoke softly but with firm tones; there would be no debate.

"Nobody owns anyone here in this house. You do not own me; I do not own you. My body is mine. You are welcome to share in the joy it can bring you, but it is not yours."

Aria spoke softly, but with determination in her voice, "But I am asking you to strip for me. I am asking you to lay yourself bare for me, completely naked, so that I can see every inch of your perfect body. So that I can feel that you are doing this because you want to please me, because you want to show me that you are willing to do anything to make me happy, to make me feel loved."

Ragden spoke softly to Aria, "I think you may need to re-evaluate what you think love is, and what it takes for you to feel loved, but I will grant you this request."

Ragden placed a single hand in the middle of Aria's chest, keeping her at arm's length while he used the other to unbuckle his shorts. They dropped to the floor around his ankles. Then he slipped off his boxers. His cock throbbed in the open air. Large, fully erect, and throbbing before them.

"There, I stand before you naked. This is my body, and I love all of you. I want you all to be happy, and if I can please you, then you need but ask."

Aria's heart raced faster; her breath caught in her throat. She looked at his large, fully erect dick standing at attention in between them. She reached out and ran her fingers along the length of it. She felt the heat and pulse of life that flowed through it. She gazed up at him, her cheeks flushed, her eyes focused on his, filled with adoration and love.

"Oh my God... It's beautiful," she whispered.

Sarah peeked around his side to gaze longingly at his cock. She unclasped

her hands to reach out and feel the hard length of it. Ragden closed his eyes, letting them feel it. He felt Emily step up to his side. He could feel her energy swirling, her desire burning red hot. He reached out and placed a hand in hers and squeezed. He could feel his energy reaching out to hers and entwining it. Something was happening between them. He gasped softly as he could feel her heartbeat; without touching her, he could feel her breath. He could feel the pulse of her love as it flowed through her body. He could feel her fluids flowing as if they were his own. Separate but there. He opened his eyes and looked at her. She looked up at him, and he knew that she could feel him feeling her.

Aria sensed something happening between Emily and Ragden, and she could feel their connection. She looked at Ragden's cock, then back at Emily, her heart racing, her body trembling in anticipation.

She pleaded, "Do it. Touch it."

Ragden pulled Emily around in front of him, and pulled her into a warm embrace, wrapping his arms around her. He kissed her softly on the lips, slipped his tongue into her mouth, and tasted her sweetness. He whispered against her lips, feeling the charge of energy in the air.

"We do this on your terms, my dear..."

All of them felt the charge of energy in the air, and they knew that what was about to happen was something incredibly intimate and special. All three women felt the sudden rush of arousal flooding through them. Sarah and Aria realized that this was something that Emily wanted to show them and share with them. Emily looked up at Ragden, her cheeks flushed, her heart racing.

"On my terms, huh?" Emily asked, her voice soft.

Ragden nodded slowly, feeling the charge in the air thicken. He smiled into Emily's lips. Enjoyed the sensation of her body pressed to his. He slid his hands to her back and over her backside. He slipped his hands under her skirt, running them over the edges of her panties, gripping her firm ass. He sighed contentedly.

"We only do what you want to do..."

Aria's blue eyes sparkled, and her body trembled with desire as she watched Ragden's hands slide under Emily's skirt, gripping her firm ass through her panties. She felt a mix of fear and excitement, a sense of vulnerability that consumed her very being. She looked at Emily, her cheeks flushed, her heart racing, her eyes wide with anticipation.

"Take them off," Aria whispered, pleading.

Emily hesitated for a moment and looked up at Ragden with a knowing smile and desire. She nodded slowly, and with a gentle movement, she removed her panties, leaving her smooth, perfect bottom bare for all to see. Sarah pressed herself against his back, her arms reaching around to find Emily's hips, to slide under her skirt and gently caress her bare bottom. Emily sighed and leaned around Ragden's side to kiss Sarah softly on the lips. Sarah leaned into the kiss, tasting Emily. Then she drew back and giggled. Sarah

pulled her hands back and ran them down Ragden's firm legs, then up his inner thighs to run her hands over his hard dick. One hand wrapped around the base of it, while the other gently cupped his balls. She sighed contentedly. Emily leaned against Ragden, pushing her whole body against him, trapping his cock against her abdomen. Sarah's hands pinned against him. Both girls sighed with pleasure at the intimate contact. Aria plopped down hard on the edge of the bed, her heart racing, her mouth agape. She wanted to take part, to be filled, but she also wanted to watch.

Ragden kissed Emily even more passionately, his tongue delving into her mouth, exploring her, savoring her, tasting the incredible flavor that was her. Meanwhile, his hands slipped around her firm ass. His fingers gently curled around her bottom, teasing her asshole. They spread her moist lips and slipped between them. Emily moaned with pleasure and gasped with surprise and delight.

Ragden gently cupped Emily's ass, lifting her off the ground. Sarah stepped back as Emily's legs wrapped around him, as his fingers slipped around her ass, spreading her pussy. Sarah stepped forward and gently pulled on his cock, angling it towards Emily's pussy as he poised her over it. Emily breathed heavily, her eyes sparkling with desire. Then he leaned forward and nuzzled her chest softly. Emily smiled, and pulled her blouse over her head, revealing her bra. Then she reached behind her back, and unclasped it, dropping it at Aria's feet. Ragden smiled happily and kissed her chest. His tongue found her firm nipples and pulled each into his mouth to gently suckle them one at a time. Then he slowly lowered her onto his cock, held out by Sarah. As Emily's juices dripped down his dick, Sarah giggled as her hands got wet. Emily moaned softly as his cock slid up into her. He slowly lowered her until her groin slid against Sarah's hands.

"God, I never get tired of the feeling of you," he whispered against Emily's lips as he kissed her again.

Aria trembled as she watched Emily's now exposed, round and full breasts, which were standing proudly against her chest. Her rosy, pink nipples begged for attention. Emily gazed down at Aria, seeing the mixture of anticipation and fear in her eyes. Then she looked up at Ragden, her cheeks flushed. Aria felt her mind whirling with lust and desire.

"You're so beautiful," Aria whispered, slowly standing, and walking over to Emily. She stepped up behind her. Aria reached up and softly caressed Emily's breasts. Emily moaned softly as Ragden's cock filled her, gasping as his cock caressed her cervix. She smiled at Ragden, then bit her lip.

"And I never get tired of you filling me," Emily sighed against him. Her arms grasped his shoulders so she could rock her hips against his. Pressing his cock against her cervix. She moaned softly in pleasure.

Ragden leaned forward and kissed her passionately again, tasting her sweetness. His heart thumped with excitement as he gently lifted her half-way off his cock and slid her back down again. His eyes slipped closed as her pussy

clenched around his cock, squeezing it tightly as it slipped through her depths to press against her cervix again. Then he turned and smiled down at Sarah, whose hands were still wrapped around the base of his cock. He saw the greedy, hungry look on her face. Then he turned to Aria, whose hands held Emily's breasts, gently pinching her nipples as Emily moaned softly. Aria's eyes were filled with need and desire. He nipped at Aria's hands with his teeth; her eyes flashed to his.

Ragden smiled at her hungrily and whispered, "Is this what you wanted to see?"

Aria gazed up at Ragden. Her cheeks were flushed. Her heart raced. Her mind whirled with lust and desire. "Yes," she replied softly. She released Emily's breasts and turned to look at Sarah, who was still stroking Ragden's cock with a hunger that seemed insatiable.

Ragden leaned back slightly, letting Emily's hips rest on his own, her legs wrapped around him tightly, holding her in place. Then he reached out and placed his hands on Aria's hips, sliding them up to her breasts. He gently cupped them through her shirt and thumbed her nipples. He felt them go erect under his soft touch. Then he released her and slid his hands over her stomach to the top of her skirt. He ran his fingers around the inside of it, tugging on it gently, pulling her against Emily's back. Emily sighed, ground her hips against Ragden, and felt his throbbing cock against her cervix. A soft moan slipped from his lips at the sheer pleasure of Emily on him. His hands slipped back to Emily's ass, gripping her cheeks gently. He straightened up and lifted her partly off his cock. Then slid her down again. He gently bucked his hips into her as she came down, driving his cock into her cervix with a little more force. Her breasts jiggled gently with the impact.

Ragden reached back around Emily and grasped the bottom edge of Aria's blouse. Aria lifted her arms, allowing him to pull her blouse over her head. She reached behind her and unclasped her bra, letting it drop to the floor at her feet. Her breasts were revealed, round and full, her dark nipples taught. She looked up at Ragden. Her cheeks were flushed, and her heart was racing.

"You like my tits, don't you?" Aria whispered seductively.

Holding Emily against him with one hand around her waist, Ragden turned to Aria. He leaned over and kissed Aria's nipples, one and then the other. He leaned his shoulder against her and kissed her softly on the lips. He slid one hand around her waist to grab her ass, closing his eyes to savor the texture of it.

"I do love them," he whispered huskily against her lips.

"Mm... You like having them in your hands, don't you?" Aria purred, her voice barely above a whisper.

Ragden bucked his hips against Emily, causing her to gasp slightly as she slid up and came down hard against his cock. He turned from Aria and kissed Emily fiercely, bucking her again, watching her smile as she slid up and down on his cock once again. He felt the shock of pleasure as his cock hit her

cervix. Then he turned to Aria, reached out, and cupped her breast with his right hand, thumbing her erect nipples. He smiled lustily at Aria. Emily watched through half-closed eyes as she ground her hips against his groin, feeling his cock sliding inside her and filling her. Emily bit her lip as she watched him fondle Aria's beautiful chest.

"I do," he sighed to Aria as he softly kissed her lips.

"Good," Aria whispered.

Ragden wrapped one hand around Emily's waist, gripping her ass firmly. He lifted and lowered her on his cock. He could hear her moaning with pleasure as his dick slid in and out of her depths. His other hand slid down Aria's flat stomach and down to her groin. He reached inside her panties, slid his fingers through her wet folds, and slipped them up into her. He looked her in the eyes as he slipped two fingers up into her tight pussy. He felt her juices flow out onto his hand. He continued to bounce Emily on his cock as he withdrew his hand from Aria's pussy and licked his fingers clean. Aria gasped softly. Her body trembled with desire.

He whispered to her huskily, "You taste wonderful."

Sarah released Ragden's cock and came around to look at Aria. She approached her cautiously and timidly, reaching up to gently cup her breasts. Aria's eyes slipped shut as Sarah kissed her nipples. Aria gasped slightly. Sarah looked at Ragden and grinned, then leaned over and kissed him softly on the lips. He returned her kiss, parting her lips, and slipping his tongue into her mouth. She stepped back, breathless, her heart pounding. Then Sarah turned to Aria.

Sarah looked at Ragden and whispered, "Does she taste good?"

He smiled and nodded. Sarah turned back to Aria, placed her hands on Aria's hips, gazed at her lustily, and whispered, "Can I taste you? I've always wanted to taste you... Please?"

"Go ahead," Aria whispered, her voice full of desire.

Ragden pulled his hands back and gripped Emily's ass in both hands, gently lifting and lowering her along his cock. He felt it bottom out against her cervix gently. Emily moaned softly with each impact and rolled her hips against him, heightening the experience. Her hands on his shoulders allowed her to move with him. He moaned softly at the feel of her pussy squeezing his throbbing cock as she slid up and down.

Both Emily and Ragden watched in fascination as Sarah knelt in front of Aria, her hands sliding down Aria's hips, slipping her panties down her thighs to the floor, exposing her perfectly shaved mound. Then Sarah looked up at Aria hungrily. She slowly slid a hand up Aria's inner thigh. Slipped her fingers through Aria's tight, wet folds. Aria moaned softly as Sarah slid her fingers up inside her. Sarah slipped her fingers out and sucked on them. Aria gasped as Sarah removed her fingers from her mouth. Sarah moaned softly as she looked up at Aria. Then Sarah looked at Emily and Ragden and smiled broadly, stark hunger and need on her face.

"She does taste amazing..." She turned to Aria, a huge grin on her face, "I want more... please."

"Oh, God yes!" Aria exclaimed softly, "Taste me."

Emily smiled brilliantly to Ragden as she continued to move with his gentle thrusts, his cock sliding in and out of her tight pussy, gently pushing against her cervix with each thrust. He leaned forward and kissed Emily hungrily, savoring the taste of her. Then they both turned and watched as Sarah pushed Aria against the bed; Aria stumbled backward and sprawled out on the bed. Sarah giggled playfully as she crawled between her legs and put her face into Aria's pussy. Sarah hungrily slid her tongue through Aria's lips, pulling on her clit, and suckling it. Then she slid lower to dip her tongue inside Aria, who gasped loudly at the sudden invasion.

Emily and Ragden chuckled softly, enjoying the feel of his cock sliding in and out of her tight pussy. He continued to lift and lower Emily, who ground her hips, and used his shoulders to drive herself against his thrusts. His cock slid harder against her, pushing harder against her cervix. Their breath coordinated; their movements matched. They felt the joined climaxes building within each other. The air around them crackled with the energy of it.

Aria's blue eyes sparkled, her body trembling with desire as Sarah pushed her against the bed, her fingers gripping her hips, forcing her to spread her legs wide apart. She gazed up at Sarah. Her cheeks flushed. Her heart raced. Her mind whirled with lust and desire. Sarah moved down between her legs, her tongue flicking out. Sarah teased her entrance, before diving deeper. Then she pulled back and swirled her tongue around Aria's engorged clit.

Ragden continued to lift and thrust into Emily, as she rolled her hips against his, their bodies in perfect rhythm. He smiled up at her beautiful face and saw her moan with each stroke. Her face in the throes of ecstasy was so incredibly stunning in its beauty. His heart thundered harder in his chest. He felt her heartbeat responding to his. He paused for a moment, letting their groins press together. He leaned in to kiss her fiercely. Then he pulled back breathless, his heart pounding in his chest.

"God damn woman..." He whispered against her lips, breathless, amazed, and dumbfounded. "How did I get so lucky to have you in my life? You are so beautiful."

Then they looked over at Sarah and watched her as she buried her face in Aria's bald pussy. Using her fingers to spread those swollen pink lips, she inserted two fingers in her pussy, her tongue stroking and licking it. Sarah paused for a moment, sliding more of her hand up into Aria as she turned to look at Ragden and Emily. Sarah grinned wickedly, clearly enjoying herself. Ragden whispered against Emily's lip huskily, "Shall we join them?"

Aria's blue eyes sparkled, and her body trembled with desire as Sarah's fingers dug into her thighs, holding her in place. She gazed up at Emily. Sarah paused briefly, looking up at Emily and Ragden before diving back into Aria's wet pussy, stroking her walls, and playing with her sensitive nub. Sarah's

cheeks were flushed, her eyes bright with lust, her breath coming in short gasps as she worked to please Aria. Emily smiled at the scene of Sarah and Aria, then looked at Ragden and shyly whispered, "Join them?"

Ragden ground his hips against Emily's groin, sliding his cock into her cervix and kissing her deeply. Then he pulled his head back just a tad and whispered to her softly, "Yeah... give Aria an afternoon she will never forget. What do you think?"

Sarah continued to work Aria's pussy with relentless passion. Her fingers slid deep inside her, as her tongue flickered in and out. Her cheeks were flushed, her heart raced, and her mind focused on the pleasure of the moment. Aria gazed up at Ragden. Her cheeks flushed. Her mind whirled with lust and desire.

"Please... let Sarah have her way with me. Let her make me cum like only she can..."

Ragden smiled down at Aria writhing under Sarah's relentless assault on her most private parts.

"As you wish, my dear," he smiled as he pulled Emily against him and felt the press of her breasts against his chest. His cock throbbed deep inside her, causing her to moan against him. "I just thought we might be able to heighten your experience..."

Aria's breath came in short bursts as she spoke softly, "Just by watching Sarah pleasure me, knowing how much she wants to taste me... It makes everything even more intense." Sarah glanced up at Ragden. Her cheeks flushed, her eyes bright with lust. Her fingers were still buried deep inside Aria's wet pussy, her tongue still stroking her swollen clit.

Ragden smiled happily, looking at her state. "Of course... I just thought... What if I slipped my cock up your ass while Sarah ate you, and Emily played with your breasts?"

Aria's body continued to tremble as Sarah continued to work her pussy with relentless passion. Sarah's fingers slid deep inside Aria. Her tongue flickered in and out. Aria's eyes glazed over as she tried to imagine what it would feel like. The thoughts played over her mind. Her body twitched with desire.

"Yes... that sounds perfect. Just thinking about it already has me so wet."

He turned to Emily and kissed her deeply, his tongue exploring her mouth while he lifted her up his cock and slid it back home against her cervix again. He broke away from her mouth to whisper against her lips.

"And what of you, my love? Does that sound like fun? We can finish this..." He lifted her and slid her down, savoring the feel of her on his throbbing cock, "...later."

Emily smiled softly. A look of sadness crossed her face. Then she ground her hips against his and bit her lip, savoring the feel of his cock on her cervix. Then she smiled, the desire and need on her face tempered with the knowledge that she could have him later. She nodded softly.

"Yes," she whispered, her lips pressing against his, "I would like to see that."

Emily's eyes twinkled as she licked her lips, then his. Ragden smiled and kissed Emily passionately. Not wanting to part with her, but eager to blow Aria's mind. He gently lifted Emily until his cock slid free of her tight pussy. She moaned softly, as it slid out, her fluids dripping out as it did. Ragden could see the look of disappointment on her face. He kissed her softly and winked, a promise that he would finish what they had started. Then he carried her over to the bed and set her next to Aria, who watched, her eyes filled with lust and desire. Ragden stepped around behind Sarah, gently lifted her skirt, and pulled her panties down. She giggled against Aria's pussy as she kept licking while he slipped her panties off her feet.

Sarah's wet pussy was exposed. It glistened with excitement and anticipation. Sarah's cheeks flushed. Her eyes were bright with lust. Her fingers gripped Aria's hips as she continued to eat her out.

"Mm," Sarah moaned into Aria's flesh.

Ragden knelt behind Sarah and slid his cock through her wet folds, putting pressure against her clitoris. His cock throbbed against her. He gently grasped her hips and pulled her ass against his groin. Emily straddled Aria's stomach, her dripping wet pussy over Aria's swollen lips. Then she leaned down and kissed Aria on the lips, while gently fondling her breasts, her thumbs flicking across Aria's hardened nipples.

Ragden grasped his cock in one hand and pushed it through Sarah's wet folds, gently sliding it into her pussy. He grunted as it slid into her tight depths. Sarah gasped hard as it bottomed out in her and pushed against her cervix. The gentle pressure against her pushed her face into Aria's dripping folds. Aria gasped at the sudden impact of Sarah's face on her. Emily smiled and licked Aria's lips, then moved down to kiss her breasts. Ragden gently pulled his cock back and slid into Sarah again, pushing her into Aria's pussy again. Both women gasped from the impact.

He stroked two more times, deep and hard into Sarah, who moaned against Aria's clit with each stroke. Then he pulled out and slapped her ass playfully. Sarah glanced over her shoulder at Ragden, as her tongue flicked over Aria's clit, disappointment in her eyes. He nodded to her, a promise to finish that later with her. Then he reached down and took her hand, lifting her off Aria. He leaned over and kissed Emily on the lips and nudged her over. Emily climbed off Aria as well. Aria lay on the edge of the bed, panting, her cheeks flushed, her eyes wild with desire. Ragden crawled up on the bed next to her, and kissed her softly on the lips, tasting her desire and need. Then he picked her up and set her hips on his stomach. Her hands reached back to his chest to brace herself. He reached down and slid his cock through her folds, down to her ass. The tip pressed hard against her, and he pushed it in a slow circle around her tight hole.

He whispered, "Are you sure you want to do this? It is a lot to take..."

"Yes... I want this," she moaned softly, her body twitching with desire.

Ragden gently slid his hips up towards her and pushed the head of his cock into her ass. The head slipped in, and he stopped. Her body shook and twitched at the invasion of her most restricted area. Sarah crawled up between their legs. She ran her tongue over Ragden's balls, up his shaft, across Aria's asshole, and into Aria's lips. She dipped her tongue into Aria's pussy. She pulled back and giggled as she saw Aria's whole body shuddering with pleasure.

"So tasty," she sighed as she dropped her face into Aria's folds, sinking her tongue deep into Aria. Aria gasped loudly, her hips bucked, sunk Ragden's cock deeper into her ass.

Aria's body twitched and trembled, sliding a fraction down onto Ragden's throbbing cock. Sarah continued to push her tongue into Aria's slick pussy.

"Oh, God..." Aria groaned as she slid a little farther down onto his cock.

Ragden smiled as his throbbing cock slid a little deeper into Aria's tight ass. He reached over, grabbed Emily's hand, and pulled her over to him. He grabbed her by the hips and lowered her pussy to his face so he could lick her sweet folds, slipping his tongue into her while his cock slid a little deeper into Aria's ass. He could hear Aria moaning loudly as Sarah licked and plunged her tongue into her pussy; each stroke pushed her down onto his cock.

Aria trembled with desire as Sarah's tongue continued to work its magic on her swollen pussy. Her fingers gripped Aria's hips tightly. Sarah's mouth watered as she eagerly lapped at every drop of wetness that escaped from Aria's dripping folds. She gazed up at Emily, her cheeks flushed, her heart racing.

"Oh fuck!" Aria gasped as she spasmed against Sarah's tongue, causing her hips to sink lower down onto Ragden's cock. It slid deeper into her asshole, filling her bowels.

Ragden slowly lifted his hips and pushed his cock up her ass. Feeling her body convulse at the sudden intrusion. Her bowels were filled with all of his pulsing meat. He could feel her ass clenching against him. He reached up and spread Emily's lips further, slipped his tongue through her delicious folds. He licked her clitoris, then slipped his tongue as deep into her as he could, probing her tight walls. He could feel her moan softly above him. Emily reached out and wrapped her arms around Aria. She gently grasped Aria's breasts, pinching her nipples as Sarah ate her pussy, and Ragden's cock throbbed in her ass. Aria cried out, the flurry of sensations too much for her to bear.

"Fuuucccckkkk!" Aria cried out in pleasure, unable to hold back any longer; her body twitched with the immense pleasure that washed over her.

Ragden gently thrust up into her, causing her hips to rise off his groin. Then he dropped his hips down, his cock sliding back until just the tip remained in her ass. Then he thrust it up into her again, driving it home against her. Aria's whole body shook with the gentle impact. Sarah grasped

Aria's hips, keeping her face firmly planted in Aria's pussy while riding up and down on his cock. Emily sighed, feeling her pussy clench on his tongue as he continued to lick her dripping wet folds, swallowing her juices as they leaked out of her.

Aria's whole body shook with the impact of each thrust, her pussy clenched tightly around Sarah's fingers as she rode up and down on his thick, throbbing member. Ragden continued to gently buck his hips, sliding his cock in and out of Aria's tight ass. Her body rocked as Sarah continued to finger her pussy and lick her clit. Emily sighed in pleasure as she cupped Aria's breasts, pinching her nipples as her whole body rocked against Ragden's cock.

Aria's whole body trembled. The pressure and pleasure suddenly built and built within her. Sarah continued to finger her pussy. Her tongue stroked Aria's swollen clit. Her fingers worked their magic deep inside her slick walls.

"Mm... I'm so close." Aria moaned as she felt her climax building. Her body was overwhelmed by the sensations of everything at once.

Ragden licked Emily's pussy more fiercely, feeling Aria's impending climax, his heart rate starting to increase. His thrusts picked up a faster rhythm, driving his cock harder into her ass. Then sliding back, and up into her again. Sarah let herself go limp, bouncing along for the ride. Her face buried in Aria's pussy, lapping, licking, and flicking anything she could get her tongue on.

Aria trembled from head to toe, as Sarah continued to work her pussy. Ragden continued to plunge his cock into Aria's tight ass, filling her bowels with the enormity of his throbbing cock.

"Yes... Oh, God, yes!" Aria exclaimed as she felt the rush of pleasure wash over her body. Her climax loomed over her, threatening to wash everything away.

Ragden could start to feel his starting to build in response to Aria's climax. He licked Emily, sliding his fingers into her, stroking her depths as he ran his tongue over her clit. He thrust his hips more forcefully up into Aria. His cock drove into her depths, then dropped down to the mattress, almost coming out of her, and then thrust up into her hard again. The impact of his groin against her ass sent his balls up into Sarah's chin as she buried her face in Aria's pussy. Sarah licked and lapped, her fingers delving into Aria's tight walls. Ragden could feel her fingers through Aria's soft walls, pushing against the swell of his throbbing cock deep in Aria's ass.

Aria's orgasm built and built, her pussy clenching and releasing involuntarily as she felt Sarah's fingers push against the swell of Ragden's cock deep inside her ass.

"Fuuuuccckkk," Aria moaned softly, as her heart raced. Her mind was lost in a haze of pleasure.

Emily's pussy started to clench and release on Ragden's tongue, as he felt her orgasm building as well in response to everything else in the room. Emily's hands involuntarily clenched on Aria's breasts. Her fingers pinched

Aria's nipples forcefully as Ragden's cock slammed harder into Aria's ass. He went deeper, then dropped back, only to slam up into her again. Ragden's tongue drove over Emily's clitoris, licking as his fingers deep in her pussy folds, stroking her walls, trying to drive her climax harder.

"Oh, God, yes! Fuck me harder, Ragden!" Aria cried out as her orgasm continued to swell.

Ragden slid his hands out of Emily's tight pussy, feeling her moan in disappointment. Then he slid his hands under Aria's ass, to hold her in place so he could thrust into her harder and faster. He drove his cock into her bowels with renewed force. He continued to lick and suck on Emily's clit and pussy lips, feeling her moan softly on him.

Aria's body trembled and spasmed as Sarah continued to work her pussy with relentless passion. Her fingers slid deep inside her. Sarah's tongue flickered in and out. Her mind focused on the pleasure of the moment. Aria's eyes rolled back into her head. Her mouth hung agape as she panted. Her body pushed beyond the limits of anything she had expected or experienced before.

"Oh, God... Yes... Fuck me hard... Make me cum like only you can," Aria cried out.

Ragden held her hips more firmly, thrusting up into her with more force, then slid back and thrust up into her again. Each thrust shook her entire body. His throbbing cock filled her ass. He felt her tighten and clench on him as he slid in and out of her bowels. While doing that, he continued to lick and suckle Emily's incredible folds over his face. He could hear her breathing speeding up above him, her climax starting to boil over within her.

"Fuuuuccckkk!" Aria cried out, her voice shaky as she felt the incredible fullness of Ragden's cock filling her tight ass. Her body trembled, and her legs started to quiver and shake. Her arms twitched. Her muscles started to spasm as her climax threatened to roll over her.

Ragden continued to lick Emily's tight pussy, slipping his tongue as deep into her as he could, probing her inner walls. Then he slid his tongue over her clitoris, twisted around it, and flicked at it. He could hear her moaning above him. While holding Aria's hips steady, he pounded his throbbing cock harder into her ass. Each impact sent his cock deep into her bowels and shook her whole body. He could hear her breath exploding out at each impact. Her moans as he slid back and then slammed into her again. He could feel her body starting to spasm, her climax beyond her control to contain. He could feel his climax building with hers, threatening to overwhelm him.

"Fuck me harder! Fuck me faster!" Aria cried out. Sarah increased her pace. Her fingers worked harder inside Aria's pussy. Her tongue slid in and out, and her cheeks flushed. Her eyes bright with lust as she watched Ragden pumping his cock in Aria's ass. Emily grasped Aria's breasts tightly, pinching Aria's nipples.

Ragden licked at Emily's pussy more furiously, feeling her body quiver and

shake above him. He held Aria's hips in place while he thrust up into her harder, faster, feeling her entire body shake with each impact of his hips into hers. He thrust his massive throbbing cock deeper and harder into her bowels. His climax scratched at the edges of his awareness. He could feel the pressure building and the need for release becoming more insistent. He could feel Aria's body at the edge of what she could take. Her breath ragged gasps. Her heart pounded in her chest like a caged animal. He smashed his cock into her ass harder and faster. Her ass clenched against him.

Aria craned her neck to look at Emily behind her. She saw the pleasure etched across her face, as she saw the sight of her lover sliding into another woman's ass while being pleasured by him. Aria's eyes rolled back into her head again as her body spasmed. She could feel the incredible length of Ragden's cock sliding deep in her bowels. It felt like it was filling her entire body and soul with his power, his energy, and his love. She shuddered as it washed over her.

"Fuck me hard," she gasped, her voice breaking as she felt her orgasm starting to overcome all reason, "Make me cum with Sarah eating my pussy."

Ragden continued to lick and probe Emily's sublime pussy while he jackhammered his cock into Aria's ass. His body started to spasm with effort. He could feel Aria's body clench, every muscle going rigid as the force of her climax rolled over her. He continued to pump his cock into her ass again, and again until suddenly his orgasm broke over him like a storm. His body spasmed, and he slammed into her one more time, thrusting as deep into her as possible. His arms went limp, and his groin dropped to the bed. Aria's legs gave out, and she collapsed on top of him, slamming her ass down on his cock, forcing it deep into her bowels. She cried out as she felt it fill her up so suddenly again. The pressure and suddenness of it caused another explosion of cum to shoot out of his throbbing cock into her bowels. She cried out with the force of it. Her body shuddered. Her legs convulsed as the juice burst forth into Sarah's waiting mouth. Sarah thrust her face into Aria's orgasm, lapping up her juices as they spilled forth.

Aria gazed down at Sarah and watched as she eagerly took in her cum, her eyes fixed on Aria's pulsating hole. Sarah eagerly took in her love's essence, her tongue flicking in and out. Her cheeks flushed. Her eyes were bright with lust. Her fingers played with Aria's engorged clit as she slammed her face into Aria's pussy. Her mouth was full of Aria's delicious nectar.

"Oh, God!" Aria cried out. Her voice was hoarse with the power of her orgasm still riding over her. She collapsed back against Ragden's chest, going limp against him. Her body shuddered with the feeling of his cock shooting cum into her bowels. Emily sat up, pulled her engorged pussy off Ragden's face. Her own body twitched and shuddered as she lay down next to Aria. She snuggled against her, kissing Aria's breasts. Then she kissed her lips softly, bathing in the afterglow of Aria's orgasm.

Ragden slipped his hands out from under Aria's perfect ass and gently

cupped her breasts. He leaned forward and gently kissed her ear. His cock still throbbed in her ass. He whispered in her ear, "I hope you enjoyed that."

"It was amazing, thank you." Aria breathed softly, her body still riding the afterglow.

Ragden smiled against her head and breathed softly into her ear, "You are quite welcome. Thank you for joining us and allowing us to give you this."

Ragden watched as Sarah licked up the last of Aria's dribbling juices and pulled herself back from Aria's tight pussy. Then Sarah crawled up on the other side of Aria. Sarah softly kissed Aria's nipples, then kissed Aria softly on the lips. Aria smiled, tasting her essence on Sarah's soft lips. Both women moaned into each other's mouths at the sensation. Then Ragden gently lifted Aria's hips upwards, his throbbing cock sliding slowly out of her ass. She moaned loudly, her hands scrabbling to grab his hips. She tried to pull herself back down, but he kept lifting until his cock slipped free. Then he gently placed her next to him on the bed between Emily and him. Aria's body continued to twitch. Her muscles contracted with aftershocks. Ragden softly kissed her lips.

Then Ragden rolled over to look Sarah in the eyes as he cupped her breasts, softly kissing each. He brought his face up to hers and softly kissed her on the lips. Then he spoke softly to her, "Seems you've been neglected, my love. Would you like some attention?" He slid his hand down to her groin, and gently cupped her wet mound, slipping a finger through her lips, teasing her entrance.

Emily wrapped her arms around Aria, comforting her while her orgasm passed. Aria shivered with the force of it and snuggled into Emily's warm embrace. Emily leaned down and kissed Aria softly on the forehead, then on the lips. Emily looked over at Ragden and smiled serenely, then nodded once to let him know she was okay. Sarah's eyes widened, and she giggled to herself.

"Did I do good?"

Ragden kissed her lips softly and nodded, "You did amazing, my dear."

He slipped his fingers through her swollen pussy lips, stroked along the insides of her lips, felt her wetness. Then he slipped a finger into her vagina and gently stroked her walls. His cock throbbed against her abdomen, still wet from Aria. Sarah reached down and wrapped her fingers around it, feeling it throb in her hands. Her eyes lit up with desire and need.

"Yes," she whispered shyly, "Please... I need this in me."

"Of course," Ragden whispered to her. Then he rolled over on top of her, his knees spreading her legs, his cock slipped through her folds. Her eyes slipped closed at the feeling of it pressing against her.

Emily rolled Aria over on her side, pulling Aria's back against her stomach and chest, her erect nipples pressed into Aria's back. She gently grasped Aria's breasts, ran her fingers over her nipples, and kissed her shoulder softly as she watched Ragden and Sarah.

Sarah licked her lips, tasting Aria's juices on them, and giggled. Then she looked up at Ragden with need and desire on her face. She rocked her hips gently, feeling the head of his cock pushing against her tight entrance, and moaned softly. Then she reached back and grabbed his ass, trying to pull him into her. Failing, she bit her lip.

"Please... I am ready."

Ragden smiled down at her, leaned in, and gently kissed her on the lips as he slid the massive, thick head of his cock into her vagina. She gasped, her fingers digging into his ass.

"Oh, God," she moaned as she pulled against him, thrusting her hips forward, forcing more of his cock into her. He leaned into her, gently sliding it inside her, feeling her tight pussy clenching around his thick shaft as he continued to slide deeper into her. It filled her vagina and pushed into the back of her. She moaned as it gently pushed against her cervix.

Sarah moaned, feeling his massive cock filling every inch of her tight, wet pussy. She wrapped her arms around him and pulled him down against her. His body pressed against every inch of hers. His chest against her breasts, his breath on her cheek. She shivered with the sheer joy of having him in her and on her. Then she rocked her hips, feeling the pressure of his cock pressing across her cervix. The pressure and pleasure filled her up inside. She smiled and bit her lip. Then kissed him passionately, slipping her tongue into his mouth and tasting the love and passion that boiled off him.

"Fuck me," she whispered, "I need you to fuck me."

Emily licked her lips as she pulled Aria against her tighter, feeling the other woman's shuddering body pressed against her; a shiver ran down her back. Her pussy was suddenly damp with arousal. She was jealous of Sarah; she wanted that magnificent cock to fill her again. She was also happy for Sarah. Sarah who had been fucked to the point of not walking. Sarah had brought so much pleasure and ecstasy to Aria. Sarah, who had been so patient and yearned so much for Ragden's cock that it was almost painful to see. Emily smiled. She had had her chance with Ragden, and would again, but now it was Sarah's turn, and it brought her joy to watch.

CHAPTER 15

Aria's vision was so blurred, that she could hardly see straight. The afterglow of her incredible orgasm still blotted out the world. Her vision cleared enough to see Ragden on top of Sarah, his cock buried in her swollen pussy, and Sarah's ecstatic joy of being filled by him. She knew that feeling. She wanted more of it, but it brought her joy to see Sarah getting her chance. Her heart swelled with the love of it. She could feel Emily's body pressed against her, and she snuggled into the warm comfort of the other woman. She had seen the love on Emily's face and could feel it against her back. Her muscles relaxed, and she sighed contentedly. She reached back and slipped her hands into Emily's groin, felt the dampness there, and slipped her fingers into Emily's pussy. Emily moaned softly in her ear.

Ragden propped himself up on his elbows and smiled down at Sarah. Then he kissed her gently on the lips as he slowly slid his cock back but not out. Then he gently slid it into her again, filling her up and caressing her cervix lovingly. Sarah moaned at the sensation of it. As he drew back again, she sighed. Then as he slid in, she rolled her hips to meet his, bouncing her cervix off the head of his cock.

Sarah moaned, and bit her lip, feeling the heat and pressure build up inside her. She gazed up at Ragden. Her cheeks were flushed. Her heart raced. Her mind whirled with lust and desire. She dug her hands into his ass, trying to pull him against her harder.

"Fuck me hard. Make me scream for more."

Emily licked her lips, feeling her arousal and desire climbing as Aria's fingers caressed her pussy, and fingered her clitoris. Her nipples were firm, and her breathing and pulse escalating. She kissed Aria's shoulder, neck, and earlobe. Aria smiled at the attention, feeling Emily's hands gently squeezing her breasts as she slipped her fingers deeper into Emily. She watched with hungry eyes as Ragden slid his massive cock deep into Sarah. Then slowly withdrew and slid into her again. She could feel her hips moving with the

motion as she watched. Ragden gently drew his hips back and slid his massive cock out of Sarah, then slid back into her. Sarah quickly matched his slow rhythm, moving her hips in time. Rolling back as he withdrew and rolling forward to drive her cervix into his cock. Feeling her insistence, her need, her desire, he increased the pace. He slid in and out marginally faster, the impacts gently rocking her breasts.

Sarah moaned and clutched her breasts. She felt the pleasure and pressure inside her stoking the furnace of her desire. It filled her up with ecstasy. She felt her heart beating faster.

"Yes... Oh, God, yes," Sarah gasped. Her voice was soft, as she matched each thrust with her hips. Her body rocked with each impact. Ragden's pulse and thrusts matched hers. They moved in harmony. His big dick slid deep into her. He leaned down and kissed her passionately, slipping his tongue into her mouth. He tasted her sweetness and felt her breath against him.

Emily sighed with pleasure and pulled Aria against her chest, feeling her breasts squeeze against Aria's back. She gripped Aria's breasts tighter as she watched the intensity of Ragden sliding his cock in and out of Sarah's tight, wet pussy. Aria moaned at the pressure on her chest, and slipped her fingers deeper into Emily's tight pussy, causing Emily to moan against Aria's back.

"Oh, God," Sarah whispered between kisses. Her voice was breathy. Her body trembled with anticipation, "Fuck me hard... Fuck me like only you can."

Ragden slid his hands along Sarah's sides. He felt the swell of her chest, the smoothness of her abdomen, the swell of her hips against the mattress. He pushed down into the mattress along her sides and raised his body off hers. He changed the angle of entry and gave himself some leverage. He slid his cock against her mound, pushed deeper. His thrusts picked up a little more speed. Sarah quickly matched the new rhythm. The intensity in the air notched up a level.

Emily kissed Aria's neck and grazed her soft flesh with her teeth. Her hands squeezed Aria's full breasts, pinching her nipples. Aria moaned softly in response, slipping her fingers out of Emily's pussy, and gently rubbing across her clitoris. Emily moaned around Aria's neck. All the while, Emily's eyes were locked on the scene of Ragden thrusting deep into Sarah's tight, engorged pussy. His cock came free, then slid its full length back into her. Emily felt the intensity in the air increasing as Ragden thrust into Sarah faster. Sarah's body rocked with each meeting of their hips. Sarah kept pace with Ragden and rocked her hips in time to his thrusts. Her breath became ragged with the effort. Emily could sense Ragden's climax starting to build and knew from the frantic expression on Sarah's face that she would not be able to contain herself much longer.

Sarah felt her climax looming over her. The pressure and pleasure inside her built and built. Her body shuddered with it, needing that release. She tried to contain it as best she could but knew she did not have long. She rocked her

hips in time to Ragden's thrusts and felt his cock pushing against her cervix with each thrust. Her body rocked and that old familiar ache inside her filled her with incredible pleasure. She felt her eyes starting to roll back into her head and forced herself to refocus on Ragden over her. The sensations threatened to overwhelm her. She reached out and grabbed his ass, clinging to him, pulling him into her.

"Harder... Please," She begged him between gasps for breath. She never wanted it to end.

Ragden continued to thrust deep into Sarah's tight pussy. Each thrust met with the thrust of her hips. Their hips collided, driving his dick deep through her pussy, filling every inch of her. His cock thumped into her cervix. Each impact rocked her body, her breasts rolling. He could feel his climax quickly building and wondered how much longer she could last at this pace. He could feel the energy in the room becoming thick. The love and passion flowed over everything. He glanced over and saw Emily curled around Aria, the two of them enjoying their bodies. It warmed his heart. He smiled at them, then refocused on Sarah. He could feel her energy swirling, her climax building. He closed his eyes and reached out to her. Her energy reacted instantly. Sarah's entire body shuddered. Her climax intensified. His eyes flashed open, and he looked down at her. He watched as she gasped for air, her thrusts becoming almost wild; he could see her barely holding on. He continued to thrust into her, gaining speed and intensity. He could feel her fingers digging into his back, her hands like claws, as she started to lose her sense of reason. He kept thrusting into her, stoked by her energy. Faster. Harder. The pleasure and pressure building.

Emily's eyes widened in surprise as she felt the energy levels in the room suddenly escalate. She could feel the swirling maelstrom inside Sarah. Somehow, her connection with Ragden let her feel it. She could also feel him reaching out to it, stoking it, and responding in kind. She felt it inside her, and through her connection, her own suddenly caught up in it as well. She felt Aria's fingers in her pussy and on her clit, and her body was suddenly climaxing. Her limbs shuddered. Her pussy clenched on Aria's hand.

"Oh, God," she gasped as she felt fluid flowing out of her pussy over Aria's hand. She clenched Aria tightly to her as she rode out the shuddering orgasm through her body, gasping for breath.

Aria felt the sudden change in Emily, and her own body twitched and shuddered with the feel of Emily's climax against her. She felt the waves of energy pulsing through her own body, and closed her eyes, feeling her body responding to it. She felt the waves of pleasure washing over her and wished it were her being filled by Ragden's massive cock, but she felt the sublime pleasure washing over her and smiled, sinking into it.

Sarah felt something change in her. She felt Ragden touching her in a way that she had never felt. She felt his cock thrusting rapidly in and out of her tight pussy, pushing against her cervix, rocking her body, but this was

different. Her mind drifted for a second, as she felt his presence, his passion, his love touching her. Suddenly, her climax intensified. Her eyes flashed open, wide, and staring as her body was suddenly overcome with such an intense climax that she opened her mouth and screamed. Sarah's body went rigid; her legs kicked and locked. Her pussy clenched so tight on Ragden's cock that she felt his cum exploding out of him and filling her up. He gasped at the sudden intensity of her reaction. As his cum exploded into her, she felt her orgasm explode over her again. The waves of pleasure rolled over her. Her muscles shuddered, twitched, and convulsed.

Ragden thrust once more into her, as he felt the orgasm roll over him. His muscles clenched, and cum exploded out of his throbbing cock as he pushed against her cervix. He could feel her fluids flowing down over him. Her body thrashed, twitched, and shuddered against him. He rolled over onto his back, pulled her over on top of him, and cradled her body against his own. He kissed her softly and watched her eyes flutter as he kissed her neck, her ear, her chin, then her lips softly. He waited for her to recover. He felt his cock still throbbing within her. Her pussy still clenched tight on it.

Emily lay against Aria as her orgasm passed. She took deep breaths of air, trying to calm herself. Aria slipped her fingers out of Emily's pussy. Emily gasped at the sensation, then kissed Aria's shoulder tenderly.

"Thank you. That was... very nice," Emily whispered against Aria's back. Aria smiled, happy she could provide some pleasure for Emily. She bathed in the afterglow, feeling the passion and love in the room.

Sarah was only barely aware of what was going on. She could not keep her eyes open. Her orgasm was still riding over her. She could feel her muscles still twitching. She knew she was on top of Ragden, and she tried to snuggle closer to him, feeling his heart beating against her chest. She slipped her arms around him and pulled herself more firmly against him. She felt his love filling her, making her feel incredibly beautiful, desired, and loved. She also felt his cock, throbbing so deep inside her. She could feel the gentle flow of fluids leaking out of her. The feeling was so incredibly pleasureful. She kissed his chest, then tried to speak, her voice hoarse, barely a whisper.

"Thank... thank you."

Ragden cradled Sarah's body against his. He could feel her pulse slowing to a more normal rate. Her breathing became normal. The spasms in her muscles were slowing. Her pussy finally released his cock. He felt it slide around in her, free to move again. He moaned softly against her.

"Of course, Sarah," he replied softly to her. He gently ran a hand through her hair, down her back to rest on her firm ass. He smiled at her, savoring the feeling of her against him. Enjoying being with her, under her, in her.

Sarah looked at Ragden, her breath returning to normal. Her cheeks were still flushed, her eyes bright with lust, her skin glowing with excitement. Then Sarah looked over at Emily and Aria and giggled softly.

"That was... incredible," Sarah said.

Ragden leaned up and kissed Sarah softly on the lips, slipping his tongue into her mouth. He tasted her sweetness. Then he pulled back and smiled at her.

"Yes. It was."

Then he gently sat up, cradling Sarah in his lap. Her body was still mostly limp and weak. He hugged her against him and kissed her forehead. Then he gently lifted her out of his lap. As his cock slipped from her wet folds, she moaned, a look of utter disappointment on her face.

"No. I'm not ready... oooh," She moaned as he sat her next to him on the bed. She pouted at him, then reached out and ran her hands over his throbbing cock, feeling it still slick with her juices. She giggled, then quickly bent over and took it into her mouth and down her throat, gagging softly but pressing her lips against his groin.

"Oh god," he gasped at her suddenness. Then she pulled her head back, popping it out of her mouth, and ran her tongue over the full length of his cock. She licked her juices off. She smiled hungrily, her tongue running over its head. As she stroked it once, squeezing more cum out onto her tongue, which she quickly swallowed.

"I needed that," she said, licking her lips. Then she settled down onto the bed, on her side, looking up at him. Her fingers still playing down the length of his cock, causing it to throb in her hands.

"You are insatiable!" He laughed, then bent down and kissed her softly on the lips.

"I know," she whispered sultrily and winked up at him.

Then he turned to Aria and Emily. He smiled at the two of them, seeing how close they were pulled together. He could see by the look on Emily's face that she had almost recovered from her orgasm. He reached out to Aria and pulled her towards him. Aria smiled. Her eyes hungry as she saw his throbbing cock. He hugged her to him, her hand grasped his cock, stroking its length. He kissed her softly on the lips, then moved her around him next to Sarah.

"Later, love," he said softly to her, comfortingly, "I need to spend some time with Emily."

Aria pouted and snuggled up next to Sarah, who snaked her arms around Aria, pulling the other woman to her chest. Aria rolled over onto her side, letting Sarah spoon around her. Sarah slipped her hands along Aria's side, cupped her firm ass. She snaked her arm down along her thigh to rest there. Aria smiled happily, grasping Sarah's hand on her own. Ragden smiled at the two of them. Then he leaned over and kissed each on the lips softly. Then he turned to Emily laying down on his side and pulled her across the bed to him.

Emily sighed and reached out to Ragden wrapping her arms around him, hugging him to her. She buried her face in his chest, breathing deeply in his scent. Then she pulled her entire body against his, feeling his muscles against hers. His cock pressed against her abdomen. Her legs slipped around his, curling around him, trying to press to as much of his flesh as she could. She

looked up at Ragden's face and smiled, then kissed his lips tenderly. He leaned into her, his tongue slipped into her mouth, their kiss deepening as they pulled each other closer. Their arms wrapped around each other.

Ragden felt Emily's energy, her passion, her love pouring over him. He drank it up, soaked in it, reveled in it. His heart fluttered in his chest. He felt her energy as it washed over him, his energy responding. The air around them felt charged with power, passion, and love. He slid his hands across her back and cupped Emily's ass. He pulled her groin against his, feeling her tight strong muscles, and smiled against her lips. Ragden whispered to Emily, "Would you like to see if we can replicate what happened at lunch today?"

Emily blushed slightly, thinking about what had happened at Sarah's house during lunch. She looked down at Ragden's throbbing cock, reached out, and gently ran her fingers down its length, feeling the heat and energy pulsing off it. She looked over at Sarah cradled around Aria. Sarah's eyes sparkled with curiosity and hunger. Aria still looked burned out but comfortably enjoyed the view.

Emily looked back up at Ragden and smiled softly, her eyes twinkling with desire as she nodded slowly. She did want it again, the feeling had been unbelievable, but the intensity was almost frightening. She placed a hand on his chest softly and kissed his lips tenderly. She could feel the intensity of his heart beating. She closed her eyes and could feel his energy pulsing through the room. She felt her energy mirror his. She reached out and felt her heartbeat start to race as her energy intensified at the proximity. Their energy swirled and pulsed together. She felt the wash of warmth, passion, and love flowing from them across the room.

Aria and Sarah felt the wash of energy, their bodies responding, their heart rates increasing, knowing they were about to witness something amazing. Sarah licked her lips and found her hand sliding down across Aria's stomach to her wet folds, gently dipping her fingers in. Aria moaned softly, her hands reaching behind to cup Sarah's ass and pull her against her back.

Ragden felt Emily's energy touch his and felt his body respond. His heart started to beat faster. His cock throbbed hard under her touch. He opened his eyes and looked down at her and licked his lips, then he kissed her passionately and slipped his tongue between her lips as he rolled over on top of her. Emily moaned softly against his lips, as he slid between her legs. His cock throbbed against her abdomen, a small amount of precum leaking out onto her. Where it touched her, her skin tingled, and she shivered at it. Ragden slid his hands over Emily's ass and around the insides of her thighs. She moaned again at the sensation of his touch, her skin tingling everywhere he touched her. He slid his knees up under her thighs. His cock rubbed against her sensitive folds, pushing against her clitoris. She reached out and grabbed his back, trying to pull her against him. Her hips ground against him. Ragden leaned down and kissed her passionately as he rolled his hips against her, his cock sliding through her folds. The head of it slipped between her

lips. Emily groaned, pulled against him harder as the head of it pushed against her entrance.

Emily moaned softly, feeling the heat and pressure pressed against the entrance into her vagina. She rocked her hips gently and felt it slip inside her. She shivered at the feeling of it. Her vagina clenched tightly against it. She bit her lip as she looked up at Ragden, seeing the look of pure pleasure in his eyes. His desire and hunger for her. The look on his face made her feel so incredibly desired, cherished, and loved. She never wanted it to end. Her eyes slipped closed as she felt his throbbing cock slowly sliding deeper into her. The pressure and pleasure of it slowly filled every inch of her. It slid deeper and deeper. She felt his energy mixing with hers and felt a fullness at that. She moaned softly as she felt the head of his cock gently press against her cervix, striking that deepest part of her. Emily opened her eyes and looked up at Ragden. She saw the look of ecstasy on his face. She knew he loved how her body made him feel, and she could see and feel his love for her pouring over her. She rolled her hips against his, pushed against him, felt his cock push against her cervix, and she moaned again at the sensation.

Ragden gently caressed her inner thighs, felt the muscles flexing and squeezing against him. Her legs wrapped tightly around his waist, pulling him against her. His cock pressed firmly against her cervix. He leaned down and kissed her passionately on the lips, feeling the intensity filling the air. His skin tingled with the rush of energy filling the air. His tongue slipped inside her mouth, exploring her, tasting her, feeling the rush of her. He gently slid his cock backward out of her, then slid it back in. Savoring how tight she clenched against him. His cock throbbed deep inside her. He pressed it against her cervix, marveling at the pleasure of it. Their kiss broke, and she moaned softly against his lips, her back arching, pressing his dick against her cervix with even more pressure. Her hips rolled, gently sliding along his cock. A shudder ran down his back at the feel of it. Then she clenched on him again, so hard he gasped. His eyes opened, and saw her wry smile as her muscles relaxed and his cock pressed against her cervix again. She bit her lip, her hands pulled against his back as she clenched hard on him again.

Sarah put her chin on Aria's shoulder, watching Ragden and Emily, her pussy clenched and released as she watched. As they built a slow rhythm, Sarah found her hips moving in time to their gentle thrusts against each other. She realized that what she was watching was not just two people fucking, but two people deeply in love with each other and the physical manifestation of that love. Her heart swelled. All she had ever wanted was sex, and to get fucked. The urge for it was a primal thing inside her. Watching Emily and Ragden, she realized she wanted to feel that too. She smiled to herself, knowing that if she asked him, he would give it to her, because he loved her, and a tear slipped down her cheek. The realization slowly dawned on her that she had stumbled into something so much more amazing than she had ever anticipated.

Aria felt Sarah's shuddering breath on her back. She wondered at it briefly as she slid her hand along Sarah's thigh against her own. She felt the other woman's love and shuddered at the sensation of the emotion filling the room. Her own heart swelled with it. She placed her hand on top of Sarah's along her wet pussy folds, feeling the other woman's gentle touch on her. Aria's body shuddered softly at the feel of it, the love of it. Aria smiled to herself, feeling content and loved.

Emily felt the pressure and pleasure as it started to build within her. She closed her eyes and bit her lip, feeling the energy of it filling the room. She could feel Sarah's energy changing subtly, some change coming over the other woman. She could also feel Aria's contentment. Emily smiled to herself. Ragden's energy pulsed like a sun before them, pouring rays of passion and love over them. They all drank it up, feeling their hearts swell. Emily rolled her hips, sliding herself along his thick cock, buried so deep inside her. She clenched her vagina on it and felt it throb inside her. The pressure continued to build within her. She looked up at Ragden and saw the love on his face, the depths of it in his eyes. Then she felt him slowly withdrawing his throbbing cock from her pussy, only to slide it back in. She moaned as it filled her again, then out and back in to caress her cervix again.

Ragden reached down and gently grasped Emily's incredible breasts, feeling her heartbeat beneath his fingertips, as he ran his thumbs over her nipples, feeling them go taught. He smiled down at her, slowly sliding his cock the full length of her, out, then back in to caress her cervix. She rolled her hips in time to his slow thrust, meeting him in the middle; his cock bumped against her cervix with a little more pressure. He felt the pressure and pleasure building inside them. He continued at a slow pace, gently stoking that fire within them. Emily's hands slipped around his back to hold his arms, felt the muscles flex gently as he squeezed her breasts in time to each gentle thrust into her. Emily's eyes slipped closed with each meeting of their groins, his cock bumping into her cervix, causing her to gasp softly.

Emily felt the energy surging through the room, but it did not have the same edge it did earlier that day. It was amazing and felt wonderful, but it was not the same. She felt nervous about asking Ragden for the same thing, but at the same time, she wanted to feel that incredible release again. Amazingly, her ass had not been sore, much as she had expected it would be. The more she thought about it, the more she could feel the muscles in her ass start to clench at the expectation of his cock filling her. She shivered at the memory of it. She wanted it.

Emily bit her lip, planted her feet on the mattress behind Ragden, and lifted her groin off his. She moaned loudly as his cock slid out of her. She bit her lip again, looking at his surprised expression. Her pussy ached from the loss of his thick meat. She looked at it hungrily, wanting it back inside her. She wanted to clench her pussy around it, feel the fullness inside her, but right at this moment; she wanted it in her ass so much she could not wait. Emily

reached down and wrapped her hand around his throbbing cock, her fluids making it slippery. It throbbed in her hands as she pointed it at herself and lowered her hips against it. She watched the surprised look on his face as his eyes slipped closed, feeling her flesh pushing against him. She slid it around against her folds, trying to find the right spot. Then she found it, the tip of his cock pressed to her asshole. She gasped at the pressure. The anticipation built, and her body shook with it. She pushed her hips down, while holding his cock steady and felt the tip of it entering her.

"Oh, God," she moaned loudly, as she felt her asshole stretching, the pain of it causing her to sweat and grit her teeth. She could not wait; she had to have it in her. She pushed harder, feeling the tip working its way into her. Then it suddenly popped into her, and she gasped loudly, "Holy fuck!"

Emily opened her eyes and looked up at Ragden. The look of painful pleasure she felt echoed on his face. His eyes were wide looking down at her. She shuddered under that hungry gaze. She reached up and caressed his face, gently cupping his chin. He leaned into her hand, kissing her softly. She nodded slowly to him, as she rolled her hips, sliding him a hair deeper into her. Both shuddered from the ecstasy of it.

Ragden moaned softly as her ass clenched on the head of his cock where it had slipped into her. She was so incredibly tight. The pressure within him compounded. He ached from the desire to slide it deeper into her, but he resisted. He gently caressed her breasts, then leaned down and kissed her on the lips passionately, slipping his tongue in to taste her desire. Her body shuddered under his touch. Every muscle clenched. He drew a shuddering breath and whispered against her lips. "Emily, my love, are you sure this is what you want?"

Emily bit her lip, tears in her eyes. The pain and pleasure swirled within her. The pressure building, she nodded vigorously. "Oh, God," she breathed, "fill my ass. oh, God. Please."

Sarah looked on, unable to tear her eyes from the spectacle before her. The intensity of it washed over her, making her body shiver with it. She felt her ass clench; her muscles shuddered with the imagined feeling of Ragden's massive cock sliding into her. She did not think she could handle it, but she suddenly wanted it. Craved it. Had to have it. But first, she wanted to watch Emily take it. She had seen Aria take it, and she shivered at the feel of Aria's body under her hands as he had filled her. She knew that she would have to ask him for that someday, but for now, she was content to watch. She shivered again, watching Emily begging for him to fill her ass. Sarah continued to rest her chin on Aria's shoulder, pulling Aria's body against her, feeling her snuggle against her.

Aria watched with rapt attention, licking her lips. She felt her muscles ache from the feel of Ragden filling her ass in the very same way. The position had been different, but the result was the same. She felt his cum in her bowels and smiled. The sensation of it had been more than she had been prepared for,

but something she would never forget. She felt her muscles clenching as Ragden slipped his cock a little deeper into Emily. She wanted to trade places with her, to feel that massive dick filling her again. She shuddered and shivered at the thought of it. Aria smiled as Sarah pulled her body back against her. She felt Sarah's firm nipples pressed against her back and sighed, contentedly. It was so soft, so comforting. She felt loved and cherished. Sarah's fingers slipped through her wet folds, and she moaned softly, her eyes fixed on the sight of Emily and Ragden.

Ragden rolled his hips forward, slowly, gently sliding his cock deeper into Emily's bowels. Emily moaned loudly. Her body clenched against Ragden's. He could feel her ass squeezing around his cock, so tight, so hard. He felt like he was about to burst. Then she would relax, and he would slide another inch, and she would clench again. He took a deep shuddering breath; his body shivered with the ecstasy of her. Then pushed another inch into her. She moaned loudly again. Her body shuddered. He paused and kissed her again, passionately; her response was almost manic, her tongue swirling around his chaotically, reflecting how close she was to climaxing. He could sense her on the verge of losing it.

Ragden closed his eyes and reached out to her energy. It was a wild chaotic maelstrom that threatened to overwhelm her. He tried to calm it, but instead felt himself getting caught up in it.

"Oh God," he breathed as his body shuddered. He tried to contain it through sheer force of will and only marginally succeeded. He felt her racing pulse, her intense desire like a storm surge near to bursting through the dams of her self-control. He tried to reinforce them, with his love and passion. The interaction was like adding kerosene to a wildfire.

Emily cried out and bucked her hips against his, forcing his cock deep into her. She cried out again as his hips slid against her. His cock filled her bowels. Ragden felt Emily's dams bursting, her climax running rampant across her, and consuming him in the process. He could sense the dark cloud looming in his psyche and had only a heartbeat to react. He felt Emily's presence beside him, adding her strength and love to the smashing blow he gave the cloud, sending it into the recesses of his existence. The cloud was gone; her climax rolled over him. He pulled her tight against him, as he withdrew and thrust his cock into her. He drew back and thrust into her again. After the second thrust, she rolled her hips away as he withdrew, then rolled forward to meet him. The impact rocked both of their bodies. Both gasping, their bodies twitched and shuddered with intense feeling as their climax deepened and spread. The air of the room crackled with the power of it.

Ragden could feel the sensation of ants crawling on his skin. He looked down and saw the blue electric sparks running over his skin again. He saw them rolling up his legs, and down his abdomen toward his groin. He looked at Emily and saw her eyes wide as they both prepared for what would come next. Ragden felt the sparks rolling through his body, as they suddenly ran the

length of his cock, and burst into Emily. He felt their discharge, along with an explosion of cum from his throbbing cock. He cried out as the pleasure of it consumed him. Emily cried out as the energy surged through her body.

The energy surged through her abdomen; the sparks rolled through her body to collect on her skin and roll back down into her abdomen. Emily felt the energy collecting in her abdomen, building, and building. Then she felt the charges of energy sinking through her body into her uterus and down into her pussy. With Ragden's next thrust, they leaped through her groin into his, causing her to cry out with the force of it. She felt her juices flowing as her muscles convulsed. Her pussy and ass clenched together. She felt every inch of Ragden's throbbing cock as it slid faster in and out of her ass. She opened her eyes, and looked through the tears down at Ragden's body, watching the sparks pass up his legs, popping up along the firm muscles of his abdomen. She tried to brace herself but was wholly unprepared for the force of them bursting out of his cock into her again.

Ragden cried out again, as the energy surged through his cock and deep into Emily's bowels again. Then his body went rigid as his loins once again shot loads of cum up into her. This time, the energy flowed through her whole body and rolled out of her in a wave that rocked the entire bed. She cried out again, as it flowed out of her, rolling across the room.

Aria and Sarah stared with wide eyes as the wave of energy rolled into them. Both cried out as their bodies climaxed with the force of it. Sarah shuddered and twitched, pulling Aria against her so hard her breasts hurt from the force of it. She could feel her fluids suddenly flowing out of her pussy, soaking her legs. Her pussy and ass clenched and released of their own volition. Aria felt the wave crash over her, her body shuddering and twitching as she felt her juices flowing, soaking Sarah's hand on her mound. She moaned at the feeling of it.

Ragden collapsed on top of Emily; his muscles gave out, his body spent. He sucked air in greedily, trying to catch his breath. Emily moaned in pleasure beneath him. Her arms circled him, weakly embracing him.

Aria and Sarah lay panting on the bed, their hearts racing. Their bodies still quivered with the aftershocks of the intense orgasm that had overtaken them all. Aria's pussy was dripping with her juices, and her clit throbbed with need. Her heart pounded with desire. Sarah's pussy was glistening with her release, her face flushed with pleasure and satisfaction. They both looked up at Ragden and Emily, who lay entwined together on top of each other, their bodies in a tangled heap of sweaty limbs and heaving chests.

Aria gazed at Sarah, her eyes burning with lust and admiration. Her voice was breathless and hoarse, "That was ..."

"Fucking AMAZING!" Sarah exclaimed, breathless. Then she giggled at the sound of her voice. Her body ached with a bone-deep weariness, but she felt overcome with the joy and pleasure of the moment. She wanted to dance for joy but knew she did not have the energy now. Sarah leaned against Aria

and kissed her shoulder softly. Then she giggled again as she looked at Ragden and Emily, neither of whom moved much.

Love & Nature

CHAPTER 16

Emily giggled softly, feeling the shuddering within her muscles subsiding. She looked over at Sarah and smiled. She reached out to Sarah and Aria. Sarah reached out and grasped her hand, squeezing her fingers. Aria blushed and put her hand in theirs as well. Ragden slowly lifted his head and looked over at Sarah and Aria. He kissed Emily softly on the lips, his heart still thundering in his chest. He tenderly reached out and put his hand on top of all of theirs. At his touch, an electric charge passed through all of them. All the women moaned as Ragden gasped softly, then he wrapped his hand around all of theirs.

"I love you all so much," he whispered, his voice carrying just enough to be heard by all of them. Emily blushed and kissed his cheek, smiling.

Sarah giggled and smiled, whispering back, "I love you too."

Aria whimpered as tears spilled from her eyes. Overcome with the moment, she sighed softly, "I love you too... God, I love all of you."

Ragden turned his head and kissed Emily on the lips tenderly, feeling his muscles starting to recover. He then looked over at Sarah and Aria again and smiled. He spoke softly, "Shall we go down and see if dinner is ready?"

At his words, Sarah suddenly felt ravenously hungry. Her stomach grumbled loudly. She giggled and nodded, pulling Aria against her tightly in response. Aria, too, realized she was hungry, her body responding with a rumble of its own. She also nodded. Emily smiled and kissed Ragden's cheek again, nodding against his flesh. She did not want to release him, though. She could feel his massive cock in her bowels, and she did not want that to end. She could dimly feel the ache of her sore muscles, but she savored the feeling of it. Raden turned to Emily and searched her expression, quickly realizing what she was thinking. He gently ground his hips against her groin, pushing his big dick deeper into her bowels. Emily clutched him tightly, pulling his body against her, moaning in pleasure at the feel of him pushing into her.

Ragden kissed her again, then broke away and spoke softly, "I know love.

This feels amazing, but we need to eat."

Emily groaned, not wanting this incredible sensation to end. She knew she would get to experience it again. She knew that Ragden enjoyed being inside her as much as she enjoyed him being there. It made her feel so cherished, desired, and loved. She could part, knowing she would get to sleep by his side, to feel his presence in her life and her body. She smiled, feeling his love surrounding her. She closed her eyes, and felt him there with her, surrounding her and inside her. It was the most marvelous feeling in the universe. She smiled and nodded, her nose brushing his face.

Emily answered quietly, "Yes, love, I'm hungry. Let's get some food."

Aria smiled at the scene, knowing she had witnessed something truly incredible. Her body ached from it; every muscle felt exhausted. At the same time, she felt the love washing over her, and she felt content and happier than she could ever remember feeling before. Tears welled up in her eyes, as she realized that this was what it was like to be genuinely loved, and in love. She pulled Sarah tighter against her, feeling the comfort of her presence against her body. Sarah giggled and kissed Aria's shoulder, her ear and her neck. Aria sighed in pleasure at her touch. Sarah smiled at Aria, enjoying the feel of her naked body against hers.

Sarah watched Emily and Ragden, not wanting to get up, but knowing that this would end soon. She also knew that this was a beginning, not an ending. There would be more of that, she was sure.

Aria's blue eyes sparkled as she murmured, "Mm... Yes, let's go down and eat."

Ragden turned to look Emily in the eyes. He smiled as he spoke softly, "Shower first?"

Emily giggled and blushed, remembering the last time they had gone down this road. Then she felt his cock softening within her and moaned. She rocked her hips against him, feeling it slide inside of her. Then she clenched the muscles of her ass around his cock and felt it throb within her. She smiled at his expression of pleasure.

"Stay hard in me... please," she whispered.

Ragden laughed softly, an edge of desire in his voice. Then he nodded slowly, and she felt his cock throb and swell within her. She closed her eyes as she felt it filling her bowels again. She was not sure how he did that, but she loved it. She bit her lip, as she rocked her hips, feeling the full size of it slide in and out of her. Then she raised her head and kissed him on the lips passionately, tasting his strength, his passion and his love. She sighed in pleasure against his lips.

"Okay... Okay," Emily sighed softly, pushing Ragden up off her, "Let's go take a shower and get some food..."

Ragden chuckled again, slowly raising himself off Emily. She looked up at him with a soft pleading look in her eyes. He sensed that there was indeed a part of her that did not want to leave this bed or this room, but he could feel

the hunger in him. Ragden gently rolled his hips back from Emily. His dick slowly slid from her bowels, from her ass, until it slipped out. A stream of fluids followed it. Emily moaned loudly. Her body shuddered at his withdrawal. She smiled serenely and sighed.

Ragden turned and slowly crawled towards Aria and Sarah. Both reached out to him as he crawled over them to the edge of the bed. Aria ran her fingers over his cock, feeling Emily's fluids still there, running her fingers the length of it. She marveled at its firmness, the pulse of his life within it. Sarah watched him with a hungry look in her eyes, licking her lips. Ragden chuckled and kissed both girls on the lips as he crawled over them. He lowered himself to the floor and stood, stretching his muscles.

Sarah kissed Aria's shoulder one last time, then scrambled off the bed. She dropped to her knees in front of Ragden and slipped his cock into her mouth before he could say or do anything about it. Ragden gasped softly as Sarah sucked the length of his cock down her throat, her tongue swirling around the base of it. Her lips gently hit his groin. Then she withdrew and gently stroked his cock, squeezing out any cum she could get. Then she pulled it out of her mouth and smiled up at Ragden.

Aria slipped off the bed and spied Sarah at Ragden's feet. She dropped gently to her knees next to Sarah and nudged her softly, "Can I... Can I taste it?"

Sarah turned to her, smiled, and nodded. "Of course."

Aria gently grasped Ragden's big dick and slipped the head of it into her mouth. Ragden moaned softly as she sucked on the tip, unable to get it down her throat. She tried a couple of times but could not get it. Then she pulled it out of her mouth and looked at Sarah questioningly, "How... How do you do that?"

Sarah laughed lustily, grabbed his cock from Aria's hands, and slipped it down her throat in one massive gulp. Then she pulled it from her mouth and giggled. "Practice. I can show you later if you want..."

Aria and Sarah both looked up at Ragden who moaned softly at their attentions. Aria smiled softly, turned to Sarah, and nodded, "I'd like that."

Emily slipped off the bed and stood next to Ragden, slipping one arm around his waist as she looked down at Sarah and Aria. She giggled softly, then hugged Ragden, burying her face in his side. Then she leaned up and kissed him softly on the lips. He turned to look at her and smiled.

"Shower?" Emily asked softly, "Dinner?"

Ragden laughed and nodded. He reached down and pulled Aria and Sarah to their feet, hugging them around him. His hands slipped down to cup their asses. Each sighed in turn. Emily giggled again. Sarah giggled in response, and Aria smiled. Ragden slowly disentangled himself, stepped up, and opened the door. He walked across the hall and into the bathroom, turning on the light.

Aria and Sarah followed Ragden across the hall, holding hands. Ragden went into the bathroom, opened the shower, and started the water. Then he

turned as the two women followed him. Then he walked back to the doorway and waited for Emily to follow, holding his hand out for her. She walked across and took his hand. He pulled her into the room and against him, softly kissing her on the lips.

"Oh wow," Sarah gasped behind them, "This shower is amazing."

Sarah walked into the shower, pulling Aria in behind her. Emily looked past Ragden and giggled as the two women got under the water and started rinsing off. Ragden turned to watch as Sarah grabbed the soap and started lathering Aria down, paying special attention to her chest, then slipping the bar of soap between Aria's legs and across her pussy lips. Sarah giggled as Aria moaned in response. Then Sarah spun Aria around and lathered up her back, slipping her hands between Aria's ass cheeks and slipping a finger into Aria's asshole. Aria leaned against the wall, moaning as Sarah fingered her ass, giggling.

Ragden's dick hardened watching them. Emily reached down and gently stroked his cock, causing him to sigh softly. Sarah turned and saw Ragden and Emily standing outside the shower. She reached out to them and beckoned for them to join her. Ragden opened the door and stepped back as Emily walked in to join them.

"Little tight for four," Ragden said, his eyes sparkling as he watched them soaping each other down, "I'll just watch from here."

Emily and Sarah pouted sadly at Ragden, then turned back to Aria, who was rinsing the soap off her body. Then Aria grabbed the soap, lathered up her hands, and started to work down Sarah's back. Sarah stuck out her backside into Aria's groin. Aria laughed and slid her hand through Sarah's ass cheeks, and ran her fingers through her folds, slipping her fingers up into her pussy. Sarah looked at Ragden, licked her lips, and blew him a kiss, then sighed with pleasure as Aria gently fingered her. Then Aria stuck a couple fingers into Sarah's ass, and Sarah clenched and darted forward, pulling off Aria's hand. Aria laughed coyly and turned her attention to Emily. Sarah moaned softly as she gently rubbed her ass.

Aria soaped up Emily's chest, then let the water rinse the soap off. Emily sighed softly, as Aria licked her nipples and slid a hand between her legs, running her fingers through Emily's slippery folds. Then Sarah walked up next to Emily and soaped up her back, sliding her hands up and down Emily's back. Emily sighed in pleasure as the other two women massaged her tired muscles and worked the soap in. Once Sarah had rinsed herself clean, she stepped over to the door, pushed it open, and reached out towards Ragden.

Ragden raised an eyebrow as Sarah grabbed his hand and pulled him into the shower. Aria and Emily giggled as Sarah pulled him in. Ragden sighed as the hot water cascaded over his face and ran down his back. The women all lathered up their hands and proceeded to rub soap into his arms, chest, and back at once. He closed his eyes and relaxed into the feeling of six hands working his muscles at the same time. Then a pair of hands ran over his

buttocks, another went over his groin, while the third went down his thighs.

His eyes closed, Ragden did not see which one of them it was, but one of the women pushed him against the wall while another took his cock into their mouth. He moaned softly as another licked his balls. He opened his eyes just as Sarah took his cock down her throat, her lips kissing his groin. She quickly backed off, winking at him as she giggled. Then Aria tried to do the same but failed to completely relax her throat and choked on the head of his cock. Emily giggled while watching. Then Aria backed off, and Emily took a turn, easily swallowing his entire cock and kissing his groin. She flexed her throat on his cock, squeezing him in a way he did not entirely think possible as she bobbed her throat on him. Then she backed off and took a big gulp of air. She smiled up at Ragden as Sarah nudged her and gave her a big thumbs up, obviously impressed. Emily giggled shyly.

Ragden reached down and pulled Aria to her feet, kissing her softly on the lips. Then he turned her and gently patted her firm ass towards the shower door. Aria pouted, then stepped out, grabbed a towel, and started drying herself off. Then Ragden reached down for Sarah's hand. She grabbed his hand and put it in Emily's hand. Sarah grabbed his cock again and deep-throated him.

"Oh god," he groaned as she took his cock down her throat and tried to replicate what Emily had done. It was not the same, but remarkably close. Sarah pulled back, coughed once, then giggled to herself. Emily stood, giggled at Sarah and then pulled herself against Ragden and kissed him softly on the lips. Then she turned and waggled her ass at Ragden, who cupped her firm ass and squeezed it playfully as she stepped out, grabbed a towel, and started drying herself off.

Then Sarah stood and wrapped herself around Ragden, kissing him passionately, slipping her tongue into his mouth, and squeezing her body against him as hard as she could. Ragden thumped against the wall hard, his cock throbbing against Sarah's abdomen. Sarah broke off from the kiss, giggling. She turned and planted her ass against his cock, and rubbed it up and down, moaning softly. Ragden reached out to caress her hips, just as she grabbed his cock and backed her ass into it, his cock slipping into her asshole.

"Oh, God... Oh, God, that's so much cock in my ass," Sarah squealed as she slid back against Ragden, forcing his cock up her ass as she moaned. She rocked her body against his, sliding his cock in and out of her ass, while his hands clutched at her. Both Aria and Emily stood with their backs to the vanity, watching in shock as Sarah slid herself back and forth on Ragden's cock. His eyes were squeezed shut, clearly enjoying the moment as she stepped back fully against him, sliding his cock fully into her bowels. She gasped and moaned, writhing with his cock in her ass. Then she stepped forward, off his cock. She moaned loudly as it slid free. She spun on the spot, dropped to her knees and gave his cock a little kiss on the head, then stood and stepped out of the shower. Ragden stood there in shock.

Aria and Emily looked at each other, their eyes wide, after watching Sarah walk out. Aria hesitated for a moment, then turned to Emily and whispered, "Do you think... I could try that too?" Emily bit her lip nervously, looking at Aria and then glancing over at Ragden, who was still standing there, stunned by what had just happened.

Emily turned to Aria and whispered, "I'm sure you could ask..."

Sarah practically danced her way out of the shower; she was so excited and happy. She walked up to Emily, kissed her on the lips, then turned to Aria and kissed her on the lips. Then she licked her fingers and slid them up her ass, and moaned. Then she withdrew her fingers, licked them clean, and sighed.

"Nope, not the same. Nothing quite like Ragden's dick up my ass." She shivered and wiggled her ass at Ragden. "You are welcome to fuck my ass any time you want." With that, she grabbed a towel and dried herself off, nonchalantly shaking her ass for Ragden.

Ragden stood in the shower, his mind reeling from Sarah's sudden actions. Then he gained his senses, finished rinsing himself off, turned off the water, and stepped out of the shower. He closed the door, grabbed the last towel, and dried himself off. Ragden shook his head, watching Sarah. Then he opened a drawer and pulled out three brushes, handing one to each of the women. Then he grabbed a comb and quickly ran it through his hair. Then he dropped it into the drawer and reached for the robes. He noted that instead of the two he had seen here last night, there were four. He pulled each down and turned to the women.

"Mm... thank you," Aria said softly, her voice barely above a whisper as she accepted the robe from Ragden. She wrapped it around her, tying it securely, hiding her nakedness from view. She glanced at Sarah, who was now toweling off.

As Sarah finished drying herself, Ragden stepped up behind her, holding the robe open for her. Sarah slipped her arms into the holes, and pulled it around her, then turned and wrapped herself around Ragden, reaching around behind him and grasping his bare ass. She kissed him passionately, squeezing herself against him, her bare flesh against his softening cock, which throbbed against her. She giggled against his lips and pulled back just enough to look down at his cock. Then she looked up at him hungrily.

"I think your cock is hungry for me... I'm hungry for it..."

With that, she dropped to her knees and slipped it into her mouth. Still soft, it easily slipped down her throat as she sucked on it fiercely. Ragden moaned as his cock throbbed in her mouth, growing larger and firmer. Sarah's eyes widened as his cock went fully erect in her mouth, its length going down her throat. She slid her mouth back off, licked the head, then kissed the tip. Then she stood, pulled her robe around her, tying it shut under her firm breasts. She smiled and winked at Ragden. He shuddered, then stepped over to Emily, who stood blushing and giggling. Ragden held the robe open for her, and she slipped her arms in. Ragden stepped forward and wrapped it

Love & Nature

around her body, tying it around her waist from behind. She leaned back against him, feeling his body through the robe.

"Thanks, lover," she whispered huskily into his ear.

Ragden secured his robe around him, tying it neatly around his waist. His cock pressed against the front. He tried to reposition the robe to try to hide it but failed to and sighed as the three women giggled at him. Then he stepped to the door and pulled it open. He held the door for his three perfect women and smiled at them.

Aria and Sarah giggled, their faces flushed with amusement as they saw Ragden struggle to properly position his robe, trying to hide his throbbing member from view. They could not help but find it endearing, knowing full well that it was impossible to conceal such a large and impressive piece of equipment. As Ragden opened the door for them, they walked through towards him, Aria's hand lightly trailing across Sarah's ass, Sarah's hand gripping Emily's hip possessively, leading the way.

"So, where to first?" Aria asked, her voice playful and teasing.

Ragden laughed, his heart swelling as he watched the three of them walk. "Downstairs to the dining room... I'm guessing Jennifer has something cooking for us already..."

As the three stepped through the door, he walked out, letting the door slip mostly closed behind him, as he turned off the light. Then he stepped past the women, leading the way. He went down the stairs, through the foyer, and across the living room into the dining room. Emily's hand snaked into his as he walked through the living room. She squeezed his hand and smiled as he turned to look at her. The warmth of her at his side made him feel complete.

"There you guys are!" Jennifer called from the kitchen as the four of them came walking in. She gestured to the table where six places were set. "Take a seat; dinner will be ready in a moment."

"I hope everyone likes pasta," Michael's voice boomed through the dining room as he came walking in from the pantry. He was wearing a pair of sweatpants and no shirt. He smiled broadly at the women as he walked over to introduce himself.

Ragden stepped forward and introduced Aria and Sara. Michael took each woman's hand in his and kissed their knuckles softly. Aria blushed, her cheeks turning crimson while Sarah giggled, whispering to Aria.

Michael smiled, his voice deeply masculine, sending a shiver through Sarah's body, "Oh, I do wear shirts, darling, just not often at home." He winked at Sarah, who blushed darkly. Then he turned and pulled Ragden into a warm embrace. He also reached out and pulled Emily against him, in a warm hug. He spoke softly to her, "Good to see you again, my dear. Feeling better, I hope?"

Emily blushed and smiled at him, feeling a deep affection for his concern for her well-being. She sighed softly in his embrace, "Yes. Thank you." He released her and stepped towards the kitchen to help Jennifer with dinner.

Ragden took Emily's hand and pulled her against him, hugging her. Then he turned to Sarah and Aria and asked, "Where would you like to sit?"

Sarah walked seductively up to Ragden, shaking her hips with each step, her eyes locked on his. Then she threw herself against him, wrapping her arms around his neck and pulling his head down to her lips. She whispered huskily into his lips, "I don't care where I sit as long as I can sit my ass down on that fat cock and feel it in my bowels."

Jennifer and Michael burst out laughing in the kitchen. Sarah blushed darkly and giggled, then kissed Ragden softly on the lips before releasing him and taking a step back, still blushing darkly. Emily laughed while Aria blushed and giggled softly. Sarah pulled up a chair and sank into it, pulling Aria into the seat next to her. She buried her face in her hands, giggling softly to herself, "I'm so embarrassed, I could die right now."

Ragden walked around the other side of the table, with Emily in tow, and took the seat opposite Sarah. Emily slipped into the chair next to him. Emily squeezed his hand gently and smiled at him. Ragden brought her hand to his lips and softly kissed it. At that point, Michael and Jennifer came out of the kitchen carrying steaming plates of food. There was a pile of pasta, with spinach and chicken in an Alfredo sauce with a side of broccoli. The smell was heavenly. Plates were placed in front of Sarah, Aria, Emily, and Ragden. Then Jennifer and Michael went back to grab their plates. They sat at opposite ends of the table. Sarah and Aria looked from one end of the table to the other, waiting for some clue as to what the protocol was. Michael looked at them and laughed, "Please. Dig in."

Jennifer smiled at their confusion, "We don't do grace, or give thanks before eating. The only thanks you need to give in this house is to the person who cooked your food."

Jennifer nodded to Michael and spoke softly, seductively, her voice full of innuendo and sex, "Michael, thank you for preparing this feast that I will devour and love every minute. Your sauce fills me with such joy, I just cannot get enough..." She noisily slurped some of the sauce off her fork and winked at Michael. Michael laughed. It was a deep sound that vibrated around the room, causing everyone to shiver slightly as it curled down their backs, caressing them. Everyone in the room felt their arousal caressed by the sound.

Michael's eyes twinkled as his voice filled the room seductively caressing them, "Ah, my darling Jennifer, with your hands, our meat has been prepared and we give thanks for your love and company."

Then he laughed again, and Jennifer joined in with him. Ragden, Emily, Sarah, and Aria looked from Michael to Jennifer, feeling the sexual energy in the air. All their hearts beat a little faster. Michael and Jennifer returned to their meals as if nothing had happened. Sarah giggled to herself and continued eating. Slowly, the other three did the same. Then Jennifer set her fork down and looked at Sarah, who felt her soft gaze and blinked around a mouthful of food as Jennifer addressed her.

"My dear Sarah, never be embarrassed to express what you really want. Your timing and place were extremely amusing, but to express what you want is a gift of incredible value. You will never be genuinely happy if you cannot feel free to ask for what you want. Never be embarrassed about that."

Sarah blushed, blinked hard, then spoke softly, "Thank you... I will try to remember that." Jennifer smiled and resumed eating.

They finished eating their meal in silence. The food was simply too good and nourishing for any conversation to take place. As they finished their food, Jennifer and Michael gathered up the plates and carried them into the kitchen to clean. Ragden got up and joined them, leaving the three women to sit at the table and discuss the day's activities, and their plans for the night. Jennifer came walking back to the table, gently putting a hand on Aria's shoulder, "Aria, I spoke with your mom as you asked me to. Everything is fine; she knows you are here and is not expecting you home tonight." Jennifer turned to Emily and Sarah including them in her next statement, "You three are all welcome to spend the night. Unless you have some pressing need to go home, we would be overjoyed to have you stay with us tonight."

Aria sat quietly at the table, her heart pounding in her chest. She felt a wave of relief wash over her, knowing that she did not have to worry about getting in trouble for spending the night. She felt a newfound sense of freedom, and happiness, knowing that she could fully indulge in her desires without having to hide anything from her parents. She felt a warm glow of happiness fill her entire being.

"Thank you so much, Jennifer. That means a lot to me. I appreciate your taking care of things like that."

Aria turned to Emily and Sarah, smiling at them warmly, feeling incredibly grateful for their presence in her life.

Jennifer turned to Sarah and Emily, and she smiled warmly, "And what about you, Emily, Sarah? Are you young ladies staying as well?"

Sarah nodded vigorously, "Oh, I'm not going anywhere..."

Emily smiled shyly, as she nodded softly, "I'll stay. Thank you, Jennifer, for making us welcome in your home, and letting us stay with Ragden."

Jennifer smiled warmly as she turned to Emily, "Oh, darlin', you know you are always welcome in our home. It is you I need to thank for taking a chance with my son. I know he is a little strange sometimes, but he has a big heart."

Jennifer turned to Sarah and Aria, taking their hands in hers, "I need to thank all of you for taking a chance with him. It means so much to Michael and I that you all decided to spend the time to enjoy his company and his... gifts."

Jennifer winked at them, a knowing smile on her lips. Then she took a deep breath," Please enjoy your night here. I am sad to say that we will not be in town tomorrow night. We have a family trip this weekend to the beach. I would invite you to join us, but it is a family thing. We will reach out to you on Sunday about the following week."

Ragden came back to the table, Michael following close behind. Michael spoke softly, filling the space with warmth and affection, "I am sorry you women cannot join us this weekend, but it is the Spring Equinox, and that is a special date for our family."

All three girls slumped in their chairs, sad that they would not be able to spend the weekend with Ragden and his family. They had been so caught up in the activities of the evening, that they had given no thought as to what would come next. Michael spoke softly, "Oh, come now. Don't be glum. You still have an evening together, and whatever you get up to in school tomorrow. Though, I would ask that you pay attention to your classes."

Michael wrapped one arm around Jennifer's shoulders, pulling her body along his side. She smiled at him. Then he placed a hand on Sarah's shoulder and winked at her. Sarah giggled shyly, looking up at him. She felt the warmth of his touch, and her body relaxed, feeling his love and affection wash over her.

"Go... have fun. Just don't stay up too late."

CHAPTER 17

Ragden stepped around the table to take Emily's hand. As she stood, he pulled her into a hug, kissing her softly on the lips. He then turned to Aria and Sarah and spoke softly.

"It has been a long day. I do not know about the rest of you, but I could use a good night's sleep. Shall we retire for the night?"

Emily buried her face in the robe around Ragden and snuggled against him. Sarah giggled and grabbed Aria's hand in hers, then turned to Ragden and nodded. Aria looked from Sarah to Emily and then at Ragden, then nodded as well. Sarah stood and pulled Aria to her feet with her. Sarah wrapped her arms around Aria, and pulled her against her, savoring the feel of her body against her. Then she stepped away from her, took two steps into the living room, and yawned sleepily. She stretched for the ceiling and realized just how sore and tired she was. Maybe sleep was not such a terrible idea. Then she looked at Emily wrapped around Ragden, and she smiled to herself. Sleep would be good, but not yet.

Aria saw Sarah yawn and felt herself joining her. She also stretched as she realized how emotionally exhausting the day had been. She felt her muscles aching and realized it was a good kind of ache. The ache was full of delicious memories. Feelings of contentment, comfort, and love flowed over her.

Ragden and Emily stepped around the table, hand in hand, walking towards the living room. Ragden reached back for Sarah's hand, who took it eagerly as she snuggled up against his side. Aria followed Emily, taking her hand and squeezing it softly.

Ragden led the way through the living room, up the stairs, and opened the door to his room, standing back to allow the ladies to enter first. Then he followed in and closed the door behind them.

Aria stepped into Ragden's room, taking in the atmosphere of luxury and comfort. She gazed around the room at the plush furniture, the soft lighting and the large king-sized bed dominating one corner of the room. Her heart

raced with anticipation as she remembered the pleasures she had already experienced there. Aria walked over to the bed, then turned back to Ragden and smiled coyly, opening the top of her robe to show her cleavage.

Emily stepped past the doorway and over to the desk where all their clothes had been washed and neatly folded. She saw Aria holding open the top of her robe and blushed softly as she turned back to watch Sarah and Ragden enter. Sarah walked in ahead of Ragden and started to untie her robe. She smiled seductively at Aria, then let her robe fall open, as she turned back to Ragden. As the door slipped shut, she cupped her breasts and blew a kiss to Ragden.

Ragden blinked once, slowly watching Sarah. His arousal became increasingly evident as Sarah slowly walked towards him. As she came within a few feet of him, she shrugged her shoulders back, letting the robe fall to the floor behind her. Ragden gazed into her face, tense with desire, as she licked her lips, and moved closer to him. Then he looked at her round breasts, swaying slightly as she closed the gap to him and started to untie his robe. He looked down at her perfect snatch, the dark patch of hair damp with her arousal, hiding those luscious lips from view. He leaned in and kissed her face, slipping his tongue in and tasting her desire as she finished untying his robe and slipped her hands in to grasp his throbbing cock.

Sarah gently stroked Ragden's cock, feeling the heat coming off it as it throbbed with his pulse in her hands. As she broke from the kiss, her cheeks flushed with desire, slightly breathless, she whispered, "I want you in my ass..."

Ragden shivered, remembering the feel of her ass on his cock in the shower. He reached out and cupped her ass, pulling her against him. His fingers curled around her firm cheeks, grazing over her asshole, and through her damp folds. Sarah sighed at him, letting him pull her body against his. His cock pressed against her abdomen, throbbing at the touch of her skin.

Emily felt her pulse beating hard in her chest, watching Sarah handle Ragden's manhood, hearing her request. She remembered what it had felt like to have that enormous cock fill her ass, and she quivered at the memory. She longed for it again, but she smiled, knowing Sarah wanted it, and she was sure Ragden would grant that request. She would get to watch. Emily untied the front of her robe and slipped her hands inside her robe to gently fondle her breasts, which ached to be touched. Then she slipped a hand between her legs, feeling her arousal, and how damp she was. She slipped a finger into her folds and sighed with pleasure. It was not Ragden's cock, but it would do for now.

Sarah pulled back from Ragden, a pleading look on her face, biting her lip, "Please...?"

Aria blushed, watching the scene from behind Sarah. She felt the heat on her face as she watched Ragden's hands curl around Sarah's cheeks, slipping into her folds. Aria shivered, knowing what that felt like, longing for it herself.

Her pussy clenched at the memory of Ragden filling her as Sarah had asked. Aria's ass still felt tender and sore from his massive cock filling her bowels. She closed her eyes and licked her lips, remembering what it felt like to have his seed filling her bowels and dripping out. She shivered at the memory, then opened her eyes to watch as Ragden nodded to Sarah. Aria opened her robe, her body suddenly hot and flushed. She would get to watch Ragden and Sarah, and she wanted some cool air on her skin when she did.

Ragden nodded slowly, his cock throbbed painfully against her abdomen. She smiled and looked down at it, licking her lips. Ragden shivered again, and nodded to Sarah, granting her permission to do what she wanted.

Sarah leaned against Ragden, pressing her supple body against his as she kissed him passionately on the lips, enjoying his taste. Enjoying the heat coming off his body, the feel of his pounding pulse against her chest. She stepped back away from him, her skin tingling, wanting that contact again, but she had other plans. She grinned wickedly as she stroked his cock, feeling it throb in her hands. Ragden sighed with pleasure as she did. Then she slowly crouched down in front of him. She grasped his cock and pulled the head of it into her mouth. He moaned as she licked the tip, tasting the bit of precum that had leaked out. Then she slipped it into her mouth, and sucked on it fiercely, causing Ragden to gasp. She ran her tongue around it, swirling it in her mouth, sucking on it hard. Ragden groaned again. Sarah ran one hand down her chest and between her legs, slipping it between her folds and into her wet pussy as she leaned into Ragden's groin, taking his throbbing, massive cock down her throat. She flexed her throat as she had seen Emily do before and gently bobbed her head back and forth on it. Ragden moaned again, his cock throbbing inside of her. Then Sarah slowly withdrew it from her throat and her mouth, a line of saliva still connecting her lips to its throbbing head. She pulled her hand out of her pussy and ran her juices over his cock, smiling wickedly as she slipped the head into her mouth and sucked fiercely. Ragden moaned again in response.

She slid it from her mouth and smiled up at him. "I love the taste of your cock with my juices on it." Then she stood and took a step backward towards the bed, pulling him towards her with his cock. Ragden staggered forward, following her as she stroked his throbbing cock.

Aria scrambled out of the way, as Sarah almost backed into her, pulling Ragden towards her. Sarah went back into the bed, feeling it pressed against the backs of her legs. She fell backward onto the bed, still stroking Ragden's cock as he stepped up against her. She spread her legs wide, pulling his cock into her damp folds, moaning loudly. Ragden sighed, echoing Sarah as his cock slid into her lips, brushed across her clit, and into her vagina. Her hands squeezed tightly around his shaft as it slid deep into her. She moaned loudly, her fingers sliding along the shaft of his throbbing cock as he leaned into her and lowered himself down on top of her to kiss her passionately as his cock slid home. His groin pressed against her perfect mound; the tip of his cock

pressed gently against her cervix.

Aria's blue eyes sparkled, and her body trembled with desire as Sarah pulled Ragden onto the bed, their groins pressed together, his cock sliding deep into her wet folds. Their tongues tangling together in a desperate dance of passion.

Sarah felt Ragden's hands squeezing her tightly, his fingers intertwining with hers as they both struggled to maintain control of their raging passions. She could feel his cock pressed against her cervix, sending shivers down her spine, causing her heart to race faster and faster.

"This is... amazing," she gasped between kisses, her voice barely audible, her breath coming in short gasps, her heart racing, her mind consumed by the intensity of the moment.

Emily gasped, watching Ragden slide the entire length of his manhood into Sarah's dripping, wet pussy, her own fingers sliding deeper into her own folds. She gently stroked herself, closing her eyes as she ran her other hand across the top of her mound, putting pressure on her clitoris. She opened her eyes to watch Sarah's spread legs quiver with ecstasy as she ground her hips against him, sliding his cock around inside of her. Emily shivered, knowing exactly what that felt like. She stroked herself a little faster, the pleasure was comforting, but she ached for the real thing...

Ragden kissed Sarah passionately, his tongue slipping into her mouth, tasting her sweetness as he ground his hips against hers, sliding his cock into her cervix. She moaned into his mouth, grinding her groin against his, causing his cock to slide back and into her again. Ragden rolled his hips back, sliding his cock back out of her until just the tip remained in her lips, then he slowly slid back into her, his entire length filling her. Sarah moaned loudly, her legs shaking as he pressed his groin into hers again, his cock gently pressing against her cervix, then he withdrew again. As he did so, Sarah rolled her hips, sliding back away from him, his cock almost slipping out. Then they rolled their hips together, his cock thumping against her cervix solidly, causing her breasts to rock, and her thighs to shake with the gentle impact. Sarah moaned in ecstasy as Ragden sighed in pleasure against her lips.

Aria slipped out of her robe, letting it fall to the floor at the edge of the bed. The cool air felt so refreshing as it blew across her skin from the slightly open window. Her nipples grew firm watching Ragden and Sarah gently slide their hips together and apart, in a slow synchronized rhythm. Each gentle impact shook Sarah's body, her breasts rocking, her hips flexing. Sarah moaned softly with each impact; her face flushed.

Ragden raised himself upright, standing at the edge of the bed, gently thrusting into Sarah as he looked over at Aria and smiled. Ragden placed his hands on Sarah's hips, gently pulling her against him with each thrust. Aria smiled as Ragden leaned over and kissed her softly on the lips, his tongue gently tasting her, then slipping out. Aria blushed, then bent over and kissed Sarah softly on the lips. Sarah greedily thrust her tongue into Aria's mouth,

causing her to gasp in surprise as Sarah ran her tongue roughly around the inside of Aria's mouth. Then Sarah slipped her right hand between Aria's legs, and slipped two fingers into her damp pussy, stroking deeply into her. Aria moaned at the contact, feeling her muscles quiver and shiver in delight. Sarah pulled back from kissing Aria and slipped her fingers out of her pussy. Sarah brought her hand back and licked her fingers clean while gazing lustily into Aria's eyes. Aria shivered under that gaze. Sarah giggled, then reached up and gently caressed Aria's face, running her thumb over Aria's lips. Aria sighed softly, her lips parting and licking Sarah's finger. Sarah moaned, with each gentle impact of her hips against Ragden's. His throbbing cock slid deeper into her on each stroke, caressing her cervix. Sarah reached out and took Aria's hands, pulling her over on top of her.

Aria let herself be drawn over on top of Sarah, straddling her waist, her groin poised over Sarah's. Sarah slid her hands up Aria's arms, and gently pulled her down to her lips, kissing her passionately. Aria melted against Sarah. Their bodies pressed together. Ragden smiled at the scene before him as he continued to gently slide his hips against Sarah's. Aria's feet slipped under Sarah's thighs, hanging just off the edge of the bed. Ragden leaned down and ran his tongue through Aria's pussy lips, and up across her asshole. Aria moaned against Sarah's lips at his gentle touch, a thrill ran down her spine. Sarah smiled and slid her arms down Aria's back, firmly gripping her ass and pulling it down against her groin.

Emily watched, leaning against the desk, her robe open, her fingers gently working across her clitoris and inside her wet pussy. She moaned softly, her hips rocking to the thrusts of Ragden's and Sarah's hips.

Aria's blue eyes sparkled, and her body trembled with desire as Sarah pulled her down onto her lips, their tongues intertwining in a passionate dance of lust and desire. Sarah's hands gripped Aria's ass, pulling her down onto her swollen pussy, their wet folds combining in a slick mess of heat and need. Aria gasped as Ragden's tongue found her asshole, teasing her sensitive ring of muscles, sending shivers down her spine.

Sarah grinned wickedly against Aria's lips as she reached back and pulled Aria's groin down against hers, the gentle thrusts of Ragden's hips against her rocking both women. Ragden slid back, slowly easing his throbbing cock out of Sarah's deliciously wet, tight pussy. Sarah groaned loudly, clearly not happy that her pussy was no longer filled. Ragden ran his hands across Sarah's inner thighs, and slid his hands across her pussy, his fingers teasing across her. Sarah reached down and grabbed Aria's ass, her fingers curling under her cheeks to spread her lips wide. Ragden watched and gently slipped his throbbing cock into Aria's pussy.

Aria moaned loudly, her body shivered as Ragden's cock slid deeper and deeper into her. Sarah licked Aria's lips, kissing her chin, then slipped her tongue into Aria's mouth, as she pulled Aria's pussy open wider, allowing Ragden to gently slide the entire length of his cock into her tight wet pussy.

Ragden moaned softly as she felt Aria's heat enveloping him, her tight walls squeezing on his throbbing cock as he slowly filled her with all of him. His cock gently pressed against her cervix, his body shuddering at the sheer pleasure and ecstasy.

"Oh, God..." Aria moaned softly. Sarah slipped her fingers out of Aria's pussy and grabbed her ass cheeks, spreading them, her fingers finding the edge of her ass and slipping in. Aria moaned even louder, feeling Sarah's fingers entering her ass as Ragden slowly withdrew and slid back into her, gently bumping her cervix again. Aria looked over her shoulder, her cheeks flushed, her eyes rolling wildly, her voice strained with need and desire.

"Fuck my ass... Oh, God," Aria pleaded

Ragden slowly withdrew his cock from her pussy, placing his hands on top of Sarah's on Aria's ass, holding her cheeks open as he placed the head of his cock against her asshole. Sarah pulled her fingers out of Aria's ass as Ragden slipped the head of his cock into the tight opening. Aria moaned loudly at the sudden invasion. Sarah giggled softly, then bit her lip as she pulled harder on Aria's cheeks, spreading her asshole open even wider, allowing Ragden to slide more of his cock into Aria's ass. Aria moaned louder as Ragden slowly slid the rest of his cock into her.

Tears welled in Aria's eyes. The pressure, pleasure, and pain overwhelmed her. Her breath came in gasps as his cock filled her bowels. The heat of it filled her, washed over her, drove her insane with desire. Her muscles clenched hard, making his cock feel even larger inside of her. She could feel every inch of it in her ass, and she could feel her climax building, without it even moving. Then Ragden slowly slid back until only the tip of his cock remained in her. She moaned loudly, the muscles in her ass relaxing but still straining to push the last bit of him out. Sarah looked up at Ragden and nodded as she pulled on Aria's cheeks, spreading her ass wide so he could slide back in. Aria moaned loudly again, tears slipping down her cheeks as Ragden slid his massive, throbbing cock all the way back into Aria's ass. She gasped loudly as his groin thumped gently into her ass.

"Oh, God... oh, God..." Aria moaned, her voice breaking, "Harder... Fuck me... Harder."

Emily watched it all. Her heart pounding, her own juices flowing, her arousal dripping down her legs. Her fingers deep in her pussy, watching Ragden slide his dick up Aria's ass. She shivered, knowing the feeling and wanting it, but enjoying the view. She slipped a finger into her ass and gasped. She wanted something so much bigger, but her finger felt so good. She gently stroked her pussy and ass at the same time, feeling her own pressure and pleasure building.

Aria gasped and moaned again and again. Her ass hurt. Ragden's cock was so huge and filled so much of her, going deeper into her than she could imagine. When she had sat on it, it had felt huge inside her, but having Sarah pulling her ass open and Ragden sliding in, it felt even larger. Her mind could

not handle it. Sarah's firm nipples pressed tight against hers. Her chest throbbed, her nipples hard and firm. Her ass spread so wide it hurt, but the pleasure she felt was amazing. She felt the tears on her cheeks. Were they tears of pain or ecstasy? She was not sure. She just did not want it to stop. She tried to rock her hips back against Ragden, pushing more of him into her, but found she was held firmly in place by both Sarah and Ragden's hands on her ass. She moaned loudly again. She wanted him to fuck her. This was too slow, too gentle, and too loving. She did not deserve this love that was filling her. She deserved to be used. She wanted to be used.

Feeling her desire and need, Ragden slowly slid his cock in and out of her ass at a gentle, loving pace. He gently held her hips in place as he thrust his cock deep into her bowels, then pulled it slowly back and slid deep again. He felt every inch of her body quivering and shaking against him. Her need and desire raced across her like a fever.

Aria moaned loudly. She could not find the words. Her vocal cords would not respond. She wanted to beg, to plead, but found she could not. The pleasure building within her was too much. The pain was too much. The love, unbearable. Filling her, coursing through her body with every beat of her heart. She loved it so much. Too much. She felt her own climax building with each gentle stroke of Ragden's cock into her bowels. She felt her muscles clenching and releasing faster. She balled up the blankets of the bed in her fists, clenching them as tight as she could. Sarah leaned up and kissed her softly, tenderly, passionately. As her tongue slipped into Aria's mouth, Aria forced Sarah's tongue back into her mouth, her own tongue diving into Sarah's mouth, forcibly exploring her. Sarah moaned into her lips, enjoying the invasion. Again, Aria tried to rock her hips against Ragden's gentle thrust, and this time, Sarah released her cheeks, and she rocked back into Ragden's groin hard. Her hips slammed into his, forcing his cock deep into her. Aria's lips broke from Sarah's as she gasped, incoherently.

"Oh, my... fuck me, God... Fucking... Fuuuccckk..."

Ragden laughed, but thrust against Aria harder, his hands pulling her hips against his groin. He could feel her building climax and knew she did not have long. Aria's body trembled with desire as Ragden thrust against her, pulling her hips against him, gripping his hands tightly on her waist. She could feel the intensity building within her. Her heart raced. Her mind whirled with lust and desire. She gazed down at Sarah beneath her. Sarah bit her lip and grinned wickedly up at Aria. As Ragden pulled her back, Sarah's hands gripped Aria's breasts firmly, squeezing them together, pinching her hardened nipples.

"Fuck..." Aria gasped, as her climax built up inside her, threatening to burst forth uncontrollably.

Ragden fucked her ass harder, sliding his massive throbbing cock out, then slamming it back home into her bowels. He held her hips steady, as he slammed in and out of her. His cock throbbing with each thrust. Aria's body rocked against his. Her thighs and breasts vibrated with the impact. Sarah bit

her lip, feeling her body rock with each thrust. Then Aria's climax burst over her. She cried out, as her body clenched, her muscles convulsed as fluid flowed forth from her pussy. Ragden slammed his cock home into her as more tears slid down her cheeks, her teeth clenched with the force of her climax.

Aria collapsed against Sarah. Her body shook and quivered. Ragden leaned over her, pressed his chest against her back, and reached around to gently grasp her heaving chest and kiss her softly on the neck. Sarah leaned forward and kissed Aria on the lips, a tender, caring touch. Aria moaned softly in response, her eyes closed, her body still shaking.

Hearing Aria's heartbeat slowing, her breath calming, Ragden stood up, his fingers trailing down her back to rest on her hips. Ragden gently gripped her waist as he slowly withdrew his throbbing cock from her ass. Aria moaned loudly as it slipped free from her bowels and slipped from her ass. A stream of fluid dripped from both her ass and pussy. Ragden slid his cock through Aria's lips, gently pressing against her clitoris before pressing it against Sarah's body and sliding it through Sarah's pussy lips. Sarah moaned loudly as his throbbing cock slipped into her pussy and slid deeper and deeper into her. Sarah spread her legs wider, allowing Ragden to slide his entire massive length into her, gently pressing against her cervix firmly; her whole body shuddered at the pressure of it.

Shockwaves of pleasure flowed through Sarah's body as his cock pressed against her cervix. Sarah gasped as Ragden's massive cock slid deep into her, filling her completely. Her heart raced. Her breath caught in her throat. Sarah gazed up at Ragden, her cheeks flushed, her mind whirling with lust as she felt the fullness of Ragden's thickness stretching her tight walls to their limit. She moaned.

"Fuuuuuckkk.."

Sarah pulled her hands back and slid them under her thighs. She grasped her ass cheeks, her fingertips sliding over her asshole. She sighed with pleasure as she slipped them in and pulled her asshole open.

"Now..." she moaned softly at Ragden, "You can fuck my ass... it's my turn..."

Ragden nodded, slowly withdrawing his cock from her pussy, watching the look of desire on her face, the sudden look of disappointment as his cock slipped out of her. The desire, the uncertainty, the questioning look, and the shy giggle as he pressed the head of his cock into her ass. Sarah's eyes squeezed shut as she pulled her asshole open wider, allowing the head of his cock into her. Then she slipped her fingers out and let her ass clench on his cock. She moaned at the sensation of her body fighting against the invasion of her tightest hole.

"Mm... this feels so good." Sarah sighed, looking up at Ragden, feeling the head of his cock inside her ass.

Ragden paused, only the head of his cock in Sarah's ass, as her body

clenched and pushed against him. The walls of her ass clenched and released against him, a rhythmic massage trying to push him out, and failing. Sarah bit her lip, feeling his cock just inside of her. She gripped her ass cheeks, pulling them wide as she rolled her hips, gently against Ragden, forcing his cock to slip in a little deeper. She moaned loudly as she stopped and savored the feeling of him. She reached down and ran her fingers the length of his cock, feeling just how much was not in her yet. Feeling the slickness of her and Aria's fluids along his shaft. Feeling the massive, throbbing heat. She wanted more of it in her. She wanted to feel all of it.

Sarah looked up at Ragden, her eyes pleading for more. Ragden nodded in response, seeing her need and desire. He slowly pushed against her as his cock slid into her depths. The lubrication of juices from Aria's and Sarah's wet pussies allowed him to slide deeper and deeper into her. Sarah groaned, feeling her bowels being filled. Her eyes rolled back into her head. Her heart beat harder. Her breath came in short gasps. She could feel the pressure, pleasure, and pain building within her. She could feel her climax starting to build.

Sarah moaned loudly as Ragden's hips gently pushed against her ass. She pulled her ass cheeks wider, hoping to get more of his cock inside her. More slid in, but not much. Then she rolled her hips back and forth, feeling his cock slide in and out of her bowels. Ragden smiled and matched her movements, sliding his cock out, then back into her. She moaned happily at the sensation. Her ass clenched tightly on him, allowing her to feel every inch of him filling her up. It was everything she had dreamed it would be, and more.

"Cum in my ass, please... I want to feel your seed filling me up..." She begged him.

Ragden felt his cock throb at her words. Sarah's eyes sparkled with desire. A shiver ran down his back as he picked up a slow rhythm, sliding in and out of her. She rocked her hips in time, meeting his thrusts. Aria laid on top of Sarah the whole time; her eyes closed, her breathing mellow, just enjoying the rocking sensation of Sarah's body beneath her.

Emily stood in the same place, two fingers in her pussy, one in her ass, another sliding across her clitoris. Her body twitched with desire as she watched Ragden slide his massive, throbbing cock in and out of Sarah's tight ass. The robe slid off her shoulders, pooling on the desk around her ass. Her breasts were slick with sweat. She loved it. She was comfortable, and she felt alive, desired, and loved. She could watch and enjoy the view. She had enjoyed watching Aria cum, and collapse on Sarah. Now she watched in rapt attention as Ragden slid his cock in and out of Sarah's ass at increasing speed. Sarah moaned with each thrust, her body rocking. A sheen of sweat forming on both Ragden and Sarah. Emily knew she would have her turn, and the anticipation was... wonderful.

Emily got the dim sense that Ragden's climax was building. She could feel it like a dim ache in the back of her head. The sensation felt... amazing.

Knowing that she was about to watch him finish in Sarah, just as she had asked for. Emily felt her own climax building in response to that feeling. Her fingers moved faster over her clitoris in response.

Ragden grasped Sarah's hips in his gentle hands and pulled her against him with each thrust. He could feel her climax building, her body shaking with the force of it, and his own was building in response. Her thighs flexed under his palms. He could feel her pulse racing against his body. Her ass clenched on his cock.

Ragden continued to slide his cock in and out of Sarah's incredibly tight ass, the sensation sending waves of pleasure throughout his entire body. His balls started to tighten as he felt her ass grip him. He tightened his grip on her hips and began to pump in, and out of her with greater force; his cock slammed deep into her bowels. His breathing became ragged. Sarah gasped and moaned with each thrust; her body rocked harder. Aria moaned in time to Sarah's gasps, her eyes slipped open, and her hands grasped Sarah's breasts beneath her. Sarah moaned against Aria's lips as she kissed her. Sarah felt her body on that crumbling precipice above the raging maelstrom of her climax. The pleasure and pressure building within her bowels, filling her entire being with waves of orgasmic energy.

"Oh, God..." Sarah moaned, "Harder..."

Ragden dug his fingers into her hips, pulling her against him. She rocked her hips in time to his massive thrusts. His pace increased. He slammed his cock harder and faster into her bowels.

Sarah rolled her hips against Ragden's thrusts, feeling his cock filling her bowels. Each massive thrust shook her entire body, and waves of pleasure rolled through her. Sarah's mind reeled; the sensations washing over her were too much. Her eyes rolled back into her head as the precipice she was on crumbled beneath her, and she tumbled into the whirling maelstrom of her orgasm.

Sarah's body bucked and thrashed, as she cried out. Her body clenched. Every muscle flexed as hard as it could. Ragden slammed his cock home into her bowels. His groin smashed into her ass, thrusting his cock as deep into her bowels as he could get it. His body clenched, and cum exploded out of him into her. His body clenched. All his muscles locked as he gasped for breath. Aria curled up against Sarah, cupping her face and kissing her softly on the cheek and mouth as Sarah's orgasm rolled over her, blotting out existence.

Aria rolled off Sarah's chest, and curled up along her side, resting her head on Sarah's shaking chest. Ragden leaned forward and gently kissed Aria on the lips. Aria kissed him back, softly, enjoying the tender affection. Then Ragden moved up and kissed Sarah softly on the lips. Feeling the heat against her skin, Sarah kissed him back, passionately. Her tongue slipped into his mouth and tasted his strength, his desire, and his love. She moaned softly against his lips, feeling his throbbing cock still spewing his seed into her bowels. Sarah smiled, as she shivered at the feeling in her bowels. It was everything she had

dreamed it would be and more. It made her feel so full of life, full of love and so complete. She reached up with one arm and cupped his face, pulling him back down to kiss her again.

"I love having your seed fill me up," Sarah whispered lustily to him, "Thank you..."

Ragden smiled down at her, his cock still throbbing in her ass. He could feel her bowels clenching and releasing his cock, milking the juice from it. His eyes slipped closed, savoring the feel of her on him, then he opened his eyes and smiled at Sarah.

"Of course, my dear," he kissed her softly on the lips again, then whispered softly, "And I love being able to cum in you..."

Sarah giggled and bit her lip as another muscle spasm passed through her body. Ragden's eyes slipped closed as he felt her body clench tightly on his cock, still throbbing in her ass. Sarah reached out and grabbed his neck, pulling him close, and whispered fiercely to him.

"Please leave your cock in me for a little longer... Please?"

Ragden nodded slowly, smiling at her. She grinned wickedly, enjoying the fullness in her bowels. She could feel his sticky seed filling her bowels, pouring into her tight channel. Her well-prepared depths welcomed the fluid filling her. She knew it would drip from her when he pulled from her depths, and she was not ready for that sensation yet.

Aria's blue eyes sparkled at the exchange. She felt the love and desire flowing over her, and she felt honored to be so close to it. She felt included, and it warmed her heart. She reached out and tentatively and put her hand on Ragden's shoulder. He turned to her, smiled, and kissed her lips softly.

"Did you need something, my love?" he asked softly. Tears slipped down Aria's cheeks as he spoke. The care, understanding, compassion, and love in his voice swept over her. She closed her eyes and felt a shiver run down her spine at it.

She smiled and shook her head, then spoke softly, "I... I just wanted to say... Thank you..."

Ragden smiled at her and kissed her on the lips a little more passionately than before. Aria felt her pulse stir, her body tingle, and her desire well up in her again. When the kiss broke, she felt tears in her eyes again. She blinked hard, feeling them trickle down her cheeks. Ragden saw them and softly kissed them from her face.

Aria whispered, "I... I love you."

Ragden gently wrapped an arm around Aria, pulling her closer to Sarah and him. Sarah wrapped an arm around her as well, pulling them all close together.

"I love you too, Aria. Now and forever more," Ragden spoke softly to her, watching her breath hitch at the sounds of the words. She buried her face in Sarah's bosom, hiding the tears they could all feel. Sarah ran a tender hand down her back, while Ragden kissed the top of her head, comforting her.

As things reached their conclusion, Emily stood off the desk, the shaking of her own orgasm subsiding. She stepped out of the robe, and stepped around Sarah and Ragden, pulling herself onto the bed beside them. She rested her head on Sarah's other shoulder, kissing her softly. Sarah wrapped an arm around her, pulling her into the embrace. Ragden turned to Emily and smiled warmly, kissing her softly on the lips.

"So glad you decided to join us," he whispered softly.

Aria looked up at Emily and smiled. Sarah turned and kissed Emily on the lips. Emily smiled happily, then spoke softly, "I didn't want to interrupt."

Sarah giggled and kissed Emily again, then whispered to her, "You are always welcome to interrupt. I'd have loved to grab your pussy when I came and felt your heat."

Emily blushed softly. Ragden kissed Emily softly on the lips and smiled at her, then he pulled himself upright, slowly slipping from between the three girls. He started to slide his throbbing cock from Sarah's ass. Sarah groaned loudly and whined.

"No... not yet... oh fuck... that's not fair..."

The other two women giggled at Sarah as Ragden's cock finally slid free, then all three of them turned to his throbbing member between her legs. All three women reached for it simultaneously and then laughed at each other. Ragden gazed down at the three of them and smiled, his love flowing off him like heat from a fireplace. They all snuggled closer to each other.

"The three most incredible women I have ever known, here... with me now... I cannot tell you how much I love you all."

Love & Nature

CHAPTER 18

All three women blushed and snuggled closer to each other. Then Sarah looked down at Ragden's still large, firm cock, her eyes full of hunger and desire. She licked her lips as she looked up at Ragden's face.

"Can I... Can I lick you clean? I want to taste my juices mixed with your cum on your cock. Please?" She whispered, her voice full of need and desire. Emily giggled while Aria blushed, looked at Ragden's cock, and nodded in agreement with Sarah's request.

Ragden laughed and nodded, stepping back from the bed to give them room.

Sarah disentangled herself from Emily and Aria and slid off the bed hungrily, dropping to her knees in front of Ragden as Aria scrambled to follow. Emily lay on her side of the bed, watching as Sarah grasped his cock in her hands and slipped the head into her mouth. Ragden sighed as she swirled her tongue around the tip, sucking hard on it. Then she slipped it out of her mouth and handed it to Aria.

Aria blushed and gently ran her hands along the wet, throbbing length of his cock. She teased the tip with her tongue and gingerly slipped it into her mouth. Aria's eyes went wide as she swirled her tongue around the tip of his cock, pulling the head into her mouth. Aria tried to slip it deeper into her mouth and gagged. Then she backed off of it and slipped it from her mouth, coughing softly. Then she smiled and let Sarah grasp it again.

Aria spoke softly to Sarah, "I never thought it would taste like that."

Sarah giggled and spoke in a rush, "I know, right? It tastes so good..."

With that, she slipped it into her mouth and down her throat. Sarah relaxed her throat and slipped its entire length down her throat until her lips pressed against Ragden's groin. He moaned as she bobbed her head on his cock, sliding it along her throat. Then she backed off, swirled her tongue around the tip, and she slipped it from her mouth.

Aria watched Sarah in fascination. She blushed slightly as Sarah passed it

back to her. Aria stroked the length of his cock, gently running her fingers down to the base and cupping his balls as she slipped it into her mouth again. She relaxed her throat as she had seen Sarah do and tried to slip the head down her throat. Her eyes bulged with effort, tears leaking out. She strained for a moment, going red in the face, then her eyes lit up as it passed into her throat. She got half of it into her mouth before she started to turn blue and pulled it out of her mouth, gasping for air.

Ragden moaned as his cock slipped from her mouth, his cock throbbing in their hands, a small bit of precum leaking from the tip. Sarah grabbed his cock and stroked it firmly, coaxing more cum out before licking it off deftly, smacking her lips. Then she turned to Aria and wrapped her arms around her, pulling their chests together and kissing her passionately on the lips, tasting her. Aria broke off giggling, feeling the heat in her face, and her pulse started to race. Sarah grinned and grabbed Aria's breasts, gently pinching her nipples.

Sarah whispered huskily to Aria, "Oh, that was hot, girl. I love watching you choke on his massive meat."

Both women laughed furiously, falling over against the side of the bed. Ragden beamed down at them, enjoying the amusement. Then he looked over at Emily, who beckoned him over with one finger. As he walked over to the edge of the bed, Emily crawled backward, her eyes burning with desire.

Sarah turned and noticed Ragden crawling up onto the bed again. She groaned loudly, complaining, "Hey! I wasn't done sucking your cock!"

Aria laughed again, grabbing Sarah, and slipping a hand between her legs to feel her damp pussy. Sarah moaned in pleasure and slipped her hand between Aria's legs. Aria moaned in response. The two of them leaned forward, kissing softly as they fingered each other.

Meanwhile, Ragden crawled over the bed to Emily, who lay on her back, her legs slightly spread, her arms outstretched to him. He crawled into her arms and kissed her passionately, his tongue slipping into her mouth, tasting her sweetness. The length of his cock pressed against her groin and abdomen. Emily moaned in pleasure at the press of heat against her. Emily wrapped her arms around him and pulled him down against her. She felt his entire body pressed against hers. She sighed with pleasure. With him against her, she felt complete, like a missing piece of her very soul had been rejoined to her. She spread her legs wider, allowing his knees to slide up under her thighs.

"My turn," she whispered huskily as she kissed him again. Ragden smiled down at her and nodded, clearly enjoying the feel of her body against his.

Emily slipped one hand down Ragden's chest, his abdomen, running over his firm muscles, then over his groin, and softly down the length of his cock. Ragden sighed at her touch. Then she grasped it firmly, stroked it once, and guided it into her dripping-wet pussy. As the head slid into her, she gasped softly. Her mouth slipped open, her neck and back arching. Ragden leaned in and kissed her neck, his teeth softly grazing her soft tender skin, causing her to moan again. His cock continued to slide deeper into her. She felt her body

stretching as it filled her. Her walls gripped around him tightly. Emily's cheeks flushed, her eyes rolling as she lost herself in the sensation. She knew it had only been a few hours since he had been inside her, but it felt like she had waited a lifetime for this moment.

Her fingers wrapped around his cock, as it continued to slide into her. She moaned louder as his groin pressed her hand against her folds. His cock pushed into her deepest depths and pushed against her cervix. She felt her pussy clench and release him once, twice, three times. The pleasure of being so incredibly stretched and full of him almost overwhelmed her.

"Oh, God," she moaned softly, "Yes."

Hearing the soft moans coming from Emily, Sarah's head popped up over the edge of the bed to see Ragden and Emily. Her eyes hungry, she crawled up onto the bed, closely followed by Aria. Sarah crawled up within reach of Emily and Ragden, and she stopped to watch, licking her lips hungrily. Aria crawled up behind Sarah, watching her plump ass wiggle as she crawled. Aria's eyes locked on Sarah's slick folds. When Sarah stopped and lay on her side, Aria crawled up and buried her face in Sarah's wet folds. Sarah gasped in surprise, then moaned in pleasure as Aria slipped her tongue inside Sarah. Sarah rolled over onto her back, spreading her legs so Aria could get easier access to her. Aria smiled at Sarah hungrily, and slipped her fingers into Sarah's wet folds, stroking her clitoris, then slipping a finger into her pussy. Sarah moaned, her eyes rolling back and her head flopping back on a pillow as Aria ran her tongue the length of her wet folds, pulling her clitoris into her mouth.

Ragden kissed Emily passionately and slipped his hand down along her side, as he raised his chest off hers so he could cup her breasts as his cock throbbed against her cervix. She moaned softly as he licked her nipples and pulled them into his mouth, pinching them between his teeth. Then Ragden slowly rolled his hips back, sliding most of his cock out of her twitching pussy, then slowly slid it back in. Emily matched his movements; she rolled her hips against his and met him halfway. His cock thumped against her cervix, causing both of them to moan in pleasure. Emily's eyes flashed, and she smiled up at Ragden. She reached out and wrapped her arms around his neck and pulled him down to kiss her as they built a slow rhythm, their hips sliding apart and then together.

Meanwhile, Aria slipped a finger up Sarah's ass, as she continued to stroke her pussy with another finger, her tongue swirled around Sarah's clitoris. Sarah moaned loudly, her hips bucking gently against Aria, driving her fingers deeper into her tight holes. Sarah marveled at the gentle feel of Aria probing her tight holes. The love and care Aria expressed for her made her feel vulnerable, desired, cherished, and loved. Her heart beat faster. It was different from having Ragden in her, but it still felt amazing. Sarah looked to her right and spied Emily and Ragden, their hips sliding together, his cock filling every inch of her pussy. Sarah's heart beat faster, her desire growing.

She could feel the waves of pleasure and love rolling off them and felt herself caught in its magnetic draw. She wanted more but knew she could settle for what Aria would give her. She smiled to herself, loving every moment of Aria's pleasuring her.

Aria focused on Sarah, even though out of the corner of her eye, she could spy Ragden's massive cock sliding into and filling Emily's tight pussy. She could see Emily's pussy lips stretching to accommodate the massive size of his cock going into her. She shivered, seeing it again. She had had that inside her. It seemed impossible that something so large would fit. She could clearly remember the feel of her body stretching painfully to let him fill her. Her insides ached from it, ached for it. She smiled, knowing that she would get another opportunity to feel that beast between her legs. Aria refocused on Sarah, driving her fingers deep into both her tight holes, feeling Sarah clench against her. Sarah felt so good on her fingers, she had seen Sarah stretch to fit Ragden in her but marveled that her body still felt so tight after. Aria licked Sarah's clitoris, pulled it into her mouth, ran her teeth over it, and gently tugged on it, hearing Sarah moan in pleasure.

Ragden continued to roll his hips against Emily's. Their rhythm was coordinated. Their pulses matched. Their breath in time to one another's. The pace was slow, rhythmic, and full of passion, desire, and love. Emily reached up and cupped Ragden's cheek as they continued, their hips parting, meeting, parting, and meeting again. His cock slid out, then gently pushed against her cervix, then slid out to do it again. Each gentle contact caused Emily's chest to roll gently, her thighs to vibrate, and her legs to flex.

Ragden placed his hands on her chest and grasped her incredible breasts. Gently, his thumbs grazed over her nipples. He felt her nipples tighten and firm up against his gentle caress. Emily moaned in pleasure.

"Gods... I love... this..." Emily spoke softly between thrusts.

Ragden nodded, speaking between thrusts, "I love... being... in you."

Emily closed her eyes and felt Ragden's energy enveloping her, surrounding her, permeating her entire being. She could feel him on her, around her, in her. She loved every moment of it, and never wanted it to end. She could feel the pressure as it started to build within her, the pleasure and pressure building on itself. She could feel his touch on it, like a gentle caress, nurturing it, feeding it, changing it subtly into something even more powerful that filled her being with love and compassion.

Ragden closed his eyes, as he continued to roll his hips with Emily's. He could feel her energy, a perfect match to his. She felt like the missing piece of his soul. He could feel everything that was her, and he loved every bit of it. He could feel her building climax, could feel his energy feeding it, and he smiled. Ragden felt like he could manipulate her climax and chose not to. He could feel his own, like his heart, beating along with hers. Like two lovers walking down a lane, hand in hand. Ragden felt Emily's body responding to his, her heart beating faster, her breath becoming rapid. As hers increased, so

did his own. He felt his body responding to her every movement. Her hand twitched on his chest, and he caressed her nipples in response, heightening her arousal. He could feel the twitch in her left leg and shifted his hips to rub across that spot. He felt her moan and could feel his moan in response to hers. Her pussy clenched, and his cock throbbed in response. Her hips pressed against his more insistently, and he pressed back to match.

Sarah felt her body responding to Aria's fingers and mouth. The pressure and pleasure built within her. She knew she would not last much longer. It seemed Aria could sense it, too, as she worked her body even more furiously. Her tongue flicked faster. Her fingers dug deeper. Sarah felt her body clenching and releasing on Aria's, and she moaned, urging Aria while knowing it would not be long for her.

Aria could sense Sarah's need and desire building. She could feel Sarah's pulse quicken, her breathing growing more rapid. She felt Sarah's ass clench on her fingers, squeezing painfully; then her pussy clenched on her other fingers, equally as hard and painful. Aria flexed her fingers once Sarah let up, and stroked her faster, urging her on. She wanted to taste Sarah's climax and feel it bursting over her face. She flicked her tongue faster.

Ragden felt the energy in the room starting to build, his compassion and love filling the room. He could feel Sarah's climax building. He could feel Emily's building rapidly. He could feel his own building as well. Ragden felt Emily's pulse quicken again, his own matching it. Their hips rolled faster. His cock thumped against her cervix more insistently. Her gasps of pleasure came faster; he answered in time. He squeezed Emily's breasts in time to her heartbeats; his thumbs flicked across her nipples at the same strike of her pulse.

Emily felt the building energy, the quickening of her pulse, and Ragden's against her skin. She felt the pressure on her chest, matching the pressure between her legs. She moaned louder, feeling everything adding together. She knew she was on the verge of losing control. Emily felt Ragden's loving caress across her energy, across her skin, on her chest, around her, and deep inside her. Her climax was building and building.

Ragden felt Emily hitting the edge of what she could take, knew she was moments away, and knew he was right there with her. He rolled his hips faster, feeling her match him. Their hips rolled faster, met, and parted and met again. Each meeting caused his cock to push firmly against her cervix. Sent surges of pleasure through both their bodies.

Aria felt her body tremble with desire as Sarah's climax built. Her heart raced. Her breath came in short gasps. Her body tense with pleasure.

Emily cried out, her orgasm rolling over her so fiercely that she inadvertently pulled her fingers across Ragden's chest, leaving red lines on his skin. Her hips bucked hard against his, slammed his cock against her cervix. Ragden cried out, as his seed exploded out of him in a torrent. The force of it caused Emily to cry out again as her pussy filled, and it all came rushing out

over Ragden's groin.

Sarah cried out as her juices ran down over Aria's hands. Aria felt her juices releasing at the sudden wave of pleasure that filled the room. She sighed and collapsed, face first into Sarah's pussy, just as a gush of Sarah's juice came flowing out. Aria latched her mouth onto Sarah's pussy and swallowed everything she could. Sarah convulsed at the sensation. Her hips drove against Aria's face.

Aria's body trembled with pleasure as Sarah's pussy flooded with juices, gushing over Aria's mouth as she eagerly lapped at every drop. Aria felt her pussy release violently, spraying down her legs with thick ropes of her arousal. She gasped and collapsed onto Sarah's hot, wet folds, pressing her face against them as Sarah convulsed, her hips bucking wildly against Aria's mouth. Sarah's fingers dug into Aria's back, her nails biting into her skin as she rode out her explosive orgasm.

Ragden collapsed against Emily, as his muscles gave out. He broke his fall and gently laid his chest against hers, his face in her hair, his lips against her ear. Her arms slipped around his body and pulled him against her. He sighed at her, as the twitching of his body started to subside. He kissed her ear softly, relished in the spasms of her pussy on his thick cock buried so deep inside her. He could feel himself still leaking cum into her. His cock started to soften. Emily moaned softly at the feeling of him filling her up. She knew this was inevitable, but she still loved the feel of him inside her, soft or hard; it was still marvelous. She kissed his ear softly. Then Emily reached over and clasped Sarah's hand gently in hers and squeezed. Sarah's eyes fluttered open, and she smiled back at Emily.

Sarah's cheeks flushed. Her heart was still beating hard but calming. Sarah reached over and placed a hand on Ragden's shoulder. He lifted his head slowly, looked over at her, and smiled. She grinned back and licked her lips. Then she spoke softly.

"When you pull that marvelous piece of meat out of Emily, I want to taste it. Please?"

Ragden laughed. Emily blushed. Aria pulled herself off Sarah, and lay down next to her, smiling happily.

"Sure," Ragden breathed softly.

Emily kissed his lips tenderly. He smiled down at her, then cocked an eyebrow. She shook her head. He chuckled softly, feeling his manhood still softening, but still filling most of Emily's tight pussy. He could feel her still clenching and releasing him. Her insides milked all the cum out of his cock it could get. It felt amazing, and he smiled at it. She smiled back and kissed him softly on the lips. Aria crawled over and laid down next to Emily and Ragden, curling her side along Emily. Sarah crawled around them and lay on the other side, curled up against them. The closeness of their naked bodies added heat and intimacy. Ragden kissed Emily softly, then slowly lifted himself off her, slowly sliding his cock out of her. She moaned softly, her legs twitching as his

cock slipped out of her. She bit her lip as she looked down at his limp dick hanging between her legs.

Aria gazed down at Emily, her blue eyes sparkling with delight as she saw the evidence of Ragden's recent pleasure from her friend. She reached out and ran a finger lightly along the tip of his cock, admiring its warmth and softness. She could feel the last traces of Emily's juice still clinging to it, adding to the sensation of intimacy and shared experience.

Sarah sat up and crawled over to Ragden, lowering herself to slip his cock into her mouth. She sucked on it softly, tasting the texture and mix of his and Emily's cum still on it. She smiled up at Ragden as she sucked it clean.

"Mmm," she sighed contentedly, "Delicious."

She slipped it back into her mouth, marveling at the soft feeling of his cock in her mouth. Ragden's eyes slipped closed as he moaned while she sucked on his cock. Then she released it and smiled at him.

"All clean."

"Thanks."

Sarah licked her lips seductively, inviting him to put it back into her mouth.

Ragden laughed and cupped her chin, leaning down to kiss her softly on the lips. Then he spoke softly, "It is getting late, and we have school in the morning. Probably best if we got some rest."

Aria, Sarah, and Emily pouted. Then they cleared off the bed and pulled back the covers. Emily slipped in, followed by Aria. Ragden crawled over Aria and laid down on his back between the two of them. Emily and Aria snuggled up against him, resting their heads on his chest. Ragden slipped his arms down their backs, gently caressing them. Sarah giggled and bit her lip. Her eyes twinkled with mischief. Sarah crawled under the covers, then across Aria to lay down on top of Ragden. She rested her head in the center of his chest, her breasts resting on his abdomen. She stroked his cock and cupped his balls playfully and giggled. Both Aria and Emily reached over and caressed Sarah, who sighed contentedly. Ragden reached down and grabbed the covers, pulling them up across his chest. Aria and Emily pulled the covers up to their shoulders, completely covering Sarah, who giggled under the covers. They all snuggled up against Ragden, settling in comfortably.

Ragden basked in the feeling of their bodies against his, his body relaxing. He felt sleep tickling the edges of his awareness. He spoke softly, sleepily, around a yawn.

"Is everyone comfortable?"

Emily and Aria sighed softly against Ragden's chest. They felt his heartbeat against their cheeks. Their bodies calmed, their eyelids growing heavy.

"Oh... yes..." Aria breathed softly.

She felt so divinely loved and comforted. Emily smiled, basking in the warmth of his heart against her cheek. She nodded softly and kissed his chest tenderly. From under the covers, Sarah giggled and nodded her head against

his upper abdomen. Ragden smiled happily, gently caressing Aria and Emily's backs, gently pulling them against him, savoring the feel of their bodies against his.

"Good night, my loves," he whispered as his eyes slipped closed, and he drifted off to sleep.

Emily listened to his slowing heartbeat, feeling hers slowing with it. Her eyes grew heavy, as she listened to his slow, steady breath as she slipped off to sleep.

Aria felt sleep slipping over her, her mind still overwhelmed by how included and loved she felt. The warmth and comfort of the embrace and presence around her pulled her into a deep, dreamless sleep.

Sarah lay quietly against Ragden, hearing everyone else drifting off to sleep. Their breathing and hearts slowing. She marveled at the warmth and love of lying against Ragden as he slept. Her heart slowed as she sank into the comfort of his flesh against her. She ran a finger down his limp cock, wondering at the soft skin under her touch. She kissed the head softly, whispering to it, "Good night," as she finally slipped into sleep.

CHAPTER 19

Friday...

Sarah was the first to wake in the dark, predawn hours. She felt something hard against her chest; her eyes slipped open. For a moment, she panicked when she could not see anything, but then she remembered the eventful night before. She was still under the covers. She felt the warmth of the bodies around her and smiled to herself. She could feel Ragden's slow, even breaths against her cheek. Around her, she could sense Aria and Emily, still deep asleep. What had woken her?

Then she realized it was Ragden's massive cock, large and firm against her chest, poking into one of her breasts. She tried to stifle the giggle that rose to her lips and only managed to keep the sound quiet. She ran one hand down its length, feeling it throb to her touch. Ragden must be dreaming about something interesting, or maybe this was just the 'morning wood' that she had heard about.

She bent her head down and ran her tongue over the tip and felt it throb against her soft touch. She could barely hear Ragden's soft moan in his sleep. She bobbed her head a little lower, taking the head of his cock into her mouth and gently sucking on it. She sighed at the sensation of it in her mouth. The massive head of his cock filled her mouth. She shuddered in delight, and sucked on it gently, tasting a tiny bit of precum oozing from the tip. She stopped as she heard him moan again softly in his sleep. She did not want to wake him, as she had no idea what time it was, but her desire to swallow his cock was too strong to resist.

She bobbed her head lower and slipped the head of it deeper into her mouth. She relaxed and slipped it past her gag reflex and into her throat. She bobbed up and down on it, feeling it fill her throat, choking her airway off. She felt tears in her eyes but continued bobbing, marveling at the sensation of his cock filling her throat. She tried to flex her throat against it, swallowing the small bits of cum reflexively as it leaked out. Then she backed it out of her mouth, taking in air and breathing. She felt light-headed from the loss of air

but overjoyed at the sensation of it.

She ran her tongue over it again as she caught her breath. She gently cupped his balls and felt their texture in her hand as she slipped his cock back into her mouth and down her throat. This time she was prepared, and she bobbed gently up and down, flexing her throat on his cock. She could hear him softly moaning in his sleep, his body tensing against her. His pulse quickened. His cock throbbed in her throat. Then she backed it into her mouth, and sucked in air greedily, her tongue swirling around the tip of his dick.

Sarah gently wrapped one hand around the massive base of his cock, the other cupping his balls as she took it down her throat a third time. This time, she kept sliding it down her throat until her lips pressed against her fingers around the base. Then she bobbed gently, flexing her throat while stroking the base of his cock and gently squeezing his balls. She felt his breath catch in his throat; his balls tensed under her fingers. Then, suddenly, his cum was exploding down her throat. She swallowed reflexively, his cum going straight into her stomach. She bobbed faster, flexing her throat on his cock, stroking his cock harder while squeezing the cum down her throat. When she grew light-headed again, she slid her head up his cock until only the head was still in her mouth, so she could breathe.

She could still feel his cum spilling into her mouth, and she did not want to waste a single drop. She continued to gently stroke his cock, from base to head, feeling his sticky seed squeezing out into her mouth. She rested there, the head of his cock still in her mouth, as it throbbed under her hands. Less cum leaked out. She ran her tongue over the tip of his cock, catching what little she could, and quickly swallowing it. She felt satisfied, content, and full of his cock, her belly warm and satisfied. Now, that was a wonderful way to start the day. She smiled to herself, then giggled softly, her pulse still racing. Once Sarah was satisfied that she had gotten all the cum out of his throbbing cock that she could, she rested her head back on his stomach, feeling his soft, even breaths beneath her. It seemed nobody else had woken. His cock was still rock hard beneath her hands, against her breasts. She wondered what else she could get away with before anyone woke.

Sarah gently lifted herself off Ragden's abdomen. She placed a hand between each of his sides and Aria and Emily, sliding her body up along his. She tenderly slid a knee down along his hip on either side. Aria and Emily both groaned in their sleep and moved just enough to let her legs slip into the place she wanted. She straddled his groin and placed her dripping-wet pussy over his big dick. She leaned forward, sliding along him, until her pussy lips were right above the head of his cock. She reached down with one hand and gently wrapped her hands around his throbbing length and angled it into her lips. Sighing at the pressure against her, she slid down against it, slowly, easing it through her lips. A soft moan slipped from her lips as she did.

Ragden's eyes fluttered open. He felt Sarah on top of him, his throbbing

cock in her gentle hands, slipping through her pussy lips. He smiled, leaned forward, and gently kissed her on the lips. Sarah gasped in surprise and drew her head back, turning to look at him.

Ragden smiled up at her and whispered, "Just what do you think you are doing?"

Sarah blushed darkly, blinking her dark eyes at him. She tried to smile sweetly, but her lips quivered as his cock throbbed at her entrance. She fumbled for words, her jaw moving, but no sound came out. She bit her lip, then whispered, "I... You... I just wanted to feel you inside me to... start the day."

Ragden chuckled softly. Then kissed her softly on the lips, "Well, don't stop now."

Sarah smiled broadly as she slid her hips down, her hand still guiding his cock into her. She gasped softly as her walls stretched to accommodate the massive size of him. Her mind reeled. How was she this tight? She had just had him inside her not twelve hours ago. Then she stopped caring as her groin pressed against his, and his cock slid against her cervix. She moaned, louder than she had intended. Ragden moaned softly in response. Sarah quickly looked to her right and left, checking on Emily and Aria. Neither had stirred, yet. Though she was not sure how long that would last. She looked down into Ragden's face and saw his eyes sparkle with lust, desire, and love. She felt her heart swell and knew she was exactly where she wanted to be. Sarah leaned forward and kissed Ragden passionately, feeling her heart beating faster. She rolled her hips gently, feeling his cock push against her cervix. She moaned at the feeling. The pressure of it sent waves of pleasure through her whole body. A shiver ran down her spine. She laid her body down against his, resting her head on his chest between Aria's and Emily's. She sighed, content and happy, as she felt his big dick filling her pussy as it pressed against her cervix. She loved it.

Ragden sighed and kissed the top of her head, feeling her body clenched on his cock. He felt every inch of her insides pressed along his throbbing manhood. It felt amazing. This was an enjoyable way to wake up. He relaxed and let himself sink into the bed, his muscles relaxing, well, most of them, anyway.

Sarah tried to relax; her body pressed against Ragden's. It felt heavenly, but her pulse was a little too fast. Her arms and legs relaxed, feeling the warmth and love of the close embrace. Her pussy clenched on his cock, pressed deep into her. The head of it throbbing against her cervix. She moaned softly, feeling it inside her. Then she pressed a finger to her lips, trying not to wake anyone else. She wanted to stay this way all day. To never leave the bed. Just lay there, filled with his magnificent massive cock.

Sarah slipped a hand down along her belly, across her mound. She felt her labia stretched around the base of his cock. She heard him sigh softly at her touch. Sarah slid her hand a little lower, felt his balls, and gently cupped them.

She heard him moan softly again. Then she slid her hands up to her chest and tried to still her pounding heart.

Sarah looked to her left and saw Emily sleeping next to her. She reached over and ran her hand up Emily's thigh, feeling the firm muscles under the soft skin. She ran her hand over her ass, feeling the marvelous curve of her. Then slid her hand up her side to the swell of her breast. As she looked up higher, she saw Emily's eyes open, and she looked at her with love. Emily leaned over and kissed Sarah softly on the lips.

"Sorry," Sarah whispered, "I didn't mean to wake you."

Emily smiled and whispered back, "It's okay. That was the kindest, sweetest way to be woken."

Emily looked down at Sarah's body and saw her thighs spread over Ragden's groin, her eyes widened, and she giggled softly. Emily placed a hand on Sarah's back and ran it down to her ass. Sarah sighed at the soft caress as Emily slid her hand over Sarah's ass, and to her labial lips, feeling them stretched around Ragden's cock. She gently circled her hand around the base of his cock and squeezed gently. It throbbed deep inside Sarah in response, causing Sarah to moan softly again. Emily looked over at Ragden and saw him gazing at her lovingly. She leaned over and kissed him softly on the lips.

"Good morning, lover," his voice rumbled softly, sending a thrill down her back.

She smiled and whispered back, "Good morning, my love."

Then she kissed him on the lips again with a little more passion. Then she turned and saw Sarah watching them, and she kissed her softly on the lips as well. Sarah returned the kiss passionately, slipping her tongue into Emily's mouth. Emily gasped softly and smiled back into her.

Aria slowly drifted awake. She heard the soft rumble of Ragden's voice and felt his pulse against her skin. A thrill ran down her back, her pulse quickening as she realized where she was. She sighed softly, feeling the warmth and love over her body. She felt her breasts pressed against his side, his arm along her back. Then she felt the leg between her and Ragden's hips. She reached out softly and felt the leg. Ran her hand up it to cup the ass attached.

Aria opened her eyes and saw Sarah looking at her. Aria giggled, and Sarah smiled at her lovingly. Aria ran her hand up Sarah's thigh, over her ass, and gasped as she felt Sarah's lips stretched over Ragden's cock. She felt a wash of jealousy. His cock was fully seated inside Sarah's tight pussy. She cupped his balls and felt the throbbing of his body inside her. Aria bit her lip, then looked at Sarah's face, saw her flushed cheeks and her rapid breath. She leaned forward and gently kissed Sarah on the lips as Sarah pressed back against her. Aria could taste her desire, her passion, and her love. Her jealousy washed away in Sarah's love.

Aria looked over and saw Ragden watching her. His gaze was full of compassion, desire, and love. She blushed slightly as he leaned over and kissed her softly on the lips.

"Good morning, my love," his voice rumbled softly, sending a thrill down her back. She blushed again, then leaned over and kissed him more passionately. He returned it with just as much passion.

Sarah smiled, and spoke huskily, "Well... now that everyone is awake..."

She sat up, pushed the covers off everyone, and ground her hips against Ragden's groin. The change in angle caused his cock to push against her insides in a new spot. She moaned at the sensation, then gently raised herself, and sat down heavily, feeling his cock push into her cervix again. Ragden moaned softly at the impact, feeling it reverberate through his entire body. Aria giggled, her eyes sparkling with desire as she watched Sarah ride Ragden's cock. She snuggled closer to his chest. She reached out and ran her hand down Sarah's thigh along Ragden's side and gazed up at Sarah. Ragden gently rocked his hips up into Sarah, pushing his cock against her cervix. Sarah moaned in response.

Sarah's eyes sparkled. Her body trembled with desire as she rode Ragden's cock. Her pussy gripped him tightly. Her walls clenched and released around him as she climbed up and down on him. Her breasts bounced with each movement. Sarah gazed down at Ragden. Her cheeks were flushed, her eyes bright with lust as her heart raced. Her mind whirled with pleasure and excitement. She bit her lip and looked at Ragden's strong chest and muscular form as she leaned in to kiss him passionately.

"Mm... I love feeling you inside me like this, Ragden." Sarah whispered huskily.

Ragden placed his hands gently on her waist, felt her body flex as she lifted herself partially off his throbbing cock, and sat back down on it. He matched her movements, thrusting up into her as she came down and drew back as she lifted. Each thrust caused his cock to push into her cervix more insistently. He moaned with the impact, feeling the waves of pleasure through his body.

Sarah gazed down at Ragden as he placed his hands on her waist, feeling her body flex with each thrust and release. Sarah's pussy gripped Ragden's cock tightly, pulling him deeper into her every time she lifted off and fell back onto him. The sensation sent shivers of pleasure coursing through her entire body.

"Fuck," she moaned.

Emily watched, her head resting on Ragden's chest, hearing his heart beat faster in his chest. She could feel her own heart starting to race with the energy in the room. She smiled up at Sarah, watching her ride his massive cock. She slipped one hand down between her legs, feeling her damp arousal, and slipped a finger into her pussy, feeling her muscles clenching in time to Ragden's thrusts into Sarah. Emily moaned softly.

Aria watched, licking her lips, as Sarah rode his cock harder. She watched him thrust up into her, her chest and hips bouncing with each impact. She slid a hand up Sarah's thigh, feeling the taught, strong muscles of her legs working in tandem with Ragden's. He matched Sarah's movements as the pace

increased, his thrusts harder against hers. The collisions of their groins increased in intensity. He felt each impact reverberate through his entire body, his cock pushing harder against her cervix. Each impact caused both to exhale sharply.

Aria's blue eyes sparkled. Her body trembled with desire as Sarah continued to ride Ragden's cock. Her hips bounced with each impact. Aria gazed over at Emily, and saw her cheeks flushed, as her hand slid up Sarah's thigh, gripping tightly. Sarah's pussy gripped Ragden's thick cock tightly, her walls pulsing with each impact, as she continued to ride him more forcefully. Sarah moaned, loving every bit of it. Feeling her insides stretched to their limits, his massive cock filled her and pushed against her cervix with each impact of their hips. She felt her breasts bouncing, her hips vibrating with the impact. She felt her heart racing faster and could feel Ragden's pulse through his cock, matching hers. His breath exhaled at the same speed as hers. She felt her climax growing within her as the pressure and pleasure started to build and build.

"Oh, God," Sarah moaned loudly, "Fuck me harder."

Ragden pushed his feet down into the bed, pushing his groin forcefully up into Sarah, pushing her slightly forward. A small surprised, "Oh!" slipped from her lips. From this new angle, Ragden started to pound his cock into her pussy faster and harder. Each impact rocked her entire body, sending massive waves of pleasure through both. Ragden moaned happily, feeling his climax quickly building along with Sarah's. He looked up and saw her eyes go wide with delight as her body reached the tipping point.

Sarah's eyes sparkled. Her body trembled with desire as her pussy was pounded relentlessly. Sarah gasped in surprise and pleasure as Ragden's powerful thrusts sent waves of ecstasy through her body, her orgasm rapidly approaching. Sarah's eyes locked onto Ragden's.

"Fuuuckkk," she moaned loudly; her voice was audible, even over the pounding of their hearts and the slapping of skin against skin. Sarah reached down and put her hands on his chest, bracing herself so she could push back against his groin, increasing the power of the impact of his cock against her cervix. Her eyes rolled back into her head as her climax exploded over her.

Aria grinned widely, as she spied the condition of Sarah. She watched in admiration as her body bucked against his thrusts. She crawled around behind to get a better view of his cock slamming into her. She whistled softly to herself, feeling her juices starting to drip down her legs. She tentatively placed a hand on Sarah's back, feeling the other woman's body tensing and the pulsing of her heart.

Emily watched, smiling, her hand on Ragden's chest, her head on his shoulder. She could feel his pounding heartbeat as he fucked Sarah harder and faster. Being so close, she felt her own body responding to the intense energy washing over her. Her pussy clenched on her hand, the muscles of her body quivering with pleasure. As she watched Sarah climax, her own body clenched

hard, her fluids flowing over her hand. She sighed happily.

Ragden felt Sarah's muscles go rigid, her motion stopping as her eyes rolled back into her head. He held her hips steady as he continued to thrust into her, her body rocking hard as he slammed his cock into her cervix again and again. Then his climax rode over him, as he slammed his cock into her one more time. His climax exploded out of him, filling her up. He could feel their mixed juices running down over his cock and shivered with the ecstasy of it. He relaxed his muscles, letting his ass fall back onto the mattress. He let go of her hips, and she sat heavily down upon his cock, slamming it into her cervix again, moaning loudly at the sensation. He moaned in response as she collapsed on him, her head thumping hard against his chest. Her pulse was still racing as she gasped for air.

Aria's blue eyes sparkled, and her body trembled with desire as Sarah's motions suddenly stopped, her pussy emptying as Ragden's cock spurted hot cum into her. Sarah's orgasm crashed over her, sending her body into convulsions. She gasped and moaned loudly, her hands grabbing onto anything she could find as she slammed back onto Ragden's cock, driving herself into him once more. Her heart pounded in her chest. Her breath was ragged and uneven. Aria crawled closer to Sarah's twitching body; she dipped her head between her legs and ran her tongue over Ragden's swollen balls, licking the mixed juices off them. Then she ran her tongue up across Sarah's lips and to her ass. Aria pressed her tongue against Sarah's ass and slipped it into her. Sarah cried out at the sudden invasion, her body convulsing again as she climaxed again. She felt Aria's tongue exploring her ass, and waves of pleasure rolled over her. Her pussy clenched so hard on Ragden's cock that another spray of cum exploded into her. She moaned again as Aria withdraw her tongue and proceeded to lap up the mixed juices dribbling out of Sarah's pussy over Ragden's balls.

Ragden moaned softly at the feel of Aria's soft tongue on his balls. He felt his balls tighten up and shoot more cum into Sarah's clenched pussy. Sarah moaned again, feeling even more of his seed filling her.

Emily watched, giggling to herself. Then she leaned over and kissed Sarah softly on the lips, tasting the woman's exhaustion, her sweetness, and her love. Sarah moaned again, reaching out and caressing Emily's cheek. Emily then broke from the kiss with Sarah, breathless. She took a moment to catch her breath, her eyes closed. When she opened them, she saw Ragden looking at her, his eyes full of love, desire, and compassion, which were all the things that she loved about him. She felt her heart swell, as she leaned in to kiss him passionately. She could taste his love, his desire, his exotic flavor that sent her heart fluttering. She felt his tongue dip into her mouth, and her heart raced. She broke off from the kiss, even more breathless than before. Emily could feel her juices dripping down her leg, and she knew she wanted him inside her, desperately.

Ragden wrapped his arms gently around Sarah, pulling her body close to

his as he kissed her on the forehead. Sarah moaned softly in response, her body still twitching, her heart calming but still beating hard. She looked up at him, a pleading look in her eyes. She giggled, her body still clenching and releasing on his massive cock. She loved the feeling of how full she was with him in her. She never wanted it to end. Sarah looked at Emily and saw the desire and need on her face, the twitching of her muscles, the dampness between her legs. Sarah smiled at her, and gently caressed her face and neck, cupping her breast. Emily sighed against her touch. Sarah nodded to her.

Aria drew back, sensing something was about to change. She slid back a little farther to give them room. Then Ragden rolled to his left, slipping Sarah beneath him as he did so. She moaned in pleasure, feeling his weight against her. She reached up and ran her hand up to his side. She nodded but could not keep the disappointment from her face as he slowly withdrew his still throbbing cock from her depths. She groaned softly as it exited her. Ragden leaned down and kissed her softly on the lips. A tear slipped down her cheek as he moved off her and crawled over to Emily. Aria crawled between Sarah's legs and ran her tongue over Sarah's folds. Sarah moaned loudly, clutching her breasts hard, feeling her body convulse at the soft touch. Aria slipped a finger into Sarah's damp folds as she licked up the fluids still draining from within her. Sarah moaned again.

Ragden crawled over to Emily, who lay on her back, waiting for him. She reached out and grasped his strong shoulders as he slipped between her legs, his massive cock slipping into her wet folds and inside her. She moaned loudly as he filled her up.

Emily watched as Ragden moved between her legs, her pussy glistening with excitement and desire, her juices flowing freely as she gazed up at him adoringly. Emily moaned loudly as Ragden's thick cock penetrated her completely, filling her to the brim with his thickness and heat. Emily clung to Ragden's shoulders, her hands gripping tightly as she reveled in the pleasure of being filled by his powerful erection. Emily arched her back, her chest heaving as she tried to take in deep breaths to control the intensity of the sensations coursing through her body.

Sarah felt Aria's soft tongue slipping through her folds, swirling around her clitoris, dipping inside her vagina. Aria caught every drop of her cum as it slipped from her. Her mind reeled at the soft sensation of it, after having just been filled with Ragden's massive cock. Aria's tongue was soft and sensual and the perfect thing to soothe her sore walls and muscles. She moaned softly at the feeling of it. Aria smiled, sensing how much Sarah was enjoying her soft touch. She felt happy to be able to please her so much. She looked over and saw Emily getting filled with Ragden's cock and felt the desire to be filled. She was okay waiting though. She was enjoying herself and knew Ragden would be there for her when she was ready.

Ragden moaned softly as his cock slid up into Emily's tight wet pussy. He slid his knees up under her thighs and rolled his hips against hers, his cock

sliding against her cervix. Emily's body clenched on the entirety of his cock, causing him to moan softly in response. She smiled up at him, her hands on his shoulders as she kissed his lips passionately, slipping her tongue into his mouth to taste him. Emily moaned softly feeling his thick cock fill her and gently push against her deepest depths. She felt the pressure against her cervix and moaned in pleasure, as she felt the warmth and pleasure flowing through her whole body. She felt like every fiber of her being was waking up and drinking in the love and ecstasy of the sensation. Emily gently rolled her hips against Ragden's, feeling his cock push firmly against her cervix. She moaned again, the pressure inside her building. She felt his cock throbbing inside her and smiled. Ragden smiled at her, kissing her softly on the lips as he slid his cock partially out of her and then slid it back in. It gently pressed against her cervix in a loving caress. As he rolled back again, she matched his movement, causing his cock to slide out of her and up through her folds against her clitoris. She blushed and rolled her hips back as he chuckled and pushed his cock down with one hand to get the head of it back into her lips. Ragden moaned softly as his cock slid up into her again. Emily rolled against him, pushing her cervix against the head of his cock, moaning at the pleasure of it. Ragden withdrew partially and slid back in, matching her movements.

Emily moaned in pleasure as Ragden's cock slid up into her and pressed against her cervix. She matched his slow rhythm, enjoying the feeling of his cock stretching her tight walls, then them closing around the gap left behind, and him filling them again. She matched his slow rhythm, their bodies moved in unison. Their hearts beating as one. She felt the immense pleasure and pressure building within her. She gazed into his eyes and saw the deep depths of his love reflected there. An endless sea of beauty, grace, compassion, and boundless love. Emily rocked her hips back as he withdrew, sliding back far enough for his cock to slip out of her. She groaned at the emptiness she felt, the ache within her to be filled.

Then she looked up at him, and a shiver ran down her spine as she smiled seductively and whispered, "Put it in my ass. I want to feel you in my bowels. Please?"

Ragden looked at her questioningly, and she nodded. He smiled and kissed her as he took one hand and slipped his throbbing cock through her folds to her asshole. He slid the head of it in a tight circle around her asshole, teasing her. She moaned and rolled her hips against him, pushing the head of his cock into her ass. She moaned loudly, as she felt her ass puckering against him, tightly clenched, not allowing him in. The pressure was building and building against her ass. She pressed her groin harder against him, feeling it start to slip in. Emily took a deep breath, closed her eyes, and forced herself to relax. She gasped loudly as the head of his cock slipped into her. Immediately, her body clenched on his cock. Ragden moaned as her ass clenched on his throbbing cock. He looked down at her and saw her biting her lip. Ragden leaned down and gently kissed her on the lips, feeling her body tense and clench against

him. As he softly slipped his tongue into her mouth, he felt her starting to relax, his cock sliding into her. She gasped as it slid deeper and deeper into her. Ragden moaned softly as she clenched on him again, then released, allowing him to fully slide his massive throbbing cock up into her bowels.

Emily moaned loudly as his cock filled her bowels. She squeezed her eyes shut, feeling his massiveness filling her. She felt her body pulsing against his. Her ass clenched and released his cock. She felt her pulse racing, her breath catching in her throat. The waves of pleasure filled her entire body, her entire being. She felt so full of life, compassion, love, and his cock. It was almost too much to bear. She could feel the pain of her asshole stretched so wide to let him in. The walls of her intestinal tract stretched by his massiveness. A small voice in the back of her head cried out, saying this was not right, her body was not supposed to stretch like that. She silenced that voice in a snap. It may hurt, and be uncomfortable in the extreme, but the pleasure was so intense and overwhelming that she never wanted it to stop. Emily rolled her hips away from Ragden's, sliding his cock partially out of her. She groaned at the intense feeling of pressure that welled up. Then she rolled back against him, her groin touching his, sliding his cock as deep in her bowels as it would go. She moaned softly, squeezing his shoulders with her hands, digging her fingers into his flesh.

Ragden gently rolled his hips back, sliding most of his cock out of her ass before sliding back into her. She rolled her hips with his, pressing their groins firmly together. Then they rolled apart as one, and back together. Their pulses raced, their breathing faster as their bodies moved in synchronized motion. Ragden could feel her climax building rapidly, the waves of pleasure filling both of their bodies. Her tight ass squeezed on his cock, urging him to drive into her faster. He fought that urge and maintained a slow steady pace. Their hips met with some force, then parted, and met again.

Emily moaned, feeling Ragden's throbbing cock sliding in and out of her ass. Her mind whirled, her body pulsed with pressure and pleasure. She felt her climax roaring up within her. She could feel Ragden's swelling to meet hers. She knew it would not take much to push that over the edge. As much as she would enjoy that, she was not ready for that just yet. She stopped rolling her hips and placed a hand on his chest. He stopped and looked at her questioningly, concern on his face.

She smiled, and spoke softly, "This is AMAZING... But... I... I want your cum in my pussy."

Ragden smiled and hugged her to him, pulling her body firmly against his. His cock throbbed in her bowels, and she moaned softly at the feel of it.

"Of course, my love," he whispered, sliding his cock slowly out of her bowels.

Emily groaned and moaned as it slid back until it finally slid free. Emily looked down at his cock throbbing in his hand, dripping with her juice. Her ass ached from the feel of him being inside her. It had felt so good, so

amazing to have him filling her up, but she wanted him in her pussy now. Ragden smiled and slowly slid his cock into her pussy. Her walls clenched against him, so tight he had to press with some force to slide in. She moaned loudly as he filled her up. It slid deeper and deeper into her. So impossibly deep. Her body clenched so hard; that it made him feel even larger within her. Finally, his cock pressed against her cervix. Her pussy was so full of him. Ragden moaned at the tightness of her on him. The smoothness, the silkiness of her tight pussy. She was so incredibly damp with her desire for him. He looked down at her, questioningly, to make sure this was what she wanted. Emily smiled back and winked, nodding. Then he ground his hips against hers, watched as her eyes slipped closed, and she moaned at the sensation of his cock pushing against her cervix. He closed his eyes and savored the feeling, moaning softly at it.

Emily rolled her hips to meet his, sliding back and away, picking up a gentle rhythm that Ragden quickly matched. She felt her pulse starting to race again. Her breath came in gasps, as their hips collided with increased force. His cock first caressed her cervix. Then pressing against it insistently. Then pushing against it harder as they moved faster against each other. She felt her climax building impossibly fast. Her body responded to all the stimuli it had received in the last ten minutes. She felt like she was going to burst with all the pressure, pleasure, and love that filled her.

"Oh, God..." she moaned, "Harder."

Ragden braced himself against the bed and leaned into her. His hands leveraged his body and changed his angle, letting his hips roll faster. His strokes became longer, deeper, faster. Emily found her rhythm and matched his. The sounds of their groins colliding got louder and filled the room.

"Yes! Yes!" Emily hissed, between strokes, "Faster! Please!"

Ragden responded by increasing his pace, feeling her body twitching with the edges of her climax. He felt the energy building up within him. The air around him felt thick. In his mind, he could see a swirling ball of energy forming. His energy merged with Emily's to form a ball of swirling energy that pulsed with electrical sparks. He felt it gathering within him. He opened his eyes and looked down at Emily. Her eyes were wide, and he knew she could feel it, too. Still, their pace did not slow. They moved faster against each other. The bodies slapped together harder. The energy within them surged and grew, the ball growing larger as they continued to feed it with their desire, their love, and their sexual power. Ragden felt it collecting in his groin, in his balls. They felt charged, full, and ready to explode. He looked down at Emily, whose eyes were even larger, and she nodded softly as she thrust her hips against his. He thrust back into her; then, as he withdrew and prepared to push into her again, he felt the energy surge through his body, up out of his balls and into his groin. As his cock hit her cervix, the energy blasted out of him into her.

Emily felt the energy blast into her body. Every muscle went rigid as it filled her uterus. She could feel her ovaries collecting the energy, felt it

flooding through her body. Every nerve ending felt like it was on fire. Everything in the room felt brighter. The textures of the bed felt sharper. The details of the ceiling came into sharp relief. She could see every pore on Ragden's face, every spot where he needed to shave, clearly visible to her. She heard the rustling of the bushes outside, the leaves tickling each other, the birds in the tree outside looking at the house, wondering what was going on.

She could sense Sarah next to her. She could feel her heart beating, the texture of her skin where she was sweating as Aria's tongue slipped through her tight, wet folds. How Aria's tongue felt inside her. She felt Aria's love, her desires, her needs. Emily also felt Sarah's desires and needs. All of it washed over Emily in harsh relief. An assault on her sense that was too much to bear. Within her, she could sense the ball of energy building. She rocked her hips against Ragden, who was drawing back, getting ready to slide into her again. Everything moved impossibly slowly. She could feel every muscle fiber as they stretched and contracted to create the movement of her hips against his. Every inch of his cock as it slid along her vaginal walls. The ball of energy built within her uterus. Building and building. As his cock slid back towards it, she felt herself release it back to him. She cried out with the force of it; she could feel her climax riding her. The juices flowed inside her. His cock struck her cervix, and the energy shot back through his dick into him. Her back arched with the power of it. Her head craned back. She felt her whole body arching off the bed. Her arms were thrown back with the force of it. Everything was at the point in her cervix where the energy charged into Ragden's throbbing cock inside her.

Ragden cried out as the energy surged through his cock back into his body. He felt the energy come up through his groin into his chest. Where he caught it, caressed it, nurtured it. He filled it with his love, and as he drew back from Emily, preparing to thrust into her again, he felt the energy surge down through his body into his groin. He felt his balls tense up as he slid forward into her. As his cock smashed into her cervix again, he felt the energy unleash into her, along with the most massive load of cum he had ever felt himself release before. He cried out with the force of it. His back was arched. His legs convulsed. His head was thrown back. He felt locked into position as the energy and cum left his body.

Emily cried out again as the energy rode back into her. It felt different somehow than last time. She felt Ragden's ejaculation inside of her. The massive amount of fluid that filled her up and poured out of her. Every muscle in her body went rigid again. She felt the energy roll up through her body into her chest. She felt herself catch it, caress it, own it. Her body went limp as she absorbed most of the energy but felt more than she could handle. What she could not process, she felt it pulse out of her in a wave. As the wave of energy rolled out of her, she felt the blankets ripple with it, thrown off the bed. The pillows slid back from her head.

Sarah felt the wave of energy roll over her and felt every muscle in her

body clenched with the force of it. Her fluids ran freely from her pussy as she climaxed again. Her back arched, and she cried out, then fell limply against the bed.

Aria felt the wave of energy roll through her, and she felt Sarah climax beneath her; she felt her body climaxing again. She shivered and twitched with the force of it. Her body convulsed. She felt Sarah climaxing beneath her, and as more fluid rolled out of Sarah's pussy, Aria tried to lap it up but found her body having difficulty as her climax rolled through her. Eventually, she collapsed against Sarah's leg, and rolled over on her side, trying to catch her breath.

Ragden collapsed on Emily, laying his body across hers. He kissed her softly on the lips. She returned the kiss but barely moved. Her eyes fluttered but remained closed. Her body twitched and quivered beneath him. He could feel her pussy as it clenched and released on his dick, milking the cum from him. He lay his head on her shoulder, relaxed, trying to catch his breath. He felt Emily's arms wrapped around him, gently hugging him against her. He felt her firm nipples pressed against his chest. Her heart was still pounding against her ribcage. Ragden smiled at the feeling of her beneath him. He felt cum still oozing from his cock into her depths. The sensation was incredibly relaxing and sensual. He kissed her again, more deeply this time, and she responded to him, welcoming his tongue into her. She pulled him tightly against her with her arms. As the last of his spasms passed, Ragden raised himself off Emily, who pouted at him, then smiled beatifically. He leaned down and kissed her softly on the lips, lingering, feeling the fullness of her lips against his. Then he pulled back and smiled again. He slowly backed himself out of her, until his cock slipped from her pussy. She moaned and pouted.

"It is a school day, after all, and we need to start getting ready for school," he spoke softly, but his voice carried through the room. Emily nodded but lay where he left her, smiling, basking in the afterglow of her intense orgasm. Ragden crawled across the bed and softly kissed Sarah and Aria before standing and stretching his muscles.

CHAPTER 20

Ragden held his hand out as Aria crawled across the bed. She took his hand and crawled down off the bed, allowing him to steady her as she stood and stretched, then she turned and pulled herself against his body while pressing every bit of herself to his skin that she could. She felt his limp cock pressed against her abdomen, firm and hot, but still large against her. She shivered at the sensation of having it against her skin. She kissed him deeply on the lips, savoring the feel of his heat, passion, and love.

"Thank you," Aria whispered as she drew back from him.

Her hands lingered on his waist, then his cock. Ragden sighed with pleasure as she gently stroked his cock, which pulsed with life in her hand. Aria then dropped to her knees and took the head of his cock into her mouth, gently swirling her tongue around the soft skin of it. She could taste Emily on him still and shivered at the texture and taste of it. Then she bobbed the soft cock down her throat and pulled back, taking a deep breath. She then smiled, stood, and kissed Ragden lightly on the lips before she stepped towards the doorway. She stopped just short of the door, turned, and leaned against the wall as Sarah crawled to the edge of the bed. Ragden smiled at Aria, then held his hand out for Sarah.

Sarah reached out and firmly took Ragden's hand as she slid off the bed and stood. She stretched and sighed in pleasure, then turned and wrapped herself around Ragden. She pressed herself to him, much as Aria had done before her. She looked up at him and pulled his head down to kiss her. She pressed her lips to him passionately, her tongue darting in and tasting him. He then darted into her mouth and she moaned softly as his tongue explored her mouth. A shiver ran down Sarah's back as he pulled her closer to him. She could feel his cock throb against her stomach, growing harder as she pressed herself against him.

Sarah grinned into his lips and giggled as she pulled her head back from his. She stroked his cock as she took a small step back from him. Ragden moaned softly as she stroked his cock harder, feeling it stiffen in her hands

and throb at her touch.

"Hm..." She whispered seductively as she continued to stroke his cock, "I think I'll want to play with this later..."

Then she dropped to her knees and slipped the head of his cock into her mouth. Ragden moaned softly as she took it down her throat, pressing her lips to his groin. She bobbed her head back and forth, sucking as hard as she could, before slipping it out of her mouth with a huge smile. She flicked her tongue across the tip of it before she stood. She kept one hand on it, stroking gently as she stepped up to Ragden again. This time she straddled his cock, forcing it through her pussy lips as she pulled herself against him. Ragden moaned softly, feeling her wet juices slide along the length of his cock as she kissed him fiercely.

Then Sarah stepped back and winked at him. He held her firmly for a moment, not letting her get away from him before he finally let her step back. His cock throbbed through her lips as she did. She shivered briefly, then stepped over to Aria, giggling. She wrapped herself around Aria, hugging and kissing her tightly. Ragden shivered; his cock throbbing as he turned to Emily. Emily slowly crawled across the bed, having watched everything that had just played out. She giggled to herself as she took Ragden's hand and stood up, stretching her muscles.

Then she too turned to him and pulled herself against him. She felt his cock press against her and smiled into his lips as she kissed him. She dipped her tongue into his mouth, tasting his desire, his need and his love. She pressed her body against him, feeling her nipples firm up against his skin. She felt his heart beating against her chest, his cock throbbing against her abdomen. Emily drew her body reluctantly away from his. She felt his need, his cock throbbing against her with it. She looked down at his throbbing cock and then up at him.

"Shall we do something about this before we take a shower?" Emily asked softly.

Ragden's eyes glittered with desire, but he shrugged nonchalantly. His voice was mild, only his cock throbbed as he spoke to show his need, "If you wish, but if not, I'll be fine."

Emily pouted at Ragden, not hearing the confirmation she wanted. She looked down at his cock, throbbing in her hands, a bead of precum forming at the tip. She stroked it once, causing more precum to form on the tip.

"As you wish dear..." she whispered as she took a step back and turned her back to him. She waggled her ass as she took a step away from him.

Ragden groaned and grabbed her by the waist, pulling her back to him. She bent over at the waist, reaching between her legs to grab his cock and point it at her pussy as he pulled her back. The effect sent his cock straight into her pussy. She sighed in pleasure as Ragden moaned. His cock sank deep into her pussy. She ground her hips against his while Aria and Sarah giggled. She looked at them and winked.

Emily looked over her shoulder at Ragden and sighed softly, "I thought you didn't want to take care of that..."

Ragden laughed softly as he held her steady and thrust into her, his cock sliding against her cervix. She moaned in pleasure as he drew back and thrust into her again. Emily gasped in pleasure, feeling the fullness of his thick cock stretching her tight sheath, her back arching in pleasure. Then she stepped forward, groaning as his cock slipped out of her wet folds.

While Sarah and Aria giggled at the scene, Emily spun around and faced Ragden. She kept one hand on his cock, which was slick with her arousal. She looked at him sternly and shook a finger at him, "I thought you said you would be fine."

"I did," he groaned.

"If you want release then ask for it, otherwise it's shower time... your words," Emily said sternly.

Ragden sighed, and chuckled to himself, "Emily, my love, would you help me get some release before our shower?"

She smiled beatifically as she dropped to her knees before him, "Of course my dear."

With that, she grabbed his cock firmly in both hands, slipped the head of it into her mouth, and stroked it up and down. She squeezed as hard as she could. Ragden moaned loudly as she sucked on the tip of his cock, feeling his climax quickly approaching. Emily could sense his balls starting to tighten as she stroked him harder and harder. Just as she sensed his muscles starting to clench, she slammed her mouth against his cock, the head of it easily slipping down her throat. Her lips pressed against his groin and she grabbed his ass and pulled him against her as she flexed her throat against him. Ragden cried out as his climax rode over him, his throbbing cock so far down Emily's throat, his cum bursting out and straight into her stomach. She released his ass and bobbed her head on his cock, squeezing every last drop of cum out of him. She bobbed repeatedly as he clenched and moaned at the sensation of her throat clenching on his cock. Then she backed off, gasped for air, and sucked on the tip of his cock. Again, she wrapped her hands around his cock and stroked up and down, squeezing his cum out into her mouth. Another burst of cum exploded into her mouth, but she was ready and swallowed it easily.

Aria and Sarah stood at the door, their mouths hanging open as Emily swallowed every drop of cum that she could squeeze out of him. Ragden sank onto the bed and flopped onto his back while Emily continued to suck and stroke his cock, still squeezing out cum. As his muscles stopped convulsing and he sat back up, Emily drew back, running her tongue over the tip of his cock and smiled up at him. Ragden smiled down at her, his body still quaking softly at the sudden orgasm she had coaxed out of him.

"Thank you," he said while taking large, deep breaths as he tried to catch his breath. "That was amazing."

Emily smiled coyly as she stood between his legs. "All you had to do was ask..."

Emily wrapped her arms around him, pulling his head against her chest. He nuzzled her breasts affectionately, kissing her as she hugged him. . Emily stepped back and pulled him to his feet. Ragden chuckled as he stood, letting her pull him up. He smiled and allowed her to pull him to the door. Sarah and Aria giggled as Ragden pulled the door open and stepped across the hall, the three ladies close on his heels. He stepped in and turned on the water, holding the door open as Sarah and Aria slipped in together and began rinsing and cleaning each other.

Ragden leaned against the vanity watching. Emily stepped in front of him and leaned against him, kissing him softly on the lips. She gently stroked his limp cock and looked up at him, "Feeling better now, lover?"

Ragden chuckled softly, his voice full of amusement and pleasure. "Yes. Thank you" he replied. He leaned down and kissed her on the lips softly. The shower door opened and Sarah and Aria grabbed Ragden's arms and pulled him into the shower. He laughed and let himself get pulled in, as Emily turned and watched, giggling.

"Okay, ladies, you got me in here... what now?"

Aria and Sarah giggled to themselves as they lathered their hands up with soap. They proceeded to soap up Ragden one woman in front of him, the other at the back. Sarah ran her hands over his shoulders and chest, then over his abdomen. She soaped up his groin, then ran soap down his legs, massaging his large muscles. Aria worked down his back, working the soap into his muscles and then kneading his ass. As the soap was rinsing off, Sarah ducked down in front of Ragden, and slipped his soft cock into her mouth. She slipped his cock down her throat while Aria cupped his balls, squeezing gently. Ragden sighed in pleasure as he shampooed and rinsed his hair out.

Sarah stood, kissed him softly on the chin, and whispered, "Can you get hard for me? I want to suck your cock."

Aria pressed herself against his back, reaching around and stroking his cock as she giggled.

A shiver ran down his back as he looked down into Sarah's hungry eyes. Aria giggled as his cock throbbed in her hands, growing large and stiff. Sarah smiled hungrily as she dropped down in front of him and slipped his cock into her mouth. He moaned softly as she took it down her throat and bobbed her head on it, flexing her throat. Ragden moaned with pleasure as her lips pressed against his groin. Aria then stepped around him and nudged Sarah. Sarah bobbed again, then backed off, wiping her chin as Aria grasped his cock and slipped it into her mouth. She sucked hard, swirling her tongue around the tip as she tried to relax her throat and slip it deeper into her mouth. Ragden groaned as she managed to get the head into her throat. She gagged softly and coughed, pulling it out. She licked the tip greedily, sucking on the small amount of precum that had collected there.

Sarah slipped it into her mouth and sucked it down her throat, pressing her lips to his groin as Ragden moaned in pleasure. She bobbed once, then backed off, grinning up at Ragden hungrily.

Ragden moaned softly as Sarah let go of his cock and Aria slipped it into her mouth again. She took a deep breath and slipped the head of it into her mouth, sucking gently, then tried to relax and pull the head down her throat. She choked softly then slipped it into her throat. Her eyes went wild as she pressed forward, grabbing his ass and pulling him into her mouth. Her lips kissed his groin and she quickly backed off, coughing, and gasping for breath. She blushed darkly as she moved back to allow Sarah to take it. Sarah smiled wickedly, then slipped his cock down her throat again, bobbing up and down on it, while Ragden moaned in pleasure, Then Sarah backed off, taking deep breaths.

Sarah stood, grasping Ragden's cock firmly as she stepped up against him and kissed his lips softly. Aria stepped out of the shower and started drying herself off while Emily stepped in. Aria paused to kiss Emily softly on the lips, then slapped her ass playfully as she grabbed her towel. Emily blushed, then stepped up next to Ragden in the water. She smiled up at him as Sarah stroked his cock and kissed him. Sarah stepped back and kissed Emily on the lips softly, then she turned back to Ragden and winked.

"Thanks for that," she giggled mischievously as she started to step away from Ragden. Then she bent over, touched her toes, and let her ass slip backward and thump heavily against Ragden's groin. Her ass cheeks slipped around his throbbing cock. She stood, looking over her shoulder with an almost innocent smile on her face as she ground her hips against his cock. Then she reached back, grasped his cock and pressed it against her asshole. Ragden gasped softly as she pressed herself back against it. Emily giggled as it slipped into her ass.

Ragden reached down and firmly gripped her ass, pulling her against him. Sarah moaned in pleasure as his cock slipped deeper and deeper into her. She stood up, arching her back, and thrust her ass against him, her ass cheeks pushing firmly against his groin. She moaned, realizing that his entire cock was up her ass, then she slid herself forward and back along it. Ragden moaned, then gripped her ass and held her firmly while he thrust deeply into her. She moaned in pleasure, clutching her chest. Emily giggled as she finished soaping herself down, then stepped around Sarah and grasped her breasts, pushing her back against Ragden. Sarah moaned at the pressure on her chest as Ragden thrust into her ass harder.

"Oh God," she moaned in pleasure, feeling each thrust going deeper into her, shaking her whole body. Sarah felt the pressure on her breasts and gasped as Emily licked her nipples, then pulled on them with her teeth as Ragden continued to slam his cock up her ass. She felt her body responding to all the sensations and knew she was reaching her limit.

Sarah's mind whirled, her heart racing, her breath exploding out of her in

great gasps with each massive thrust of Ragden into her bowels. She felt the pain, pressure and pleasure building within her. She knew she could not last long with this onslaught on her body. She felt Emily grasping her breasts firmly, pinching her nipples, adding more to the ecstasy. Her bowels throbbed, clenched, and released as Ragden pounded his cock into her.

"This is... what you... wanted," Ragden grunted between thrusts, "isn't it?"

"Yes... Oh God... Yes!!" Sarah exclaimed in response, "Harder! Oh God... Fuck me harder!!"

Emily pushed more firmly against Sarah's breasts, pinching her nipples as she pushed her upright. She then leaned in and kissed her passionately, thrusting her tongue into Sarah's mouth. Sarah moaned in response. Ragden dug his fingers into her hips, grasping her firmly as he thrust against her harder, his cock throbbing inside her, then pulling back and slamming into her harder. Each thrust was accentuated with the slapping of his groin against her ass cheeks. Sarah gasped in pleasure and pain. Her body rocked. Her senses were overwhelmed. Emily grinned against her lips, sensing her impending climax. She looked at Ragden, caught his gaze and nodded. Ragden grinned back at her. They both closed their eyes and as Ragden continued to thrust against her, they both reached out with their energy and found Sarah, caressed her climax, fed it, and felt it grow.

Aria watched, her mouth agape as a bit of drool collected on her chin. Her pussy dripped with need and desire as she watched Sarah twitch and spasm between Emily and Ragden. She could sense something happening and could feel the energy level in the room increasing, with Sarah in the middle of it. She reached down and cupped her mound. She felt her damp arousal and slipped a finger into her wet folds, feeling the tightness of her pussy. She groaned softly as she slid a finger in and out of herself as she watched Sarah get fucked.

Sarah felt her body trembling with pleasure, her climax threatening to overwhelm her senses. She felt Ragden's massive cock sliding in and out of her bowels with a ferocity she had not felt before. Her body quivered and shook, her muscles twitching. The pressure building within her was more than she could contain. Each time he thrust into her; she could feel her climax building even more.

Ragden felt the energy building up within his body, his balls tingled with it. His legs felt like ants were crawling on them. He grasped her hips firmly and continued to thrust into her as deep and hard as he could. Her ass squeezed on his cock, the pressure building up in him, escalating and building. The pleasure compounded on itself and built faster. Ragden felt himself about to burst as he focused his mind on the energy collecting in him and pushed it into his balls and as he thrust into Sarah, he thrust the energy up through his cock and into her. He cried out as the energy burst out of his cock into her bowels. Every muscle in his body went rigid with the force of it pushing out of him. His fingers convulsed into her hips, digging deep, locking her in place.

His legs flexed and locked, his back arched, his arms convulsed. His cum exploded out with it, filling her bowels with his hot, sticky seed.

Sarah cried out as his cum and his energy exploded into her. She felt it surge through her bowels, filling up her abdomen with his massive load of cum. Her climax rolled over her in response, as fluid flooded out of her pussy, dripping down her legs into the shower. Her body convulsed, her legs buckled, her hips pressed hard against his groin. Her back arched and her head was thrown back against his chest as she cried out to the ceiling as her orgasm rolled over her.

Then Emily grabbed her neck and pulled her lips down to hers. She kissed her deeply, and while doing that, sucked the energy out of her. Sarah's eyes went wide as she felt the roiling energy in her abdomen surge up through her chest, into her throat, and Emily's mouth. Her body convulsed, her legs twitched, her arms thrashed as she felt it rush out of her. Then Emily drew back from her.

The energy flowed down into Emily's chest. Emily closed her eyes as she pulled the energy into her chest, feeling it collecting, then she opened her eyes and pushed it down her arms back into Sarah's chest. Sarah cried out again as Emily squeezed her breasts tightly, the energy flowing back into her. Sarah felt her senses heighten, her pulse raced and she gasped for breath as she felt like her chest was full of so much compassion, desire, lust, and love. She felt like a ball of fire had been stuffed into her chest and she clutched Emily's hands on her chest as the energy rolled down into her abdomen. She felt it roll down into her bowels. She shook her head, not ready for what was coming next as it collected in her uterus. She felt it building and building inside her. Ragden suddenly drew back his cock out of her ass and plunged it into her pussy, sliding deep up into her, striking her cervix. At that moment of contact, she felt the energy flow out of her and into Ragden's massive cock. She cried out as the release of energy caused her to climax again. Fluid flowed freely out of her pussy. As the energy rolled out of her, she felt her senses return to normal and the world felt a little less bright, as if someone had dimmed the lights. She felt her muscles clenching and convulsing as Ragden withdrew his cock from her pussy. She groaned as her pussy clenched on the empty space left behind.

Ragden grasped her hips firmly and placed the head of his cock against her asshole again. She moaned at the pressure as he slammed it home into her bowels. She cried out again, as the energy exploded into her again, along with another load of his sticky seed filling her bowels. She felt the energy flow up into her body, every nerve in her body felt like it had been lit on fire. Her legs buckled, and she would have fallen if Ragden had not been holding her hips firm. Emily leaned forward and kissed her passionately, breathing something into her. She felt more than just her tongue and lips pressing against her. That something flowed into Sarah and mixed with the roiling energy in her abdomen, calming it. Sarah felt it absorbed in her. Hot tears slipped from her eyes at the incredible amount of pleasure and love that filled her being. Her

body went completely limp. Emily held her body in place, while Ragden wrapped one arm around her waist, the other snaking up her chest to pull her body against his.

Sarah gasped for breath, trying to reconcile what had just happened to her. She had no strength to hold herself up. She felt her back against Ragden's chest. The water of the shower cascaded over her, rinsing the fluids from her legs that were leaking down from her pussy and ass. She could still feel Ragden's massive, throbbing dick deep in her bowels. Her ass ached from being stretched by him, yet it was an ache that felt so good, so amazingly powerfully wonderful. She smiled and giggled. Sarah's eyes fluttered open. In front of her, stood Emily watching her carefully. A mild look of concern on her face. Sarah tried to reach out and reassure her, but her arm would not move. Everything felt so heavy.

Emily reached out and placed her hands on her breasts again. She felt the warmth, compassion, desire, and love flowing into her. Her muscles tingled, and she felt strength filling her body again. Sarah reached out and pulled Emily against her. Emily smiled happily and wrapped her arms around Sarah, hugging her warmly. Sarah felt her legs find footing beneath her and she stood up tall, testing her muscles.

Ragden slipped his hands to her waist, holding her steady while she stretched her legs. She smiled, feeling so very much alive. Sarah started to step forward and immediately stopped, the massive cock in her ass throbbed and she moaned loudly as it started to slide out of her. Sarah pressed her back against Ragden's chest, feeling his heat, compassion, and love pulsing against her. She felt his cock throbbing inside her, his cum still filling her bowels. She smiled. Emily stepped back and giggled to herself.

Emily spoke softly, "If you two don't mind, I'd like to wash off now If you are done?"

Sarah laughed and nodded, "Yes. I think I am done. But... I have this... COCK in my ASS." She shivered with pleasure and licked her lips.

Ragden leaned down and kissed her shoulder, her neck, then her ear. He whispered to her, "Are you quite satisfied, my love?"

Sarah nodded happily, loving every throb of his cock in her ass, "Yes, I am... but... Do you have to...?"

Ragden laughed, a deep wonderful sound that sent shivers down her back. Emily looked at him and smiled, a finger drifting across her groin, tickling her lips.

"If we did not have school today, I would consider it. However, I am not sure I want to turn into any more of a prune than we already have..."

He laughed again, this time it sounded more normal with less sexual edge to it, just deep humor as he bent his knees and slowly lowered himself out of her bowels. He did it slowly, sliding inch after inch out of her. She groaned, feeling her ass clench on the space he had occupied within her.

After he finished pulling out of her, she tried to turn around and found

herself unsteady. His hands grabbed her hips, holding her steady so that she would not fall. Emily moved closer and placed a hand on Sarah's shoulder. Her touch was soft and loving. Sarah looked up and leaned into Emily, kissed her on the lips softly. Emily smiled and stepped back under the water, washing herself off.

Sarah turned and wrapped her arms around Ragden, pulling herself against his body. His cock throbbed against her abdomen and she sighed in pleasure. She could feel the heat and intensity of it against her. She looked down at it, saw it still slick with her cum and his. She looked up at Ragden questioningly. He cocked an eyebrow at her, then nodded. Sarah slowly lowered herself to her knees, then slipped his cock into her mouth and moaned at the pleasure of it slipping into her throat. She slid it in, her lips pressed against his groin. Ragden moaned in pleasure as she bobbed once on his cock, then pulled back slowly, easing it out of her mouth. Then she sucked all the cum and juice off it. She nodded slowly and Ragden took her hand and pulled her back to her feet.

"Jesus, fuck me sideways, that tasted good..."

She smiled at Ragden, then she wrapped herself around him, hugging him fiercely. He tilted her head back gently and kissed her on the lips. She smiled in pleasure, then she released him and stepped gingerly to the edge of the shower. Ragden followed behind her, his hands trailing on her hips to make sure she did not fall. Sarah stepped out of the shower, grabbed a towel, and started to dry herself off. Ragden followed, grabbed a towel for himself and started drying off as well. Aria stood transfixed against the vanity. She blinked slowly at both. Then she snapped her mouth shut and walked up to Ragden.

Ragden put his towel back on the hanger and looked at Aria. Then slipped his arms around her and hugged her warmly. He kissed her softly on the lips, then spoke softly to her, "Can I do something for you, my love?"

Aria's blue eyes sparkled and her body trembled with desire as she snuggled close to Ragden, feeling the warmth of his embrace enveloping her. She gazed up at him lovingly. Her cheeks were flushed. Her heart raced. Her mind whirled with lust and desire. She felt the weight of his cock pressed against her stomach, the hardness of it filling her with anticipation and need.

"Yes, my love," she whispered, her voice barely audible, "please... give me what I need."

He kissed her softly on the lips, one hand caressing her cheek as the other drifted down her back, "And what is it that you think you need?"

Aria's blue eyes sparkled; her body trembled with desire. She gazed up at Ragden, as he kissed her softly on the lips, one hand caressing her back, the other drifting down her spine, causing Aria to shiver with pleasure.

"I need you to fill me up completely," Aria whispered, her voice barely audible, as she looked up at Ragden with pleading eyes, yearning for him to give her everything she craved.

"Oh... I suppose I could do that," he whispered huskily. His hand trailed

down over her ass, slipping between her ass cheeks, gently caressing her asshole, then sliding through her pussy lips, feeling the dampness there. "Just one question love... Where do you want it?"

She gazed up at Ragden. Her cheeks flushed, her heart racing, her mind focused on the pleasure of the moment.

"You can put it wherever you want," she whispered breathlessly, her voice barely audible.

Ragden chuckled softly, then he slid both hands down her back and gripped her ass firmly, lifting her to his body. She sighed in his embrace, draping her hands around his neck. His fingers slipped into her folds, pulling her pussy open as he stepped over to the vanity.

Sarah stepped out of the way, watching hungrily. Then she stopped, giggled and grabbed a washcloth, wiping a trail of cum off her thighs that dribbled from her asshole. She shivered with pleasure, then pulled a brush from a drawer and started brushing her long dark hair.

Ragden lowered Aria onto his cock, her lips spread and his cock slid into her. He moaned softly as he lowered her onto his groin, his cock sliding up into her tight pussy, and pushed against her cervix.

Aria gazed up at Ragden and she sighed deeply. Her pussy stretched to accommodate his thick, throbbing length. She gasped as he slid deeper into her. Her walls gripped him tightly, pulling at his length, pulling at his balls.

Ragden gently lowered Aria onto the counter, setting her hips down softly. He kissed her gently as he slid his cock out of her pussy, then slid the entire length of it back into her, pressing gently against her cervix. He placed his hands on the vanity under her thighs, holding her legs spread as he gently slid in and out of her, each gentle stroke pressing against her cervix.

"Is this what you wanted?" He sighed huskily into her lips as he kissed her again.

"Yes... Oh yes," she whispered breathlessly. Her hips bucked against his as she tried to increase the pace of their lovemaking, driving herself closer to the edge of ecstasy. "Fuck me... fuck me hard."

Ragden picked up his pace, matching the bucking of her hips. Then he increased the pace, forcing her to work to keep up with his fast thrusting into her. Each long, deep, hard stroke pushed hard against her cervix. Her body rocked with each impact.

"Is this better?" he asked between thrusts as he kissed her passionately.

Aria gasped in pleasure and matched Ragden's pace, their groins slapping together with each powerful thrust. Aria's breath quickened, her heart racing as she felt Ragden's strong presence filling her up completely. It drove her wild with lust and desire. She gazed up at Ragden, her mind whirled with pleasure and anticipation.

"Yes... Oh yes... it feels incredible."

Ragden thrust into her faster. His cock pushed forcefully against her cervix. Her body rocked with each impact. The vanity shook beneath them.

Aria's body trembled with desire as Ragden's cock slid faster into her pussy. His cock pushed against Aria's walls with every thrust, driving her wild with lust. Ragden's hips bucked against Aria's pussy, his cock pushing deeper into her tight, slick folds with each powerful movement. Aria gasped with each impact, her body shuddering with pleasure as she felt his thick member filling her up completely, driving her to the edge of orgasmic bliss.

Sensing her impending orgasm, Ragden slid back, his cock slipping out of her. He leaned into her, rolling her back on her hips, her legs going up into the air. He kissed her passionately as he pressed the head of his cock against her ass.

"Does your ass need to be filled too?" He whispered huskily against her lips.

Aria gasped in pleasure as Ragden pulled back, releasing his cock from her pussy, leaving her aching for more. Aria nodded enthusiastically, biting her lip in anticipation of feeling his cock pressing against her tight rear entrance.

"Yes... please."

Ragden pressed his cock against her ass, the head digging into her tight muscles, forcing her to accept his size. Her ass slowly stretched open for him. As the head slipped in, he moaned softly as her tight depths squeezed against the head of his cock.

Aria trembled with desire as Ragden's cock pressed against her ass, the head slowly pushing inside her tight, slick depths. She gasped in surprise and pleasure as her ass slowly stretched to accommodate his large girth. Aria's pussy dripped with arousal, her juices flowing down her thighs as she felt his fingers grip her hips, urging her to take more of his thick cock.

"Fuuuckkk...."

Ragden slowly slid more and more of his cock up her tight ass. He moaned louder as more of it slipped into her. He kept working it slowly until his groin pushed against her firm ass.

"Is this what you wanted?" He whispered breathlessly from the effort of filling her.

Aria gasped with pleasure as his thick member filled her, causing her to moan in pleasure. Aria's pussy dripped with desire, as her mind whirled with the pleasure of feeling Ragden's cock fill her up.

"Fuck, yes... This is exactly what I wanted."

Feeling her dripping fluid from her pussy flowing over his cock, Ragden slowly slid his cock almost out of her ass. Then he gently slid it back in, slid it almost out again and then slid it back in more rapidly. He kissed her softly on the lips as he slid it out and into her again.

Aria's blue eyes sparkled and her body trembled with desire as Ragden's massive cock slid deep inside her driving her wild with lust and desire. Aria's hips bucked against his groin. His cock pulsed with every stroke, filling Aria with pleasure as she gasped with delight. Sarah's cheeks flushed, her eyes bright with excitement, as she gazed at Ragden, her lover, and admired the

sight of him fucking her best friend.

"Fuck... Oh, God."

Ragden felt Aria matching his pace and started moving against her faster. He more urgently filled her ass with his throbbing cock. Then sliding out and filled her again, and again.

As Ragden's thick cock drove into her ass at an increasing tempo, their movements became more frantic, more urgent. They both lost themselves in the pleasure of the moment. Aria gasped and moaned with each thrust, her hands gripping tightly onto the edge of the vanity as she felt Ragden's powerful thrusts sending waves of pleasure coursing through her body. Aria's ass clenched and unclenched around Ragden's invading cock, her juices flowing freely as she arched her back and cried out in ecstasy.

Ragden thrust into her faster. His cock slid in and out of her. His groin slapped against her ass, shaking her whole body, and the vanity underneath her.

Aria felt Ragden's hips buck against her, his cock drove deeper into her tight, slick depths. Aria gasped in pleasure and moaned louder. Aria's ass gripped his thick member tightly, her fluids flowing as she felt the pleasure intensify. Ragden's cock rubbed against Aria's walls with every stroke. Aria could feel the heat radiating from her bowels, burning with lust and desire.

Ragden rolled his hips back, sliding his cock out of her ass, then pressed it into her wet pussy, sliding up into her and pressed it firmly against her cervix. He moaned in pleasure, then slid out and pressed it against her ass again. He moaned again as the head slipped in and then he thrusted it up into her bowels until his groin pressed firmly against her ass. Then he rolled back and slid it out of her. He pressed it to her pussy, slipped it through her folds, then thrust it up into her pussy, all the way up into her until it pressed against her cervix again. Then Ragden repositioned his hands under her thighs and started to thrust rapidly into her pussy, feeling her muscles clenching against his throbbing cock as he slammed it into her cervix hard, again and again. Each impact rocked her entire body. Her breasts rolled wildly. The whole vanity shook with each massive impact.

Aria gasped as Ragden's cock pressed against her cervix, the impact sent shockwaves of pleasure throughout her entire body, causing her to arch her back and cry out in delight. Aria's breasts heaved with each gasp, her heart racing.

"Oh fuck!"

Ragden thrusted into her hard and fast, feeling his climax building rapidly. Each thrust shook her body. Each impact of his cock against her cervix sent waves of pleasure through his body. He moaned with each, his breath bursting out of him.

Aria's body shook with each powerful thrust of Ragden's cock as he drove it hard into her pussy. Her heart raced with each impact. Her breath came in short gasps. Her mind reeled with the overwhelming pleasure of it. Aria

moaned, feeling her climax building quickly within her.

Ragden felt his climax building rapidly within him. His balls started to clench and his muscles started to twitch with the force of it. He clenched his teeth and proceeded to thrust into her with renewed force and vigor. Her entire body rocked, shaking the vanity with the force of each thrust. His cock smashed into her cervix repeatedly, sending shockwaves of ecstasy through his entire body. Then he rolled back, yanking his cock out of her pussy, and slammed it into her ass. Both gasped at the sudden change, feeling their bodies clenching up at the ecstasy of it.

Aria's body shook with each powerful thrust of Ragden's cock as it slammed into her ass. Her pussy dripped with each impact. Her heart raced with each pulse of pleasure. Her whole body trembled with the force of his powerful thrusts. Her breath caught in her throat as she felt her climax building within her.

"Ahh! Fuck!" Aria cried out. She felt her insides tighten and contract around Ragden's pulsing length.

Ragden's cock slammed into her bowels. Her entire body shook with the force of each impact. Aria's breath came in short bursts of pleasure and effort. She felt pleasure building within her, threatening to consume her.

Ragden continued to pound into her, struggling to maintain his pace and ferocity. His muscles twitched, his balls clenched, his body on the edge of an explosion. He continued to pound his cock up her ass repeatedly. He could feel her body tense against his. Her pulse raced. Her muscles clenched and released his massive cock inside of her. He knew she would not last much longer and wanted to see her climax with him.

"Oh fuck!" Aria cried out, as she felt her climax crashing over her, sending waves of ecstasy throughout her entire being.

As Ragden felt Aria's climax crash over her, he slammed in again and felt his climax explode out of him. Cum burst out of his cock into her insides. He drew back and slammed home one last time, pulling her close against him as his cock pressed deep into her ass. His body convulsed against her. The muscles of his legs twitched erratically. He leaned against her. His arms circled her back. He pulled her body tight against his. Her breasts pushed into his chest. His heart thundered against hers. He kissed her passionately and slipped his tongue into her mouth. He tasted her desire and need, savored the flavor of her sated by his massive cock.

Aria breathed heavily and rapidly as she felt the enormous surge of pleasure wash over her, the enormity of Ragden's cock pulsing deep within her ass, sending her spiraling into ecstasy. She cried out in pleasure as her body convulsed against his. Her hips bucked against his as she climaxed with him. Her orgasm washed over her in waves of pure bliss.

She cried out, her voice inaudible over the roaring in her ears. She felt the incredible power of Ragden's load flooding her insides, filling her bowels with his thick, creamy seed.

Ragden continued to hold Aria against him. He felt her body calming down. He could still feel cum leaking from his cock into her bowels. Her bowels clenched and released on his cock, squeezing the cum from him. The sensation was incredible. He gently kissed her on the lips and felt her hot breath against his. Then he pulled her against him again and whispered in her ear.

"Was that what you wanted?"

Aria gazed up at Ragden, her blue eyes sparkling with satisfaction. Her skin flushed with pleasure. Her heart raced. Her mind whirled with the intensity of the moment. She could feel her body still quivering with aftershocks of her orgasm, as she rested against his chest. Her pussy still throbbed with desire. Her ass still gripped tightly around his cock.

"That was... amazing," she murmured, as she looked up at him. Her eyes shone with gratitude and lust.

Ragden kissed her softly on the lips, lingering there, feeling her pulse, her passion, her satisfaction and her love. He pulled her close against him, Feeling the texture of her body against his. He smiled into her lips and savored the touch of her skin, then he kissed her softly again.

Emily stepped out of the shower and wrapped her arms around Ragden's waist. She hugged him back and then released him and came around his side and kissed Aria softly on the lips.

She spoke softly, huskily, satisfaction in her voice, "Well... looks like you two had a good time."

Then Emily pulled a drawer open, grabbed a brush and brushed out her wavy red hair, smiling at Ragden in the mirror as she did. Sarah came over to the other side and leaned in to kiss Aria on the lips softly. She gently grasped Ragden's ass and caressed it softly.

Sarah spoke softly, "That was amazing to watch... I hope you both enjoyed yourselves."

Ragden smiled and kissed Sarah softly, then leaned into Aria and pulled her against him. He slowly let go and slid his cock out, one agonizing inch at a time. He moaned softly as it slipped from her ass, a stream of fluid running out of her.

Aria moaned loudly as his cock slipped out of her ass. Her body clenched on the space he had occupied. She felt like her bowels had become his permanent home and she missed the feeling of him so deep in her body. She felt the fluids running out of her and sighed in pleasure.

Sarah stepped around Aria and kneeled between her legs, placing her tongue against Aria's ass. Aria moaned loudly as Sarah lapped up the juice spilling out of her. Aria's body twitched in pleasure as Sarah gently ran her tongue over her asshole, sucking up the spilling fluids. She then ran her tongue through her damp pussy lips.

Sarah then turned and grabbed Ragden's softening cock and slipped it into her mouth, sucking on it fiercely. She slipped it down her throat, savoring the

soft feel of him in her mouth and throat. Ragden moaned loudly as she sucked everything off him, then Sarah pulled back and let his cock slip from her mouth. She stood with a mischievous grin and giggled as she kissed him on the lips softly.

Aria watched, wondering what his cock tasted like and was about to slip off the vanity to taste it when Sarah turned back to her. Sarah leaned into Aria, kissing her passionately on the lips. Aria moaned softly as she could taste the flavor of Ragden's cum on Sarah's tongue. Sarah pulled Aria against her and lifted her gently off the vanity. Aria's feet found the floor, and she stood shakily as Sarah released her. Ragden put a steadying hand on her hip, grasping her waist lovingly. She looked down at his hand on her hip and sighed. She felt his warmth, his compassion and his love swelling inside her. She could still feel his seed sliding around in her bowels and shivered at the feeling of it.

Ragden smiled at Aria, Emily and Sarah, enjoying their affection, their presence and their love. Then he looked at the clock and sighed. "We really do need to get going..."

CHAPTER 21

He laughed softly, as he opened the door and walked across the hall to his room. He grabbed some clothes from his dresser and started getting dressed.

Emily sighed, then followed. She walked into the room, walked over to the desk, and leaned against it, watching him get dressed. She loved watching the muscles move under his skin. The way the clothes hid the bulges of his strength and his manhood. She found herself amazed by the fact that he had so much strength but when dressed, there did not seem to be anything that special about him. She closed her eyes and she could feel his energy pulsing through the room. She could feel it pulsing in her. She sighed contentedly, opened her eyes and started getting dressed. After Emily had fit her panties around her waist and had finished getting her bra in place, Ragden came up behind her and wrapped his arms around her waist, pulling her against him. She sighed in pleasure as his hands came up and cupped her breasts softly. His breath was soft in her ear as he looked down into her cleavage.

His voice was soft, "I think you might need a new bra. This one seems a bit... tight."

Emily sighed against Ragden, enjoying his presence against her back. She could feel the thickness of his cock pressed against her ass and licked her lips. Then she looked at her cleavage, her breasts, the tightness of her bra around her chest. She tried to adjust it but still found it a bit tight.

"You're right, this seems... tight. I wonder how that happened."

"I suppose you could ask your folks to take you shopping this weekend while I'm at the beach, or we can go together when I get back."

Ragden smiled mischievously as he released her and stepped back.

Ragden turned to the doorway and spied Aria there, watching. He walked over to her and took her hands in his, pulled her into the room and hugged her tightly. He felt her naked body against him. He kissed her softly on the lips, then he drew back from her and nodded to his desk. "Time to get dressed, love. We'll have time to play later. Promise."

Aria gazed up at Ragden, her blue eyes sparkling with desire. Her skin flushed with the intensity of the emotions coursing through her. She felt his strong embrace envelop her and she sighed deeply. She felt safe and secure in his arms. She felt the weight of his promise in her heart and knew that she would be able to indulge in all the pleasure he had to offer her later. She smiled up at him, her cheeks flushed, her breath catching in her throat as she gazed up at him.

"Okay, I will get dressed," Aria whispered, as she stepped away from him, turning towards her clothes that lay neatly folded on the floor beside the bed.

Ragden followed her, his hands trailing along her waist, cupping her ass softly. He leaned against her bare back and kissed her on the shoulder. Then he stepped away as Sarah came walking into the room. He stepped over to Sarah.

Sarah walked into the room. She looked over and saw Emily mostly dressed, just fixing her blouse around her bosom, straining to get it tied properly into place. She saw Aria just slipping her panties up her legs and licking her lips. Then her eyes found Ragden, sauntering over to her, fully clothed. At first, she thought him meek, small and someone easily missed when looking over a crowd. Then she blinked, and his power and strength flowed over her. She sighed in pleasure as his hands curled around her waist and pulled her body against his. She could feel the bulge of his cock in his shorts pressed against her as she wrapped her arms around him and hugged him tightly.

Ragden drew back softly from Sarah, looked her in the eyes and kissed her softly. Then he pulled back from her and gestured to her clothes. "You need to get dressed my love. We need to get going. Breakfast and school..."

Aria gazed up at Ragden. Her body still trembled with the aftermath of the intense pleasure she had just experienced. She nodded in agreement, understanding the need to get ready for the day ahead. She quickly dressed herself. Pulled on her skirt and socks, leaving her breasts bare. She glanced over at Emily, who was also getting dressed.

"Alright, we should probably get moving,"

Ragden stepped back from Sarah and handed her the neatly folded pile of clothes, then leaned against the wall and watched the three women get dressed. His smile never left his face. He watched the clothes cover their breasts and their asses. He loved watching every inch of them. His eyes lingered on Aria's bare chest, waiting for her to cover herself.

Aria gazed back at Ragden, her blue eyes sparkling with lust and satisfaction. Her body still quivered with the aftermath of the intense pleasure she had just experienced. She carefully put on her top, covering her breasts. She looked at him over her shoulder, biting her lower lip slightly.

"There. I'm dressed now."

As Aria turned to face him fully, Emily followed suit, putting on her top and fastening her skirt, giving her ample cleavage and a hint of her curves

underneath.

Ragden smiled in satisfaction, eyeing them both with love. Then he turned to Sarah, laughed, and slapped her bare ass playfully. "Sarah, you really need to dress darlin'."

Sarah put a hand to her chest and batted her eyelashes in mock outrage. "Me? Am I holding you up?" Sarah giggled and shook her ass just out of reach of Ragden. Then grabbed her panties and sexily slid them up halfway up her legs. Then she bent over and reached between her legs and spread her labial lips for Ragden to see. "Oh... Darling," she moaned softly, "My hole is so empty without you."

Ragden eyed her pussy, watching its dampness drip down her legs. His cock throbbed against his shorts. He stepped forward and slapped her ass, hard, leaving a red mark. She gasped in pleasure. Then Ragden slipped a finger into her pussy, stroked her insides, then slipped his finger out and stepped back.

Ragden laughed lustily, "Get dressed."

Sarah moaned softly, pouting. Then she stood, pulled up her panties and giggled. She grabbed the rest of her clothing and dressed quickly. Emily laughed at Sarah as she walked over and wrapped herself around Ragden. Her right arm circled his waist. She leaned into him and kissed him softly on the lips. Aria finished dressing, walked over, pulled herself against Ragden's right side, and slipped her left arm around his waist. As she pulled herself against him, he leaned down and kissed her softly on the lips. Sarah finished getting dressed, turned, and pouted. She strutted up to him, shaking her hips with each step in an exaggerated, sexual walk. Then she spun in place and pushed her ass against his groin. She ground herself against him, feeling his cock throb through his shorts.

"I'm dressed now," she purred, rubbing her ass against his groin.

Ragden laughed lustily, placed his hands on her ass and gripped her hips firmly. He slapped her ass playfully again. Causing her to gasp softly in pleasure. Then he reached down and pulled her up against him. She sighed in pleasure as he kissed her softly on the lips. Then he released her and opened the door, stepping into the hall. Sarah groaned and waited for Aria and Emily to follow Ragden, then followed.

Ragden led the way down the stairs through the living room into the kitchen. Jennifer was busy making food. She had four plates prepared and was bringing them to the table as they walked in.

"Good morning lovers!" Jennifer said cheerfully as she set the plates down. Then she walked over and hugged each of them in turn, squeezing them tightly against her firm bosom. "Eat! Eat! or you will be late for school!"

"Good morning, Jennifer!" Aria called cheerfully; her voice bright with happiness. She turned to Jennifer, her eyes twinkling with mischief. "Did you make breakfast especially for us? We are starving!"

"Of course!" Jennifer said cheerfully as she went back into the kitchen to

clean up the pans. "Now eat!"

Ragden slid into a chair and started eating ravenously. Aria sank into the chair next to him, while Sarah and Emily sat across. They all consumed their meal quickly and in silence. Then they handed their plates to Jennifer, who started cleaning them. As they headed for the door, Jennifer called out, "Have a great day at school! Ragden, do not forget, we will pick you up after school!"

The four of them headed out the front door, down the walkway to the sidewalk and headed to school. They walked close together, enjoying the proximity to each other. "Where would everyone like to meet up for lunch?"

Aria smiled brightly, her blue eyes twinkling with excitement as she walked alongside Sarah and Emily towards school, her heart racing with anticipation. She could not wait to spend more time with her friends and share more intimate moments with them. She loved the feeling of being so close to them and the knowledge that they were all in this together.

"We could just find an empty classroom or something," Aria suggested, her voice light and inviting, as she thought about how much fun it would be to have more private time with Sarah and Emily during the day. "Or maybe even just sit outside in the courtyard if it's nice out – that always feels good on a day like today."

Ragden pulled Emily against his side, his lips brushing her forehead, "What about you love? What sounds good to you?"

Emily smiled up at Ragden, her arm snaking around his waist as they walked. She rested her head against his side and shrugged against him, "Doesn't really matter to me, as long as we are all together."

Ragden smiled then reached out and grabbed Sarah's ass playfully, cupping the firmness of her. "What about you, Sarah? Do you have a preference?"

Sarah gasped in pleasure and spun on the spot. She grinned mischievously and flashed her skirt up at Ragden and Emily, showing her pink panties, damp with her desire. She bit her lip as she dropped her skirt back in place. Sarah's voice was low with desire and sexual tension, "Why don't we go back to my place and fuck on the kitchen table?"

Ragden laughed, reached out and pulled Sarah against his body. His cock throbbed against her through his shorts. He reached down and cupped her ass, pulling her firmly against him, making sure she could feel his cock. He kissed her softly on the lips and smiled down at her.

"That sounds like an entertaining option, as long as everyone else is okay with it."

Aria's blue eyes sparkled at the thought, as she bit her lip and looked from Sarah to Emily and then Ragden, "Mm... I think we can do that."

Ragden smiled, as they kept walking towards school. He playfully slapped Sarah's ass with one hand while he squeezed Emily's waist along his side with the other. "Sounds like a plan, then. Shall we meet at Emily's locker and head that way then at lunch?"

All three women nodded. Sarah giggled and then dashed off into the halls

towards her first class. Aria pulled herself against Ragden, her arms reaching around his waist, and pulling herself against his body. Her breasts pressed against his chest as she kissed him passionately on the lips. Aria smiled and licked her lips, then turned and walked off to her class.

Ragden turned to Emily and pulled her against him. Feeling her warmth and passion, her love. He leaned in and kissed her softly on the lips. Then deeper as she pulled him against her, her lips parting, her tongue dancing with his. They stood embracing for a minute, other students whistling at them and making comments as they walked by. Neither Ragden nor Emily paid them any mind. Then they broke, breathless, their bodies throbbing for each other. Ragden took a soft step back from her, not wanting to leave. Then the bell rang. He stepped forward and gave her one last kiss before dashing off to his class.

Emily stood for a moment in the hall, watching as Ragden jogged off to his class. So much had happened in such a short amount of time. Her life had been turned upside down. She could not remember a time when she felt so loved, cherished, or desired. Her heartbeat was in her throat as Ragden went around the corner. Once he was out of sight, it was like the spell was broken. She suddenly noticed other students watching her. She blushed, pulled her bag against her chest and hurried off to class.

The first couple of classes flew by for Ragden. He found the texts easy to read, the lectures made sense. He did not find himself struggling to keep up with the material. The only problem he did have was staying focused on the material. His mind kept wandering to the experiences of the previous night, and that morning. He had never imagined that all three women would want to spend so much time with him. Each was incredible and unique. He was eager to see them again and see where things went. He was a little sad that he would not be able to spend the weekend with them. His dad had been a bit mysterious about the weekend. He knew something major was going on this weekend, but neither Jennifer nor Michael would say much about it. He hoped to learn more on the way there after school. After third period, Ragden gathered his stuff and headed to his next class. As he rounded the corner, hugging the wall to avoid the crowd, he almost ran over Sarah. He stopped just short. She stood there coyly, her hands clasped in front of her, blinking demurely up at him.

Aria stepped around the corner, cozying up to Sarah, and looking up at Ragden. Sarah looked at Ragden with a seductive gaze, her hands clasped demurely before her, her body tense with expectation, and her heart racing with excitement.

"Hey Ragden," Aria said softly, her voice barely audible over the noise of the hallway, "We wanted to talk to you about something important."

Ragden blinked looking from Sarah to Aria. He gulped slowly and found his voice, "Of course. What can I do for you?"

Aria gazed up at him, her hands resting on his chest, her fingers lightly

tracing patterns on his shirt.

"Mm... Please make Sarah feel good too," she said softly, her voice barely audible, but filled with sincerity.

Ragden cocked an eyebrow at Sarah. Then he looked at Aria. He leaned over and kissed Aria softly on the forehead. Then he did the same for Sarah. "Don't you two have a class you need to get to? Can this wait until lunch? We only have one more class."

"Yeah, we do. But we can just skip it. No one will notice if we're a few minutes late." Aria said, her voice breathless with anticipation. Sarah bit her lower lip nervously but nodded in agreement. Sarah looked back at Ragden, and then back at Aria, both wanting this moment together.

"Actually, everyone noticed when I was late yesterday. If it happens again, well... that would be bad. I'm sorry. Just... wait an hour? Please?"

"An hour," Aria whispered, her voice barely audible, "I promise. I won't be late again."

Ragden laughed, then pulled Aria into a warm hug and squeezed her against him. Then he kissed her softly on the lips and released her. Then he reached over and pulled Sarah against him. Sarah moaned softly her hands caressing his groin, feeling the size of his cock through his shorts. Ragden kissed her softly on the lips. "Go, get to class. I'll see you at lunch."

Aria and Sarah pouted but hurried off. Sarah kept looking over her shoulder as Aria pulled her along. Ragden smiled at them, then rushed off to his next classroom.

Ragden hurried to class and got through the door as the bell rang. The teacher glared at him as he moved quickly to his seat.

As Ragden took his seat, the large football player in the seat next to him elbowed him, snickering. "Bathroom issues again, eh Rag?"

Ragden glared at him for a moment. The other man snickered to himself as the teacher rapped his knuckles on the chalkboard calling everyone's attention to the work written there. The rest of the class went well enough. Math was not a hard subject for Ragden, and it came easily enough to him. As the bell rang, the teacher reminded them about the test on Monday. Ragden nodded as he grabbed his bag and headed towards Emily's locker. He could hear the football player, Roy, snickering behind his back. Ragden ignored him as he headed to Emily's locker.

Ragden walked to Emily's locker, feeling an extra spring in his step. They had a whole ninety minutes before their next class started. Lots of time for whatever the women had in mind. As he rounded the corner, he saw that only Emily was at her locker. Sarah and Aria were nowhere to be seen, yet. Ragden walked up and Emily turned to see him at the last minute, a huge grin spreading across her face. She reached out to him and draped her arms around his neck as he came up to her. His arms slipped around her waist as she drew him down to kiss her lips. Her red hair danced along her back as she pressed her lips firmly against his. He pulled her body tight against him,

feeling his loins stirring against her. Their kiss was passionate, their tongues tasting each other, their pulses speeding up. They broke away breathlessly but kept their bodies firmly against each other.

Emily smiled, her whole face lighting up. "Hey there lover," she whispered breathlessly, "Ready for lunch?"

Ragden nodded, his hands cupping her ass and pulling her groin against his, his cock throbbing against her. She looked down and a knowing smile spread across her face. She licked her lips seductively. Ragden laughed and kissed her again, not as passionately.

Ragden smiled at Emily as he felt Sarah's presence coming up behind him. Sarah wrapped her arms around his waist and pulled herself against his back. Her body pressed tightly against him. She drank in his warmth and love, feeling it pulse off him. She needed his presence, she had felt empty without him, and being here now, against him, made her heartbeat with joy.

Sarah whispered against his back, softly, her voice muffled through his clothes, "I missed you. Can we go now?"

Emily smiled, looking down at Sarah's arms, watching her hands snake down over Ragden's groin, and stroke his cock through his shorts. Ragden laughed softly, the sound sensual, sending shivers down both women's backs.

"Not yet. We are still waiting for Aria."

Emily stepped back from Ragden, pouting softly as Sarah slipped around the front and buried her face in his chest. She took a hitched breath. A concerned look slipped across Emily's face, and she bent down and kissed Sarah softly on the cheek, resting her hand on her back.

Aria came around the corner and spied Ragden, Emily, and Sarah. She felt her heart swell, her pulse quickened, and her breath grew short. She ran to them and threw her arms around all of them hugging them. She kissed Sarah and Emily softly on the lips. Then looked up at Ragden, apologetically. "Sorry, I'm late. I had to collect homework assignments."

Ragden smiled down at her, cupping her cheek softly. She nuzzled into his warm hand, kissing his hand softly. "It's okay love. We are just glad you made it."

Ragden pulled Aria against him, Sarah moved reluctantly to the side, allowing Aria to hug Ragden. He kissed her softly on the lips, feeling her pulse beat faster, the desire on her skin. He smiled at her.

"Okay, now we can go."

He pulled Aria and Sarah along behind him, as Emily walked a half step ahead of them as they headed to Sarah's house.

Aria snuggled close to Ragden, feeling his strong warmth envelop her. She felt safe and secure in his embrace. She felt Sarah move away, giving her space to be closer to Ragden. Aria gazed up at Ragden, her eyes filled with gratitude and love as he held her close, feeling the beats of her heart accelerate in his chest. She felt Sarah's disappointment but understood that they needed this time together. "Thank you," Aria whispered, her voice barely audible, as they

Love & Nature

walked towards Sarah's house, Emily leading the way.

CHAPTER 22

Ragden followed the girls into the house, then stepped away from them and walked into the living room. He knelt and ran his hand over the carpet. After a moment, he found the holes his fingers had left the last time he had been there with Emily. His eyes got a little wide as he found them.

Sarah walked over and looked down at him, "What are you looking at?"

Emily and Aria walked up behind Sarah and watched Ragden on the floor. Emily blushed slightly. Aria looked from Ragden to Emily and giggled. Aria nudged Emily and caught her attention.

"You two fucked right here?" Aria whispered, a hint of jealousy in her voice. Emily blushed a little darker.

"Yeah... When we climaxed, my hand sunk into the floor..." Ragden said softly, his hands over the holes, "Right here, actually; I thought maybe I had imagined that part, but the holes are here..."

Sarah walked over and knelt beside Ragden, running her fingers over the holes. Her eyes got a little wider.

"How...?" Sarah breathed softly. Ragden shrugged in response.

Sarah grinned mischievously and bit her lower lip, "Think you can do it again?"

"I... Maybe? I don't want to do any damage to your house."

Sarah pouted, then stood and walked back over to Aria and Emily, shaking her ass as she did. Ragden watched her ass shake. Aria wrapped her arms around Sarah, reached under her skirt, and grabbed her ass while winking at Ragden.

A shiver ran down Ragden's back, watching Aria squeeze Sarah's ass as she licked her lips. He stood as Emily walked around Aria and Sarah and wrapped herself around Ragden. He sighed in pleasure at her embrace. She smiled at him and kissed his lips softly. Then she looked down at the carpet, the holes, then back up at Ragden. He shrugged again, then pulled her tighter against him.

Love & Nature

"Sarah, do you have anything we can eat for lunch?" Ragden asked.

"Just me," Sarah looked over her shoulder and shook her ass for Ragden. He laughed, watching her, as Aria slipped her hand inside Sarah's panties and slid them down her legs. Aria stared at Ragden as she slipped her fingers over Sarah's asshole. Sarah thrust her butt out, leaning into Aria as she slipped a finger into her ass and another between her pussy lips. Sarah moaned in pleasure.

Emily felt Ragden's cock throb against his shorts, looked up to meet his gaze, and turned to look over at Aria and Sarah; then she started giggling. Emily grabbed Ragden's ass, pulling his groin against her hard. Ragden looked down at her. She winked at him and gestured to Sarah and Aria with her head.

"Go," she said softly, "I'll find some food."

Ragden leaned down and kissed her passionately. Emily felt her heart start beating harder. She wanted to feel him inside her but also wanted the satisfaction of bringing him food. To watch him eat something from her hand. That idea brought a smile to her face. As he stepped away from her, she pressed herself against his back, reached around his waist, and undid his belt.

Ragden laughed, enjoying her hands on him, the press of her against his back. Emily felt her hunger surging with his. First, she wanted to help him just a bit. She opened his belt, and dropped his trousers, freeing his massive cock. It throbbed in the air in front of him. She reached around him and gently stroked it, listening to him moan softly. Aria and Sarah both turned to look; their eyes transfixed on his massive, throbbing member.

Emily stepped back from Ragden, to watch for a moment as he stepped free of his shorts and boxers. Then she stepped into the kitchen to look for food.

Ragden stepped free of his shorts, his cock fully erect, throbbing in full view. Emily giggled and walked off into the kitchen. Aria's eyes sparkled with delight and hunger as she watched him stalk closer. Ragden pulled his shirt over his head and dropped it to the floor as Aria spread Sarah's cheeks.

Sarah looked over her shoulder. Her face flushed. Her pulse raced. Her pussy dripped with need and desire as Ragden stepped closer. Then she turned and slipped Aria's panties down her legs and slipped her fingers into her. Aria moaned in pleasure, gripping Sarah's ass and spreading her cheeks.

Aria's blue eyes sparkled with delight, and her body trembled with anticipation as Sarah bent over, her panties discarded, her naked bottom exposed to Ragden. She gazed up at Ragden, her cheeks flushed, her heart racing, her mind whirling with lust and desire.

Sarah felt Aria's excitement building, her pussy dripping with need and desire as Ragden approached, his massive cock throbbing with uncontainable energy. Sarah wiggled her ass, waiting for Ragden to fill her. Her heart raced with excitement. This was what she wanted. To be filled by his magnificent cock. Aria reached down and spread Sarah's ass cheeks wide, spreading both her holes.

Love & Nature

"Fuck her in the ass while she eats me... Please," Aria moaned.

Aria lay back on the floor, her legs spread, giving Sarah better access to her. Sarah dipped her face into Aria's pussy, one finger slipping up Aria's ass as she parted her lips and dipped her tongue deep into her. Aria moaned loudly, her body bucking against Sarah's face.

Ragden got down on his knees behind Sarah, grasped her ass firmly, and slid his cock through her labial lips, dampening it with her arousal. Then he slid it back and pressed it against her asshole, sliding it in slow circles around her tight entrance. Slowly increasing the pressure, forcing her ass to accept the massive head of his cock into her.

Sarah gasped, feeling Aria's pussy clenching tightly against her face, her juice flowing down her chin as she sucked greedily. She felt Ragden's cock press against her ass, and she looked back at him over her shoulder, her eyes wide with excitement and lust. Sarah lowered her mouth even further, taking more of Aria's swollen folds into her mouth, sucking and licking enthusiastically.

"Yes... Yes... Fuck her... I want to feel you filling her up with your thick, hot cum."

Aria moaned, looking at the scene in front of her.

Ragden pushed his cock against her ass, sliding the tip of it in slow circles around her tight entrance. Sarah moaned at the pressure. She pushed her ass backward, forcing the tip of it into her. As it slid in, Ragden moaned in pleasure, feeling the tight pressure of her muscles squeezing his thick meat. The head slipped in, and he paused, savoring the feel of her around him.

Sarah gasped, feeling the head of Ragden's cock slip into her ass. Her heart thundered in her chest. Her breath caught in her throat. She looked at Aria with a mixture of lust and need, her eyes burning with desire. She turned her head towards Aria and gave her a seductive glance before looking back at Ragden.

"I'm yours... do whatever you want with me... I'm yours," Sarah moaned softly.

Ragden slapped her ass hard, leaving a red mark on her right ass cheek.

Sarah's ass clenched and jiggled, the smack making her entire body quiver with delight. She gasped and arched her back, her pussy dripping with need. Her eyes locked onto Ragden's. She looked at him with adoration and desire, her heart beating wildly. Her mind was consumed by lust and passion for him.

"Do it... Sarah... Please eat me while he fucks you," Aria moaned, watching.

Ragden grabbed her waist and pulled her back against him, as he slid his cock deeper into her. He started slowly, sliding into her an inch at a time. Sarah's heart raced, and she rammed her ass backward into him, taking all of him into her. Ragden gasped in pleasure as his hips slammed into her ass, his cock sliding deep into her bowels.

Aria's blue eyes sparkled. Her body trembled with excitement. Her pussy

dripped with arousal. Her heart raced with desire as Sarah continued to work her pussy. Her fingers slid in deep. Her tongue flicked in and out. She looked up at Ragden, her eyes pleading, her voice breathless with need.

"Yes... Fuck her... make her take all that thick, delicious cock," Aria moaned, feeling her climax building.

Ragden slowly drew his cock back, almost slipping from her, but stopping just short. Sarah waited until he started to slide forward, then rammed her ass back against his groin again. Feeling her insistent need, Ragden drew back faster and slammed it back into her. Both moaned at the pleasure of it. Sarah and Ragden quickly built a fast rhythm, she drew forward while he drew back, and then they slammed their groins together, ramming his cock deep into her bowels.

Aria's pussy dripped with need as Sarah continued to work her fingers deep inside Aria's swollen cunt. She gazed up at Ragden, her mind focused on the pleasure of the moment. She watched Ragden's massive cock driving into Sarah's depths, and the thought of it made her pant with need.

"Fuck... Yes... I want to watch her eat me while she takes all your thick, delicious cock."

Ragden continued to match Sarah's insistent rhythm. He slid his cock out, then rammed it into her bowels. The sound of their groins slamming filled the room. Ragden felt Sarah's heart racing. He watched her lick Aria's cunt as she tried to keep her breathing normal and failed. Sarah panted into Aria's pussy lips, her fingers working inside her, but unable to keep her tongue in. Her face flushed with need. Their hips continued to slam together, his cock ramming deep into her bowels with each massive thrust. He could feel her body clenching and releasing him, her climax quickly approaching. He felt his building rapidly as her tight body squeezed him, driving him to slam into her faster and harder.

Aria's eyes sparkled with lust and excitement, her voice breathy, her body trembling with need as Sarah continued to work her pussy, her fingers sliding deep inside her, her tongue flicking against Aria's sensitive nub, her cheeks flushed, her heart racing, her mind consumed by the pleasure of the moment.

Ragden grabbed Sarah's ass cheeks and spread them wider, allowing him to drive his massive cock deeper into her. His strokes picked up more speed. He felt her body starting to convulse, her legs twitch. His muscles were starting to ache from the strain. He pounded his cock into her ass harder and faster.

Sarah's eyes were wide with lust and need. Her cheeks were flushed. Her breath was heavy, and her voice ragged. Her body trembled with desire. She looked over her shoulder at Ragden. Her heart raced.

"Yes... Fuck me," Sarah moaned.

As Ragden's cock pounded into Sarah's ass. It drove her wild with pleasure. Sarah lifted her head and looked at Aria. Her eyes burned with need. Her mouth hung open with want and lust.

Ragden pounded his dick harder into Sarah. He felt her moving against

him. Her hips rolled back against his massive thrusts. His balls clenched with the need to release. He felt her body tensing in response. Her ass clenched harder on his cock, her breath fast and heavy.

Sarah's eyes flashed with excitement. Her cheeks were flushed. Her breath was hot and heavy. She gripped Aria's thighs tightly. She felt the slickness of Aria's pussy against her palm, her juice dripping down onto her hands.

Ragden pounded his cock into Sarah's ass and matched her thrusts. Their groins slammed together harder. Her ass clenched on his cock as his groin slammed into her. His muscles clenched, and cum exploded into her depths.

Aria's eyes widened as her body shook with the force of Ragden's powerful thrusts. Sarah felt the hot spurt of cum shoot up her tight ass, filling her. Aria looked down and saw Sarah panting, her skin glistening with sweat. Sarah's hips bucked against Ragden's as she took everything he had to offer.

"Yes! Yes! Oh fuck, I'm cumming too!"

As Ragden's cock filled Sarah's ass, she gasped and arched her back. Her muscles clenched as her juices flowed from her dripping pussy. Her clit throbbed with need and desire.

Ragden pulled back and stroked into her again, his body twitching, his muscles convulsing from the effort. He stroked one more time, then rammed his cock deep into her bowels and leaned down against her back. His hands draped around her body and clutched at her breasts, squeezing them tight. He kissed her back, her shoulders, and the back of her neck. His cock throbbed in her ass, cum still leaking out.

Sarah cried out as her orgasm rode over her. Her muscles twitched and convulsed. Her hand inside Aria clenched, causing Aria to moan in pleasure. Sarah bucked her hips against Ragden. A small burst of fluid squirted from her pussy onto the floor between her legs. She moaned in pleasure, feeling his cock still buried inside her.

Aria watched, transfixed by the scene in front of her. She felt her climax building rapidly. Her pussy clenched on Sarah's hand as it rode over her. She moaned in pleasure as her fluids slipped from inside her, releasing over Sarah's hand. Sarah opened her mouth and lapped up Aria's juices as they ran over her hand. She pulled her hand out and latched her mouth onto Aria's pussy, swallowing whatever she could. Sarah moaned in pleasure as Ragden's cock throbbed in her ass while he watched her doing her best to lap up Aria's juices.

Ragden slowly slid his throbbing cock from Sarah's ass, an inch at a time, savoring the feeling of her squeezing him as he withdrew. Sarah groaned, feeling her body collapse over the gap left behind. Slowly, he slipped it out of her. It glistened in the air, damp with her fluids. Ragden shivered at the sensation of the chilly air in the room after being somewhere so warm. A slight shiver ran down Ragden's back as he looked down at Sarah's incredible ass and watched as her asshole clenched tight.

Sarah gasped at the emptiness inside her, the burning need in her bowels.

She let out a long, low moan, her eyes closed in bliss. She turned her head and looked at Ragden, her voice breathy, "God... I need you to put your cock back in me... I need to be filled again."

Ragden licked a finger and slid it up her ass, feeling her tight depths. He stroked it twice, then pulled it out, smiling at her. "Later, love, I think it's time for someone else to get filled. Wouldn't you agree?"

Ragden stood, looking down at Aria and Sarah. He reached his hand down to Sarah. She took his hand and sat up to her knees. Sarah crawled seductively towards Ragden, shaking her ass in front of Aria's face. Then she sat on her heels in front of him, reached out, and pulled his cock into her mouth. Ragden moaned softly as she slipped the head into her mouth. Then she licked and sucked at it. Ragden moaned again as she slipped his cock down her throat, sliding the entire length into her mouth, her lips pressing softly against his groin. She then backed up and grinned wickedly up at him

Aria's eyes gleamed with pure delight. Her cheeks flushed with excitement. She watched Sarah's throat work as she eagerly sucked Ragden's cock. Sarah's hands gripped his thighs tightly. She looked up at him with a sinful smile. Her dark eyes burned with lust and desire as her heart raced with the thrill of pleasuring him. The sight of Sarah's plump lips engulfing his cock made Aria's pussy wet with need and desire. "Yes... Yes... I want to watch her take all of you."

Ragden moaned softly as Sarah slipped his cock down her throat, her lips once again pressed against his groin. He closed his eyes, letting the feel of her throat working his cock wash over him. She bobbed back and forth, using her throat to fuck him. He moaned as she grazed his skin softly with her teeth. She backed off him slowly, savoring every inch of him as she slipped his cock from her mouth, then she took big gasps of air while she licked her lips.

"God..." Sarah whispered, "I never tire of that taste."

Aria's eyes sparkled with lust and excitement, her heart raced, her pussy dripped with need, and her body trembled with desire. She gazed up at Sarah, her cheeks flushed, her breath heavy with arousal; her mind focused on the incredible sight of Sarah sucking Ragden's cock and the thought of what was coming next. Sarah looked up at Ragden with a mix of determination and passion in her eyes, her cheeks flushed, her heart racing, her breath heavy with need.

"Can you cum for me again? I want to swallow your cum... I want to feel it still dripping from my ass while you fill my stomach with more..."

Sarah's eyes gleamed with lust, her breathing heavy, her voice breathy. Her body was tense with anticipation. She gazed up at Ragden. Her cheeks flushed, her eyes bright with desire. She bit her lower lip, her eyes never leaving his face as she waited for his nod of approval. Ragden smiled down at Sarah and softly caressed her cheek with his hand. He nodded softly as his cock throbbed in her hands. Sarah's eyes lit up with joy. She reached out, grasped his throbbing cock, and ran her tongue over the tip, then down along

the shaft to his balls. She gently sucked on each, taking them into her mouth and suckling them softly before dragging her tongue along the length of him again.

Ragden moaned softly at the feel of her plump lips and soft tongue playing along his manhood. He moaned a little louder as she slipped the head of it into her mouth, sucking on it, then she wrapped both hands around the shaft and gently stroked it, as she sucked on the head. Ragden groaned, feeling his balls tighten. Sarah sensed the slight change in him and opened her mouth wide, slipping the head of his cock down her throat and thrust herself forward along his cock. She released the shaft as it disappeared down her throat and grabbed his ass, pulling him into her.

Sarah's eyes watered slightly as she took Ragden's cock into her throat, her nose brushing against the base of it. She gripped his ass tightly and pulled him even deeper into her. Sarah's eyes were wide with excitement. She looked up at him, her cheeks flushed, her eyes glistening with lust and desire. She flexed her throat, feeling the massiveness of him there. Then she bobbed her body back and forth along his cock. Her eyes watered from the effort and the loss of air. Her cheeks turned red as she fucked his cock with her throat. Ragden moaned loudly, feeling his climax building rapidly.

Then Sarah backed off, pushing him back away from her so she could breathe. She took two deep breaths, grinning wickedly, then she grabbed his ass and pulled him into her again, slipping his cock down her throat. She bobbed hard and fast along it, flexing her throat while he moaned loudly.

Ragden felt her throat tighten on his cock, and his balls clenched up. Cum exploded out of him down her throat. He could feel her convulsively swallowing as she continued to fuck his cock with her throat. Another load exploded inside her as his body shuddered and his legs twitched. He felt his balls clench up again as she pulled back, taking a breath, as another load of cum exploded into her mouth. She swallowed reflexively, her tongue stroking over the head of his cock. Ragden staggered and dropped to his knees. Sarah lowered herself with him, keeping her mouth locked onto his cock, sucking fiercely. She stroked his cock and tried to squeeze every drop of cum out she could. Ragden lay backward on the floor, his body shuddering with the ecstasy of Sarah continuing to suck and stroke his cock. He felt another load of cum explode into her mouth. He lifted his head off the floor and saw her swallowing and sucking while his body shuddered and twitched.

As Sarah continued to suck and stroke Ragden's cock, swallowing his hot, sticky load, her cheeks were flushed with pleasure. Her throat worked with determination. She looked up at him. Her dark eyes bright with excitement and lust, her mouth full of his cum-smeared cock. She gazed at him, her eyes pleading for more.

"Give me more; I want to taste more of your hot, thick cum."

Ragden lay back on the floor, feeling drained as his body twitched and convulsed softly under Sarah's continued ministrations. He felt his balls

clench again as another load of cum exploded into her mouth. Sarah moaned in pleasure, sucking it up, and swallowing every bit she could. Ragden groaned as his cock started to soften in her mouth. She kept squeezing, stroking, and sucking until there was nothing left for her to get. She groaned as his cock started to go soft in her hands, then she slipped it deep into her mouth again, sucking it down her throat as far as it would go. Ragden moaned in pleasure, feeling his softened cock sucked into her throat. Sarah gently slipped it out of her mouth and ran her tongue down over his balls, gently licking each, making sure she did not miss anything. She slid her tongue along his cock, taking the head into her mouth again and sucking long and hard before releasing it.

Right at that moment, Emily came walking back into the living room, carrying a tray of food. She spied the scene and giggled to herself. She sat down on the floor next to Ragden and laid a hand on his chest, feeling his steady heartbeat. She smiled at him as he sat up. She kissed him softly on the lips, then giggled at Sarah between his legs.

"I found some apples and cut them up, along with some carrots. I also found some sandwich meat and cheese. I hope this is alright?"

Ragden sat up and leaned against her, wrapping his arms around her and kissing her softly on the lips.

"Looks amazing," he said as he took a piece of apple and ate it.

Emily lay the tray of food next to him, picking up another piece of apple and slipping it into her mouth. As Ragden swallowed the first one, she turned to him, half a slice hanging from her mouth. Emily giggled as Ragden slipped his mouth around the piece of apple and kissed her as he bit it in half, taking it from her.

Sarah crawled over and grabbed a slice of cheese and a roll of meat. She slipped the roll of meat into her mouth and sucked on it while staring at Ragden. Ragden shivered slightly under that gaze as Sarah giggled and started chewing it up.

Aria crawled over and sat between Sarah and Emily. She reached in and grabbed some slices of carrot, and ate them. The four of them sat in silence, enjoying a quiet meal together. Once the food was gone, Sarah turned to Ragden and gently wrapped her hands around his soft cock. She leaned over and kissed the head of it, feeling it throb under her grasp. She grinned wickedly as she released it and kissed Ragden softly on the lips. Then she grabbed the empty tray and stood with it in her hands.

"I'll take care of this." Sarah shook her ass in front of Ragden and walked out of the room. Emily and Aria giggled as she left. Ragden shivered as he watched her bare ass shaking as she walked out of the room.

Aria giggled with Emily as Sarah left the room, her ass swaying enticingly. She turned to Emily and winked, "God, I love how she does that..."

The two women laughed together, sharing a moment of intimacy and amusement. Emily softly kissed Aria on the lips, then looked over at Ragden. She crawled closer to him and kissed him softly on the lips, then she leaned

over his groin, gently grasped his soft cock in her hands. She looked up at him and smiled, "Save any for me?"

A shiver ran down Ragden's body at Emily's soft touch. He felt his cock thickening, throbbing, growing harder in Emily's hands. She smiled happily, feeling him grow hard under her grasp. She loved being able to do that. Ragden nodded slowly, watching her. Emily bent over and kissed the head of his cock softly, her lips grazing the tip of it. It throbbed under her soft touch, then she opened her mouth and slowly slid it in. She suckled the tip softly, then kept going down, the head of it slipping into her throat. She kept going until her lips pressed softly against his groin. She moaned softly as she felt his cock throbbing in her throat and chest. She slowly raised herself off it and licked her lips.

Emily turned and slowly crawled down along his side. Aria reached under her skirt and pulled her panties down her legs as she kept moving. Then Emily sat on her heels between his legs. She reached up and slowly untied the front of her shirt, slipping it off and laying it on the floor behind her. Then she unclasped her bra and let it slip off her breasts. She took a deep breath and smiled happily, cupping her incredible, large breasts. She then slowly crawled up over Ragden. He shivered, watching her come up to his face. She straddled his groin, sitting her pussy on top of the base of his cock, her damp folds caressing his balls. Ragden shivered again, his hips bucking softly against her.

Aria giggled as Emily leaned down and laid her body against Ragden's. She kissed him passionately, slipping her tongue into his mouth, tasting him. He reached up and pulled her down against him, feeling her body pressed against his, enjoying every inch of her against him. His skin tingled at the feel of her touch.

Aria gazed into Ragden's eyes, her blue orbs shimmering with desire, her heart racing. Her breath quickened, her mind whirling with lust and anticipation. She looked down at Emily, who was gazing at her with adoration and love in her eyes. She smiled back at Emily, feeling the incredible intimacy of the moment, the three of them sharing such an intense, passionate experience. Aria then crawled around behind Emily and laid down between Ragden's legs. She ran her tongue over his balls, feeling them tingle beneath her soft touch, then she ran her tongue up along the base of his cock and into Emily's soft, wet folds. She continued to run her tongue up along Emily, feeling Emily moan at her touch. She dipped her tongue into Emily's ass, feeling her clench against her. Aria pushed her tongue into Emily's tight ass, feeling the soft skin inside, probing her ass. Emily moaned loudly at the feeling.

Ragden reached back and spread Emily's ass cheeks, giving Aria better access. Emily moaned even louder, her hips rocking gently back and forth, sliding her wet pussy along Ragden's cock. Ragden moaned in pleasure at the sensation as Aria continued to lick and probe Emily's ass with her tongue.

Emily kissed Ragden fiercely, her tongue pushing into his mouth. He welcomed her passionate embrace, feeling her tongue delve into his mouth. Emily rocked back and forth with more force, driving her hips against Aria's mouth, feeling her tongue go deeper up her ass as she moaned loudly again.

Aria's blue eyes sparkled, her mouth full of Emily's ass, her tongue sliding deep. She sucked and probed at Emily's ass, feeling the heat and wetness envelop her tongue. She could taste the musk and the tanginess of Emily's ass on her tongue, feeling the combination of pleasure and power surge through her.

Emily moaned, her hips bucking against Aria's mouth, her hands gripping the carpet as she felt the pleasure wash over her.

Emily's eyes flashed open and stared into Ragden's with fierce need and burning desire. "I need you in me; I need your cock inside me."

Then she kissed him again, even fiercer than before, her need driving her. She raised her hips, letting his cock throb free. Aria reached in and grabbed his cock, pointing it up into Emily's folds. Emily felt the tip of it graze through her labia and sat down hard on it, driving it up into her.

"Oh, God!" She moaned loudly as his cock slammed into her cervix. She sat up and clutched at her chest. Her body shuddered in ecstasy, as she felt herself filled with Ragden's throbbing cock. Emily moaned loudly again, her muscles vibrating with her pleasure.

Aria whistled appreciatively, then placed her tongue against Emily's ass again. Emily's eyes flew wide, and she leaned forward, putting her hands on Ragden's chest to brace herself, rocking her ass into Aria's mouth. Aria slipped her tongue into Emily's ass again, feeling her narrow tract further restricted by the presence of Ragden in her pussy. Aria shivered at the feeling and pressed her tongue deeper into Emily's ass. She grasped Ragden's balls and gently squeezed them, feeling his cock throb in response inside Emily. She could feel the throb on her tongue and shivered at the feeling of it. Emily moaned loudly again.

As Emily's ass clenched and unclenched around Aria's tongue, her eyes were wild with passion. She gazed up at Ragden, her eyes feral with lust, her mouth open in a silent scream of pleasure, her body convulsing with ecstasy.

"Fuck me... fuck me hard... make me cum," Emily's voice rose in volume as she pleaded with Ragden, her need driving her speech. Emily's ass clenched and unclenched around Aria's tongue.

Ragden reached down and gently lifted Emily's groin off him, then he slid his cock up into her, gently pushing against her cervix. Emily moaned loudly as Aria continued to lick and probe her ass with her tongue, then Ragden dropped his hips down and gently thrust it up into her again.

Emily's eyes flashed open; she glared down at Ragden, her face full of need and desperation. "I said to fuck me hard. Goddamnit, man, FUCK ME!"

Ragden stopped, abashed for a moment. Then he laughed bawdily, the sound full of sexual tension. Aria felt herself go damp at the sound of it. She

felt like Ragden had just run his tongue over her body, teasing and caressing her ass, her pussy, her breasts. Her entire body twitched with desire and the need for sex. Then Ragden slammed his cock up into Emily so hard her entire body lifted out of his hands. Then he dropped his groin heavily into the floor. The whole room reverberated with the sound. He then slammed up into her again, even harder. Emily gasped in pleasure and moaned; her breasts rocked upwards so hard they slapped down against her chest as she came down into his hands again.

"Is that hard enough?" Ragden whispered. He dropped his hips to the floor and rammed up into her again, lifting her off his hands, then dropped to the floor again.

Aria watched in fascination, her blue eyes wide, as Emily's body was used as a receptacle for Ragden's raw sexuality. She saw the intensity on Emily's face, the need and desire etched there. She felt a surge of jealousy, a mix of lust and possessiveness. She wanted to be filled by Ragden like that, to have him use her body in such an intimate way. She wanted to feel his power and dominance flowing through her.

Emily's eyes squeezed shut, tears on her face as Ragden slammed up into her again, lifting her, then dropping back. His hands easily caught her as his ass hit the floor with a solid thump, then he slammed up into her again, just as hard. Emily nodded, gasping for breath, clutching her chest to keep her breasts from painfully bouncing as Ragden slammed into her again.

Aria's pussy dripped with arousal, her juices flowing freely, the carpet beneath her soaked. Her hips bucked along the floor, her clit throbbing with need as she gazed up at Ragden. She wanted to see everything, to be part of everything, to feel everything.

"Oh, God," Emily moaned between thrusts, "Don't... Stop."

Ragden started to thrust faster, feeling Emily's body tense. He could feel her energy starting to collect, her orgasm building. He could see the tensing of her muscles, her stomach going taught, her arms and legs quivering with need. Ragden slammed into her faster, harder, the floor reverberating with each impact of his ass against it. The room filled with the thunder of his ass bouncing off the floor. Emily moaned louder and louder with each incredible impact. Her body rocked, her hips vibrated, her insides clenched and released with each thrust.

Sarah's breath caught in her throat, as she walked into the room, witnessing Ragden fucking Emily so hard. She stood in the doorway, transfixed, her eyes locked on Emily's incredible body bouncing off Ragden's incredible thrusts. Her body quivered, her pussy clenched as she imagined herself in Emily's place. She licked her lips, and slipped her hand between her legs, spreading her lips and slipping three fingers into her tight pussy. She felt her slick walls clench on her hand as she watched Emily riding Ragden's thrusts.

Emily's voice grew louder with each incredible impact. Her breathing was

ragged. Her voice strained, her body trembling with need.

"Fuck. Fuck. Fuck. Fuck. Fuck," Emily moaned with each impact, completely at Ragden's mercy.

She surrendered herself to it. Let herself ride it. It was like the first time he had fucked her, at the school, only this was so much better. She felt connected to him on a spiritual level. He was not just fucking her body but making love to her soul, and it made her feel complete.

She closed her eyes and felt her energy. She also felt Ragden's energy riding over her. She felt herself surrounded by his care, his desire, his compassion, and his love. There was so much love she felt overwhelmed by it. For a moment, she wondered if she was worthy of it, but that thought was batted away in a blink because it did not matter. It was there. She drank it in. She felt tears of joy on her face as his energy suffused her very being, becoming part of her, as she was part of him.

Emily felt something inside of her swelling, blossoming, like the world's most incredible flower, full of her sexual energy, her life energy, everything that was her. Inside that blossoming flower, she felt him with her. So deeply a part of her, she was not sure where she stopped and he began. Her breath hitched, and she started crying in earnest; the joy of it so completely overwhelmed her. She felt herself swelling, filling with his love and the sexual energy building inside her. She felt her orgasm being nurtured by that incredible blossom in her soul. The joy and ecstasy of it radiated through her entire being. She felt every pour in her body filling with that energy, that joy, that sex, that love. She felt like something was being awakened in her that she never knew existed. The feeling of it was the most amazing thing she had ever felt. She felt her body bouncing off his incredible thrusts, his jackhammering into her cervix with such force it was lifting her into the air; then it would drop back, he would catch her hips in his hands, then slam into her again, lifting her. She felt herself airborne, then caught, then airborne again.

Ragden felt the energy in the room changing, deepening. The air felt thick around him. He kept his eyes focused on Emily and watched her body. He kept his hands in place to hold her as he thrust into her with such force it lifted her out of his hands. He saw her gaze go inward and felt something changing in her. He felt his energy seeping into her, as something changed in her. He felt himself with her, in that incredible blossom of love, and he felt it subtly changing the very core of her being. He could not explain it, or even understand what was happening. He watched her incredible red hair bouncing with her. Her hands clamped on her large breasts, keeping them from smacking her body. The amazing swell of her hips as they vibrated with each impact of his groin into hers. The feel of her pussy clenching on his cock as it slid up into her and crashed into her cervix, lifting her into the air.

Then he felt his energy blossoming, his balls tightening, his entire body starting to wind up like a spring ready to explode. He dropped his hips to the floor and felt something crunch beneath him, hearing the thunderous hammer

of his heart in his chest as he thrust up into her. The room seemed to fill with light as his cock smashed into her cervix. Her entire body seemed to glow with an inner light as his orgasm exploded out of him. He felt his balls loose, as cum exploded into her with force unlike anything he had ever felt before. He felt her lift off him, hovering in the air. Her arms were thrown back, her legs convulsed, her incredible breasts rising into the air. She floated there for a moment; her body suffused with light. Then she came down against him, and cried out at the force of it, her orgasm exploding over her. She screamed as fluid poured out of her, her arms and legs convulsing as she landed on Ragden's cock. It slammed into her cervix again, more cum exploding out of Ragden as he collapsed against the floor. Emily collapsed on top of him as the lights in the room went out.

Aria's blue eyes were wide with excitement, as she gazed at Emily. Her pussy dripped with excitement, her breasts heaving with each breath. She gasped as she felt Ragden's cock slamming into Emily, and the room filled with the sound of their combined pleasure. She looked down at her pussy, seeing it glistening with her juice.

Emily lay against Ragden, feeling her body trembling with the aftershocks of her orgasm. She rested her head against his chest, listening to his strong heartbeat. She drew a ragged breath, trying to catch her breath. Her vocal cords hurt from crying out. She felt the dampness on her face from her tears. Her legs quivered as spasms still ran through them. Emily smiled as she felt his throbbing cock still pressed against her cervix, the length of her pussy still clenching and releasing around his massive girth. She could still feel his seed filling her up inside. Her insides swelled with it. Their ejaculation collecting, mixing, and spilling out of her over his groin. She felt complete, whole, and satisfied in a way she had only dreamed of. She gently kissed his chest, tried to raise her head, and found she barely had the strength to do even that. Emily pulled her arms along his sides, groaning with the effort, trying to hug him.

She whispered against his chest, "Gods... I... I love you... so much."

His arms draped around her, hugging her to him. She felt his warmth, his passion, his love washing over her. He kissed the top of her head softly. His cock throbbed inside her.

Ragden closed his eyes, savoring the feel of Emily against his skin. His cock pulsed inside of her. He could still feel her fluids slipping out of her over him. His cock still leaking inside of her. The twitching in his muscles slowed, and his breath returned to normal. He could feel her heart beating against him, slowing to match his own. He cradled her against him, feeling her calm.

Ragden kissed the top of Emily's head softly, then whispered, "Are you okay?"

Emily nodded. She felt the flush of her cheeks. Her breathing slowed and steadied. Her heart rate calmed; her body relaxed. She gazed up at Ragden, her eyes filled with love and trust, her hands resting on his thighs. Her fingers lightly caressed his skin. "I'm fine, Ragden.... Thanks for asking."

Ragden sighed contentedly. Aria crawled up next to them and draped herself along his side. He smiled happily as she leaned over and kissed him on the lips softly. He smiled at her. Then Sarah came into the room and laid down along his other side. She leaned over and kissed him softly on the lips, then laid down, resting her head on his shoulder. They lay together, basking in the afterglow of the incredible climax for a few minutes, just enjoying being next to each other.

Then Ragden checked the time and groaned. "We need to clean up and get going. Class starts soon."

Aria and Sarah groaned audibly. Emily sighed, feeling her insides still clenching on Ragden's massive cock. She felt it starting to soften inside her and groaned. She was not ready for that to happen just yet. Aria sat up, grabbed her panties, and slid them on. She frowned, then stomped over to the couch and sat down in a huff. Ragden looked at Aria and chuckled softly to himself. Aria caught him chuckling and scowled at him.

"It's not fair," Aria stomped her foot, "I didn't get to feel you inside me."

Ragden watched her and smiled, "Your tantrum does not fit you well, my dear. You will get a chance. I'm sorry it didn't happen today, but I promise you will get your turn."

Aria's face lit up at his kind words. She settled back onto the couch, knowing she would get a chance. Sarah giggled softly against Ragden's side. Ragden looked at her and cocked an eyebrow. She shrugged, then reached over and found her panties, sliding them up her legs. She sat on the floor watching, licking her lips.

Ragden ran his hand down Emily's back and cupped her ass softly. She lifted her head and looked at him, a wonderful smile on her face. She lifted herself gingerly and kissed him on the lips. She sighed against him, savoring the feel of his body against her. Then she slowly sat up, feeling his cock slide around inside of her. She moaned softly, then slowly stood, allowing his cock to slide out of her. Emily gathered up her clothes and started putting them on.

Sarah crawled over Ragden and slipped his cock into her mouth. Aria and Emily both giggled as Sarah greedily sucked hard on his softening cock. Ragden moaned softly as she slipped his cock down her throat, her tongue twisting around its base, her lips kissing his groin. She bobbed him twice, then slipped his cock out, licking her lips. Then she gently kissed the head of his cock and stood, satisfied.

Ragden chuckled, then sat up and grabbed his clothes, slipping them on. He then stood and flexed his muscles, stretching them. Feeling refreshed, he walked over and hugged Emily. Then he pulled Aria up off the couch and hugged her. Aria blushed as she took a step back from him, her heart beating hard in her chest. Then Sarah ran up and wrapped herself around him, pulling her body fiercely against him. She kissed him on the lips, then rested her head against his chest, sighing contentedly. Emily giggled and then pulled on Ragden's arm, gesturing towards the door. Ragden nodded and pulled himself

away from Sarah. He took Sarah by the hand and let Emily pull them towards the door. Aria smiled and dashed ahead of them, running out the door and down to the street where she waited for them.

Aria stood on the sidewalk, her hands clasped together, and her whole body trembling with anticipation. She heard footsteps behind her and turned just as Sarah and Ragden came into view. She ran forward and threw her arms around Sarah, hugging her tightly, and then stepped back and held Sarah at arm's length, looking at Ragden.

Ragden chuckled at her enthusiasm as he pulled Emily against his side. Emily blushed and sighed at him. As they walked, she whispered to him, "What happened back there? Was it just me, or... did... something happen?"

Ragden squeezed her hand, feeling her warmth against his skin. He looked down into her eyes and nodded. "Yeah, I felt it too... I... I don't know. It was kind of amazing."

Aria giggled, "She floated. I saw her glow and float... How did you do that?"

Emily shrugged, "I... don't know how to explain it. I feel... different, but... amazing. It felt amazing."

Sarah danced away from Ragden's side and spun in place, her skirt flaring, showing her panties. Then she stopped and pushed her skirt down with a mischievous grin. She giggled, "Ragden... you fucked her so hard you made her float... Can you make me float too? Can you fuck me so hard I float too??"

Aria watched Sarah with a mixture of envy and excitement; she felt her panties growing damp with desire. She could not wait to see Sarah get everything she wanted, and more. Sarah gazed back at Aria with a determined expression, her eyes bright with determination, her body tense with anticipation. She took a deep breath and looked at Ragden, waiting for him to respond.

Ragden shrugged, "I don't know how that happened. I'm not sure how to repeat it. I suppose we can try, but not today. I'm afraid we probably won't have time for more fun today."

All three women pouted as they walked onto the school campus. The warning bell rang, letting them know they had 5 minutes to get to class. Aria and Sarah dashed off to their classes as Emily and Ragden walked towards theirs. They stopped where they needed to part, hugging tightly. They kissed softly, pressing their bodies against each other. Ragden whispered, "I'll call you as soon as I get back into town. I hope you have a great weekend, my love."

Emily looked up at Ragden, trying to stop the tears from welling. She nodded as she stepped away from him. She whispered as he ran off to his class, "Love you too..."

CHAPTER 23

Ragden's classes after lunch went well. His body felt refreshed. His stomach sated. The lectures went well, and the texts were easy to read. Everything made sense, for the first time in a long time. He did catch his mind wandering occasionally, thinking about the experiences during lunch. He was not sure what had happened to Emily. Only that it had been amazing. He wondered if he had broken the floor. He would have to check that later. Ragden did hope he did not have to explain that to Sarah's parents. That would be a terribly awkward conversation. He tried to imagine explaining it and cringed. Hopefully, that would be something he could avoid.

As he was approaching his last class, he turned the hall corner and spotted Sarah leaning against the bank of lockers along the right side of the hall. He smiled at her and watched her face light up as she stood and sauntered over to him. Her hips swayed seductively.

"Hey, lover," he said softly as he wrapped his arms around her, pulling her against him.

Sarah hugged Ragden close against her, pressing her firm body tightly against him. She looked up at him, tears in the corners of her eyes.

"Do you really have to go away for the weekend?" she whispered, pleading.

Ragden nodded slowly, "' Fraid so... It's a family thing. I can't skip it and it is family only. Sorry."

Sarah buried her face in his chest, tears leaking out of her eyes. Then she looked up, the pleading look in her eyes even more intense, "Okay... But... I... Can I have your cum in me one more time before you go? Please?"

Ragden shook his head sadly. He leaned down and kissed her softly on the lips, "Sorry, love, no time. I must get to class. We will have more time when I get back. I promise."

Sarah buried her face in his chest again. Her breath hitched. Hot tears

trailed down her cheeks. Sarah could not shake the feeling that something terrible was going to happen over the weekend. She had just found Ragden and all the amazing experiences she had had in the last couple of days. She did not want it to end. She thought she might die if she could not have those experiences again. She did not know how to convey her fears but wanted desperately not to have this be the end. Ragden patted her back comfortingly.

"It's only two days, love. It will be over before you know it," he said soothingly.

"It's too long!" Sarah moaned.

Ragden gently put his hands on her shoulders and pushed her back from him. He smiled at her. Then kissed her softly on the mouth. She smiled back.

"Two days," He said softly, "You can wait two days."

Sarah nodded slowly, "Okay..."

She pulled him against her again, hugging him fiercely. Then she stepped back, kissed him on the lips softly, then dashed off to class. Ragden smiled to himself as he headed off to class. Sarah was a bit clingy, but he understood. He would find a way to make it up to her when he got back.

Ragden's last class went by in a rush and was over before he knew it. After the bell rang, he headed to his locker to drop off books he would not need over the weekend. He kept his math book so he could look over the most recent assignments. He did have a test on Monday, and it would help to go over everything one more time. He double-checked he had everything he needed, then slung his bag over his shoulder and closed his locker.

As he headed off campus, he looked around one last time, wondering if he would catch sight of the three women of his life. He ached to see them, to hold them but knew his dad was waiting for him. As he reached the edge of campus, he saw the family car parked at the curb, his dad behind the wheel. Jennifer was sitting in the passenger seat reading something on her phone.

Michael waved as Ragden approached. Ragden returned the wave and slipped into the back seat. As he got in, he fastened his seatbelt. Michael pulled the car away from the curb.

"How was school?" Michael asked as he pulled the car into traffic.

"Good, actually, very good."

"Really? Not having any issues with your classes? I know some of them have been a bit hard for you these last couple of years."

"Yeah, I know. But... I feel like something... changed. The problems I used to have seem to be... resolving themselves?"

"That is great news," Michael beamed from the front seat as they took a turn, making their way to the freeway.

"It's like... I don't know how to explain this. I feel like... uh... the ... experiences with... Emily, Sarah, and Aria... fixed me?"

Michael laughed in the front seat. Jennifer looked up from her phone and turned to look at Michael, then at Ragden in the back seat. She smiled softly and nodded. Ragden furrowed his brow, confused.

"That actually makes sense," Michael said from the front seat.

"How does that make sense?" Ragden asked, confused.

"Well... That is something we need to talk about. And now seems like as good a time as any..."

"Dad. Can I get a straight answer?"

"Sorry. This is a subject we have been dancing around since you were old enough to talk. Hard to find the right words now. The reason you have a problem with books, and school in general, is because of something you inherited from me. That is the easiest explanation."

"Oh?" Ragden cocked an eyebrow at his dad. "That... doesn't really explain anything."

Michael laughed, "No. It does not. I am getting to the part where it does. Bear with me."

Ragden sighed and nodded, waiting.

Michael turned to Jennifer with a soft pleading look on his face. She giggled and shrugged, "You'd think, after all this time, that we would have figured out how to explain this."

Jennifer laughed again, softly, her voice like the tinkling of bells. Ragden felt himself smiling along with her, then frowned. This was not helping.

"Mom?"

"Yes, dear. Sorry. I met your dad over two thousand years ago, right about the time Jesus Christ was reported to have been born. You know, they never did get the date right. To think, all the calendars we use are based on that. The Chinese calendar was much more accurate."

"Wait, what? Did you say you met Dad the year Jesus Christ was born?" Ragden scratched his head.

"No, what I said was that I met him right about the time it was reported that he was born. Not the same thing. Semantics, but yes." She laughed again.

"Is this some kind of joke?" Ragden asked softly, wondering if his head was going to explode.

"Nope."

"You are over two thousand years old?"

"Yes. But your dad...," she laughed again, "Michael is older."

Ragden scoffed. Surely this was some kind of joke. He looked at Michael driving the car as if nothing had changed. Ragden peered at him.

"Okay... How old are you, Dad?"

Michael looked over his shoulder, smiled, then shrugged. "I don't know."

"How can you not know?"

"Excellent question," he laughed softly to himself. Then he said, "Well... I have existed since animals first started falling in love with each other. I was not able to take a physical form until humankind started worshipping the Gods of Love, and then I manifested as the form of that god."

Michael looked over his shoulder, seeing the astounded look on Ragden's face, "No, Rag, I am not a god. Never met one. I am... something else. I think

the parlance that would make the most sense to you is... Force of Nature. I am Love, given physical form."

Ragden scoffed. Michael smiled in the front seat. Then spoke softly, "I know this is hard to believe. I get it. That does not change the truth, though. You are force-born. Which comes with its own special challenges. Mainly reading and writing, and some of the technological stuff will always be hard for you."

Ragden mouthed the phrase... force-born. Something about that just... felt right. It made sense in a strange sort of way. He looked up at Michael, nodded, and then spoke softly, "Okay, let's say I believe you. What does that mean?"

"Well...," Michael smiled softly, "When the force-born reach their eighteenth birthday, that is when their abilities start to manifest."

"Abilities?" Ragden asked.

"Yes," Michael continued, "Each different force tends to manifest different abilities. For you, it would be... well... love and sex. Some enhanced physical strength, especially around those you love. I think you have already discovered some of the sexual benefits."

Michael chuckled softly to himself, "When was the last time you remember being sick?"

Ragden pondered for a moment, trying to recall. He shrugged, "I don't remember..."

Michael nodded, "The force-born do not get sick from the kinds of things most people do. You won't catch diseases or pass them on to others."

Ragden thought about it for a moment, then asked, "What about getting someone pregnant? Do I need to worry about that?"

Michael chuckled, "You haven't been using protection, have you?"

Ragden blushed, sighed, and spoke softly, "No."

Michael spoke soothingly, "Not something to worry about. I cannot explain why this is the case, but Jennifer and I, we had to make the conscious choice that that was what we wanted. I imagine it will be the same for you. Unless you AND your partner choose it, it will not happen."

Ragden sighed, he was not ready to be a father just yet and preventing that had not been something he had even considered with everything that had been going on. He looked out the window and saw the landscape flying by. He ran over the events of the past week in his mind. It all fit. Strangely, it did. Part of him did not want to believe it was true, but in his soul, he knew it to be so.

"Are there... others? Like me?" Ragden asked quietly.

Michael nodded, "There are. Few, though. There are also the descendants of the force-born. Those are called force-touched. Jennifer is force-touched. Which complicates things."

Jennifer turned and smiled at Ragden, sadness in her eyes. She spoke softly, "Sorry, love."

Ragden looked at her, then asked, "If Dad is the embodiment of love, what force are you from, Mom?"

"Earth."

Ragden sighed. That made sense. His mother was always in the garden, her hands in the soil. She smiled at him, seeing the realization dawning in his eyes, and she nodded. Ragden thought about it. Their garden was always lush, the plants always healthy, the flowers always blooming. The grass never needed to be cut or the bushes trimmed.

"How does that complicate things?" Ragden asked.

"A long time ago, there were a lot more force-born, and they caused a lot of problems. Unchecked, they caused chaos in the world. The Primal Forces decreed that all force-born must be presented before them. Since powers manifest after their eighteenth birthday, the first presentation is on the spring equinox following your eighteenth birthday. That is this weekend."

"Oh," Ragden stated. "Wait... Primal Forces?"

"Earth, Fire, Wind and Water."

That clicked for Ragden. The ocean. He was going to meet the embodiment of Water. Why did that make him nervous? He felt like his father was not telling him something. He wanted to ask, but he sat quietly, trying to grapple with what he had just learned.

"Michael, do I still call you that? Or do you prefer Dad? Or... do I call you Love?" Ragden stammered, not sure how to continue.

Michael laughed, "Dad is fine. Or Michael. I've used this name since the day you were born. It has grown on me."

He reached over and clasped Jennifer's hand in his. She smiled and brought his hand up and kissed it softly, then rested it on her thigh, smiling at his touch.

"You've used other names?"

Michael laughed. Jennifer giggled.

"I've used many names. Some, you may even recognize. The Norse called me Freyja. The Greeks called me Aphrodite. The Romans named me Venus...."

"Wait... You... You were a woman?"

Michael laughed, a deep sexual sound that sent a shiver down Ragden's back, his loins tingled. Jennifer shivered and slapped his hand playfully, "Stop. Not while you are driving."

Michael's laugh suddenly became very female and coy, sending another shiver down Ragden's back. For a moment, he saw an incredibly beautiful woman driving the car. She was completely naked, with flowing, curled blonde hair that draped over her shoulders. She had large, plump breasts, a flat stomach, her groin shaved, her hips round, and shapely legs tapering to small ankles. Ragden felt his cock throb. He blinked again and saw his father sitting there laughing.

Jennifer reached over and slapped his hand harder, "I said not in the car!

Not while you are driving!!"

He looked at her apologetically, "Sorry."

Michael looked over his shoulder at Ragden, shrugged and winked.

"I'm... That's... Wow, okay, that is a LOT to grapple with, Dad."

"I'm not apologizing for that. That would be like asking the ocean to apologize for being wet." Michael laughed softly at the thought. "I am what I am. Regardless of anything else, I love you, and always will."

Ragden smiled. Love. Yes. He could accept that. Ragden looked up at Michael, saw the love in his eyes, and felt the car full of it as he realized it had always been there. He smiled at his dad and saw him smile back.

"I do have... another question..." Ragden started. Michael looked back at the road but nodded to Ragden to continue, "What about the ... energy thing?"

"Energy thing?" Michael asked. Ragden explained the times energy had surged over the room, the time Emily had seemed to float. Michael listened attentively, then looked at Jennifer.

She shrugged, "I thought you might know something about that."

Michael pulled the car off on the next off-ramp. Found a parking lot and stopped the car. He sat up and turned around to look at Ragden in the back seat.

"I have seen that before, but it has been a very long time. Emily, she is the one you gave part of your soul to, right?"

"Wait, what?"

"The one you thought was dying."

"Yes... Wait, I gave her part of my soul?"

Michael nodded, "Yes."

"What does that even mean?"

"In short, you bound her to you. Do me a favor and close your eyes. Think about Emily, focus on the first image that comes to mind, and..." He shrugged, "It's hard to explain, but... If you focus your heart and mind on her, you will see her, and you can see where she is. Depending on... how much she loves you, how much you gave her, you might be able to feel what she is feeling, hear what she is hearing, be there with her..."

Ragden's jaw dropped. Then he snapped it shut. He raised his eyebrows, looking at his dad.

"I know, it sounds crazy, but try it. I want to see what happens if you will let me."

"What do you mean see?"

"If I put my hand on you, I can share your vision."

"How does THAT work?"

Michael laughed, "You are my son. Your soul is connected to mine; I cannot explain it better than that. Just... try."

He sighed, then closed his eyes, "Okay, Dad. I'll try."

Ragden focused his thoughts on Emily and tried to reach out to her. In his

mind's eye, he saw a filament of love from the core of his being running away from him. He followed it and felt something coming rushing towards him. He found her. In all her radiant beauty. She was walking through a department store, the ladies section. She was with her mom, looking at bras.

"Are you sure you need a new bra? We just bought some last week..." Emily's mother asked, looking over at Emily, furrowing her brow.

"Yes, Mom, this bra is killing me; I can hardly breathe. Just... Can we try this one?" Emily pulled a bra off the rack. Her mom looked at the bra, aghast.

"That is a C-cup; you were in A's last week. How on Earth would that fit you?"

Emily looked at her pleadingly. Her mother sighed and took the bra, leading them to the changing room. The woman at the counter looked at them questioningly, then handed them a key. Emily grabbed the bra, moved down the hall, and pulled the door open.

Once inside, she quickly removed her shirt and popped her current bra off. Her chest heaved as she took a deep breath. She looked at her chest in the mirror, gently cupping each breast. Then she pulled the bra off the hanger and slipped it around her chest. She fitted the bra to her chest and sighed in delight. She cupped each breast again and blew a kiss to her reflection.

Ragden felt himself sigh in pleasure; his cock throbbed in his pants. He could feel the caress of her chest, the fingers cupping her breasts. Ragden felt like he was standing behind her, his head over her shoulder, his hands gently cupping her breasts. He sighed with pleasure. Her face flushed suddenly and she looked at the mirror, straight into his eyes. She felt herself go damp as she mouthed his name. She whirled around in the dressing room, her heart hammering in her chest. Ragden felt himself draw back while Emily spun in the room, searching for him.

Then she grabbed her shirt, slipped it over her chest, and walked out of the changing room, her face flushed, her heart hammering in her chest. She walked up to her mom and handed her the old bra. Her mother's eyebrows climbed up her forehead.

"How... What... It fits?"

"Perfectly."

"That's... That is insane. Are you pregnant?"

"What... No!"

"Look, I know you are a full-grown woman now. An adult. I get it. You have that boyfriend, what is his name, Rag... Ragden?"

"Yes. That is his name. But I only started sleeping with him this week..."

"What!?" Emily blushed. Her mother blushed, grabbed Emily by the hand, and dragged her back away from the counter.

"Did you use protection?"

Emily blushed even more and shook her head. Her mother scowled.

"How do you know you aren't pregnant?"

"I... I just know. But..."

"Go get tested."

"Fine. But even if I am, it's too early for there to be any physical changes. That takes a month at least... right?"

"True... Really dear? Unprotected sex? Have I taught you nothing?"

"I love him, Mom. I really, really love him. Oh, God, I love him so much, my chest hurts. I cannot think straight without him. I... Oh, God, Mom." Tears sprang to her eyes. Her mom looked shocked and then pulled her into a comforting hug, holding her head against her chest and gently patting her on the back.

"This still doesn't make any sense... But fine. We can get you a new set of bras. We'll get you seven, one for each day. What kind do you think he would like to see you in?"

"I... I..." Emily blinked back her tears and looked at her mom gratefully, "I have no idea... I think he prefers it when I take them off."

Her mother laughed, "Of course he does. But I think we can find some that might be more fun to take off... What do you think of lace? Or silk? Spendy, but they feel amazing..."

Ragden pulled away and felt himself returning to... himself. He opened his eyes and saw Michael staring at him, smiling. Ragden picked up his hand and flexed his fingers. It felt like his hand. The sensation of cupping her breasts had felt so incredibly real. His heart thundered in his chest.

"That was... I... Wow."

Michael laughed and then spoke softly, "Your connection with her is... Incredibly strong. I have only seen a connection that strong once or twice."

He reached over and patted Jennifer on the thigh, squeezing her softly. She smiled happily, leaned over, and kissed him on the lips. Michael beamed at her, then turned back to Ragden.

"My connection with Jennifer is like that, but we have lived together for..."

Ragden laughed, "Two thousand years? Yes, that makes sense."

Michael nodded, smiling. "That you have a connection that strong after such a brief time speaks to a couple of different possibilities. One, you gave you more of your soul than you realized. Two, she is force-touched herself and does not realize it. Three, something else entirely."

Michael scratched his chin, deep in thought for a moment, then continued, "I have seen someone do that once before... Conjure energy and pass it to someone else like that. Though, not during sex. They had given a portion of their soul to someone and managed to conjure their life force and pass it between them. The results were... spectacular. I would encourage you to exercise caution while doing this. From the sounds of it, you just conjured some incredible sex, which is fine. Just... be mindful that energy can be used for... other things too."

"What about her... physical changes?" Ragden asked, blushing slightly.

"Oh, totally your fault." Michael laughed. He patted Jennifer's thigh. Then looked back at Ragden, "I will explain. As the physical embodiment of love,

when I manifest a physical form, it is always the idealized form of beauty for the current culture I am in. If we were in Africa, my skin complexion would match theirs. If we were in China, I would look Chinese. However, we are in America. And Americans like their women with small waists, big breasts, and nice butts. I will not complain; it is one of the reasons why we live here."

He laughed again, a rich, warm sound. Jennifer giggled, and Ragden found himself chuckling along with him. Then he looked at Ragden again: "You gave her part of your soul, so her body is changing to reflect your ideal of perfection, along with societies. You can override it, but that would take concentration. It's not worth it. Just enjoy it. I am sure she is."

Michael smiled wolfishly, "Haven't you noticed your physical changes since your birthday? You were a scrawny fellow; now, you have gained almost 30 pounds of muscle. Look in the mirror when we get to the house. Really look. You can still see the old you if you concentrate, but again, why."

Ragden raised an eyebrow. He had noticed that he felt different, but he had not really looked at himself. He looked down at his body, his arms felt ... larger? His shoulders did seem broader than he recalled. He looked back at his dad.

"Is this... cosmetic? Will it change back to how it was?"

"Only if you want it to. Now, Emily's changes could... if she were away from you long enough. Not a couple of days. It would take years and would be so gradual she would not even notice right away. Now, I would not be surprised if you caused physical changes in Sarah and Aria as well. Though, it sounds like you fucked Sarah more than Aria. I would expect her to be more affected."

Ragden blushed. Then spoke softly, "Sarah really likes... swallowing my cum."

Michael laughed, nodding. "Yeah, that will affect her. Though, not as fast as Emily's changes."

Ragden blinked, not sure how to take that. He looked up at Michael and raised an eyebrow, "Would it be better to stop her..."

"Oh, hell no..." Michael laughed, "She enjoys it, you enjoy it. Just... don't worry about it."

Jennifer giggled from her seat. She looked at Ragden, reached over, and squeezed his shoulder affectionately. She spoke softly, her voice sensual and carrying in the quiet car, "It's just sex, dear. Sex with amazing rewards for those who choose to partake of it. It is a gift; one you give with your love. If they are willing to accept, then never, ever regret giving it."

Ragden smiled, a tear slipping down his cheek, "Thanks, mom."

Michael smiled and climbed back into his seat, "Shall we head to the beach house now? I am hungry. Or... I can sense both of you are hungry..."

Ragden nodded, paused, "Wait... You don't get hungry?"

Michael laughed, "Nope. This physical form is a manifestation of love. I don't need food. I eat because I enjoy the sensation and the look on Jennifer's

face when she serves a delicious meal."

Jennifer blushed and squeezed his hand.

Ragden pondered for a moment, then asked, "Does that mean I don't..."

"NO!" Both Jennifer and Michael answered at once, in unison.

Ragden looked shocked at their sudden passion and blinked from one to the other. Michael looked back at him, then pulled the car back onto the road, heading for the freeway again.

"Sorry. You are only force-born. You are still very mortal. Your body does things that no normal person can. You need more fuel than the normal person does to continue doing those things."

"Oh, okay. That makes sense. I guess."

Ragden sat back and looked out the window. The sun had slipped under the horizon, and the world was full of flashing lights and the blur of buildings going by. His mind drifted, trying to puzzle over all the things they had discussed. He felt like there were things that they were not telling him. It had been a lot, and he felt he needed time to come to grips with it all.

Ragden sat quietly, his thoughts wandering from one subject to the next. Then he thought about school and his math test on Monday. He pulled out his math book and started flipping through it until he found the chapter they were working on. He read the pages, going over the equations in his mind.

"Oh," Michael said into the quiet of the car, "I forgot to mention. George and Stacy will be renting the house next to ours. Do you remember them?"

Ragden looked up from his book and thought for a minute. "Has it been five years since we last saw them?"

Michael nodded, "Sounds about right. We will have dinner with them on Saturday night. They are arriving sometime around noon tomorrow."

"Are they here for the equinox too?"

"Oh, no. They are normal." Ragden paused for a moment, realizing his entire world was now pushing people into three categories. Force-born, Force-touched, and normal. He shook his head; that was going to take some getting used to.

"Do you remember their daughter?" Michael asked quietly. Ragden thought for a moment. He vaguely recalled they had a daughter several years older than him. She had been a little taller than him, with dark hair, and green eyes.

"Barely," Ragden answered.

"I am not sure if she will be joining us. She went off to college, and George did not say if she would be joining them or not." Michael shrugged.

"Anything I need to be concerned about?" Ragden asked.

"Oh. No. Not at all. Just thought you would want to know."

"Oh, okay. Dad... why did no one try to stop me during that day in school? No teachers ever came. The whole thing just... played out."

Michael chuckled in the front seat. "That is not unusual. Most mortals simply will not notice such a blatant use of your gifts in public. It is like some

kind of glamour. You could have sex in the middle of Times Square, and hardly anyone would notice. That is not to say that I would recommend doing that. Since there are sometimes ones who will. There are rules against such public displays of gifts like that for a good reason."

"Oh, and... the black cloud I sometimes sense?"

"That... is the dark side of our gifts. Sex without love. All-consuming lust. The selfish desire for self-gratification. It can consume you and destroy those around you. You must always remember the ones you are with. Never embrace the darkness."

"Yeah, that sounds bad."

They pulled off the freeway and started making their way through the back roads toward the beach community they were staying in. Another half-hour in, they stopped at a small restaurant and ate dinner. Michael ate sparingly, but Ragden found himself ravenously hungry. Michael shared his leftovers, smiling the whole time. Their server was a young twenty-something with a pretty figure. She flirted with both Ragden and Michael the whole time. Ragden found himself watching her walk away. Jennifer giggled at them.

Ragden looked at Jennifer, "Mom, don't you get jealous of Dad flirting with other women?"

Jennifer shook her head. "I came to terms with him a long, long time ago. I love him for who he is and what he does. I would not get upset if he fucked that poor waitress's brains out in the back. I know he is thinking about it; I can feel it."

Michael grinned wolfishly as Jennifer squeezed his leg affectionately. "What do you say, Ragden? Shall we go two-man her? I know you'd like to see what she looks like without those clothes on."

Ragden blushed and shook his head. "Not sure I'm ready for that."

Michael smiled softly, "I understand." He reached over and patted his hand reassuringly. As the waitress came by again, he flashed a huge smile. Watching her cheeks flush at his attention, he leaned over and whispered to her, "Check, please?"

She blushed as if he had said something else entirely and scurried off to get their check. Ragden chuckled to himself as Jennifer giggled. When she returned with the check, Michael handed her a credit card, and she grabbed it, her hand lingering in his for a moment. He gently squeezed her fingers. She almost swooned, looking like her knees were going to give out. She caught herself, took his card, and scrambled off again.

The waitress came back moments later and handed back the card along with a receipt. Michael smiled at her pleasantly, as she stood there waiting, her hands clasped lightly in front of her. Michael stood and stepped up to her. The poor woman's eyes got big as saucers as he leaned into her and gently whispered, "Thank you." in her ear. He placed a hand on her waist as she started to fall backward. He kept her standing and softly kissed her on the cheek. She blinked, tears in her eyes, her breath coming fast, her cheeks

flushed.

Jennifer slipped out of the booth as Ragden stood. Michael turned the waitress and gently pushed her down onto the seat. Her legs shook as she sat down, looking up at him adoringly. He kissed her softly on the lips. She moaned in pleasure and fell backward across the seat. Michael held her hand gently, easing her down. Then he smiled at Ragden and pressed a finger to his lips, making a shushing motion. Ragden looked down at the sleeping waitress and shook his head; then, he followed his parents out of the diner.

Once they were back in the car, Ragden looked from Jennifer to Michael. Jennifer looked at Michael and laughed.

"Okay, what was that?" Ragden asked.

Michael chucked from behind the wheel. "Okay. I will explain. I can feel people in love, or in need of love. In her case, she needed love. That poor girl, Amelia, was dumped by her girlfriend last month. Her dog died two weeks ago. One of her cats ran away. Just a bad string of luck. She works hours on end at that Diner, taking on extra shifts because she would rather work than think about her home life.

"Since you did not want to partake, I gave her a dream. A dream filled with love. She will wake up in a bit, feeling happy for the first time in months. Will it last? I have no idea. She left her number on the receipt. Not that I would need it to find her again."

Jennifer smiled happily in the seat next to him. "I love you, Michael; that was so kind."

Michael smiled at her and blew her a kiss, whispered huskily back to her, "I love you more..."

Michael looked into the mirror and saw confusion on Ragden's face and chuckled. "It is part of what I am. I often find myself drawn to couples who are deeply in love with one another. I will just hang out in their vicinity, basking in their love. Other times I find women, or men, like Amelia who just need a little love to get through their lives. Sometimes a dream is all they need. Sometimes they need mind-blowing sex. Other times they just need to hear a kind word from a stranger and a little love. Or sometimes a lot of love."

Michael winked at Ragden, then he spoke softly, "In fact, Rag, I bet that is what happened with Aria, Sarah, and Emily. That is what you found so attractive about them. They needed your love, and you gave it to them without reservation or condition. It changed their lives and who they were. That is the gift we can give to those willing to receive it and do not be surprised if you find it happening with other women or even men. Love is unconditional, and everyone finds that they need a little love from time to time."

Ragden pondered this in silence for a bit, then he looked up at Michael, "Dad... How did you know all those things about the waitress, Amelia?"

Michael smiled, "The closer I got to her, the more I learned of her life. People who really, truly need love, you will learn why, either by proximity or

by touch. My advice is to trust your gut when that happens. Do not fight it; just do what feels right."

Ragden sat back in silence, pondering this. They drove for another hour, before pulling up at the beach house. Ragden got out and looked over the area. He remembered this place, but it had been so long since he had been there. In the dark, it looked familiar, but he could not remember from when.

"Dad, when was the last time we were here?"

"The year you were born."

"What? Why?"

"To present you before Mother Ocean, of course."

"Oh. Of course..." Ragden answered, then, "Wait, what?"

"Same reason. All force-born are presented before Mother Ocean on the equinox following their birth, then again on the year of their eighteenth birthday."

"Oh. Okay."

They headed into the house. Michael pointed out his bedroom down the hall. They walked through the large house, which looked to be built for a family of eight. There was a game room, a theatre, a massive kitchen, a living room, and a dining area on the top floor. Ragden's room was not overly large and had a double bed. His parents got the largest room with a king-sized bed. Ragden looked at his room and sighed. The last two nights he had not slept alone and was not relishing the idea.

As he settled in, Michael stuck his head in the doorway and smiled. "I know it is not what you want, but get some rest. Tomorrow is going to be a long day."

"Okay, Dad. Thanks... thanks for explaining everything."

"Of course. I have been looking forward to this since you were born. Rest well son."

"Thanks."

Michael closed the door and Ragden heard his footsteps heading upstairs. He could hear Michael's voice and his mother's musical laughter. He stripped down and crawled into the bed. Ragden lay there staring at the ceiling. His mind ran in circles trying to wrap his head around all the things that had been revealed to him. Eventually, his eyelids grew heavy, and he slipped off into sleep...

CHAPTER 24

Saturday...
    Ragden woke in the early morning hours. He groped across the bed, searching for the lovely ladies who had shared his bed the night before. His arm went off the edge of the bed and he sighed sadly. He reached out the other way and found the bed equally empty. He sighed even more heavily. He remembered where he was and what he was doing there and groaned again.
    This was important, his dad had said it was and there was a weight to the way he had phrased it that sat heavily on Ragden. The presentation to Mother Ocean. He sensed danger there but could not figure out exactly what it was. He lay in bed, listening to the silence of the house, an exceptionally large house for three people. He imagined during peak season this house would be bustling with activity, so many people could stay there.
    He rolled over, pulled the pillow over his face and tried to go back to sleep. He did not want to deal with the world without Emily, Sarah, and Aria there. He sighed, his heart heavy, trying to force himself back to sleep. He lay on his back, clasped his hands over his navel, and took deep, calming breaths. He imagined his muscles relaxing, one at a time, working his way from his shoulders down his arms, then down his legs. By the time he got to his toes, his eyelids felt heavy and he slipped off to sleep again.
    The sounds of clinking dishes reached his ears, as Ragden came back to the waking world. He groaned, then looked out the window. The sun was up, and it looked like it would be a glorious day. Though, perhaps not as glorious as it could have been. He sighed heavily, then threw back the covers and pulled himself to the edge of the bed.
    He dropped his feet to the floor and walked over to the bathroom. He looked in the mirror at himself. Blinked and looked again. The figure staring back at him was, not one he was familiar with. The broad shoulders, the strong muscles across the chest, the chiseled abdominal muscles. The large muscular thighs. He cocked an eyebrow and watched his reflection match his

gaze. It was him. This was not the body he remembered. His dad was right. He looked like some kind of movie star or supermodel. Yet the eyes and face were much the same. His jaw seemed more squared; his skin clean of blemishes. He smiled and blinked. His teeth were perfect and almost shined in the light.

He sighed and went back into the bedroom, rummaging through some drawers to find some clothes. He pulled out a bathing suit and a T-shirt. Both fit, though a little snug. He shrugged and headed upstairs to the dining room.

As Ragden stepped onto the top floor he spotted Jennifer and Michael in the kitchen cooking. They were talking softly and laughing with each other. Jennifer spotted him, dried her hands and came running over to him. He stopped and watched her. She had her hair pulled back in a bun, stray hairs sticking out. She was wearing a loose-fitting T-shirt that could not hide her ample bosom. He could see the straps of a bikini top across her shoulders. She was wearing a pair of tight jeans that nicely complimented her shapely legs. She ran across the floor barefoot and threw her arms around him. He felt her breasts press against his chest as she hugged him tightly.

"Good morning, dear," she said softly into his ear. He blushed as she pulled back. She looked down at her figure and laughed. Then she posed seductively for him. Ragden felt his body responding. Jennifer giggled and grabbed his cock. She whistled nicely, then turned and walked back into the kitchen, her hips swaying seductively with each step.

Michael stood at the island, watching the whole thing play out. He laughed to himself as Jennifer came around the island and hugged herself to him. He reached down and pulled her tightly against him, squeezing her ass and kissing her passionately. Then he looked at Ragden and winked.

As Ragden came walking up to the island, hoping his erection was not too visible, Michael smiled and spoke softly to him, "You know... It is okay to be attracted to her. She is a two-thousand-year-old hottie who loves good sex. She might be able to teach you a thing or two..."

Jennifer looked up at Ragden and licked her lips, then winked. Ragden shook his head, not prepared to deal with this.

"I... But... Mom?"

Jennifer laughed. Then leaned against the island, letting her shirt dip down so he could see her cleavage down the front of her shirt. She smiled seductively, "Your silly societal taboos don't hold with me dear. We both know those 'laws' don't apply to us."

A shiver ran down Ragden's back at the thought of what that implied. He thought about it for a minute and realized some of what he had learned and simply accepted did not apply anymore. Still, having sex with his own mother seemed like a bit of a leap right now.

Seeing the look on his face, Jennifer started laughing.

"Is this all a joke to you? Are you messing with me?" Ragden asked, a touch of anger in his voice.

Jennifer pouted, "No, dear. No joke. It is just sex. You could not make me pregnant if you wanted to. I can see you aren't ready to explore that yet. When you are, let me know."

She smiled and turned back to the stove, rocking her hips from side to side as if hearing music he could not. Michael turned and slapped her ass sharply. She gasped loudly, then turned to him and winked. Michael laughed and stepped up against her back, rocking his hips with hers.

Ragden shook his head and walked around the kitchen, grabbing dishes and silverware. Then he placed them on the dining room table and sat down in the spot he had set for himself. Not a minute later, Michael and Jennifer came walking over with steaming plates of food in their hands. There was bacon, sausage, scrambled eggs, toast, and oatmeal. Ragden looked at the sheer quantity of food and blinked.

He looked questioningly at Jennifer and Michael. His father laughed, "Eat your fill. You may find you are hungrier than you think you are..."

Ragden filled his plate with servings of all the different things and dug in. His mother ate a fair portion, while Michael only ate a few items. With each bite Michael took, he would look at Jennifer and smile, give her a thumbs-up, or comment on how tasty it was. He ate a piece of sausage and smiled like it was the most wonderful thing in the world.

After swallowing, Michael turned and took Jennifer's hand in his and said huskily, "My God, woman, you cooked my meat so perfectly, it is a joy to put it in my mouth... It's like you made love to my tongue..."

Jennifer blushed and whispered back hotly, "Oh. dear, we can do that later..."

Ragden stared intently at his plate, trying not to listen to his parents flirting. After eating all that was on his plate, Ragden cleared off all the other plates and consumed what was on them as well. Before he realized what he had done, he had eaten all the food on the table. He felt pleasantly full. It had not been too much; the portion had been exactly right. Michael smiled a knowing smile at Ragden and patted his hand.

"It will take some time to adjust to. Don't worry."

Jennifer smiled happily, then turned to Michael, "I think I'd like to go swim in the ocean; care to join me?"

Michael raised his eyebrows, then smiled, "No, I need to run a few errands. But I'm sure Ragden could use some time in the sun." Michael winked at Ragden, then picked up all the dishes and headed into the kitchen to start cleaning them. Jennifer turned to Ragden and smiled. She stood and came around the table, offering him her hand.

"If you would be so kind as to escort me to the beach. I really could use a dashing young man to keep me company."

Ragden laughed, took her hand, and stood. She squeezed his fingers and pulled him along behind her as she headed to the stairs.

"Have fun, you two!" Michael called after them as he cleaned up the

kitchen. As they got to the bottom floor, Jennifer opened a closet and pulled out a couple of beach chairs, handing them to Ragden. Then she grabbed an umbrella and a couple of towels. They stopped at the door, slipped on some sandals, and then headed out.

The sun was blazing brilliantly up in the sky. Ragden had not realized it was so late. Jennifer danced along the path down to the beach, her ass shaking as she went. Ragden felt his loins stirring but tried to ignore it.

Jennifer followed the trail to the crest of the dune and stopped, waiting for Ragden. She slid an arm around his waist and leaned against him. Ragden smiled down at her. She pointed out a spot just down the beach. "I think that will be a great spot to set up the chairs and umbrella."

Ragden nodded and carried the stuff over. He set up the chairs and umbrella to shield them from the sun. Jennifer pulled her shirt over her head and dropped it onto one of the chairs. Then she stared at Ragden as she shimmied her shorts down her legs. She was wearing a tiny bikini bottom that accentuated her curves. Ragden found himself staring at her bottom, seeing the tight line of it against her skin, the folds of her pussy almost visible through the tight fabric.

Jennifer reached out and tapped his chin, bringing his eyes up to hers. Then she kissed him on the lips softly. She shook her finger back and forth, then licked it and placed it on her ass, making a sizzling sound through her teeth. Ragden blinked and sat down hard in the other chair as Jennifer laughed, turned, and ran off into the water.

Ragden sat back and watched her run down the beach, step high into the water, then dive under a small wave as it broke. She popped up on the other side, threw her hair back, and laughed loudly. She turned around and looked back at Ragden and blew him a kiss, then she turned and started to swim out to sea. Ragden leaned back in the chair, his mind reeling.

A shiver ran down his back. Ragden stood, dragged his chair into the sunlight, and sat down again. He quickly found himself sweating and peeled off his shirt. He closed his eyes and leaned back, letting the sun warm his skin. His mind wandered as his eyes drifted shut.

Ragden heard splashing in the water and another voice he did not recognize gasping. He opened his eyes to see a beautiful brunette emerging from the sea; beads of water clung to her smooth tan skin, glistening in the scorching sun. She shook her hair, like a dog and unzipped the top of her bikini a little, letting her gorgeous tits breathe.

Ragden caught himself staring and tried to play it cool as she approached him from the water.

"Hey Ragden!" she greeted him, with a warm smile, and a twinkle in her eye. Her bathing suit struggled to contain her breasts as she bent over to pick up a towel at Ragden's feet. Ragden's mind reeled, searching for who this beauty was.

"Selina?" he asked. He tried to search his memory, but the girl he

remembered only barely resembled this incredible woman before him.

Selina laughed, "Who else? Where did Jennifer go?"

As she dried herself off, she turned to look at the ocean, giving him a perfect view of her ass.

Ragden choked a bit on his words, hoping she didn't notice his sudden erection, "Not... sure?" His memory slipped as all he could think about was the gorgeous body in front of him. Nothing else really mattered.

She heard something in his voice and turned around quickly, worried that something might be wrong. She saw his obvious arousal and could not help but feel both curious and proud of herself.

"Ragden...?" she asked softly, concerned about his well-being. Her eyes roamed over his crotch, noticing the tell-tale signs of arousal. She wanted nothing more than to satisfy his desires and tease him even more.

"Is everything okay down there?" she asked with a mischievous grin, knowing the answer full well. She bent over in front of him, her cleavage right in front of his face as she rested her hands on the sides of the beach chair next to his hips. She looked at him and licked her lips.

"You know," she whispered seductively into his ear, "If you need release, I wouldn't mind helping you out."

Her gaze and attention between his legs caused his cock to throb and strain against his shorts, like some giant beast ready to devour the world. His voice lost, he could only nod and bite his lip.

Selina took this as a cue to continue teasing him, running her fingers along the bulge in his shorts and feeling the heat emanating from his throbbing member. With a sly grin, she leaned in closer and whispered into his ear, "Well then, I guess I have a job to do then, don't I?"

Her voice was full of temptation and desire as she slowly started undoing the tie on the front of his swim trunks, freeing his hard cock from its confines. Once they were completely open, she reached in and wrapped her hands around his thick shaft, stroking it gently and feeling how hot it was against her palm.

"Mm... looks like someone needs some attention."

Ragden's eyes squeezed shut, as his cock throbbed in her hands. He nodded, begging for more without saying a word.

She smiled and continued to stroke his cock gently, her other hand moving to wrap around the base and squeeze gently. As she watched his reaction, she felt a surge of excitement. She watched his cock throb and pulse in her hand.

"You're so responsive," she whispered into his ear.

Without warning, she took him deep into her mouth. She swirled her tongue around his length, pulled every drop of pre-cum onto her tongue, and slurped it. Her hand moved faster on his shaft, pumping his thick meat expertly as she took her as far back into her throat as she could manage.

"Mm-hm..." she hummed between sucks. Ragden leaned back and surrendered to the feeling.

Selina heard his submission and took it as her signal to continue pleasuring him, pushing him deeper into the realm of pleasure. Her hand worked faster and more confidently now, pumping his thick shaft expertly as her mouth engulfed every inch of him. She could taste his precum and the musk of his masculinity as she sucked eagerly. Her cheeks hollowed out as she took more of his length into her throat. She loved the feel of him inside her mouth, and she wanted nothing more than to see how far she could take him.

"Gonna cum for Mommy, huh?" she teased playfully as he saw the precum dripping from her lips onto her chin, "That's a good baby."

"You are amazing…" Ragden moaned softly.

She heard his praise and felt her arousal grow stronger, her hand working even faster as she felt his throbbing cock pulsing against her lips. She pulled off for a moment, looked up at him with a seductive smile, and licked her lips clean before answering, "Thank you, sweetie. I'm glad you're enjoying this."

She took him back into her mouth again, taking more of him each time she pushed forward until her nose was buried deep in his public hair and her cheeks stretched tight. As she felt his climax building, she increased her pace, determined to bring him to the edge and watch him lose control completely.

"Come for Mommy, you little slut," she whispered encouragingly, "let it all out."

Ragden relaxed and surrendered, letting the climax wash over him. She heard his surrender and saw the warmth and release flooding from him, and she loved it. She relished the feeling of his trust and submission as she worked to bring him an intense orgasm. Her hand moved faster still, pumping his thick shaft expertly as her mouth swirled around his throbbing head, and took in every drop of his essence. She swallowed eagerly, savoring the taste of his cum as it filled her mouth, and she squealed with delight.

"There we go, Ragsy... my pretty boy came home," she teased playfully as she finally pulled off his throbbing cock and looked up at him with a satisfied smile.

Ragden stuttered and stammered, almost unable to find the words, "That was amazing..."

She smiled triumphantly, seeing the effect her administration had on him, and knowing that she had taken him there. "I'm so happy to hear that, Ragsy. I love being able to give my baby boy something so incredible."

Her hand moved to wipe away the last traces of his cum from her lips and chin, and she leaned in close to whisper into his ear, "And there's so much more where that came from. Don't worry, Mommy's little boy won't ever have to be unsatisfied again."

She ran her finger gently over his sensitive tip, teasing and stroking it lightly as she watched him recover from the powerful climax.

"Now, I think it's time for round two."

She stood up, towering over him with her perfect figure and teasing him with a playful grin. Her hand moved to undo her bikini bottoms, revealing her

perfectly toned ass, and the hint of her pussy beneath the fabric. With a wicked gleam in her eye, she lowered them slowly, letting them fall to the ground, revealing her naked from the waist down.

"Feast your eyes on Mommy's sexy body, Ragsy." She commanded, "And don't forget who is in control. I decide when I let you have a taste."

Ragden's cock immediately jumped to full attention, throbbing painfully. He gazed at her perfection, licking his lip, "What do you wish of me?"

Seeing his reaction and her arousal growing. Her hand moved to stroke her smooth thighs together, reveling in the sensation of her desire.

"I want you to admire my beauty, Ragsy," she told him firmly, "and I want you to know that I'm in charge of when you get to have a taste."

With a wicked grin, she stepped closer to him, letting him get a better look at her perfectly round ass and plump pussy glistening with excitement and desire.

"But first," she adds, "I want you to show me how much you appreciate everything I've done for you so far. Beg for it, Ragsy," she demanded.

Ragden sighed, "You are one of the most beautiful women I've ever seen. You have one of the most incredible bodies. Please let me touch you. Please let me lick your perfection. Please let me fuck that ass raw."

Selina gasped at his enthusiastic response, feeling her desire intensify as she watched him beg for her touch. Her hand moved to gently cup her perfect ass, feeling the heat radiating from within.

"Oh, Ragsy... You really are such a good boy, aren't you?" She teased, "And I know you'll be rewarded for being so obedient."

With a playful smile, she leaned down to permit him, allowing him to touch and explore her body however he pleased.

"Go ahead, baby," she whispered, "Lick every inch of Mommy. Taste my sweetness, and when you're ready, I'll let you put that big thick cock of yours inside my tight little hole."

Ragden stood up and staggered forward on weak legs to caress her breasts. He took the perfect nipples into his mouth, suckling and licking them. He pinched them between his teeth, flicking the tip of it with his tongue.

She gasped in pleasure, feeling his warm mouth enveloping her sensitive nipples, and the gentle pressure of his teeth against them sending shivers down her spine. As he suckled and played with them, she could not help but let out a small moan of delight.

"Oh, Ragsy... such a good boy," she murmured, "Just like that... just the way I like it."

She closed her eyes and let the sensation wash over her, feeling his obsession with her body coursing through his actions. When he released her aching peaks from his hungry mouth, she gazed at him with gratitude and approval in her eyes.

"Good boy," she repeated firmly, "Now show me how much you want Mommy's ass."

Ragden grabbed her, almost frantic in his desire to please her, and spun her around. She gasped in surprise and pleasure. He placed a hand on her lower back and bent her over, exposing her ass. He spread her cheeks and buried his face in her ass, his tongue running through her pussy lips, and back up to her asshole. Slowly he circled her asshole with his tongue.

She felt his hot breath on her sensitive cheeks and the gentle pressure of his tongue exploring her delicate folds and entrance. She let out a soft moan of delight, feeling his obsession with pleasuring her rear.

"Yes, Ragsy... That's it," she whispered encouragingly, "Show Mommy how much you crave her tight little ass." She lifted her hips slightly, offering more access to his eager mouth and allowing him to explore every inch of her vulnerable flesh.

Leaning against her, Ragden pushed his face deeper between her ass cheeks. He ran his tongue down through her pussy lips, swirled it around her clit, across her vaginal opening then up to her ass. He did two slow circles around her ass, then plunged his tongue into her asshole. Pushing as hard as he could into her tight hole. He slipped as much of his tongue in as he could.

She felt his persistent tongue probing her most intimate areas, diving deep into her slick folds, and exploring every crevice with determination. Her body trembled with anticipation and desire as she felt his tongue slide into her tight asshole, pushing past the resistance and filling her entire cavity with his warmth and wetness. She gasped in pleasure and excitement, feeling his hunger for her most hidden depths.

"Oh, Ragsy... You're going to make Mommy so dirty," she teased, "And I love it."

Her hips rocked back involuntarily against his face, driving him further into her tight, needy depths.

He pushed his tongue deeper, then slipped it out. Then he pushed deeper again, fucking her ass with his tongue. He flicked and twisted it, pushing against the walls of her ass as he drove it as deep as he could, then sucked it out, then pushed it in again. While doing this, he grabbed her ass cheeks and spread them farther, allowing him to push even deeper into her.

She felt his insistent tongue fucking her tight asshole, driving deep into her bowels, and filling her with his saliva and passionate energy. Her body quaked with pleasure and excitement as she felt his strong hands grabbing hold of her ass cheeks and spreading them wider, giving him unrestricted access to her most vulnerable areas. As he pushed his tongue in and out, she let out a low moan of pleasure with need and submission, feeling his total focus on pleasuring her most intimate regions.

"Yes, Ragsy... make Mommy your filthy plaything," she whispered, "I love how dirty you're making me."

Ragden drove his tongue deeper into her until his entire tongue was inside her. He spread her cheeks wider, pushing even deeper.

Selina felt his relentless tongue driving deep into her bowels, pushing past

the very limits of her body and into the darkest recesses of her soul. Her body trembled with ecstasy and abandonment as she surrendered fully to his masterful control, feeling his hands spreading her cheeks wide and claiming every inch of her naked form. As he pushed his tongue even deeper, she cried out in pleasure, feeling the exquisite combination of pain and pleasure coursing through her veins. Her pussy leaked copious amounts of liquid, evidence of her arousal and the intensity of the experience they were sharing.

"Fuck me, Ragsy," she moaned, "You little filthy whore."

She gasped in pleasure and pain, feeling her body pushed to the brink of ecstasy as he continued to probe her most hidden depths with his insistent tongue. Her pussy dripped with desire and need, and she could barely continue the overwhelming urge to come as she felt his relentless assault. As he pushed deeper and faster, she moaned loudly, feeling her very core threatened by his unrelenting exploration. Her body trembled with anticipation and excitement, and she knew she was about to reach the point of no return.

"Yes, Ragsy... Yes!" She cried out.

Ragden spread her cheeks even wider. Pushed his tongue even deeper. His tongue was a miniature jackhammer on her ass, driving into her deepest depths.

Selina felt his tongue driving deeper into her, pushing past every boundary and barrier as he probed her most hidden recesses with reckless abandon. Her body trembled with pleasure and pain, feeling his insistent assault on her most vulnerable areas. She could hardly believe the intensity of the sensations coursing through her entire being. As he continued to push his tongue into her, she could not help but scream in pleasure and submission, feeling her very core threatened by his unrelenting desire to claim every inch of her body. Her pussy dripped with need and desire, and she knew that she was about to break apart under the weight of his total domination.

"Oh, God. Oh, God... YES!" She cried out.

As her climax suddenly burst over her, a gush of fluid streamed from her pussy. He let go of her ass cheeks and pulled his mouth off her ass, and clamped over her pussy. His tongue ran over her clit and into her pussy, catching the fluid and lapping it up. He licked the slick folds of her pussy, dipping his tongue into her vagina and catching all she had to offer.

She gasped in surprise and delight, feeling his mouth clamped over her sensitive folds and his tongue devouring every drop of her juice. As he lapped up her sweet nectar and tasted the essence of her pleasure, she let out a soft moan, feeling the intensity of his hunger for her most intimate flavors.

"Mm... good boy," she cooed.

Ragden licked the last drops of her cum from her pussy lips and lifted himself out of her. Selina stepped forward and turned to face him as he leaned forward, placing his face in front of hers.

"Did I do good?" he whispered into her face, his face drenched with her

juices. His rock-hard, throbbing cock inadvertently slid against her folds, causing him to close his eyes in momentary ecstasy.

She smiled seductively, feeling his lips and tongue covered in her sweet nectar. She loved the way it made him look and feel. She reached down and caressed his rock-hard cock, feeling the heat and pulsing desire emanating from within.

"You were incredible, Ragsy," she whispered, "But now it's time for me to take care of this big, bad boy."

With a mischievous grin, she grabbed his erection, stroking it gently before kneeling and taking it into her mouth. She looked up at him with a hungry gaze, showing him that she was ready to fulfill his every desire and indulge in his most primal needs. Then she released it and stood before him, pushing him back onto the ground.

"I want you to lay back and let me fuck you..." She said softly as she stepped over him. Ragden relaxed and let her lead him back into the sand. She positioned herself above him, straddling his hips and looking down at him with a mix of desire and determination in her eyes.

"Just relax, baby boy," she told him, "And let me show you how much I love pleasuring you."

Ragden relaxed and lay down in the sand; his hands reached up and slid over her firm ass, enjoying the feel of it under his fingers. She felt his hands on her ass and smiled, knowing that he appreciated the way her body felt. She leaned down, giving him a quick kiss before sitting up and straddling his hips, her slick pussy hovering inches above his eager cock.

"Are you ready for me to fuck you?" she asked, her voice low and seductive.

"Yes, Mommy, fuck me," Ragden whispered, "Ride me as hard as you can, Mommy, I can take it."

Selina heard the desire in his voice, and she felt a surge of excitement and arousal coursing through her veins. She nodded, then lowered herself onto his throbbing cock, feeling the way it filled her tight, slick pussy. She started to ride him slowly, at first, getting used to the feeling of being filled by his thickness.

"Yes," she breathed, "This is exactly what I want to do."

She picked up the pace, moving faster and harder, driving herself down onto him with each powerful thrust. She felt the way his cock slammed against her walls, sending waves of pleasure throughout her body, and she let out a soft moan with each impact.

Ragden bucked his hips in time to her thrusts, meeting her halfway. His cock slid deep into her, hitting her cervix, jarring her. He placed his hands under her thighs to help her maintain position and move faster.

She felt his hands holding her thighs, and she loved the way they added to the intensity of the experience. She increased the speed and force of her movements, driving herself down onto him with even more fervor, feeling the

way his cock slammed against her cervix and sent shockwaves of pleasure throughout her entire body.

"Faster," she panted, "Harder... I need more of you, baby boy."

She reached down and put her hands on his chest to balance herself as she continued to ride him with wild abandon, feeling the way his sweat mixed with her own and created a tangible bond between them.

Ragden bucked against her harder, driving his cock against her cervix. He lifted her hips, in time to her movements, speeding her up, driving harder into her. He punched into her insides with his massive cock. She felt his big dick pounding against her cervix, and she let loose a loud cry of pleasure mixed with pain. His power drove her wild with desire.

"Yes," she gasped, "Fuck Mommy harder."

She wrapped her hands around his waist, pulling herself down against him. Ragden drove up into her, his cock bouncing off her cervix. She let out a gasp of surprise and delight. At that moment, he rolled forward, rolling with her, placing her on her back. Her ass rolled high in the air. He held her knees down, pinning her into the sand. He slid his cock completely out and slammed it down into her rocking her entire body.

"Wow," she breathed, "That's... intense."

She felt his hands holding her knees down, and she felt vulnerable and exposed. She felt a mix of fear and excitement run through her veins.

"Do it again," she pleaded, "Mommy needs it all."

Ragden pulled back and slammed home again. Harder. Just as deep, filling her abdomen with his massive throbbing cock. Then he pulled back and did it again, and again. He started to build up a frenetic rhythm. She felt his cock slamming into her abdomen, and she let out another gasp of pleasure mixed with pain. She loved the way he pushed her limits. More fear and excitement coursed through her veins.

"Yes!" she cried out, "Faster!"

She felt his hands holding her down and knew she was at his mercy. He slammed harder, deeper, pushing into her depths, and then drawing out and doing it again. Then he suddenly pulled out completely, and pushed his cock against her asshole, sliding in, riding his weight into her. Filling her bowels suddenly and completely.

As his cock slid into her asshole, she gasped in surprise, feeling a mix of pleasure and discomfort. She loved the feeling of him filling her body. Fear and excitement coursed through her equally. She felt his weight pressing down into her bowels, and she knew that he was claiming her, filling her with his thick, hot presence. She loved it.

Ragden slammed his cock into her ass, then drew back and slammed home again. He built a rhythm of massive, powerful body-shaking thrusts, his cock filling her bowels, then drawing out and filling them again and again. She let out a gasp of surprised delight.

"Yes, baby boy," she breathed, "Fuck Mommy like this forever."

He chuckled softly as his cock slammed home into her ass again, rocking her entire body. He pushed her hips harder into the sand, shifting her position again, letting him slam her even harder. Her incredible breasts bounced with each impact. He slammed home again, and again. Deeper. Harder.

Each massive impact on her body caused her to gasp again with delight. A huge grin crossed her face as her body coursed with the sheer incredible pleasure of it. She felt him filling her body and soul.

Ragden slammed his cock home again into her ass. Harder than the last time, pushing even deeper into her. He paused, his weight pressed firmly against her ass, his cock pushed incredibly deep into her. He ground his groin against her ass, forcing his cock to shift around in her bowels, pushing at her organs, sliding around the inside of her ass.

"I want you to stay deep inside me. I want you to fuck me until I can't walk straight for days..." She whispered huskily, licking her lips as she looked up at him, feeling his throbbing cock in her bowels. She closed her eyes, feeling the pulsing so deep in her body. She marveled at the feel of it.

He slid his cock nearly out, until just the head was still in her ass, then slapped her ass hard, causing her to yelp in surprise. She opened her eyes, looked up at him, and bit her lip as he drove down into her the hardest he had done yet. She gasped loudly. Then watched, her eyes wild as he pulled up and slammed home even harder.

She moaned loudly in pleasure, feeling a mix of pride and pleasure coursing through her veins, feeling claimed. She felt his cock slamming into her asshole and loved it. Even as fear and excitement coursed through her, the sheer joy and pleasure of it washed over her. He slid nearly out, slapped her ass sharply, then drove into her again, even harder, somehow getting even deeper.

She gasped in surprise, feeling the stinging red mark on her ass cheek. She felt pride and pleasure coursing through her as his cock slammed deeper into her asshole.

"Deeper," she said again, "I want you as deep as you can go."

He slid his cock almost out, then slapped her ass again, even harder, and drove his cock into her again, getting even deeper. She felt a burning sensation that spread across her entire bottom, causing her to moan in pleasure. Then he rolled her up onto her shoulders, putting her ass high in the air. He spun around, facing the other direction. He crouched over, then drove his cock down into her ass again, the angle causing his cock to slide against the back of her ass, driving deep into her. Again, her body rocked with the impact.

From his new angle, Ragden started to build a new rhythm of incredibly deep strokes. He struck deep into her depths, then withdrew and slammed home again. Each incredible impact rocked her entire body. Again, and again, and again. Building speed and momentum.

She felt his cock slamming into her asshole from behind and let out a gasp

of delight with each impact. She loved having her boundaries pushed; it made her feel desired and wanted. He pounded her ass harder, deep, and fast. She felt his dick penetrating places in her body and soul that she had never dreamed were even possible. Each stroke rocked her entire body. Her breasts bounced wildly as he slammed into her.

He continued to slam his cock as deep into her ass as he could get, then pulled back and did it again, harder. Then again, harder than before. He continued to go faster, slamming into her.

Then he suddenly withdrew, pulling his cock out of her. It came out of her with an audible pop, dripping wet with her juice. She felt a mix of disappointment and relief wash over her. He let her backside flop down into the sand and walked over to her. He crouched over her face, dropping his cock against her chin, her fluids sliding down over her lips.

"Taste your juices, Mommy," he said softly, the head of his cock against her lips. She opened her mouth and took it in, sucking gently and swirling her tongue around it. She loved the way he had her taste herself. Her heart was hammering in her chest. He plunged his cock down her throat, his balls bouncing off her chin. As her eyes watered, she gagged, and her throat bulged; he pulled it out, leaving her gasping for breath.

CHAPTER 25

Ragden stood and walked back around her and knelt between her legs. He placed the head of his cock against her asshole again. As he swirled his cock around her asshole, teasing her, she moaned loudly. Fear and excitement coursing through her veins again.

"Please," she pleaded, "Don't deny Mommy."

"As you wish," He answered her softly. As she heard the words, she felt a surge of excitement. She knew that he was going to fulfill her request.

"Deep," she pleaded, "Make me feel you deep inside."

She felt his cock pushing against her asshole, and she let out a gasp of pleasure and desire. He slid his cock into her. Inch by inch, sliding deeper and deeper into her. Slowly filling her bowels with the immensity of his big dick. It twitched and spasmed inside her, pushing against her bowels. She gasped as his cock slid into her, surprised and delighted. She loved how much it made her feel wanted and needed.

"I want you to cum with my cock in your ass," he whispered, as he partially withdrew his cock and slid it back into her.

"Cum," she agreed, "with your cock in my ass."

She felt his cock sliding in and out of her asshole and she let out another soft gasp of pleasure and desire. He started fucking her ass faster, stroking his cock's entire length up into her, then slid it out and back in. He slipped two fingers into her pussy, pushing down against her pussy walls, creating additional pressure against his cock filling her bowels. With his thumb and forefinger, he pinched her clit. With his other hand, he reached up and grabbed her right breast, squeezing tightly, pinching her nipple.

She gasped with each thrust, her breath coming faster, her heart pounding in her chest. She loved having her boundaries pushed and how much she felt desired. She felt his fingers in her pussy, stroking her insides, the pressure building inside her.

"Please, baby boy," she pleaded, "Make Mommy cum for you."

He fucked her harder, his cock sliding in and out of her ass, filling her bowels. He twisted her clit, pushed against her pussy and squeezed her nipple. All in a continuous rhythm, driving her wild. He rode her harder, faster, and his rhythm increased. Her climax started to build, creeping like a monster in the dark to claim her soul. He rode her, filling her bowels with his monstrous cock. He could sense her impending climax and his own started to build with it.

She felt his cock slamming into her asshole and she gasped with each impact, loving the way it felt to have her body pushed and his cock slamming into it. She felt his hands in her pussy, working her, driving her, the pressure building within her.

"Cum," she moaned softly, "For you... only for you... I'm cumming!"

He rode her faster, driving deeper, feeling his climax matching hers. It felt like two monstrous creatures in the darkness of their minds. His eyes found hers and he stared into her, as her breasts rocked in time to each pounding thrust.

"I'm cumming! I'm cumming! I'm cumming!" she moaned louder and louder as her sudden climax hit her like a freight train, shattering her psyche. As her body quivered and shook beneath him, Ragden's climax overrode all sense and he suddenly started to fuck her with wild abandon. His body thrashed to its own rhythm. His cock slammed into her wildly. He cried out with the force of it.

Her body convulsed beneath him as she came, she felt his cock slamming into her asshole and felt her world coming apart at the seams. The pleasure, pain, excitement, and fear overriding her sense of the world around her.

Their bodies continued to thrash against each other. His cock still slamming into her with reckless abandon. Her hips rocked against him, driving him deeper than he thought he could go. Her pussy overflowed with her juice as it washed over him. He felt an explosion of cum release out of his cock, filling her bowels. It flowed down out of her, over his cock, and into the sand forming a pool between his legs. Yet he still did not stop. He kept pounding into her.

Her body continued to convulse as she came and she felt his cock slamming into her asshole. Her mind reeled, her eyes rolled and she lost all sense of what was going on around her. The only thing she could focus on was his cock, in her ass, pounding into her. She could feel his cum sliding out of her and the sensation added one more thing to the burgeoning sensorium that overwhelmed her.

Ragden slammed his cock into her ass, grinding his hips against her so deep it hurt. He still felt streams of cum pouring into her bowels. He slid his fingers out of her pussy, his hand soaked with her fluids. He released her breast, to see his fingerprints deep into her skin, leaving angry red marks. He pulled his soaked hand up to his face and licked it, tasting her cum. Then he held out his hand to her, dripping her fluids across her chin and lips. She

licked his fingers clean, savoring the taste of their shared climax.

He leaned forward against her, and kissed her passionately on the mouth, his tongue diving into her, tasting her cum in her mouth. His hips continued to grind against her ass, his cock still painfully deep. In the back of her mind, she registered the pain in her bowels, and her ass, and knew she would be sore later. Possibly unable to walk, she smiled. She had asked for it, got it and it filled her with such joy and satisfaction.

"Cum," she whispered, her voice hoarse, "I came. We came. We came together."

She wrapped her arms around his neck, pulling him closer to her and deepening the kiss even further. Ragden collapsed into her embrace, savoring the feel of his dick lodged so deeply in her bowels. The taste of her on his tongue and her cum mixing with her saliva. The feel of her slick breasts against his chest. He shuddered at the ecstasy of it all.

She held him close, feeling his cock still buried deep in her ass. She was not sure she would be able to walk right ever again.

"We came," she spoke softly. "We came together. Our cum mingled. Our bodies are joined forever. I love you. I love being with you. I love being one with you, baby boy."

She felt his heartbeat against her chest and she knew that he was as much a part of her as she was a part of him.

Ragden smiled, and whispered against her lips, "We did. I hope you enjoyed that as much as I did, Mommy."

He wiggled his hips, causing his dick to shift around inside her. Still hard, still so deep.

She giggled, "Oh yes, baby. I loved it. I love being filled by you, being filled by your big cock. I have never felt so full before. So happy. So, content."

She felt his cock moving around in her asshole and she was sure she would be walking funny for a week, if not longer.

"I love you," she added, "And I love being one with you, being connected like this."

Ragden smiled happily, kissing her passionately on the lips again. He tasted her, tasting him, tasting mixed cum and saliva.

"Thanks for having me," he whispered back to her. He wiggled his hips gain, causing his cock to shift around inside her bowels again, relishing the feel of her tight ass squeezing the last bits of juice from him as it started to soften inside her. She giggled, feeling his cock moving, knowing it would have to come out eventually, but not yet.

Ragden kissed her on the nose, then licked her nose playfully. He wiggled his hips again, feeling his softening cock moving around inside her. He shivered again at the pressure of her bowels pressing against him. She giggled again, feeling his lips on her nose, and his cock moving inside her. He did not want to take it out, not yet.

"Mm," she moaned softly, "I don't want you to leave just yet. I want to feel you inside me."

She wrapped her arms around his neck, holding onto him tightly and sighed in contentment as she felt his cock inside her. Smaller, but still there.

"Maybe. Maybe if we wait long enough. My cock will get hard again, and we can just keep fucking?" Ragden asked softly.

Selina smiled, feeling his cock inside her. "Yes," she agreed, "That sounds perfect. Just us. Together. Fucking... Loving. Being one with each other."

She pulled him tighter against her, sighing in contentment as she felt his cock inside her.

"Well, let me try this, then. Maybe..." He said quietly as he ran his arms down her back, cupping her perfect ass, then he grabbed the base of his cock, squeezing fiercely. He grunted with the effort, but his cock throbbed painfully inside her, starting to thicken, harden, and fill her up again. She felt his cock growing inside her, and she gasped in surprise delight.

"You're doing it," she breathed. "You're making yourself hard again. Staying inside me. I love you. I love feeling you inside me."

His cock throbbed inside her, growing, lengthening, hardening, filling her bowels. Somehow becoming larger than it was before, filling her up. Selina felt him getting bigger and she felt nervous, not sure she could handle the size. His cock, now rock hard, throbbed within her bowels. He grinned, as he ground his hips against her, feeling her tightness squeezing around him.

He slid partially out of her and slid back home. Slowly, purposely, savoring every tight bit of her around him. Her heart started to beat faster, her breath getting pushed out of her as his cock slid deep into her again. She felt the pressure and pleasure starting to build again and reveled in the sensations.

Ragden pumped his cock nearly out of her ass, then slid it home again, grinding his hips against her ass. Then he pumped in and out slightly faster. He kissed her on the cheeks, the chin, the neck. He kissed her breasts as they rolled with each impact of his cock, filling her up.

She felt his cock sliding in and out of her and she felt the same fear and excitement building in her, the pressure and pleasure building in her core. She knew he was taking his time, and she was not sure she could handle it, but she wanted it slow because she never wanted it to end.

Ragden wrapped his arms around her, pulling her against him as he sat up, pulling her into his lap, his cock still firmly in her bowels. He laid back, placing his hands under her thighs, balancing her above him. He lifted her thighs with his hands, lifting her slightly off his cock, allowing it to slide back partially out of her bowels. Then he thrust upwards into her, watching her gasp with the impact as it shook her perfect tits, her ass bouncing off his groin, which dropped back down into the sand, only to thrust up into her again, harder, deeper and with more force.

She gasped at the hard thrust up into her bowels. She watched his cock slide out of her, feeling a mix of disappointment and anticipation, then it slid

back in and she gasped at the feeling of his cock filling her bowels.

Ragden thrust his groin up against her, slamming his cock up into her bowels, then pulled back and thrust again; then again, faster. The sensation of her tight ass convulsing on his throbbing cock caused his eyes to water and his vision to gray. He could feel wildness starting to consume him. He thrusted up into her again, and again. Harder, loving the bounce of her breasts, the feel of her flesh against his.

Selina gasped as she felt his cock slamming into her asshole. She felt him getting more intense and she was nervous about whether she could handle it, but she pushed that aside because she did not want him to stop. She wanted it to continue forever. Her mind was caught in a loop, the same word repeating itself over and over, "forever." She whispered it to herself over and over, each impact into her bowels. She felt that word solidify in her consciousness. Her fear gave way to confidence and her anxiety was replaced with assurance. She would have this experience forever, and ever, and nothing else mattered.

Ragden thrust faster, holding her thighs above his groin, as her legs trembled. His cock slammed deeper into her as her magnificent breasts bounced with each incredible impact. Her asshole clenched around his cock, and she could feel herself getting wetter as he kept thrusting deeper into her bowels. She could feel the intensity building, the pressure, and the pleasure building with it.

He reached up and grabbed her ample breasts, letting her groin slam heavily down upon him. She gasped loudly at the sudden attention on her chest. He thrust up to meet her halfway, his cock slamming deep into her bowels. He lowered his ass to the sand, under her weight. He squeezed her breasts, pinching her nipples as he ground his hips against her, pushing his cock deeper into her ass, sliding it around in her bowels and pushing at her inner organs.

He grasped her breasts more firmly, digging his fingers in and pinching her nipples. Then he thrust hard against her, lifting her off the sand and then he dropped his groin down and slammed back up into her, her entire body rocking with the impact. He did it again, using her weight to slam his throbbing cock deeper and harder into her ass.

Selina's mind reeled; the limits of her body being pushed even further. Her eyes rolled. She felt every inch of his cock sliding in and out of her ass with such force it shook her entire body. She felt her inner organs being pushed around, her breath catching, her heart thundering in her chest. The intensity washed over her, blotting out everything else. She clutched his hands on her chest and felt his fingers digging into her soft skin. The pain mixed with the incredible pressure, and pleasure in her ass. She could feel her ass stretching around the immensity of his cock being forced impossibly wide with each massive stroke into her.

Each thrust into her forcing her to gasp, words bursting from her lips at each impact, "Forever. God. Forever. Forever, baby boy."

He squeezed her breasts harder, as he slammed his cock into her even harder, bouncing her entire body. Her legs clenching, her thighs flexing trying to work with each massive thrust that lifted her. The intensity was building and building. The pressure and pleasure filled her, overwhelming her. It was too much; it was never enough. She never wanted it to end. Her heart thundered in her chest, she gasped for air at each impact into her. She was overwhelmed and loved it.

Ragden sat up, wrapping an arm around her waist. His other hand reached behind him to brace against the ground as he thrust up into her even harder. Selina's head rolled back, her body bucking against each impact. She clenched her eyes shut as she tried to find a way to work with Ragden's incredible thrusts. She tried to plant her feet on the ground, but her muscles trembled, her body shaking. The pressure and pleasure were too much. The intensity overwhelmed her senses and her ability to do simple things. She focused on the only thing she could do, breathe, and ride it.

Ragden slid his feet back, folding his legs under himself to sit on his heels. He roughly rolled her backward, lowering her onto her back, her ass in his lap, his cock deep inside her. Then he rolled forward, sliding his cock in, repositioning her with her ass in the air, his groin pushing her into the ground. From his new position, he slid his cock out and then plunged it into her ass again. Then he pulled it out, ran the tip around her asshole, then slammed it home again.

Selina shuddered, her legs twitching, her heart racing. Her mind reeled at the assault of sensations. She felt the grains of sand against her shoulders, the cool ocean air blowing across her soaking pussy. Her body rocked with each incredible impact of Ragden's cock deep into her bowels. Ragden grabbed her legs, holding her ass in the air, her shoulders against the sand as he continuously slammed his cock into her ass, pushing deeper, driving harder into her. He squeezed her calves tightly, as he continued to drive his massive throbbing cock down into her ass, filling her bowels. He licked his lips, as he watched her body rock with each deep impact, her breasts bouncing, her legs shaking. She reached back and grabbed her ass cheeks, spreading them, urging him to go deeper.

Each massive thrust rocked her entire body, her bowels stretched beyond the limits of what she thought possible, her heart like a stampeding bull. She felt her climax swelling, consuming her. She pulled harder on her cheeks, relishing in the pain as his cock seemed to go even deeper into her. The heat of it filled so much of her that she felt her world washing away. The only thing that mattered was her ass and the cock that filled it.

"Oh fuck. Oh fuck. Oh fuck. Fuck. Fuck. FUUCCKK... FUUCCCKKK ME!!" Her voice broke into gasps with each pounding thrust into her.

Ragden continued to slam him his cock into her bowels, harder, faster, deeper. Each thrust rocked her incredible body. He could not help but marvel at her incredible chest as it rolled with each impact. Her ass squeezed around

him, her muscles starting to contract and release. The sensation was a sudden surprise and he gasped slightly. The tight squeezing of her bowels as he tried to draw back made his dick feel somehow longer, larger, filling more of her.

She could feel his hands squeezing her calves and his cock driving deeper into her bowels. She could feel her asshole clenching around his thick member. She smiled at the look of surprise on his face. She squeezed again, feeling every inch of his throbbing cock in her tight bowels, then her eyes went wide as she felt his cock swell within her. Her eyes rolled back into her head at the sudden sensation of even more of him in her bowels. She felt her limits being stretched and loved every minute of it. She reached up and grabbed her ass cheeks, spreading them further, allowing him to push even deeper into her.

"Oh fuck... How... Is... That... BIGGER... FUUUCCCCCKKK ME!!"

Her voice turned into a scream filled with passion, pleasure, and pain. Ragden could not help but drive into her harder, deeper, his cock seeming to swell and fill her bowels, growing larger, harder. His eyes went wide at the incredible sensation of her ass getting tighter around his swollen, throbbing cock. He felt her pulse under his hands, beating harder, faster. His pulse quickened to match. He drove into her harder, deeper.

Her voice became more desperate as he drove his cock deeper into her bowels, and she could feel her ass clamping down harder around his throbbing member. She could feel her insides stretching, her limits being pushed even further than she ever thought possible. She could feel his cock swelling even more, and she knew she was about to get fucked harder than she ever had before.

"Oh god. Oh fuck... Stretch me... Fill me up... Make me yours... FUUUCCCKKK!!"

She stretched her ass cheeks wider, his cock going deeper into her bowels, her ass feeling even tighter, making him feel like it was going to burst with each thrust. Her body rocking wildly, her breasts bouncing. He fucked her like a crazy man, his body pounding into her like a jackhammer. His balls bouncing off her perfect ass.

Feeling her spread her cheeks wider, he drove deeper and harder. Her ass felt even tighter, clenching harder on his cock. He could not tell if she was somehow squeezing her bowels on him, or if his throbbing cock was somehow swelling in her. He felt an electric charge on her skin, coursing through them. Sparks of energy started to ripple along their bodies. He had only a moment to marvel at them before he felt her climax start to roll over her. His own was suddenly there to match it.

Her ass stretched wide, she tried to buck her hips against his strokes, trying to get even more of him into her, her breathing ragged, her pulse racing beneath his grip on her calves. Her bowels clenched tighter, his cock feeling even tighter in her. Her climax crashed over her like a thunderclap, the ground around her vibrating with the force of it. The muscles of her legs convulsed,

her fingertips digging into her ass, drawing blood as her muscles convulsed.

"Fuck. Oh fuck. I'm cumming!"

Feeling the thunderclap of her climax, Ragden's climax crashed over him. His hips continued to drive against her as he could feel cum exploding from the tip of his cock into her bowels. He drove in again, and again, feeling her muscles convulsing on his, milking the cum out of him with each thrust. Her breasts were still rocking. Then he drove home one last time, as the muscles in his legs seized, pushing him deeper into her than he thought possible. His cock felt stretched, swollen, and pushed so deep into her bowels that he felt like her intestines were filled with his cock. His seed was still flooding into her. He slowly settled down and sat on his heels, lowering her ass to the sand. He lay her legs in the sand, as the muscles continued to spasm beneath his grasp. He leaned forward and gently kissed her breasts, savoring the taste of her sweat, the mix of salt and sand on them. Her heart beat frantically as her orgasm continued to roll over her. He kept his cock pressed into her, feeling her convulse on it, squeezing it, milking it. He looked down and saw her juices freely flowing from her pussy, leaking out and washing over his groin.

The waves of pleasure crashed over her, and she could feel her muscles spasming, her insides clenching and releasing, her mind lost in a haze of pleasure. She felt his cock stretching her bowels, and she could feel her intestines filled with his thick member. She could feel her pussy dripping and she could feel the sand and salt on her swollen labia. She knew that she was being filled with his hot, sticky seed.

Ragden leaned over her, his cock still throbbing in her ass and kissed her breasts, gently suckling on each. Then he kissed her softly on the lips. He felt her heartbeat still frantic but slowing. Her breath was no longer ragged but evening out. He could still feel the waves of her orgasm crashing over her. He could still feel her fluids flowing over him. He reached down and gently caressed her cheek. She turned her head against his hand, nuzzling it gently. Her eyes were still closed.

Selina's body still trembled from the aftermath of her orgasm, her insides still clenching and releasing as her bowels tried to absorb every drop of his seed. She could feel his cock still buried deep in her bowels. She could also feel his mouth on her breasts, and she knew he was waiting for her to open her eyes, but she did not know why. She trusted him, and opened her eyes, looking up at him with desire and vulnerability.

"Mm. Kiss me." She said, "I want you to fill me with your tongue."

He leaned into her, resting his body on top of hers. Feeling her large breasts pressed against his chest. He felt his cock throb inside her, pulsing with desire as she clenched on it, another load of cum bursting up into her. Then he kissed her passionately, his tongue exploring every inch of her mouth, savoring her salty sweetness

She felt his tongue exploring her mouth and his cock pulsing inside her bowels. She also felt her bowels filling with his cum and the feeling was so

amazing, that she shivered at the ecstasy of it. She let out a low moan, at the pulsing in her bowels. She looked up at him and saw the hunger in his eyes.

"Yes. Kiss me more. Fill me with your tongue. I want to taste your seed. I want to taste you. I need you."

Just then Ragden heard a voice from behind him, "Hey! You! What are you doing!?"

He turned and looked over his shoulder to see his dad standing at the top of the dune above them, smiling. Standing next to him was an overweight older man, in a t-shirt and shorts. Ragden recognized him. George, Selina's father. He was red in the face, shaking his fist. He came running, and stumbled down the dune towards them, shaking his fist in the air.

"Get off her! Get off her right this minute, damn you!"

Michael lazily walked beside him, matching his pace easily, almost seeming to glide over the dunes. Shocked, Ragden drew back from Selina, his cock sliding out of her ass. He gasped slightly as his swollen, massive cock flopped into the sand. It did indeed somehow look larger, but it quickly wilted, returning to its normal size. He grabbed his shorts, pulling them up over his legs as he stood.

Selina sat up, her face flushed with pleasure, her body still trembling from the aftermath of her orgasm, and she saw both Michael and George coming down the dune. She saw Michael, the serene smile on his face, and George, running and stumbling next to him, red in the face. She could see that he was furious.

"Dad. George. I, umm, I think I just needed some space and some fresh air," she lied. "It's really hot today and I just needed to cool off. Can we please go back now? I promise everything is okay. Please."

George spluttered, almost yelling. Ragden took a step back from them. "You lying BITCH, you are FUCKING NAKED with his CUM dripping out of your goddamn ASS!"

Selina curled into a ball, her fluids still leaking out of her pussy, Ragden's cum leaking out of her ass. She started crying, her voice hitching.

"I'm sorry! I needed his cum. I needed it in my ass. I needed all of it. I'm sorry. I had to have it. Please. I need more. Let him fuck me in the ass, Daddy... Please."

She started crying, clutching at his feet. He rounded on Ragden and started to shake his fist when Michael put his hand on George's arm. George rounded on Michael; his fists raised. When he looked him in the face, his anger wilted. Michael smiled at him and gently squeezed his arm.

"George, surely this is a misunderstanding. The poor girl needed some comfort and my son provided it. No harm in that."

Amazingly, George's anger drifted away, like it had never been. A strange look passed over his face. Then he looked down at his crying, naked daughter.

Michael spoke softly, his voice full of calm reason. "As you can see, she needs your help now. Take her back to the house, get her some rest. I am sure

she will be fine after a little nap."

George nodded, pulling his daughter to her feet. An arm around her waist to support her as her legs trembled. He grabbed her discarded bathing suit and shoved it into his pocket. He whispered kindly to her, "Come on, let's get you home."

Selina's eyes welled up with tears of relief as her father helped her to her feet. She felt her legs tremble beneath her, but with his support, she did not fall. She saw, absentmindedly, her father slipping her bathing suit into his pocket, and knew she was stuck naked, but she did not care. She wanted Ragden to see his cum dripping from her ass because she wanted more. As another spasm of muscles clenching shot through her, she stumbled in the sand, but George caught her and supported her. She looked over her shoulder at Ragden, her gaze hungry as they stepped over the dune and out of sight.

Michael slipped his arm around Ragden's shoulders, hugging him softly.

"It certainly looked like you were enjoying yourself there. Be careful, I suspect she will come looking for more."

He laughed softly to himself, then ruffled his hair playfully. Jennifer came jogging up the beach, grabbed her towel and wrapped it around herself. She walked over, saw them, spotted the mess in the sand, and giggled.

"Ready to head back?" she asked softly. Michael winked at her and nodded. Michael grabbed the two chairs and umbrella and the three of them walked back to the house together.

CHAPTER 26

The walk back to the beach house was a quiet one. Jennifer could sense something had taken place but did not pry. Michael smiled, his presence comforting and benign. As they got back into the house, they stowed the beach stuff and dropped off their sandals.

Michael turned to Ragden, "Hey bud, get yourself a shower, and some rest. I suspect tonight will be a long night. We do not head out to meet with Mother Ocean until midnight."

Ragden nodded and headed off to his room. He heard Michael and Jennifer heading upstairs, their voices fading as they went. He went into his room and stripped, then he went into the bathroom and started the shower. He got the water as hot as he could stand it and stepped under it.

Ragden stood under the water, feeling the heat pounding against his face. He closed his eyes and turned to let it drum heavily against his neck and shoulders. He longed for Emily and Sarah, even Aria, who still vexed him. He hoped she could get past her jealousy and her demands. She wanted to own everyone and that was not healthy. Though he was not sure how to reach her and hoped that she would learn.

He built up a lather in his hands with the soap and wrinkled his nose at the smell. Not his usual brand. It would do, but he wanted his soap at home. Ragden sighed heavily, finishing his shower, and toweling himself off. He paused in front of the mirror and looked at himself again. He grabbed a comb and ran it through his hair, then looked at himself again. The stranger in the mirror smiled back at him. The face was his, but the physique was not what he was used to seeing.

He gently lifted his flaccid penis. When it had been inside Selina, it had grown or felt like it had grown. He had stopped wondering what was possible. The gifts from his father had been more than he was prepared for. What else could he do? What else did he want to do? His memory of his experience with Selina left him a little frightened of his potential. He never wanted to hurt

anyone, and that... could have done real damage to her body. He hoped she was all right.

Part of him longed to check on her and make sure she was okay, but the look on George's face, red and filled with rage, charging down the dune towards him, haunted him. Perhaps it was best not to try.

Ragden went back to his bedroom and crawled onto the bed. He collapsed, his head on the pillow. He spread his arms and legs, stretching to the edges of the bed on all sides. This bed was large enough for him, but not really for company. Oh, how he wanted to curl up around Emily, feel her skin against his. The smell of her hair, the feel of her skin against his. He did not want sex, just the comfort of her presence. However, sex with her was always amazing. Even though he had just had some pretty wild sex, the thought of Emily in his arms caused his cock to throb and grow, until it was standing fully erect off his groin.

He casually placed his right hand between his legs, feeling his cock. He ran his fingers down its length, feeling it throb at his touch. He closed his eyes and gently stroked himself. Not the same. He sighed and placed his hand back at his side.

There was a soft knock at the door, and before he could say anything, Jennifer came walking in and closed the door behind her. Ragden's eyes went wide; he looked at her in shock. She stood, her back against the door, looking at him. Her gaze caught his whole body and lingered on his throbbing cock. She smiled softly and licked her lips, but remained at the door. Her eyes raised to his face, and her gaze was soft, comforting.

"Michael told me about what happened on the beach." She spoke softly, her voice soothing, motherly, exactly what he needed to hear. His erection wilted, his cock shrinking back to its more normal size. She smiled, "Are you okay?"

For a moment, Ragden considered trying to cover himself, embarrassed at his nakedness. Then he pushed the thought away; she had seen everything already. It did not matter. He sighed heavily and spoke softly, "I guess so. I... Don't really know how things got so crazy so quickly."

Jennifer giggled softly, her voice musical, comforting, "Darling. It happens. You gave her something she needed. Something you needed. Do not be ashamed. Search your feelings. What does your heart tell you?"

Ragden smiled, closed his eyes, let his thoughts roam, and searched his feelings. He was sad Emily, Sarah and Aria were not there. But how did he feel about Selina? He pondered the encounter. Looked inwardly to see how he felt about it. He sighed softly. The only emotion he could feel for her was love. Though, not the same kind of love he felt for Emily, Sarah, or even Aria, but it was love, nonetheless. He opened his eyes and smiled at his mother.

"I... I feel love for her. But... I don't know her. I haven't seen her in years."

Jennifer shook her head, her voice soft and soothing. "That doesn't matter, dear. You are the son of the embodiment of Love. As such, you are

going to love almost everyone you meet, and sex is a part of that. Never shy from it. Your love is a gift you give freely to anyone who welcomes it. It is a gift; never forget that."

Jennifer walked slowly forward, her hips swaying from side to side as she did. Ragden realized suddenly that his father was not there. His mother was so incredibly gorgeous. Her white t-shirt stuck to her chest, still damp from the ocean. Her bathing suit top was clearly visible through it. Her breasts were large, firm pressed against it. Her hips swayed seductively. Ragden swallowed hard. He felt his cock starting to harden as she sat down on the bed next to him.

She rested a hand on his and looked at him, love in her eyes. Ragden felt a spark of energy jump from her hand to his. The hairs on his arms stood as he felt that spark pass up his arm into his body. A shiver ran down his back.

"Mom? Where is Dad?"

Jennifer smiled. Her smile was full of beauty, love, and a hint of sex. "He went to get some food for dinner. He will not be back for a little bit."

She closed her eyes and hummed softly to herself, then she opened them again. She had a far-off look in her eyes, like she was seeing something that he could not. "He is at the butcher's shop. The butcher and his wife have been having some problems. They wish to have a child but have been having issues. Michael is... helping."

She smiled again, her eyes returning to focus on Ragden's. He gulped. She placed a hand on his chest and caressed the muscles softly. His skin tingled at her touch. He felt something inside him stirring—something he did not understand. It did not feel like love; it felt... earthy. He looked at her with a curious expression on his face.

"Mom, what are you doing to me?"

She smiled sweetly, innocently. Then she giggled shyly. "As my son, you are Earth-Touched. None of the gifts you have described have been earth-related. I wanted to see if I could ... waken them."

"How would you do that?" Ragden asked with a gulp, suddenly nervous about her intentions.

Jennifer giggled again, a tinkling sound that sent a shiver down Ragden's back. "Well, dear, as with most things for you, sex holds the key." She winked and licked her lips. Then, seeing his expression, she smiled softly. "I can see you are still not sure you want to have sex with me. I understand. American taboos are hard to break sometimes. Just know that I will be ready whenever you are."

She stood, her movements feline and graceful. He watched her ass shake as she walked to the door. His erection throbbed. She looked over her shoulder and spoke softly, "Your father knows this, and welcomes it. He does not get jealous. It is not in his nature. You do not need to worry about offending him. The only thing in the way of this is you. I will not pressure you into this. It is your choice to explore, or not to."

She opened the door, silkily moved through the opening, and pulled the door mostly shut behind her. Her eyes glowed through the doorway at him. Her voice cooed, softly, full of love, sex, and things he could not describe, "I'll be ready when you are."

Then she shut the door. Ragden lay on the bed, his cock fully erect and throbbing between his legs as he stared at the door. Part of him longed to see what she could offer, what she could show him. Another part of him rebelled against these thoughts, screaming it was not right. This was his mother. You do not have sex with your relatives.

He turned the idea over in his head. Where did that come from? He wondered. Society. Taboos were a societal norm. An unspoken rule. That was how societies worked. Why was that a rule? To prevent inbreeding. The danger of inbred children was something taught at an early age. Tales in the bible of such things happening and causing the downfall of entire kingdoms. The ensuing chaos. Why would they teach that lesson? Who did that serve? Logically, he could find the argument and understood the purpose. He could rationalize it. He could not make her pregnant, so where was the harm? Who did it hurt? Nobody.

Still, the thought of having sexual intercourse with his mother made his skin crawl. He could rationalize the arguments and understand where the ideas came from, but he could not quite get past them. He knew his body would respond to the stimulus. She was incredibly attractive; she had the body of a supermodel, a porn star, the ideal woman of every man's dreams. His body would respond and do what bodies do, but his head got in the way.

Ragden slumped back against the bed, his head pressed into the pillow. A problem for another day, perhaps. He tried to clear his mind, tried to rest. His thoughts kept coming back to Emily. His dear, precious Emily, the keeper of some part of his soul. He sighed; his heart heavy with the need to touch her. His eyes drifted closed, and sleep claimed him.

Ragden was aware of Michael's presence before he heard or saw him. He opened his eyes, and Michael was standing in the room. The door was closed behind him. Ragden blinked, glanced at the clock, and saw it was after 5 pm. He had been asleep for a few more hours than he had anticipated.

Michael smiled at him, "Slept well, I hope?"

Ragden nodded.

"I heard Jennifer tried to seduce you."

Ragden blushed and nodded slowly. Michael laughed softly.

"I thought she might. You cannot fault her. We are both curious if you will manifest any kind of Earth-related powers. Do not think too harshly of her for it."

Ragden's blush darkened. "I understand. I... Want to... But..."

Michael smiled softly, "Oh, I understand. Those Puritanistic views are hard to shake. I get it. You cannot fault her for trying."

He chuckled again, then said, "George, Stacy, and Selina will be joining us for dinner."

Ragden glanced up quickly, his eyes wide. Michael spoke soothingly, "Do not worry about George. His daughter is a grown woman. He may not accept her choices, but they are hers to make. Besides, I do not think he will try anything foolish tonight. Fret not. Come, dinner will be ready soon. Oh... and... before you head upstairs, you might want to put some clothes on."

Michael chuckled to himself as he walked out of the room. Ragden glanced down at his body. He had fallen asleep with no clothes on, on top of the covers. Yet, his nudity before his father had seemed like the most natural thing in the world. Probably because his dad did not look at his dick like he wanted to eat it. He shrugged, went to the dresser, and pulled out a pair of boxers, shorts, and a T-shirt. Everything fit fine, except for the T-shirt, which was stretched tight over his chest and shoulders. He looked in the mirror and sighed. He looked like a model, with massive shoulders and the chest of a bodybuilder.

As Ragden made his way up the stairs, he heard voices. The tinkling of glasses and laughter. As he got to the top floor, he heard his mother's voice, "And there he is! Good evening, sleepy head!"

He waved to Jennifer, who winked at him as he came up the stairs. She was behind the island, cutting something up on the cutting board. Michael stood behind her at the stove, in his usual sweats and no shirt. His broad back flexed periodically, the muscles rippling. Ragden shook his head then he saw George and Stacy. George, he recognized immediately. The older man glared at him. Ragden waved and George continued to glower in his general direction. Stacy elbowed George hard in the gut. He winced and rubbed the spot.

Stacy was a middle-aged woman, her hair sandy, with a sprinkling of grey. She was around five foot five, maybe five foot six. She was an attractive older woman, but the crinkles in her eyes were sad and showed that her life had not been easy. She smiled and walked over and hugged him. She was wearing a knee-length skirt and had a soft blouse on. Ragden could see that once, many years ago, she had been an incredibly attractive woman.

"Thanks for looking after Selina on the beach today," she said softly, "I know George is not happy, but I'm glad you were there when she needed you."

"Uh... Of course." Ragden wondered what she believed had happened, but decided it was best not to pry. Then he heard movement on one of the couches.

"Ragsy!" Selina spoke as she jumped to her feet. She started to run towards him, saw her dad, stopped short, walked over calmly, and gave him a chaste hug. "Hi," she said softly as she pulled back from him. He could see the hunger in her eyes, the need, the fast breathing. Her pupils were slightly dilated, her nostrils flaring. He could sense her rapid pulse, the dampness

between her legs.

Ragden blushed, looked at his feet, and tried to calm himself. He felt his loins stir and tried to think of something else. He spoke softly, "Hi back."

Michael laughed from the kitchen. All eyes turned toward him. His voice boomed across the room, commanding their attention, "Now that we are all here, dinner can be served. Please take your seats..."

Ragden walked to the dining room table and found himself a seat. Selina followed close behind and sank into the chair next to him. George started to take the seat across from him, but Stacy elbowed him again and slid into the chair as he pulled it out. He glared at her and took the seat next to her, frowning at Ragden.

Jennifer walked out to the table carrying dishes and utensils. She hummed a soft song to herself while walking seductively around the table and placing items in each place. George could not keep his eyes off her. Stacy watched him watching her and shook her head. Selina watched her just as closely. Ragden found himself watching her move around as well, unable to take his eyes off her swaying hips. As she finished, he blinked hard and shook his head to clear the image.

Selina noticed Ragden's movement and giggled to herself. Then she whispered to Ragden, "Does she always do that?"

Ragden looked at Selina and saw her big brown eyes boring into his. Selina looked at Jennifer sashaying back into the kitchen and then at Ragden. Ragden glanced at Jennifer, watched her hips sway, and then back at Selina, "What? Oh... No. Only for company. Apparently."

Selina's eyes sparkled with amusement, "Oh." Then she giggled again and spoke even quieter, just barely loud enough to be heard, "She is so beautiful, I could watch her do that for hours." Then she giggled again, looked down at her lap where she clasped her hands and fidgeted.

Then Jennifer and Michael came back to the table carrying large plates with food on them. There was a plate of mashed potatoes, asparagus, green bean casserole, and a plate of shredded chicken and sausages. It was a small feast. Ragden's eyes got big as Jennifer and Michael took their seats.

George looked at all the food on the table, then looked at Jennifer, and Michael, "Uh... That is a lot of food."

Michael laughed, "Yes, well, we do have a growing boy at the table." He looked at Ragden fondly. George glared again. Stacy chuckled softly, then elbowed George again. He rubbed his side, looked at her, and apologized.

Michael looked at them all, cocked an eyebrow, "Well, dig in."

They all reached for different platters and put servings onto their plates. Each time Ragden picked up a plate, he gave Selina a small serving as well. She blushed and thanked him. He piled food on his plate until it was nearly falling off.

Selina giggled, watching him push things around to make room for other things, "Are you really going to eat all that?"

Ragden shrugged, "Probably."

Jennifer spoke from her end of the table as she served herself some chicken, "Selina, you are in college, no? What are you studying?"

Selina looked at Jennifer surprised, then spoke softly, "Yeah... Second year. I had wanted to study psychology, but I'm thinking of changing my major to Engineering."

"Fascinating," Jennifer answered, smiling, "Why the change?"

Selina smiled, her face lit up, "Well... I decided I did not want to sit around talking to people all day. I want to get out and do things."

"Lots of Engineering fields," George grumbled, "Which one interests you?"

Selina smiled sweetly at her dad, "So many interesting choices. I am thinking about Mechanical Engineering. Or maybe Nuclear Engineering? Electrical Engineering is so cool too."

George sighed. This had the sound of an argument that had been going on for some time. George took a deep breath, appearing to try to calm himself. He smiled at his daughter and stuffed a bite of sausage in his mouth, rather than comment. Stacy smiled at George, then smiled happily at her daughter.

Ragden watched the whole scene unfold, devouring his meal. He glanced at his plate, saw it almost empty, and took the last few bites. Then, as he was refilling his plate, he said, "I always thought college was a fantastic opportunity to learn what things interested you. A place to figure out what you want to learn."

George glared at Ragden and mumbled something about money but kept eating. Michael chuckled to himself, then his deep voice filled the room, "Quite right." He looked at Selina and smiled, "I would recommend taking as many different courses as that interest you. You never know what you are going to genuinely enjoy until you have tried it and figured it out."

George choked on his food. Stacy thumped his back roughly. George swallowed whatever he was having an issue with, then took a deep drink of water. He scowled but did not have anything to add to the conversation.

Once Michael and Jennifer had finished their plates, they started collecting the empty dishes. Ragden was still finishing off the last of the things left on the table. Selina sat next to him, awestruck by the amount of food he was putting away. Stacy raised an eyebrow, watching. George excused himself and went to sit in front of the television. Stacy joined him shortly after.

Selina whispered, "How can you eat that much food?"

Ragden shrugged, "I just do. Hungry, I guess."

Selina chuckled, "I guess..." She picked up her empty plate and took it into the kitchen, where Michael and Jennifer cleaned it. Once Ragden was done, he followed her into the kitchen and handed his dishes over as well.

While Ragden stood at the island, offering to help, Selina wrapped her arms around his waist, and leaned against his back, resting her head against the back of his shoulder. Ragden patted her hands absently as he asked if he

could help. Michael handed him a dishrag, and he stepped away from Selina, who groaned, following him like a sad puppy while he dried dishes. He would dry one, hand it to her, and she would then put it away.

"Selina!" George barked from the couch, "Can I talk to you?"

Selina sighed, put away the plate in her hand, and walked into the living room.

"When do you head back to campus?" George asked kindly.

"Tuesday."

"We only have the house through tomorrow afternoon; what are you planning to do? Are you coming back with us?"

"Oh... I thought you were here for the week. Short trip?"

"No, work stuff. Sorry."

"Oh darn. Can I think about it? Need to make some calls."

"Sure."

They all heard Selina pull out her phone and start calling people as she stepped out onto the deck. Ragden, Jennifer, and Michael finished cleaning up the dishes and cleaning up the kitchen. Michael leaned over and spoke softly to Ragden, his voice low, and quiet, "Why don't you go downstairs and watch a movie? We have a few hours before we must head out. It'll probably be easier if we don't antagonize George further."

"Sure. Thanks."

Michael winked and squeezed Ragden's shoulder. Michael and Jennifer headed into the living room while Ragden headed down the stairs.

"So, George, how is work going these days?" Michael asked.

"About the same as usual. Lots of meetings, man... so many meetings."

"That is what happens when they put you in charge. You did realize that before you agreed, right?"

"Yeah..."

Their voices trailed off as Ragden headed down to the theatre. The theatre was not very large. It could comfortably seat 10 people. The screen took up the whole wall, with speakers lining the room. Ragden found the remotes and flipped them on, turning the volume down. He surfed through numerous different streaming service options. Eventually settled on HBO and started going through numerous different movies and television shows. There were so many things he had not had a chance to watch. He chuckled to himself, hard to keep up with things when you have school and three girlfriends. He made his way into the middle seat of the middle row and got comfortable. With the lights off, he settled in and started watching something quietly.

CHAPTER 27

Ragden sat quietly in the theatre, mostly zoned out, when he heard the door open behind him. He heard soft footsteps coming into the room but did not bother to look up as someone dropped down onto the seat next to him. He looked over and sat up a little straighter. His loins stirred as he saw Selina sitting next to him. Her shirt was tight across her top, shorts hanging loosely around her waist.

"Is this seat taken?" She whispered, her voice like silk. Her lips were plump and ready to be kissed. Ragden felt his cock hardening as he looked at her and shook his head.

"Nope. All yours..."

Selina could feel his eyes on her and felt her pulse beating harder. She looked over at him in the dark and could barely see the bulge of his growing erection and smiled. A warm sensation filled her body at the thought of the activities from the afternoon, and the possibility of what might come next.

"Thank you," she whispered, "for helping me earlier. I needed that. I needed all your cum in my ass."

Ragden gulped hard, his eyes on her incredible bosom. He sat up a little straighter, not bothering to hide his erection as his cock strained against his pants.

"What about your dad? Isn't he going to come looking for you?"

Selina noticed the bulge in his pants and smiled hungrily. Fear and excitement coursing through her veins. She wanted to have more fun with him, knew she wanted to feel his cock filling her ass again. She needed to be filled with his hot, sticky seed.

"My dad will be checking on me soon, but he thinks that I am just taking a nap. He is really worried about me, so he is being extra nice. He wants me to get better, but I think I'm feeling better now."

Ragden leaned over and kissed her softly on the lips, enjoying how soft and pliable her lips were against his. He smiled softly at her, slipping his hand

around her shoulder and leaning into her.

"I am glad you enjoyed that. It did feel amazing. Have you ever done anything like that before? I mean... You are in college, right? You do all kinds of crazy things in college, right?"

She smiled at the soft kiss, and shook her head, "No, I have not done anything like that before. I have never felt so... so... needy or dirty... or so... turned on in my life."

She nestled against him, snuggling against his chest, and looked up into his eyes, "But I liked it. I like feeling like this. I like feeling dirty and I like feeling needy. I also like feeling turned on by you, Ragden."

Ragden blushed as his cock throbbed in his pants. He looked back into her eyes, wondering, "Do you have a boyfriend back in college? A woman as incredibly beautiful as you, surely no man can resist you."

Selina saw the flush in his eyes, and her heart beat a little stronger. She felt nervous and excited to be so close to him. "No, I do not have a boyfriend. I have never had a boyfriend. Guys always seemed so boring, but I always wanted a bad boyfriend—someone who would take me to the edge of danger and push me over. I always wanted a guy who would make me feel like I was living on the edge."

Ragden blinked hard, trying to figure out how something like this had happened. "Wait, are you trying to tell me that you... were a virgin before today?"

Selina looked at him, her green eyes wide and innocent, and she could not help but feel a mix of fear and excitement coursing through her as she answered him.

"Yes. Yes, I was a virgin before today. I know it is weird, but ever since I saw your cock and ever since I've felt your hot, sticky seed fill me up, I have been so...so thirsty for more. I've been so thirsty for more of you, Ragden."

At her words, his cock throbbed painfully. His shorts suddenly felt too tight. He had the almost uncontrollable urge to adjust them, to shift them, and let his cock free. Still, she was a virgin? Impossible.

"How. I am sorry... but HOW were you a virgin? Surely you had guys throwing themselves at you? I just... This is hard to swallow."

Selina saw his cock throbbing in his shorts, and she felt a mix of fear and excitement coursing through her as she answered, "I know, it's hard to believe, isn't it? But it is true. Guys never really interested me. They always wanted to take me out on dates or buy me flowers, and they always wanted to have sex with me, but they never really turned me on. They never made me feel like I wanted to be filled, like you did, and I know that is hard to swallow."

Ragden laughed at the double meaning of her words. No wonder her dad had been so upset. That made sense now. He looked at her and smiled softly. "I'm sorry I was rough with you. I just... assumed you knew what you were getting yourself into. Knew what you wanted. Knew what it would be like."

Selina saw the warmth in his eyes and felt it spreading inside her. Filling her with affection and care.

"Please don't be sorry, Ragden. I wanted it. I asked for it. I wanted all your roughness. I wanted it all."

"Well, you got it."

He laughed again, a deeper, sensual sound. Ragden leaned over and kissed her softly on the lips, pulling her body against him in the chair. He looked down, saw the armrest between them, reached down, and pulled it up out of the way.

"Do you realize you are about 2 years older than me? Do you have a problem being with a... younger man?" He chuckled as the words left his mouth.

Selina felt his warm breath on her lips, and her pulse quickened, her face flushed with excitement.

"Two years? Really? You are only two years younger than me, Ragden? You feel so much older than that. You feel like the perfect age for me. Mature, experienced, and rough."

She felt his arms wrap around her, pulling her body against his in the chair, "And no, I don't have a problem being with a younger man. I find it exciting."

"Mature?" He laughed at the idea. "I haven't even graduated from high school yet."

Selina felt his laughter against her lips and she felt fear and excitement coursing through her as she added, "Yeah, but you feel so mature, Ragden. So much more mature than any of the boys at my school. So much more mature than any of the guys who have tried to take me out on dates. So much more mature than any of the guys that have tried to get in my pants, and I love that you're so rough with me, Ragden."

"Just to be perfectly transparent. I want you to know I have a girlfriend... three, actually.

He hefted her up and dropped her into his lap, his cock pressing against her ass through his pants. Ragden reached around her and slid his arms up under her shirt, gently cupping her breasts. He kissed the back of her neck softly.

"Is that going to be a problem?"

Selina felt his strength as he lifted her, her heart fluttered in her chest, and the press of his cock against her ass sent shivers down her back. She felt turned on by him, and she also knew that she wanted more of his roughness and more of his cock filling her.

"No, that's not a problem. I'm simply happy for you, Ragden. I'm happy that you have three girls that love you. I'm just... happy to be here with you."

"I don't think you understand." He said as he slipped his hands up her shirt and unclasped her bra. Then reached around her again and pulled her bra forward off her.

"We have an... open agreement. I do not restrict who they engage with and

they simply enjoy the time we get to spend together."

Selina gasped in surprise as his hands pulled her bra off, revealing her perky, pink nipples to the cool night air. She felt his fingers graze against them, sending shivers down her spine.

"I see. Well, that sounds nice. I'm happy that you have such an arrangement with them."

She felt his arms wrapping around her, pulling her close. Her heart beat harder, feeling his skin against hers. A shiver ran down her spine as she added, "And I'm happy to be part of that arrangement, Ragden."

"Happy to include you." He whispered into her ear as he kissed her neck. He slipped one hand down the front of her shorts, gently cupping her soft mound, feeling her dampness. He gently pressed a finger against her clitoris as he kissed her ear.

Selina felt his breath against her ear, and she gasped in surprise and pleasure, arching her back, pressing her groin against his cock, as she added, "Oh. Oh, Ragden, that feels so good."

She could feel his wet finger gently probing her entrance, and she felt her pulse race with excitement at the prospect it what might come next.

Ragden gently slid his hands under her shorts and panties, slipping them down her thighs as he continued to kiss her neck, nipping softly at the tender skin in front of him. He leaned against her, sliding her garments down over her knees and down to her ankles. He slid his hands up her legs, gently spreading them so he could slip his fingers through her damp folds. His cock throbbed against her ass through his shorts.

Selina felt her shorts and panties slide down her legs, leaving her completely bare before him. She felt his hands gently spreading her legs apart, and she could not help but feel a mix of fear and excitement coursing through her. She felt his large, heavy cock pressing against the cheeks of her bottom, her heart beating frantically, her cheeks flushed as she moaned, "I want this. I want all of this. Please."

She felt his thumb gently parting her folds. He could feel the beat of fear in her pulse, the frantic beating like a wild rabbit chased by wolves. He kissed her softly on the back of her neck. He slid his hands up her body, lifting her shirt over her head. Then he gently cupped her breasts, his fingers gently caressing her nipples as he kissed the back of her neck, then her spine, working his way down her back. "You have nothing to fear from me, love. Tonight, I'll show you tender love and care."

Selina felt his lips kissing her neck, and she felt his hands gently cupping her breasts. She heard his tender words and tried to slow her breath, to calm herself, but failing, she whispered, "Thank you, Ragden. I've always been afraid of... of being touched."

She shivered at the tender touch of his lips on her back; every nerve felt alive under his touch; she moaned softly as she added, "I trust you, Ragden. I know that you will not hurt me. I know that you'll take care of me."

Ragden slowly slipped his shorts and boxers off, sliding them down his legs. His cock throbbed and slipped between her legs. The length of it pressed against her mound, the head standing up between her spread legs. He cupped her breasts again, gently feeling the weight of them as he kissed her neck softly.

Selina looked down at the massive piece of meat between her legs. Her breath caught in her throat. Her mind reeled, 'that had been inside me?' She reached out and tentatively put a hand on it, feeling it throb at her touch. Her heart thundered in her chest; a sweat broke out on her brow.

"Oh. Oh, Ragden. You are so big and so heavy. So thick. I hope that I am not too small or too tight. I want this, Ragden. I want all of you."

"Too small?" He laughed softly, his voice sensual, sending a shiver down her back. "But you've already had this inside you, on the beach. Or have you forgotten already?"

Selina felt his sensual laughter against her back, felt the shiver of excitement that ran through her. She felt his large, heavy head press against her mound, her clitoris, and she let out a small gasp of fear and excitement, "I want... I want you, Ragden. I want to be filled by you."

Ragden gently lifted her, his fingers spreading her lips as he set her on his cock. He lowered her inch by inch, his cock sliding up into her lips, parting them and sliding deeper and deeper into her slick pussy. He kept lowering her until his cock was fully seated inside her. Pressing softly against her cervix. Then he slid his hands up her flat stomach to cup her breasts again as he kissed her neck, her ear, and the side of her jaw.

Selina let out a long, low moan of fear and pleasure as he pushed her walls apart. She could feel the heavy weight of it as it pressed against her cervix. She moaned, "Fuck... it hurts so good."

He gently cupped her breasts, squeezing softly, as his fingers brushed across her nipples. He kissed the back of her neck, a soft brushing of his lips across her tender skin.

"We do not have to do anything you are not comfortable with. If it hurts, then we can stay like this until you are comfortable with doing more."

Selina moaned softly, the pleasure and pain coursing through her. She felt the aches inside her from the activities earlier in the day. She wanted more but had not thought the pain would be so intense.

She whispered, pleading with Ragden, "Doing more feels good... and hurts, but it feels so fucking good."

Ragden gently slid his hands around the underside of her thighs, lifting her above his groin. Then he gently slid his groin up into hers, sliding his cock up against her cervix. Then he gently lowered his hips into the seat and then raised into her again. Slowly, purposefully, gently pressing his cock against her cervix. Selina let out a long, low gasp of pleasure.

"Fuck. Shit. That hurts... so good."

He gently lowered himself back into the seat, lowering her down onto his

cock. Selina moaned in pleasure, her hand clutching her stomach. He leaned his chest against her back and turned her head to him so he could softly kiss her lips. "Where does it hurt?"

"It hurts in my stomach and deep down in my pussy, but it feels so good."

Selina moaned, long and low, feeling the throbbing of his cock inside her. She clutched at her chest, grasping her breasts fiercely, digging in her fingers. "Everything. Everything about this feels so good and so bad at the same time."

"I'm sorry it hurts. Do you want me to... see if I can do something about the pain?"

Selina looked into his eyes, and she could see the concern and the desire to please her in his gaze, "Yes, please. I want you to make it better."

She felt his cock moving within her, pressing against her sensitive areas, and she moaned again in pleasure. Ragden closed his eyes and slipped his hands over her hips, placing his fingertips along her soft folds. He reached out with his energy, feeling her body, feeling where the pain hit her. He reached out and caressed those parts of her, filling them with love, easing the sore muscles. He could feel her muscles, the soreness in them, the aches of her insides. He caressed those parts with love, encouraging the strained muscle fibers to heal back stronger. The bruised bones to heal.

Selina felt his hands on her hips, and she could feel the warmth and the energy flowing from them. She moaned in pleasure as she whispered, "Oh fuck. That feels good."

She felt his energy flowing into her, filling her with a sense of peace and well-being, and she felt a mix of fear and anticipation coursing through her.

Ragden smiled against her neck and kissed her softly. "Does that feel better?"

Selina felt his smile against her neck, and she felt herself smiling in return, her heart thumping heavily in her chest. She whispered, "Much, much better."

She felt his cock pressing against the deepest depths of her. She could feel it throbbing inside her. His pulse was so deep inside; she shivered at the sensation of so much of him so deep inside her. She moaned softly, "It feels full and good."

Once again, Ragden slid his hands under her thighs, lifting her partially out of his lap, his cock sliding halfway out of her tight wet pussy. Then he gently thrust up into her, his cock gently pressing against her cervix, then he slowly lowered his groin to the seat and pushed up into her again.

Selina gasped in pleasure as Ragden lifted her, and she could feel his thickness pressing against her sensitive areas. She let out a long, low gasp of pleasure as he thrust into her, feeling her insides stretch around his massive cock. She felt it press deep into her, and she shuddered at the feeling.

Selina moaned softly, "I feel so full."

Ragden slowly stood up, pushing his groin against her, putting her on her feet in front of him. He gently cupped her breasts as he slowly slid his cock

almost out, and gently slid it back in to touch her cervix. All the while he continued to cup her breasts, pulling her back against his chest, feeling her skin against his. He kissed the back of her neck as he slowly withdrew and slid into her again.

Selina stood in front of him, her pussy dripping with need, and she let out another long, low gasp of pleasure as he pulled his cock from her, only to slide it back against her cervix.

She moaned with need and pleasure, "Fuck. Please."

She moaned softly as she felt the heat and pressure of his palms against her sensitive flesh, her heart thundering in her chest, "I need... I need more."

"More?" He asked huskily against her skin, his teeth nipping at her earlobe as he drew back from her and slowly slid back in, the tip of his cock kissing her cervix before he drew back and slid in again. "I'm not sure I could fit more without hurting you."

Selina took a deep shuddering breath and let it out slowly, savoring the feeling of his monstrous cock sliding in and out of her. She could feel every inch of it passing through her, pressing gently against her innermost depths, then sliding out and in again. She moaned in pleasure, feeling the pressure building within her.

She moaned softly, "Yeah, I know, but I need more. I don't care if it hurts. I want everything."

Ragden softly kissed the back of her neck, as he slowly withdrew his throbbing cock from against her cervix, sliding back into her pussy and easing his cock from her wet folds. He stepped back from her and gently turned her to face him. Ragden leaned into her, pulling her body against his, one hand on her ass, pressing it against his groin, trapping his dick against her groin, the tip of it leaving a wet trail along her waistline. He kissed her passionately, slipping his tongue into her mouth and tasting her sweetness. He pulled back, pulling his lips from hers, feeling her breathless against him, her pulse racing. "Are you sure you want to do this?"

Selina looked down at his thick meat pressed against her body. She shivered at the feeling of it against her skin, the wet trail it left on her. Her skin tingled at its touch. She moaned softly, "I want everything. Every fucking thing."

She kissed him softly, moaning into his mouth, "Kiss me...kiss me like you mean it..."

Ragden wrapped his arms around her, pulling her body fiercely against him, kissing her passionately, slipping his tongue into her mouth, exploring her, as he pressed her groin against his, pulling her chest against his, pulling her body against his. He could feel her heart thundering in her chest against him. Ragden's pulse was slow, steady, and calming.

Selina felt his arms wrapping around her, pulling her fiercely against him, and she let out a long, low gasp of pleasure as she moaned softly, "Oh. Fuck. Yes."

Ragden slipped his hands around to cup her ass, lifting her against him. Her legs wrapped around his waist. He slipped his fingers into her folds, spreading her open as he lowered her onto his cock. It slipped through her folds, sliding up into her, as he kissed her deeply again.

Selina moaned in pleasure as she felt his cock sliding up into her, "Fuck."

She tightened her legs around his waist, holding onto him tightly as she felt his cock filling her. She moaned again, "Oh. Fuck."

Ragden slowly lowered her to the ground, laying her down on her back, his cock pressing against her cervix. He gently ground his hips against her, pressing his cock harder against her cervix.

He spoke softly, his voice sensual, "You wanted deeper?"

Selina moaned softly, "Yes."

"This afternoon, I pushed deeper into your bowels than with any other woman I've ever done that with. I don't know how it happened... It was insane."

Ragden slid his hips against hers, his cock pushing harder against her cervix. Then he gently pulled back and slowly slid back into her, pushing at the same angle, hitting the same spot on her cervix.

"Oh. Fuck," Selina moaned as his cock slid back into her again. She felt his cock pressing against her delicate inner walls. She felt the pressure building within her, waves of ecstasy surging through her body, "It feels so good. Can you keep doing that? Can you fill me with your cum until I can't take anymore?"

"If this is what you want, then yes."

Ragden smiled at her kindly, then leaned forward and pressed his chest against her, letting his weight rest against her chest. He kissed her lips softly as he ground his hips against her. Then he slowly slid out, and back in again. Ragden raised himself and sat on his heels. He softly placed his hand on her abdomen, feeling the bulge as his cock slid in and out of her. He lifted his hand, gently picked up one of hers, and placed it on the spot in her abdomen where the bulge of his cock could be felt. Then he gently slid out and stroked back into her again so she could feel it under her hand.

Selina pressed her hand against her abdomen, feeling the throbbing of his cock both inside her and under her palm. Her mind rolled at the sensation. She felt his hand on hers and smiled at the tender affection of it. She felt his cock sliding inside of her, and moaned in pleasure, the waves of it flooding through her.

She looked up at him, batted her eyelashes, moaned in pleasure, then whispered, "Can you fill me up with your cum? I want to feel your cum filling my insides until I cannot contain it."

Ragden kissed her softly as he continued to slowly slide his cock in and out of her.

"Yes. We can get there."

Then he sat back on his heels and started to build a slow rhythm of

pumping into her, then sliding out and sliding back in again. He could feel the pressure building within her, the waves of pleasure building in her core. His cock throbbed with each gentle thrust into her.

Selina felt the pressure building inside within her, the waves of pleasure growing stronger with each gentle thrust. She moaned softly.

He continued his slow rhythm, pumping the entire length of his cock into her, sliding it out, then back in again. Ragden reached down and gently grasped her breasts, running his thumbs over her nipples as he continued to slide in and out of her. He could feel the waves of pleasure building through both.

Selina moaned loudly, "Oh, fuck."

She felt his thumbs on her sensitive nipples, the intensity building from his movements, and urged him on, "Faster. Faster."

Ragden continued to slide in and out of her, building momentum, moving marginally faster. The entire length of his cock slid up into her. Long gentle strokes filled all of her. He placed his hands under her hips, gently raising her as he stroked into her, then lowering her as he slid back, moving her groin against his, adding to the pressure and pleasure of it. He started to move a little bit faster inside her.

She felt his heavy cock pressing against her sensitive walls, driving deeper into her, and she moaned in pleasure. She whispered insistently, "Faster... Faster..."

Ragden moved inside her a little bit faster, feeling her pulse against his skin, the waves of pleasure filling her body. He continued to slide in and out of her. As he continued to move inside of her, he reached around behind him and unlocked her ankles from behind his back. He put her feet on the floor and slid his hands up her legs to her thighs. He gently stroked the insides of her thighs, feeling the trembling of her muscles as he continued to slide his big dick in and out of her.

Selina felt his cock moving faster, as she felt the waves of pleasure flowing over her. She felt his powerful movements, her body rocking with them. She moaned softly, urging him on.

He gently pressed her thighs to the floor, pinning them in place as he changed his angle slightly, letting him drive down into her, feeling his cock slide along the back of her pussy, pushing up into her cervix. Then he slid back and slid up into her again, pushing hard against her cervix.

Selina moaned in pleasure, feeling pinned to the floor, unable to do anything but surrender to the sensations of his cock pushing into her, sliding into her cervix. She felt the pressure and pleasure building within her. She wanted more.

Ragden slid in and out of her faster, his cock thumping against her cervix, rocking her body with each gentle impact. Her breasts gently rocked with the vibration inside her. Each impact caused a surge of pleasure back through Ragden's body. He moaned softly in pleasure.

She felt the continued striking of his cock against her cervix, the pressure and pleasure building and building within her. She was unsure how much she could take, and the words slipped from her lips, "Oh, fuck."

Ragden drove into her faster, his cock thumping solidly against her cervix, her body vibrating with each impact, her breasts rocking harder. He felt her legs flexing with each impact, the strong muscles clenching beneath his grasp. He could feel her pulse against his skin, beating hard and fast. Her breath became ragged with the intensity.

Selina felt her body rocking with the massive thrusts against her. As they increased in speed, she felt her heart racing and her muscles trembling. She felt his dick pressing against her sensitive walls. The pleasure of it was almost overwhelming. She felt her legs pinned, the massive thrusts causing her legs to flex against his hands. She put her hands on his and looked up into his eyes, "My... my legs... please."

"What? Oh. Sorry." Ragden released her legs and sat back on his heels. He slid his cock up into her, pressing solidly against her cervix. He gently brought them up against his chest, squeezing them together as he slid his cock in and out of her, rocking his hips against hers as he nipped his teeth across her calf. With one hand, he held her legs against his chest; with the other, he reached down and gently squeezed one breast, then the other. Then he reached down and caressed her cheek as he kissed her ankles.

Selina felt his cock thrusting against her cervix, each impact rocking her body gently, sending waves of pleasure washing over her. She felt his teeth on her calves and moaned in pleasure, the combination of sensations threatening to overwhelm her.

He clasped her legs to his chest more firmly, gripping her calf with his teeth, gently grinding his teeth into her while he continued to thrust the length of his cock out and into her cervix, gently shaking her body with each thrust. He gently pressed down on her abdomen with his other hand, increasing the pressure of his cock pushing into her. Selina moaned in pleasure, feeling the pressure and pleasure building within her.

Ragden continued to slide in and out of her tight, wet pussy, building momentum, sliding slightly faster. His cock thumped against her cervix, sending waves of pleasure back up his cock and into him. He moaned softly at the sensation. He continued to clamp her legs against his chest, kissing her ankles softly, his teeth grazing across her soft skin.

He slid in and out of her slightly faster, his hips thumping against her thighs more solidly, her body vibrating with the impact. He kissed the bottoms of her feet, his teeth scraping across the balls of her feet.

Selina felt his cock pressing against her even more powerfully, and she let out a long, low gasp of pleasure. She felt his teeth scraping against the soles of her feet. The waves of pleasure surging through her grew increasingly powerful with each new sensation she felt. Her eyes rolled back into her head, as she clasped her breasts, feeling them rock with each impact against her

cervix. She closed her eyes, feeling her grip on sanity slipping.

Ragden continued to stroke into her faster, his cock thumping against her cervix, shaking her body with each impact. He felt her body clenching against him, pressing him tight inside her. He moaned at the pleasure of it. He kissed her ankles again, gently suckling them.

He stroked into her even faster, his cock bouncing off her cervix, her body shaking with each impact, her breasts rocking, her thighs vibrating. He clamped his teeth down on her calf, grinding into her soft muscles. He pulled her thighs hard against his abdomen, as he thrust into her harder.

Ragden slammed his cock into her pussy, his groin slamming into her ass, his cock smashing against her cervix hard. He gently spread her legs and leaned between them against her. His chest pressed against her supple breasts. He kissed her passionately, slipping his tongue into her mouth as he gently ground his hips against her, causing his cock to push into her cervix.

Selina whispered to him as his lips pressed against hers, "I want nothing else but you. I need only you."

Ragden kissed her softly, then sat back on his heels, pulling his chest up off hers. He placed a hand on his cock and slowly deliberately slid it out of her wet pussy. Selina groaned in disappointment, her eyes desperate, she glared at him. Damp with her juice, he ran the tip of it through her folds, pressing against her clitoris, then through her folds to tease the opening into her pussy. Then lower, he slid it in a tight circle around her asshole, gently teasing the opening. Selina moaned, feeling him pressing against her, but not inside her.

He gently pressed the head of his cock against her asshole, tracing tight circles around her opening, stretching it to fit the massive head of his cock. He continued to trace circles around it, easing it wider and wider, increasing the pressure, and pushing harder with each tight circle.

Selina moaned with need and desperation. She whispered, "I want your cock deep inside me... Please."

Ragden kept pushing the tip of his cock in tight circles against her asshole until the tip of it slid in. Then he increased the pressure, easing the head fully into her. Then he paused and took a deep breath. He leaned forward and kissed her passionately, slipping his tongue into her mouth as he eased his cock another inch into her.

Selina moaned in pleasure, feeling his cock sliding into her ass. She felt her muscles clenching around the thick meat squeezing into her tight asshole, and she moaned again. Feeling her ass stretching to accommodate his size. As her ass stretched wider and wider, her eyes got large; her breath came in desperate gasps. The pain and pleasure swelling in her bowels.

"Oh. Oh," she moaned, "Fuck. Fuck. Fuck me."

Ragden gently slid his cock in another inch, then slid it back to just the head, then in another inch, plus a little more. He kept gently sliding his cock back and forth, easing it into her. Deeper and deeper until his groin gently

Love & Nature

thumped against her perfect ass. Then, with his hips firmly against her groin, he leaned forward and kissed her again.

Selina felt his powerful presence filling her, and she moaned in pleasure. Feeling her stretched innards, the pain, the pleasure swelling within her. She remembered him entering her ass on the beach, but this felt even more intense. She gasped loudly as his groin pressed against her ass.

Ragden gently slid most of his cock out of her, then slid it back into her tight ass, feeling her bowels clench against him, savoring the tight pressure of her squeezing against him. He gently slid it in and out of her, building a slow rhythm as he ran his hands up the insides of her thighs, then slipped his fingers through her soft folds, caressing her clitoris.

Selina's eyes rolled into the back of her head again, as she felt his fingers on her sensitive folds with his cock gently sliding in and out of her ass. She felt him throbbing in her bowels. Each slow, steady beat of his heart caused hers to stampede in her chest. Each throb of his cock causing her muscles to squeeze and clench on him.

He slid his massive throbbing cock in and out of her ass, sliding almost out, then back in, feeling his cock going deep into her bowels. He slid in and out of her, savoring her tightness. All the while, he gently ran his fingers over her clitoris, slipping two fingers into her pussy, feeling the muscles clench on his fingers.

Selina felt his massive, powerful presence filling her, and she moaned even louder, her voice filled with need and desperation, "Only yours. All for you. Rule me. Fuck me."

He slid his cock fully into her bowels, his groin pushed against her ass. He leaned forward and kissed her on the lips passionately, his tongue slipping into her mouth. Ragden ran his hands down along her sides, feeling the swell of her breasts, the smoothness of her stomach, the swell of her hips.

Selina felt his cock filling her bowels, and she moaned against his mouth in pleasure. She felt his powerful presence and his passionate kiss; she moaned louder, "Fill me! Fuck me! Oh, God!"

Then Ragden sat back on his heels and slowly slid his cock back, inch after inch slipping out of her ass until finally it fully slipped free. Selina looked down between her legs, watching his cock slip from her ass, and she groaned in disappointment. She felt the hole he left in her closing, collapsing, and she felt empty and desperate for more.

Ragden placed a hand on his cock and guided it in slow circles around her puckered ass, watching as it squeezed tightly shut. Selina groaned loudly in disappointment. Then he slipped the head up through her lips, pushing it against her clitoris, sliding around her clit, then back through her folds, teasing the entrance to her pussy. "Tell me, his dear Selina," he whispered, "Which do you prefer?"

Selina groaned, waiting for him to fill her, begging for him to fill her. She heard the question, her mind reeling. She just wanted him inside her, but she

knew she had to pick something, anything. She moaned softly, "Pussy. Please... Please, cum in my pussy."

Ragden smiled down at her and gently slipped his cock into her pussy, sliding deeper and deeper into her. Feeling the walls of her vagina squeeze against his massive throbbing cock as it slid deeper into her, filling her, pushing her walls out, pressing firmly against her cervix.

Selina felt his massive cock filling her, and she smiled, feeling her body stretch to accommodate his size. She felt his powerful presence filling her, and she felt complete. She smiled up at him, and whispered, "Yes. Yes. Fill me."

He slowly slid out of her, then slid back in, filling her up. His cock throbbed deep inside her, sending waves of pleasure through her body. He could feel her clenching around him, squeezing his cock inside her. He slid back and into her again, pressing gently against her cervix.

Ragden placed his hands on the ground beneath her thighs, keeping her legs gently spread, bracing himself so he could gently thrust up into her. His throbbing member slid deep into her and thumped her cervix softly. He then withdrew almost completely out and slid back in more quickly, thumping into her with a little more force. Then again, watching as her breasts gently rolled, her thighs vibrating, her breath in short gasps accentuated with each bump into her deepest depths.

Selina felt his powerful thrusts as her body rocked with each impact. She moaned in pleasure, feeling the pressure building within her. She felt his repeated impacts inside her and felt the waves of pleasure filling her. She loved every moment of it.

He leaned into her and kissed her fiercely, slipping his tongue into her mouth as he gently stroked in and out of her. His tongue explored her mouth as his cock slid into her cervix, then drew out and slid in again, building a steady rhythm. Selina felt the waves of pressure and pleasure building within her.

Ragden slid in and out of her faster, his thrusts picking up momentum. He sat up and rocked his hips into hers, taking deep breaths to maintain his rhythm. He moved faster, maintaining long, hard strokes into her. His cock bouncing solidly off her cervix. Her body rocked with each impact, her legs shaking, her breasts rolling. He could feel her pulse quickening, her breath becoming ragged, her climax building.

Selina felt his powerful thrusts, the deep penetration, and the increasing rhythm and speed. Her heart raced, and she moaned in time to his thrusts. She felt the pressure inside her spreading, filling her. The pleasure flowing out of her vagina and filling her entire body.

He stroked into her harder, faster, his cock now solidly thumping against her cervix. The pleasure of that repeated impact spread through his body. He could see the pressure and pleasure building within her, the waves of pleasure rolling over her body. He felt his climax building within him, his balls starting to clench and tingle.

Love & Nature

Ragden placed his hands on her waist, pulling her against him as he thrust into her harder. His cock now bounced off her cervix with each thrust. He drew back, then thrust into her harder. Her breasts rocked, her thighs shook, and her breath was forced out of her with each impact. He felt her pussy clenching on his cock as he stroked into her, releasing as he slid out. Her breath came faster, her heart racing as her climax built and built within her. He felt his own climax building with speed to meet hers.

Selina moaned in pleasure, her breath now rushing out of her with each incredible impact. Her legs squeezed around him and spread to let him push into her. She felt the pressure and pleasure building within her. The waves of ecstasy washed over her. She knew she was nearing the edge of what she could handle, and she wanted more.

Ragden thrust into her faster, feeling his impending climax, feeling each impact of his cock against her cervix, pushing her closer and closer to release. His climax threatened to overwhelm him. He slammed his cock into her harder, his cock smashing into her cervix.

Selina felt that smashing impact, felt the waves of pleasure overwhelming her. Her climax surged and built. She felt his powerful thrusts, and she let out a long, low moan of pleasure. She felt his cock driving her towards her climax. She moaned loudly, "Cum... inside...me."

As Selina's sudden climax exploded over her, Ragden felt his balls clench and tingle as he stroked into her. Then he pulled back and slammed his cock into her cervix again. His body clenched, and his balls released. Cum exploded out of him and into her. He let out a loud gasp at the feeling, pulled back, and thrust into her one more time, more cum exploding out of him. His back arched, his legs seized, his arms vibrating with the force of it. As his muscles released their tension, cum flowed out of him; he lay himself down upon her, feeling her vibrating body against his.

Selina felt his powerful climax, and she let out a long, low gasp of pleasure. She felt his cock spurting his hot, thick cum into her. She moaned in response.

He kissed her softly on the lips, as he felt her body vibrating beneath him. Her climax caused her insides to clench and release as her body twitched and convulsed against him. He pulled her against him, feeling her magnificent breasts pressed against his chest. He gently lifted himself off her and kissed each of her breasts, gently suckling her nipples, savoring the flavor of her sweat and the feel of her heart beating against his mouth. Then he placed his chest against her again and kissed her softly on the mouth. He took a few deep, calming breaths, feeling his body starting to relax. His cock still throbbed within her, but with less urgency, still large and firm within her, but starting to soften. He smiled as he looked into her eyes. "Was that what you hoped it would be?"

She looked into his eyes and whispered, "Yes. Yes. Perfect."

Just then, the door to the theater opened, and they heard Michael's voice

call out, "Hey, Rag... It's getting late. We have things to do. Selina needs to head back to their house."

Ragden sat up and looked over at the seats. Michael stood in the doorway and smiled. He winked. "Get her dressed; her father is waiting on her."

Ragden nodded, then lowered himself to kiss her softly on the lips as he heard the door shut. Selina smiled into the kiss, enjoying the feeling of him inside her. Then, he slowly withdrew himself from her. Selina groaned in disappointment, her insides aching to be stretched by his size. He gathered up his clothes and started getting dressed, handing Selina her clothes.

Selina started getting herself organized, grabbing her clothing, and slipping into her clothes, dressing quickly. She whispered to Ragden, "Thanks for everything."

Ragden watched calmly as she put her clothes on. He watched her cover all her wonderful body. As she started to go, he grabbed her wrist and pulled her against him, kissing her softly on the lips. Then he whispered into her ear, "We might have to do this again sometime."

Selina felt his kiss and gasped in pleasure. She smiled back at him, "Mm. This was not enough. Maybe when I get a break between classes. Could we meet up sometime?"

"Sure, give me a call when you have some free time; we can figure something out."

As she turned to walk to the door, he softly slapped her ass, enjoying the firm feel of it in his hand. She gasped softly in surprise and pleasure. He waited a moment then followed her up the walk.

"Mm. Okay, I'll call you," She said, before turning around to look at him and sighed softly, "Thank you."

She turned, walked away from him, and headed towards the door, feeling his strong presence lingering behind her. She could still feel his hand on her ass, she whispered as she walked to the door, "It was amazing. Thank you. Goodbye."

She left, walking towards where her dad was waiting for her.

CHAPTER 28

Ragden waited in the theatre for a minute, then followed Selina out. He caught a glimpse of Selina and George stepping out the door. George glared at him balefully as the door closed. Ragden took a deep breath and then turned to Michael, who snickered.

"Well timed," Michael said as he turned and put an arm around Ragden's shoulders.

"Thanks."

"We will head down to the beach in about an hour or so. We need to be there at midnight. Come, I have something special for you to wear during this."

"Oh?"

Michael led Ragden up to the master bedroom. Jennifer had just stepped out of the room into the bathroom as they walked in. Ragden caught a glimpse of her slender leg going through the doorway. He blinked once, hard. He shook his head, trying to focus on what Michael had just said. Had Jennifer been naked?

"I'm sorry, Dad, what?"

Michael laughed softly, looked at the doorway, and then back at Ragden. He spoke softly, "Yes, she was naked. Have you reconsidered your earlier decision?"

"Huh? Yes. I mean," He looked at Michael, amusement in his eyes, a half-smile on his face, "No. Maybe another time."

Michael nodded. Walked him over to the walk-in closet. Hanging inside were three large white bathrobes. He pulled one out and handed it to Ragden. Ragden looked at him quizzically.

"A bathrobe?"

"Yup, and nothing underneath."

"Oh." He said sarcastically, "That makes more sense."

Michael laughed. Then nodded.

"Go downstairs, take a shower. No soap. No shampoo. Just water. Then dress in the robe, and we will meet at the front door at fifteen-till midnight."

Ragden looked at his father, saw that he was serious, and nodded in response. Ragden took the robe and went downstairs. As he walked out of the room, he caught a glimpse of Michael heading into the other room where Jennifer was. He did not feel jealous; he felt more curious. He would have to take her up on that offer one of these days—just not today.

Ragden went down to his room, stripped out of his clothes, and walked into the bathroom. He started the shower, then turned and looked at himself in the mirror. He shook his head, still having a tough time grasping his physical changes.

He walked into the shower and rinsed himself off. He stood under the water, letting the hot water beat against his sore muscles. Sighing softly, he enjoyed the drumming across his shoulders and back. Then he sighed, turned off the water, grabbed a towel, and dried himself off. He walked into the bedroom and pulled the robe around him. It was a perfect fit. Soft and plush against his skin, it felt quite comfortable.

Ragden looked at the clock in the room and noted he had a good thirty minutes before he was meeting up with Michael and Jennifer to head to the beach. He sat on the edge of the bed, pondering what was coming next. Meeting a Primal Force. He had no idea what to expect.

His thoughts, instead, turned to Emily. He wondered how she was doing. This late at night, she was probably sleeping. He was curious but was not sure what would happen if he tried to reach out to her while she slept. Something to ask his dad about, later.

Ragden flopped back on the bed, staring up at the ceiling. His mind wandered, his thoughts drifting. He felt the cool air of the air conditioner upon his exposed skin and shivered slightly. It was not an unpleasant sensation.

He thought about his mother Jennifer. Her age defied reason. How had she lived to be that old? Had Michael done something that had enabled her to live that long? Or was that part of being earth-touched? If her appearance had changed due to Michael's powers, what had she looked like when they had met? What had he looked like? Where had they met? So many questions.

Michael had lived for so long and seen so many things—the things he must have seen, the stories he could tell. Ragden did not find history overly interesting, but having someone who had seen so much of it, he had so many questions.

Ragden heard movement on the stairs and sat up. He looked over at the clock and realized that it was time. He stood, pulled the robe around him, and tied it shut. Michael walked into the doorway and smiled at Ragden.

"Time to go."

Ragden nodded and followed Michael out the doorway. They walked down to the front door, slipped on sandals, and walked out of the house. As

they walked down the path to the beach dunes, Ragden noticed a full moon high overhead. A light breeze blew in across the ocean bringing with it the smells of the sea. Ragden took a deep breath, feeling it calm his nerves.

As they crested the dune, they were able to view the expanse of the ocean before them. The water was calm; small waves lapped at the shore; the reflection of the moon shone on the surface before them. Ragden was struck by the utter beauty of it. Michael and Jennifer stopped and slipped off their sandals. Ragden followed their lead, placing his next to theirs. Then they untied their robes, neatly folded them, and put them on top of their sandals. Ragden blinked for a moment, then did the same.

Jennifer and Michael turned to Ragden and smiled softly, reaching out to take his hands. Ragden looked at them questioningly and then took their hands. Michael stood on his right, while Jennifer was on his left, as they walked to the water's edge. The waves lapped the shore at their feet, not touching.

Michael and Jennifer spoke in unison, softly, intoning the words as if some kind of ritual, "Mother. We come before you to present our son, Ragden. Please, welcome him, and make your judgment."

Ragden felt his heart beat a little faster. Michael turned his head and whispered, "Present yourself."

Ragden coughed and found his throat dry. Nervous, not sure what to say. Then he closed his eyes and felt the words come to him. "Mother. I present myself for your judgment."

A small wave crashed across the shore at his feet; words almost too soft to hear seemed to come from the crashing sound, "Yyyeeesss... Come... Closer... Boy."

Ragden looked to his father, who nodded. Ragden took a step forward, the water lapping across his feet. It felt icy cold, and he felt goosebumps prickle his skin, but he took another step in. The water swirled around his ankles, like a soft caress. Another wave lapped against his feet, "Closer..."

Ragden walked slowly into the water, feeling it lap around his ankles, then his calves, then his knees. Once the water lapped around his thighs, he stopped. The water swirled around him with the tide, gently pushing and pulling against him. He heard the water gurgling around him; little eddies of it swirled. He looked down and noticed what looked like small tendrils, made entirely of water, snaking up his legs.

His heart thundered in his chest. He took a deep breath and relaxed himself. The water trickled up his legs, more small tendrils caressing his skin softly. He felt their cold, gentle touch come up over his hips, encircling his waist. The water trickled down his groin, to his soft cock. He felt the tendrils building up, encircling his cock. His balls tingled at the sensation, his cock starting to harden and lengthen at the attention. He took a deep steadying breath.

Before him, the water bubbled and swirled, starting to form a shape that

rose out of the water. The shape rose higher, taking on form, until it was level with his eyes. Definition slowly trickled into the form. A head took shape, almond-shaped eyes, a small nose, and pouty, plump lips. Hair took on shape, water that trickled and dripped down the back of it. Her shoulders formed; a chest, breasts, a flat stomach, a small waist, and hips formed into legs before him. The proportions were that of a cartoon figure. The breasts were entirely too large to be real, the waist too small, and the hips also overly large. The mouth pouted, the lips moved, and a voice like the soft lapping of the water along the shore.

"I see you, Ragden, and I greet you."

She moved closer to him, her arms draped down into the water. She came up to him and walked around him, observing him. Then she stopped in front of him, and reached out, her hand grasping his firm cock. He looked down and saw that his cock was inside her arm. He could feel her squeezing, pulling, and sucking on his cock all at the same time. The sensation was incredible. He moaned softly at it. She looked at him, a soft smile playing across her features.

"Does that feel good?" she asked, her voice soft and seductive.

"Yes," he replied

The squeezing on his cock strengthened, the suction intensified, and he felt it pulling on him ferociously. His body responded; his cock throbbed, and his balls tingled. He looked down and saw small bits of precum slipping out of him, clearly visible in her arm. The bits were swept up her arm, into her body, where they swirled and mixed with other things visible through her chest. He marveled at the vision of it.

Then he felt his balls clench, the pressure building, the waves of pleasure flowing over his body, pulsing from his cock. His eyes went wide as he watched cum explode out of his cock into her. He watched as it was also swept up into her body. The intensity of the motion on his cock softened, but her arm continued to hold him within her, softly massaging his cock, stroking him, pulling more cum from him, massaging his balls. He moaned softly at the sensation.

Her eyes glowed, and he could feel her in his head. Her voice was soft and mellow within his skull. He closed his eyes as he felt her presence washing over him, engulfing him. He surrendered himself to it.

"You have come to be judged little loveling." Her voice was soft but filled his skull and reverberated within every fiber of his being. He could feel her sifting through his mind. He felt his memories play out for her. The events at the school played in perfect clarity and everything that came after.

When she came to the night of his encounter with Emily, she paused. He felt something change in the intensity of her presence in him. She watched him pour his soul into Emily. His memories stopped playing for her. He felt her withdraw from his mind. He opened his eyes and gazed at her watery form before him. He looked down and saw that he was up to his chest in the water. The tide gently lapped across the broad expanse of his chest. Her eyes

floated inches away from him. Her incredible chest nearly touched his.

Her voice was soft, inquisitive, questioning, "You... gave a piece of your soul to her. Why?"

"I thought she was dying."

"She was."

Tears sprang into Ragden's eyes. His voice hitched, "It was the only thing I could think of to do."

She leaned in and Ragden closed his eyes as she kissed the tears from his face. She spoke softly, her voice like the soft lapping of the waves on a beach, "You gave away a piece of your soul to save a mortal you hardly even knew. You bound yourself to her and bound her fate to yours. Why?"

"I... I did not know. I love her."

"Of course you do. You are Love's son..." She laughed, a harsh sound, like the crashing of waves on rocks. Then she stopped and moved her face inches from his, gazing into his eyes. He felt her going into his memories again; his eyes slipped closed as he felt her presence in his mind. The rest of the events of the week played out in seconds. Then she withdrew from him.

He opened his eyes and saw her hovering before his face. The water had receded to his knees. He could see the shapes of her thighs, and her breasts, inches from him. She looked at him, considering.

"You are not like the others, little loveling. Washing her away with you... Tsk, I cannot do that."

Ragden could sense the loneliness in her voice, the aching for times past. His heart swelled with love for her. For this entity of raw power. He wanted to comfort her, hold her in his arms, and share with her. He sighed, surrendering himself to her judgment. He reached out, caressed the side of her thigh with his hand, feeling the silky smoothness, and firmness of her form. His cock throbbed within her, precum leaking out of him. Her eyes flashed a brilliant blue, glowing at him. Then her form collapsed, all the water splashing back into the ocean. The water suddenly pulled back away from him, leaving him standing on dry land.

Ragden blinked and looked around him. He stood in a dry column, surrounded by water. He turned and saw a clear path leading back up the beach to where his parents stood. He turned back to the ocean. He heard her soft voice in the swirling eddies of the water around him.

"You... You... DARE to... Touch me." He heard anger, awe, and affection in that soft voice. He heard a soft sighing in the water around him, a sense of wonderment in it, "Go.... worthy loveling... The first... in a thousand years."

Ragden turned and walked up the beach to Michael and Jennifer. Jennifer had tears in her eyes. As he stepped clear of the tide line, the water washed back into place, as if nothing had happened. Jennifer grabbed him and pulled him into her embrace, her breasts pressing against his chest as she cried into his chest. He hugged her, feeling her firm supple skin against his. He felt his cock throb softly against her, and she laughed between hitches in her breath.

Ragden turned and saw pride on Michael's face. He clasped his shoulder and squeezed it firmly. Michael turned and picked up their robes. He stepped behind Ragden and draped his robe around him. Then Michael reached in and gently grasped Jennifer's shoulder. She turned, looked at him, and smiled. She stepped back from Ragden and let Michael place the robe around her shoulders. She slipped her arms into it then slipped her arms around Ragden's waist, slipping her hands under his robe, pulling his skin against hers. She kissed his chest softly and squeezed him against her. Ragden hugged her back gently.

Ragden looked at Michael and spoke softly, "Dad... Mother Ocean, she said I was the first 'worthy' loveling in the last thousand years... I am not your first child, am I?"

"No."

"How many others before me?"

"More than I care to count."

"And... what happened to the ... others before me?"

"Mother Ocean... took them."

"Took?"

"Drowned them, cast their bodies into the ocean. Never to be seen again."

"Oh." Ragden stared, a bit wide-eyed. He knew there had been danger there but had not suspected his life had been on the line. "She killed them. Why?"

"Yes... Well... As I said, previous force-borns caused great trouble and the Primes decided that all force-borns would be judged before being allowed to live out their lives. Those that were found wanting were killed."

"Oh. You... Did not think to mention this before?"

"You did not ask. Part of the rules. We cannot give that information if you do not ask. Sorry."

Jennifer's voice hitched, tears still leaking from her eyes, "The important thing is that you passed."

They wrapped their robes around them as they headed back up towards the house. As they walked back, Ragden tightened his robe around him and looked over his shoulder at the ocean. Its beauty was startling. He took a deep breath of the ocean breeze as he stepped over the dune and walked up the path to the house. As they stepped inside, Michael and Jennifer turned to Ragden in the foyer.

"You are going to have to meet the rest of the Primes. Not tonight, but soon."

"Oh."

"This will be something you will have to do on your own. I can tell you where to go, but nothing more."

"Are... Are they going to judge me? Kill me if they do not find me to their liking?"

"Not likely. Though, nobody else has done this in thousands of years. So, I

cannot say what will happen."

"That's... not exactly comforting, Dad."

"I know." Michael stepped in and hugged Ragden to him. Ragden sighed into his arms, feeling the warmth and comfort of him. Michael softly kissed his forehead as Jennifer came in and hugged him from the other side.

"Get some rest, Rag; it's been a long day."

Ragden nodded and walked towards his room, weariness consuming him. His eyelids felt so heavy, his limbs dragging. As the door closed behind him, he untied his bathrobe, let it fall on the floor behind him, and fell face-first into his bed, asleep before he made contact.

Sunday...

Ragden awoke sometime in the early morning hours. The room was dark, light from the moon coming in the window, across half the bed. His eyes fluttered open, wondering what had woken him. The smell of the ocean, salty and fresh, tickled his nose. He felt his cock stir, his loins aching. He looked up at the ceiling, realizing he was on his back, still on top of the covers. His cock stood up straight from his groin, twitching in the cool air.

Ragden felt his skin prickle and realized someone was watching him. He turned and looked at the doorway. A figure stood there, in the shadows. He felt a kind of curiosity from the figure as it stepped closer to him. Its movements were fluid and sensual. He heard the soft splashing of water as it walked closer to him. As he watched, he was able to make out the edges of the figure: round hips, soft shoulders, large breasts.

It was a woman, naked, walking into his room. As he looked, he was able to make out more details. She had kelp in her dark hair, and a line of fish scales down her arms. Ragden watched as she walked over to the side of the bed and looked down at him. The woman's body shivered, her form wavering for a moment before becoming solid again.

Ragden sat up and swung his legs off the side of the bed. The woman took a step back as if she were afraid to touch him. He reached out a hand to her. She hesitated, and as she reached out to him, he felt a small spark of electricity. His eyes closed as images swept through his head. He saw this form taking shape at the edge of the ocean, staggering up the shore before finding its footing, each step more details of her body becoming solid.

Ragden blinked, opened his eyes. The woman smiled down at him. Her plump lips opened, as her soft tongue licked them. Her voice was soft, like the rolling of tiny waves against the beach, "It has been... so long since... I have done this."

Ragden smiled at her, feeling her hesitant timidity. He squeezed her cold fingers. He felt her skin starting to warm at his touch. Her hand becoming firmer, more solid in his. She smiled as she felt his hand in hers. Blinked her eyes at him.

"Mother..." Ragden started to say softly, but she shook her head.

"No... Oceana will do. Please. Call me Oceana," Her voice took on shape and sounded more human, and less like the waves of the ocean. She shook her head, and drops of water flew from her. She blushed.

"Oceana," Ragden said softly. She smiled. "That is a beautiful name."

A shiver ran down her figure. She leaned forward, her lips brushing his, "No one has called me that in a millennium. You offered yourself to me. I want to feel your touch as a woman feels a lover. Would you... indulge me?"

Ragden smiled up at her. He nodded softly, "I would be honored to."

Oceana smiled back at him. Then kissed him softly on the lips. She tasted like salt, ocean spray and desire. Ragden reached up and put his hands on her hips. Her skin felt cool to the touch and too soft. Then her skin firmed up beneath his touch and started to grow warm. She pushed gently against him, and he laid back on the bed and scooted back to give her room.

She crawled onto the bed over him, her legs brushing against his. He felt the tingle of her touch, leaving his skin slightly damp. Ragden lay back on the bed, letting her crawl over him. She planted her knees on either side of his waist and placed her hands on his shoulders. She leaned down and gently pressed her lips against his. He tasted the ocean on her lips and shivered slightly as her tongue dipped into his mouth. It was forked like a snake, but as it brushed his, it became rounded and more human feeling. Her body warmed at his touch. Her tongue explored his mouth, tasting him. He felt his heart beating hard as she kissed him.

Ragden ran his hands along her back, feeling the firm skin, with occasional fish scales growing out of it. His hands ran over her firm ass, and she sighed against him, breaking from his kiss, her eyes flashing. He gripped her firm ass, his fingers slipping between her cheeks. She moaned softly against his mouth, her breasts pressing against his chest. His cock throbbed against her.

He slipped his fingers deeper between her cheeks. He furrowed his brow as he felt no asshole. Then he slid his fingers deeper and felt her labial lips, soft and warm to his touch. They moved against his fingers, wrapping around them, pulling them into her. He blinked in surprise and pulled his hand back. She winked at him coyly. She gently rocked her hips forward, poising her groin over the head of his cock. He reached under her and pointed it up at her. She slid back against him; her pussy lips grabbed his cock and pulled him into her.

Oceana settled down against his groin, his cock sliding up into her. It reminded him of slipping his cock into a cool bath, her insides swirling around his cock. He felt like his dick had been pulled into a watery vacuum, her insides sucking on his cock. He felt pressure along his entire cock as her insides took shape, formed around him, squeezing him, stroking him. He moaned in pleasure, his eyes squeezed shut, feeling her body working his cock inside her.

He opened his eyes and saw her staring at him. Her insides stroked,

squeezed, and sucked on his cock. He felt his balls starting to clench, his climax fast approaching. Then it stopped. Her insides became more solid against him, squeezing his cock.

"This... this isn't how humans have sex, is it?" she asked softly, her lips inches from his.

Ragden shook his head, "Not normally, no. Our bodies... cannot do that."

She blushed and licked his lips. "But you enjoy it, yes?"

"Oh, my goodness, it feels amazing."

She giggled at him. Her body vibrated with her humor. Her insides squeezed his cock tighter, gently stroking him. He sighed with pleasure. Then she stopped. Her insides went still around him. She rocked her hips gently forward, sliding her body partially off him. Her insides felt silky smooth against him. His dick throbbed inside her, and she smiled at the sensation.

Oceana smiled at him and nodded, "I watched you... and Selina... Can you fuck me like you did her?"

Ragden chuckled, and nodded, "If that is what you want."

"It is," she purred. Her voice was a deep rumble like the crashing of monstrous waves across the shore. Ragden gently thrust his hips against hers. He felt his cock sliding deep into her, meeting no resistance. He expected to hit her cervix but only felt more silky-smooth softness inside her. Then he drew back, and her insides sucked along his cock as he did. The sensation caused his dick to throb hard, and his balls to clench.

"Wow, that's... insane," He moaned softly.

"Do you like that?" She whispered. Ragden nodded, his eyes wide. He then gently thrust back up into her, and she rocked her hips back to meet his, his cock going deeper into her than he thought possible. Again, he expected to hit something but felt only the silky-smooth suction of her insides. She smiled as their groins thumped together; her breasts gently rocked against his chest.

"Oh," she moaned softly, "That felt nice. Again..."

Ragden smiled and chuckled softly. He slid his hips back as she rocked her hips forward, sliding most of his cock out of her, then he slid forward again, and she rocked back into him. Her body rocked with the gentle impact, his dick sliding deeper into her than any other woman he had ever done that with. She grinned at him as they moved their bodies apart, then thumped together again.

She sat up, her hips grinding against his, her insides squeezing his cock and stroking it inside her. She rocked her hips forward, and Ragden rocked his hips back, feeling her insides pulling at his cock; he moaned in pleasure. Then they rocked gently together. She grabbed his hands and placed them on her. He grabbed her incredible breasts, feeling how soft and supple they were. Her nipples tightened beneath his touch, and she moaned softly. Then she placed her hands on his chest, bracing herself as she lifted her groin off his, and sat down hard on him.

Ragden moaned in pleasure. He thrust up into her, his dick sliding deep into her. She moaned again. They started to build a steady rhythm, as Ragden rolled his hips back, and she rocked hers up, and they slammed their groins together. Her body shook with the impact. They started to pick up speed, moving faster with each other. Ragden gently grasped her breasts, holding them, feeling them rock with each impact of their groins crashing together.

Ragden found his climax fast approaching, his body shuddering at the pleasure of her on him. Her skin was firm and warm beneath his touch, her insides smooth, firm, squeezing and sucking along his length. His cock throbbed, and his balls clenched. He continued to thrust with her, his hips meeting hers, parting, and meeting again, harder.

They moved faster, her breath coming in soft gasps, his becoming ragged with the effort to keep the pace. Their hips slamming together. The waves of pressure and pleasure crashed over Ragden. He felt his balls clenching, as he slammed into her. Then suddenly, his climax hit him, and she sat down heavily against him as his cum exploded up into her. He looked up at her and saw a sublime smile play across her face. His legs spasmed and convulsed, the muscles of his stomach going rigid as his cum pour out of his cock. Her pussy gripped his cock, stroked it, sucked it, milked the cum from him.

Ragden moaned loudly, feeling her draining his cock into her. She leaned forward, laying her soft body against his. She kissed his lips softly, her tongue dipping into his mouth. Then, breaking away from him. He gasped for breath, his arms wrapping around her body, holding her tight.

"That... That was wonderful," she purred against him. A shiver of ecstasy ran down through her body. He felt her insides still squeezing his cock, and gently stroking it. His dick throbbed in pleasure; his balls ached.

"Thank you," she whispered, "For the gift of your seed."

She slowly raised herself off him, his cock slipping from her folds. Then she leaned down and kissed him softly on the lips before she slid off the bed and stood. She gently grasped his hand in hers and squeezed it.

"I won't forget your kindness or your love, Ragden."

Then she turned and walked from the room. Ragden sat up and got off the bed. He walked to the door, but she was already gone. The only sign that she had been there was the damp footprints on the floor. He scratched his head. He could still smell the ocean on his skin as he walked back to the bed.

The bed was damp with his sweat and her water. He chuckled, then peeled the bedding off the bed. He piled it in a corner of the room, then got out fresh sheets. He made the bed, then crawled under the covers. He lay on his back, staring up at the ceiling. His mind reeled at the encounter. This would be fun to explain to Michael. Then he drifted off to sleep.

CHAPTER 29

Ragden woke up the next morning when someone bounced onto the bed next to him. He groaned and tried to roll over, but found he was at the edge of the bed, and someone giggled beside him. He opened his eyes only to find Selina staring at him, her face inches from his, her lips spread in a huge grin.

Selina smiled from ear to ear and breathed huskily, "You're awake. Good morning."

She licked her lips seductively, as she spoke softly, "Can I stay here with you?" She looked into his eyes with a hopeful expression on her face.

"We aren't staying. We are heading home soon."

He groaned, his body stiff and sore. He tried to roll away from her but found himself pinned under the covers by her weight and the edge of the bed. He looked at her and furrowed his brow. "Where is your dad? I'm sure he will beat my ass if he catches you in here with me..."

Selina's eyes widened as she whispered, "He's upstairs, watching TV with your parents. He doesn't know I came down here."

She spoke softly, pleading, "Please don't send me away. I want to stay here with you. I just want to be close to you."

Ragden groaned and sighed, "Fine, but not for long. Get off the bed."

He grumbled as she stood up, and then he lifted the covers so she could climb in. Selina's eyes widened in surprise as she caught a glimpse of his naked body under the covers. She felt her heart quicken, her breath racing.

"Really? You are not going to kick me out?" she asked, hopefully, "Thank you. Thank you so much."

She climbed into the bed next to him, turning her back to him and curling up on the side of the bed, "I will just lie here with you, close to you. Feel your warmth. I just want to be near you."

"Fine," Ragden grumbled. He pulled her against him. Feeling her warmth. Then he dropped the covers over both and spooned his body around hers. He placed one hand on her waist, pulling her back against his bare chest.

Selina felt his arm wrap around her, and she let out a long, low gasp of pleasure as she spoke quietly, "Thank you. Thank you so much. This feels... amazing. Your warmth is incredible."

"I get it. You are welcome."

He pulled her body closer to his, his groin snugly against her ass. His cock slipped between her cheeks, still limp, but large. He felt her shirt and shorts against his skin. He breathed in the smell of her hair, and her nervous anxiety. He gently cupped her breasts, as he buried his face in her hair and gently nuzzled her neck. He closed his eyes and tried to relax against her, his heart slowing, his breath calming.

Selina felt his arm around her, and she let out a long, low gasp of pleasure as she whispered, "Mm. Thank you. This feels... incredible."

She felt his cock between her ass cheeks, pressing against her, and moaned softly in pleasure. Her voice was quiet but insistent, trembling with desire, "I cannot believe I'm lying here with you and feeling your heat. I never thought something like this could happen. I just want to stay here... with you."

"You are here, with me. Now shut your cake hole and let me rest," He sighed against her back, feeling her heart beating hard against his chest. His cock started to stir poking between her cheeks against her groin through her shorts. It throbbed, growing, pressing against her.

Selina moaned softly in pleasure, then spoke quietly, "Okay. I'll be quiet. I'll just lie here and admire your body and listen to your heartbeat."

As she felt his cock growing between her legs, she gasped softly. She looked down at it under the covers, "Mm. I can feel it. It is so big and warm. I wish I could touch it."

His cock throbbed at her words, pressing against her insistently. He sighed. "If you want to touch it, go ahead..."

Selina gasped softly. She spoke in a rush, "Really? You don't mind? Can I really touch it? Please tell me I can..."

She reached down between his legs and carefully took hold of his cock. She gently wrapped her fingers around it, marveling at the texture of the flesh beneath her touch. She moaned softly, feeling it throb beneath her fingers, feeling his quickening pulse at her touch.

Ragden moaned softly at her gentle touch. He slipped his hands under her shirt and gently cupped her breasts. He then noticed that she was not wearing a bra; he ran his fingers over her nipples, feeling them harden at his touch. Then he slid one hand down her stomach, under her shorts and panties, to slip a finger between her damp folds.

"Little excited?" he asked softly, whispering into her ear.

Selina let out a long, low gasp of pleasure as she answered the question, "Yeah. I'm a bit overwhelmed. I'm not used to all of this."

"You are the one who crawled into my bed. What do you really want?"

Selina gushed, eager to tell him everything, "I want. I want everything. I want to feel everything. I want to be yours completely. I want to be filled by

your cock. I want to feel it pushing into me and filling me."

"We did that yesterday. I came inside of you four times. You sucked me off, I came in your ass, twice, then I came in your pussy in the theater room last night."

He slid his finger deeper into her pussy, testing her walls, stroking deeper into her.

"We do not have much time. What do you WANT?"

Selina gasped at his question, fear pulsing across her skin, "I remember. I remember everything. I remember being filled up and having your cum pouring inside of me. I remember feeling your hot, thick, heavy load filling me up and feeling your power over me. I want more of that. I want to feel it again."

Ragden slid his hands along her sides, slipping them under her shorts and panties, sliding them down her hips, around her knees. He pressed his cock against her folds, feeling it throb against her.

"Can you be my lover? I want a partner who fucks me as hard as I fuck her. Can you do that?"

Selina moaned in pleasure as he removed her shorts and panties. Then she whispered, her voice trembling with desire and need, "Yes. I can be your lover. I can be whatever you want me to be. I want to feel your cock pushing into me and filling me up. I want to be your perfect partner. Just tell me what to do... I will do anything for you.

"Take my cock then. Put it inside you. Ride it."

Selina sighed softly, "Yes... I can do that."

Ragden rolled over onto his back as Selina positioned herself over his dick, looking down at him with a mix of fear and desire in her eyes, and she slowly began to lower herself down, taking his thick, heavy meat deep into her tight pussy.

Ragden gently rolled his hips against her, pushing his cock the rest of the way up into her, gently pressing against her cervix. Selina gasped in pleasure as she felt his cock pressing deep inside her. Then he dropped back, sliding most of the way out. He looked up at her, expectantly.

He sharply slapped her ass. "Are you going to do anything, or sit there like a bump on a log?"

Selina winched, feeling her ass sting under his hand. She felt the pleasure of it, felt her body quivering with desire. She spoke softly, "No. Sir... I am sorry. I will start moving."

Selina started to move, slowly at first, but then faster, riding his cock with a mix of fear and desire in her eyes. Her hips bounced slightly as she added, "Faster. Sir. I want you to fill me up."

He waited for her to find a rhythm, then matched it, thrust against her as she sat down hard, his cock thumping against her cervix. Selina gaped in pleasure as she felt his cock bumping against her cervix.

"Fuck," She moaned, "Fuucck."

Ragden reached up and gently grasped her breasts, matching her movements, thrust against her motion, his cock bouncing off her cervix, jarring her with each impact. She moaned with pleasure, feeling his hands on her amazing chest. Selina continued to ride his cock, her pussy clenching tightly around him, and she let out a long, low gasp of fear and pleasure as she added, "More. More."

He thrust against her movements, harder, his cock slamming into her cervix with each thrust, her breasts rocking hard under his grasp.

Selina moaned in pleasure as he slammed into her cervix. She felt the waves of pleasure filling her womb and her abdomen, pulsing out through her body. She continued to ride his cock, her pussy clenching tightly around him

"Fuck," She moaned loudly, her body vibrating with pressure and pleasure.

He continued to match her rhythm, then pushed a bit faster, slamming into her harder, ramming his dick against her cervix with even more force, feeling her body clench and convulse against his. Selina gasped in pleasure, her body rocking with each massive thrust. She moaned with pleasure as she felt her inside clenching around his throbbing meat inside her.

He released her breasts and slapped her ass hard, leaving a stinging red mark on her soft flesh. She winced hard. A shiver of ecstasy ran through her body, a mix of pain and pleasure. She paused, feeling his cock throbbing inside her, and moaned softly.

"Keep riding; I'm waiting on you," Ragden said softly, an edge of command in his voice.

"Yes, Sir. I'm riding for you," Selina started bucking again, trying to ride his cock, her hips bouncing slightly. She moaned softly, "Fill me with your cum."

"Bounce harder," Ragden said softly.

Selina gasped in pleasure, taking it as an order, "Yes, Sir. Bouncing harder." Her hips bounced harder, her pussy clenching tighter around his cock.

"Harder!"

"Yes! Harder, Sir! I'm bouncing harder for you!" Selina's hips bounced harder, her pussy clenching tighter around his cock. She moaned in pleasure, feeling her actions driving his cock deep into her pussy, feeling him hit her cervix with her movements. She clutched her chest, her heart pounding.

"Harder. Keep that intensity right there, as long as you can."

He matched her rhythm, slamming his cock into her with each of her hard thrusts, feeling his cock smash into her cervix, the impact sending waves of pleasure down his cock and up into her body.

Selina moaned in pleasure, feeling the waves of pleasure surging through her. She felt her heart thundering in her chest. She felt her pussy clenching with more force, squeezing his cock inside her. She heard his words, the response barking out of her, "Yes! Fucking harder, Sir!"

"I didn't say you could stop. Keep riding. Keep rocking those hips. Fuck

that cock, if that's what you want."

Selina moaned in pleasure, her heart hammering in her chest. Selina's hips kept bouncing, her pussy clenching tighter around his cock, "Yes! I won't stop, Sir. I'll keep riding. I'll keep fucking your cock."

Ragden thrust against her thrusts, matched her speed, then pushed her faster, thrusting harder, his cock slamming into her cervix with even more intensity. He could feel her climax building, the waves of pleasure sweeping over her, spreading to consume her entire body.

Selina let out a long, low gasp of pleasure as he pushed her faster. Her pussy clenched tighter around his cock as she continued to bounce her hips faster. Her voice trembled with desire, "Yes! Faster! Yes! Yes!"

Maintaining that frenetic pace, he slammed his cock into her, striking deep. Matching her thrusts, slamming his cock into her cervix. He watched her body rock with each impact. Waited for her to move, then matched her movements and smashed his cock into her cervix again. He slapped her ass sharply, as he continued to push her faster.

Selina cried out in pleasure, feeling his cock slamming into her cervix, "Ahh! Yes! Fuck."

She bounced her hips faster, her pussy clenching tighter around his cock as she moaned in pleasure. She could feel the pressure building up within her. She felt the waves of ecstasy starting to pulse through her body.

Ragden moaned softly, feeling her pussy tightly clenched on his cock as he thrust hard against her movements. He felt his climax building. The pressure in his balls increased, the waves of pleasure building. He looked up at her, grabbed her breasts, and squeezed them tightly, his fingers pinching her nipples. He held her chest as he rammed his cock into her cervix, feeling her entire body bounce and convulse against his. Selina moaned in pleasure, feeling his hands squeezing her breasts.

"Ahh! Ahh! Yes! Yes! Yes!" She cried out in pleasure.

As her climax exploded over her, Ragden felt his exploding upwards into her. His legs convulsed as she sat down heavily on his cock. He slammed up into her cervix one more time and remained pressed against her as cum exploded out of his cock into her. His hands clenched on her chest, squeezing tightly as his body convulsed.

Selina continued to bounce against his groin, riding out her climax, her body bucking and convulsing against his. She moaned in pleasure, feeling his cum filling her. She panted heavily, trying to catch her breath as she felt her pussy clenched tightly around his cock inside her.

"Ahh! Ahh! Yes! Yes!"

Ragden's muscles released, and he slumped back into the bed, his arms dropping limply to his sides. Selina moaned in pleasure, watching him. His cock pressed against her cervix, throbbing inside her. Cum still pumping out of him into her. Her pussy still clenched around his throbbing cock tightly, squeezing it inside her. He gently laid a hand on her thigh and felt the

vibrations of her climax riding through her.

Then he sat up, wrapped his arms around her, and pivoted, dropping her onto the bed beneath him. He slipped his throbbing cock from her pussy and pressed the head of it against her ass, pushing hard against her.

Selina moaned in pleasure, feeling his arms around her as he placed her on the bed. She felt the pressure against her ass and felt a shiver of excitement run down her back. Her body shook, her ass quivering in anticipation as she felt his cock pushing against her.

"Ahh! Yes! Oh God," She cried softly.

Ragden pressed harder, the head of his cock slipping in. The fluids leaking out of her pussy dripped down over his cock, providing the lubrication needed. He slid his throbbing cock into her ass, deeper and deeper, his cock throbbing up into her bowels until his groin bumped against her incredible ass. He moaned softly at the sensation of her body quivering and clenching against him. His cock throbbed inside her ass.

Selina moaned in pleasure, feeling his cock filling her ass. Her eyes rolled into the back of her head, her back arching, pressing her ass against his groin as it sank deeper and deeper into her. She moaned loudly, "Ahh! Yes! Yes! Yes!"

He slid back, his cock nearly slipping out of her, then rammed it back in, hard, driving deep into her ass. He grabbed her hands and slid them to her ass cheeks, spreading them as he slid out and slammed home again, going deeper this time, pressing his cock into her bowels.

"Work with me here, roll your ass into my cock as I fuck you."

He slid his cock back, then slammed home into her again. Then he slid back and waited for her to move.

Selina rolled her ass towards his cock, and she let out a long, low gasp of fear and pleasure, "I am doing as you ask."

"Now, work with me," he said softly as he slammed his cock back into her bowels. Then he drew back, and slammed into her again, harder, shaking her whole body. Selina's ass shook with each impact, causing her to moan in pleasure. She bit her lip, looking up at him, and nodding her head, urging him to continue.

Ragden drew his cock back to the edge of her, then waited for her to move. Selina obliged, rolling her hips against his groin, feeling his cock fill her bowels at her movement. She moaned loudly at the sensation. She could feel her empty pussy clenching and releasing, spasming with her pleasure. The waves of ecstasy rolled over her. Her bowels filled with his massive cock, making her feel so full of life and love. So full of him.

As her ass moved towards his cock, he slammed it into her, riding her movements up into her bowels. He drew back and slammed into her again, building a slow rhythm of massive, deep strokes into her. Selina gasped in pleasure as she felt his cock slamming into her bowels. She moaned loudly, then cried out.

He pounded into her faster, harder, feeling her climax building again, her muscles starting to spasm, her breasts rocking with each impact. His climax built rapidly with hers. He felt the pressure building within him, and his balls started to clench. Selina's ass clenched and unclenched with each impact as she felt her climax building, blotting out her reality. Her eyes rolled back into her head, her back arched, her hips rolled against him of their own accord. She felt the incredible waves of pleasure emanating from her bowels and crashing through the rest of her body.

He slammed into her harder and faster, feeling everything building to a breaking point. Her muscles started to twitch and convulse against him. He felt her ass clenching on his cock, and his balls clenched up tighter, the muscles in his legs straining to keep moving as his climax built and built.

Selina moaned in pleasure, feeling the waves of ecstasy surging over her. She felt the pounding in her bowels and did her best to match his movements, but her muscles started to twitch and spasm. She felt her ass clenching and releasing with each impact. Her pussy clenched even tighter. The pressure building up inside her, threatening to overwhelm her.

Ragden slammed into her harder, faster, and then his body convulsed. He lost all rhythm and slammed into her like a madman as his climax rode over him. His body convulsed and slammed hard into her sporadically as his climax exploded out of him. Her body lost all rhythm, and she cried out as her climax exploded over her. Selina's legs kicked and spasmed, her muscles convulsing.

"Oh God!" Selina cried out loudly, as her climax rode over her. Her head rolled back, pressing her head into the bed; her back arched, and her legs convulsed. Her body twitched and spasmed with the force of it. Cum erupted from her pussy, flowing down over her groin, coating his cock lodged in her ass. She reached out, clawing at the blankets around her, trying to find something to grab onto. Her body twitched and convulsed, her muscles clenching on his cock, squeezing it within her bowels. She released it and slumped against the bed, her breath ragged, her heart beating wildly in her chest. She took great gulps of air, trying to catch her breath.

"Oh God," she said again, her body still racked with spasms.

Ragden smiled, then collapsed on top of her, pressing his body against hers. He kissed her softly on the mouth, feeling his cock still lodged in her bowels, twitching and throbbing within her. He moaned softly as her ass clenched on it, squeezing it hard inside her.

Selina gasped, surprised by the sudden weight on top of her and she looked up at him, her eyes wide with surprise. She could feel his cock throbbing against her insides, and she let out a long, low gasp of pleasure as she whispered, "My God."

The spasms in her ass continued to clench and release as she added, "You're still inside me."

Selina's pussy continued to leak, coating her inner thighs with her fluids as she added, "And you're still hard."

Selina's breath hitched in her chest as she added, "Isn't that amazing?"

Ragden smiled against her lips, "It is, but it won't last. We are expected at breakfast."

He sat up, and slid his softening cock from her ass, watching the fluids slipping out of her. Then he playfully slapped her ass as he crawled off the bed, stood and stretched.

Selina watched him carefully, her eyes wide with surprise and curiosity. She groaned softly, "Breakfast? Already?"

She looked at him curiously, her ass still quivering with the aftershocks of her orgasm, and said softly, "But you're still hard. Can't you stay inside me a bit longer? Please."

"Nope. That is enough for today. I must get back home. We have things to do tonight."

He offered her his hand to help her get off the bed. Selina took his hand and slipped off the bed. She stood in front of him and pouted, looking at his mostly hard cock, "But. I want more. I need more. Please don't leave me like this. I'll suck you off if that's what it takes to keep you here."

Ragden shook his head, and spoke softly, comfortingly, "Nope, sorry. I mean, you can if you want, but that won't keep me here. We have to get going, and I'm hungry."

Selina's face fell, and she whispered, pleading, "But I want to keep you here. I want to make you stay. Please, Ragden. I'll do anything... I'll give you anything."

Ragden gently leaned into her and kissed her on the lips softly. "I don't need anything from you. This has been wonderful fun, and I hope you enjoyed it, but I really must get going."

He stepped around her and headed into the bathroom, turning on the shower as he did. Selina stood there watching him go into the other room; her lips parted slightly as she whispered to herself, "It hasn't been enough. I need more of you. Please, Ragden... Stay with me."

She stood there alone in the bedroom, her body quaking with need, her pussy dripping with desire as she talked softly to herself, "Please come back soon..."

CHAPTER 30

Ragden took his time in the shower, rinsing the sweat and fluids from his body, using copious amounts of soap and shampoo to get clean. He stepped out and dried himself off. He stopped in front of the mirror and combed out his hair, then walked back into the bedroom and spied Selina standing there in only a T-shirt, straining to keep her breasts contained and no other clothes on. He noticed the need on her face, the arousal dripping from her pussy. He cocked an eyebrow at her as he stepped up to her and gently kissed her on the lips.

"You really are in a state, aren't you?"

Selina looked at him, her eyes wide with surprise and pleasure as he appeared in front of her. She had been standing there, lost in her thoughts, her body still quaking with need, her pussy leaking with desire. She gasped softly and whispered, "Yes... I am completely undone."

Selina stepped closer to him and spoke softly, "Kiss me like you did before. Kiss me like you're never going to stop."

Ragden kissed her softly, the passion building. He slipped his tongue into her mouth, tasting her need and desire. He pulled her body against him, feeling her breasts against his chest. He cupped her perfect ass, pulling her groin against his. His soft cock gently grazed her groin.

Ragden pulled back from her, looked her in the eyes, and spoke softly, "I love you, Selina... but I cannot stay. You are welcome to visit sometime, but your parents are waiting upstairs."

Selina closed her eyes, feeling the warmth of his tongue and the passion building between them. She gasped softly, then added, "I love you too, Ragden."

Selina's voice trembled with both love and need. Her body clung to his, her groin pressed against his cock, her pussy leaking with need. She looked up at him pleadingly and whispered, "Please don't go. Stay with me. Please do not leave me like this. Make love to me one more time. Just one more time."

Ragden laughed and turned her towards the bed. He pushed her back against it and watched her stumble and fall onto the bed. He stepped up between her legs, his cock thickening, hardening, and swelling to a monstrous size between her legs. He pushed the head of it against her lips, the tip pushing against her clitoris.

"Is this really what you want?"

Selina gasped with surprise, her eyes growing large as she saw the size of his cock. Her mind reeled, trying to grasp how it had gotten so large. Surely it had not been that large before. She moaned with need and desire as she whispered, her voice trembling with fear and excitement, "Yes... Yes! Please put it in me. Fuck me, Ragden. Fuck me like you are never going to stop. I need you to fill me up. Put your cock in me now."

Selina looked at him eagerly, waiting for him to enter her and to feel his heat and power surging through her body. She spread her legs, placing her hands on her thighs, and opened herself to allow him in.

Ragden pushed the head of his cock through her pussy lips, its enormous size pressing against her opening, but too big to fit. He pressed it against her, forcing her vagina to stretch to fit it in. He pushed harder, stretching her more.

"Last time, love, then I really must go."

The head finally slipped in, leaving her gasping at the pain and intensity of it inside her. Selina gasped, her breath ragged, her chest heaving. Her voice trembled with both shock and pleasure, "Oh, my God. You are so big. Fill me up... fill me."

Her breath hitched, her pussy contracted, and she looked at him desperately, her body quaking with need, "Make love to me."

He pressed harder, sliding his cock into her deeper, stretching her farther and farther until it bumped into her cervix. He looked down and laughed at the length of his cock still not inside her. He took her hand and pulled it down between her legs for her to feel how stretched her pussy was and how much of his cock could not even fit inside her.

"Are you sure you want this?"

Selina gasped with surprise and pleasure and moaned, her voice trembling with excitement, "Yes! Yes! I want all of it... I want every inch of you, Ragden."

Selina's pussy clenched and unclenched with each inch of his cock that entered her, and she added, "I need every inch of you inside me."

"It won't fit here."

Ragden gently slid his cock back and then thrust into her, sliding up into her cervix, savagely, pushing her into the bed. His cock filled every inch of her pussy, and still could not fit all of it.

"If you want every inch, you're gonna have to put it somewhere else."

Selina moaned in pleasure, feeling herself fill up with all of him inside her. She felt her walls stretching around his massive cock. She wondered what he

meant, her mind overwhelmed with the sensation of him, "What do you mean? Where else can you fit?"

Her voice trembled with both anticipation and curiosity, and she whispered, "Show me where else..."

Ragden slowly slid his dick back, then thrust into her again, slamming it into her cervix. He grabbed her hips to keep her from sliding off the bed. He pulled her against him as he slammed it into her again, then slid it back and slipped it out of her vagina. He pushed the head against her lips, against her clitoris, then slid it down and pressed it against her ass, the head of it pressed hard against her tight hole.

Selina felt the incredible pressure against her ass; her body quivered in anticipation. She felt the heat against her, the pressure increasing. Her heart started beating harder, and her breath rate increased. She sat up on her elbows and looked down between her legs at the massive meat of his cock pushing against her. She moaned in pleasure and pain, feeling it push against her harder and harder.

"What... What are you doing?" She whispered, her voice trembling with confusion as she felt her pussy clench and unclench with each moment of contact between his cock and her ass, and she moaned, "You're not going to fuck me in the ass. Oh fuck... make love to my ass. Please. Please fuck my ass... Oh, God."

Ragden pressed his cock against her asshole, watching as it stretched and stretched, trying to fit the enormity of his cock. He pressed and pressed, and only the very tip slipped in. He pulled back and slid his cock through the dripping wet folds of her pussy, collecting her arousal, and then pressed against her ass again, harder. He gritted his teeth as he pressed it against her, stretching her ass open until it finally slipped in. He gasped at the pressure of her ass on his cock, then grabbed her hips and pulled her gently towards him, forcing her bowels to stretch as his cock slid up her ass. Deeper and deeper, he pressed it in until his groin bumped into her ass. His enormous, throbbing cock was fully seated in her bowels.

Selina felt her heart racing. The enormous heat and pressure in her bowels caused her eyes to cross and roll back into her head. Her mouth dropped open as she panted heavily, the pressure inside her unlike anything she had ever felt, "Oh, my God... Oh, my God."

Selina's voice trembled with both amazement and arousal, "You're in my ass. Oh, God. Fuck my ass... Oh, God."

"Last time, love. Shall we make this quick, so we can get to breakfast?"

He gently slid back until only the head of his cock remained in her, then slid it forward, fully embedding his cock in her ass.

Selina gasped in surprise and pleasure; her voice hissed between her teeth as she gasped for air, "Yes."

Her pussy leaked with need; her body clenched around the enormous cock in her ass. She felt the heat in her bowels, the pressure building within her, the

waves of pleasure consuming her. Her mind reeled; her thoughts scattered. She looked at him in desperation, feeling his enormous cock pulsing deep in her ass. She moaned, loudly, "Fuck me in my ass. Fuck me like you are never going to stop."

Ragden grabbed her hips tightly, holding her in place as he slid back, then thrust into her. He felt her body stretch to accommodate his massive size. He slid back and thrust into her again, harder, then again, harder still. He held her in place as he stroked back and forth faster, harder, slamming his cock into her bowels. He felt the waves of pressure and pleasure building within her and within himself as well.

Selina gasped in pleasure, feeling his cock filling her bowels and pulsing within her, as well as the pain of her body stretching around his incredible size. The mix of pain and pleasure formed an ecstasy so exquisite that she could not help but moan louder with each thrust into her. She felt the heat in her bowels, the pressure building within her, her pussy clenching and releasing.

She moaned in pleasure, "Ohh. Fuck. Mmmph!" She clenched her jaws, gritted her teeth, then gasped for breath as her heart started beating faster, "Yes. Fuck me. Fuck me harder. Fuck my ass. Oh... Fuck. Fuck. Fuck."

Ragden pulled back and slammed into her harder, faster, his groin smacking against her ass with a loud slap at each impact. Her body rocked with the force of it. The only thing holding her in place was his hands on her hips, pulling her against him as he thrust into her again, again and again.

Selina pushed her head back into the mattress, her back arching, her ass thrusting against his groin. She felt his enormous cock stretching her asshole, her intestinal tract, and her bowels. The pain of it mixed with the pleasure into a potent cocktail of ecstasy that threatened to overwhelm all her senses. She moaned loudly, gasping for breath, "Ahh. Fuck. Ahh."

She felt her pussy dripping, her juices slipping down through her folds and over her asshole. She felt it slipping around his cock as it slid in and out of her ass. She felt him slamming into her. Her entire body rocked with each incredible impact. Her gorgeous, wonderful breasts rocked back and forth as he continued to pound her ass with his cock. She moaned louder, "Fuck me. Fuck me harder."

Ragden pulled back and slammed into her harder, faster, driving deep into her. He pulled her hands to her ass cheeks, spreading them. He grabbed her hips and pulled her against him as he slammed into her harder, going even deeper, while she used her hands to spread her ass cheeks for him. His massive cock stroked so deep into her that her bowels clenched and spasmed at the feel of it.

Selina moaned in pleasure, feeling her body rocking, his hands holding her in place as he thrust against her. She pulled on her ass cheeks, keeping her ass spread wide, feeling his incredible cock sliding in and out of her bowels. The massive size of him stretched the walls of her ass, filling her bowels with his

heat, pressure and love. She felt the pressure filling her bowels, the pleasure crashing over her in waves. She panted heavily, trying to catch her breath, her pussy and ass clenching and releasing as he slid in and out of her. She looked down at his enormous cock driving into her ass and her eyes rolled at the sight of it. She looked up at him, her eyes wide and desperate, "Fuck. Fuck me. Fuck me harder."

Ragden slammed his cock into her ass harder, deeper, faster. He could feel the waves of pleasure riding over her body, her ass clenching against each massive thrust, releasing as he slid back and thrust into her again. He could feel her breath exploding in and out of her, her heart beating frantically against his hands on her legs. Her muscles were starting to convulse under his hands. All the while, he continued to slam his cock into her, then draw back and slam into her again, faster and harder than before.

Selina felt his powerful hands holding her in place as he slammed his massive cock in and out of her ass. She felt the waves of pressure and pleasure building within her. Her bowels filled with his heat. She moaned at the feeling. She felt her ass clench against each powerful thrust of his cock and she moaned in pleasure. She looked up at him as she held her ass open so he could fuck her harder and she begged him, "Ahh. Fuck. Ahh. Yes. Fuck my ass. Faster. Harder."

Ragden obliged her request and turned the intensity up another notch, slamming the incredible length of his enormous cock deeper into her bowels. Slamming against her harder and faster, a frenetic rhythm in time to her frantic pulse. He started to feel his climax building again, like a monster in the darkness threatening to overwhelm both of them. He felt her climax building, her body tensing, her muscles starting to twitch and convulse beneath his touch. He continued to slam his cock up her ass, harder, deeper and faster.

Selina felt her body rock even harder. His thrusts stronger, deeper, faster into her. She felt her heart racing in her chest. She moaned in pleasure, feeling her pussy leaking with her desire. Her juice dripped down over his cock, sliding up her ass onto him. Her ass clenched against each powerful thrust, her body vibrating with his power and desire. Words slipped through her lips with each exhalation as she gasped for breath, "Ahh! Ahh! Yes! Fuck me! Faster. Harder."

At her urging, he thrust into her harder and faster, driving into her at the pace of a madman, his muscles burning to keep pace. His fingers dug into her thighs, pulling her against him and driving his cock deep into her bowels.

Ragden continued to thrust into her as hard and fast as he could. He felt her bowels squeezing his cock, increasing the intensity, making his cock feel even larger in her. He felt the waves of pleasure consuming her, her body quivering and convulsing against him.

Selina moaned loudly in pleasure. She felt all the sensations washing over her, filling her, drowning her in pleasure and ecstasy. Her body rocked, her thighs shook and her breasts bounced with each incredible impact. She felt his

cock sliding almost out, then slamming back into her bowels. Stretching her, pushing into her bowels, filling her with his passion, power and love. She felt it flowing into her, filling her up. She felt every cell in her being overflowing with all that was him.

She looked up at him, her eyes brimming with tears at the sheer ecstatic joy of what she felt. Her breath was hot and heavy as she exhaled, the words slipping from her lips, "Ahh! Ahh! Fuck me! Yes. Fuck my ass. Faster."

Ragden continued to drive into her as hard and fast as he could, his pace frenetic, his cock slamming into her bowels wildly. He pulled her hips against each thrust, his cock slamming deep into her bowels. He felt her clenching against him, her muscles convulsing and twitching against his throbbing cock in her ass. He felt her climax building and building within her.

Selina felt her heart racing in her chest, feeling like it was about to burst. Every muscle in her body clenched and spasmed as his cock slid in and out of her bowels. The incredible heat, pressure and pleasure filled her bowels, chest, heart and every single cell in her body.

She looked up at Ragden, tears slipping down her cheeks from the sheer joy of the pleasure filling her. She felt her pussy leaking with need, coating his cock. She felt her ass clenching and releasing him, her pussy clenched in response. Her breath raced in and out of her, in time to the cock filling her, "Ahh! Ahh! Fuck me!"

As he continued to thrust into her hard and fast, Ragden suddenly felt her climax roll over her like a thunderclap. She cried out with the force of it, her fingers digging into her ass, drawing blood as her hands clenched. He felt her ass clench on his cock so hard, he exploded inside of her. Cum burst forth from his cock to fill her bowels. He thrust into her one more time, feeling his legs and back convulsing with the effort. He leaned onto her, pressed against her legs and collapsed on top of her.

Selina moaned in pleasure, feeling her body clenching and releasing, the cum flowing into her bowels. She moaned loudly as her muscles twitched and convulsed. She pulled her fingers out of her ass cheeks, letting them clasp around his cock. She wrapped her arms around him, pulling him against her large breasts. She moaned in pleasure, feeling all the sensations of her ass stretched around his enormous cock.

"Thank you," she whispered huskily.

Ragden kissed her lips softly, "You are welcome."

He lay there on top of her for another few minutes, letting his body calm, basking in the afterglow of her incredible climax. His cock throbbed in her ass, still large, but softening, slowly.

Selina nuzzled against his chest, feeling the afterglow of her orgasm washing over her. She could feel his cock throbbing in her ass and she knew that she would be sore, but she did not care. She was happy that he was inside of her, filling her up completely.

"Ragden, thank you." she whispered, "That felt amazing."

"I'm glad you liked that. Now we really must get to breakfast and get on the road."

He gently raised himself off her, slowly standing up. He looked down at his cock still in her ass and slowly slid it back, easing it gently out of her, watching as inch after inch slipped out until the whole thing finally slipped out of her.

Selina watched as his cock slipped out of her ass, feeling relief mixed with sadness. She loved having him inside of her, but now it was gone. She got up quickly, grabbing some tissues to clean herself up.

"We need to go to breakfast," she said quickly, trying not to show how emotional she felt.

Ragden grabbed her wrist and pulled her against him, kissing her softly on the lips. He ran his hands down her back, gently cupping her incredible ass, then slid them up her back, holding her against him.

"It's okay," he whispered into her ear as he hugged her gently. "You can come visit when you get a break between classes."

Selina felt his hands on her back and she smiled, feeling comforted. She looked up into his face and she felt his lips against hers.

"Thank you, Ragden," she whispered back, feeling her heart swell with gratitude. She felt his hands caressing her backside and she felt a wave of desire wash over her, despite knowing that he was being gentlemanly.

"I would love to visit you," she added, "But I also wouldn't mind if you came to see me sometimes... You know, since we're friends now."

Ragden laughed softly, "Friends? Is that what we are?"

He stepped away from her, found some clean clothes and started dressing himself. He looked over at her and chuckled, then he picked up her shorts and panties and tossed them to her.

"As beautiful as I find your pussy, you might want to cover it."

Selina blushed deeply, feeling her face heat up at his comment. She quickly picked up her shorts and panties, feeling the wetness against the fabric. She nodded in agreement, feeling a mix of embarrassment and arousal.

"Yeah, I guess I need to cover up," she said quietly, trying not to sound too vulnerable. She dressed quickly, putting on her shorts and panties and feeling the fabric stick to her damp skin.

"There, that's better," she added, looking at him hopefully.

Once dressed, Ragden walked over and wrapped his arms around her, pulling her body against his, feeling her warmth and the swell of her large breasts pressing against his chest. Selina felt his arms around her and sighed contentedly. She felt safe and protected in his embrace. He kissed her softly on the lips, then stepped back, his hands trailing along her waist as he moved towards the door. He took her hand in his and pulled her along behind him. She felt his large hands guide her through the house and up the stairs as she found herself walking beside him, feeling a mix of happiness and longing.

"Where are we going?" she asked curiously, feeling a new sense of

boldness within her.

Ragden laughed softly as they headed up the stairs. As they reached the top landing, they spotted Michael, Jennifer, George, and Stacy. Ragden walked into the kitchen and spoke to everyone, "Sorry I'm late; look who I found wandering around the house like a lost puppy."

Selina stood behind him, feeling a mix of nervousness and excitement. She heard him speaking to everyone, and she felt a sudden rush of desire wash over her. She knew that they did not suspect anything, but she knew that they would be able to sense something different about her.

"Hi, everyone," she said quietly, trying not to draw attention to herself, but feeling a new sense of confidence within her. Selina noticed their eyes linger on her, and she felt a wave of arousal wash over her, feeling her pussy grow wet with need. "It's good to see everyone," she added, trying to sound normal, but feeling her heart race in anticipation of what may happen next.

Michael's eyes glittered knowingly as he smiled at them, his voice warm with affection, "Good morning Ragden, Selina."

Selina looked at Michael and felt the heat in his gaze. She felt herself growing damp, her heart beating faster. She smiled back and waved with her free hand, feeling the heat on her cheeks. Jennifer looked at Michael, chuckled to herself, then elbowed Michael gently. He looked down at her, laughed softly, and kissed her on the lips.

George glared at Ragden and Selina. He opened his mouth to say something, but Stacy grabbed his wrist and pulled on his arm. He turned to look at her, saw the look on her face, and his features softened. He took a deep breath and sighed slowly, then he turned back to Ragden and nodded curtly. Stacy stepped over and gave Ragden a gentle hug. She slipped a hand around his back, grabbed Selina's wrist, and squeezed it. Stacy released Ragden and stepped around him to hug Selina.

Stacy hugged Selina tightly and whispered in her ear, "I see you had a good morning with your friend here," then she stepped back from her and smiled knowingly.

"Ragden, can you help me set the table?" Michael asked. Ragden nodded and stepped into the kitchen to assist. He grabbed enough plates for everyone and a handful of silverware. Ragden walked over and set the table, then walked back into the kitchen. Jennifer smiled sweetly at Ragden and shook her head, "Go. Take a seat. We'll have the food out in a minute."

Ragden nodded, walked over to the table, and found a seat. Selina smiled at Stacy, then stepped away from her to sit next to Ragden. George and Stacy sat across from them. George kept his face passive, as he struggled with his emotions. He could see that his daughter was happy, as she radiated her happiness and he wanted to be happy for her, but he was not sure he liked how she got there.

Jennifer and Michael brought out steaming plates with hot food. There were pancakes, waffles, scrambled eggs, sausage and bacon. George's eyes got

wide at the sheer amount of food. Ragden smiled, feeling his belly rumble. Selina heard the rumble and giggled, feeling that she had contributed to him being hungry and it made her feel satisfied, a warmth deep in her body. She could still feel his seed in her bowels and it sent a shiver of ecstasy down her back.

As Jennifer and Michael sat, everyone started placing portions from the plates in the middle onto their plates. Ragden piled food on his plate, far more than anyone else. George watched; his eyes wide. Stacy shook her head, then got to eating her portion. They ate quietly, enjoying the meal prepared by Michael and Jennifer. Ragden cleared his plate and then proceeded to fill his plate a second time, clearing all of that as well. By the time he was finishing his second helping, almost everyone else were sitting and watching him devour all the food that was left on the table.

Michael pushed his chair back and started gathering dishes. Jennifer stood up to assist. Ragden finished clearing off the last of the food on the table, then also started gathering up dishes and moving them into the kitchen. He stepped around to the sink and started washing the dishes, as Jennifer and Michael brought him the rest.

George stood and stepped over to the other side of the island.

"Thanks for the fine meal, as always, Michael. It was nice to hang out for the weekend." George said.

Michael turned to him and smiled, "Of course, old friend. Any time. We are glad you could make it out to join us."

"Thank you for the invite. We are heading back to pack the house. Next time?"

"Of course."

George and Stacy walked down the stairs, slipping from view. Selina waited until they had left, then came over to the island and sat down, watching as Ragden cleaned the dishes. Her heart was beating hard in her chest. He looked up at her and smiled as he finished what he was doing.

"Have you decided what you are going to do with your break from school?" Ragden asked.

"I... No," she answered shyly, "I was hoping you would stay here with me. You folks did rent the house for the week, right?"

"No. Sorry. We spoke with the owner and only got it for the weekend." Michael said softly, "Besides, Ragden must get back to school tomorrow. Big math test, right?"

"Yeah," Ragden's eyes got big, "I need to study. Great. Not how I wanted to spend my Sunday afternoon."

Selina looked crestfallen. She had hoped she could have more time with Ragden. Her heart ached. Michael came around the island and hugged her. She sank against him, burying her face in his chest. He gently patted her back, comforting her. Ragden finished the dishes and then dried off his hands.

Michael gently rubbed Selina's back. She straightened up and smiled at

him. He kissed her softly on the forehead.

"Thanks," she said softly, then turned and ran over to Ragden, giving him a tight hug. She sobbed softly against him. Ragden hugged her tightly, feeling her body sink against his. He kissed her head softly, whispering to her, "I am sure we will meet again soon. It is okay. You are going to be all right."

She pulled back and looked at him, smiling softly, "Promise you'll come see me?"

Ragden smiled back at her, "As soon as I can find the time. I promise."

She hugged him tightly, her heart swelling. She softly kissed his lips, feeling him respond to her. She could feel his cock starting to harden against her, and her heart beat a little faster; she felt herself growing damp again. She blushed and pulled back, afraid Jennifer and Michael might notice. She smiled shyly, then ran off down the stairs.

Michael chuckled softly, turning to Ragden, "I think you have a new fan."

"Yeah. That is one way of putting it."

Michael laughed. Jennifer came up and hugged Ragden, pulling herself against him. She looked down at his hard cock and laughed. Ragden blushed. Then she looked up at him, her eyes twinkling, "I'd say you were a fan of her too, yes?"

"Yeah, we had fun."

Jennifer let go of Ragden and headed over to the bedroom. Michael walked Ragden down to his room, "Let's get your room cleaned up."

As they entered the room, Michael stopped just inside the doorway. His eyebrows furrowed. He took a deep sniff of the air, then turned to Ragden, his eyes questioning.

"Ragden, why do I smell the Ocean in your room?"

Ragden blushed and looked at the pile of dirty sheets in the corner. Michael took another deep breath through his nose and looked at the corner, then at Ragden.

"Tell me."

"Uh. Oceana. I mean. Mother Ocean."

Michael's eyes got wide, "Oceana?"

"Yeah. That is what she asked me to call her."

"Mother Ocean came to you in the night?"

"Yeah. She... she said she wanted to feel love like one of us. We had sex. It was amazing."

Michael laughed, long and hard. His voice was full of love, sex, and sensual things. Ragden felt his cock throb in response, a shiver running down his spine. He looked at Michael, watching him laugh, and a smile started to spread across his face. Michael walked over, picked up the dirty sheets, sniffed them, laughed, and carried them to the laundry room. Ragden stood in the middle of the room, confused.

As Michael came back into the room, he walked over and started pulling the bed apart. Ragden grabbed the blankets, helping.

"You must have left quite the impression. I have not heard of... Oceana taking a lover in an exceptionally long time. She has used that name before, but I struggle to remember the last time I heard it spoken aloud."

"Am I in trouble?"

"Oh. No. Quite the opposite. I would not be surprised if she left a mark on you, a blessing of some kind. She... tends to do that with mortals she takes a fancy to. I would not be surprised if she comes to you again."

Ragden blushed, remembering his encounter with her. Michael walked over to Ragden, looking at him. He walked around him, examining him. Not seeming to find what he was looking for, Michael frowned.

"Can you remove your shirt, please? If she marked you, it is not in an obvious place."

Ragden removed his shirt, looking down at his chest and stomach, his arms, while Michael walked around behind him looking at his back. Ragden shrugged, not finding anything out of the ordinary, then Ragden noticed something on the inside of his right wrist. He turned it over and showed it to his dad. A tiny fish scale was embedded in the skin. It sparkled in the light, a soft blue color. In the light, it changed color, refracting the light.

"It's beautiful," Ragden said softly, about to run his finger over it. Michael snatched his hand back.

"Careful, Ragden, there is no telling what exactly will happen when you do that. That is a mark from Mother Ocean. Touching it could do... well, I have no idea."

Michael laughed, thought for a moment, then smiled at Ragden, "On second thought, go ahead. Let's see what happens."

"Is it safe? You do not think it would be dangerous?"

Michael laughed, "She is fond of you. I doubt she would give you a gift dangerous to you without telling you what it was. You do not recall it being placed there, I am guessing."

Ragden shook his head. Then licked his finger and gently ran it across the scale. The instant his saliva-slicked finger touched the scale, he felt a surge across his body. The smell of the ocean filled his nostrils; a shiver ran down his back. He felt her presence fill his mind. His eyes rolled back in his head.

In his mind's eye, he drifted in the ocean; gentle waves caressed his skin like lover's hands gently holding him and caressing his skin. He felt her presence all around him. Her hands were on his back, her hands holding his. Her hands caressed his legs and feet. He saw the woman he had seen in his room, walking across the water to him. Her hips swayed seductively. She smiled at him, her eyes sparkling with love and desire.

Her voice was soft, and sultry, sending a shiver of joy down his back, his loins ached, his balls tingled, and his cock throbbed in response, "I see you have found my mark. Any time you are feeling lonely, or in need of me, touch this, and I will be there for you."

She leaned down, took his hand in hers, and pulled him to his feet. He

blinked for a moment, realizing that he was standing on the water, and it felt as firm as any ground. Then she hugged him, leaned into him, pressed her cool flesh against his, and kissed him passionately. His mouth filled with the taste of salt, desire, power and love.

He blinked hard and found himself standing in the bedroom. Michael was watching him with a bemused look on his face. Ragden touched his lips and felt the remnants of salt water there. Michael raised an eyebrow and chuckled softly.

"Not dangerous, I presume."

"No."

Michael smiled, "What did she tell you? I assumed it was a message when your eyes went blank."

"Yeah. She said... touching this would summon her."

Michael's eyes got wide, an astonished look on his face. "Wow. That is unexpected. I have heard of her temporarily granting her lovers powers over water, but never summoning her to them... You must have let QUITE the impression indeed."

Michael laughed again as he turned to walk out of the room. Ragden stood dazed for a moment, considering the implications, then he hurried to follow Michael. Jennifer was coming down the stairs. She stopped when she hit the landing, taking a deep smell. She turned to Michael and looked at him, questioning. Michael pointed a thumb over his shoulder at Ragden. Jennifer giggled and shook her head. Ragden held up his arm, the small scale catching the light. Jennifer hurried over and took a closer look at it.

"Oh Ragden, it is beautiful. What does it do?"

Michael called over his shoulder as he went down the stairs to the lower level, "Nothing special. Just summons her to him."

Jennifer's eyes got wide as saucers; then she hugged Ragden fiercely. She pulled back, looked him in the eyes, and smiled ear to ear.

"That is amazing. Congratulations."

Ragden blushed as Jennifer took his hand and headed after Michael. He felt there was some deeper meaning to all of this but could not figure it out. They walked out the front door and climbed into the car. Once their seat belts were strapped in, Michael started the car, pulling out onto the road to head home.

As they pulled out onto the highway, Ragden leaned forward in his seat, "Dad. Why do I feel like there is more going on here?"

"Well. There is. Your instincts are right. Now that you have met one of the Primal Forces, you will need to meet the other three. Earth makes the most sense for you to seek out next. Mother Ocean is always easy to find, the others... not so much."

"Oh," Ragden said softly. "How is that going to work?"

Jennifer turned in her seat and smiled softly, "I can help you find Mother Earth. I have some ideas of where they might be. I would say you can start

your journey next Friday. Worry about your schooling for now. Until you graduate, you need to continue with your normal studies."

"Graduate? Isn't this more important?"

Michael chuckled from the front seat. Then spoke, "No. You still must find your way in the world. You could use your gifts to make a living, but I would not recommend that. If you use them too blatantly, it can turn against you. Yes, there are ways to do that, but it is important not to lean too heavily on that."

Ragden nodded, "I had not thought of that."

Michael said warmly from the front seat, "You are welcome to live with us until you get it figured out. You still have plenty of time."

"Thanks, Dad."

"Of course."

The rest of the ride was quiet as Ragden pondered over the day and the events of the last 24 hours. So much had happened. So much had changed. He had a lot to think about. He ran his finger over the fish scale on his wrist, feeling the soft ridges of it. The promise it held, the gift. He shook his head. He looked out the window, watching the landscape fly by as they sped down the freeway. Eventually, Ragden fished his math book out of his bag and flipped to the chapter he needed to refresh on for the test on Monday.

CHAPTER 31

Ragden sat in the backseat of the car, reading his math book. He paused occasionally, closed his eyes and worked over the problems in his mind, feeling the numbers and how the equations fit together. As the car slowed, Ragden looked around and realized they were back in town. He stowed his book back in his backpack and watched the neighborhood slip by.

"Is that someone in our driveway?" Michael asked.

"Is that Emily?" Jennifer asked.

Ragden leaned over to the window and saw the young woman sitting in the driveway, her knees pulled to her chest, rocking back and forth. As the car pulled into the driveway, Michael stopped it and Ragden jumped out of the car, running over to her.

Emily sat in the driveway watching the car coming. Her heart thumped heavily in her chest. She felt him growing nearer and knew he was there, unharmed. She knew something had changed and had felt it the previous night. The memory of it was seared into her brain.

***

Emily had been sleeping peacefully when suddenly she was wide awake, staring at the ceiling. It took her a moment to realize why she was awake, but very quickly she sensed something was wrong, terribly wrong. She could not feel Ragden's presence anymore. One moment she could feel his love radiating through her and the next, it was gone; yanked out of her like someone pulled the tablecloth out from under a table crowded with dishes, sending them crashing to the floor. She felt like she was the crystal glasses and dishware shattering.

Tears leaped to her eyes as she cried out into the night, "NOOOooo...."

She threw the blankets from her bed and fell out of it in her mad rush to find him. She crashed heavily to the floor. As her eyes closed at the pain of

hitting the ground, a picture flashed through her mind. Ragden.. in the ocean, the water rising around him, his body slipping under the waves...

She felt like her heart was going to explode. The tears streamed from her eyes as she cried out again. She heard movement in the house as someone called to her, but it was not Ragden. It was not his voice and she did not care who it was, or what they wanted.

Her door crashed open and someone came running to her. Arms wrapped around her, but she tried to push them away. She tried to pull herself to her feet and found someone helping her. She could not see who it was through the tears in her eyes. They tried to pull her back to bed, but she fought them. She pushed, shoved and broke loose. She ran for the doorway, someone in hot pursuit behind her. She ran down the hall, her robe flapping around her as she ran down the stairs towards the front door.

Someone behind her called her name, but she ignored them. She had to go to him. She had to find him. The only thought in her head was of the man she had fallen in love with, whose presence had been omnipresent with her since that Wednesday night but was now gone. She did not know how or why it had happened. She ran down the sidewalk. She heard footsteps behind her, that voice calling out to her.

All she could hear was the pounding of her heart and the pulse in her ears. She had to know. Had to find him. She saw his house, ran down the sidewalk and turned up the way. The plants reached out to her and caressed her bare legs, lovingly, soft and gentle. She ignored them as she ran up and started pounding on the door.

"Ragden!!! RAAAGDEN!! Oh God... Please," She collapsed against the door, slumped to the mat in front of it, her voice breaking and hitching as she sobbed, "Please... God... Ragden."

Warm hands embraced Emily from behind. She tried to shrug them off, but they were insistent, wrapping around her, comforting her. She turned into them, buried her face in the chest of the woman holding her and sobbed uncontrollably. She let herself be pulled to her feet, but when they tried to pull her from the door, she tried to push them off, tried to get back to the door.

Then something changed. She felt warmth in her chest. Like the tide flowing back into a cove, she felt his love filling her again. Her eyes swelled and fresh tears spilled down her cheeks.

"Ragden?" she asked softly. She closed her eyes and let herself be guided as she tried to probe her heart, the place where she always felt him. He was there, but there was something different about the way it felt. There was something else there too. She puzzled over it. She could not feel him the way she had before. It was like there was something in the way. She closed her eyes tightly, tried to reach out to him, tried to feel where he was, what was going on.

She saw him standing in the ocean. The water receded away from him, leaving a clear path up the beach. She watched as he slowly walked up the

beach to where his parents stood. She sighed, her heart swelling with love as she watched the muscles in his back ripple with his movements. She pulled back and felt strong hands guiding her back to her room. She heard comforting words, hands guiding her back to bed, pulling her covers up. None of that mattered. She could feel his presence in her heart and soul. She did not understand how he had disappeared out of her, but he was there now. That was all that mattered.

Emily settled into her bed and felt the warmth and comfort of her blankets, but more importantly, she felt his love and comfort filling her soul. Content, she slipped back into dreamland.

When Emily awoke, the first thing she did was look inward, searching for his presence within her. Her heart swelled with joy when she felt his familiar presence in her soul. His love and warmth spread through her. As she lay in bed, she felt his presence swell within her. She felt his arousal. She giggled, as his arousal made her damp. She reached down and felt her damp mound, her fingers slipping between her wet folds.

She looked inward, following the line to his presence. In her mind's eye, she saw him in bed with a voluptuous dark-haired woman. She watched as he pulled his cock from her pussy and slipped it up her ass, rocking her body with his massive thrusts. She felt the heat on her cheeks, her pulse increasing. She watched as they climaxed together, feeling her own body responding to the intensity of the moment.

She gently fingered herself as she watched him break from her and step into the shower. She sighed with affection as she watched him clean up and then come back into the room. She saw them embrace again. She felt his attraction, his love, his passion, and his desire. She watched as his cock swelled larger than anything she had seen before. She felt her eyes going wide at the sheer size of his manhood.

"Oh, God," she whispered, wondering if she could handle something so large. She watched in fascination as he tried to put it into the woman. The woman's name slipped into her mind: Selina. She smiled to herself; a pretty name for a pretty woman. She watched as Ragden forced his oversized cock into Selina's ass. Emily moaned, watching it. She could almost feel her ass stretching to fit something so large. She slipped a finger into her ass, feeling her tightness, stroking herself as Ragden fucked Selina.

She pulled back to herself. The imagery in her head filled her with arousal and desire. She slipped her other hand down her abdomen and stroked her clitoris as she slipped two fingers into her pussy and stroked herself. She moaned with pleasure as she brought herself to climax. Then she pulled herself out of her bed, slipped her nightgown off, and walked into the shower.

She paused in front of the mirror and looked at herself. She stared at the woman in the mirror. Her hair was full of natural waves and beauty; her eyes sparkled with intensity. Her cheeks were flushed, her lips plump and full. Her breasts were large and perky, her stomach flat, her hips round and full. She

turned and looked at her ass and giggled. Her ass was perfectly round, toned, and jiggled with her movements. She blew herself a kiss.

This was not the body she remembered having just weeks ago, but she was in love with what she saw in the mirror. She stepped into the shower and stood under the hot water. Her mind wandered as she cleaned herself up. Being able to see where Ragden was and to feel his presence was... something new. She felt like she was eavesdropping on him, but she did not suspect that he would mind. She was curious about Selina, but not jealous. She was happy that he had found someone to have fun with, and she was eager to see him later that day. The sex was always amazing, but she just wanted to feel his skin against hers, hear his heart beating against her chest.

She got out of the shower and toweled herself off. The texture of the soft towel against her skin felt wonderful. She cupped her large breasts and marveled at their weight and tenderness in her hands. She looked in the mirror, giggled, and blew herself another kiss; then, she grabbed a brush and brushed her hair. As her hair dried and brushed it out, it started to build its waves and body again. The color was a vibrant red. She had thought it duller once, but now it was shiny and vibrant.

She giggled again, as she walked back into her bedroom. Walking around the house naked was not something her family allowed, but she did not care if they saw her. Once in her room, she shut the door and fished through the new underwear she had gotten with her mom. She picked through the different ones, wondering what she wanted to show Ragden later that day. Finally, she settled on a black lace set that was slightly transparent in all the right places. She fastened the bra on, then looked in her mirror, admiring how it looked over her chest, her nipples visible through the sheer fabric.

She looked down at her pussy, noting the apparent lack of hair. She did not shave there, never had. She had remembered having pubic hair, but now there was only a fine layer of transparent fuzz there. She slipped her fingers through it, feeling its softness. She moaned softly at the feel of it, then slipped the matching pair of panties over her body. Again, she looked in the mirror and giggled at the near-transparent lace over her pussy. It looked solid enough over her labial lips but was translucent over the rest of her. She turned and looked at her ass, giggling as she saw her ass crack.

She grabbed a pair of pants and a T-shirt, then she pulled out a sweatshirt and zipped it up the front over her chest. Again, she turned and looked in the mirror, and admired how incredibly beautiful she looked. Then she headed downstairs to breakfast.

"Darling," her mother called out as she came into the kitchen, "What happened last night? Why did you go running off in the night?"

Emily blushed and looked at the floor. She was not sure how to explain what had happened in a way that would make sense to her mother, "It... I... I had a bad dream."

"That must have been one hell of a dream. Feeling better now, I hope?"

"Oh, yes. Very much so. I am so sorry for last night."

"Okay. Let's just... not do that again, please?"

"Okay."

"Get yourself some breakfast. I have a few things to do today, shopping to get done, and the like. You can come with me if you want or stay home. Your call."

"I will stay home. I have some things I need to do. Thanks."

Emily walked into the kitchen, got a bowl and a spoon out, then found the box of cereal and got some milk out of the refrigerator. She ate casually, her mind drifting as she did. Her mother came by and gave her a gentle hug.

"You look beautiful today. Special occasion?"

"No. Ragden gets home today, and I will probably meet up with him later."

"Well, that is special enough. Have fun then, dear. I will see you later then."

Her mother gathered up her keys and headed out the door. Once she was gone, Emily finished eating, cleaned up her dishes, and put them away. Once she was done with that, she put on her shoes and walked over to Ragden's house. Once there, she sat down in the driveway and waited. She could feel him drawing nearer. She tucked up her knees to her chest and waited.

***

As Ragden jumped out of the car and ran towards her, Emily jumped to her feet and ran to meet him. They collided midway up the driveway, hugging fiercely. Ragden pulled her to the side as Michael pulled the car into the garage. Emily buried her face in his chest, her breath hitching softly. Tears leaked out of her eyes. She looked up at him and felt her heart swell.

Ragden looked down at Emily and felt her warmth against him. He felt complete with her in his arms. He saw the tears on her face and leaned down to kiss them gently from her cheeks. She smiled, then pulled his head down to kiss him fiercely on the lips. She slipped her tongue into his mouth, tasting him. Ragden smiled and pulled back from her, catching his breath.

Emily licked her lips and looked up at him questioningly, "You taste salty, like the ocean."

Ragden chuckled, "I need to explain a few things. Come, let's go inside."

Emily smiled happily and circled his waist with her left arm, walking by his side up the way. Ragden dragged his fingers through the bushes, their leaves curling around his fingers. Emily noticed, watching. Then she reached out as well and felt their soft caress. She smiled up at Ragden as they approached the door.

They heard the locks turn from the inside, and Michael pulled the door open. He smiled down at Emily and offered her his hand. She stepped away from Ragden, and Michael pulled her into the house and hugged her gently.

She gasped softly in surprise, then hugged him back. Ragden smiled as he came through the door and shut it behind him.

"Come, join us in the living room," Michael said softly. Emily looked back at Ragden, a quizzical look in her eyes. He nodded as he followed them. Michael released Emily and sank into the loveseat next to Jennifer, who was already seated. Ragden and Emily sat on the couch across from them.

Emily turned to Ragden, "What happened last night? I couldn't feel you anymore. I thought you died."

Ragden smiled softly, placing an arm around her shoulder, pulling her against him. She rested her head on his chest and heard the solid thumping of his heart against her ear. Her breath hitched as she took a deep, calming breath.

"I very nearly did. It is hard to explain, but that danger is past us now."

"I was scared. I thought I was going to die, then I felt you again."

"I know. I am sorry. I did not mean to scare you like that."

She lifted her head off his chest and kissed him softly on the lips, then smiled at him, "Please don't do that again."

"I'll do my best."

"You better!" She softly, playfully, punched him in the arm. She felt the solidness of the muscles there and looked up at him, "What really did happen?"

Michael leaned forward. Spoke softly, his voice gentle, "That was our fault, sort of. Ragden is not a normal young man. I am not even a man. Not really."

Emily looked from Ragden to Michael, confused. "What are you saying? Are you some kind of Alien?"

Michael laughed softly. Jennifer giggled beside him, patting his shoulder. She looked at Emily and shook her head. "No, silly."

Michael sighed and looked at Jennifer. She shrugged back at him. He turned to Emily and took a deep breath, "This is never easy to explain. The forces of nature, as you think of them, occasionally take human form. I am Love."

Emily giggled. She looked at Ragden and saw the serious look on his face. She furrowed her brows and looked at Jennifer, who smiled back at her and nodded.

"You are joking, right?" Emily said softly.

Ragden gently squeezed her shoulder, pulling her body against his, and shook his head. "It is not a joke."

Michael smiled softly. "This can be hard to grasp, but we have rules among us. The forces of nature, that is. Our children are not permitted to run free without being tested. After their eighteenth birthday, any child of a force of nature must meet the four Prime Forces. Last night, Ragden met Mother Ocean. She tested him, and he passed, or he would not be here with us now."

"It is possible," Michael continued, "That that test interrupted your bond."

"The Ocean?" Emily asked, she looked from Michael to Jennifer, then

Ragden. Ragden nodded.

"That is why I taste like salt water and the ocean. She left a mark on me. Though, that happened later."

Emily raised an eyebrow. Ragden held up his right hand, the light catching the small fish scale on the inside of his wrist. Emily furrowed her brow and brushed her finger across it. Ragden closed his eyes; the sensation of her touching it sent a shiver down his spine. Emily tried to hook a fingernail under the edge but could not find an edge to it. She ran her finger over it again.

"Is that a fish scale?"

"Yes."

"Why is there a fish scale in your wrist?"

"Oceana... Mother Ocean gave it to me."

"Oceana?"

Ragden nodded. "That is what she asked me to call her when she came to me in her physical form."

"She... went to you?"

"Yeah... She wanted to... feel the touch of a man."

Emily giggled, "Are you saying you had sex with... the Ocean?"

Ragden nodded. Emily saw that Ragden was serious and tried to stop giggling.

"What was that like?" Emily asked softly.

Ragden leaned in and kissed Emily softly on the lips, then smiled, "Unreal. She did things with her body that I have a tough time putting into words."

"And what about me? After an experience like that, do you still want... normal women?"

Ragden laughed and pulled her close, then kissed her softly on the lips. He whispered huskily to her, "I'll always want you, love."

Emily blushed and smiled softly, returning his kiss. She leaned back and peered up at him, "Who is Selina?"

Ragden blushed and spoke softly, "How do you know that name?"

This time, Emily blushed, looked down into his lap, and spoke quietly, "I might have... spied on you... through our bond."

Ragden laughed, then kissed her on the forehead.

"You aren't mad?" Emily asked, looking up into his face, seeing the humor there. Ragden shook his head.

"No, of course not. Are you jealous?"

Emily shook her head, "No. But... how did your cock get so big? I have never seen it get that large before."

Ragden shrugged. Jennifer sat forward on the couch, looking at Emily. She licked her lips, "How big was it, Emily? Would you take a guess?"

Ragden turned to look at Jennifer and saw the heat in her gaze. He blushed and felt his loins stirring. Emily giggled softly and looked at Jennifer, "I don't know, at least a foot long, probably two or three inches in diameter."

Jennifer sighed softly; her eyes big. She looked at Ragden, considering for a moment. Then she spoke softly, "Physical changes are not unheard of among the Love-touched or Earth-touched, though that does seem quite dramatic. I would be curious to see what you can do, Ragden."

Emily looked at the intensity on Jennifer's face and giggled. She looked up at Ragden and saw the heat on his face. She saw the growing bulge in his shorts. She reached down and put her hand on it. Ragden moaned softly at her touch, his gaze turning to her. She felt the heat of his gaze and felt her own body growing aroused.

Michael laughed. "If you keep doing that, things are going to get very interesting."

Michael leaned over and kissed Jennifer softly on the lips, one large hand fondling her breast. Jennifer moaned softly into his lips. His other hand slid down between her legs, which she spread, letting him rub across her crotch. Both Emily and Ragden watched her shiver with ecstasy under his touch. Michael drew back and laughed lustily. Jennifer blinked, closed her legs, and giggled, then leaned in and kissed Michael passionately on the lips.

Emily blushed, watching them as she looked down and saw her hand still on Ragden's throbbing cock. She pulled her hand back and looked up to see the heat in Ragden's gaze. She leaned in and kissed him softly. He pulled her against him, his tongue slipping into her mouth. She moaned softly, feeling his passion and desire wash over her. Then he released her, catching his breath. She took a deep breath, feeling her body quaking with desire.

Emily looked up at him again, batted her eyelashes, and asked coyly, "So... who is Selina?"

Ragden laughed, "Family friend I ran into while we were at the beach. I had not seen her in five years."

Emily giggled, "Ran into? You fucked the shit out of her."

Emily covered her mouth and saw Jennifer and Michael chuckling softly. Emily pointed at Ragden, talking to his parents, "Well, he did."

Michael nodded, "I know. I felt the energy throughout the whole house. You would have laughed if you had seen the look on her father's face. The poor man could not decide what to do with himself. That man has issues."

Jennifer giggled, then leaned forward, "Overprotective."

Emily smiled, looked up at Ragden, and licked her lips, "Oh. Got it. He did not want Ragden's big dick to ruin his precious little slut of a daughter?"

Ragden's eyes got wide. Michael and Jennifer laughed. Ragden relaxed as Emily giggled. Jennifer nodded, agreeing, "Something like that, yeah."

Emily smiled and hugged Ragden, then turned and looked over at Michael and Jennifer, "This... nature thing... that's why I can feel him even when you folks are hours and hours away? That's how this bond got formed?"

Michael nodded. "When he nearly killed you that first night, he gave you part of his soul. You two are connected in ways most mortals will never understand. You will always be able to feel the other. Their moods, their

feelings, their pains, their strength. You can see the other if you concentrate on them. See where they are, feel what they are feeling. There are some other benefits as well. Some of which you have already noticed."

Emily looked down at her chest, and giggled, "I wondered how that happened. Not sure how to explain that to my mother."

Michael chuckled, "Don't bother. One other thing you need to know is that he can only make you pregnant if it is something you both agree upon. If that is not something you are TRYING to do, it cannot happen. Something about the way the forces of nature work. I never really understood it myself."

Emily blushed and looked down into her lap, "Right, good to know."

Jennifer smiled and spoke softly, "The same is true for you now, Emily. If you were to sleep with another man, you would never get pregnant, unless that was what you wanted. It is now a conscious decision you must make."

Emily looked up at Ragden and laughed. "I cannot see myself sleeping with another man. I... No," She laughed again.

Ragden smiled at her, placing his hand on hers. "If you wanted to sleep with another man, I would not stop you."

Emily blushed and shook her head, "I don't see that happening, but if it does, we can discuss it."

Ragden smiled at her. Michael grasped Jennifer's hand firmly and squeezed it, then he turned to Emily and smiled, "You took this better than I had expected you to. Welcome to the family. Our home is yours whenever you need it."

Jennifer smiled and stood. "I'll get you a copy of the key."

Emily smiled, then furrowed her brow, "Wait, I have a question... Ragden's bedroom. It did not have a king-sized bed the first night I slept in it. But then it did. Can you explain that?"

Jennifer stopped, turned, and smiled. "Yes. I made it bigger."

Emily gawked at her for a moment. "How?"

Jennifer giggled softly, "I am earth-touched; I can manipulate things made with natural materials. It is part of my gift."

Emily's eyes lit up, "Really? Like what?"

"Well, like changing the size of his bed because it is made from wood. Come, let me show you how I make a new key."

Emily stood and followed Jennifer into the garage. Ragden stood to follow, but Michael gestured for him to sit down. Once the garage door closed, Michael winked at Ragden.

"You picked a winner with that woman," he smiled, "You do still have to meet the other Prime Forces. They are not to be trifled with. Each could just as easily snuff out your life. Treat them with respect and kindness, and you will be fine."

Ragden nodded. His heart beat a little harder with nervousness.

Michael continued, "Next weekend, you will go to meet Earth. I cannot tell you much more than I already have. Jennifer will tell you where to go. She

has a surprising relationship with Earth. Most of her ancestors have passed away and she is probably the oldest earth-touched alive today. As such, she has a closer connection to Earth than anyone else. You would do well to heed her words."

Ragden nodded. Just then, the garage door opened, and Emily came running into the room. In her hands, she held a shiny silver key. She held it out to Ragden. He had never seen a key quite like it before, not that he spent a lot of time checking out his parents' key chains. The key was made of a silvery metal that changed color as the light hit it. The teeth were irregularly shaped. Only the teeth had hard edges; the rest of the metal was smooth, like a river-polished stone.

"Feel it," Emily said giddily pressing it into his hand. The key was warm to the touch. It radiated its own heat. Jennifer smiled casually and kissed Emily on the forehead as she walked past her to settle into the love seat next to Michael. He wrapped an arm around her, pulling her against his side. Jennifer leaned over and rested her head on his chest.

"That is really cool," Ragden said, handing the key back to Emily. With a huge grin on her face, Emily slipped the key into her pocket. She turned to Jennifer and smiled broadly, "Thank you so much. That was amazing."

Jennifer waved her hand dismissively, "Don't worry about it. Nothing to it. Ragden, don't you have a test to study for?"

Ragden's eyes got wide as he remembered. "Yeah... I do."

"Well, go study then." Jennifer said softly, then followed it up sharply with, "And no sex until you finish studying!"

Ragden stood, chuckled, and pulled his backpack up over his shoulder. Emily stood next to him and slipped her arm around his waist. Jennifer looked at Emily and shook a finger at her, "You better not distract him too badly. He needs to pass this test."

Emily giggled, then saluted, "Yes, ma'am."

Jennifer smiled happily and waved them out of the room. As they walked into the foyer, Ragden cast a glance back and saw Jennifer lift herself into Michael's lap, grinding her hips against his crotch. Ragden paused for a moment watching Jennifer's ass grind against him. Then Emily giggled and pushed him up the stairs.

"Perv," Emily whispered, as she giggled at him. "Trying to watch your parents have sex."

"You know... Jennifer wants to have sex with me, too."

"Really? She said that?" Emily rushed past him, put her back against his door, standing in his way. She looked into his face, searching, "You refused her more than once. Wow... Why?"

"She is my mom!"

Emily laughed. Poked him in the chest, "With everything else going on, that seems like a small thing. You totally need to fuck her. Rock her world, big man. She is so beautiful. I bet she is a monster in bed."

Ragden's jaw dropped open. He stared at Emily. Emily giggled and stepped up against him, placing one hand against his groin, feeling his cock throbbing, the other she placed on the back of his neck as she pulled him down to kiss her. Their lips met with a spark of energy. Emily stroked the length of his manhood through his shorts as she kissed him passionately, her tongue dancing with his. She stepped back breathlessly, licking her lips.

Emily grinned wickedly as she opened the door and backed into the room, her eyes on Ragden's, "I would love to watch you fuck her. I bet it would be so goddamn hot."

Ragden blushed darkly. He felt the heat in his cheeks, his cock throbbing in his pants. He wanted to protest, but her insistence crushed the barriers left in his psyche. He nodded to her. She grinned ear-to-ear. Ragden lifted his backpack and shook it. Emily laughed, turned, jogged into the room, and dove onto the bed.

"God, I love your bed," She rolled onto it, throwing out her arms and laid on her back. She craned her head back and looked at Ragden. He laughed, shaking his head as he went to his desk and sat down, his back to the bed. He fished through his backpack and pulled out his math book.

"Ooh. Math." Emily giggled, rolling over onto her chest, kicking her feet in the air, her hands on her chin. Ragden looked over his shoulder and looked down the front of her shirt. His eyes got large, as he saw the black of her bra. She looked down and giggled, then looked at him, smiled and licked her lips.

Emily shook her head, "Nope. No looking until you are done. I will show you everything WHEN you are done." Emily giggled and zipped the front of her sweatshirt to her chin.

Ragden sighed and turned back to his desk. He opened the book and flipped through the pages until he found the right chapter. As he read the material, he could hear Emily humming to herself as she watched him. It was something tuneless, just noise in the background, but it warmed his heart to hear it.

Ragden bent over the pages, pulling out a piece of note paper and writing equations down. He read the chapter and took some more notes, then flipped through the book to the page of the test on that chapter. He wrote down the questions, slipped a bookmark into the page, then worked through them.

Emily rolled over on her back on the bed, relishing the soft comfort of laying in Ragden's bed. She pulled out her phone and sent a message to Sarah, informing her of Ragden's return and well-being. They bounced messages back and forth while Ragden worked through his test. Sarah wanted to come over, but Emily asked if she could wait until dinner time. Sarah grudgingly agreed.

Then Emily flipped through her phone to find Aria's number. She paused. Her relationship with Aria had always been a little strange. They had been best friends once, but once they had gotten into high school, things had not been the same. Aria had been the attractive one. She had used those looks to garner

fame and became the bully everyone feared. Emily had never wanted to be a part of that but had been swept up in it. Once it had started, she could not figure out how to break free.

Until Ragden turned everything on its head. She thought about that day and felt herself growing damp again. It had been so incredible, watching him fuck her in front of everyone. Then she had had her chance, and nothing was ever the same again. She looked at Aria's number again and decided to shoot her a message. Aria responded immediately. Emily let Aria know Ragden had returned, and she wanted to come over as well. Emily pondered that for a minute, then craned her head to look back at Ragden.

"Shall I invite Aria over?" Emily asked.

"Hm?" Ragden responded. He turned in his chair and looked at Emily. "Sure, after dinner."

"Okay," Emily smiled, looked back to her phone, and sent the message to Aria. She agreed.

CHAPTER 32

Emily tucked her phone away and rolled over to the side of the bed, standing up. She sauntered over to Ragden's desk and looked over his shoulder at the test. She watched for a moment, then walked out of his line of sight.

She spoke softly to him, "Looks like you are almost done there."

"Depends on how this test goes..."

Emily smiled to herself, then bit her lip, "How about a little incentive?"

"Hm..." Ragden asked, "How do you mean?"

"For each problem you get right, I'll take off a piece of my clothes..."

Ragden's eyes got wide. He turned and looked at her. She stood demurely, her legs crossed, her hands on the zipper to her sweatshirt. Her eyes twinkled as she shook her hair. The gentle waves of it danced around her shoulders. She looked at him seductively and sucked on one finger; then, she slid it down the zipper of her sweatshirt. Ragden gulped and turned back to his practice test.

As he finished the last problem, Emily walked over and placed her hand on it. She smiled and winked at him. Then pulled the piece of paper off the desk.

"All done?"

Ragden gulped, "Yes."

"Guess I need to check this."

She grabbed his textbook and moved over to the bed. She set the textbook down and opened it to where his bookmark was. Then, she flipped a couple of pages over to find the answer key. She placed his paper down next to it and started comparing the problem with the answers he had written.

She looked at the first problem and saw that he had written the correct answer. She turned and looked at him. She smiled and bit her finger. Then she spoke softly, "First one is right..." Then she reached down and pulled one foot up so she could slip her sock off. She flexed her toes, reached out her

foot towards him, then set it down on the carpet.

She looked back at the test, found the second problem, and checked it against what was in the book. She looked over at him and winked, "This one is right too..." Then she lifted her other foot, slipped her sock off, and set that foot down on the carpet.

Emily turned back to the test, bent over it, and gently shook her ass as she checked the next problem. She looked over at the textbook and grinned. "This one is right too..." She stood up and turned towards Ragden. She gently grabbed the zipper to her sweatshirt and gently pulled it down. Once it hit the bottom, she pulled it open and slipped it off her shoulders. Her tight T-shirt showed the shape of her breasts, the shape of her nipples clearly visible through the thin material. She cupped her chest and blew him a kiss, then turned back to the test.

Out of the corner of her eye, she could see the effect her slow striptease was having on Ragden. His eyes had gotten wide, his cheeks flushed, and she could see the bulge of his cock in his shorts. She giggled to herself as she bent over the test. She gently shook her ass as she looked at the problem and compared it to what was in the textbook.

She turned to Ragden and bit her lip, then smiled and ran her tongue across them, "This one seems to be right too..."

She grabbed the bottom edge of her shirt and lifted it over her head. She held her shirt over her chest for a moment, hiding her bra and chest, then she dropped it to her feet. She watched his reaction as his eyes looked at her incredible chest. Her nipples tightened under his gaze. The lace bra did little to hide her actual chest, just emphasizing her size. Ragden licked his lips, his cock throbbing in his pants. Emily cupped her ample chest and blew him a kiss, then she turned back to the test.

She shook her ass as she looked at his test, found the next problem, and compared it with the textbook answer. She smiled, then stood up straight and turned to face Ragden. "Oh my, I do believe this one is right too..."

While watching Ragden's face, she unbuckled her belt and slipped it through the loops of her pants. She held the belt up and dropped it to the floor at her feet. Then she turned and looked at the test. She counted the number of problems and smiled. Emily looked at the last problem. Then checked it against the book. She smiled and then shook her ass again as she giggled.

She stood up and closed the book, then turned to Ragden and sighed seductively, "This one is right too..."

She slowly unbuttoned the top of her pants and pulled the zipper down, then bent over towards him as she slid the pants down over her hips. She looked at him and licked her lips as she slipped them down over her knees. She lifted one leg out, then lifted the other leg and pulled the pants off her foot. She stood, holding the pants in front of her groin. She slowly ran her tongue along her lips as she let go of her pants, letting them fall to the floor at

her feet. She stood up straight and posed for Ragden, cocking one leg to the side, thrusting her chest and hips out. She watched as Ragden's eyes got big, and his cock bulged in his pants. She giggled to herself as she noticed a small damp spot forming on his pants.

"Do you like what you see?" she asked

Ragden nodded, his heart in his throat. His eyes watched her ample breasts, accentuated by the lace bra. Her nipples were clearly visible. He looked down at the lace panties, their mostly transparent front showing the gentle smooth slope of her mound, but still covering her labial lips.

Emily turned to the bed and picked up the test, set it on top of the book, then picked up both and walked over to the desk. She set both on the desk and then bit her finger as she looked down at Ragden. He looked up at her with a hungry look in his eyes. Her heart fluttered in her chest.

She smiled at him, seeing his hungry look. Ragden stood, running his hands over her lace undergarments. His cock throbbed in his pants at the soft feel of her garments. He leaned forward and kissed her softly on the lips. He could taste her need and desire. He pulled his shirt off and tossed it aside.

Emily took Ragden's hands and stepped back from him, pulling him to his feet. She placed his hands on her chest, shivering in pleasure at the feel of his warm hands on her breasts. She licked her lips as she reached down and cupped his balls through his shorts. She gently ran her hand up the bulge of his cock in his shorts and smiled up at him. She leaned into him and kissed him hard, pushing her tongue into his mouth. She tasted the salt of the ocean on his tongue, the strength of his passion, desire and his love. His powerful, all-encompassing love for her. She moaned into his lips, feeling herself go damp at the powerful emotions rolling off him. As she kissed him, she slipped her hands inside the back of his shorts, cupping his bare ass. She pulled him against her, feeling his body press against hers. She moaned into his mouth in pleasure.

Ragden smiled against her lips, feeling her hands cupping his ass. He reached down and undid the front of his shorts, letting them slide down his legs. He leaned down and ran his tongue over her nipples through the lace bra. He smiled at the feel of the lace against his tongue. He reached down and gently cupped her mound. He looked into her eyes and watched her shiver with pleasure as his hand pressed against her sensitive folds. He could feel her dampness through the material.

"This lingerie is amazing. Please thank your Mom for buying them when you get a chance."

Emily looked down at his throbbing cock and licked her lips. She heard his request, and she nodded absently, "Yes... Of course... I will tell her."

Then she bent down and licked the head of his cock, taking it gently into her mouth. She suckled the tender, soft skin, running her tongue over it as he moaned in pleasure. She dropped to her knees and wrapped her hands around the meat of his cock, pulling it into her mouth, widening her throat and

slipping all of it down her throat. She kept pressing forward until her lips gently brushed against his groin. She bobbed back and forth on his cock, taking it down her throat, then she backed off and took a deep breath, licking the cum and saliva from her lips. She looked up at him and smiled, then stood and kissed him passionately on the lips.

Ragden leaned into Emily, pulling her body against his, feeling the lace of her bra against his bare chest. He reached down and cupped her incredible ass, feeling the sheer fabric in his hands. He lifted her by her ass. Her legs curled around his waist, pulling her firmly against his throbbing cock. He carried her over to the bed and laid her down on the edge of the bed.

Emily lay on the bed. She looked up at him, biting her lip. She smiled and licked her lips, then reached up and slid her hands along his chest to gently grasp his massive throbbing cock in her hands. He moaned softly at her light touch. She grabbed it firmly and stroked it, a bead of precum forming on the tip. She smiled while watching it form, then she guided his hands to her hips.

Ragden gently ran his hands along Emily's waist and slipped them under her panties, then he slid them down her legs. As they slipped off her feet, he lifted them and sniffed them; enjoying the smell of her sex and desire. He dropped them on top of the rest of her clothes. Emily looked up at him and bit her lip as she spread her legs. Ragden knelt between her legs and ran his tongue through her tight, wet folds. He slipped his tongue over her asshole, then through her folds, dipping into her lightly. She moaned loudly as his tongue grazed over her clitoris, then dipped lower and slipped deeper into her, probing her tight, wet depths. She moaned loudly as he stroked in and out of her pussy with his tongue, then he drew back and ran his tongue over her clitoris again. He sucked her clitoris into his mouth and gently ran his teeth over it. His jaw worked slowly as he sucked on her most sensitive bit, gently sucking on it while she moaned in pleasure.

Emily moaned, enjoying his slow, gentle tongue on her body. She clutched at her ample bosom, enjoying the feel of the lace on her skin. Her heart raced, the pressure building up inside her. The waves of pleasure flowed over her body. Then she reached down and took him by the chin and gently lifted his face out of her pussy. She looked him in the eyes and winked, gesturing for him to rise, "That feels incredible love, but I really want to feel you filling me up. I want your body on top of mine... Please."

Ragden smiled down at her as he stood up, his throbbing cock visible. She gasped at the size of it, biting her lip. She reached out and gently ran her fingers down it, then crawled backward on the bed. He crawled up onto the bed with her, sliding his knees under her thighs. He gently pushed the head of his cock through her damp folds, feeling the incredible heat of her tight pussy. She moaned loudly at the contact, her body quivering with anticipation and excitement. He slid the tip of his cock through her folds, slipping down to her asshole. He circled around her asshole, softly pushing against her, then pulled it up through her folds to press against her clit.

He leaned forward against her body and kissed her passionately. She clutched at his body, pulling him down against her. He felt the lace of her bra against his chest and smiled, then reached under her back. She arched her back against him, thrusting her breasts into his chest as he unclasped her bra. He slipped it off her shoulders and pulled it off her, tossing it aside. Her perky nipples were hard and dark in color from her arousal. He leaned in and kissed her again, feeling her bare breasts against his chest.

Emily moaned in pleasure. She looked up at him now that she was completely naked and she smiled. She could remember a time when being naked in front of someone was quite possibly her worst nightmare, but now she reveled in it. She loved her body. The way it felt and the way he reacted to it. Her heart swelled with love and passion. She loved the way his eyes watched her breasts move as she breathed, the way his eyes caressed the flatness of her stomach, the softness of her bald pussy. She reached out and cupped his face, bringing his eyes back level with hers. She kissed him softly, her lips brushing his.

Emily shook her head, "I said I wanted to feel you filling me up, not your cock against my stomach."

Ragden laughed softly, then kissed her passionately as he rocked his hips back. He felt her hands on his cock, guiding it towards her folds. He gently rolled his hips forward, his dick sliding through her folds into her pussy. She moaned against his mouth as it entered her. He felt the heat of her insides across his cock and moaned into her mouth at the sheer pleasure of her around him. He paused, his dick halfway into her. He kissed her again, then he drew back and looked into her eyes. He saw her love, her passion, her comfort, and her pleasure. He shivered softly at how it felt to be inside her. The ecstasy of her soft pussy wrapped around his throbbing cock. He leaned down and kissed her again.

"I love you so much," he whispered, his heart swelling with love for her, "And I love being inside you. Nobody feels quite like this."

Emily's green eyes sparkled, her heart raced, and her body trembled with desire as Ragden's cock entered her slick, hot pussy. She felt his warmth envelop her, his thickness filled her, and she moaned into his mouth, her tongue tangling with his as he paused before thrusting into her fully. She gasped, her hands clutching at his back, her nails biting into his skin ever so slightly, feeling the power and strength that emanated from him.

"I love you too," she whispered. As his cock slid fully into her, Emily felt like the missing part of her soul had finally slipped into place. Her eyes flashed open, and the world took on a crisper feel as if she had been living in a haze until that moment. She looked at Ragden again, seeing his body illuminated with light and energy. She lifted her hand off his back and saw the same light playing across her skin. She felt warmth emanating from the core of her being, suffusing every pore in her body. The love that flowed through her brought tears to her eyes.

"Oh God, Ragden," she moaned in pleasure, "Do you feel that? It feels so incredible... Oh, God."

He smiled down at her as his cock slid fully into her, their groins bumping together, as a wash of pleasure filled his body. He felt their souls connecting, and the world became crisp and clear. He felt her heart beating as if it were his own. Their breath coordinated, their hearts beating as one. He saw the energy radiating through her body. Her skin glowed with a soft blue luminescence. Her beauty was overwhelming. He felt tears slipping from his eyes.

"I feel it," he whispered, as he leaned down and kissed her. As their lips met, he felt a spark of energy pass between them. He felt his tongue in her mouth and hers in his. He felt the sensation from both sides. Every sensation she felt, he felt simultaneously. He felt his heartbeat heavily in his chest, their chest. The pressure and pleasure continued to build without their bodies moving. He moaned into her mouth, as she moaned into his. He gently slid his cock back, halfway out of her, and then slid it back in. The incredible pleasure of it made his eyes water. He looked down and saw tears on her face. Did they come from his eyes or hers? He did not know, nor did he care. He kissed her again, feeling that twinned feeling. His cock thumped against her cervix, and he felt a wave of incredible pleasure wash over them both. Her body shivered and quivered against his, and he realized he was doing the same.

"Oh, God," he moaned into her mouth, as she nodded against him, feeling the same.

Emily moaned in pleasure, feeling an overwhelming sense of peace, passion, desire, and pleasure wash over her. She felt his cock filling her insides and thumping against her cervix. She felt the wave of ecstasy that emanated from that contact to fill her whole body. She still saw the light suffusing his body and hers. It was the most wonderful feeling she had ever felt. She wrapped her arms around him and pulled his body against her. Every place his skin touched hers, she felt that surge of electrical energy. It tickled and played across her skin. She moaned at it, feeling its gentle caress as it filled her with love.

She gently rolled her hips back, sliding her pussy along his length. She watched the pleasure of it roll across his face, then she rolled back against him, gently rocking her cervix onto his cock. The impact sent another incredible wave of pleasure through her body. She could feel her pussy clenching and releasing along the shaft of his cock. She felt her climax building within her. Emily pouted; she did not want this to end so soon. It felt so amazing that she wanted to feel this way forever. She kissed his soft lips, feeling his tongue slip between them to caress her own. She rolled her hips again, feeling him slide with her. Their joined motion caused her heart to beat faster in her chest and her breath to come faster. She looked at him and saw the same effect. She felt his heart beating with hers.

Ragden felt her hips moving and moved with her. Their hips gently

bumping together, his cock pushing against her cervix. Again, that contact was incredible. The waves of pleasure washed over both their bodies. He felt her pussy clenching on his cock, and he felt his balls clench up, tingling with their intensity. He did not want it to end. He gently slid back, feeling her roll her hips away from his at the same time, then they rolled together, their hips meeting, pressing his cock against her cervix with slightly more force. The impact was so full of ecstasy that he almost lost control of his orgasm. He felt her body gently convulsing against his. Her body twitched with her climax almost upon her. He raised an eyebrow, questioning her.

Emily moaned loudly in pleasure, her body vibrating with the force of her impending climax. She felt his cock sliding into her, bumping into her cervix, and her body convulsed. Her muscles twitched, her legs spasmed. She saw the question in his eyes and rolled her hips back faster and slid against him, pressing his cock against her cervix more forcefully.

"Oh, God," She moaned loudly, "Don't stop. Please. Don't stop."

Ragden leaned down and kissed her throat as she craned her head back, exposing her throat to him. He suckled gently on her throat as he slid his cock back, and her hips rolled away from him, then slid back together, his cock thumping solidly against her cervix. The pleasure burst over them. Ragden felt his climax building steadily. He felt her body quivering with desire beneath his. The waves of pleasure spilled over them both. He felt her heart beating to match his, her breath coordinated with his. They moved their hips at the same time, drawing apart and thrusting together. Meeting with a little more force, his cock thumped against her cervix as their hips met, then slid apart, to meet again. Their rhythm increased, the pace more insistent, the impact more forceful. Emily moaned in pleasure as she exhaled with the collision of their groins, his cock thumping against her cervix. She felt her hips vibrating with the impact, her breasts rolling gently. She felt her back arching with each impact, pushing her hips against his with more force.

Emily rolled her hips faster, feeling the intensity of the moment increasing. Their hearts beat faster; their breath became more explosive. Each impact of their hips drove his cock against her cervix. Each thump deep inside her sent another wave of ecstasy crashing through their bodies. Emily found herself moaning with each impact, the volume of her voice rising as their pace increased. His cock was no longer caressing her cervix but thumping into it solidly. Each impact rocked her entire body. She looked down at her glowing body. The light softly emanated from her skin. She felt the love pouring into her from deep inside. Ragden's cock seemed to be filling her with love going directly into the core of her being. Every place their skin touched, she felt his love entering her. She felt her climax building and building, her muscles quivering with the need for release. Her pussy clenched against every roll of his cock into her, releasing as it slid out, then clenching again as it thumped into her. She rolled her hips with his, increasing the intensity of each impact. She could not believe how incredible it felt.

Ragden matched her pace, then increased, feeling her move faster to match him. Their hips parted and slid together, his cock thumping hard against her cervix. She moaned loudly with each impact, the volume increasing as they moved faster. Their joint climaxes, building, and building. The waves of pressure and pleasure were building impossibly stronger with them. Ragden looked down at their softly glowing bodies and wondered about it, but he did not care. Everything felt so amazing. He thrust into her faster, feeling her match his pace. Their hearts beat hard together; their breath exhaled hotly against each other as his cock crashed into her cervix. He felt her pussy clenching harder around his cock, his balls clenching tighter and tighter like a wound spring ready to burst.

Emily's green eyes sparkled; the glowing of her body pulsed with her heart. Her breath exhaled hard at each impact of their groins together, his cock crashing into her cervix. She felt the waves of pleasure hitting that threshold inside her that she could no longer contain. She looked up at his face and saw the strain, the fight to control himself and to push himself further. She tried to reach out to caress his face, but her muscles twitched and convulsed as she felt her climax starting to take hold of her. She fought and tried to take a breath.

"Oh, God. Ragden, I'm going to come. I can't hold it any longer."

Ragden nodded, gritting his teeth as he continued to slide in and out of her. Their hips sliding apart and thrusting together. Each impact of his cock into her cervix brought him closer to climax. He could feel her climax building and building beyond her ability to contain it. He drew back and thrust into her one more time, then his body convulsed, his muscles seized. For a moment, he felt himself go wild. Thrusting against her like a madman, then drawing back and crashing into her cervix repeatedly. His muscles locked up, and he thrust into her, his cock crashing into her cervix as cum exploded out of him into her. His body locked up, his back arching, his legs convulsing.

Emily's green eyes sparkled with delight, her pussy dripping with Ragden's cum and her arousal. She felt her orgasm crash over her. Her body convulsing, quivering, and shuddering against him. She felt her pussy clench on his throbbing cock inside her. She felt his cum erupt into her, and she felt herself cum again at the sensation. She reached out and grabbed Ragden, pulling him down against her. His body convulsed with the force of his orgasm; then he collapsed upon her. His body lay down on hers, his cock buried inside her, throbbing against her cervix. She felt each pulse of his body against hers and felt it reverberating throughout her soul. She felt so magnificently alive. Cherished, desired, and loved. As her orgasm faded, she noticed the glow of her skin started to fade away. She groaned as the crispness of the world around her started to fade as well. She looked at Ragden and saw that he, too, was no longer glowing the same way. She held him tight, feeling his heart thumping heavily against her chest. Emily reached up and guided Ragden's face to hers, kissed him passionately as their tongues danced with

each other. They parted, and he lay upon her, breathing hard while echoing her hard breaths.

"Oh, God," she said softly, "That was amazing."

Ragden smiled down at her, then kissed her neck, her chin, and her lips softly.

"Yes. Yes, it was."

Ragden sat up, his cock still pressed firmly into her. He gently rolled her onto her side. She looked at him questioningly, and he just smiled. She let herself be rolled over onto her side, then Ragden spooned himself around her body and lay down against her back. He slipped an arm around her, pulling her back firmly against his chest. His cock still throbbed inside her. Not losing any size, she could still feel cum pumping out of it into her. She shivered at the sensation. She clutched his arm against her, pulling him against her back firmly. She felt every inch of his chest pressed against her back. Feeling him there was so comforting, so incredible, that her eyes slipped closed, and she lay there savoring the feel of him with her.

Ragden lay his head in her hair, his arms around her, pulling her against him. His cock continued to gently pulse inside her. He felt her heart beating against his chest, and it was the most wonderful feeling in the world. He closed his eyes and savored the feel of her against him. Laying there, he drifted off to sleep.

Emily felt Ragden pressed against her back, his breathing even and slow, his pulse a gentle thump against her. She felt his cock inside her throbbing gently with his pulse, cum still leaking into her. She blinked tears from her eyes. She felt so incredibly wonderful, so content. She closed her eyes, savoring all of the sensations, and drifted off to sleep...

Love & Nature

CHAPTER 33

Ragden found himself walking on a beach, his feet straddling the tide line. The water was cool as it washed across his feet, then receded only to gently come up and wash against him again. The sand was soft and warm under his bare feet. The sun was high overhead and a light breeze blew down the beach into his face, caressing his skin and pushing his hair back. The water was an incredible, translucent blue. He could see rocks and coral just past the tide line through the clear water.

On his right, Emily walked beside him, her hand in his. He turned and looked at her and saw her smiling back at him. As the breeze blew her hair back, she closed her eyes, letting the wind caress her skin. She stood next to him, naked, the sun reflecting off her skin. Ragden looked down and noticed he wore nothing as well. His cock stood at attention, firm, hard and ready for action.

Emily looked over at his cock and giggled softly. She started to reach for it, then stopped as she looked to Ragden's left. Curious, Ragden turned his head and saw Oceana standing next to him in her radiant, naked beauty. Her hand was in his, cool to the touch. Her eyes sparkled in the light as she smiled at him. The fish scales in her arms refracted the light, sparkling. The kelp twisted in her hair and waved gently with the breeze. Her overly large breasts bounced with each soft step she took. She looked down at her body and giggled. Where she should have had feet, her legs disappeared into the water. With each "step" she took, her legs moved like she was walking, but she never broke contact with the water. It flowed up into her with the movements of the tide, then back as the tide drew out. Oceana waved shyly at Emily.

Emily giggled and waved, "You must be Oceana."

Her voice was soft and melodious, "I am. It is such a pleasure to... meet you, Emily."

They stopped walking, and Emily stepped around Ragden to get a better look at Oceana. She stepped up to her, reached out and ran her hand down

Oceana's arm, gently running her fingertips over the fish scales and then grasping her hand. Oceana sighed softly at the touch and smiled. Her pure blue eyes sparkled.

Oceana blushed softly as she looked at Emily, "I'm sorry if I gave you a fright."

Emily frowned, then looked sad, "The part where I could not feel Ragden... That was terrible. Why did you do that?"

Oceana looked at Ragden, then back at Emily. She spoke softly, almost embarrassed, "I had to know how connected you two were. I had to test him. I did not want to cause you grief. I am sorry."

A tear slipped down Emily's cheek. She stepped forward and hugged Oceana, pulling herself tightly against her. Oceana looked at Ragden, surprised, then smiled, wrapping her arms around her. Emily felt Oceana's supple body against hers. At first, she felt like a water balloon, but then her body firmed up against her, feeling increasingly real. Emily breathed in the smell of her; the salty spray, the cool freshness of the ocean. She felt Oceana's overly large breasts pressed against her own and felt herself growing damp with arousal. She pulled back and blushed.

Then Emily looked at Oceana and spoke softly, "Thank you. Thank you for... not killing us, and... letting us be together."

Oceana smiled broadly, squeezing Emily's hand tightly in her own, "Of course, and... thank you for letting me have time with him."

Emily blushed and giggled, "Oh, yes. That is totally okay. But... maybe... can I watch next time?"

Emily felt her arousal increasing as the words slipped from her mouth. Her heart beat hard in her chest at the suggestion. She licked her lips and felt herself growing damp between her legs. Oceana looked at her coyly and smiled, then nodded. Emily took a deep breath, not realizing she had been holding her breath, waiting for an answer. They both looked at Ragden, saw his throbbing cock and laughed.

Ragden stood, watching the two women talk as if he were not there. He smiled at the interaction, happy to see the two of them getting along. As their discussion turned to him, he felt his cock thickening, growing harder and throbbing in response. He blushed darkly as they both turned and looked at him, then at his throbbing cock.

He blinked, and they were sitting at a coffee table, mugs of steaming fluid in their hands. People bustled around them, paying them no heed. They were still naked and comfortable in their nakedness. Then he blinked again, and they were in bed. He was lying on his back, Emily on one side, Oceana on the other. Their hands rested gently on his chest as they whispered to each other over him. He blinked again, and they were back on the beach, the tide line gently brushing across their feet.

A slight expression of surprise passed over Emily's face. Ragden cocked an eye at Oceana, who stood there with one hand in Ragden's and the other on

Emily's shoulder. She looked slightly abashed.

"Sorry," she said softly, "I invaded your dreams and it is starting to fall apart. I must go now, but it was wonderful to meet you Emily and I look forward to... meeting you in the real world. Ragden, beware the other Primals. They are not happy right now. You must seek out Father Earth, and soon."

With that, her form collapsed into the ocean with a splash.

Ragden blinked and opened his eyes, finding himself back in bed, curled around Emily. His cock was still firmly lodged deep in her exquisite pussy. He felt his cock throb inside her and moaned in pleasure. Her pussy clenched on him tightly, and he felt his cock throb even harder. She turned her head and rolled her shoulder so she could look at him.

"Was that... Did you..."

"Yeah, that was a dream, but more than a dream."

Emily blushed, "Was that how she appeared to you?"

Ragden nodded, "Yes."

"Her body is incredible."

"A bit exaggerated, but yes."

Emily giggled, then moaned softly, feeling Ragden's cock throb inside her. She looked down her body, to where his groin was pressed against her ass. She slipped a hand down her abdomen to her groin. She ran her fingers through her pussy and felt where her lips were stretched wide around his cock inside her. She ran her fingers around the base of his cock, feeling the firmness of him. Ragden moaned softly at her touch. His hips bucked softly, pushing against her. She closed her eyes at the sensation and moaned softly.

Ragden gently rolled his hips back from her, sliding most of his cock out of her, then slid it back into her. As he slid forward, Emily rolled her hips back into him, their groins thrusting together, his cock thumping against her cervix. They both exhaled sharply at the impact, a wave of pleasure overcoming them.

Emily looked up at Ragden and smiled, licking her lips. Ragden leaned down and kissed her softly, and then she glanced at the clock on the nightstand. Her eyes got a little bit wider. She looked back at Ragden.

"We slept for hours!"

Ragden leaned against her, looking over at the clock. He shrugged. "It is Sunday, and we finished studying for Math. Why does it matter?"

"Because Sarah is coming over for dinner," Emily exclaimed.

"Oh. Any idea what time she is due to arrive?" Ragden asked her.

"If I had to guess, I'd say we probably have twenty, maybe thirty minutes?" Emily replied.

Ragden smiled at Emily, kissed her softly on the lips, then gently rolled his hips away from hers. As he slid back towards her, she thrust her ass against him, his cock thumping into her solidly. She nodded, her eyes closed, enjoying the wave of pleasure that ran up through her body.

"Plenty of time then," Ragden said softly as he slid his hips back away

from Emily and slid into her again. Their hips met, his cock thumping hard against her cervix. Emily moaned in pleasure, then rolled onto her shoulder so she could thrust her hips against him with more force. Ragden sat up and slid one bent knee along her back, the other along the undersides of her thighs. He placed a hand on her hip and thrust into her solidly, his cock bumping into her cervix.

Emily felt his body pressed against hers, and she moaned softly. She propped herself up on one elbow and looked down her side at Ragden. She watched as he drew his hips back and slid into her with more force. She closed her eyes and rolled her hips against his thrust, feeling his cock slide deep into her and push into her cervix. She moaned at the impact, feeling it resonate deep within her. The waves of pleasure flowed through her body. She felt the pressure building inside her.

Emily looked up at Ragden and bit her lip softly, nodding as he thrust into her. She gasped as his cock thumped into her cervix. This was a new angle, and it hit somewhere slightly different inside her. It felt amazing, feeling his throbbing cock deep inside her. She felt the walls of her pussy clenching along his length, squeezing his cock inside her. She looked at his face and saw his eyes close with the sheer pleasure of her body on his.

Ragden rolled his hips with more force, seeing the look of need and desire on Emily's face. He pulled back and thrust against her harder, feeling her pussy clenching along the length of his cock as it hit her cervix again. She rolled her hips away from him as he pulled back, and then they thrust together once again. The impact caused both to exhale sharply. Emily moaned in pleasure as she rolled her hips away from his. He drew back and thrust into her harder. She matched his movement, and his cock thumped heavily against her cervix.

Emily moaned in pleasure, feeling his cock sliding in and out of her pussy. She felt her body clenching as it slid in and releasing as it slid out. She watched him over her shoulder, the way the muscles in his stomach flexed, his chest as he pulled her against him. She loved watching him. She looked down at his hands on her hips, pulling her against him with each thrust. She continued to roll with him, increasing the intensity of each of his thrusts.

"Harder," she pleaded softly as she rolled her hips against his. She felt the pressure building within her. The waves of pleasure surged across her, building in strength. She felt her heart thumping hard in her chest. She could feel his pulse along his cock as it thrust deep inside her.

Ragden looked down at Emily and saw the look of pleasure on her face. He felt her pulse beating beneath his hands. He heard her request and responded. He smiled as he increased the pace, thrusting more forcefully against her. She matched his pace, driving her hips against him harder, his cock thumping hard against her cervix. Each impact caused the pressure to build inside him. His balls started to tingle and clench with the force of it. He felt her climax building within her, his echoing it.

Emily felt her climax building within her. Her heart raced, her breath rushed in and out of her with each thrust of his massive cock into her cervix. Each thump against her caused her body to vibrate and roll. Her breasts bounced, her thighs shook and her muscles vibrated with the ecstasy of it. She moaned in pleasure, feeling his cock sliding in and out of her faster, more insistently. She matched his movements, rolling her hips to meet his, his cock hitting her harder.

"Yeeesss..." she hissed in pleasure, feeling the pressure building within her. She reached down and placed a hand on her ass, pulling her cheek up, giving him better access to her. His cock hit her harder, rolling her body with more force. She rocked her hips against his movement harder, moaning in pleasure as his cock hit her cervix.

Ragden grabbed her ass firmly, assisting her in her movements against his thrusts, pulling her against him. She moaned in pleasure as his strong hands gripped her soft skin. He pounded his cock against her thrusts, his cock slamming into her cervix deep inside her. Each impact caused another wave of ecstasy to wash over them both. He felt the vibrations going back up his cock, into the core of his being. The pressure was building, his balls clenching with the force of it.

Emily moaned in pleasure, feeling his cock sliding faster in and out of her tight pussy. She felt her body clenching with each thrust and releasing as he pulled back. She rocked her hips with his motion, meeting him halfway, then pulling back and slamming into him again. Their hips clapped together solidly, the sound of it adding to the sensory overload of pleasure. Emily felt the pressure building in her pussy, the waves of that pressure permeating her being, filling her soul with incredible pleasure.

As Ragden started to pull back, Emily placed a hand on his chest. He stopped, only the head of his dick still inside her. Emily took a deep breath, her chest heaving. She gently pushed him back from her. Ragden obliged and withdrew his cock from her. She groaned loudly as it slipped from inside her.

Ragden looked at her questioningly, "Are you okay?"

Emily rolled onto her back and spread her legs around him, "Never better. Just ready to change things up."

She looked down at his large dick, dripping with her arousal over her. She felt each drip as it landed on her groin. She ran her hands over her mound, smearing the moisture across her body, then she brought it up to her lips and licked her fingers clean as she looked up at Ragden. He watched, his eyes burning with desire. She grinned.

Then she reached down and wrapped her hand around his meat. Ragden closed his eyes as she stroked him, coaxing a bead of cum to form on the tip of it. She watched the muscles in his stomach tense and flex. She planted her feet and lifted her groin as she pointed his cock at her. She pulled him forward, placing the head of his cock against her ass.

Ragden inched forward on his knees, pushing the head of his dick into her

ass. He inhaled sharply as the tip of it slipped into her. She slowly lowered her groin to the bed before him, sliding him deeper into her as she did. Ragden moaned loudly as his cock slid deeper into her.

Emily reached up and grabbed his hands, pulled him down on top of her. Ragden smiled as he laid his chest against her. He felt her breasts pressing against his muscular chest. She reached up and pulled his face to hers. A spark of energy passed between them as their lips met. They kissed each other hard, their tongues pushing into each other as their hips slid closer together. His cock slipped deeper into her. She exhaled sharply as her body stretched around his girth.

"Oh, God," she moaned into his mouth, "Fuck my ass... Please."

Ragden laughed, then kissed her. Breaking away, he spoke softly, "Of course, my love."

He slid his hips against her ass, his dick sliding up into her. She exhaled loudly, feeling the heat and pressure filling her. As his groin bumped into her, she felt that completeness again, that crispness of reality. She felt the world becoming sharper around her. Ragden looked down at her and saw the soft glow of her green eyes on his. Her body suffused with light again. He felt the play of energy along the shaft of his cock, pulsing inside her. He felt her energy flowing through her bowels, filling his cock, and flowing back into his body. Ragden moaned in pleasure.

Emily put her hands on his chest and saw the soft glow of her skin. She also saw the soft glow of his. She felt the energy pulsing inside of him, filling her insides. She felt the pressure and pleasure building inside her. Her very soul was filled with his love and passion. She kissed him again, slipping her tongue into his mouth. She could still taste the salt in him, the kiss of the ocean. She felt a spark of energy pass from his mouth into hers. It flowed down her throat into her chest, where it blossomed inside her, filling her chest.

Ragden rolled his hips back, sliding his cock partially out of her. Emily closed her eyes, feeling the heat of him sliding out of her. She rolled her hips away from him, almost sliding his dick out, then they rolled their hips together, and he slid deep into her as his groin bumped into her hips. Emily exhaled sharply, feeling the pressure and heat filling her bowels.

Emily turned her focus inward. She could feel the energy coursing through her body, filling every bit of her awareness. She felt Ragden gently sliding his cock in and out of her bowels. She rocked her hips counter to his movements, sliding her hips against his as he slid into her. Each gentle impact filled her with his power, energy, and love. She felt it filling every bit of who she was.

Each time their hips met, she felt the swell of his power inside her. His love filled her. She felt her heart beating faster in her chest. She could feel his pulse against her, the pulse of his meat inside her as it slid in and out of her. The pace was slow and steady. She felt the pleasure and ecstasy of it filling her.

Ragden closed his eyes, enjoying the feel of Emily under his hands and against his body. He felt her heart as it beat hard in her chest. Ragden gently slid his cock in and out of her, feeling her body tightly squeezing the length of him. He moaned softly as their hips bumped together, thrusting his meat deep into her body. He felt the energy coursing through his body. He felt her energy merging with his, filling him. He felt the pressure building up inside his body; his balls started to tighten with the need to release.

Emily wrapped her legs around his waist, pulling his groin tightly against hers. He thrust once more up into her; their groins pressed firmly together. She moaned softly as she kissed his lips again. She felt another surge of energy pass from his mouth into hers. She felt the sparks of energy coursing over her body. She opened her eyes and saw arcs of energy between their bodies. The room was lit with them. Everywhere their bodies touched, her skin tingled with energy. Everywhere they did not, the energy arced between them. Her entire body felt alive with his energy. Her heart swelled with love. There was so much of it, she felt like she was going to burst.

Ragden continued to roll his hips back and forth, sliding his cock in and out of Emily's ass. He felt her body squeezing the length of his dick. As their lips parted, he opened his eyes and looked down into her beautiful face. Her eyes were squeezed shut as she arched her neck and back, pushing her groin against his. He felt the energy starting to collect in his abdomen. The pressure swelled within him. He felt his balls clenching and swelling with the need to release.

He turned his gaze to look at where their groins were pressed together and saw the energy flickering down their bodies, passing into his body and collecting in his groin. He looked up and found Emily looking at the same place. She moaned in pleasure, but a slightly nervous look passed through her eyes. Emily could feel the energy collecting within him; she could sense the pressure building and knew that once it peaked, it would explode into her. She felt excited and nervous about what that would do to her. Deep within her, she prepared herself to receive it. She took deep, steadying breaths, then she reached up and placed her hands on his face and pulled him down to kiss her.

Ragden smiled in pleasure, the sensual feel of her hands on his face, her lips to his. He pressed against her and slipped his tongue into her mouth. He savored the sweet taste of her. He felt the pressure building within him. He drew his groin back from her until only the head of his dick throbbed in her ass. He waited, feeling his muscles start to tense and clench. Just as the pressure started to become unbearable, he thrust it into her.

As Ragden's groin slammed into Emily's ass, he felt the pressure release. Their lips broke as he cried out, and the built-up energy exploded into her. He felt his orgasm thunder over him as fluid and energy poured into her bowels. Every muscle in Emily's body clenched. Her back arched, thrusting her against his groin, pushing his cock deeper into her. She felt her orgasm release in time to his and felt the fluid pouring through her vagina. She felt the energy

flow up into her body, lighting her nerves on fire.

Sparks of energy burst up along her skin, throwing light around the room. Emily moaned in pleasure, feeling his cock thrust so fully into her bowels. Everything felt complete. Every fiber of her being was suffused with love and desire. She felt the combination of his energy and hers swirling within her. She felt it building in her bowels, filling her stomach, and swelling into her chest. Her heart thundered with the power of it.

Emily opened her eyes and looked up into Ragden's face. She could see the light thrown off her body reflected against his skin. Each beat of her heart increased the pressure building within her. She felt the energy tingling and creeping along her arms and legs as it crawled up into her chest. She moaned in pleasure, feeling it swell and built within her.

Ragden gazed down at Emily, watching the play of light across her skin. He watched as the sparks of energy crawled up her arms and sunk into her chest. The light playing off her chest started to grow brighter as more energy collected inside her. He could feel the pulse of energy coming off her. Emily felt the pressure of the energy in her chest becoming almost unbearable in its intensity. She felt like her chest was about to explode with all the love and energy that had been collected there. She felt it surging through her body, looking for somewhere to go. She closed her eyes and concentrated on pulling it together inside her.

Then she reached up and grabbed Ragden's face and pulled him down to her face to kiss him. Their lips met, and their kiss became fiercely passionate. She felt the energy shift inside her and then pour up through her throat into her mouth and into Ragden.

Ragden's eyes went wide as he felt the energy suddenly pouring into him. His body shuddered and convulsed with the sudden flood. His arms jerked, and his legs twitched, then he pulled his groin back from her and slammed back into her. His pace suddenly frantic, he slammed his throbbing cock in and out of her bowels as hard and fast as he could manage. She released his face and fell back against the bed, gasping for breath as she thrust her hips against his. They threw their bodies against each other, feeling the energy level in the room suddenly increasing dramatically. The air felt charged as the energy coursed down through Ragden's body. For a brief moment, Ragden saw the same incredible light being cast from his body as a roiling ball of energy passed down his abdomen and into his groin.

He thrust into her bowels again, and every muscle in his body seized and strained, trying to push his cock deeper into Emily as his climax exploded into her. The energy slammed through him and back up into her body. Emily cried out as the energy surged up into her. Her body writhed, her hips rocked back from Ragden, sliding her ass almost off his cock, then she arched her back and slammed her groin back against him, smashing his cock up into her bowels. The energy rolled back through her bowels and into Ragden's body. Emily cried out as her climax rode with the energy. Fluid burst from her

pussy, splashing against Ragden's groin.

Ragden's body again went rigid, his back arched, his head thrown back as the energy surged up into him. He shuddered, his body jerked, and his hips slid back as he slammed into her again. More cum and energy exploded out of him up into her bowels. Emily felt the explosion inside of her and cried out again. Ragden went limp and collapsed on top of her as her body twitched and spasmed. She felt the energy roiling inside her. She wrapped her arms and legs around Ragden and squeezed him against her as tightly as she could. She felt the energy spreading down her arms and legs. Everywhere her body touched Ragden, she could feel the energy passing through her skin into him.

Emily turned her head, found Ragden's face and kissed him again, as she felt the energy passing through their skin between them. She could feel a steady flow of it back and forth. This was not orgasmic, or climatic, but a gentle sharing of the very essence of who they were. The lights in the room started to dim as Emily started to catch her breath.

Ragden lay atop Emily, feeling his thundering heart calming. He could feel the energy passing between them. It filled him with joy, love and everything that was her. His heart thundered with the ecstasy of whatever it was that had just happened to them. He smiled and kissed her, slipping his tongue into her mouth and tasting her sweet flavor. He felt his dick still pulsing with energy in her bowels. He could feel her body clenching around his cock, squeezing him. It was the most incredible feeling he had ever felt.

Slowly, Emily started to relax, releasing her tight grasp around Ragden. He lifted his head and looked down into her face and smiled at her. Emily looked up at him and smiled back. He kissed her softly on the lips, feeling the passion burning between them. Their lips parted and their tongues twisted around each other, then they parted and smiled again. Ragden pushed his face against her cheek, kissed her softly on the chin, then her neck and ear.

"I love you," he whispered. She nodded, a tear slipping down her cheek from the sheer joy of the moment.

"I love you too," she whispered back.

Ragden felt his cock starting to soften within her. Emily moaned softly as she felt her bowels clench around his softening member. She could still feel its size, but she did not want it to get smaller just yet. Ragden chuckled softly, then whistled through his teeth as she clenched as tightly on him as she could.

"Do you have to go soft now?" Emily asked quietly.

Ragden sighed, "When is Sarah due to arrive?"

"Oh shit!" Emily exclaimed, "I almost forgot."

Emily closed her eyes and thought about Sarah. She felt the energy inside her stretching and awakening. She felt Ragden's incredible presence in her heart and soul. In her mind's eye, she clasped hands with him, and they turned their gaze to Sarah. They saw her walking up the street and turning onto the walk up to Ragden's house. Emily's eyes flashed open. She looked up at Ragden and saw him smiling down at her.

"Is she..." Emily started to ask.

Ragden finished her sentence, "...almost here. Yes, I think so."

"How..." Emily started again. Ragden shrugged. Emily bit her lip and peered at Ragden. "Does she have a part of your soul as well?"

"No," Ragden answered, "But we have pushed our energy through her, and she has swallowed our essence. If I had to guess, I would say that residue inside her allows us to... feel her presence. We are linked with her, but not as strongly as with each other."

Emily nodded, not entirely understanding the how or the why, but the words had a ring of truth to them that she could not deny. Emily reached up and grasped Ragden's face and pulled him down to kiss her again. Their lips parted, and their tongues danced. She felt her heart swelling with love and affection. Her body responded, her pulse quickening. She felt her desire for his love swelling. The warmth in her chest spread out into her limbs.

Ragden kissed her harder, feeling the passion building between them. He felt her energy spreading through her, and his own responded. He felt his cock starting to harden within her. He moaned in pleasure, as her ass clenched hard on him. They broke the kiss, gasping in pleasure. Ragden smiled down at her as he rocked his hips, sliding his now rock-hard erection back from her ass, then he slid it back into her until his hips bumped into hers. They both moaned in ecstasy, their eyes closing, their bodies wrapped around each other.

Ragden set his forehead against Emily's. He closed his eyes and in his mind's eye, he saw Sarah walking up to the front door of their house. He felt Emily beside him, watching. She giggled as they watched her finger push the doorbell and heard it ring through the house. Their eyes flashed open, and they gazed lovingly at each other.

Ragden pulled back from Emily and lifted his chest off hers. He looked down at her magnificent chest and sighed in pleasure. She smiled at him and licked her lips. Ragden leaned down and kissed her, sensing that was her desire, then pulled back again.

"What are we going to tell her?" Emily asked as she watched Ragden lift his chest off hers. She ached to feel him against her but wanted to see Sarah too. For a moment she considered pulling Ragden back down on top of her and letting her walk in on them entwined. She giggled at the mental image of the look on Sarah's face as she saw Ragden's dick throbbing deep in Emily's ass. However, it would not be the first time she had seen that. She giggled again. So much had changed in such a brief period. She felt the pressure in her bowels, the need for release. She wanted to feel Ragden climaxing in her ass again. She longed for it so badly she could feel the moisture dripping through the delicate folds of her pussy.

Ragden watched the thoughts play across Emily's face. He fought the urge to laugh and won. His dick throbbed inside her. He wanted to finish what he had started. He fought the desire to fuck her ass with every ounce of his being. He smiled, chuckled and then slid back from Emily, sliding his cock

from her ass.

Emily moaned loudly, grabbing Ragden's shoulders and trying to pull him back into her. She did not try hard but put on the show of not wanting him to stop. Ragden chuckled, knowing it was all for show. He heard the voices downstairs. They both heard the door shut and the soft footsteps coming up the stairs. Emily playfully punched Ragden in the shoulder and laughed.

"What are going to tell her?" she asked again. Ragden shrugged. Ragden sat back on his heels, his cock throbbing, wet and dripping with Emily's fluids. Emily looked down at it. She felt her desire surging, her heart beating rapidly. She licked her lips and fought not to dive onto it and suck it down her throat. The urge was so powerful she started to salivate. Ragden looked at her and saw the drool collecting at the corners of her gaping mouth as she panted. He leaned over and kissed her. Emily pulled back, laughing.

Ragden spooned around Emily and pulled the covers up over their naked bodies as they heard Sarah's footsteps outside the door. Just as the covers settled, they heard a soft knock. Ragden reached around Emily and pulled her body against his chest. She sighed, feeling his cock slip between her legs and press against her mound. She slipped a hand down between her legs and pushed him into her lips, feeling his hot meat slide into her. She moaned as his cock slipped deeper and deeper inside her. She gasped as it pressed against her cervix. She felt her body surge with energy, her limbs shaking softly. A soft spasm ran down through her legs. It felt so incredible.

"Come in," Ragden called. His voice was steady and strong, though Emily could hear the hint of his desire in it. She could feel his pulse against her back, the throbbing of his cock deep inside her. She closed her eyes and clenched her vaginal walls on his cock. She heard him gasp as she squeezed him as hard as she could, then she stopped as the door opened.

Sarah stood in the doorway, watching the door slowly swing open. As she spied the scene before her, she started laughing. The floor was strewn with clothes, both Emily's and Ragden's. She spotted the semi-transparent lace bra and underwear and she wanted so much to see Emily wearing it. She wanted to run her hands over, feel her body beneath the sheer fabric. She felt herself grow damp with desire as she pictured Emily and what she wanted to do with her.

Then she looked at the bed and saw Ragden & Emily watching her. The covers were pulled over them, but she could imagine their naked bodies spooned together. She felt her cheeks go hot as she pictured that incredible dick planted somewhere deep inside Emily. Sarah felt her arousal starting to soak through her underwear. She stepped into the room, turned her back to them and closed the door.

Sarah took a deep breath and tried to calm her frantically beating heart, then she pulled her blouse over her head. She unclasped her bra and dropped it to the floor, then unzipped her skirt and let it drop down her legs. She slipped her soaked panties off, then knelt and slipped her socks off. She heard

Emily gasp softly behind her. She smiled as she turned back to them. Sarah bounded across the room and dove under the covers as Emily lifted them for her. Sarah laughed to herself as she saw Emily's naked body.

Sarah snuggled up against Emily, wrapping her arms around her. She pulled herself against her naked body, feeling her large breasts push against her. She kissed Emily on the lips, pressing herself into her. She slipped her tongue into Emily's mouth and marveled at her taste, then she broke off, gasping for breath and looked at Ragden's face over Emily's shoulder. She leaned forward and kissed him just as passionately. She blinked for a moment, tasting the hint of salt and seawater on his tongue, then she broke from that, her heart thundering in her chest. She leaned back so she could see both their faces.

"Oh, God," she exclaimed, "I've missed you both so much."

Sarah slid her hands down Emily's body, feeling the softness of her flat stomach. Emily moaned in pleasure at her touch. Sarah slid her hand down into Emily's groin and felt her pussy lips spread wide around Ragden's throbbing cock. She felt it pulse and throb at her touch. Her eyes went a little wider, and she panted with lust for a moment.

"And I especially missed this!" Sarah wrapped her fingers around the base of Ragden's cock and squeezed it. Ragden's eyes slipped closed for a moment at the feeling of it. Sarah giggled, watching his face, then she snuggled up against Emily's body, pressing herself against her. Emily wrapped her arms around Sarah, pulling her tight against her. Sarah buried her face in the crook of Emily's neck and started to cry.

"Sarah," Ragden asked softly, "What is wrong?"

Ragden reached around Emily to gently pat Sarah, running his hands through her hair. He stroked down her back, then pulled his hand back up to her shoulder and ran it down her back again in soft, soothing movements against her skin. She shuddered, her breath hitching with her soft sobs. Sarah pulled her head back, tears still slipping down her cheeks.

"Where were you!?" She looked Ragden in the eyes and demanded. Her gaze was fierce with anger and desperation. More tears slipped down her cheeks. Her lips trembled as she spoke, "I had a dream... the most horrible dream." Her voice broke, and she sobbed. She blinked her eyes, trying to shake the tears loose as she looked up at Ragden.

"I woke up, and the house was quiet, and I felt... empty. So empty. Like all the joy in the world had been sucked out of it. I lay in bed and cried for no reason that I could fathom. I thought about what you said on Friday, and I could not stop crying. I fell asleep, somehow. When I woke up in the morning, I felt better, but I had this nagging feeling that I was never going to see you again, like the past week had just been a dream, and now I was trapped in this reality without you."

Sarah's voice started to take on strength. Tears still sparkled in her eyes, trickling down her cheeks. Ragden's heart ached for her. Emily felt Ragden's

sadness herself. Neither of them had thought the events of Saturday night would have affected Sarah so strongly.

"This morning was like a terrible dream, until Emily called me. Then I had to come. I had to see you again. I had to know for sure."

Sarah leaned forward and kissed Ragden again. She pressed her lips against his fiercely, forcing her tongue into his mouth. She pushed her tongue into him. He yielded and allowed her passion to ride over him. When she broke from him, he smiled sadly at her.

"I am sorry, Sarah," Ragden spoke softly, his voice even, full of love and compassion. Sarah felt more tears trickling down her face, "I had to do something out of town. I never wanted to hurt you. I am sorry this happened, but I love you, and I am here. It is okay. You are okay. We are okay."

Sarah smiled, then leaned in and kissed his lips again. She nuzzled his face and felt his breath on her cheek, then pulled back and snuggled up against Emily. Sarah's heart soared. She could not be angry with him; she loved him too much and wanted him too much. She leaned down and kissed Emily softly on the lips.

Sarah looked back up at Ragden, "I don't care what happened. You do not need to explain it to me. I do not understand what is going on with me, or my body." She grabbed her breasts and squeezed them fiercely, digging her nails into herself. She gasped at the pain, then licked her chest. She shuddered in pleasure, "I love you both. Please do not leave me. Please."

Ragden smiled at Sarah, "As long as it is within my power, I will always be here for you. I will always love you."

Sarah smiled, content with the answer. She reached up and caressed Ragden's face. She ran her fingers along the line of his jaw. He kissed her fingertips as she pulled her hand back. Sarah felt the sincerity of his words. Her heart swelled with the love she felt from both Emily and Ragden. Never in all her life had she ever dreamed she would end up in a sexual relationship that included Ragden, Emily and Aria, but here she was, and she could not get enough of it. She cupped her breasts again, marveling at their size and beauty. She knew they were changing and could not understand why, but she did not care. As long as she had the love of her three favorite people, everything else was secondary.

Love & Nature

CHAPTER 34

Sarah smiled happily at Ragden and Emily. She felt the heat coming off their bodies. She felt the dampness between her legs. She wanted him inside her so much it hurt. Her insides screamed with the need to get fucked so hard that the entire world melted into an orgasm that would blow her mind. She knew Ragden could do that for her. He had done it before. She wanted it again. Now.

"Can I have a turn with him, please?" Sarah asked Emily. Emily smiled and nodded, tears leaking from her eyes. Sarah and Emily kissed again, more passionately, as Ragden withdrew from Emily. As his cock slipped from her, Emily groaned. Sarah giggled, watching the play of emotions across Emily's face, then crawled over Emily and lay down between Emily and Ragden.

Emily turned to face Sarah, smiling happily at her. She wiped the tears off her face and kissed Sarah softly on the lips. Sarah leaned into Emily, pressing their lips together. She reached out and cupped Emily's breasts, then pulled back and looked down at her chest. She thumbed her nipples, smiling as Emily gasped softly.

"Your breasts are even larger than they were on Friday," Sarah said in awe. "How?"

"That is a long story," Emily whispered as Ragden threw the covers back and crawled over Sarah, his knees spreading her legs, and sliding up under her thighs. Sarah spread her legs even further, closing her eyes as she felt Ragden's rock-hard erection slide up along her groin.

"We can explain later," Ragden said softly as he pressed his hands into the mattress under Sarah's armpits and lowered himself on top of her. He kissed her neck, then moved along her jawline to her ear and kissed her ear.

"Later," Sarah said softly in response. She moaned in pleasure as Ragden kissed along her jaw, then her lips. She licked his lips, and they kissed, Ragden slipping his tongue into her mouth while she reached out and grabbed his cock, pulling it into her pussy.

"Oh God," Sarah sighed in pleasure as his cock slid deeper and deeper into her, eventually pressing against her cervix. She felt that pressure so deep within her and moaned loudly in pleasure. Ragden ground his hips against her, pressing his cock harder against her cervix. She moaned again, squeezing her eyes shut as her body shuddered in ecstasy; then she opened her eyes and looked over at Emily lying next to her.

Emily smiled, watching Sarah get filled by Ragden. She looked at him and saw the pleasure in his eyes. She felt the waves of his love pulsing along his skin, filling the room. She shuddered softly at the caress of his energy across her body. As Sarah looked at her, Emily smiled happily. Sarah reached over and caressed Emily's face. Emily nuzzled her hand, kissing her fingers. Sarah giggled and then pulled Emily to her so she could kiss her again. Ragden sat back on his heels, giving the women room to embrace.

Ragden savored the delicious depths of Sarah's pussy. She was incredibly tight, but so aroused and wet that he easily slid into her. Her body squeezed around him, the walls of her vagina clenching around his length, yet as he drew back and slid into her again, he was able to easily push back into her.

Sarah moaned in pleasure as she felt Ragden's cock sliding in and out of her pussy. His pace was slow and methodical. She wanted it hard and fast, but there was a sensual pleasure in the slow building of pressure inside her that she could not bring herself to stop. Emily continued to kiss her, their tongues slipping past each other and exploring each other's mouths. She could sense Emily's arousal and feel her desire. Sarah felt the waves of pleasure coursing through her body with each gentle thump of Ragden's cock into her cervix. Her body rocked with each impact inside her. She no longer felt the dull ache of it from the week before. Now it was sensual, and she shivered at the exquisite ecstasy of it.

Sarah reached out and slid a hand down Emily's stomach to her groin. She slipped her fingers through the wisps of her pubic hair and slid a finger into her damp folds. Emily moaned into Sarah's mouth as she slipped two fingers into her pussy. Emily gently rocked her hips as Sarah stroked inside her, then Sarah withdrew her fingers. She slipped her hand up to Emily's clitoris and ran her fingers around it. Emily gasped at the sudden pressure.

Ragden continued to slowly slide his throbbing member in and out of Sarah. He watched the way her body rolled with each gentle impact deep inside her. He smiled down at Emily as she gasped and ground her hips against Sarah's hand, then he reached over and cupped her ass with his right hand. He slipped his fingers between her cheeks and cupped her slippery mound, then slipped his fingers through her folds, feeling Sarah's hand on her clitoris. He moved his hand a little higher and applied pressure to her asshole, slipping a finger into her. Emily gasped even louder.

Emily kissed Sarah harder, forcing her tongue deeper into her mouth. Sarah moaned in pleasure, opening her mouth to let her in. Emily felt the pressure on her clitoris and asshole, and her body shuddered with pleasure.

The gentle hands between her legs, applying pressure, filled her with such pleasure. Her body shuddered, and she felt the pressure building inside her.

Ragden continued to slide his big dick in and out of Sarah's tight pussy. Each stroke was a soft caress against her cervix. Her body gently rocked with each impact. Her breasts rolled, and her thighs shook with the gentle impacts. Ragden slipped his finger deeper into Emily's asshole, stroking in and out of her. He watched her body twitch with pleasure. Emily's thighs shook, and her asshole clenched on Ragden's fingers. He slipped his fingers from her ass, then leaned over and gently kissed her ass cheek, grazing his teeth across the firm skin. Emily moaned in pleasure, breaking from her kiss with Sarah to look over her shoulder at Ragden.

The desire and passion that burned in Emily's eyes was palpable. Sarah squeezed Emily's clitoris, slipping her fingers into her pussy and stroking inside her. Emily gasped, her eyes slipping closed as her body shuddered. Emily turned back to Sarah and kissed the other woman passionately, slipping her tongue into her mouth. Sarah withdrew her hand from Emily's wet folds, then grasped Emily by the hips and tried to coax her to sit on her stomach. Emily complied, straddling Sarah's groin, her wet folds dripping down onto Sarah. Sarah giggled, slipped her hand down to her groin, and slid the small pool of fluids around on top of it.

Ragden continued to gently stroke in and out of Sarah's wet folds as he watched the two girls kiss and nip at each other. He placed his hands on Emily's waist and ran his thumbs across her ass. Emily broke from Sarah and looked over her shoulder at Ragden.

Emily raised her ass towards Ragden and spoke huskily, "Kiss me."

Sarah turned Emily's face back to her and kissed her. Ragden chuckled, then leaned down and kissed one ass-cheek, then the other. He nipped his teeth across her perfect ass, then leaned between her cheeks and ran his tongue through her folds. Emily shuddered at the feeling as Ragden slipped his tongue inside her pussy.

Ragden continued to slide his thick meat in and out of Sarah's tight pussy. Her body rocked gently with each impact of him against her cervix. Her body shuddered, and her muscles clenched around the big dick inside her. She panted against Emily's mouth as she tried to kiss her, feeling the waves of pleasure starting to roll over her. Sarah felt the pressure building within her. She had always wanted to get fucked, but the sheer pleasure and ecstasy of the slow pace Ragden now set blew her mind. She felt her climax slowly building within her. She felt the waves of love coming off Ragden and Emily pouring through her. Sarah reached up and cupped Emily's incredible breasts, gently pinching her firm nipples. Emily sighed in pleasure.

Sarah looked down at her chest, then up at Emily's. Her mind reeled. Emily had always been the least endowed of the three of them. Aria had sprouted breasts before any of them and then Sarah had grown a pair, but never quite as large. Emily had always been the one who wore clothes that hid

the fact that her breasts were the smallest of the three. Not now. Emily's breasts were easily larger than Aria's or Sarah's. Sarah did not care how it had happened. It made her so happy to see Emily getting everything she had always wanted. Most of all, she was happy to see her with Ragden, and overjoyed that she was able to be included in that.

Emily kissed Sarah, parting her lips and pushing her tongue forcefully into her mouth. Sarah moaned against her as her body gently rocked to each thrust from Ragden. She felt his lips on her pussy, his tongue delving into her while Sarah held her breasts, pinching her nipples. The assault on her body drove her wild. Her body shook with the pleasure of it. She felt her climax building, her body shuddering and twitching with it. She placed her hands on Sarah's ample chest, squeezing her breasts, feeling the rocking of Ragden against her body. She broke her lips from Sarah's and gasped as Ragden ran his tongue around her clitoris, sucking on it, pulling it into his mouth. She looked down at Sarah and saw the ecstasy written across her face.

Ragden continued to gently pump his manhood in and out of Sarah's deliciously tight pussy. He could feel her body shuddering with pleasure. Her tight walls started to clench around his big dick. He closed his eyes and could feel her barriers starting to slip, her control breaking down. He could sense her climax building steadily within her. The waves of pleasure flowed over her like the incoming tide; gentle, slow, unstoppable.

Ragden opened his eyes and grabbed Emily's hips. He spread her cheeks wider as she gasped, then buried his face in her pussy. He stroked his tongue across her clitoris, then slipped it deep into her vagina, stroking and licking at her wet walls. He could feel her sharp gasp as her body twitched and spasmed in ecstasy. He could feel her climax fast approaching. Her body was on edge from all the stimulation.

He closed his eyes again and reached down into the core of his being. The dark cloud of reckless abandon surged forward, seeking to claim him, but he swatted it aside like a gnat, sending it screaming into the depths. Then he found the energy that filled the core of who he was. He focused on it, summoning its power and intensity. He felt his heart start to pound harder in his chest. His skin started to tingle as he pulled it to the surface. He felt the sharp change in the air of the room, and the air became thick with it.

Emily gasped, feeling the sudden change in the room. She felt the change coming from Ragden and gasped again, as her skin started to tingle. She felt goosebumps break out across her skin. She sensed his intent and smiled to herself as she kissed Sarah even more passionately. She wrapped her arms around Sarah's chest, pulling their breasts together as she kissed her hard, pushing her tongue deep into Sarah's mouth. Sarah gasped, moaned, and tried to pull back, but had nowhere to go. Emily bucked her hips against Ragden's face, felt the intensity increase, and her body started to shudder. She felt the muscles in her legs and arms starting to twitch. She felt her core swelling, her climax ready to burst over her. She tried to hold it off, to wait for Ragden's

queue. She hoped she was ready for what was to come.

Sarah felt the intensity of the room changing. She could feel Ragden doing something, her skin tingling with the power of it. The air in the room was thick and hard to breathe. Emily had her tongue so far down her throat that she could not pull away. She felt Emily exploring every bit of her mouth, and for a moment, she was afraid the other woman would suffocate her with her love. She felt the urge to fight or flee. She felt trapped between them and struggled for a moment, then felt the love and passion emanating from the two of them. She felt the gentle pressure of Ragden's magnificent dick still sliding in and out of her. The pleasure of it felt so incredible that her body surrendered to it. Emily was down her throat while Ragden filled her pussy.

Sarah started to buck her hips against Ragden's strokes, her hips bumping into his, driving his cock harder against her cervix. Each impact sent waves of pleasure through her body. She felt the pressure escalating so fast within her. She wanted to scream for him to go faster, to hit her with that intensity of action that blew her mind. She opened her mouth, and Emily just pushed deeper into her. Sarah's eyes went wide as she realized she had to wait for them. She was at their mercy. Her body shuddered and twitched. She felt the power in the air, like the hand of a lover, caressing her skin so softly. She wanted to brush it off, but at the same time, there was something so incredibly sensual about the gentle feel of it. She did not want gentleness, though. She desperately wanted the roughness, the power, and the domination that Ragden could give her.

Ragden continued his slow, methodical pace as he felt the energy surging to the surface of his being. He felt the thickness in the air, the charge crawling his skin. He found himself struggling to maintain the slow pace he had set. His body twitched with the desire for release. He felt the swelling in his groin, the pressure building, and his balls starting to clench with the power he had summoned. He felt his pace starting to increase; he could not stop himself. Ragden leaned forward and ran his tongue through Emily's tight folds and felt a spark of energy leap from her to him. He shuddered, and his pace increased. His hips thumped against Sarah's harder. He drew back and took a deep breath. He grabbed Sarah's thighs, held her steady, and started to thrust into her harder. Each stroke was a little harder than the last.

Emily twitched and shuddered. She had felt the spark of energy leap from her folds to Ragden, and her eyes went wide. Her body rocked with the increased intensity of Ragden thrusting into Sarah. Emily felt Sarah's body rolling beneath her, and she squeezed her tighter. Her breasts rocked with each movement. Emily broke her lips from Sarah's mouth, and they both gasped as Ragden started to pound his cock into Sarah harder. Emily watched Sarah's eyes roll back into her head as the sensations consumed her. As Sarah arched her neck and back, thrusting her hips against Ragden's groin, Emily leaned down and latched her mouth onto Sarah's throat. Sarah moaned in pleasure.

Sarah felt the tender brush of Emily's lips and teeth across her neck. Between her legs, she felt the rhythmic pounding of Ragden's big dick into her body. Each time his hips pushed against her thighs, his dick pounded into her cervix. Gone was the soft caress. This was closer to the intensity she craved. She knew he could go harder, and she wanted to scream for it. She could feel the pressure building within her. The tease of what she could have was just out of her grasp. She felt the change in the room, the thickness of the air. She could feel the energy emanating off Ragden's body, filling her vagina, her womb, her entire body. She also felt an echo of the same energy coming from Emily. Sarah knew something had changed between Emily and Ragden. She had been between them before, but it had never been this intense.

Ragden felt the energy coursing through his body. He could feel it reaching out to Emily. Their connection caused it to shift and pulse. He could feel it welling up and trying to go to her. He could also feel her energy responding and starting to reach out to him. Ragden continued to pound his hips against Sarah's legs. His throbbing cock slammed against her cervix with each stroke. Her whole body shuddered and shook with each impact. He could feel her climax building, her body aching for that incredible release. Ragden could also feel something within the core of her start to shift and grow, responding to the buildup of energy.

Emily smiled as she felt the change in rhythm of Ragden's movements. Her body shuddered, feeling Sarah twitching beneath her. She could feel the swell of energy inside Ragden. She closed her eyes as she suckled on Sarah's neck, feeling the prickle of energy across her skin. Emily felt the pressure building within her, the need for release. Her heart thundered in her chest in anticipation of what was to come. Her body was ready, and her need for release swelled with the energy and power she felt. She rocked her hips and body in time to Ragden's thrusts. She could feel Sarah's heart slamming against her ribcage. She knew how badly Sarah needed the release. She could feel her desperation clawing its way out of her.

Ragden felt the energy swelling inside him. The blood thundered in his ears as his heart hammered in his chest. He closed his eyes as he slammed his groin against Sarah. As he drew back, he felt the energy shift and pulse within him. His loins clenched, and every muscle in his body tingled, then he thrust forward, and everything clenched. His cock smashed into her cervix, and with that impact, the energy released, exploding into Sarah. She cried out as the energy rode into her body, filling her. Ragden felt his muscles twitch and spasm with the force of it. His climax exploded, an incredible load of cum bursting up into Sarah. She cried out again as it filled her.

Sarah spasmed, her muscles twitching uncontrollably as the energy rolled through her body. She felt her insides filling with Ragden's seed, and her climax exploded. Her fluids filled her pussy and flowed over Ragden. Every fiber of her being felt like it was on fire. Love and passion rode over her entire existence. She felt Ragden's passion and love filling her. She felt it blossoming

inside her, filling her in ways she had never experienced. Her muscles thrashed with the ecstasy of it.

Emily felt Ragden's release into Sarah. She clenched to her, feeling his energy flow into her body. She pulled back from Sarah's neck and clamped her mouth over Sarah's. She kissed her, thrusting her tongue into Sarah's mouth. Sarah tried to pull back, but Emily pulled her head against her. She felt Ragden's energy inside Sarah, roiling and churning within her. Emily felt the energy inside her responding, pulling that power in Sarah towards her. Without knowing how she did it, she pulled that energy from Sarah, sucking it into her body.

Sarah gasped, feeling that incredible energy in her body swelling up into her chest, and then into her throat as it flowed into Emily. As it left her, Emily finally released her head, and she fell back. Sarah felt weak, drained as if Emily had drained her very life force. She gasped and moaned in pleasure but ached to feel that energy in her again. She felt her muscles go slack as she collapsed against the bed. She felt Ragden's dick filling her insides, the fluids of their joint climax filling her insides and slipping from her. She felt like she had died and gone to Heaven.

Emily felt an incredible surge of power and energy as she pulled it into her. Emily's muscles twitched and spasmed as she pulled it into her core. The energy within her welcomed it and joined with it. It swirled and combined inside her, filling her with such incredible ecstasy. Her muscles twitched and spasmed as she felt it crawling over her skin. She felt that energy moving into her core. She thrust her hips back and found Ragden had lowered his face to her folds again. She ground her hips against his face and felt that surge of energy go flow out of her.

Ragden kissed Emily's silken folds, sensing what was to come. As his tongue slipped into her, she thrust herself against his face. As his tongue went deep into her, she climaxed, and the energy surged into him. He felt it ride down his throat and into his body. His muscles clenched, as he felt that power filling him again. It flowed down into him, and he slid his cock back from Sarah as the energy went down into his loins, filling him with the need to release. He thrust forward into her, and the energy exploded out of him into Sarah again. He felt himself climax again, another load of cum bursting up into her.

Sarah felt the energy riding up into her again, and she cried out. She suddenly felt incredibly alive again. The muscles in her body surged with strength, love, and passion. She wrapped her arms around Emily and pulled her mouth down onto her. As their lips met, Sarah felt the energy in her body surge forward through her again and into Emily. This time, as it left her, she did not feel weak and drained but invigorated. She felt as if something had been left behind inside her. A heat that filled the core of her. She felt a blossom of something opening inside her, filling her.

Emily felt the surge of energy pass from Sarah's mouth down into her. She

smiled and pulled back from Sarah, feeling that incredible warmth filling her being again. She moaned in pleasure as her muscles shuddered and twitched with the feel of it filling her. She felt it churning within her, combining with the core of who she was. She felt her arousal deepening, her need for release swelling within her. She looked over her shoulder and bit her lip as she looked at Ragden.

Ragden met Emily's gaze and saw the heat in her eyes. He chuckled to himself, knowing what she wanted. He placed his hands on Sarah's hips, squeezed her gently, and held her in place as he slid his massive cock from her soft folds. Sarah moaned loudly in disappointment, a soft curse on her lips as she looked up at him. He blew her a kiss, then placed the head of his cock against Emily's dripping-wet pussy.

Emily moaned loudly, feeling the heat and pressure at her entrance. She could not wait any longer, and she thrust her hips backward as Ragden slid into her. She felt his incredible size and heat filling her. His cock thrust hard against her cervix, and her body convulsed. She felt herself climax immediately. She cried out as the energy suddenly rushed out of her and into him. Her body twitched and spasmed as she collapsed on Sarah, her head resting on the other woman's shoulder.

Ragden groaned loudly, feeling the rush of her fluid over him as the energy rode into him again. His body twitched and spasmed. He thrust hard into her multiple times, feeling her twitch and spasm with each impact into that deepest part of her. He pulled back, his cock slipping from her folds, dripping with her fluids, then pressed his cock into Sarah, easily sliding deep into her.

"Oh God!" Sarah exclaimed as Ragden's cock slammed up into her cervix. Her whole body shuddered once more as the energy rode up into her again. Ragden climaxed again, filling her pussy with his thick seed. She felt like her vagina was going to burst from the pressure, as it flowed back over him, soaking the bed. She felt the energy roar over her again. Her pulse thundered in her ears. Emily squeezed her tightly and kissed her hard on the lips. Sarah felt a surge of energy from Emily as well, washing over her. The two waves crashed together inside her, as she felt a tumultuous whirling, which then slowed and started to settle.

Emily released Sarah and rolled over to one side of her, curling along her, cupping her breasts, and kissing her shoulder. Ragden lay down on top of her, pressing the length of his body against her. Ragden pressed his lips against her, his tongue invading her mouth. Sarah moaned in pleasure. The feel of his body against hers was pure ecstasy. She had never felt so loved and cherished. She wrapped her arms around him and pulled him against her as tightly as she could.

Ragden gently pulled back, then leaned over and kissed Emily tenderly on the lips. He lingered against her, savoring her. Sarah smiled at the tenderness of it, then Ragden turned back to Sarah and softly kissed her on the lips again. He turned his head and kissed her chin, her neck, then her shoulder. He

rested his head on her left shoulder, as Emily rested on her right. They lay there for several minutes, basking in the afterglow of their incredible climax.

Sarah thought about what she had just experienced. She felt different. Something profound had shifted inside her. She felt his energy within her. She felt the hardness of his cock in her pussy, throbbing gently with his pulse. It pressed against her cervix, gently filling her with heat and love. This had been what she had craved so desperately, and she felt tears welling in her eyes at the joy of it.

Then she giggled. She thought about that massive meat in her, and she had the undeniable urge to taste it. She wanted to feel that texture on her tongue. She wanted to taste the flavor of Emily on him and the sweet taste of her sex mixed with his. She felt so full of him and loved every moment of it, but the urge to suck on that fat cock was overwhelming her.

Sarah turned to Ragden, kissed his jaw softly, then whispered in his ear, "Can I suck your big dick?"

Emily giggled, listening to Sarah. Ragden chuckled, then kissed Sarah softly on the lips before answering her, "Of course."

Ragden raised himself off Sarah, who moaned as he pulled back. She had asked, and been granted her wish, but she still wanted to feel him against her. That desire in her burned brighter. Ragden sat back on his heels and slowly withdrew from her. She felt him sliding from her and moaned even louder. She had not realized just how stretched she had been. She felt so empty as his cock slipped free. For a moment, she lay there gasping. Then she remembered what she wanted and sat up. She scrambled forward and almost dove into his cock.

Ragden blinked hard as Sarah fell onto him. Emily continued to giggle as she watched Sarah ram her face into Ragden's groin. Sarah felt her body twitching with desire as his cock slipped down her throat. She relaxed and sucked on it as hard as she could. She felt fresh cum slipping into her mouth, and the flavor of it made her twitch even harder. She pulled her mouth back, sliding the meat of his cock back into her mouth. She grasped the thick shaft with both hands and squeezed and stroked as hard as she could.

Ragden gasped at her fierceness, feeling his cock throb in her hands. He felt the sudden pressure building within him, his loins aching again. She swirled her tongue around the head of his cock, then sucked as hard as she could while stroking up and down his cock, while squeezing. Ragden loudly moaned. His body shuddered as another climax exploded out of him. Sarah greedily sucked it down her throat, feeling her skin tingling, her muscles twitching, her own body nearing climax again. She clamped her legs together, and her thighs began quaking as she stroked him harder, feeling another welling within under her grasp.

Ragden gasped again as he climaxed again, even harder. Sarah released his cock from her hands and drove her head down his shaft. Her lips kissed his groin as his seed exploded down her throat. She bobbed and sucked,

swallowing everything he had to give her. Then she backed off and grabbed his cock again, holding it steady in her mouth as she licked and sucked on the tip, stroking and squeezing every bit of cum she could from it.

Sarah felt her body climax as another burst of his cum exploded in her mouth. She shuddered and twitched, forcing herself to stay focused as her body writhed on the bed. She kept her lips locked on his cock so that she would not spill a drop as more cum oozed from him.

When she felt satisfied, she gently released his softening cock and pulled her legs under her, kneeling before him. She kept her hands on his cock as she leaned forward and kissed him softly on the lips. Ragden moaned in pleasure and kissed her fiercely, his cock softening, but still large in her hands. She continued to hold him in her hands, her fingers slipping over the soft skin, cupping his balls in her hands. She leaned back, broke the tender kiss and smiled. She licked her lips.

"Thank you," she whispered.

Ragden chuckled again and nodded, "You are welcome."

Then he collapsed onto the bed between Emily and Sarah. Sarah lay down along his side, curling against him. Her head rested on his shoulder. Feeling her body against his, she felt at peace. One hand was still on his cock, feeling the size and heat of it in her hands. Emily curled along his other side as she also rested her head on his other shoulder. One of her hands rested on his chest, the other slipped down between his legs and wrapped around his manhood, gently clasping Sarah's hand as well.

Emily and Sarah looked at each other and giggled. Ragden slipped his arms around both women, gently cradling them against him. He took a deep breath and let it out slowly, then he looked at the clock and let out a bark of a laugh.

"I am sure dinner will be on the table very soon. We may want to head down." Ragden said. Emily nodded, and Sarah giggled to herself.

"Shower?" Ragden asked as he sat up. Emily smiled and nodded, sitting up and kissing Ragden's shoulder softly. Sarah giggled as she also sat up.

"Can't we just go down like this?" She said, batting her eyelashes as she ran her fingers down Ragden's cock.

Ragden laughed, then cupped her chin and brought her face up to his. He kissed her softly on the lips, then said, "I'm sure we could, though I doubt we would spend much time eating the meal prepared."

Sarah giggled and nodded. She pouted slightly as Ragden moved past her and got off the bed. He stood and stretched, then turned back to the two women. Sarah beamed as she took his hand and stood. Emily followed. Ragden pulled both women against him, hugging them tightly, then disentangled himself and moved towards the door. Sarah and Emily each held a hand, walking with him as he got to the door. Emily grasped the handle, pulled the door open, and led the way across the hall into the bathroom.

CHAPTER 35

Once in the bathroom, Emily opened the shower door. She reached in and turned on the water, then stepped back and closed the door while she waited for the water to heat up. Sarah watched Emily, hungrily licking her lips as she watched the other woman's ass jiggle with each step, then she turned to Ragden. She looked up at him as she cupped his balls and kissed his lips softly. He sighed in pleasure and their kiss deepened, their tongues twisting around each other. Sarah released his balls and slipped her arms around him, pulling her body against his. She felt the pulse of his heart in his chest against her breasts as she squeezed herself against him.

Ragden slipped his hands down her back and grasped her ass, pulling her against him. She moaned into him as his fingers squeezed her ass. Her heart rate accelerated as she felt his manhood growing hard against her belly. As she pulled her lips back from his, she saw that hungry look in his eyes. A thrill ran down her back and she felt her arousal growing. That tight spot between her legs grew damp. She felt something deep within her awakening and she shivered in pleasure.

Sarah heard the water running behind her and turned to look. Emily felt Ragden's arousal growing and felt herself going damp in response. She turned and saw Sarah pressed against Ragden. She felt his energy awakening within her. She sighed in pleasure as she felt the energy uncoiling inside her, stretching like a cat, getting ready to pounce. Emily licked her lips and stepped closer to Sarah.

Emily kissed Sarah on the shoulder as she slipped her hand between Sarah's cheeks and slipped her fingers into her wet folds. A shiver ran down Emily's back as she felt how damp Sarah was. She slipped two fingers through her folds and up into her. Sarah moaned in pleasure, pressing herself more firmly against Ragden. Ragden kissed her passionately, his tongue slipping into her mouth. Emily slid her fingers deeper into Sarah, feeling her tight pussy contract on her hand. Emily grinned and kissed Sarah on the neck as she slid

her fingers out of her. Sarah moaned into Ragden's mouth.

Ragden spread Sarah's cheeks as Emily slipped a finger into Sarah's asshole. Sarah moaned into Ragden's mouth and thrust her ass against Emily's hand, pushing her fingers deeper into her. Sarah's muscles twitched and shuddered in pleasure as she felt Emily's fingers sliding into her tight hole. Emily suckled on Sarah's neck as she gently finger-fucked Sarah's ass. Sarah moaned and spasmed against Ragden, thrusting her ass against Emily's hand.

Sarah broke from Ragden's mouth, gasping for breath. She felt his cock throbbing against her stomach, Emily's fingers in her ass. Her body shuddered with pleasure. She turned and put her back against Ragden's chest, his cock sliding between her ass cheeks. Emily's fingers slipped from her ass and she groaned. It felt so good to have Emily's fingers inside her, but she wanted something bigger. Emily stepped back, giving Sarah room to turn. Sarah twerked her ass against Ragden's cock, feeling the thick meat of it between her cheeks.

Emily leaned in and kissed Sarah passionately on the mouth. Sarah moaned into Emily's mouth, as her tongue slipped into her. Emily placed one hand on Sarah's mound, her fingers slipping through Sarah's dripping pussy. Sarah took a step forward against Emily, pushing their bodies together. Sarah reached back and grasped Ragden's big dick and pulled it against her asshole. Sarah moaned loudly as she felt the hot pressure against her ass. Her body quaked, her knees shook, and her thighs trembled with desire.

Ragden placed one hand on his cock and guided it into Sarah's ass. The head of his cock pressed hard against her, the tip starting to slip in. Sarah shuddered as Emily withdrew her fingers from Sarah's pussy and slipped her hand down to Ragden's cock. She spread the fluids from Sarah's pussy along the length of his shaft. Ragden moaned softly, then pressed more firmly against Sarah's ass. Sarah gasped, her mouth dropping open as she panted.

"Oh fuck!" Sarah exclaimed as his cock slid deeper into her bowels. She thrust her ass back against him, feeling his hips press against hers. She felt the enormity of him filling her. She closed her eyes, craning her neck as she arched her back and pressed her ass against him as hard as she could. She felt the length of his cock throbbing inside her. She could feel every pulse of his heart along the shaft of his cock as she pressed her ass against his groin. That slow steady beat inside her and against her back was in stark contrast to the frantic beat in her chest.

Emily felt herself going damp with arousal as she watched Sarah writhe in pleasure. Emily leaned forward and cupped Sarah's breasts as she kissed her on the lips. Sarah's tongue darted into Emily's mouth as she moaned in pleasure. Emily squeezed Sarah's breasts as she broke from the kiss and licked her lips. Sarah's eyes were wide in shock as she panted, then Ragden drew himself back from her and thrust into her. Sarah's legs shook and she staggered forward at the force of the impact. Her eyes watered and she panted as she looked over her shoulder at Ragden.

Sarah's mind reeled. Her world exploded with color and vibrance. She could feel every texture of Emily's fingers on her chest. The pressure around her nipples caused her heart to skip a beat. She felt the heat in her chest blossoming and flooding through her being. Every cell of her being was filled with love and compassion. She felt Ragden's incredible manhood filling her body. Her ass burned at the invasion. Her tight sphincter of muscles stretched so wide around him. She had had him in her like this before, but this time felt different. It felt like the first time. He was so large, and her body felt stretched to its limits to allow that invasion of her most private parts. The parts that were never designed to allow something so large in.

Yet, at the same time, she felt her body welcoming it. He was a familiar lover. This was the same giant cock in her ass. It burned. There was pain. Her ass hurt, but there was pleasure. The likes of which she had dreamed of. Feeling him inside her, filling her, was the most exquisite thing she had ever experienced. She felt that blossom in her heart opening, welcoming him into her. She felt his love and passion flowing up into her. His cock in her ass was the doorway for his energy to pour into her.

Ragden gently gripped Sarah's hips, holding her steady while he slid his cock back from her ass, then slid it back up into her. He sighed in pleasure as her silky insides squeezed tight around his throbbing manhood. He held her steady as he slid his hips up against her ass cheeks, his cock going deep into her bowels. She thrust back against him, pushing him deeper into her, sucking air into her lungs sharply as the pressure and pleasure washed over them.

Ragden felt the energy inside himself awakening again. It spread from deep in his chest down into his abdomen, filling his groin with heat. A tingling sensation ran across his skin as the power filled him. He looked over Sarah's shoulder as she craned her head back to rest against his chest. Emily stood there, her eyes filled with need and desire. Emily licked her lips as she locked eyes with Ragden. Emily stepped forward, slipping her hand between Sarah's legs, running her fingers through her dripping folds to caress Ragden's balls. Emily leaned forward and kissed Ragden on the lips. Sarah panted, her breath coming in gasps, as her heart thundered in her chest. Emily and Ragden thrust their tongues together, their passion and love crashing over the three of them. Ragden ground his hips against Sarah's ass, his cock pushing a hair deeper into her. Sarah reached back and grabbed Ragden by the ass, pulling him against her, trying to get more of him inside her.

As Emily broke the kiss from Ragden, she felt his heat, strength, love and passion flowing over Sarah and to her. She felt like she stood before a thunderstorm, from which Sarah was only partially blocking her exposure. Emily leaned down and kissed Sarah's breast, gently pulling the nipple into her mouth and suckling it as she slipped her right hand back from Ragden's balls and into Sarah's dripping pussy. She slipped two fingers through Sarah's wet folds, sliding them up into her. Sarah gasped as Emily gently pushed deeper into her. Emily smiled and kissed Sarah's other nipple as she felt the pressure

of Ragden's big dick through the wall of Sarah's vagina. Emily could feel his pulse through Sarah's walls. She gently pushed against his cock, relishing the small noises the two of them made at the change in pressure. Emily stood up straight, slipping her fingers from inside Sarah. She placed her left hand on Sarah's cheek and guided her face to her. She kissed her softly, then brought her hand up to Sarah's lips and moistened them with her fluids.

"Taste," Emily said softly. Sarah's eyes flashed open and she sucked Emily's fingers into her mouth, greedily sucking hard on them. Emily smiled and started to pull back. Sarah grabbed Emily's arm and kept her hand in her mouth. When Sarah was sure that Emily would not withdraw her hand, she released Emily's arm and grabbed her ample bosom. Emily's eyes closed as Sarah cupped her breasts and thumbed her nipples, then slipped her hand down Emily's flat stomach and into her groin. Emily moaned softly as Sarah slipped a finger into her.

Ragden moved his hands up to Sarah's breasts, cupped them, and pulled her back against his chest. He gently stroked in and out of her ass as he kissed her on the shoulder. Sarah moaned in pleasure. She withdrew her hands from Emily's wet pussy and clamped them over Ragden's hands on her chest, squeezing her chest tighter. She relished in the pressure in her chest as his dick filled her ass. She felt his presence filling her body and soul. Her eyes rolled and her mind reeled.

Ragden looked at Emily and smiled. She met his eyes and leaned against Sarah, pressing her breasts against hers as she kissed Ragden on the lips. Both Sarah and Ragden reached out to Emily, pulling her body against Sarah. Sarah moaned in pleasure, as she felt pressed between the two of them. Ragden's dick throbbed inside her, and she sucked in air at the feeling of it. Emily broke the kiss and licked her lips, then she turned and thrust her ass into Sarah's groin. Sarah slapped her ass playfully as Emily rubbed her ass against her. Sarah reached down and slipped her hand between Emily's ass cheeks, two fingers slipping through her wet folds, while another finger pushed into her asshole. Emily craned her neck and thrust her ass backward into Sarah, sliding her fingers up into her. Emily moaned in pleasure as Sarah fucked both her holes with her hand.

Emily stood up straight and stepped forward off Sarah's hand. Sarah giggled playfully, then gasped again as Ragden withdrew and thrust hard up into her again. Sarah staggered forward another step, then thrust her ass back against Ragden's big dick. Emily took Sarah's hand and pulled her forward as she opened the shower and stepped in. Sarah giggled as she stepped forward, Ragden's dick sliding from her ass. She stopped for a moment, halfway through the doorway into the shower and turned and looked at Ragden. His dick throbbed in the air, her fluids running down its length. She saw the hungry look in his eyes and felt the powerful urge to suck that magnificent cock. She started to step towards him when Emily pulled her into the shower.

Emily stepped into the water and turned her face into the water. She let it

cascade through her hair, down her back. She leaned back and let the water run down over her bosom. It ran over her stomach and trickled between her legs. Sarah stood in awe of her beauty, watching the water rinse her; then Emily turned to Sarah and smiled. The spell was broken, and Sarah stepped forward and wrapped her arms around her, pulling her body against the other woman. Sarah stepped in front of Emily, letting the water hit her in the back and shoulder, washing down over her. She stood there for a moment, enjoying the sensation of the water beating on her skin.

Sarah closed her eyes and savored the moment; then she felt the ache between her legs, in her ass, and her bowels. She opened her eyes and looked towards where Ragden stood watching them. His dick stood at attention: large, firm, and throbbing in anticipation. She looked at that amazing piece of meat and started drooling. She wanted to taste it and feel it with her tongue. She wanted to feel the pressure in her throat as she deep-throated him and sucked every bit of him down she could. Her ass ached from being penetrated by him. It had hurt so good. Her body quaked and shivered at the memory of it.

Sarah looked Ragden in the eyes and mouthed the words, "Fuck my ass. Please."

Emily watched the play of emotions across Sarah's face. She giggled to herself, watching Sarah drool as she gazed at Ragden hungrily. When she saw Sarah talking without making any noise, she reached out to Ragden and gestured for him to join them.

Ragden smiled and stepped towards the shower. Emily leaned back against the wall as she grabbed a bar of soap, built up a lather, and started cleaning herself. As soon as Ragden was within reach, Sarah dropped to her knees in front of him, grasped his cock, and slipped it into her mouth. Ragden moaned in pleasure as she sucked hard on his cock. She swirled her tongue around the tip, then leaned forward and kissed his groin, his cock going all the way down her throat. Ragden put his hands out to the wall to steady himself as the pleasure consumed him. Sarah grasped his ass cheeks, pulling him deeper into her as she bobbed her head up and down on his cock.

Sarah felt his cock throbbing in her throat. This was one thing she could never get enough of. She felt her pussy dripping with her arousal as she continued to bob up and down on his cock. Her body shuddered and the room started to go grey from lack of oxygen. The feeling of him so deep down in her throat, filling her with his manhood, passion and love, was almost more than she could bear. Finally, as she was almost afraid she would black out, she backed off his cock and let it slip from her lips. She collapsed on the floor of the shower, gasping for air. Her body shuddered and quivered in ecstasy. She weakly reached out and grasped his cock, feeling the life and power throbbing in it. She smiled as she tried to catch her breath.

Ragden and Emily knelt around her, letting the water cascade over them. Ragden took one of her hands in his and gently slipped his other hand under

her arm. Emily took her other hand as they lifted her back to her feet. Sarah smiled and giggled as her legs wobbled beneath her.

"Thanks," she sighed once she was back on her feet, one hand on the wall to brace herself. Ragden placed a hand on her hip to steady her, while Emily did the same on the other side.

"Are you okay?" Ragden asked softly. Sarah nodded, feeling her strength return. The concern in Ragden's voice warmed her heart. She felt his love filling her entire being and she ached to hold him in her arms, to press herself against him. She staggered forward and he caught her. She wrapped her arms around him and buried her face in his chest. Hot tears slipped down her cheeks.

"Please," she begged, looking up at him, blinking the tears from her eyes, "Please love me. Love me like the world is dying. Love me like we are the last people in the world."

"Of course, my love," Ragden replied softly.

Sarah turned to Emily. She reached out to her and pulled her against them. Then she turned back to Ragden and blinked at him.

"Fill me," she pleaded softly, her voice cracking as more tears slipped down her cheeks, "Fill my ass with your big dick. Fill my bowels with your seed and your love. Fill us both with everything you have. I never want to be separated from you again. I want to feel you inside me for all time..."

Ragden leaned into her and kissed her lips, interrupting her. Sarah wrapped her arms around him and pulled herself against him. She pressed every bit of her flesh to his body as she could. She felt the steady, strong beat of his heart against her chest. The rock-hard throbbing of his dick against her abdomen. Then she felt Emily pressing against her back. Emily's arms circled them. Emily kissed her cheek, brushing the tears away. She felt their love, passion, and their energy surrounding her. Sarah felt cherished and loved. She sighed in pleasure, but it was not enough. She needed something more that she could not explain.

Emily placed a hand on Ragden's shoulder. He broke the kiss from Sarah and looked at Emily. Sarah sobbed and buried her face in Ragden's chest. Emily kissed Ragden softly on the lips. She pulled back and smiled at him, then nodded.

Emily placed a hand on Sarah's shoulder and turned the woman to face her. She moved her hand to her face and cupped her cheek. She leaned in and kissed her softly on the lips.

"Sarah," Emily said softly, tenderly, "We cannot give you the connection Ragden and I have. It is too dangerous..."

Sarah sobbed harder, fresh tears streaming down her face. She was crestfallen. She saw the look of love on Emily's face and saw the other women had more to say. She tried to catch her breath and looked at Emily.

"There is something else we can give you, though," Emily smiled tenderly as Sarah looked up into her eyes. The pleading look on Sarah's face nearly

broke Emily's heart, "You already have a connection to Ragden. We can try to strengthen that. If you would like?"

Sarah turned to look at Ragden. He nodded to her and kissed her softly on the lips. Their kiss deepened, their lips parting, their tongues dancing. Sarah pulled herself against his body. When they broke, her breath hitched, but she smiled at him. Emily smiled happily, then stepped back to rinse the soap from her body.

Emily grabbed the shampoo and worked it into her hair. Ragden watched her for a moment, then turned back to Sarah. He looked her in the eyes and smiled. She smiled timidly back, then blushed under his hungry gaze. He kissed her again, softly, then pulled back.

"We have already started down this path," he said, "Emily and I have shared some of our energy, love, whatever you want to call it. We felt you coming to the house. You felt the events that took place last night. We can strengthen that. I will need to consult with my father, but I know we can do it."

Sarah nodded vigorously. She remembered what that night had felt like; the loss, the agony, the despair. There had been more, though. The way she had felt when she had woken up this morning and the things she had felt as she had gotten closer to the house. She had felt something. It had been faint, but there. She opened her eyes and looked at Ragden. He smiled at her and nodded.

"Yes," she said huskily, "Please. I want that... I want that connection. I want to feel you with me always..."

Ragden kissed her again, interrupting her words. She melted into his embrace. His arms wrapped around her, grasping her by the ass, pulling her body against his. Her legs became weak and her knees trembled. He held her against him easily as her knees bent and her feet came off the ground.

Emily giggled and slapped Sarah on the ass playfully. Sarah put her feet down and Ragden released her. Sarah looked at Emily and giggled. Emily leaned in and kissed Sarah softly on the lips. Sarah turned to Emily and wrapped her arms around her, pulling their bodies together. Ragden left a hand on Sarah's hip, wondering if he would need to steady her. As the two girls squeezed against each other, his dick throbbed. He felt Emily's sexual energy pulse to life. He responded to it. The air in the room became thick with energy.

As Sarah continued to kiss Emily, thrusting her tongue into the other woman's mouth, Emily reached around behind her and grasped her ass cheeks firmly. Ragden stepped up to her, his hands on his cock, angling it between her cheeks. Sarah moaned loudly as she broke her lips from Emily's mouth. Her head turned to the side, to see Ragden stepping up against her. She bent over slightly, leaning into Emily as he put the head of his cock against her asshole.

"Oh God," Sarah moaned, "Fuck my ass."

Ragden smiled as he pushed the head of his cock against her. Sarah squeezed her eyes shut as she felt the heat and pressure against her tight hole. She tried to relax herself. She wanted him in her so badly she ached. Her heart thundered in her chest. She could feel the fluids dripping from her pussy. Emily held her hands tightly as Sarah took a deep breath, trying to relax her muscles. She pushed her ass back against Ragden as he held her hips and pushed against her. Sarah groaned as the pressure started to cross that border between pleasure and pain.

Sarah panted as she eased herself forward, away from Ragden. She felt hot tears in her eyes. Her body burned with the desire to feel him in her, but her body had denied her. She looked up at Emily, as the shower rinsed the tears from her face. Emily knelt and kissed her lips softly, tenderly. Sarah basked in the love and compassion she felt coming from her.

Ragden placed one hand on Sarah's back, gently caressing the soft skin and reassuring her. With his other hand, he guided the head of his cock into her dripping-wet lips. Sarah gasped and inhaled sharply, as Ragden's big dick slipped into her wet pussy. Her eyes went wide as she gazed into Emily's face. Emily smiled and kissed Sarah more passionately as Ragden's throbbing meat slid deeper into her. Sarah moaned in pleasure as she felt her pussy being stretched open. She felt him throbbing inside her and her body quivered and shuddered at the ecstasy of it.

Sarah groaned loudly, as Ragden started to withdraw from her. She felt him slipping out, the walls of her pussy collapsing on the space he had occupied. Emily drew back from her, and Sarah looked at her pleadingly. Emily smiled reassuringly and put a finger to Sarah's lips.

Ragden slid his dripping wet cock up to Sarah's ass and slid it around her tight hole. Sarah felt fresh tears trickling from her eyes as she felt his cock teasing her ass. Her body shuddered in anticipation. She looked at Emily, pleading for her help in some way. Emily smiled and kissed her again, softly, her lips parting and her tongue slipping into her mouth. Sarah moaned in pleasure.

Ragden continued to slide the head of his cock around Sarah's asshole, gently applying more pressure with each circle he made. Sarah moaned loudly as she felt the pressure increasing against her backside. She took deep breaths, trying to relax herself and calm her frantically beating heart. Emily leaned into Sarah, kissing her shoulder, and reaching down to gently grasp her butt cheeks. Emily pulled on Sarah's ass, pulling her cheeks apart, spreading her open. Ragden slipped the head of his cock into Sarah's ass.

Sarah gasped loudly as she felt Emily release her ass cheeks and lean back from her. She mouthed the words 'thank you,' to Emily. Emily smiled back at her and kissed her softly on the lips. Sarah melted into the tenderness of Emily's lips. The softness of the kiss at sharp contrast to the pressure and heat of Ragden's big dick slowly sliding deeper into her ass.

Ragden held Sarah's hips gently, his fingers kneading her supple skin as he

pulled her back against him. His dick continued to gently slide deeper into her. He marveled at how tight she felt around him. Her body quivered and quaked with pleasure. He could feel her pulse pounding against his hands and around his dick.

Emily broke her kiss with Sarah and looked over Sarah's shoulder at Ragden. Their eyes met for a moment and Emily smiled beatifically. Ragden felt his heart soar as he witnessed that smile. Emily stood, cupping Sarah's breasts as she did. Sarah pulled herself upright, feeling the shifting of Ragden's immensity in her bowels as she did. She looked over her shoulder and saw that he was still not fully inside her. As she saw the length of him protruding from her ass, she shivered. Sarah turned back to Emily and cupped her breasts, thumbing her sublime nipples. Emily smiled and closed her eyes.

Emily turned her focus inward and found that part of herself that was so intimately connected to Ragden. She felt the energy stirring within her, reaching out to him. That bond they shared started to come alive. The energy within her reached out for Ragden, filling every pore of her being. Her skin felt alive, every drop of water a symphony of feeling. She felt the texture of Sarah's fingertips on her nipples. She squeezed Sarah's chest, feeling the energy roll down her arms.

Ragden watched Emily reach into herself and summon her connection to him. He felt his body responding. The energy within him uncoiled itself and came alive. It filled his abdomen. The warmth of pleasure and love slowly spread out his arms and down his legs. He felt it collecting in his groin, filling his balls. Ragden's cock throbbed with the intensity of it.

He partially withdrew his cock from Sarah's ass, then slowly slid it back in. He felt her body clenching around his thick member, her ass squeezing him tightly. Sarah moaned in pleasure. She felt his cock throbbing inside her. Each pulse of his heart down the length of his cock caused her body to shudder with pleasure. As he slowly stroked in and out of Sarah, he felt the energy building within him.

Sarah pushed against Emily's chest, thrusting her ass against Ragden's groin. She moved counter to his movements, causing his dick to slam into her bowels with more force. He immediately matched her pace, moving with her movements, matching her intensity. She gasped as she felt him match her. Each stroke shook her whole body. Emily pushed against her chest, squeezing her nipples. Sarah panted, trying to catch her breath, feeling her climax building within her. The pressure and pleasure threatened to overwhelm her.

"Harder!" she gasped as she thrust herself against Ragden. She clenched her teeth, feeling his cock riding up into her bowels with each stroke. It was not enough. She wanted more. She wanted to feel his seed filling her bowels. She felt her body clenching against him, the size of him stretching her out. She felt tears in her eyes from the sheer pleasure of it.

Sarah opened her eyes and gazed into Emily's face. Emily smiled and kissed her passionately. Emily felt the intensity of Ragden's thrusts, shaking

Sarah's body beneath her hands. Through her bond, she could feel the tightness of Sarah's body clenched around Ragden's throbbing meat. Emily felt herself responding to that sensation. Her climax was suddenly building, and her need for release started to become more than she could handle.

Then Emily felt the tickle of energy coursing over her skin. It crawled over her chest and down her arms. She opened her eyes and saw the soft blue sparks trickling along her skin. She looked over and saw the same thing happening on Ragden's arms and legs. She felt the energy starting to pulse with the intensity of their encroaching orgasms. Emily looked at Ragden's face and saw that his eyes were starting to glow softly.

Ragden felt the intensity of the room increasing. He felt the tickle of the sparks of energy crawling up his legs. As they encroached upon his groin, they sank into his flesh, and he felt the pressure in his balls increasing. He thrust harder into Sarah. He squeezed her hips harder, pulling her against him with renewed force. She pushed against Emily, then thrust herself against him harder than before. Ragden felt his cock riding up into her bowels in deep, powerful strokes. Her ass squeezed tightly around his cock. He inhaled sharply and started to move even faster. He felt the energy coiling up in his balls like a spring, winding tighter and tighter. His climax built with each thrust into her.

Ragden felt the urgency of his climax as it pushed past the point of his control. He thrust like a madman as it suddenly broke loose. He thrust into her one more time, pulling her against him as hard as he could. She pushed back against him, sliding his cock as deep into her bowels as was possible. All three of them climaxed at the same moment. Sarah cried out. Emily gasped. The energy suddenly released from its dams and exploded into Sarah.

Emily felt the energy that had coiled up within her suddenly coursing down her arms into Sarah's chest. She moaned loudly as she felt her fluids gushing down her legs. Her knees became weak and she stumbled back against the wall of the shower. She kept her grip on Sarah and used her hips to push herself back into a standing position.

Ragden felt cum exploding out of him and filling Sarah's bowels in a torrent. The energy rode over him, flowing from him into Sarah. He felt it riding up his legs, through his abdomen, and pouring into Sarah. She was like an empty vessel that Emily and he poured their energy into.

Sarah felt the energy coursing into her from two fronts. Her orgasm exploded over her and she clenched her eyes shut as the sensation of it overwhelmed her beyond anything she could believe. Her legs folded underneath her. She would have fallen, but Ragden held her hips in place and Emily's hands on her chest kept her upright. Her body twitched and thrashed as fluid gushed down her legs. She felt Ragden's seed filling her bowels and something else filling the core of her being. She felt the energy flowing into her chest from Emily's hands and riding up into her bowels was more energy from Ragden. The two collided in her core, filling her with passion, life, and

love. It swirled within her like a maelstrom, then flowed out to fill every pore of her being. She kept her eyes closed as she felt it riding over and through her.

Emily leaned against Sarah, pushing her body against Ragden's. Ragden held Sarah steady as Emily pushed them together. Emily leaned over Sarah's shoulder and pushed her lips against Ragden's. Ragden returned her kiss, their lips parting, their tongues intertwining. Ragden felt the energy in him stirring again. It swirled within him and surged up through his chest into Emily's waiting mouth. He felt her suck it down, gaining strength.

Emily felt the energy filling her up. She felt her legs become steady, her strength returning rapidly. She stood up straight and wrapped her arms around Sarah, pulling their bodies tightly together. Ragden leaned against Sarah's back, still holding her hips firmly against his. He kissed Emily again, tenderly and lovingly. As she pulled back and their lips parted, she smiled and licked her lips. She turned to Sarah, who was held up and panting hard, trying to catch her breath. Emily closed her eyes and could sense the swirling maelstrom of power and energy within Sarah. She giggled softly to herself, then caressed Sarah's face tenderly. Sarah leaned into her hand as Emily kissed her softly on the lips.

Sarah slowly opened her eyes. She saw Emily looking at her. Sarah still felt the swirling maelstrom within her. She took a deep breath and felt her body still quaking with the aftershocks of her orgasm. She could still feel Ragden's throbbing cock in her bowels. It felt like heaven. She had died, and this was heaven. She smiled serenely to herself, savoring all the sensations of her body. She felt so full of passion, love, and the giant dick in her bowels. She put her feet on the ground and felt Ragden's grip on her hips loosen. Sarah stood on trembling legs but was able to support her weight. She leaned her back against Ragden's firm chest and felt the beat of his heart against her. She turned her head to the side and kissed her jaw softly.

"Thanks," Sarah whispered, her throat still raw from her scream earlier. She giggled to herself, remembering the passion that had created that scream. Ragden slid one hand up along her side, then crept across her chest to gently grasp one breast as he turned into her face and kissed her softly on the lips.

Sarah moaned in pleasure, feeling his heart beat a little harder against her back. She felt his cock throb inside her and her breath caught in her throat. Everything inside her swirled a little faster at that sensation. She felt her heart racing again. She placed a hand on top of his and took another deep breath, trying to find some sense of calm in all the chaos inside of her. Emily leaned in and gently kissed her cheek. Sarah felt Emily's breasts brush against hers.

Emily spoke softly, "We need food."

As Sarah heard the words, she felt her stomach rumble loudly. Ragden's echoed hers. His deep chuckle shook her body. Sarah nodded and turned to look at Emily. Emily smiled sadly and nodded to her.

"You cannot go downstairs like that... You need to finish cleaning up,"

Emily said, a hint of sadness in her voice.

Sarah took another deep breath and nodded, "I know. I just... I..."

Emily kissed Sarah on the lips, interrupting her. Emily's tongue slipped into Sarah's mouth, and Sarah moaned in response. Emily broke contact and stepped back into the water, letting it cascade over her face and run down her incredible chest, "I know. There will be time for that later."

Sarah pouted and took a deep sigh. Ragden slid his hands back down Sarah's sides to grip her hips gently as he slid himself out of her. Sarah felt every inch of his throbbing cock sliding out of her, and she cried out at the feeling. Her body shook, her legs trembled, and her knees went weak. Sarah's legs almost folded under her, and she would have fallen if not for Ragden's strong hands holding her in place. The withdrawal of his cock left her body aching for more. She started to turn to him, but Emily grabbed her arms and pulled her into the water. Sarah staggered forward and leaned heavily against Emily.

Ragden stood for a moment, watching as Sarah trembled in Emily's arms, then he stepped up next to them and let the water course over his body. He grabbed a bar of soap and worked up a lather in his hands, then cleaned himself. When he came down to his groin, he worked the soap over his stiff shaft, then rinsed himself clean. As the water rinsed the last of the soap from his body, he looked over at Sarah and Emily and saw them still holding each other. Sarah rested her head on Emily's shoulder. Emily held her tenderly.

Sarah felt Ragden's presence near her. She continued to rest her head on Emily's shoulder, letting her body calm. She could still feel the energy roiling within her. She longed to feel his touch again but was afraid she would not be able to stop herself if she started. She had so much of him inside her already; she was not sure she could take any more. She wanted it, though. She opened her eyes and watched him clean himself. She saw his stiff cock, the water running down its length. She could feel herself salivating and licked her lips.

Emily leaned against the wall, cradling Sarah in her arms. She could feel the other woman's desire rampaging over her. She watched Ragden clean himself and knew she wanted him. Her heart thudded heavily in her chest with her desire. She saw his stiff meat and wanted to put her hands on it, taste it, and slip it deep inside her. She felt her arousal growing. She could feel him as well. Emily could also feel Sarah's body responding. She could feel the swirling maelstrom within her. Emily closed her eyes and she could sense her energy mixing with Ragden's inside Sarah. She sensed Sarah on the brink of some change and was not sure what would happen next.

Emily took a loofah off the shelf on the wall and held it out to Ragden. Sarah watched as Ragden poured body wash onto it, then grabbed another and did the same. Emily and Ragden ran the two loofahs over Sarah's body, tenderly scrubbing the sweat and dried fluids from her body. Once her back was clean, Emily turned Sarah to the wall so that they could clean her chest and abdomen.

Sarah leaned against the wall of the shower, letting the water cascade around her as Emily and Ragden gently worked the soap into her skin, kneading the sore muscles and cleaning her, then Emily kneeled before Sarah and kissed her stomach. Her soft lips pressed against her flat stomach as her tongue dipped into Sarah's navel. Sarah moaned in pleasure as Emily worked her tongue down into her groin.

Ragden watched for a moment, then sat down on his heels on the floor behind Emily. She turned and looked at him over her shoulder and grinned, then she reached back and spread her ass cheeks as she angled herself over his stiff cock. Ragden pointed his cock into her and she slid herself down on his meat. She inhaled sharply as his cock rode up into her tight pussy. Ragden leaned forward and wrapped his arms around her, cupping her magnificent breasts as he kissed the back of her ear. She continued to lower herself until his cock pressed firmly against her cervix.

Emily sighed in pleasure. She felt the throbbing of his cock against her deepest depths and moaned in pleasure. Her lips stretched out around his meat felt so amazing. She felt the walls of her pussy stretch around him, clenching hard on him. She turned to Sarah and leaned into her groin. Emily ran her tongue through Sarah's folds, up to her clit and sucked softly on her.

Sarah moaned loudly at the soft touch of Emily's tongue. Her legs quivered and her thighs twitched in pleasure. She would have fallen if she had not been already leaning against the wall. Emily suckled on Sarah's tight nub and Sarah grabbed her chest and squeezed it. Sarah's entire body pulsed with desire. She felt her orgasm rapidly building. It was almost too much to bear after all that she had experienced in so short a time.

Emily gently raised her hips up and down on Ragden's groin, sliding along his shaft. She felt his dick hitting her cervix, and the pleasure and pressure built rapidly within her. Ragden gently thrust against her, increasing the intensity of the experience. She wanted him to fill her insides with his seed. She wanted to feel it running down out of her. She could feel his powerful desire for the same, his cock throbbing inside her with need.

Ragden thumbed Emily's nipples as he gently thrust against her movements. He could feel her increasing the pace, her heart beating hard beneath his hands. His pulse increased to match hers. His thrust became more insistent. The impact inside her started to cause her breasts to rock with each impact. All the while, Emily slipped her tongue along Sarah's silky folds. Sarah moaned, clutching at her chest, her body twitching as Emily slipped a finger up Sarah's ass, another into her pussy. Sarah cried out at the sudden invasion; her voice hoarse. Emily stroked her fingers in and out of Sarah's holes as she continued to lick and suck Sarah's clitoris.

Emily felt her climax rapidly approaching, her body starting to vibrate with the need for release. She continued to stroke her fingers in Sarah, matching the pace of her own heart, lifting her hips faster. She flicked her tongue across Sarah's clitoris, then sucked it hard into her mouth, grazing it with her teeth.

Sarah cried out again as fluid burst from pussy, flooding down over Emily's hand. Emily latched her mouth into Sarah's mound, her tongue lapping at the copious fluids pouring out of her. Sarah could taste the unmistakable flavor of Ragden's seed still flowing out of Sarah. A shiver of ecstasy ran down Emily's back as she sat down hard on Ragden's cock and ground her hips against his groin. His cock slammed into her cervix, and she felt him explode inside her. His sudden, sharp exhalation against her back. He pulled her hard against his chest, and she leaned back into him, feeling his body shuddering inside her.

Emily groaned, feeling unsatisfied by her climax. Her pulse still raced, her pussy clenched and released on Ragden's thick cock. She continued to grind herself against him, savoring the feel of his throbbing ejaculation inside her. She could tell his shaft was still rock-hard inside her and knew she could get more from him if she just gave him a moment to recover.

Ragden kissed the back of Emily's neck. His body shuddered as cum continued to pulse out of him into her. He had finished too quickly and knew she wanted more. His cock throbbed inside her. He squeezed her chest and felt her desire still building.

Emily placed her hands on the floor between her legs and slowly raised herself off Ragden. She bent over, his ass in his face, and looked down at his cock. She watched as a small trickle of cum slipped from the tip. He was still rock-hard. Ragden leaned forward and kissed her mound, slipping his tongue between her lips. He tasted his seed and her sweet nectar, then leaned his head back and slipped his tongue across her asshole. Emily gasped and quickly lowered herself down against him, her ass pressing into his groin. His cock slipped between her cheeks as the tip pressed against her back.

Emily groaned, then reached between her legs and firmly grasped his cock. She raised herself and placed the tip of his cock against her asshole. She pressed herself down onto him, feeling the tip of his cock start to slide into her. Emily moaned loudly as she felt her ass stretching around the immensity of his cock.

Ragden took deep breaths, trying to steady himself as his big dick slipped into Emily's ass. She was so incredibly tight. The muscles of her anus squeezed so hard on his shaft that he almost exploded again. He continued to take deep breaths, straining every muscle he could to stave off another climax. He felt his eyes getting wider as she continued to press herself down onto him. He squeezed his eyes shut as her body clenched so tightly around him, then opened them as her ass finally pressed against his groin.

Emily moaned loudly as she felt his cock throbbing in her bowels. It felt so amazing to have him so deep inside her. Every inch of him squeezed into her tight hole. She felt a shiver of ecstasy run down her back. Her legs spasmed in pleasure. She looked at Sarah and saw a twinge of jealousy pass over her face. Sarah sank to her knees on the floor. She leaned forward and kissed Emily on the lips, softly, tenderly.

Sarah saw the stark desire on Emily's face and understood how badly she

wanted what she had right now. Sarah could not help but feel a little jealous. She wanted that big dick back up her ass too. Seeing how much pleasure it gave Emily, though, made her feel good. She loved that they could share this, and Ragden was perfectly capable of giving them both as much as they wanted. Sarah leaned back against the wall, enjoying the water that rained down on her as she watched Emily grind herself into Ragden's lap, riding that big dick in her ass.

Emily's legs shook as she sat her knees down on the hard tile floor of the shower. Ragden waited until Emily raised herself just a hair, a fraction of that big dick sliding from her, before thrusting against her. His groin pressed hard against her ass, his cock going deep into her. Emily's head rocked back, a soft cry on her lips.

"Oh yes!" Emily said while she raised and Ragden lowered his groin, then they slammed their bodies together again. Emily exhaled sharply at the impact while Ragden grunted softly. Sarah smiled as she cupped one breast and slipped a hand down between her legs, a finger dipping into her wet folds. She loved watching them and felt her arousal growing.

Ragden placed his hands on Emily's waist as they pulled apart again. When they slammed back together, he pulled her against him, increasing the pressure and slamming his dick deeper into her. Emily moaned in pleasure, feeling him going so deep into her. She felt his presence deep inside her body and the energy and love in her soul pulsed with joy and ecstasy. Their pace increased, their hips rocking apart and slamming together. Sarah lay against the wall, watching as Ragden and Emily fucked like the two horny young adults they were.

Ragden's breath was ragged as he matched Emily's desperate pace. Her breasts rocked and her thighs vibrated with each incredible impact. Sweat flowed over their bodies, mixing with the water cascading down around them. Emily's mind reeled at the incredible sensation of Ragden filling her bowels. She continued to thrust herself against him with renewed vigor, driving her hips into his, feeling the impact of his hips against her ass. His dick drove deep into her. She had watched him love Sarah, filling her bowels with his seed; now it was her turn, and she relished every moment of it. She felt her climax swiftly approaching, that pressure building up deep within her. The need for release started to overwhelm her. She could sense it swelling within Ragden as well. Distantly, she felt the same thing happening to Sarah.

Emily looked at Sarah as she continued to drive her hips into Ragden again and again. Sarah lay against the wall, her mouth slightly agape, her fingers working her clit feverishly as her legs twitched. Emily smiled to herself, then gasped at the next impact against her. As Ragden's dick withdrew and slammed into her again. Her mind shifted back to the amazing sensations in her own body. Her eyes rolled shut as she felt the energy within her burst into life. She felt the sudden electrical charge filling her and pulsing in her womb. Each stroke of Ragden's dick into her caused that energy to ratch up another

notch.

Ragden felt the growing pressure within him. The energy made his balls feel swollen. He felt the sparks of energy collecting inside him. His orgasm swelled, causing him to clench up. He thrust into Emily hard; then, as he drew back for another thrust, he felt the dam break loose. He cried out as he pulled her against him one more time and thrust into her. His balls cut loose, and cum exploded into her. He felt the energy explode out of him, filling her with everything he had to give.

Emily cried out as she felt him cum in her bowels. His sticky seed filled her. His energy exploded into her. Her orgasm erupted like a volcano, sending fluid and energy out of her pussy. The energy crashed into Ragden's balls, causing him to jerk, pull back, and thrust into her again, another burst of cum exploding up her ass.

Ragden sat down heavily on his heels and leaned back until he lay on the floor. Emily twitched and spasmed as fluid continued to leak out of her pussy. Her cum mixed with the water from the shower and swirled down the drain. Sarah watched, his body spasming with her orgasm, fluid leaking from her drenched pussy. She withdrew her fingers and licked them clean. She watched as Emily sat on Ragden's groin, her body shaking with her orgasm, his dick still deep in her ass.

Sarah crawled forward and kissed Emily on the lips. Emily moaned softly and kissed her back, then Sarah put a gentle hand on Emily's chest and pushed her back. Emily groaned loudly, then lifted herself off Ragden's cock. As it slipped from her ass, Emily moaned loudly again, as a stream of fluid leaked out of her. Emily crawled over to Ragden and kissed his lips as he lay on the floor. Sarah bent down over Ragden's waist, grasped his cock tenderly and slipped it into her mouth.

Ragden moaned loudly as she sucked it down her throat. She could taste the nectar of Emily's orgasm and the cum still leaking out. She pumped his cock, drawing out more and quickly swallowed it. She pushed her head down into his groin, her nose touching his abdomen as she took his entire cock down her throat. She gagged softly, then bobbed twice on it, drawing out everything she could, then she slid it from her mouth and licked her lips. She was shocked at how incredibly delicious he tasted. The flavor of Emily mixed with his thick musk. She smiled wickedly, then crawled over him and kissed him on the lips.

Ragden smiled as Sarah broke from his lips. Sarah saw that smile and felt genuinely loved. Her heart fluttered in her chest. She laid her head down on his chest and listened to his heart beating. Ragden laughed softly as his stomach grumbled. Both women both giggled. Ragden sat up slowly. Emily and Sarah sat around him, enjoying being in his presence and the hot water of the shower. Ragden gently pulled himself to his feet, then helped both women stand around him.

He reached for the soap again and they took turns lathering each other up

and rinsing off. Next, they shampooed each other's hair and then rinsed. When they were done, Ragden turned off the water, opened the door and grabbed the towels. He handed one to Emily, then Sarah and took the last for himself. The three toweled off without saying a word, then stepped from the shower and hung up their wet towels.

They stood shoulder to shoulder in front of the mirror, admiring each other, then pulled out brushes and took turns brushing each other's hair. When they finished, Ragden fetched the robes and helped each woman into one. He stood naked between them for a moment, enjoying their presence, then shouldered his way into his robe. The women giggled softly as he tied his robe shut. Emily pouted for a moment as Sarah bit her lip, watching.

Ragden's stomach rumbled again as he pulled open the door and held it for them, then the three of them headed down for dinner.

CHAPTER 36

Ragden walked quietly behind Sarah and Emily as they headed down the stairs. He could hear Jennifer and Michael in the kitchen preparing food. Sarah and Emily giggled; their heads were close together as they talked passionately about something. Ragden caught bits and pieces of the conversation, but not enough to catch the thread of their discussion. His thoughts wandered the events of the afternoon. The gift he had tried to figure out how to give Sarah. He knew she wanted to share in his bond with Emily, but the thought of exposing her to the dark cloud in his subconscious made him nervous. It had nearly killed Emily and he had saved her. He did not want to risk that with Sarah. It had been an accident and one he would not repeat if he could help it.

Still, Sarah wanted that connection. She wanted to feel his presence in her even when he was not there. His bond with Emily allowed that. How did he create that same kind of connection without threatening her? He sensed that Emily was open to doing that for Sarah, but the how felt just beyond his reach. He had thought that if he could conjure the energy with Emily and somehow trap Sarah in the middle, maybe that would create that same bond? They had tried that. It had been a wonderful experience, but had it achieved the result she so desperately craved? He did not know.

As they rounded the corner in the living room to the kitchen, Michael came walking into the room. As was his usual attire at home, he had no shirt on. His broad, hairy chest was exposed, though partially covered with his thick beard. His eyes twinkled with mischief and a large grin spread across his face. His eyes lit as he saw Emily and Sarah, and he pulled them both into a warm embrace. Michael winked at Ragden as he hugged the two women.

"Emily! Sarah! How good to see you both again so soon!" His voice was low but filled with his contagious good humor. Both women smiled and blushed at his attention. They stood with their arms around him smiling. Michael kissed both on the forehead, then gestured to the couch. "Sit. Sit. We

must talk."

Sarah and Emily drew their robes about them and sat on the couch side by side. Michael turned to Ragden and gestured to the same couch. Ragden walked over and Emily and Sarah made space between them so he could sit. They both leaned against him, draping arms around him and leaning their heads on his shoulder as he settled into the couch. Ragden draped his arms around both, pulling them snugly against him.

Michael sat across from them, his eyes twinkling with mischief.

"Well, don't you make the cozy threesome," he mused. Ragden blushed as the women giggled softly. Michael looked at Sarah and smiled. "What have they told you?"

Sarah shook her head and spoke softly, "Nothing. Only that you had a family trip this weekend."

Michael smiled with a sad look in his eyes. He spoke softly, "While this is true, it only scratches the surface of what happened. I know it affected you, and I am sorry for what you went through."

Sarah blinked, her eyes damp as tears started to trickle down her cheeks. "It does not matter. I am glad it turned out to be a bad dream."

Sarah snuggled closer to Ragden, her arm squeezing him protectively and possessively around him. Ragden smiled and kissed her forehead.

Michael's voice was soft and sad, "It was no dream, Sarah. Ragden nearly died. We almost lost him. The important thing is that we did not. He passed the test."

Sarah sat in shock, as the words washed over her. Her mind reeled. She could not bear to think about what could have happened. Sarah turned and buried her face in Ragden's chest as more tears streamed down her face. Michael stood and walked over to the couch. He kneeled in front of Sarah and put one hand on her knee. Sarah turned and looked at him.

"Your bond with Ragden is not strong enough for you to have experienced all that transpired. You felt a fraction of that loss."

Michael looked at Ragden, then back to Sarah. His voice was low and mild but held weight to it. "You asked him to strengthen that connection."

Sarah nodded.

"I do not blame you. He has given you the tools to do that. The next step is for you to accept it. I will caution you though, before you do, you need to consider the consequences of this decision."

Sarah sat up straighter and looked at Michael. She weighed his words, wondering if the rewards would be worth the cost.

"What consequences?" Sarah asked softly.

Michael smiled and squeezed her leg gently, then he spoke in a soft level tone, "If you accept, you will be changed. You will be bound to him for the rest of your life. You will always feel his presence, but you will also feel his emotions and his physical condition. If he stubs his toe, you will feel it. Not as sharply as he does, but you will feel it."

Sarah gulped, "If he dies..."

"You may not survive the experience."

Sarah looked at Michael's face and saw that he was deadly serious. She turned to look at Ragden, then buried her face in his chest again. Her voice was muffled as she said, "Good, I don't want to live in a world without him in it..."

Ragden rubbed her back soothingly with one hand as he turned to look at Emily. Emily giggled and shrugged. Michael rolled his eyes. Sarah wiped the tears from her face and turned back to Michael.

"I accept. One hundred and ten percent. Wholeheartedly. I accept. Now and forever. Please... What do I have to do?"

Michael chuckled to himself and squeezed her leg again. Shaking his head, he stood and walked back over to the loveseat. Sinking into it, he looked back at Sarah and said, "Nothing more than that. Close your eyes. Look inward. Feel the roiling mass of energy that Emily and Ragden have given you and accept it. Let it become part of you. That is all you must do."

"I...," Sarah stammered, "I can do that."

Sarah closed her eyes. She felt Ragden's presence next to her. She could sense Emily on the other side of him. She could feel them around her and within her. She let her mind wander and felt the roiling mass of energy within the core of her being. Her stomach felt unsettled by how things kept swirling within her. She could sense the bits of it that belonged to Emily and Ragden. It was alien to her body, like an invasion into her very soul. It was something that did not belong.

Sarah took a deep breath, and in her mind's eye, opened her arms and welcomed it. The mass of energy stopped swirling and roiling. Instead, it swept into her arms like the lover sitting next to her and embraced her. As it did, it sank into her. The parts that she could distinctly identify as both Ragden and Emily started to merge within her to become something more. At first, it was like a warm blanket wrapped around her, comforting, soothing, loving. Then it felt like a second skin, soothing and cool. Then it was deeper than that, sinking into the very core of what and who she was. For a moment, her heart thundered frantically. This invasion, this beast, this OTHERness was taking her over. She wanted to scream, to reject it, because it was not HER.

Sarah took another deep breath and decided that she wanted it to be hers. At that moment, her heart slowed, her breath calmed. The strange, otherworldly energy that had seemed so foreign was now hers. She owned it. It felt different. She felt different. She felt complete, like she had been missing something she never knew she needed. She tried to explore this new sensation within her and found it pulsed with a life of its own. It was her, but it was more than just her.

Sarah's stomach rumbled loudly. She realized she was famished. She opened her eyes and realized that Ragden, Emily, and Michael had been

talking about something, but she had not heard a word. She felt exhausted. Her body ached. Her ass hurt. Her pussy felt like it had been stretched around a football field. She wanted to lie down and sleep for the rest of her days.

"Why..." Sarah yawned, blinked, and yawned again. "Why am I so tired?"

Michael laughed. Emily and Ragden looked at Sarah. Michael spoke softly, "What you have gone through is a lot. The emotional turmoil of what you have experienced will probably take you weeks to puzzle through. Though, I would encourage you to explore that newness you sense in you."

Sarah blinked and peered at Michael. He smiled back at her, a knowing smile. He tapped his right temple and winked at her. Sarah saw the way his eyes seemed to peer into her very soul. She got the impression that he knew everything she had experienced.

Michael stood and nodded towards the kitchen. "If I'm not mistaken, I do believe dinner is about ready. Come, you will feel better with some food in that stomach of yours."

Emily and Ragden stood. Sarah sat for a moment, then Ragden pulled her to her feet. She giggled and draped her arms around his waist, snuggling her face against his side. Ragden smiled at her and kissed her softly on the top of her head. Emily giggled to herself and turned to follow as Michael walked into the dining room, then Michael turned back to look at Sarah and Ragden.

"Ragden, can you let Aria in?"

Ragden looked at Michael questioningly, and then the doorbell rang.

"You did invite her for dinner, did you not?"

Ragden nodded. Sarah stepped back as he headed for the door. Sarah watched Ragden walk into the foyer, then turned and followed Michael into the dining room. Sarah chased after Emily and wrapped herself around the other woman. Emily giggled and hugged her back, then kissed her softly on the lips. Michael watched them and smiled when they noticed him watching them, then they found two chairs at the table to sink into. Michael went into the kitchen to help Jennifer finish making dinner.

Ragden padded barefoot to the front door. He turned the knob and pulled the door open. Aria stood on the step, looking over the front yard. As the door opened, she turned to look at him and smiled. Aria was wearing a knee-length skirt, striped black and white. She had short socks and sneakers on her feet. Her shirt was a button-down with only a few buttons in the middle holding it closed over her bosom. He could easily see a dark bra holding her breasts in place. Her hair hung loosely over her shoulders. Aria grinned, then looked down at her outfit, then back at Ragden. She stepped up close to him and wrapped her arms around him, hugging him tightly. She buried her face in his chest and held him tighter. Ragden wrapped his arms around her and pulled her against him.

"Hello, handsome," she whispered breathily. "I missed you. Wait... Are you wearing anything underneath that?"

She pulled on the front of his robe, looked down and started giggling.

Ragden chuckled and shook his head. Taking a step back, he allowed her entry into the foyer. She bent down, flashing him a beautiful view down the front of her shirt as she picked up a small gym bag and stepped inside. She dropped the bag by the shoe rack and slipped her shoes off.

Aria stepped up the Ragden and wrapped her arms around him. He leaned into her and kissed her passionately on the lips. Their lips parted and their tongues danced, then Aria stepped back, her heart racing and she giggled again. She took a deep breath and smiled.

"Smells like dinner is ready," Aria grabbed his hand and pulled him towards the dining room, "Shall we?"

Ragden chuckled as he followed her, "Sure."

As they rounded the corner of the living room, Aria spotted Emily and Sarah. She let go of Ragden's hand and ran over to them. She hugged and kissed each of them, then went into the kitchen to hug Jennifer and Michael. Ragden pulled out a chair for her as she came back to the table. She thanked him politely, then sank into the chair reaching for his hand as he sat.

Ragden took Aria's hand as he sat down next to her. He turned to her and asked, "How was your weekend?"

"Oh my. Utterly Boring!" Aria exclaimed. Both Sarah and Emily giggled in response. Aria squeezed Ragden's hand as she spoke, "How was the beach? I hope you had more fun than I did sitting around waiting for you to get home!"

"The beach was... eventful," Ragden stated, trying to figure out how to explain everything that had happened over the last two days. He shook his head and shrugged. Aria watched him, then turned and looked at Sarah and Emily. Aria noted the matching robes and a look of jealousy passed over her face. She turned back to Ragden, her cheeks flushed, her pulse beating hard in her throat.

Ragden saw the intense look of jealousy on Aria's face. The firm set of her jaw, the anger beating in her throat. Before she could open her mouth to say another word, he leaned into her and kissed her hard on the lips. He pushed his tongue into her mouth and pulled her body against his. She melted into his embrace. He swept his arms around her, pulling her off the chair into his lap.

Aria melted into him. Her heart thundered in her chest as all the anger and outrage melted away. She wanted to be angry with Ragden. He had promised she would get her turn with him, but he had already been with both of her best friends. She wanted to scream at him for dismissing her and passing her by. She felt for a moment like she did not matter, then she felt his heart beating against her chest. His strong arms wrapped around her. She pulled him closer to her and felt his love.

Aria leaned back and broke from his embrace. She scooted back and sat in her chair, her heart hammering in her chest. She felt the dampness of her arousal and feared everyone at the table could see it. She looked at Sarah and Emily and tried to feel angry at them, but when she saw the looks of

happiness and love on their faces, her heart melted. She turned to Ragden and playfully hit him in the chest.

"That is not fair," she said softly.

At that moment, Jennifer and Michael came walking into the dining room carrying plates of food. They set down plates in front of Emily, Sarah, and Aria, then went back into the kitchen to get more food. On the plates was a mix of sauteed ground beef with broccoli mixed in, braised vegetables and a sweet potato mash. Jennifer and Michael sat at the ends of the table.

"Dig in," Michael stated as he took his seat.

"This looks amazing," Aria said, looking over the meal, "Thank you for having me over."

"Oh my god," Sarah said breathily, "I am so hungry. Thank you!"

"Of course. Of course. Eat!" Michael laughed as he reached over and grasped Aria's hand. She looked up at him, startled. He smiled at her as he squeezed her fingers. "Glad you could join us, my dear."

Aria blushed and looked down at her plate shyly before resuming eating. Sarah and Emily giggled and then resumed eating as well. The rest of the meal was eaten in the quiet of a delicious meal shared among friends and family.

As Sarah and Emily finished their food, they stood and took the plates into the kitchen. Jennifer finished about the same time and tried to stop them from cleaning, but they insisted, and all three women went into the kitchen together to clean and put away dishes. Michael finished soon after and joined them. Aria had finished her food a while ago, but sat next to Ragden, watching him eat and just enjoying being in his presence. He eyed her from time to time as he finished his food.

As Ragden ate the last of his food, Aria picked up his plate and carried it into the kitchen. The four women laughed and joked as they put away the dishes, then they made their way back to the table and took their seats.

As Jennifer sat again, she looked at Ragden. "Did you finish studying for your math test tomorrow?"

"Yes, I did," Ragden answered.

Jennifer smiled. "Good. I did not doubt that you had. We heard you and Emily having an enjoyable time up there and just wanted to make sure you finished your studying."

Emily blushed a deep shade of scarlet, and looking at the table, spoke softly, "Of course, we did not start until I made sure he had all of his answers right on his study test."

Aria giggled and Sarah laughed throatily. Jennifer smiled and patted Emily's hand.

"Thank you, dear. I appreciate that," Jennifer answered softly. Emily looked up at Jennifer and smiled, still blushing. Emily still had a challenging time coping with how open Ragden's parents were about their sexual lives. It was refreshing, but she still had difficulty wrapping her head around it.

Emily turned to Sarah and spoke softly. Sarah giggled and nodded. Emily

turned back to everyone else.

"If you will excuse us, we are going to head out."

Jennifer looked at them questioningly. "Are you not staying the night, dear?"

Sarah shook her head, and Emily spoke, "No. We are going to give Aria and Ragden some time together. We will be back tomorrow for dinner if that is okay?"

Jennifer smiled and nodded. "Of course, dear."

Aria beamed, looking at Sarah and Emily. "Thank you."

Ragden looked from Aria to Sarah and Emily. He looked at Emily and raised an eyebrow, "Are you sure?"

Emily walked around the table to Ragden, who stood as she approached. She wrapped her arms around him and hugged him tightly, then spoke softly to him as she turned her face to his, "Yes, Love. Meet for lunch at my locker?"

Ragden kissed Emily softly on the lips, brushing her hair from her face. He nodded and smiled at her. "Of course."

Then Emily stepped back from Ragden. Sarah pressed herself against Ragden, hugging him fiercely, then kissing him tenderly. As they broke, Sarah whispered, "Thanks for everything. I love you."

"Love you too, dear," Ragden said as he kissed her again. She giggled and stepped around Ragden to hug Aria.

Sarah kissed Aria on the lips, then whispered into her ear, "Fuck him silly for me. Please?"

Aria blushed and nodded as Sarah stood and took Emily's hand. The two girls walked through the living room and headed upstairs. Ragden stood for a moment, wondering what had just happened. Aria took his hand and pulled him back into his chair. He sat and turned towards her. She smiled happily, pulling his hand into her lap and holding it against her thigh.

"Can you tell me more about your beach trip?" Aria asked simply.

Michael laughed. Jennifer smiled and stood. She walked over to Michael and took his hand. He smiled happily and stood, leaving Aria and Ragden at the table. They walked through the living room and headed upstairs. Ragden and Aria watched them go, then Aria gently tugged on his hand again, pulling his attention back to her.

"Your beach trip?" She prodded again. Ragden looked at her and saw her curiosity.

"It is a lot to explain," he started. Aria sat quietly, waiting for him to explain. Ragden took a deep breath, then spoke. "I learned a lot. About my parents and their history together. The truth of my heritage. Then I met... I am not sure how to explain all this. I have a tough time believing some of it and it happened to me..."

Aria smiled, "Did you get the answers you were looking for?"

Ragden looked at her. "Yes and no."

"Would you like to explain?" she questioned.

Ragden smiled, "I am not sure you would believe me if I did."

"Did you explain it to Emily and Sarah?" she asked.

"Emily, yes. Sarah, no."

Aria looked surprised. She furrowed her brows, then asked, "Why Emily and not Sarah?"

"Sarah did not ask for the details."

"Emily did?" she inquired.

"Not quite. This will take some explaining."

Aria smiled and patted his hand. "I am not going anywhere. I promise to listen and not judge. Whatever you want to tell me, I'm here for it."

Ragden looked at her, his eyebrows raised, then he took a deep breath and let it out slowly. He looked at Aria, considering how to approach this. He spoke slowly, "Can you, at least, keep an open mind?"

Aria nodded solemnly. "I promise."

"Okay," Ragden said, "I guess I will start by saying that my dad is not human. He is a force of nature given physical form. He is the embodiment of Love and has existed since the dawn of time."

Aria giggled. "Your dad? Michael?" Seeing the serious look on Ragden's face, Aria stopped laughing. "Sorry. I guess that would explain why he always looks super-hot and makes my heart beat a little harder when he looks at me."

Ragden nodded. "That would be part of who he is. He cannot help it. Michael met my mother over two thousand years ago."

Aria blinked. "She looks pretty good for her age."

Ragden laughed. "I suppose you are right. That is part of being so close to him though. They have some kind of bond where he shares his ... lifeforce with her. It keeps her young. He also explained that his appearance changes depending on the societal norms of where he is. He even explained that he used to be worshipped as the goddess of love by... many cultures of the past. He paraded the names in front of me, but I do not recall them all."

Aria chuckled. "That is a lot to swallow. I can see you believe him though. Okay. If you are his son, what does that make you?"

"Force-born. That is the term he used to describe what I am. Something halfway between a force of nature and a regular human. As he explained it, there used to be a lot more force-born, but they caused some kind of problem. The Primals wiped them out."

"Wait," Aria held up a hand. She raised an eyebrow looking at Ragden, "Primals?"

"Yeah," Ragden shrugged, "The Primal Forces of Nature. Fire. Earth. Wind. Water."

"Right. Just making sure," Aria nodded, "So, they caused issues and were wiped out. How does that relate to you? Are they coming for you?"

As the words slipped from her lips, Aria shivered. This was all silly and fantastical and made her want to laugh, but when she looked at Ragden's face,

she saw he believed it. She stuffed her humor and decided to take him at his word. She shivered again. If it was true, then Ragden was in some kind of danger and she did not want to lose him. She finally had the love of her life and she could not lose him now. Sure, she had to share him, but that was a small price to pay for how he made her feel.

Ragden shook his head. "No. They are not 'coming to get me'."

Aria breathed a sigh of relief. She had not realized she was holding her breath until that moment. She felt her heart slowing its crazy beat in her chest. She placed a hand on her chest, feeling her heart still beating hard. She realized that her body was responding to his story, even if her mind was having issues grappling with it. She searched her feelings and felt her core of love for Emily, Sarah and him still beating strong within her.

Ragden cocked an eyebrow at her. "I sound crazy, don't I?"

"Yes," Aria blurted, then she laughed. "And no. I mean, your story is too crazy to be real. Yet... I can see you believe it and I guess it does explain some things. Please go on."

Ragden sighed and smiled softly. "As my dad explained it, force-born come into their ... gifts at their eighteenth birthday. Which is why nothing ever seemed out of the ordinary until then. Which is why I... uh... responded to your taunts differently last week."

Aria smiled. That day was forever engrained in her memory. She felt warmth spreading inside her at the memory of that day's activities. Her body started to become aroused, and she felt moisture collecting between her legs. She pinched her knees shut and tried to settle her breathing. She looked at Ragden and saw him smiling at her. A thought flitted across her mind, 'he knows, damn him.'

"I'm glad you did," she said huskily. Aria grasped his hand and squeezed it, sliding it up under her skirt to grasp her bare thigh. Her muscles trembled at his touch. She closed her eyes. She wanted so much more, but curiosity had the better of her at this point. "I am glad to hear you are not in danger."

"I did not say that," Ragden said softly. Her eyes flashed and she saw something behind his eyes that gave her pause. She saw fear. He continued, "They are not coming to get me. I have to go to them. That is what took place this weekend. I met the first of the four. Water."

Aria took a deep breath. Her heart thundered in her chest. If his story were true, then these things were real, and he had met one. Too wild to be true, surely, she thought. She asked, "And?"

"Mother Ocean tested me... I passed. Or I would be dead now."

"Oh. Of course. That makes sense. Wait," Aria paused. Peered at him. "How did that work?"

Ragden's eyes went unfocused for a moment as he went through his memory of the event in question. Aria watched and waited; then Ragden spoke softly, "She sifted through my memories and decided to let me live. Emily played a part in that. I think Mother Ocean would have drowned me if

not for her."

Aria looked at him and saw the sincerity in his eyes. She asked, "How did Emily play a part in that? What makes her so special?"

Aria had tried not to sound angry, but as she heard the words leave her mouth, she realized that she was jealous of Emily again. She wanted to be the important one in his life, the special one. Emily had beat her to that, somehow. Aria gazed into Ragden's eyes and saw sorrow there. Her heart melted and her anger faded. She saw how much Ragden loved Emily. His eyes were filled with it. She was jealous, but she still felt his love for her. Aria took a deep breath and swallowed her pride and her anger. She smiled at Ragden. "Please tell me."

Ragden nodded. "The first night I slept with Emily, I..." he paused, gulped, took a deep breath, "I almost killed her. There is... a dark side to being my father's son. There is darkness inside me that wants to break loose. When I was with Emily that first night, it almost got loose. It... I... that darkness sucked her life force from her. She was dying. Lying in my arms with almost no pulse, no breath, fading right before me."

Tears leaked from his eyes. Aria felt her own eyes growing damp. A tear trickled down her cheek. His sadness at that moment was so powerful. She could not understand what he explained. It did not make sense. She shook her head. Then asked, "What did you do?"

Ragden looked at her, a soft smile played across his lips as he spoke, "I gave her part of my soul. I pushed it into her until she breathed again. I watched her come back to life in my arms."

Aria cocked an eyebrow. She saw the sincerity in his eyes. She thought back to her interactions with Emily in the latter half of the week. There had been something different about her. She had been changed. This was why. It still boggled her mind. She looked down at her hand on his hand on her thigh. It felt warm and comforting. His thumb slid across her skin and she felt a tingle run down her back. She looked back at his face.

"She isn't the same, Aria," Ragden spoke softly, "I saved her, but it changed her. She is now... bound to me. Our souls intertwined. I can feel what she feels, and she can feel me."

"How does that work?" Aria asked, genuinely curious.

"I can close my eyes and see through her eyes. I can feel what she feels, hear what she hears, see what she sees. It does not make sense, but..." Ragden shrugged, "When Mother Ocean tested me, she felt that bond and temporarily severed it. When that happened, it almost broke Emily. That was part of why I was spared."

"I guess that makes sense," Aria said. She thought about it for a moment. That made a lot of sense. If Emily possessed some part of his soul, that would explain why they were so close. She could not compete with that. Yet, Emily allowed Aria to be with him and even seemed to enjoy seeing them together, and she had left with Sarah, leaving them together. Aria had a challenging time

reconciling that. If she were connected to him like that, could she have done the same? She was not sure. She looked up into his eyes and saw the happiness there. Seeing that look on his face, she knew she would try; knew she would do anything for him. She swallowed and spoke softly, "What comes next?"

Ragden laughed, his voice light, the humor like a caress on her cheek, curling down her back. She felt herself growing more damp. There was sex in that laugh and she wanted more of that.

"Now," he whispered as he leaned forward and kissed her softly on the lips, "Now we go upstairs and spend some time together. Tomorrow is another day. Next weekend I will have to seek out Earth, but until then, we have all week to figure out how our lives fit together."

Aria gulped. She wanted this very much. She stood and groaned as his hand slid down her leg. She stepped between his legs and leaned against him, pulling his head against her chest. His arms wrapped around her, hugging her tightly. She did not care if his story was true, she wanted him.

"Can we go upstairs now?" Aria asked quietly. She felt him nod against her. A thrill ran down her back. She had not had a chance to be alone with him and she felt giddy at the opportunity. She stepped back from Ragden and took his hand. He stood and followed her through the living room. She led him to the foyer where she grabbed her gym bag and slung it over her shoulder, then she went up the stairs, shaking her hips lightly teasing him with a beautiful view of her backside as she went up the stairs.

Ragden followed up the steps, feeling his hardon grow more insistent under his robe. As they went into his room, he noted that Sarah's and Emily's clothes were gone. He sighed. He had been looking forward to another night with all three of them but was just grateful he did not have to sleep alone again.

Aria tossed her gym bag to Ragden's desk, then turned to face him as the door slipped shut behind him. She sauntered over to him and undid the tie on the front of his robe. Ragden stood watching her patiently, letting her do as she wished. Aria pulled open the front of his robe. His cock stood at attention before her. She gasped slightly at the sight of it. She knew it was large, but its size always seemed a slight surprise to her. Aria wrapped one hand around it and gently felt his pulse through it. She looked at his face and watched his eyes slip closed as she gently squeezed his manhood, then she leaned into him and kissed him softly on the lips as she stroked his cock. He made small moans as she squeezed and stroked him. She grinned, listening to him.

Ragden thrust his tongue into her mouth, kissing her passionately. He wrapped his arms around her and squeezed her against him. He felt his cock press against her body, throbbing hard against her. She squeezed his cock as her tongue danced around his. She opened her mouth wider, allowing him to explore her mouth with his tongue. Her heart thundered and she felt herself growing more damp by the second. She wanted him inside her so badly. Her

entire body shook with her need. She wanted to pace herself though and make it last as long as she could.

Aria leaned back from him, sighing in pleasure as he pulled her body against his. She could feel the heat of his dick through her clothes. A shiver ran down her spine. As their lips parted, she drew in a deep breath as Ragden's tongue slipped down over her jaw. She leaned her head back, exposing her throat. He suckled on her neck, his teeth nipping tenderly at her soft skin.

Aria moaned in pleasure as Ragden worked his way down her throat to her collarbone, softly kissing the skin. His teeth nipped softly across her skin as he moved across her collarbone to that soft spot at the base of her throat. He kissed his way down her sternum, his chin gently pushing against her bra, then he dragged his tongue up her sternum and kissed her throat again.

Aria stood up straight and lowered her chin to look at him. He brought his head up to look at her. Aria saw that hunger in his eyes and shivered again. She felt his big dick throb against her and knew she had to have it in her. She saw the sex in his eyes, the desire to consume her. She wanted nothing more. She had never truly had him to herself, and she wanted everything he could offer her. This time it was just them, alone. No one watching, no one to share him with. Just the two of them. Ever since that day in the school, this was what she had wanted more than anything else.

Ragden saw the stark desire on Aria's face. He sensed her need and wanted nothing more than to give her what she wanted. He felt a small pang in the back of his head for Emily and Sarah, but knew that they were happy and wanted him to have this time with Aria. He smiled at her and kissed her lips softly. Aria melted against him, pushing her body firmly against his again. Then she drew back, put her hands on his chest and stepped back from him.

Aria took a deep, steadying breath as she stood there before him. His robe hung open around him. His body pulsed with desire in front of her. His big dick stood at attention, throbbing with his need for her. She saw that big piece of meat and licked her lips. Her mind wandered for a moment. If he really were the spawn of Love, how many times could she bring him to climax? She grinned, determined to find out.

Ragden saw the look on her face and understood her intentions. He smiled and nodded to her. He saw her eyes sparkle with desire. She gracefully dropped to her knees before him, one hand on his cock. He closed his eyes as she ran her fingers down the length of him. Ragden took a deep breath as she softly kissed the tip of his dick, then he looked down at her and saw her looking up at him as she sucked on the head of his cock.

Aria wrapped her hands tightly around his dick and looked up at his face to watch his expression as she sucked the head of his cock into her mouth. She slid it deeper into her mouth, feeling it push against the opening of her throat. She watched as he inhaled sharply, the air whistling through his teeth as she sucked harder on his cock. She squeezed a little harder and stroked his

cock as she swirled her tongue around the shaft. Ragden closed his eyes as he enjoyed the feel of her tongue on him.

Aria took a deep breath, then relaxed his jaw and throat. She slipped the head of his cock into her throat. She closed her eyes and forced her jaw to relax, slipping more of his length down her throat. As her airway was blocked, Aria felt a moment of panic. She could not breathe. His massive cock blocked her throat. Aria blinked back the tears that started to well in her eyes. She looked up at Ragden and saw his eyes closed and his breathing shallow. She could feel his cock throbbing inside her mouth and throat. She forced herself to relax and leaned against him. She continued to push forward until her nose was pressed against his groin, her lips kissing the base of his cock. A surge of triumphant joy rang through her body. She stayed there for a moment, marveling at the feeling of his length down her throat. She convulsively tried to swallow, her throat squeezing on his cock. She felt him throb in response, sucking in the air sharply again.

Aria slowly backed herself off his cock, feeling it slide free of her throat, then back into her mouth. When the head of it was finally in her mouth, she inhaled sharply. She slipped it from her mouth and gulped air. She coughed and looked up to see his look of concern.

"Are you..." he started to ask, but she nodded and smiled up at him.

"I'm fine." She breathed softly as she stroked his cock and flicked her tongue over the head of his dick. Aria watched as his eyes slipped closed. She continued to stroke her hands up and down the length of his cock while she slipped the head of it into her mouth and sucked softly on it. She grinned as she heard the small noises he made while she stroked him.

Aria slipped the tip of his dick into her mouth again and sucked on it. She tasted a drop of pre-cum form on her tongue. A shiver ran down her spine at the flavor and texture of it as she swirled it around in her mouth, then swallowed it. She felt the warmth of it pass down her throat. She closed her eyes as the feeling spread inside her. She sucked on him harder, wanting more.

Ragden closed his eyes, feeling her hands working on the shaft of his cock. He surrendered himself to the feelings she was causing. He felt the pressure starting to build up within him. He could sense her desire and was eager to satisfy it. He cupped her cheek, feeling her jaw working on his meat. She leaned her head against his hand as she continued to suck on his cock. He moaned softly, feeling his climax building.

Aria's heart thundered in her chest. She felt her panties soaked with her arousal. She moaned softly as his fingers dug into her hair, gently cupping the back of her head. She stroked first, feeling his body starting to tense up. She took a deep breath, then leaned into him. She pushed herself forward onto his cock, feeling it slide into her throat. She was prepared for the blockage. His hand spasmed against her head as she pushed herself until her lips kissed his groin, then she moved back and forth on his cock, trying to swallow anything that came out. Her throat convulsed on his cock. She heard him moan loudly,

and his cock throbbed hard in her throat. She reached up and grabbed his ass, pulling him into her, then she released him and moved herself back and forth as fast as she could.

Ragden moaned loudly in pleasure as his balls tightened up and exploded into Aria's throat. She thrust herself forward, her lips pressed to his groin, her teeth scraping the base of his cock. She squeezed her lips tight around him, sucking hard on him. Then she slowly moved back, as cum exploded down her throat. She swallowed convulsively, her throat squeezing on his cock. More cum burst forth. She swallowed it, feeling it course through her body. The heat filled her with warmth and love.

She sat back on her heels, his throbbing dick slipping from her throat until just the tip rested in her mouth. She took a quick gulp of air, then sealed her lips around the head of his cock and sucked for all she could. She grasped his cock and squeezed it hard as she stroked it, milking it for everything she could get. Ragden gasped at the pressure on his cock and felt another load of cum explode into her mouth.

Ragden felt his legs trembling and leaned back against the door. Aria leaned forward with him, keeping her mouth locked onto the head of his dick. She continued to stroke and suck him until his dick stopped leaking cum into her mouth, then she took a deep breath, and slid him back into her, leaning forward, she took his entire length into her throat again. Her lips pressed against his groin again, and then she slowly backed off him. She heard him moaning in pleasure as she slipped his dick from her mouth. She marveled at how hard it felt in her hands. He had just cum for her and yet he was still hard and ready for action. She smiled and kissed the tip of his cock, tasting a tiny bead of pre-cum as it formed there for her. She giggled and released her hands from it. She looked up at Ragden, who eyed her with that same hungry gaze.

Then Aria stood, slowly letting her hands slide down her chest and to her waist. She cupped herself through her skirt and moaned softly. Ragden eyed her hands on her body, then he reached out and pulled her against him. His hands grasped her ass and pulled her groin fiercely against his body. His cock throbbed against her, and she could feel the heat of it through her clothing.

Their lips met, and he tried to devour her. His tongue invaded her mouth, seeking and probing every crevice of hers. She broke from him, breathless, her heart pounding. His hands dug into her ass, squeezing, and pulling them together. His mouth closed on her neck; his teeth grazed her skin as he sucked on her. She moaned in pleasure as she leaned back from him. His lips broke from her neck and he gazed at her, hungrily. She untied the front of her blouse and let it slide down her arms to drop on the floor.

Ragden's hands slid up her back to find the clasp of her bra. He deftly popped it loose. Aria cupped her breasts, holding the fabric to her chest. Ragden's hands came up to her shoulders, sliding the straps down her arms. She smiled coyly as his hands found hers and gently pulled the fabric from them. She covered her chest shyly as he leaned in and kissed her softly on the

lips.

Then he leaned down and kissed the tops of her breasts. She moved her hands out of his way as he kissed down her breast to her exposed nipple. Ragden gently took it between his teeth and licked it, then pulled it into his mouth and sucked on it softly, flicking the nipple with his tongue as he did so. He moved his hand to cup and squeeze her breast as he licked and kissed it. He released it from his mouth and blew across the damp skin. Aria shivered and sighed in pleasure, then he moved over to do the same with the other breast.

Aria moaned in pleasure as he continued to display care and affection for her chest. She reached under her skirt and slid her panties down her thighs. She left them around her knees and wiggled her legs back and forth until they dropped to her ankles. Ragden broke his lips from her chest and looked down at her feet, then he looked into her eyes and smiled. She winked back and lifted her feet out of her panties. Aria slid her hands up his arms and pushed the robe off his shoulders. It dropped to the floor around his feet.

Aria took a single step back from him. She groaned inwardly as she stepped away from the heat and radiance that came off his body. She looked down at his throbbing cock and bit her lip, then spun around and started to take a step towards the bed. Ragden's hands grasped her hips and held her in place. He stepped up behind her, pressing his body against hers. She moaned softly as she felt the heat and pressure of his cock sliding between her legs.

Aria's heart caught in her throat as she looked down and saw the head of his cock pushing her skirt between her legs. She could see the bulge of it sticking out, and the heat of it through the fabric pressed against her. She grabbed the edges of her skirt and lifted it until she could feel the heat of his cock pressed against her most precious parts. His cock slid up through her folds, the head of it pushing against the top of her mound. She shivered in pleasure, feeling it throb against her body.

Ragden held her hips in place as he ground his hips against her, sliding his cock against her. Then he moved his hands up to her chest, grasping her breasts, and pulling her back against his. He rolled his hips backward, his cock sliding through her wet folds. He could feel her arousal coating his cock and he shuddered in pleasure.

Aria moaned in pleasure as Ragden kissed the side of her neck, then reached under her skirt and pushed the head of his cock into her labial lips. He rocked his hips back a little further, allowing her to position to the tip of his cock in her lips, poised at the entrance to her vagina. Her body shuddered in anticipation. She could feel the heat and pressure building inside her. She pushed her hips against him, easing him into her. She felt the tip spreading her open as it slid into her.

Aria gasped as she felt him enter her. He stopped there, and Aria grasped his hands on her chest, squeezing it. He nuzzled her neck and kissed her right earlobe. His breath was hot in her ear as her body shuddered in pleasure. Her

heart thundered in her chest. She wanted him to fill her so badly. She bit her lip and tried to press against him. His cock slid a little deeper into her but stopped.

"Please," she moaned, "I need you in me."

Ragden kissed her ear and whispered to her, "Of course, my love."

Slowly, gently, he pressed up into her. Aria moaned loudly, her breath coming in small gasps as more of him filled her. She felt herself being stretched by his immensity. The walls of her pussy were pushed open by the size of him. More kept sliding slowly into her. Deeper and deeper into her. Slow. Methodical. Inch by inch he kept sliding into her. Her heart beat harder, her body shuddering with pleasure as she felt him press against the deepest depths of her. His cock pressed against her cervix, filling every bit of her, then he pushed into her a little harder. She felt her entire body pushed forward by the inexorable pressure inside her. Her feet slipped forward on the carpet and she giggled. His hands kept her body pressed against his. She felt the steady beat of his heart against her back.

At that moment, she felt complete. Truly and completely filled with all of him; all his love and desire. She knew then that this was what she had always wanted. She felt that incredible fullness in her throbbing in time to his beating heart against her back. A small part of her ached for Sarah and Emily to be here with them, but she was glad she had him to herself. She was eager to feel his seed filling her once more. Her belly felt warm and full of him, and now her pussy was stretched tight around his incredible manhood.

Ragden held her body still as he gently rolled his hips, sliding himself partially from her, then rolled back into her. His cock pressed against her cervix again, that gentle caress of her deepest parts. They moaned together in pleasure. That impact sent ripples of pleasure through both. Aria leaned her back against him, feeling that warmth and power against her. She relaxed and let him hold her as his hips moved slowly, that rock-hard meat between her legs sliding in and out of her. It was a gentle, slow rhythm of deep caresses.

Aria could feel the pressure starting to build up within her. She felt her pulse starting to race, her breathing coming in gasps with each gentle impact inside her. She leaned forward slightly, pushing her groin against his, feeling that pressure increase. She reached forward and put her hands on the edge of the bed. Ragden's hands trailed down her back to hold her hips. His fingers softly dug in, holding her in place.

Ragden grabbed the edge of her skirt and tossed it up onto her back. Aria looked over her shoulder at him, as he gazed down at her ass. He squeezed her cheek fondly, then smacked it lightly, leaving a red mark. Aria winced at the sudden pain, then her body tingled with pleasure. She moaned at the sensation as he pulled back and gently slid back into her. As he slid in, she thrust herself back against him, feeling the head of his dick thump into her cervix. She moaned loudly. A shockwave of pleasure rolled through her body. A shiver of ecstasy went down her spine. Ragden held her against him, his

dick pressed against her cervix. Her pussy stretched tight around his thickness. She could feel his pulse inside her.

Ragden savored the feel of her ass in his hands. The pressure of her pussy wrapped around his dick. He pulled her against him a little harder, feeling his cock pressing against her. She felt so deliciously tight and smooth against him. There was something ever so slightly different about being inside Aria versus Sarah and Emily. He stopped to ponder it for a moment, enjoying the feel of her. Then he saw the look on her face, the way she bit her lip. She pulled forward, sliding herself partially off his cock, then pushed back, her cervix thumping against his dick again. Her eyes closed as her body vibrated with the impact.

Ragden chuckled to himself, then drew back from her until he nearly came out. She looked over her shoulder as he stood poised with the head of his deck just inside her. Her eyes flashed dangerously at him. He smiled, then smacked her ass again with his right hand, a little harder than before. Her eyes closed at the impact as her body vibrated, then he smacked the other cheek with his other hand. Her mouth dropped open as she panted heavily as he thrust back into her. A fast, hard thrust; his dick slamming into her cervix. Aria started to stumble forward at the impact, but he held her hips steady, his grip tight around her waist.

"More," Aria panted, sweat breaking out on her brow, "Please..."

Ragden slapped her ass again, harder this time; leaving a red, stinging mark. Aria winced from the impact and drew herself forward. Ragden grabbed her hips and pulled her back against him as he thrust into her. His cock slammed into her cervix. Aria arched her back, throwing her head back, her hair whipping across her back. Aria felt him start to slide back and she pulled forward. Just as she felt his dick was going to slip free, she thrust back, as he thrust into her. Their hips smashed together as his dick crashed into her cervix. She arched her back again, grinding her hips against his, pressing her cervix against the head of his cock.

Ragden grabbed her hips, holding her in place as he pulled back and slammed into her again and again. His pace was fast and insistent. He felt her body tensing around him, flexing, and squeezing him. Aria could feel the pressure inside her reaching a breaking point and knew she could not take much more of this. Ragden felt his balls starting to clench, the pressure inside his body building and building. His climax was fast approaching. Aria matched his rhythm, drawing forward as he pulled back, and slamming her ass into his groin as he thrust forward.

Ragden continued to pound into her, increasing his pace. He felt his climax looming over him. Aria's breath was a series of sharp gasps, exhaling as they rammed together, inhaling as they pulled apart. Ragden could sense her climax scrambling over her senses. He clenched every muscle he could, as he pulled back, then released as he slammed into her one more time. As his dick crashed into her cervix, he felt his climax explode inside of her. Aria cried out

again, her head thrown back, her body shaking as her climax exploded over her. Fluid gushed down between her legs.

Ragden's body shook as cum spurted into Aria. He held her steady as her chest heaved with the effort to catch her breath. Her body continued to shudder and spasm. Her legs twitched, and he felt her start to lose her balance.

Ragden leaned forward, placing his chest against her back and wrapped his arms around her torso. Then he stood, lifting her against him. Her legs started to spasm. He stepped back, his dick sliding out from her dripping hole. Aria groaned loudly, her hands clutching her throbbing mound. Ragden swept her off her feet and carried her to the bed. He lay her down and then crawled over her. Aria spread her legs and wrapped them around his waist as Ragden slid up against her. His dick slid into her soaked pussy. Aria moaned loudly, her body spasming again. Her legs shuddered as she felt his heat filling her up again.

Ragden lay down against her, his body draping across her. He propped himself up on his elbows so as not to crush her and kissed her softly on the lips. Aria sucked fiercely on his tongue as he probed into her. When their kiss broke, she gasped at the air, her hips rocking and sliding forward along his cock. She could feel every inch of it throbbing inside her. She moaned, feeling so full of him. She wrapped her arms around him, pulling his body down against hers. She marveled at how firm and strong he felt against her.

In that moment, Aria felt truly complete. Everything she had gone through had been worth it. All the waiting, the anticipation. This moment made it all worthwhile. Still, she wanted more. She knew he could give it to her. Her heart still thundered in her chest and her legs shook. She tried to move herself against him, to feel that incredible presence move inside her, yet she lacked the strength to accomplish what she wanted.

Ragden looked down at her and cocked an eyebrow. He could feel her trying to move against him and knew what she wanted. He kissed her softly on the lips, then he kissed her jaw and throat. He drew back and looked down at her. She opened her eyes and saw him looking at her.

"Do I..." She swallowed, trying to catch her breath, "Do I need to worry about getting pregnant?"

Ragden shook his head and spoke softly, "Is that something you want?"

"Maybe someday. Not today. How does that work?"

Ragden shrugged. "I'm not sure, all my dad said was that if it were something we both wanted, it would happen. I'm not ready for that yet. Are you?"

Aria shook her head. "No. I just want to enjoy being with you."

Ragden smiled. "That you can have."

"Thank you," she whispered as she ran a hand through his hair. Then she closed her eyes and lay back against the bed, letting her body relax. She could still feel his hard meat between her legs, filling her. She smiled as her pussy

clenched him inside her. Ragden smiled down at her. As her heart started to beat a more normal rhythm, she looked up at this man who had changed her life. She reflected on the events of the last week. She had no regrets. This was what she had wanted. She loved it. She looked into the depths of his eyes and saw only love and compassion there. Her chest filled with warmth. How did she get this lucky? She leaned up and kissed his lips and felt their softness against her own.

"Thank you," she whispered as they broke apart, "I can never thank you enough for.... everything."

She smiled as she looked down at that incredible body of his lying on top of her, then she brought her gaze back up to his face. She saw that he was blushing. She laughed and pulled him tighter against her. She loved that he was so humble and caring with her. She lay back and looked up at him again. She saw a tear in his eye. She leaned forward and kissed it from his cheek.

"No," he said softly, "I must thank you. For welcoming me in your heart, and your bed. For showing me the other side of you. The beautiful, incredible side that I will always love."

Aria's heart soared and she blushed. She knew he could see every inch of her. She felt like he could see into her soul, and she felt vulnerable and exposed, yet she felt so loved and cared for. She felt her tears starting to well up in her eyes. She loved him so much at that moment that she felt like her heart was going to break. She pulled him down to kiss her again. Their lips met and their hearts raced.

Love & Nature

CHAPTER 37

As their kiss deepened and became more passionate, Ragden slid his knees under Aria's thighs, repositioning his groin over hers. As their lips broke, Aria looked up at him and saw the desire in his eyes. She felt the burning heat between her legs, nodded, and bit her bottom lip. She pulled up her feet and pressed down into the bed behind him, raising her groin off his. She closed her eyes as she felt his cock start to slide from within her, then she lowered herself and felt him sliding back into her. That incredible heat pressed against her cervix again and a shudder of ecstasy ran up through her body.

Aria's heart skipped a beat. She loved the way her body responded to his. She loved the way it felt to have his massive cock sliding up into her, filling every inch of her tight, wet pussy. She bit her lip and nodded at him, encouraging him to continue.

Ragden smiled down at her. He raised his groin slightly off hers, using his knees as leverage to slide in and out of her at a gentle pace. Aria closed her eyes, feeling him sliding in and out of her. A moment later, she matched his pace, raising and lowering her hips along with his movements. Their groins thumped gently together. Aria felt the pressure building inside her again.

With her eyes closed, Aria's mind wandered. She brought her hand up to her chest and cupped her small, firm breasts. She felt the gentle roundness of them and ran her thumbs over her nipples. She felt them rock softly with each thrust of him between her legs. She wondered if Emily or Sarah experienced this profound sense of bliss and pleasure when they were with him. They certainly looked like they were enjoying themselves when she watched them together. What did they feel, though? Was it the same? The incredible sensation of Ragden between her legs brought her back to reality.

Ragden continued to move gently between her legs, sliding his cock in and out of her tight pussy. His big dick gently bumping into her cervix, then drawing back. Aria rocked her hips in time to his thrusts, pulling back from him, then sliding towards him as he slid into her. Each joining of their hips

was punctuated by the impact of his dick against her cervix.

Aria felt the pressure within her building with each impact against her cervix. She felt the ripples of pleasure as they rolled through her body. Aria opened her eyes and looked up at Ragden. She saw him looking down at her, watching her. She smiled, and he smiled back at her. She reached up, wrapped her arms around his neck, and pulled him down against her. They continued to move against each other, each impact a little harder than the last. The pressure within her kept building and building.

Ragden leaned down and put his face between her breasts. He kissed her breastbone, then dragged his tongue along her sternum to that soft spot between her collarbones. Aria moaned in pleasure and thrust against him a little harder. Ragden increased his pace marginally and kissed along her throat, gently grazing her soft skin with his teeth, then he kissed her jaw and worked his way to her ear. He suckled on her earlobe and then kissed her neck under her ear. Aria moaned loudly as he kissed her neck again.

She grasped his back, pulling him down against her as his teeth dug into her neck. She arched her neck back, exposing more of her throat as she arched her back and thrust against him harder.

"Oh, God," she moaned as his thrusts became more insistent. Each impact rocked her body. She felt her legs vibrating with the impact. She let go of his back, and he raised himself to look her in the eyes. She saw the incredible desire burning in his eyes and a shiver ran down her back as she looked into the fathomless depths she saw there. Aria felt her climax fast approaching, but she was not ready for it yet.

She pressed her feet down into the bed and raised her groin off his throbbing cock. She felt it slip out of her and gasped. Ragden blinked in surprise, his cock throbbing hard outside her body. She reached down and grasped it firmly, feeling it slip around in her hand with her fluids. She shivered again. Aria looked up at him and bit her lip. She saw his questioning gaze, his raised eyebrow. She closed her eyes as she concentrated on what she was doing.

Aria stroked his cock once, feeling it throb in her hands, then slowly lowered her body onto it. She felt the tip of it push against her back. She raised herself and pointed his cock at her body, and then she lowered herself until she felt the tip of it press between her ass cheeks. She felt the incredible heat pressed against her ass.

She exhaled sharply, not realizing she had been holding her breath. She took a slow, deep breath as she looked into his eyes. She saw his desire, need, and desperation to be inside her. She wanted him so badly that her heart thundered in her chest. She wanted his big dick in her ass, filling her bowels.

Aria lowered herself slowly, feeling the head of his cock pressing against her ass. Its size and girth spread her tight hole open. She gasped as the head of it slipped into her. She paused there. Her legs shook with the effort of holding that position. She tried to prepare herself for what would come next.

She had had this before, but somehow this was different. More intimate. More personal. She knew he had seen every part of her and fucked every part of her, but still, she paused. She felt vulnerable, exposed, stripped to her core before him. Her desire pounded through her.

Aria took another deep breath and exhaled slowly. Her heart thundered as she slowly sank herself onto his waiting cock. She watched his eyes close in pleasure. The gentle sigh on his lips. She could see how much he enjoyed the way her body felt on his. A thrill ran through her. Her heart thundered in her chest.

Ragden kept his eyes closed, savoring the incredible feel of Aria's tight ass enveloping his throbbing cock. Every muscle in his body tensed. She was so tight, so incredibly silky smooth, wrapped around his dick. He felt like he was ready to explode but knew that he wanted more. That she wanted more. She had chosen this. She had placed his cock in her ass, and his arousal had increased with each inch of his cock that she forced inside it. He forced his breathing to slow down as his pulse raced with excitement.

Slowly, ever so slowly, she lowered herself until every bit of his dick was up her ass. Her cheeks rested against his groin. As she relaxed and his cock throbbed in her ass, he opened his eyes and looked down into her face. He saw tears in her eyes. He froze as he watched her open her eyes and look up at him.

"Are you in pain?" he asked quietly, not daring to move.

Aria blinked the tears from her eyes and shook her head, "No. It feels amazing. I... I'm sorry; it feels so good. I did not realize it would feel this good. I love it so much, so incredibly much."

Aria felt the lump in her throat. The joy of the moment consumed her. The sheer, incredible, ecstatic joy of it. Their groins pressed together, and she felt how full her bowels felt with all of him in there. She loved how his cock bounced off her cervix when they fucked like rabbits, but this... this was a different kind of incredible joy that just made her feel so full.

Ragden smiled at Aria, feeling her ecstatic joy. He felt his cock throbbing inside her. Her body squeezed around him so tightly. She wrapped her arms around his neck and pulled his face down to hers, their lips nearly touching as she spoke softly, huskily, "Make love to me like this. Please."

They kissed. At first, the kiss was soft and tender, but then it deepened. Their lips parted, and their tongues twisted around each other. They pressed tighter against each other, pulling their bodies tighter together. Aria's breasts pressed firmly against Ragden's broad chest. His arms wrapped around her, pulling her against him in return. Their lips broke apart, leaving them both gasping. Ragden's cock throbbed deep within Aria. She closed her eyes, savoring the feel of it inside her.

"Of course, my love," he whispered against her cheek. Ragden smiled down at her, watching the look in her eyes as he slowly drew back from her. She bit her lip, her eyes going a little wide as she felt that massive meat in her

ass sliding almost out. She gasped, sucking in air sharply when he stopped moving. She nodded vigorously as he started to slide back into her. She moaned in pleasure, feeling him fill her again.

As their hips met again, Aria took another deep breath, savoring the way her body felt with that incredible invasion in her bowels. Then, as he started to withdraw, she shifted her hips and moved away from him. They moved together, their groins gently bumping into each other. Aria moaned in pleasure at the feeling. Her bowels filled with heat and pressure as they continued to move in unison, drawing apart and meeting again.

Ragden closed his eyes, savoring how tight she felt around his dick as he slid in and out of her. He kept the pace slow and methodical. He felt her body clenching tightly on his manhood, and he opened his eyes to look down at her again. She was staring up at him; sweat had started to collect along her brow. Aria moaned in pleasure, feeling the incredible waves of pleasure rolling through her body. The heat and pressure in her bowels were spreading through her abdomen. Her heart thundered in her chest.

Aria balled her fists up in the blankets under her. She tried to use them for further leverage to rock her hips against his thrusts. She tried to move faster, to urge him to fuck her harder, but his pace continued methodically. She could feel her climax fast approaching, building, and building within her. As he drew back and started to slide into her again, she rocked her hips against his, driving him deep into her. She gasped in pleasure as his dick filled her bowels. Then he started to slide back, and she moved away from him. As he started to move into her again, she slammed her groin against his.

"Harder," she begged.

Ragden nodded and sat back on his heels, his groin pressed firmly against her. She could feel his cock throbbing inside her. She clawed at the sheets, trying to push herself against him, to no avail, as he adjusted his position. He grabbed her waist and pushed her down into the mattress as he slid almost out of her, then he drove into her, drew back, and drove into her again. His groin slammed into hers, her entire body rocking with the impact. He continued picking up the pace, slamming his groin into hers. She gasped with each impact, feeling that impact rocking her body. Her breasts rocked, her hips vibrated, and her legs shook. She cried out with the next, feeling her climax growing faster and faster. She tried to rock her hips against his movements but found herself held in place as he pounded his cock into her ass.

Aria clutched at his arms, squeezing the strong muscles in her hands as he continued to slam into her. Her heart stampeded through her chest as her climax grew and blotted out her reality. She saw his eyes, the focus, depth, and concentration in them as he fucked her ass every bit as hard as she had begged for. She felt the length of his cock sliding in and out of her ass. Her bowels clenched and released as his meat slammed into her, then just as quickly slid back and in again. Her body rocked with even more force as he moved faster.

She could see the sweat breaking out on his brow. She could feel the monster of his climax growing, getting ready to claim her. 'Take me!' She wanted to shout but could not. She gasped for breath as her body rocked beneath his.

Then he suddenly slammed into her so hard her body rocked and convulsed. He pushed his cock impossibly deep into her. She could feel it filling her, exploding within her, and she realized his climax was filling her. As that realization dawned on her, her body convulsed, her legs kicked, her climax exploded and consumed her. Aria squeezed her eyes shut so hard that tears leaked onto her face. She felt a hot fluid gush from her pussy and heard it splash against his groin. She heard him moaning as his body shuddered within her. Then he jerked and spasmed, his groin drawing back and thrust into her repeatedly.

Aria cried out again, feeling another climax explode inside her and out of her. She felt his hot, sticky load blasting up into her bowels. She clutched at her chest, digging her nails into her breasts as her legs twitched and kicked under his grasp. Her body shuddered and pulsed, her heart still beating frantically in her chest. She rode out her orgasm, letting it run over her.

Ragden clenched every muscle, as his orgasm passed through him, then went limp and lowered himself down on top of her. He saw the tears of joy on her face as he lay across her and buried his face in her hair. She draped her arms around him and hugged him gently, then caressed his face with one hand. Her eyes were still closed, her breath only now starting to return to a more normal rhythm.

Aria lay still, letting her body relax after the sudden exertion. She felt a dull ache in her muscles. Aria ran her hands over Ragden's shoulders and then across his back, feeling his strong muscles. She felt his steady breath in her ear and the beat of his heart against her chest. She could feel his massive cock buried in her bowels, still leaking fluid into her. She could feel it inside her, large, firm, and gently pulsing with his life. It made her feel so alive and full of his love and presence to feel him buried within her. She gently clenched her ass on him and heard his breath exhale sharply in her ear. She giggled at the sudden response.

Feeling herself mostly recovered, she turned and kissed his cheek lightly. Ragden turned to her and gently raised himself until his face was above hers. His body felt rested and recovered. His cock still throbbed gently inside her. He could still feel cum leaking into her. He looked down into her face and saw the joyous contentment in her features. A beautiful smile lit up her features. She drew her hands up to his face and drew his face down onto hers. They kissed tenderly, their lips barely parting, their tongues touching and then drawing back.

Aria looked up into his face and admired the strong features and the tenderness in his eyes, and the love she felt looking into his face. She felt adored and cherished. In his eyes, she saw that love pouring out into her. Her heart fluttered in her chest, and she felt fresh tears in her eyes. She blinked

furiously to clear them. Ragden leaned down and kissed the tears from her cheeks. The soft brushing of his lips across her skin made her heart swell in her chest. She wrapped her arms around him, pulled her chest against his again, and squeezed as tight as she could.

Ragden lay against her, feeling her heart beating hard against his chest. He saw the love in her eyes. He felt his heart soaring for her. To see her so happy and content made him feel overjoyed. He placed his cheek against hers and kissed her earlobe softly, then kissed her ear.

Aria held him tightly, drinking in his love. She lay feeling the weight of his body across hers and savored the feel of his skin pressed against hers. She loved him and loved the way she felt under him. Then, after laying there for several moments, she drew her arms back and pressed gently against his shoulders. He raised himself on his elbows, looking down at her. She saw the question in his eyes.

"Yes, love?" he asked. His voice sent a shiver down her back. She felt his cock throbbing inside her ass and closed her eyes, taking deep breaths to calm herself.

"Can you try something different?" she asked.

"Of course," he answered with hesitation, "What would you like?"

Aria pushed against his chest until he sat back on his heels. She sat up, feeling his cock shift in her bowels, and closed her eyes again. She watched his face carefully as she raised her groin off his. She moaned softly as his thick meat slid from her body. She watched the look of desire pass over his face, along with the slight disappointment, carefully guarded. She smiled at him and then rolled over onto her hands and knees in front of him.

Aria looked over her shoulder at him and wiggled her ass. Then she spread her knees slightly and slipped a hand between her legs, and spread her pussy lips, slipping a finger into her dripping pussy. She moaned as she fingered herself for him, then she pulled her hand back and looked over her shoulder again. She saw him watching her perfect pussy like a hawk. She saw his monstrous, throbbing member leaking a tiny bit of cum. She felt a sudden, powerful desire to suck it off him. To taste it, swirl it on her tongue and swallow it. She closed her eyes as the vision washed over her, then she looked back as he leaned into her and buried his face between her cheeks.

Aria moaned loudly as his tongue pushed through her lips, finding her clitoris. She felt the soft pleasure as he sucked on her, then his tongue pushed through her lips into her soaked vagina. She moaned loudly, her legs shaking as he licked the inside of her. Then he drew back and ran his tongue across her asshole. She cried out, her body shaking with pleasure.

"Oh, God!" She cried, "Put that meat back in my ass! Please!"

Ragden laughed and sat up, his cock sliding through her lips to press against her body. She moaned loudly at the incredible sensation of it pressing against her, then drew it back and pushed the tip of it into her ass. She cried out again as she felt herself being spread open so it could slide into her.

Ragden watched her body twitch and convulse as he slowly pushed his cock into her ass. She looked over her shoulder and moaned, then gasped as it slid a little deeper into her. Her back arched, and her neck craned. She thrust herself against him, slamming her ass into his groin. His massive cock slammed deeply into her. She cried out again, her body shaking in ecstasy. She rocked forward, feeling his cock slide to the front of her, but not out. Then she rocked back against him again.

Ragden held his body still, letting Aria fuck herself on his cock in her ass. His hands rested lightly on her ass, caressing the soft skin, feeling the muscles flex as she rocked back and forth against him. He closed his eyes, enjoying the sensation of her tight ass sliding up and down his cock. With his eyes closed, Ragden could sense her climax building deep within her. Mentally, he held his in check. He could feel it building, and with a slight shift inside his head, he pushed it back, allowing her to build her own against him. His cock throbbed with need, and he could feel the pressure building in his balls, but he held it back while she worked herself into a frenzy.

Aria felt her body twitching in ecstasy as she thrust herself against him again and again. The impact of her ass against his groin pushed that incredible cock into her bowels. She could feel the pressure building and building within her. She knew she could not possibly last much longer at this rate. Her heart thundered in her chest, and her pussy clenched and released spastically. Her arms and legs shook with the effort to keep driving herself against him.

Ragden could feel her climax approaching, her body almost at the limit of what she could do. At that moment, when she was about to collapse, he grasped her hips and pulled her roughly against him. She cried out at the sudden, forceful impact. He quickly matched her pace, increasing the force of each thrust into her. Her breath exploded out of her with each impact as her body quickly passed the point of no return. Ragden cut loose the grip he had held on his climax, and as Aria screamed with her climax, his own rode over him, exploding into her.

Ragden thrust wildly into her a few more times, then pulled her ass against his groin as his body shuddered and collapsed against her. He slumped forward, laying his chest against her back. Aria's arms collapsed under the strain, and she went into the bed face-first. She laughed and turned her head to the side, then slid her body forward into the bed. Ragden held her hips against him as he crawled forward, easing her body down onto the bed. Once she was lying flat on her chest, he lay down against her back, his cock still shoved up her ass.

Aria giggled, enjoying the feel of his body against hers. She loved the feel of his heart beating against her back, the weight of his body limp against her. Ragden softly kissed her right ear. His hands found hers and clasped them tightly, the fingers interwoven.

"Are you comfortable, my love," he asked softly.

"Oh, oh yes," Aria answered softly, "Though it is a tad hard to breathe."

Ragden laughed, then raised himself off her. Aria sighed softly, not wanting his skin to part from hers. Then he slid backward, his cock sliding from her ass. Aria pushed her chest up off the bed and looked over her shoulder.

"You did not have to do that." she scolded softly.

Ragden laughed as he stepped off the bed. He grabbed her ankle and pulled her towards him. She laughed softly as he dragged her across the bed. Then he grabbed her around the waist and pulled her groin against him. She felt his cock press against her ass, and she spread her legs around his waist. Ragden grabbed his cock and slid into her wet pussy. Aria moaned loudly as she felt him fill her, his cock sliding deeper into it, pressed firmly against her cervix. Aria looked up at him, adoration in her eyes, biting her lip. Ragden reached down and grabbed her arms, lifting her towards him. She raised an eyebrow in surprise as he lifted her off the bed. One hand slipped under her ass, holding her to him, the other around her back, pulling her chest against his.

"Oh. Oh my," Aria laughed as her weight pushed his cock firmly against her cervix, "I do like this."

Aria wrapped her arms around his neck to hold herself in position as Ragden walked around the edge of the bed. He nonchalantly threw the covers back from the bed, then grabbed her ass and lifted her partially off his cock, and lowered her back down again. Aria moaned softly in pleasure and smiled at him.

Then Ragden crawled onto the bed, still holding Aria against him as he pushed the covers back. He plopped her in the middle of the bed and slid his knees up under her thighs. He gently slid his cock in and out of her tight wet pussy. Aria moaned in pleasure, rocking her hips with his movements.

"So soon?" she asked. "Don't you need time to recover?"

Ragden shook his head and kissed her softly on the lips, then sat back on his heels and pumped his cock in and out of her pussy. Aria felt that burning pleasure deep inside her. Yes, she wanted to feel him filling her up again. They moved quickly, finding a matching rhythm. They thrust their bodies together, his cock crashing into her cervix with more and more force. She felt her breasts rocking, her body vibrating with the sudden intensity. Again, she felt her climax building and looming over her. She looked up into his eyes and saw that the same intensity there that she felt.

They threw their bodies at each other, wildly, with reckless abandon. Then, as quickly as it had started, they both cried out as their orgasms exploded over them. They collapsed onto the bed, wrapping their arms around each other and taking deep breaths to calm their sweaty bodies.

Ragden rolled onto his side next to Aria and pulled her body against him. He curled around her, spooning himself against her. Aria pulled his arms around herself and slid her body against him. Ragden folded his legs up against hers. He slid his groin against her ass. His cock, still mostly firm, slid

between her legs. She giggled and reached down between her legs to feel its large form. She adjusted herself and slid it into her waiting pussy. She could still feel her fluids leaking out of her against him. She could also feel the fluid leaking out of his cock into her. It felt like heaven.

Aria curled herself tighter against Ragden, feeling his dick slide a little deeper into her. She could feel it starting to soften and could not suppress the small groan that slipped from her lips. She turned her head and felt his presence against her cheek. She knew she could not ask more of him at that moment. She could feel his breath against her neck, even and slow. His heart thudded heavily against her back, its pace slowing, then calming. She felt her own body calming, relaxing, and recovering. She pulled his hands up to her chest and squeezed her breasts with them softly. He ran his hands over them, gently brushing her nipples, sending a shiver down her back. He gently cupped them and pulled her against his back.

"Can I ask you a question?" Aria asked softly, her voice breathy and barely a whisper.

"Of course," Ragden sighed into her ear. She could hear the approach of sleep in his voice. She felt it tugging at her eyelids. She wanted nothing more than to sink into sleep in his arms. She could die now and be happy forever, but she had questions she wanted to ask before that happened. She took a deep breath and spoke softly.

"Your... bond with Emily," she asked, "What is that like?"

Ragden took a deep breath, feeling Aria cradled against him, and thought about Emily. His heart swelled with love for her. He could see her in his mind's eye, curled around Sarah, naked in bed and half asleep. He could also feel her breasts in his hands, the silky-smooth feel of her skin against his. He saw Emily open her eyes and look at him. He saw the love in her eyes, felt her breath on his cheek, and heard her whisper his name and her undying love for him. His heart swelled, and he felt Aria against him, his dick deep inside her. He could feel her waiting for his answer. He refocused on her against him, felt her heart beating slowly, calmly, her pussy tight around his cock.

"Our bond is like..." he paused for a moment, trying to find the right words, "It is like a warm blanket around my shoulders with her smell on it. She is with me always. I can close my eyes and feel her breath on my cheek, her touch on my shoulder. Her love is always with me. I can see her lying in bed wrapped around Sarah, drifting off to sleep..."

Aria felt a pang of jealousy. She wanted to feel Emily that way. She longed to wrap her arms around her and confess her undying love for the other woman. At that moment, she did not care that Emily was somehow closer to her lover than she was, she wanted to be with both at once, to feel their love wrapping around her for all time. She felt tears starting to form in her eyes. She took a breath and it hitched in her throat.

"And... Sarah," she asked, not wanting to hear the truth of it, but knowing she had to. "You bonded her too, somehow. Didn't you?"

Ragden could feel the hitch in Aria's voice, the pain beneath. He could feel that lonely spot in her heart that longed to be a part of something she could not grasp or understand. He knew he could not lie to her and knew this would only hurt her more.

"Yes," Ragden sighed, "Not the same, but... yes, I can sense her too and feel her as well."

"Why not me?" Aria demanded, her voice soft but insistent. She felt the hot tears on her cheeks but could not stop them.

"I told you. What I did with Emily was an accident, and it nearly killed her. I could not risk that with you. I would never do that on purpose. I do not want to lose you."

"And Sarah?"

"I..." Ragden paused, trying to find the words. "That had somehow already started. The way my dad explained it. Just being together will eventually form that same bond, over time. The more sex we have, the more of my essence you absorb into your body, the more we will become bonded like that."

"You sped up that process with Sarah," Aria said softly. "I saw it. I felt it. I.... felt it."

Aria's breath froze in her throat. She had felt it. She had not realized it, but she had felt the change in the other woman. She closed her eyes and searched for what that meant. She searched for some kind of connection to the other woman. She could not find it, but she knew something was there.

Ragden lay there quietly, waiting for Aria to ask the next question. He could sense the inner turmoil within her. The desperate need for that love she thought had been denied. He felt her pulse racing, then starting to slow. Aria turned her cheek to his. Ragden raised himself slightly so he could meet her gaze. He saw the pain in her eyes, the desperation.

"How long?"

"I do not know."

"How did you speed up that process with Sarah?"

"I needed Emily's help for that."

"Why?"

Ragden smiled sadly, "Because she has part of my soul. Without her by my side, I am not complete. When we have sex, and those two parts join, energy can be passed between us. We can do things with that energy. We forced it into Sarah and gave it no other outlet. It drained both of us. It infused Sarah with our energy and our love. Once she welcomed it, it became a part of who she is."

"Can you do the same to me?"

"I suppose we could," Ragden replied, thoughtfully, "But it was draining. We need time to recover before we can do it again."

"Please. I want to be included. I love you. I love Emily and Sarah. I want to be a part of this, too. Please."

Ragden kissed her softly on the lips. "There is a cost."

"I'll pay it."

Ragden smiled and kissed her on the cheek softly, "There is a drawback. Anything that happens to one of us affects all of us. If you were hit by a car, we would all feel the injury. If one of us.... dies... we might all die."

"I don't care."

"The others might. Can we discuss it first?"

"Yes..." Aria replied, as she felt a thrill pass through her. She wanted to be included. She would do or say anything to be a part of this thing her lovers had done. They had started a journey without her, and she was desperate to join them. Consequences be damned. She heard the assurance in his voice, felt the beat of his heart, and knew she might have a chance. She settled back against him and felt the even beating of his heart against her back. She pressed herself a little tighter against him and felt his cock twitch inside her. She could feel it, soft within her, and smiled. It felt amazing. She preferred it hard and full and stretching her to the limits of what she could take, but this was pretty amazing, too.

Ragden settled back into the bed. He grabbed the blankets and pulled them up over the two of them. He sank into the mattress, letting his body relax. He felt Aria's breath evening out and slowing. She would soon be asleep. Her pussy did not feel as tight on his manhood, and he knew he had softened inside her. He smiled and kissed the back of her head lightly. He did not doubt that Emily and Sarah would agree to let Aria join them, but he wanted to talk it over with them first, especially since it was something he had to have their help to do.

Ragden felt his body relaxing, his heart slowing, his breath even. His mind drifted. He felt Aria against him. He could tell she was asleep at this point. He smiled to himself as he finally drifted off to sleep.

CHAPTER 38

While Aria and Ragden sat at the dining room table talking, Emily and Sarah went up the stairs. They walked quickly into Ragden's room and pulled the door shut behind them. Emily untied her robe and dropped it to the floor at her feet. She walked around the room picking up her clothes where she had discarded them earlier.

Sarah leaned against the door, smiling as she watched Emily. She bit her finger and admired Emily's gentle curves. Sarah whistled softly, catching Emily's attention. Emily turned and saw Sarah watching her. She stopped and put one hand on her hip. She glared at Sarah.

"Like what you see?" she asked, rather pointedly.

"Oh, my," Sarah breathed huskily, stepping away from the wall to Emily. She stopped just short of her and looked over her from head to toe. She admired the curls in her bright red hair. The gentle sweep of her neck. Her large, incredible breasts. Her flat stomach. The thin tufts of red hair between her legs. Her generous thighs and narrow ankles. As she watched, she could see moisture collecting between Emily's legs. Sarah licked her lips, "You are so beautiful; I just want to eat you right up."

Emily blushed but did not cover herself. She bent over and picked up another article of clothing and turned to toss it on the bed. Sarah grabbed Emily by the hips and pulled her to her. Emily sighed as Sarah kissed her neck and wrapped her arms around her chest, gently grasping her breasts.

Emily sighed in her arms, her heart beating a little faster, "We need to get going before those two come upstairs."

"I know. I know," Sarah whined, "but can we have some fun first?"

Emily turned in Sarah's arms and pressed herself against the other woman. Sarah blinked and stumbled back before Emily grabbed her and hugged her fiercely. Their lips met, and Sarah grabbed Emily's luscious ass and pulled their groins together. They broke, breathing hard. Emily slipped a hand between her legs and felt her arousal dripping onto her fingers. She looked up

at Sarah and smiled. Sarah grabbed her hand and pulled her damp fingers into her mouth. Emily moaned softly as Sarah sucked her fingers clean.

Sarah giggled and released Emily's hand. Emily sighed, "Really, we can play later. Let's go to my house."

Sarah nodded and untied her robe, letting it drop around her feet. Emily took a step back and admired Sarah's figure. Sarah's dark hair danced around her shoulders. Sarah's breasts were not as large as Emily's, but they were still a good handful and beautiful to behold. Emily gazed at Sarah's flat stomach and the thick dark hair between her legs. Sarah struck a pose, spreading her legs so Emily could see the arousal collecting there. Emily blushed again and stepped back to the bed.

Sarah giggled as she gathered up her clothes. She tossed them to the bed, then stood shoulder to shoulder with Emily as they started to dress.

"What do you think they are discussing down there?" Sarah asked softly.

Emily shrugged, "Probably the activities of this weekend."

"What do you think he will tell her?"

Emily looked at Sarah as she got dressed. Her gaze slid down to Sarah's chest, and Emily lost her train of thought for a moment. She had the urge to suckle Sarah's chest and had to blink twice to refocus her thoughts.

"I'm sure he will tell her whatever she wants to know."

"You think?"

"Yeah, why not?"

"I don't know. Everything has been strange with Aria, ever since... well, you know."

Emily turned to look at Sarah again. Sarah was not normally one to mince words, and her hesitation confused Emily for a moment. Emily pulled her pants up and then turned to Sarah.

"I know," Emily said softly, "But, how do you feel about Aria? With everything that has happened. What does your heart tell you?"

Sarah pondered for a moment, as she pulled her panties up onto her hips, then slid her skirt up and zipped up the zipper. She closed her eyes and let her mind wander. She searched through her feelings. Deep within her, she felt that core of her being. In that presence, she sensed that alien warmth that was Ragden within her. She could not help but smile as she felt that warmth radiating out through her. His love and compassion filled her, and then she thought about Aria. That same warmth filled her. She smiled and opened her eyes to see Emily smiling back at her.

"Love," Sarah said softly, "I love her. But... Is that what I feel for her, or what Ragden feels for her?"

Emily's smile deepened, "Does it matter?"

"I," Sarah paused, then chuckled, "I suppose not. Is this what your bond with him feels like? Always loving everyone and wanting to fuck them too?"

Emily blushed and then softly punched Sarah in the arm. "Yes and no. The sex thing is... for real, like, ALL The time. The love though," Emily

hugged herself and sighed in pleasure, "It is amazing. It feels so wonderful to just be able to love him, and you, and Aria. It fills me with love and it feels so amazing. I am so incredibly grateful. I know it was horrible what happened, but I would not change a thing."

Sarah smiled. She felt some of that, too, but not as strongly as Emily. She was happy. Sarah finished putting on the last of her clothes and then turned to Emily. She watched Emily slip the lace bra on.

"You wore this for him?"

"Oh," Emily blushed a tad, "yes."

"How did he like it?"

"I'm sure he loved it, but I think he enjoyed taking it off more."

Sarah laughed. That did not surprise her. "I need to get something like that. Think you can take me to where you got it?"

"Sure. You know, if your chest gets any larger, it might just fit you."

"Wait, is that a thing that can happen?" Sarah asked, a bit surprised.

Emily laughed and nodded, "Oh yes. You are already changing. The more of him you have in you, the more it will change you."

"So that is why you look like this," Sarah laughed. Emily nodded, and then Sarah reached out and grabbed Emily's bosom. Emily laughed and hugged Sarah. The two of them kissed softly and parted, laughing.

"Come on. Let's get going. They will be up soon."

"The bond?"

"Yeah," Emily grabbed the two robes off the floor in one hand, and Sarah's hand in the other. They stepped across the hall, hung up the robes, then headed downstairs. They hurried to the front door and slipped out without making a noise. As they stepped down the walkway, Emily dragged her hand through the bushes. She felt their leaves caressing her skin and softly wrapping around her fingers. She smiled to herself, then saw Sarah looking at her questioningly. Emily giggled then grabbed Sarah and ran down the street with her in tow.

"Why do the bushes respond to you?" Sarah asked when they had stopped running.

"Because of Ragden."

"That doesn't make any sense." Sarah laughed. "Can you explain that better?"

"Nope," Emily laughed as they walked up the step to her house. She unlocked the door and slipped in quietly. Emily and Sarah walked through the foyer and headed to the stairs. As they rounded the corner they almost ran straight into Emily's mom.

All three of them stopped in their tracks, looking at one another. Emily's mom grabbed Emily by the shoulders and pulled her into a hug. Emily stood surprised for a moment, then wrapped her arms around her mother and squeezed her tight. They stood embraced for a moment and then Emily started to pull back, but her mother held her tight, then released her.

Emily's mom grabbed Sarah and hugged her too. Sarah giggled and hugged Emily's mother tightly, then released her.

"Good evening, girls," she said after releasing Sarah, "I'm assuming you had dinner already."

Both Emily and Sarah nodded.

"At Ragden's house?"

Both nodded again.

"Oh, okay," Emily's mom said, sounding a tad disappointed, "Had a good day then?"

Emily blushed slightly, and Sarah nodded her head vigorously. Sarah smiled and laughed, "Oh yes, it was wonderful. Lots of sex. It was so nice."

Emily's mom's eyes widened for a moment. She looked at Emily, who blushed, then back to the giant grin on Sarah's face.

"Jean," Emily started to say, but her mother cut her off.

"Jean, is it now? No more Mom?" Jean said, a little touch of anger in her voice, "You get a boyfriend, and now I'm Jean?"

"Mom, yes, we had a wonderful day. What do you want me to say?" Emily blurted out.

Jean frowned. She opened her mouth to say something, then closed it. Then she spoke quietly, "You are using protection, yes? Please tell me you are."

Emily blushed, and Sarah gushed, "Oh, good God, now. I love the feel of his giant dick in all my holes," Sarah spun around, clutching her hands to her chest, her skirt flaring. Jean glared at her, "It is so wonderful; I just cannot get enough."

Jean shot daggers with her eyes at Sarah, who saw and just laughed. Emily blushed an even darker crimson. Jean turned back to Emily and scowled.

"Well, I will not try to stop you," Jean clucked her tongue in annoyance, "Just, be aware of what you are getting yourselves into."

Sarah giggled and hugged Jean. The older woman stood surprised for a moment, then hugged Sarah back. She glared at Emily the whole time. Emily looked down at the floor, then back up at her mom, embarrassed.

"Her, I get," Jean said, nodding to Sarah as the younger woman giggled and stepped back, "but you, I would have thought better of."

"It isn't like that..." Emily started to say, but Sarah cut her off.

"Oh, Jean, Ragden has a magical dick that transforms us into the best part of ourselves and will never get us pregnant. It is totally cool. We cannot get sick, and we'll stay young sluts forever!!"

Jean blinked slowly, staring at Sarah. Sarah laughed and then walked past Jean, who stood in shock as Sarah went into Emily's room. Jean shook her head and then looked back at Emily. Emily shrugged.

"You cannot be serious," Jean said to Emily, "That is a joke, right?"

Emily stood there with her hands clasped, not sure what to say. She shrugged again, then said softly, "No."

Love & Nature

"Are you on drugs?"

"No. I promise. No."

Jean sighed and pinched the bridge of her nose in frustration. Then she looked back at her daughter. She took another deep breath and let it out slowly. "Just be safe. Please."

"Of course, Mom."

Emily stepped up and hugged her mother again, who returned her embrace. From Emily's room, they could hear Sarah giggling and singing to herself. Jean shook her head as she released Emily from her embrace. Emily kissed Jean on the cheek and whispered, "I love you, Mom."

"I love you too, darling."

Then, the two women parted; Emily pushed her bedroom door open and walked in. Sarah was prancing around the room in her underwear, humming a tune to herself as she did. When Emily closed the door, Sarah stopped and sat down on the edge of Emily's bed, laughing.

"Are you trying to make my mom mad at us?" Emily asked quietly.

Sarah laughed, "No. It was the truth, though."

"A truth she is not ready to hear."

"Does not matter."

Emily sighed, then walked over to her friend and sat down next to her on the bed. She looked at Sarah and hugged her.

"You really do enjoy making my life difficult, don't you?"

"Sometimes," Sarah giggled, "It felt like the right thing to say. Your mom took it well."

"She thinks you are on drugs."

"I am," Sarah grinned, "The best drug in the universe, Ragden's magic love cum."

Emily laughed and kissed Sarah softly on the lips, then pulled back and whispered, "I love you."

Sarah giggled, "I love you too."

Emily stood and moved over to her dresser and pulled open a drawer. She started going through her clothes. Sarah stood and came over to her.

"Looking for something specific?"

Emily nodded. "Actually, Ragden has a big math test tomorrow morning, and I thought it would be fun to surprise him with a cute outfit and then drag him off somewhere for lunch to have some fun."

"Oh," Sarah's grin became devilish, "You want something that will make him want to fuck you in the ass like the slut you are. I totally get it."

Emily giggled and shook her head. Then, she looked at Sarah, laughed, and nodded.

"Well," Sarah said matter-of-factly, "I'm quite sure that man would want to fuck you three ways from Sunday regardless of what you are wearing. But if you really want to grab his attention. Why don't we wear matching short skirts and tank tops? Then we can all tease him until he busts a nut for each of us?"

Emily laughed and nodded. "Deal."

For the next few moments, Sarah and Emily went through Emily's wardrobe, picking out skirts and tops until they found outfits that matched what they were aiming for. They set their clothes out on the desk and then stood back to admire what they had picked.

"I think that will be perfect," Emily said.

"Oh, yes. I cannot wait to see his expression." Sarah giggled.

Emily grabbed Sarah and pulled her against her, grabbing her ass under her skirt, pulling their groins together. Sarah sighed in pleasure and wrapped her arms around Emily. They kissed tenderly, then more forcefully. When they broke, both were breathless. Emily stepped away from Sarah and walked over to the bed, then turned back to Sarah.

"Are you spending the night tonight?"

"Oh, fuck yeah," Sarah answered, pulling her top off and unzipping her skirt. Emily watched as Sarah stripped. When Sarah stood naked before her, Emily pulled back the covers of the bed and then took off her own clothes. Emily backed onto the bed, watching Sarah stalk towards her. Then Emily reached out and took Sarah's hand, pulling her onto the bed with her.

Sarah slid across the bed and wrapped her arms around Emily, pulling their chests together. Emily wrapped her legs around Sarah and pulled them together. Sarah kissed Emily forcefully, rolling her over onto her back. Emily moaned in pleasure as Sarah slid her hands across Emily's ample bosom. Emily arched her back, thrusting her breasts into Sarah's hands. Sarah leaned down and kissed Emily's neck, then her collarbone, and worked her way down to her breasts, suckling and licking each. Emily moaned in pleasure.

Sarah slid one hand between Emily's legs and cupped her damp mound. Emily moaned louder as Sarah slid two fingers through Emily's lips and into her pussy. Emily rocked her hips against Sarah's hand, feeling those fingers slide deeper into her. Emily moaned in pleasure as Sarah stroked her fingers in and out of her tight, wet pussy. Sarah pulled her head off of Emily's chest and looked at her, a question in her eyes.

"How does he fit that giant dick in this little hole? I cannot get a third finger into you."

Emily moaned as Sarah continued to fuck her pussy. She panted as she sat up slightly and looked at Sarah. Sarah grinned evilly, then leaned down to run her tongue through Emily's folds. Emily gasped and threw her head back, moaning in pleasure.

"It... stretches," Emily responded between gasps of pleasure as Sarah pulled her fingers out and slipped her tongue into Emily. Emily flopped back on the bed and arched her back as Sarah licked the insides of her pussy. Emily felt that pressure starting to build within her. That need for release. Sarah slid her middle finger deep into Emily's pussy, causing her to gasp and moan in pleasure again. Sarah sucked on Emily's clitoris as she stroked deep into Emily's pussy.

Sarah giggled, then ran her tongue through the length of Emily's snatch. Then she leaned lower and ran her tongue around Emily's ass. Emily gasped and moaned even louder. Sarah moved a little higher, slipped her tongue into Emily's pussy, then moved up and suckled on her clit again, sucking and running her tongue over it. She slipped a finger around Emily's ass, teasing the edges of it.

"Yes! Yes!" Emily exclaimed, rocking her hips against Sarah's face. Emily felt her climax swiftly approaching. Then Sarah plunged her finger up Emily's ass, and Emily cried out, her climax exploding at the sudden invasion. Her body bucked and shuddered. She felt hot fluid gush through her pussy. Sarah changed her position and latched her mouth over Emily's wet mound.

"Oh, fuck!" Emily exclaimed as Sarah sucked down the fluid bursting from her. Emily twitched and spasmed, her body rocking and bucking against Sarah as the other woman continued to suck down every bit of fluid that flowed out of her.

Sarah continued to suck on Emily's snatch, running her tongue up inside the other woman and enjoying the feel of her body spasming around her. She pulled her face out of Emily's pussy and looked down at her handiwork. Emily continued to twitch and spasm with the aftershocks of her orgasm. Sarah spied more fluid leaking out of her and leaned down to lap it up. Emily twitched and clapped her legs around Sarah's head. Sarah giggled into Emily's pussy, then dipped her tongue as deep into her as she could. Emily moaned in pleasure as Sarah ran her tongue deep into Emily. Sarah savored the taste of her.

As Emily started to relax and her pulse started to resume a more normal flow, her legs relaxed, and Sarah was able to extricate herself. Emily giggled as Sarah sat up. Sarah crawled forward over Emily, her face still dripping with Emily's juice. Emily reached out and pulled Sarah down to kiss her. Emily licked Sarah's face, tasting her cum on the other woman. They kissed, and Emily savored the taste of her fluids on Sarah's tongue.

They kissed passionately for a moment, then Emily rolled Sarah over onto her back. She smiled down at the other woman, then kissed her on the cheek, ear, and neck. Sarah made small noises in her throat as Emily worked her way down to her chest, gently kissing and nipping at the skin. Sarah closed her eyes, letting the sensations wash over her.

"My turn," Emily growled into Sarah's chest as she kissed her way down her abdomen. Emily kissed Sarah's navel as she squirmed beneath her. Then Emily grabbed Sarah's legs and spread them so she could get better access to her nether region. Sarah moaned as Emily kissed the top of her mound and teased her lips.

Sarah squirmed and moaned as Emily slipped her tongue through her labia, then sucked on her clitoris. Sarah moaned in pleasure as Emily slid a finger through her lips and into her pussy. Emily lifted her face and looked up at Sarah.

"You know, you aren't exactly loose down here either, love," Emily said with a smile as she slipped a second finger into Sarah's pussy. Sarah moaned in pleasure as Emily stroked in and out of Sarah's wet pussy. She ran her tongue down through her folds, briefly dipping it into her pussy, then went back to sucking on her clitoris and swirling that sweet nub around with her tongue. She stroked her fingers in and out of Sarah faster, feeling the other woman's body tremble with need and desire.

Emily closed her eyes and could feel the energy within Sarah starting to wake and respond to her. She turned her gaze inward and found that part of her that resonated with love and power. For a moment, she saw Ragden in bed with Aria, their groins thumping together, his big dick going deep up her ass. Her body vibrated and spasmed with ecstasy. Emily felt herself go suddenly damp with arousal, her ass aching to be filled by his incredible meat.

Then, she found that core of her energy that resonated with Sarah's. She tugged at it and felt it flow through her, filling her with love and passion. She opened her eyes and saw the slightly surprised look on Sarah's face. Emily ran her tongue through Sarah's folds again and tasted the slight change in her body chemistry. She could taste a hint of Ragden on her skin and in her pussy. Sarah moaned loudly, her body convulsing slightly.

Emily summoned the energy up her arm and felt it pulsing in her hand. With each beat of her heart, she could feel the heat suffusing her fingertips. She looked at her hand, seeing it glow slightly. She could feel Sarah's energy responding. She pinched her fingers together and placed all of them at the opening of Sarah's pussy.

Sarah sat up on her elbows and looked down between her legs at Emily. Emily smiled up at her and then pushed her fingers into Sarah's pussy. Sarah's eyes bulged, and she threw her head back and flopped on the bed, gasping as Emily's whole hand slid up into her.

"Oh, my God! Oh, my God!" Sarah gasped as Emily's hand slid up into her. Sarah squeezed her eyes shut, feeling the pressure between her legs grow and grow. Then she felt Emily's hand slide up into her, and she cried out. Her body shuddered, her legs spasmed, and she felt her body suddenly climax at the incredible invasion.

"Holy Fuck!" Sarah cried out, beating her arms on the bed, her body shuddering in ecstasy.

Emily giggled, feeling Sarah's juices run down her arm. Then she balled up her fist and pulled her hand back, then slid it forward into Sarah's cervix. She felt the solid impact inside Sarah's body and grinned. Sarah cried out again, her legs convulsing. Emily bent down and licked Sarah's clit as she pulled her fist back and slid it forward into Sarah's cervix again. Sarah cried out again, louder than last time. Emily pulled her hand back one last time, then tried to concentrate on the energy within Sarah, drawing it toward her, then slid her fist forward into Sarah's cervix and released the energy.

Sarah cried out again, her body shuddering as the energy surged up into

her. Emily grinned wickedly, watching Sarah thrash on her arm, then she squeezed her fingers together and slowly pulled them out of Sarah's swollen pussy. As her hand slid free, Sarah cried out again. Emily raised herself and crawled up over Sarah. Sarah lay gasping on the bed, sweat across her brow. She could barely move as Emily crawled over and kissed her lips softly. Sarah saw Emily's soaking wet hand and laughed.

"You put your whole fucking hand inside me!?" Sarah exclaimed in disbelief.

"Yeah. Your body stretches too, love," Emily laughed and lay down next to Sarah, resting her head on her shoulder. Sarah lay there gasping. Sarah thought about the experience. It was unlike anything she had felt before. She had a challenging time wrapping her mind around what Emily had just done to her. It was different from having Ragden fuck her silly, but it still felt pretty amazing.

Emily curled up against Sarah, then gently rolled her over onto her side so that her back was to her. Sarah lay there numbly, letting Emily move her around. Emily wrapped her arms around Sarah's body and pulled her against her. Emily sighed in pleasure as she pulled Sarah's ass into her groin and cradled her body. She reached around Sarah and gently cupped her breasts, pulling her back against her chest. Emily breathed in the smell of Sarah's hair and sweat. She buried her face in her hair and kissed her softly. Sarah moaned softly, her body still experiencing aftershocks of the sudden orgasm.

Emily relaxed and lay against Sarah. She could sense that core of her that held Ragden's energy. She felt it warm her and soothe her. She felt his presence within her and sighed in pleasure. Emily kissed the back of Sarah's ear. Sarah moaned softly.

"Think of Ragden," Emily whispered into Sarah's ear, "Let your mind wander, and let your heart and your love guide you. Maybe you can picture what he is doing and where he is. If your bond is strong enough, you might even feel his touch or his breath on your skin."

"That would be nice," Sarah mumbled softly as she felt sleep starting to claim her. She let her mind wander, and closed her eyes, drifting in the depths of her psyche. She felt Ragden's warm presence filling her, his love flowing through her veins.

In her mind's eye, Sarah pictured Ragden kneeling behind Aria, who was on all fours. Sweat streaked down Aria's arms and beaded her brow. Ragden held Aria's waist, pulling her back against him. His massive cock was buried in her ass. They moved frenetically, with power and speed that made Sarah's pulse race to see it. She watched as they slammed their bodies together until Aria collapsed, and she felt Ragden's incredible climax exploding out of him into Aria's tight ass. Aria collapsed onto the bed, and Ragden lay down on top of her, his big dick pressed as deep into her as he could get it. She saw the tears of joy on Aria's face. Sarah felt her ass clenching and aching for that big meat to fill her.

Sarah licked her lips and felt Emily pressed against her back. Emily's hands on her chest, squeezing her nipples. Emily kissed her ear again, and her voice was soft and soothing.

"That was amazing to watch," Emily whispered, "Maybe next time you can be on the receiving end, or I will. Or all three of us can take our turns fucking Ragden until he explodes inside of us."

Sarah sighed in pleasure, "Yes. That was awesome. I wish I could be there with them, to lick him clean, to taste her cum on my tongue. Why did we have to come here and be without him?"

Emily sighed against Sarah, "Because Aria needed some time with him. She never got a chance to have him alone like we did. Next time, we can all be together, and it will be amazing."

Sarah nodded, "That sounds amazing. I cannot wait, but I'm so tired."

Emily chuckled and kissed Sarah's neck. "Then sleep, love."

Sarah nodded once more, then drifted off to sleep. Emily lay there holding her, feeling her pulse slowing, her breath becoming soft. She held her against her, as she slept and marveled at the feel of it. She rested her head in Sarah's hair, enjoying the feel of her body against her. She desperately wanted to have Ragden inside her, but it filled her with joy to know that Aria had gotten a chance. She drifted again, her mind wandering. She could see Ragden looking down on her and Sarah. She reached out to him and whispered her love for him. She could see him cradled around Aria. Aria drifted off to sleep in his arms. She smiled at him and blew him a kiss, then slipped off into sleep herself.

CHAPTER 39

Selina sat in the front seat of her car, hands on the steering wheel as she watched Ragden and his family drive away. She resisted the urge to follow them. Her heart hammered in her chest. Her knuckles were white around the steering wheel as she fought the urge to follow. Her keys were already in the ignition. All she had to do was turn the key, put the car in drive, and follow. It would be so easy. Then she could have him again. She could put her hands on his skin to feel that heat. That power. That presence inside her that made her feel like she was the most important person in the world.

Selina closed her eyes and took a deep breath. Her body shook with need and desire. Goosebumps ran down her arms and legs. Her knees knocked together. She could feel herself growing damp between her legs. The memory of him fucking her was overpowering. The way he had taken her on the beach, her legs in his arms, his dick slamming into her ass, filling her and filling her with his life, his love, and his seed overflowing in her bowels. Then in the theatre, where he was tender, passionate, caring, and full of love. His big dick filled her pussy with all of him. Then the next morning, after his shower, the way his dick had swelled and filled her bowels. It had been unlike anything she had ever dreamed possible. Nothing had prepared her for that.

Selina panted; sweat beaded her brow. Her arms shook. Her legs felt weak. Her pussy felt stretched and abused. Her ass burned. She felt wetness leaking out of her ass, and she gasped. She threw the door open and jumped out of the car, swearing. She slipped her hand down her backside under her shorts and panties. She ran a finger around her ass and felt something sticky.

Selina cursed again and pulled her hand out so she could see what was on her finger. She expected to find blood from how savagely he had fucked her ass, but instead, she saw a white sticky substance. Her eyes widened. She sucked it off her finger and moaned in ecstasy. The taste was exquisite. Like some fine salted candy. Her entire body shook with desire.

Selina yanked her shorts down around her ankles. Then she bent over

slightly, slipped her right hand through her ass cheeks, and ran her middle finger around the edges of her asshole. Much to her surprise, her puckered hole was tight and small. Her finger would not fit. She pulled her hand back, sucked on her middle finger, then bent over and pressed it against her ass again, trying to slip her finger into herself. She moaned loudly as her finger slipped inside.

She stood there, slightly bent over, her finger up her ass twitching in ecstasy. Her finger was in her ass, up to the first knuckle. She could feel the slipperiness in her ass and, for a moment, remembered how it felt to have Ragden's swollen member filling her. Her bowels clenched at the memory, and her ass squeezed on her finger. She cursed softly and slipped her finger out. When she looked at her finger, she noticed a fine film of white across it.

Selina sucked her finger clean again, and her body convulsed again at the fine taste of Ragden's cum. She could feel more of his cum slipping from her bowels. She pulled her shorts and panties off and squatted next to her car. She placed her hand under her ass and pushed. She farted softly, and then she felt a splash of liquid land in her hand.

She brought her hand around and looked at the small pile of cum in her hand. Selina stood slowly, her body quivering with desire. She could feel her pussy lips nearly dripping with need. She slowly brought her hand up to her face and then licked it clean. She closed her eyes and let the sensation wash over her. She felt her entire body shudder again. Her arousal ran down her legs. She clutched her damp pussy and slipped two fingers into herself. Her pussy was tight but overflowing with arousal. She fingered herself slowly, moaning in pleasure.

Selina leaned back against the car and spread her legs to give herself easier access. She thumbed her clit and continued to stroke her pussy. She felt her orgasm building rapidly. She imagined Ragden's big dick filling her ass again and promptly came. Her orgasm was brief but left her shaking. Her legs buckled and she slid down the side of the car until she was sitting in the dirt next to the car. She put her hands to her face, pressing against her eyeballs, and cried softly.

It was not enough. It would never be enough. She needed that monstrous cock. That enormous, swollen member, filling her again. She could see it in her mind's eye, inhumanly large. Impossibly enormous. Something that could not possibly fit inside any woman, and yet, somehow, it fit inside her.

Selina pulled her knees up to her chest and wrapped her arms around them. She rested her forehead against her knees and cried. After several minutes, she started to calm down. As her sobs resolved into soft hitches in her breath, she realized where she was. She spotted her shorts and panties a couple of feet away. She crawled over and picked them up, then stood and slipped them back on. As she pulled her shorts up around her waist again, she felt her ass clench and spasm. She clutched at her stomach and bent over, her ass pressed against the car door, and groaned. She felt a burning need inside

her. A need to be filled. She wanted Ragden but knew she could not have him. Instead of him, she needed something... anything.

Selina looked around and spotted a few pieces of driftwood nearby but did not fancy the idea of splinters in her nether region. Selina pulled the door open and got back into her car. She put the key in the ignition and turned. The car roared to life. Selina put the car in drive and pulled out of the driveway. As she drove through the small beach town, she tried to remember if there was a sex toy shop anywhere nearby. She thought there had been one somewhere nearby, so she started on her way back towards her college dormitory.

As she drove, her body continued to spasm periodically. Her muscles continued to twitch, and she felt herself starting to sweat. She rolled down the window and felt the breeze blow through her hair. She shook her head back and forth, feeling the wind twist through her hair. She felt the wind swirl around in the car. It caressed her skin and cooled her burning desire. She felt it twist around her legs, and she shivered.

Selina caught movement out of the corner of her eye and turned to look around the car. She saw nothing out of the ordinary. The wind from the window continued to roar through the car. She felt the pressure building in her ears and hit the button to roll down the passenger side window to equalize it, then she looked into the rearview mirror and saw her reflection smile back at her.

Selina screamed and slammed on the brakes. The car skidded, and she twisted the wheel to keep control. The car slid to a halt, slightly sideways. She pressed the gas and eased the car onto the shoulder of the highway. Selina looked around the car and saw nothing out of the ordinary. She turned and looked into the mirror again, and her reflection shook its head, its lips moving as if to say, 'tsk-tsk.'

Selina shivered in fear, her eyes locked onto the figure in her mirror. The eyes of her reflection had green pupils that glowed softly back at her. The wind continued to blow through her window, billowing around the car, and whipping her hair around. She looked around the car, feeling the wind slip around her arms, like a soft caress. There was nobody else in the car that she could see. She looked back at the mirror, and her reflection smiled back at her.

"What do you want?" Selina whispered as goosebumps broke out along her arms. She was losing her grasp on reality. Surely her mind must be broken if she was talking to her reflection.

The wind in the car curled around her arm, then blew past her ear, blowing her hair back behind her. A soft voice hissed on the wind as the lips of her reflection moved.

"I want what you want. To sssee you filled by your pressssscious lover..."

Selina shivered again. The voice and presence seemed utterly alien to her. She had a strong urge to bolt out of the car and run, but curiosity held her in

place. She looked at her reflection, which waited for her to respond.

"Why do you care?" Selina asked, her voice small. The eyes of her reflection seemed to sparkle back at her. She cringed under that gaze. She felt those eyes boring into her. Selina felt naked and exposed before that penetrating gaze. She crossed her arms under her ample bosom and squeezed herself, trying to find warmth under that cold gaze.

Her reflection laughed at her. The wind whipped around her, making Selina shiver even more. The wind buffeted her face, blowing her hair back again. The voice hissed in her ear again.

"Do you want to be an Engineer, Ssselina?"

Selina looked at her reflection and saw those glowing green eyes staring at her. The smile was predatory. Selina blinked her eyes, confused.

"Y-yes. How did you know..."

"I've been watching you for sssome time. You are ssspecial... The thingsss we could do together. The thingsss I could ssshow you and teach you..."

Selina felt her curiosity growing. This thing she spoke with frightened her. Its alien presence and mannerisms made her skin crawl. Yet, she could not help but be intrigued by the possibilities. The ache between her legs was temporarily forgotten. Her mind whirled.

"What kinds of things?"

"Let me in, and I can ssshow you..."

"Okay," Selina sighed, nervous about what this might mean, but eager to learn, "Show me."

The wind suddenly blew into her face, forcing itself down her throat. Her eyes bulged, and the lights went out.

When Selina awoke, she was lying on a cloud. She looked around, and all she could see was white all around her. The cloud beneath her felt solid enough. She sat up and noticed she was wearing nothing. Her bare breasts jiggled against her chest as she stood. Selina looked around her again, noticing that the clouds were slowly shifting and moving around her. A strong wind swirled around her. She could see bits of color in the wind, little things that sparkled as it did. The wind started to collect and swirl in front of her, starting to take on shape.

In moments it took on a humanoid shape. It looked like her but was mostly transparent. A figment of wisps and wind collected into a swirling shape. Her shape. The more she looked at it, the more it looked like her. The same firm bosom, shapely legs, and slender arms. She smiled, looking at it, realizing how beautiful it was and how beautiful she was. She cupped her bosom and watched the figure before her do the same.

"Where am I?" Selina asked. Her voice sounded weak and insecure to her ears.

"Nowhere." The voice that answered was no longer a hiss of wind across her ears but inside her skull. Its strength caused her entire skull to vibrate. She clutched her head in pain. She looked at the figure which was watching her.

She got the impression that it was amused.

"Why am I here?" Selina asked. She looked at the figure and cowered slightly.

"To discuss the terms of our agreement." The voice in her head was quieter, but the strength of its presence in her mind was overwhelming.

"What agreement?" Selina asked. The figure looked at her, its eyes glowing green.

"You asked for knowledge, of the things I can show you, and teach you. I shall give you this; in return, you carry my spark."

As the voice spoke, the figure before her gestured to the clouds around them. As their arm waved, the clouds took shape. Buildings formed. Flying buttresses and arched bridges spanned between them. Their grace and beauty made Selina's heart sing.

"You spoke of Engineering. I can show you architecture that will defy logic, but I can show you how to make it work."

The figure turned back to her, and the clouds shifted back to their normal shapes. The figures' eyes glowed softly.

"Or, perhaps electronics interest you more?"

As the figure spoke, lightning jumped from cloud to cloud. The sky grew dark, and the air shook with thunder. A bolt of lightning crashed from the nearest cloud into the figure's outstretched hand. A crackling orb of electricity bounced in its hand. The figure raised its other hand, and the electricity arced between their hands, crackling with energy.

"I could show you how to manipulate electrical currents to do things you have never dreamed of..."

The figure smiled, and the electrical current jumped straight up into the clouds and vanished. The figure smiled at Selina.

"All of this could be yours," the figure said with a soft smile, "I only ask that you carry the smallest spark of my essence inside you."

Selina pondered this for a moment. This creature, this being, was so alien to her. The idea of having some part of it inside her made her skin crawl. Yet, the temptation of all that knowledge.

"If I refuse?"

"Then you go back to normal. You forget we ever had this conversation. It is your choice. But this is a one-time offer. It will never be offered again."

"Okay," Selina said softly, nodding, "I agree."

The figure before her blew apart. The myriads of lights and bits flew apart and then rushed at her. She felt the presence slam into her body, forcing its way into her ears, her nose, and her mouth. She felt it pressing against her eyeballs. She felt pressure against her ass and her pussy. Her lips pushed aside as something forcefully entered her body through every hole possible. She tried to scream in rage and terror but could not make a sound.

Selina awoke with a start, sitting in her car. The windows were open, and a soft breeze blew in from the cars blasting past her on the highway. She looked

around her car and found it empty. She looked down and saw that she was still fully clothed. She grabbed the rearview mirror and looked at her reflection. No glowing eyes. She sighed a breath of relief. Surely, what she had seen was just a fever dream caused by the events of the last two days. None of it had been real, right?

Selina turned the key, and the car roared back to life. She pulled back onto the highway and continued driving back to college. As she drove, her mind drifted, and she thought about the strange entity she had dreamed about. She had never had a dream like that before.

Thirty minutes down the road, she spotted a building off the side of the road that advertised adult merchandise. She pulled over and parked in their parking lot. She got out of the car and walked across the parking lot. As she did, she felt an ache in her bones, in her bowels, and her vagina. Her body ached from how she had been fucked. She smiled, remembering the fun she had had, and she felt her arousal starting to build in response to the memory. She still desperately wanted to fill that fullness inside her again.

Selina walked into the store. The clerk behind the counter looked up at her and smiled. His eyes followed her as she turned away from him. He was not unattractive, and for a moment, she wondered how big his dick was. Could he fill her like Ragden had? Could he fuck her and make her cum like he did? She blushed and turned away, hiding her face.

She found herself in a row of various sexual implements. She saw nipple clamps, whips, and other devices used to tie people down. She tried to imagine Ragden tying her up and applying these things to her body. She had never seen some of these things, and the thought of having them applied to her made her even more aroused. Her heart thumped hard in her chest. She looked down at the floor and kept moving. She followed the aisle to the end and turned deeper into the store.

To her left, Selina spotted movement. She turned her head and saw the clerk walking down the aisle towards her. She stopped as he approached her. He caught her eye and stopped just out of arms reach.

"Evenin' ma'am," he said politely, "Can I help ya find somethin'?"

Selina blushed, opened her mouth, and closed it. She took a deep breath and said softly, "I'm... looking for..." Her mind went blank. She looked at the clerk and noticed a swell in his pants. She looked up at his face and noticed a soft smile. He raised his eyebrows and inclined his head, encouraging her to finish her sentence.

"Dildos," she said and blushed. She looked down at the floor. Then back up to the clerk. The clerk smiled softly.

"Looking for anything specific? We have lots of different types, shapes, and sizes."

"Something big." she blurted out. The clerk looked surprised for a moment, then inclined his head and gestured for her to follow as he went down the aisle. Selina followed.

The clerk led her to the back of the store, where there was a massive selection of dildos. They had dildos of every imaginable size and shape. Some that vibrated, others that did not. They were made of rubber, plastic, latex, and metal. She gawked at the selection, unsure of what she wanted. The clerk watched her for a moment.

Out of the corner of her eye, Selina noticed the clerk gazing at her bosom, then her stomach, and down to her shapely legs and between them. She blushed, not used to such scrutiny. When the clerk noticed that she had seen him looking at her, he blushed. Then pointed to the section with the larger dildos. He pointed at a particularly large pink dildo with a slight curve in it.

"This one is our best seller for large ones, ma'am. The Fun Factory Boss. Seven-inch insertable length, 1.73 inches in circumference. These things sell like wildfire."

Selina reached out and picked up the case, looking at it. She closed her eyes and tried to picture the size of Ragden's cock and thought that he had been much larger than this. Selina opened her eyes and put it back on the shelf. A little further down, she spotted a dark leather case propped open. Within it was the largest dildo of any of the ones there. The clerk followed her gaze, and his eyes widened.

"That's the Njoy Eleven. It is 11 inches long and has a 2-inch circumference. Solid stainless steel. Quite heavy."

Selina bit her lip. She tentatively reached out for it. The clerk closed the case and handed it to her. The sheer weight of it was astonishing. She gasped slightly and clutched the case to her chest. Selina felt herself going damp at the thought of what she would do with this monstrosity. The clerk looked at her, his eyes a little wide, then shrugged.

"Anything else, ma'am?" he asked. Selina shook her head rapidly, feeling the heat on her cheek. The clerk headed back to the counter. He stopped halfway down the aisle. He turned to look at her, then pointed to the shelf.

"Do you need some lube with that, ma'am?"

Selina blushed and shrugged. The clerk looked at the box in her arms, then up at her face. He grabbed two bottles off the shelf and carried them with him towards the counter. Selina fished her wallet out of her back pocket while the clerk rang up the items. When she saw the total, she gasped.

"Five hundred dollars?" She involuntarily took a step back from the counter.

The clerk shrugged, "You did pick the most expensive dildo we have."

She looked at the box and bit her lip, then she nodded and handed him her credit card. The clerk finished the sale, handed her the card back, and then put everything into a bag for her. He smiled apologetically as he handed it back to her. As she was about to step away, the clerk cleared his throat. She turned to look back at him. He leaned against the counter towards her and spoke quietly.

"I am sorry to ask, but... are you a porn star, or a supermodel?"

"What? No!" She answered, shocked at the question.

"I'm sorry, ma'am," the clerk replied quickly, "We jus' don' get many women in here that look like you..."

"Why, would you pay to see me naked?" She countered.

"Oh, God. Yes!" The clerk blurted, then he blushed and looked away. "I am sorry. That was not appropriate..."

Selina smiled as she saw the effect she had on the clerk. She felt a slight shift inside her. A sudden hunger within her. She turned back to the counter and walked over to it. The clerk took a step back, a shocked look of surprise on his face. Selina leaned over the counter, letting her shirt hang down, giving him a view of her cleavage. The clerk blushed darker, and she could see the pulse in his neck beating rapidly.

"Care to show me how to use this thing?" She asked with a sultry voice, then licked her lips. The clerk stared at her. She could see the throbbing in his pants. The clerk's eyes were huge, and he nodded and headed for the door into the back room. Selina sauntered towards the door, her hips swaying seductively from side to side. The clerk stood at the door, his eyes wide, his jaw hanging open as she approached. He pushed the door open, and Selina walked past him.

Her eyes adjusted quickly to the dimly lit room. She walked further in and found a table. The lights flickered around her, brightening the room. She poured the contents of the bag onto the table. She popped open the box and looked in at the massive, eleven-inch metal dildo inside. She could feel her arousal dripping down her legs as she looked at it. She heard the clerk coming up behind her.

The clerk came up next to her and looked down at the massive dildo. She looked at him, and he snapped his mouth shut. His hand twitched as he reached for the lube. Then he pulled the dildo out of the case and hefted it in one hand. Then he set it back in the case. He popped open the lube and spread some on his left hand. With his right, he pulled the dildo out of the case. Then he spread the lube around one end of the dildo and turned to look at her.

Selina saw a hungry look on his face. She could see the throbbing bulge in his pants, and she laughed lustily. Then she dropped her shorts and panties. She turned and bent over, thrusting her ass into his groin as she did so. She picked up her shorts and panties and set them on the table in front of the case. Then she backed onto the table and lifted herself onto it. She scooted back and spread her legs in front of the clerk.

The clerks' eyes were glued to her tight snatch. She spread her legs wider, then reached down with one hand and spread her lips open. She bit her lip as she looked at the clerk. His eyes got even wider.

"What are you waiting for," she asked, "Put it in me."

The clerk licked his lips then he stepped between her legs. He gently pushed the massive silver head through her lips. Selina moaned loudly as she

felt the cold metal sliding up into her. The clerk tentatively pushed it deeper into her, then started to pull it back.

"Oh, Goddamnit!" Selina cursed. She grasped the hard metal and slapped his hand with her hand, then slid it all the way up into her. The clerk took a step back and stumbled as he did so. She felt the hard metal filling her, stretching her. Then it hit the back of her, and she moaned in pleasure. It was so hard inside her. Hard and cold. She pulled it back and then slid it into her cervix again. She moaned loudly in pleasure. She could feel her fluids mixing with the lube flowing across the hard metal. She pushed against her cervix, feeling it push hard against her.

It felt so good to have her pussy full of something so large. It was not as large as Ragden's dick had been the last time he had fucked her, but it still felt amazing. She groaned softly, knowing that it would feel even better the next time he fucked her. She slid the massive dildo out of her pussy and put the head against her ass. She shivered as the cold metal pushed against her. She pushed harder and wiggled it, trying to slip into her ass. She groaned loudly as the head of it slipped into her.

Selina gasped as the hard cold metal slipped into her ass. Her body shook, and the metal slipped from her fingers. It weighed too much, slipped through her grasp, and clattered to the floor.

"Fucking hell!" She cried out. Then her eyes caught the clerk standing there. His zipper was down. She could see his dick in his hands. She grinned evilly, then gestured for him to step forward. The clerk's eyes got large. He shuffled forward, his right hand gripping his cock hard.

"Pick it up," she said softly, but firmly. The clerk nodded and picked up the dildo.

"Put it in my ass." The clerk nodded and pressed the lube-slicked end of the dildo into her ass. He leaned against it, forcing it inside her.

"Oh, fuck yeah," Selina moaned as the dildo slid up inside her. The clerk slid half of it into her and stopped. Then he slid it back and up into her again. She sat up and looked between her legs. She saw his small cock throbbing between her legs. His hand gripping the dildo so tight his knuckles were white. She could see that only half of it was inside her. She glared at him.

"I want all of that fucking dildo up my goddamn ass."

The clerk looked at her, his eyes big as saucers. He nodded and slid it up her ass until only the bulb of the other end was not inside her. Selina moaned loudly and flopped back against the table as she felt the full length of it inside her. Her body vibrated with pleasure. Her legs shook, and she felt her climax suddenly roll over her. Fluid gushed out of her pussy, splashing across the table between her legs. She lay there gasping. She could feel the hard length of it inside her and loved the feel of it. It was not as good as the memory of Ragden's big dick, but it would have to do. She looked at the clerk and bit her lip.

She suddenly needed to feel the heat of him inside her. She desperately

wanted the real deal inside her. It would not be as good, or as large, or as amazing as Ragden, but it was a real dick, and she wanted it inside her so badly her body shook. She sat up and grabbed the front of his shirt, pulling him closer to her.

"Fuck me." She said huskily. The clerk fumbled with his belt, trying to undo his pants. Selina cursed again, grabbed his dick, and pulled him into her. She wrapped her legs around him, pulling him against her. His dick slid up inside her, and she cried out again.

The clerk moaned in ecstasy as her tight pussy enveloped him. She felt his heat inside her and moaned again. She could feel the cold of his zipper pressed against her lips and did not care. She wanted his dick as deep as it would go. She knew it was not big enough to hit her like the dildo or Ragden, but it would have to do for now.

Selina released her legs around him, and spread them wide, allowing him to pull back and thrust into her. She felt his hips thump against hers, and she moaned.

"Harder," she begged. The clerk nodded and drew back and thrust into her harder. He built a fast pace, drawing back and thrusting into her. She lay on her back, clutching her chest, feeling her body rock with each of his thrusts into her. She rocked her hips in time to his thrusts, meeting him halfway. She could feel his dick going deeper, but still not deep enough to hit the spot she needed.

"Harder," she commanded. The clerk grabbed her hips and pulled her against him, as he thrust into her harder and faster. She could feel her climax starting to build again. Then, suddenly, the clerk spasmed, and she felt his dick spurt inside her.

"Really?" she exclaimed. The clerk gasped and shuddered as his climax rode over him. His body spasmed, and he thrust into her twice more, then pressed himself as deep into her as he could. It was still not deep enough. She groaned in disappointment.

Then she felt something shift inside her. A sudden wind filled the room, blowing papers around the room. Packages shifted. Boxes fell over. The clerk looked at her, wide-eyed. Her legs clamped around him, squeezing him against her. She could feel his dick inside her, no longer spurting, but pouring into her. She felt her pussy filling up with... something coming out of him. She had no idea what it was, or what was going on.

Selina lay back against the table and moaned in pleasure as her pussy stretched around whatever was happening inside her.

"What are you doing to me?" the clerk cried out. He tried to pull back from her, to extricate his dick from inside her, but her legs were locked in place, and he could not move. She looked up at him feeling immense satisfaction, as she felt herself filled with something. She looked up at him and saw the color draining out of his face. His eyes lost their color. His hair started to fade. She felt so full, so amazingly full. She licked her lips as she

watched the life drain out of the clerk.

He cried out once more, and then his eyes lost their color and their focus, and he slumped backward. She released her legs, and he fell backward to the floor. She laughed in joy as she felt life and energy filling her body. She reached down and ran a finger through the folds of her pussy. She felt something sticky between her legs and brought it up to her lips to taste. She saw a reddish liquid and licked it from her fingers. It was quite possibly the second most delicious thing she had ever tasted. The first, of course, had been the taste of Ragden's seed leaking from her ass.

Selina laughed in giddy glee as she rolled around on the table. She felt so amazingly alive and full of energy. She jumped up off the table and noticed the clerk lying there, his body shriveled, feebly reaching out. His eyes were grey and unfocused. He looked like he was a hundred years old. His body wasted away. Every bit of moisture seemed to have been sucked out of him. She blew him a kiss and turned back to the table and saw the dark leather case.

It was at that point that she remembered the metal dildo still up her ass. She reached down between her legs, grasped the metal nub, and slowly pulled it out of her. She gasped and panted as it slid free, then she put it back in the box and snapped it shut. She put the case in the bag, then the two bottles of lube. She put her panties and shorts back on. Smiling and feeling immensely satisfied, she turned to the doorway and stopped in her tracks.

A small voice in the back of her head told her something was wrong with this picture. She turned and looked back at the clerk, still lying on the ground. He tried to pull up his pants to cover himself but could barely move. She blinked as she started to realize what had happened.

"Help... help me," the clerk moaned, his voice a dry rasp. Selina back from him, a scream choked in her throat. She backed away from him, watching as he swung his sightless eyes around the room, searching for her, pleading for help.

A new voice rumbled inside her skull. "Knowledge requires energy. Energy requires life."

Tears streamed down Selina's face as she looked at what remained of the clerk. Then, she heard voices in the other room. She turned, startled, and looked back to the main part of the store. She snatched up her bag and stood, looking for another exit. She moved quickly into the back of the store and found a back door. As quietly as she could, she pulled it open and stepped out into the night. Then, she ran to her car.

Once in her car, Selina threw the bag into the back of the car. She pounded on the steering wheel as tears streamed down her face.

"Why?" she cried out. She looked up into the rearview mirror at her reflection. One of her eyes was now green. Not glowing, but green. In a panic, she pulled down the visor and opened the mirror there to take a closer look at her reflection. Sure enough, her right eye was now green.

"What..."

She heard a little voice in the back of her skull. It whispered and blew through her mind.

"Everything has a price..."

Selina slammed her hands against the steering wheel again as she cried, "Nooo..."

ABOUT THE AUTHOR

Ragden Zar is a professional network engineer who supports multiple companies from the comfort of his home in Pennsylvania. He lives with his wife, son and mother. He plays online games, namely Final Fantasy XIV in his off time. When he is not busy running around the mystical world of Eorzea, he can be found painting miniatures, kitesurfing, snowboarding, or writing stories.

Made in the USA
Columbia, SC
09 August 2024

f4e6f9fe-ae85-4154-a9d5-0be866e12e6aR01